SEAFORT'S HOPE

SEAFORT'S HOPE

Midshipman's Hope
Challenger's Hope

DAVID FEINTUCH

GUILDAMERICA
B O O K S ®

Published by arrangement with
Warner Books, Inc.
1271 Avenue of the Americas
New York, New York 10020

ISBN: 1-56865-154-6

PRINTED IN THE UNITED STATES OF AMERICA

Contents

Introduction

This Science Fiction Book Club edition gives me a chance to reminisce with readers who, like me, grew up steeped in science fiction and take it seriously. And perhaps, too, those who always yearned to write.

When I was a kid we didn't have much money for books, but there was the old Yonkers public library, in all its Carnegie granite glory. Starting at about age seven I took the trolley—yes, Yonkers was a bit old-fashioned—down South Broadway to a piece of heaven on earth.

We were allowed to take home a maximum of six books. I always filled my quota.

Of course, when I was seven the Dewey Decimal System was far beyond me. But I wandered the shelves of the children's section, picking out books at random, including, once, *Little Women*, which I found a complete mystery; I gave up after a couple of pages.

Notwithstanding these occasional setbacks, I managed to come up with a thick pile to take home each week. A mound of novels stacked under my chin, I waited impatiently for the trolley homeward. By the time we reached our stop I was deep into the first of my selections.

No one really explained how books in a library were organized, but after a while I remembered where I had found a book I liked. More or less by chance I soon figured out that the book immediately adjacent was also likely to be a pretty good read. From there it was a short step to the breathtaking revelation of authors' names. Now I could actually look for good books.

I know it's fashionable these days to point out all Heinlein's flaws—and God knows they exist—but I'll never forget the thrill of coming across one of his juveniles. From then on I devoured everything Heinlein, and plowed through the science fiction section like a scythe, reaping through almost everything on the shelves. Asimov, Bradbury, Sturgeon, Blish, Van Vogt, Clarke . . . and then as I grew older, my God, the pulps!

One evening along about 1959 my father, in a fit of pique, hurled one of my Galaxy magazines across the room and demanded, "Why are you always reading this crap about rockets going to the moon, and people on other planets? It's never going to happen! Why don't you read something realistic!"

Little did we know.

I stuck with SF for a long while, but after college I drifted away. My favorite authors were dropping out, dying, or writing stuff that wasn't very good anymore. Heinlein was one. Yes, his last books became talky and preachy. But *Glory Road, Farnham's Freehold, The Moon is a Harsh Mistress, Starship Troopers*, and of course, *Stranger . . .* what a legacy.

Where Asimov, among many others, would preface his books with an excerpt from the Encyclopedia Galactica or some such tome, in effect telling the reader, "Here's the setup to my story. I need to give you a whole lot of background information, and this is the fastest way to do it," Heinlein just casually brought you into his world with occasional details of how his society functioned, and what its belief system was based on. It was so . . . well, clean. I knew that's how I'd do it, if I ever had the chance.

I knew I wanted to write.

I didn't dare.

Finally, in law school, I hammered out a novel about a revolution in Harlem. I worked hard at it, even researched my subject rather well. In those days, "cut and paste" meant exactly that: cut your typing paper with a scissors and glue or paste together the new sections. It certainly discouraged rewriting, but I managed two rewrites.

I showed my work to a couple of writers, who urged me to submit it.

I chickened out.

Two years later, I found a novel on the shelves that used exactly the gimmick I'd proposed. My novel was better.

Ah well. Too late.

That was my last stab at writing for many years. I practiced law, married, raised children, went into business . . .

And kept reading. Because I read pretty fast, it became harder and harder to find anything I really liked. Even worse, my favorites were almost all dead. James Thurber, C.S. Forrester, Ayn Rand, Sturgeon, Blish, Barbara Tuchman, Teddy White. Then Heinlein.

Sure, there was good stuff—great stuff—being written. But I wasn't coming across anyone who emotionally pulled my chain. In desperation, I tried writing again, and found that while I was a decent raconteur (or so I'm told) there was a world of difference between *saying* a good story and *writing* it. I had to learn the craft. My first efforts were abysmal and left unfinished.

WARNING! THE NEXT COUPLE OF PARAGRAPHS ARE A

SPOILER! IF YOU DON'T ALREADY KNOW WHAT *MIDSHIP-MAN'S HOPE* IS ABOUT, SKIP AHEAD TO THE PARAGRAPH THAT BEGINS, "The solution was obvious." GO ON, NOW! DON'T RUIN A GOOD READ. YOU CAN COME BACK AND READ THIS AFTER.

One day I was sitting in front of the tube with my brain in idle, when an idea struck me with great force. What if . . . Well now, isn't that science fiction in a nutshell? "What if." Historical novels are about "the time when," and present day novels are about "a fellow who." SF is about what would happen, *IF*. It's as a good a way as any to define the genre.

Anyway, what if someone were in charge of a group, but he knew himself to be incompetent and unable to lead? What if those he commanded also knew it, and he was aware they knew?

How could I set that up? It had to be important. Therefore a situation where lives were at stake. Command structures would be involved, ergo a military setting. The commander couldn't seek help from home base, else the story would collapse, so the characters had to be isolated as a group for a long period. If the commander were free to resign I'd have no story. Therefore, a hierarchical and rigid society bound by oaths of honor.

The solution was obvious: the British Navy in the Napoleonic era.

Two problems. One, it had already been done. C.S. Forrester. Alexander Kent. And Patrick O'Brian, who is still writing.

Two, I would have to know immense and intimate detail about sailing ships. I could just see some reader scornfully writing to the publisher, "*Anyone* knows the halyard brace is reefed to the gimbals, not the mizzen swansail," or some such malarkey. And the problem is, he'd be right.

Where could I set a story so I was free to arrange my society as I wished, and not stumble over the technical details?

A time that hasn't happened yet. What kind of society would be so hierarchical and rigid that my protagonist couldn't resign his command? A religious one. Where would they be so isolated the story could play itself out? Between stars. The book formed itself.

Once I fastened on my character, Nick Seafort, and began to understand him, everything else fell into place. The narrative poured out of me.

Then came the magical, never-before-experienced days when I assumed a scene was done, and Nicky or one of his companions nudged me aside. "Excuse us, but we're not quite finished." And I would type like a madman while they took the action of the book to some wonderful byway I hadn't dreamed existed. When minor characters, with a stern "ahem," tapped me on the shoulder and made clear that they weren't nearly as minor as I'd envisioned.

I finished the book, began sending it off, sought an agent.

And fell flat on my face. I didn't even get rejection slips, though a SASE was enclosed. Just the ms in a return bag.

Finally, through Delphi, an online computer service, I found other writers. One of them pointed me to a gifted novelist and teacher who reviewed and critiqued my book. She agreed with me that it started too slowly. She also taught me some simple tricks about dialogue, transitions, etc. I will say this: I'm a fast learner. Whatever mistakes I make, once I'm shown the right way, I remember it. A month later, I had a new draft of *Midshipman's Hope* to send. Out it went.

I waited, and waited, and dropped dead. Literally.

I was playing tennis and keeled over. Two doctors were on the next court. Despite their best efforts, I survived. No, that's not quite right. They breathed for me until the paramedics came and zapped me back to life. It took five shots with the defibrillator to restart my heart, and they were on the verge of giving up. I spent a month in the hospital, had major surgery, and went home to recover.

After eleven months, my novel came back, rejected.

During all this, my life was such hell (on top of everything else I was broke and divorcing) that I had no choice but to keep writing, to hold on to my sanity. *Challenger's Hope* was born, and *Prisoner's Hope* came after. Then the climactic novel, *Fisherman's Hope*. I lived in Hope Nation, and Nicky's troubles were mine. It was blessed refuge.

But because I'd never thought of writing further than the book I was doing, each novel is complete in itself. I've always felt cheated if I work my way to the end of a major novel and find that it isn't over. In fact, unless that is made abundantly clear in the cover copy, I'll allow myself to be fooled once and no more. That's IT for that author.

I call it the "ahhh." It's that "ahhh," you feel at the end of a satisfying novel. The sense of closure. I guarantee you, anything you read from me will have the "ahhh" at the end. It's keeping faith.

Anyway, something I do must be working; Warner just bought my fifth novel, and I'm starting on my sixth next month. *Midshipman* and *Challenger* both made the Locus best seller lists.

I couldn't have made it as a writer without the help and encouragement of a number of people I could never possibly pay back. In consequence, I've tried to remember the gratitude and awe I felt when some busy professional stopped to show me the way. The only way to pay them back is to do likewise. So, if you know you are a writer but have never proved it, and you want advice, direction, or critique, drop me a line. Always include a SASE, and don't expect miracles; my charming editor at Warner Books keeps me hopping to meet their deadlines.

And read on. Ain't life great?

David Feintuch
P.O. Box 366
Mason, Mi 48854
MIDAVE@DELPHI.COM

Midshipman's Hope

To Ragtime Rick of Toledo, and Ardath Mayhar, who made it possible, and to Jettie, who makes it worthwhile.

MIDSHIPMAN'S HOPE

Being the first voyage
of Nicholas Seafort, U.N.N.S.,
in the year of our Lord 2194

Part 1

October 12, in the year of our Lord 2194

1

"Stand to!" I roared, but I was too late; even as Alexi and Sandy snapped to attention, *Hibernia*'s two senior lieutenants strolled around the corridor bend.

We froze in stunned tableau: I, the senior midshipman, red with rage; a portly passenger, Mrs. Donhauser, jaw agape at the blob of shaving cream on her tunic; my two middies stiffened against the bulkhead, eyes locked front, towels and canisters still clutched in their hands; Lieutenants Cousins and Dagalow, dumbfounded that middies could be caught cavorting in the corridors of a U.N.N.S. starship, even one still moored at Ganymede Orbiting Station.

If only I'd come down from the bridge a few seconds sooner I'd have been in time, but I'd been helping Ms. Dagalow enter the last of our new stores into the puter's manifests.

Lieutenant Cousins was curt. "You too, Mr. Seafort. Against the bulkhead."

"Aye aye, sir." I stiffened to attention, eyes front, furious at my betrayal by a friend whose sense I'd thought I could trust.

Alexi Tamarov, the sweating middy at my side, was sixteen and third in seniority. When I'd first reported aboard, he'd considered challenging me but hadn't, and we'd since become comrades. Now his antics with Sandy had gotten us all in hot water.

Across the gleaming corridor Ms. Dagalow's eye betrayed a glint of humor as she pried the canister of shaving cream from Sandy Wilsky's reluctant fingers. She passed it to Lieutenant Cousins. Once again, I wished she were the senior lieutenant; Mr. Cousins seemed to take undue pleasure in the ship's discipline he dispensed.

Lieutenant Cousins snapped, "Yours, middy? Are you old enough to use it?" From close observation during the five weeks since I'd joined *Hibernia* at Earthport Station, I knew that at fourteen Sandy had not yet made the acquaintance of a razor. That meant he had, um, borrowed it. From me, perhaps. At seventeen, I was known to shave, if rarely.

"No, sir." Sandy had no choice but to answer. "It's Mr. Holser's." I bit my lip. Lord God, that was all this fiasco needed: trouble with Midshipman Vax Holser.

Vax, almost nineteen, resented me and didn't care if it showed, for he'd missed being first middy by only a few weeks. He was full-grown, shaved daily, and worked out with weights. His surly manner and ominous strength encouraged us all to give him a wide berth.

Lieutenant Cousins nodded to Mrs. Donhauser, whose outrage had subsided into wry amusement. "Madam, my sincere apologies. I assure you these children"—he spat out the word with venom—"will not trouble you again." His look of suppressed fury did not bode well.

"No harm done," Mrs. Donhauser said peaceably. "They were just playing—"

"Is that what you call it?" Mr. Cousins's grip tightened on the canister. "Officers in a Naval starship, chasing each other with shaving soap!"

Mrs. Donhauser was unfazed. "I won't tell you your duty, Lieutenant. But I will make it clear that I was not harmed and have no grievance. Good day." With that she turned on her heel toward the passenger cabins, presumably to change her tunic.

For a moment Lieutenant Cousins was speechless. Then he rounded on us. "You're the sorriest joeys I've ever seen! A seventeen-month cruise to Hope Nation, and I have to sail with *you!*"

I took a deep breath. "I'm sorry, sir. It's my responsibility."

"At least you know that much." Cousins's tone was acid. "Is this how you run your wardroom, Mr. Seafort?"

"No, sir." I wasn't sure it was the right response. Perhaps my amiable manner encouraged Sandy and Alexi to step out of line. Certainly they would never have done so under Vax Holser's tutelage.

"I expect stupidity from these young dolts, but it's your job to control them! What if the Captain had come along?"

Lord God forbid. If they'd squirted Captain Haag rather than Mrs. Donhauser, Alexi and Sandy would see the barrel, if not the brig. For good measure, the Captain might break me all the way down to ship's boy. Mr. Cousins was right. I could think of no way to placate him, so I said nothing.

It was a mistake. "Answer me, you insolent pup!"

To my surprise, Lieutenant Dagalow intervened. "Mr. Cousins, Nick was on watch. He couldn't have known—"

"It's his job to keep his juniors in line!"

I did, when I was present. What more could I do?

For some reason Ms. Dagalow persisted. "But they're young, we're moored to Ganymede Station, they were just letting off steam . . ."

"Lisa, take your nose out of the puter long enough to remember the rest of your job. We have to teach them to act like adults!" From another officer it might have been a blistering rebuke, but Mr. Cousins's acid manner was well known to all, and she took no notice.

"They'll learn."

"When our shaving cream runs out?" Cousins glared at us with withering contempt before turning back to Ms. Dagalow. "Consider that by the end of the cruise at least some of them should be fit to be officers. I grant you, it's unlikely any of these fools will ever make lieutenant. But what if one of us is transferred out at Hope Nation? Do you want silly boys standing watch, fresh from shaving cream fights?"

"We've time to teach them. Nick will issue ample demerits." I certainly would. Each demerit would have to be worked off by two hours of hard calisthenics. They'd keep Alexi and Sandy out of trouble for a while.

Lieutenant Cousins's voice grew cold. "Will he?" A chill of foreboding crept down my rigid spine. "Nicky should never have been senior, we all know that." Even Lieutenant Dagalow frowned at the blatant undercutting of my authority, but Mr. Cousins was oblivious. "He'll wag his finger at them, as always." That wasn't fair; I'd kept wardroom matters from the attention of the other officers, as was expected. Except this once.

"Will you cane the two of them, then? After all, it's a wardroom affair."

"No, I'll let Nicky handle them." From the corner of my eye I saw Alexi's shoulders slump with relief. Then Mr. Cousins added sweetly, "But perhaps I can teach Mr. Seafort more diligence." He sauntered toward his cabin. "Come along, middy."

A half hour later I stood outside our wardroom, jaw aching from my failed effort not to cry out, eyes burning from the stinging pain and mortifying humiliation Mr. Cousins had inflicted across the hated barrel.

I slapped open the hatch. Inside the cramped compartment Sandy and Alexi, on their beds, dared say nothing. I crossed slowly to my bunk, stripped off my jacket and laid it on the chair. With care, I eased myself onto my bed.

After a time Alexi said quietly, "Mr. Seafort, I'm sorry. Truly." As was the custom, Alexi called me by my surname even within our wardroom. After all, I was senior middy. Only Vax Holser had the resources to ignore that tradition and get away with it.

I fought down a smoldering rage; it should have been Alexi who was caned, not I. "Thank you." My thighs smarted with exquisite agony. "You should have known better, both of you."

"I know, Mr. Seafort."

I closed my eyes, trying to will away the pain. At Academy, sometimes, it worked. "Who started it?"

"I did," they said in unison.

My fingers throttled the pillow. "Sandy, you first."

"We were in the head, washing up. Alexi splashed me. I splashed back." He glanced up, saw my face, gulped.

Skylarking, like cadets at Academy. "Go on."

"After he flicked me with a towel I grabbed the shaving cream. He chased me so I ran outside, and I was squirting him when Mrs. Donhauser came out of the lounge." I said nothing. After a moment he blurted, "Mr. Seafort, I'm sorry I got you into troub—"

"I'll make you sorrier!" I sat up, thought better of it, eased myself back on my bunk. "No officer would look into the middy's head to see how you behave. But running out into the corridor . . . Mr. Cousins is right; you *are* dolts."

Alexi flushed; Sandy studied his fingernails.

Angry as I was, I wasn't surprised that they'd frolicked like the boys they were. What else could be expected, even on a starship? One had to go to space young to spend life as a sailor, else the risk of melanoma T was too great. Unfortunately, aboard such an immense and valuable vessel as *Hibernia,* there was no room for youngsters' folly.

I growled, "Four demerits apiece, for letting your foolishness get out of hand." Severe, but Mr. Cousins would have given much worse, and my buttocks stung like fire. "I'll write it as improper hygiene. Alexi, two extra for you."

"But I started it!" Sandy's protest was from the heart.

"You ran into the corridor, which should have ended it. Mr. Tamarov chose to follow. Alexi, how many does that give you?"

"Nine, Mr. Seafort." He was pale.

I growled, "Work them off fast, because I'm in no mood to overlook any offense." Ten would earn him a caning, like I'd just been given; Alexi would have to be vigilant while he worked down his demerits. "Start now; you have two hours before lunch."

"Aye aye, Mr. Seafort." They scrambled out of their bunks. In a moment they'd slipped on shoes and jackets and departed for the exercise room, leaving me the solitude I'd sought. I rolled onto my stomach and surrendered to my misery.

*   *   *

"It's time, Mr. Seafort." Alexi Tamarov jolted me from my fretful dream, from Father's bleak kitchen, the creaky chair, the physics text I'd struggled to master under Father's watchful eye.

I shoved away Alexi's persistent hand. "We don't cast off 'til midwatch." Groggy, I blinked myself awake.

From the hatchway, Vax Holser watched with a sardonic grin. "Let him sleep, Tamarov. Lieutenant Malstrom won't mind if he's late."

I surged out of my bunk in dizzy confusion. Reporting late to duty station would be a matter for Mr. Cousins, and after the incident two days prior, Lord God help me if I called his attention anew. I glanced at my watch. I'd slept six hours!

In frantic haste I snatched my blue jacket from the chair, thrust my arms into my sleeves as I polished the tip of a shoe against the back of my trouser leg.

"Why do we bother waking you?" Vax sounded disgusted. I didn't answer; he left for his duty station in the comm room, Sandy Wilsky tagging behind him.

"Thanks, Alexi," I muttered, and nearly collided with him in the hatchway. I scrambled into the circumference corridor and ran past the east ladder, smoothing my hair and tugging at my tie as I rounded the bend to the airlock. I'd barely reached my station when Captain Haag's voice echoed through the speaker.

"Uncouple mooring lines!"

Lieutenant Malstrom returned my salute in offhand fashion, his eye on the suited sailor untying our forward safety line from the shoreside stanchion.

"Line secured, sir," the seaman said, and by the book I repeated it to Mr. Malstrom as if he hadn't heard. The lieutenant waved me permission to proceed.

"Close inner lock, Mr. Howard. Prepare for breakaway." I tried for the tone of authority that came so naturally to *Hibernia*'s lieutenants.

"Aye aye, sir." Seaman Howard keyed the control; the thick transplex hatches slid shut smoothly, joining in the center to form a tight seal.

Lieutenant Malstrom opened a compartment, slid a lever downward. From within the airlock, a brief hum, and a click. He signaled the bridge. "Forward inner lock sealed, sir. Capture latches disengaged."

"Very well, Mr. Malstrom." Captain Haag's normally gruff voice sounded detached through the caller. The ship's whistle blew three short blasts. After a moment the Captain's remote voice sounded again. "Cast off!"

Our duties performed, Lieutenant Malstrom and I had little to do

but watch while our side thrusters alternately released tiny jets of propellant in quick spurts, rocking us gently. Our airlock suckers parted
reluctantly from their counterparts on the station lock. U.N.S. *Hibernia*
slowly drifted free of Ganymede Station. When we were clear by about
ten meters I glanced up at Lieutenant Malstrom. "Shall we secure, sir?"
He nodded.

I gave the order. The alumalloy outer hatches slid shut, barring our
view of the receding station. Lieutenant Malstrom keyed our caller.
"Forward hatch secured, sir."

"Secured; very well." The Captain seemed preoccupied, as well he
might. On the bridge he and the Pilot would be readying *Hibernia* for
Fusion. I felt a bit queasy as our weight diminished. We were slowly
losing the benefits of the station's gravitrons, and the Captain hadn't yet
brought our own on-line.

We waited in silence, each lost in his own thoughts. "Say good-bye,
Nicky." Lieutenant Malstrom's tone was soft.

"I already did, sir, back in Lunapolis." I would miss Cardiff, of
course, and aloft, the familiar warrens of Lunapolis. I would even miss
Farside Academy, where I'd trained as a cadet three years ago. But
Ganymede Station was another matter. It had been over a month since
I'd cried out my regrets in an unnoticed corner of a service bar in down-
under Lunapolis, and by now I was long ready.

The fusion drive kicked in. In the rounded porthole the stars
shifted red, then blue. As the drive reached full strength they slowly
faded to black.

We were Fused.

External sensors blind, *Hibernia* hurtled out of the Solar System on
the crest of the N-wave generated by our drive.

"All hands, stand down from launch stations." The Captain's voice
seemed husky.

I locked Seaman Howard's transmitter in the airlock safe.

"Chess, Nick?" Lieutenant Malstrom asked when the sailor had
departed.

"Sure, sir." We headed up-corridor to officers' country. In the lieutenant's bleak cabin, a windowless gray cubicle four meters square and
two and a half meters high, Mr. Malstrom tossed the chessboard onto his
bunk. I sat on the gray navy blanket at the foot of the bed; he settled by
the starched white pillow at the head.

"I'm going to learn to beat you," he said, setting up the pieces.
"Something I can concentrate on besides ship's routine." I smiled politely. I had no intention of letting him win; chess was one of my few

accomplishments. At home in Cardiff I had been semifinalist in my age group, before Father brought me to Academy at thirteen.

We played the half-minute rule, loosely enforced. In the weeks since *Hibernia* had left Earthport Station I'd won twenty-three times, he had won twice. This time it took me twenty-five moves. As was our habit we shook hands gravely after the game.

"When we get back from Hope Nation I'll be thirty-five." He sighed, perhaps a trifle morosely. "You'll be twenty."

"Yes, sir." I waited.

"What do you regret more?" he asked abruptly. "The years you'll lose, or being cooped in the ship so long?"

"I don't see them as lost years, sir. When I get back I'll have enough ship's time to make lieutenant, if I pass the boards. I wouldn't even be close if I stayed home." I didn't dare tell him how strongly the ambition burned within me.

He said nothing, and I reflected a moment. "Thirty-four months, round-trip. I don't know, sir. I tested low for claustrophobia, like all of us." I risked a grin. "It depends whether it's three years playing chess with you or being reamed out by Lieutenant Cousins." For a moment I thought I'd overstepped myself, but it was all right.

Lieutenant Malstrom let out a long, slow breath. "I won't criticize a brother officer, especially to one of junior rank like yourself. I merely wonder aloud how he ever got into Academy."

Or out of it, I added silently. If only Mr. Malstrom had been the one assigned to teach us navigation. But his primary duties were ship security and passenger liaison. Judiciously, I said nothing.

I wandered back to the wardroom. Inside, Sandy Wilsky sat attentively on the deck, legs crossed. From his bed, Vax Holser scowled. "Well?"

With a shrug of despair Sandy blurted, "I don't know, Mr. Holser."

Vax's eyes narrowed. "You're not by some chance still a cadet? Have we a genuine middy who can't find the munitions locker?"

I crossed to my bunk, ignoring the boy's hopeful look. Vax was entitled to haze him a bit. We all were; Sandy was junior and just out of Academy.

"I'm sorry." Sandy glanced to me as if for succor, but I offered none. A middy should know such things. I kicked off my shoes, flopped on my bed.

Vax demanded, "What's the Naval Mission?"

Sandy took a hopeful breath. "The mission of the United Nations Naval Service is to preserve the United Nations Government of and under Lord God, and to protect colonies and outposts of human habitation wherever established. The Naval Service is to defend the United Nations and its—its . . ." He faltered.

Vax glared, and finished for him. "—and its territories from all enemies, internal or foreign, to transport all interstellar cargoes and goods, to convey such persons to and from the colonies who may have lawful business among them, and to carry out such lawful orders as Admiralty may from time to time issue. Section 1, Article 5 of the regs."

"Yes, Mr. Holser."

Vax said, "It's worth a demerit or two, Nicky."

I made no answer. If Vax had his way, the juniors would spend their lives in the exercise room. Within the wardroom, only I could issue demerits, though Vax could make the middies' lives miserable in other ways.

"Laser controls?"

"In the gun—I mean, the comm room." The youngster wrinkled his brow. "No, it must be . . . I mean . . ."

Vax scowled. "How many push-ups would it take—"

A few push-ups wouldn't hurt Sandy—we'd all been subjected to worse hazing—but Vax got on my nerves. He even had the boy calling him "Mr. Holser," which I resented. By tradition, only the senior middy was addressed as "Mr." by the juniors.

I snapped, "Laser controls are in the comm room. You should know that—were you asleep during gunnery practice?"

"No, Mr. Seafort." A faint sheen of perspiration; now he had us both annoyed at him.

I made my tone less grating. "On some ships the lasers are in a separate compartment called the gunroom, which is also what old-fashioned ships call their middy's berth."

"Thank you." Sandy sounded appropriately humble.

Vax growled, "He should have known it."

"You're right. Not knowing your way around the ship is a disgrace, Sandy. Give me twenty push-ups." It was a kindness. Vax would have made it fifty.

Dinner, as usual, was in the ship's dining hall rather than the officers' mess. I sat at my place sipping ice water, waiting for the clink of the glass. When it came I stood with the rest of the officers and passengers, my head bowed. Captain Haag, stocky, graying, and distinguished, began the nightly ritual.

"Lord God, today is October 19, 2194, on the U.N.S. *Hibernia.* We ask you to bless us, to bless our voyage, and to bring health and well-being to all aboard."

"Amen." Chairs scraped as we sat. The Ship's Prayer has been said at evening in every United Nations vessel to sail the void for one hundred sixty-seven years, and always by the Captain, as representative of the government, and therefore of the Reunified Church. Like crewmen everywhere, our sailors considered shipping with a parson to be unlucky, and any minister who sailed in *Hibernia* did so in his private capacity. Few ships had it otherwise.

"Good evening, Mr. Seafort."

"Good evening, ma'am." Mrs. Donhauser, imposing in her elegant yet practical satin jumpsuit, was the Anabaptist envoy to our Hope Nation colony. "Did yoga go well today?"

She smiled her appreciation of my offering. Mrs. Donhauser believed that daily yoga would get her to Hope Nation sane and healthy. Her stated mission was to convert every last one of the two hundred thousand residents to her creed. Knowing her, I had no reason to disbelieve it was possible.

Our state religion was the amalgam of Protestant and Catholic ritual that had been hammered out in the Great Yahwehist Reunification after the Armies of Lord God repressed the Pentecostal heresy. Nonetheless, the U.N. Government tolerated splinter sects such as Mrs. Donhauser's. Still, I wondered how the Governor of Hope Nation would react if she succeeded too well in her mission. Like Captain Haag, the Governor was ex-officio a representative of the true Church.

Hibernia carried eleven officers on her long interstellar voyage: four middies, three lieutenants, Chief Engineer, Pilot, Ship's Doctor, and the Captain. We all took our breakfast and lunch in the spartan and simple officers' mess, but we sat with our passengers for the evening meal.

Our hundred thirty passengers, bound for the thriving Hope Nation colony or continuing on to Detour, our second stop, had their informal breakfast and lunch in the passengers' mess.

Belowdecks, our crew of seventy—engine room hands, comm specialists, recycler's mates, hydroponicists, the ship's boy, and the less skilled crewmen who toiled in the galley or in the purser's compartments caring for our many passengers—took all their meals in the seamen's mess below.

Places at dinner were assigned monthly by the purser, except at the Captain's table, where seating was by Captain Haag's invitation only. This month I was assigned to Table 7. In my regulation blues—navy-blue pants, white shirt, black tie, spit-polished black shoes, blue jacket

with insignia and medals, and ribbed cap—I always felt stiff and uncomfortable at dinner. I wished again I could wear the uniform with Vax
Holser's confident style.

At his neighboring table Chief Engineer McAndrews chatted easily
with a passenger. Grizzled and stolid, the Chief ran his engine room
with unpretentious efficiency. To me he was friendly but reserved, as he
seemed to be with all the officers.

The stewards brought each table its tureen of thick hot mushroom
soup. We dished it out ourselves. Ayah Dinh, the Pakistani merchant
directly across from me, sucked his soup greedily. Everyone else affected not to notice. Mr. Barstow, a florid sixty-year-old, glared as if
daring me to speak to him. I chose not to. Randy Carr, immaculate and
athletic, wearing an expensive pastel jumpsuit, smiled politely but
looked through me as if I were nonexistent. His aristocratic son Derek
strongly resembled him in appearance, and copied his manner. Sixteen
and haughty, he did not deign to smile at crew; what courtesy he had
was reserved for passengers.

"I started a diary, Nicky." Amanda Frowel favored me with a welcome smile. Our civilian education director was twenty, I'd learned. I'd
thought her smile was for me alone, until I'd seen her offer it to all the
other midshipmen and two of the lieutenants. Ah, well.

I focused on her comment. "What did you write in it?"

"The start of my new life," she said simply. "The end of my old."
Amanda was en route to Hope Nation to teach natural science. It was
common practice to have a passenger fill the post of education director.

"Are you sure you mean that?" I asked. "Doesn't your new life
really start when you arrive, not when you leave?" I took a bite of salad.

Theodore Hansen cut in before she could answer. "Exactly so. The
boy is correct." A soy merchant, he was investing three years of his life
to found new soy plantations with the hybrid seed in our holds. If all
went well he'd be a millionaire many times over, instead of the few
times he already was.

"No, Mr. Hansen." Her tone was calm. "That would only be true if
the voyage is a hiatus in life, just a waiting period before I get to Hope
Nation and resume living."

Young Derek Carr snorted with disdain. "What else could it be? Is
this"—he waved a hand airily—"what you call living?"

His tone offended me but I had no standing to object. Miss Frowel,
though, seemed not to notice. "Yes, I call this living," she told him. "I
have a comfortable berth, lectures to arrange, a trunkful of holovid chips
to read, enjoyable dining, and pleasant company to share the voyage."

Randy Carr poked his son ungently in the ribs. The boy glared at him; he glowered back. Some signal passed between them. After a moment Derek said coolly, "Forgive me if I was rude, Miss Frowel," not sounding greatly concerned.

She smiled and the conversation turned elsewhere. As I finished my baked chicken I closed my ears and imagined the two of us alone in her cabin. Well, it would be a long voyage. We'd see.

"So you finally got something right, Mr. Seafort!" Lieutenant Cousins examined my solution on the plotting screen, rubbing his balding head. "But Lord God, can't Mr. Tamarov even learn the basics? If he's ever let loose on a bridge he'll destroy his vessel!"

Mr. Cousins had us calculating when to Defuse to locate the derelict U.N.S. *Celestina*, lost a hundred twelve years ago with all hands. I checked Alexi's solution out of the corner of my eye. He'd made a math error matching stellar velocities. Basically correct, except for the one lapse, but his omission could have been catastrophic. Perhaps *Celestina* had foundered because of some careless navigation error. No one knew.

"I'm very sorry, sir," Alexi said meekly.

"You're very sorry indeed, Mr. Tamarov," the lieutenant echoed. "Of all the middies in the Navy, I get you! Perhaps Mr. Seafort and Mr. Holser will inspire you to study your Nav text. If they don't, I will."

Not good; it was an open invitation to Vax Holser to redouble his hazing, and there was already bad blood between the two.

I had nothing against hazing; we all had to go through it and it strengthens character, or so they say, but Vax took a sadistic pleasure in it that disturbed me. Naturally, as first middy, I'd hazed Alexi and Sandy myself. From time to time I'd had one or the other of them stand on a chair in the wardroom in his shorts for a couple of hours, reciting ship's regs, or given extra mop-up duty for minuscule infractions. As low men, they had to expect that sort of thing, and did. I decided to keep an eye open. I couldn't wholly protect Alexi from Vax, who was second in seniority, but I could try to keep the brooding middy from going too far.

"Back to work." With an irritable swipe, Mr. Cousins cleared Alexi's screen and brought up another plot.

Of course, our calculations were only simulated, with the help of Darla, the ship's puter. In reality *Hibernia* was Fused and all our outer sensors were blind.

Our first stop was to be at *Celestina*, if we could find her without too much delay. She was but a small object, and deep in interstellar space. Then, after many months, we would drop off supplies at Miningcamp, sixty-three light-years distant, before completing our run to Hope Nation. But simulation or no, Lieutenant Cousins expected perfection, and rightly so.

While the fusion drive made interstellar travel practical, the drive was inherently inaccurate by up to six percent of the distance traveled in Fusion. So, we aimed for a point at least six percent of our journey from our target system, stopped, recalculated, and Fused again, as a safeguard against blindly Fusing into a sun, which had happened at least once in the early days. During Fusion our external instruments were useless; we couldn't determine our position until we actually turned off the drive.

I tapped at the keys. So many variables. Our N-waves traversed the galaxy faster than any known form of communication. Though the Navy talked of sending out messenger drones equipped with fusion drive, in practice it didn't work well. The drones frequently disappeared, and no one knew just why. You'd think a puter could handle a ship as well as a mere human, but—

"Pay attention, Seafort!"

"Aye aye, sir!" I squinted at the screen, corrected my error.

Anyway, engineering a fusion drive was so expensive, it made more sense for the Navy to surround it with a manned ship, to ferry passengers and supplies to our colonies as well as mere messages.

Perhaps someday, if the drones were perfected, our profession would be obsolete. It would be a shame. Ours was a glamorous career, despite the slight risk of developing melanoma T, the vicious carcinoma triggered by long exposure to fusion fields.

Fortunately, humans whose cells were exposed to N-waves within five years of puberty seemed almost immune, though there were exceptions. Even for adults going interstellar for the first time, the risks weren't excessive, but they grew with each successive voyage. So, officers were started young, and crew men and women were recruited for short—

"Daydreaming again, Mr. Seafort? If it's about a young lady, you could go to your wardroom for privacy."

"No, sir. Sorry, sir." Blushing, I bent over the console, my fingers flying.

One way to determine our location was to plot our position relative to three known stars and consult the star charts in the ship's puter. We could also calculate the energy variations recorded during Fusion and estimate the percentage of error that would result. This method gave us a sphere of error; we could be at any point in the sphere. Then we merely had to calculate what our target would look like and see if we observed anything that matched.

I don't care what the textbooks say. Navigation is more art than science.

When nav drill was over at last, I chewed out Alexi and sent him to the wardroom with a chip of Lambert and Greeley's *Elements of Astronavigation* for his holovid.

2

The clock ticked against me. Blindfolded, I felt for the bulkheads, hoping not to trip over an unexpected obstacle. I groped my way to a hatch. Lockable from the inside, full-size handle. That meant I was in a passenger's cabin. I felt my way out to the corridor. I turned left, arbitrarily, and walked slowly, my arm scraping along the corridor bulkhead. I sensed I was moving upward, almost imperceptibly. It meant I was coming to a ladder.

One of our training exercises was to figure out where we were, without sight. We'd be given a Dozeoff and would wake some minutes later, Lord God knew where. If we took too long to orient ourselves, we were demerited. I suppose, if a ship's power backups and all our emergency lighting failed at once, the drill could be useful. But I couldn't imagine a situation that would cause that to happen.

I bumped into the ladder railing. It extended both up and down; that meant I was on Level 2, in passenger country. Amanda's cabin was somewhere near; as our friendship had progressed I'd finally been invited inside it.

Where was I, east or west? If east, there'd be an exercise room about twenty steps past the railing. I couldn't remember what was west, except that it wasn't the exercise room. Throwing caution aside to improve my time I staggered down the passage. If Mr. Cousins had put a chair in the corridor I was done for.

No exercise room. "Passenger quarters, second level west, about fifteen meters west of the ladder, sir."

"Very good, Nicky." Lieutenant Malstrom's voice. I took off the blindfold and blinked in the light. I grinned, and he smiled back. I could imagine how our first lieutenant would have said the same thing.

Cut out three foam rubber disks an inch thick, set them one on top of another, and stick a short pencil through the center. Now stand the pencil on end. You'd have a rough model of our ship. The engine room was within the pencil underneath the disks; below that sat the drive itself, flaring into the wave emission chamber at the stubby end of the pencil.

We, crew and passengers, lived and worked in the three disks. The portion of the pencil above the disks would be our cargo holds, full of equipment and supplies for the colony on Hope Nation and for Mining-camp.

A circular passage called the circumference corridor ran around each disk, dividing it into inner and outer segments. To either side, hatches opened onto the disk's cabins and compartments. At intervals along the corridor, airtight hatches were poised to slam shut in case of decompression; they'd seal off each section from the rest.

Two ladders—stairwells, in civilian terms—ascended from the east and west sections of Level 3 to the lofty precincts of Level 1. The bridge was on the uppermost level, along with the officers' cabins and the Captain's sacrosanct quarters I'd never been allowed to view.

Level 2 was passenger country, holding most of the passenger state-rooms. A few passengers were lodged above on Level 1, and the remainder had cabins below on Level 3, where the crew was housed.

Passenger cabins were about twice the size of those given the lieu-tenants. Below, the Level 3 crew berths made even our crowded middy wardroom seem luxurious. Naval policy was to crowd us for sleeping but allow us ample play room. The crew had a gymnasium, theater, rec room, privacy rooms, and its own mess.

The exercise over, Mr. Malstrom and I climbed up to Level 1.

I had just time enough to get ready for my docking drill on the bridge. I showered carefully before reporting to Captain Haag. I still only shaved about once a week, so I had no problem there.

I dressed, tension beginning to knot my stomach. Though I was a long way from making lieutenant, I had no hope of eventual promotion until I could demonstrate to the Captain some basic skill at pilotage.

I gave my uniform a last tuck, took a deep breath, and knocked firmly on the bridge hatch. "Permission to enter bridge, sir."

"Granted." The Captain, standing by the Nav console, didn't bother to turn around. He'd sent for me, and he knew my voice.

I stepped inside. Lieutenant Lisa Dagalow, on watch with Captain Haag, nodded civilly. Though she'd never gone out of her way to help me, neither did she lash out like First Lieutenant Cousins.

I couldn't help being overawed by the bridge. The huge simul-screen on the curved front bulkhead gave a breathtaking view from the nose of the ship—when we weren't Fused, of course. Now, the other smaller screens to either side were also blank. These screens, under our puter Darla's control, could simulate any conditions known to her mem-ory banks.

The Captain's black leather armchair was bolted to the deck behind the left console. The watch officer's chair I'd occupy was to its right. No one else ever sat in the Captain's chair, even for a drill.

"Midshipman Seafort reporting, sir." Of course Captain Haag knew me. A Captain who didn't recognize his own middies in a crew of eleven officers had problems. But regs were regs.

"Take your seat, Mr. Seafort." Unnecessarily, Captain Haag indicated the watch officer's chair. "I'll call up a simulation of Hope Nation system. You will maneuver the ship for docking at Orbit Station."

"Aye aye, sir." It was the only permissible response to an order from the Captain. Cadets or green middies fresh from Academy were sometimes confused by the difference between "Yes, sir," and "Aye aye, sir." It was simple. Asked a question to which the answer was affirmative, you said "Yes, sir." Given an order, you said "Aye aye, sir." It didn't take many trips to the first lieutenant's barrel to get it right.

Captain Haag touched his screen. "But first, you have to get to Hope Nation." My heart sank. "We'll begin at the wreck of *Celestina,* Mr. Seafort. Proceed." He tilted back in his armchair.

I picked up the caller. "Bridge to engine room, prepare to Defuse." My voice squeaked, and I blushed.

"Prepare to Defuse, aye aye, sir." Chief McAndrews's crusty voice, from the engine room below. "Control passed to bridge." Naturally, the console's indicators from the engine room were simulations; Captain Haag wasn't about to Defuse for a mere middy drill.

"Passed to bridge, aye aye." I put my index finger to the top of the drive screen and traced a line from "Full" to "Off." The simulscreens came alive with a blaze of lights, and I gasped though I'd known to expect it. Stars burned everywhere, in vastly greater numbers than could be imagined groundside.

"Confirm clear of encroachments, Lieutenant. Please," I added. After the drill she'd still be my superior officer. Lieutenant Dagalow bent to her console.

Our first priority in emerging from Fusion was to make sure there were no planetary bodies or vessels about. The chance was one in billions, but not one we took lightly. Darla always ran a sensor check, but despite the triple redundancy built into each of her systems, we didn't rely on her sensors. Navigation was based on an overriding principle: don't trust machinery. Everything was rechecked by hand.

"Clear of encroachments, Mr. Seafort." Technically Ms. Dagalow should have called me "sir" during the drill, while I acted as Captain, but I wasn't about to remind her of that.

"Plot position, please, ma'am. I mean, Lieutenant."

Lieutenant Dagalow set the puter to plot our position on her star charts. The screen filled with numbers as a cheerful feminine voice announced, "Position is plotted, Mr. Seafort."

"Thank you, Darla." The puter dimmed her screens slightly in response. I'm not going to get into the age-old question: was she really alive? That one caused more barroom fights than everything else put together. My personal opinion was—well, never mind, it doesn't matter. Ship's custom was to respond to the puter as a person. All the correct responses to polite phrases and banter were built into her. At Academy, they'd told us crewmen found it easier to relate to a puter with human mannerisms.

"Calculate the new coordinates, please," I said. Lieutenant Dagalow leaned forward to comply.

Captain Haag intervened. "The Lieutenant is ill. You'll have to plot them yourself."

"Aye aye, sir." It took twenty-five minutes, and by the time I was done I'd broken out in a sweat. I was fairly sure I was right, but fairly sure isn't good enough when the Captain is watching from the next seat. I punched in the new Fusion coordinates for the short jump that would carry us to Hope Nation.

"Coordinates received and understood, Mr. Seafort." Darla.

"Chief Engineer, Fuse, please."

"Aye aye, sir. Fusion drive is . . . on." The screens abruptly went blank as Darla simulated reentry into Fusion.

"Very well, Mr. Seafort," the Captain said smoothly. "How long did you estimate second Fusion?"

"Eighty-two days, sir."

"Eighty-two days have passed." He typed a sequence into his console. "Proceed."

Again I brought the ship out of Fusion. After screening out the overpowering presence of the G-type Hope Nation sun, we could detect Orbit Station circling the planet. Lieutenant Dagalow confirmed that we were clear of encroachments. Then she became ill again and, increasingly edgy, I had to plot manual approach myself.

"Auxiliary engine power, Chief." My tone was a bark; my grip on the caller made my wrist ache.

"Aye aye, sir. Power up." Mr. McAndrews must have been waiting for the signal. Of course he would be; Lord God knows how many midshipmen he'd put through nav drill over the years.

"Steer oh three five degrees, ahead two-thirds."

"Two-thirds, aye aye, sir." The console showed our engine power increasing. Nervously I reminded myself that *Hibernia* was still cruising in Fusion, that all this was but a drill.

I glanced at the simulscreen. "Declination ten degrees."

"Ten degrees, aye aye, sir."

I approached Orbit Station with caution. Easily visible in the screens, it grew steadily larger. I braked the ship for final approach.

"Steer oh four oh, Lieutenant."

"Aye aye, sir."

"Sir, Orbit Station reports locks ready and waiting."

"Confirm ready and waiting, understood," I repeated, trying to absorb the flood of information from our instruments.

Dagalow said, "Relative speed two hundred kilometers per hour, Mr. Seafort."

"Two hundred, understood. Maneuvering jets, brake fifteen." Propellant squirted from the jets to brake the ship's forward motion.

"Relative speed one hundred fifteen kilometers, distance twenty-one kilometers."

Still too fast. "Brake jets, eighteen." We slowed further, but the braking threw off our approach. I adjusted by tapping the side maneuvering jets.

Our conventional engines burned LH_2 and LOX as propellant; water was cheap and *Hibernia*'s fusion engines provided ample energy to convert it, but there was a limit to how much we could carry. To go faster we would spend more water. We'd spend an equal amount slowing down; nothing was free. Theoretically we could sail to Hope Nation on a few spoonfuls of LH_2 and LOX, but not in our lifetimes. How much time was worth how much loss of propellant? That depended on how much maneuvering lay ahead. A nice logistics problem with many variables.

Mine was not a smooth approach. I backed and filled, wasting precious propellant as I tried to align the ship to the two waiting airlocks. Captain Haag said nothing. Finally I was in position, our airlocks two hundred meters apart, our velocity zero relative to Orbit Station.

"Steer two seven oh, two spurts." That would move our pencil to the left, still parallel with the nearby station. It did, far too fast. I had forgotten how little fuel is needed for a correction at close quarters. *Hibernia*'s nose swung perilously close to the station's waiting airlock.

I panicked. "Brake ninety, one spurt!"

Lieutenant Dagalow entered the command, her face impassive.

Lord God in heaven! I'd compounded my error by pulling away the tail of the ship, instead of the nose. "Brake two seven oh, all jets!"

The screen darkened as Orbit Station loomed into our shadow.

Alarm bells shrilled. The screen suddenly jerked askew. My hand flew to the console to brace myself for a jolt that never came.

Darla's shrill voice overrode the screaming alarms. "Loss of seal, forward cargo compartment!"

Ms. Dagalow shouted, "Shear damage amidships!"

The main screen lurched. Darla's voice was urgent. "*EMERGENCY!* The disk has struck! Decompression in Level 2!" I was sick with horror.

Captain Haag pushed his master switch. The alarms quieted to blessed silence. "You've killed half the passengers," he said heavily. "Over a third of your crew is in the decompression zone and is most likely dead. Your ship is out of control. The rupture in the hull is bigger than the forward airlock."

I'd done more damage to my ship than even *Celestina* had sustained. I closed my eyes, unable to speak.

"Stand, Mr. Seafort."

I stumbled to my feet, managed to come to attention.

"You didn't do all that badly until the docking," the Captain said, not unkindly. "You were slow, but you got the ship into correct position. You failed to anticipate decisions, and so you had too much to do in a short time. As a result you lost your ship."

"Yes, sir." I'd lost my ship, all right. And with it any chance of making lieutenant before home port.

He surprised me. "Review the manual again, Seafort. As many times as it takes. By next drill I'll expect you to have it right."

"Aye aye, sir."

"Dismissed." I slunk out.

It was the worst day of my life.

"I don't want to talk about it, Amanda." She was perched on her bed in her ample cabin on Level 1, while I sat on the deck nearby.

I was off duty, and ship's regs permitted officers to socialize with passengers. Sensibly enough, the Naval powers had decided to endorse what they could not prevent.

"Nicky, everyone makes mistakes. Don't punish yourself, just do better next time."

My tone was bitter. "Vax and Alexi dock the ship and come out alive. I'm the senior midshipman and I can't."

"You will," she soothed. "Study and you will."

I didn't tell her how Lieutenant Cousins would have to coach me all over again to prepare for the drill. When he was done I'd be lucky if I could remember how to dress myself. I writhed in disgust. I didn't normally panic; I handled some problems reasonably well or I wouldn't have made it through Academy. But knowing everyone's life depended on me was too much. I knew I'd never be able to cope.

Morose, I settled into a chair. "I'm sorry I bothered you with this, Amanda."

"Oh, Nicky, don't be silly. We're friends, aren't we?" Yes, but that's all we were. I'd have liked to be more, but there were three long years between us and she didn't seem interested. "Why do they torture midshipmen with those drills, anyway? That's what the Pilot is for."

"The Captain is in charge of the ship," I said patiently. "Always. Pilot Haynes, like the Chief Engineer and the Doctor, is staff, not a line officer."

"What's that supposed to mean?"

"It means he's not in the chain of command. If the Captain fell ill, the first lieutenant would command, then Ms. Dagalow, then Lieutenant Malstrom."

"But you'd still have the Pilot to dock the ship. Everybody can't be sick or gone."

"But the Pilot wouldn't be ultimately responsible. It's not his ship."

"Still, it's silly to expect boys just out of cadet academy to know how to fly the ship."

"Sail. Sail the ship."

"What's the difference? You know what I mean."

I tried to explain. "Amanda, we're here to learn what the lieutenants and the Captain do. That's what the drills are for."

"I still think it's silly," Amanda said stubbornly. "And cruel." I let it be.

3

"Turn that thing down, Alexi." I got myself ready for bed. It had been a bad day all around and I was cross.

"Sorry, Mr. Seafort." Quickly he lowered the volume of his holovid. Just a year younger than I, Alexi Tamarov was everything I wanted to be: slim, graceful, good-natured, and competent. But he was addicted to his slap music, while my own taste ran to classical composers: Lennon, Jackson, and Biederbeck.

I regretted my temper, but still, I thanked Lord God I was senior and had the right to order the music turned low. I'd have managed somehow even if I weren't in charge, but life had enough trials without that. As senior, I had my choice of bunks and got first serving at morning and afternoon mess, and I supposedly controlled the wardroom, though I was aware my authority was precarious at best.

In a Naval vessel, midshipmen were thrown together with little forethought. Fresh from Academy or with years of service, we were expected to live and work together smoothly. By ship's regs it was the senior middy's duty to run the wardroom, but tradition gave any middy the right to challenge him. In that case the two would fight it out. Because conflicts were inevitable and their resolution necessary, officers turned a blind eye to the scrapes, black eyes, or bruises a midshipman might develop from interacting with his fellows.

Vax Holser and I had an unspoken understanding; he bullied the other middies, and we left each other alone. We both knew that if I pulled rank on him I'd have to back it up. I ignored his calling me "Nicky" with barely concealed contempt; beyond that, we both avoided the test.

Vax stirred, opened one eye to glare at Alexi. I hoped he wouldn't start anything, but he growled, "You're an asshole."

Alexi made no reply.

"Did you hear me?"

"I heard you." Alexi knew he couldn't tangle with Vax.

"Tell me you're an asshole." The trouble with Vax was that once he started he wouldn't let up.

Alexi glanced at me. I was noncommittal.

"I don't feel like getting up, Tamarov. Tell me."

"I'm an asshole!" Alexi snapped off the holovid and threw himself on his bed, facing the partition. His back was tight.

"I already knew that." Vax sounded annoyed.

In the unpleasant silence I glumly recalled my arrival a few weeks before. Lugging my gear, I'd reported to *Hibernia* at Earthport Station, the huge concourse orbiting above Lunapolis City. Preoccupied with loading the incoming stores, Lieutenant Cousins glanced at my sheaf of papers and sent me to find the wardroom on my own.

As I bent awkwardly to open the wardroom hatch a figure cannoned outward through the hatchway, propelling me across the corridor, duffel underfoot, papers flying. I fetched up against the far bulkhead in disarray. My shoulder felt broken.

"Wilsky, get your ass in here!" The bellow came from within.

The young middy froze in horror as I swiped helplessly at a cascade of papers. He darted forward and bent to help me pick up my documents. "You're Wilsky?" was all I could think to say.

"Yes, uh, sir," he said, glancing at my length of service pins, knowing instantly that I was his senior.

"Who's that?" I beckoned to the closed hatch.

"That's Mr. Holser, sir. He's in charge. He was going—" Wilsky grimaced as the hatch sprang open. A huge form loomed over us.

"What the devil do you think—" The muscular midshipman frowned down at me as I crouched in the corridor stuffing papers back into their folders. "Are you the new middy?"

"Yes." I stood. Automatically I checked his length of service pins. When I got my orders I was told I'd be first middy, but mistakes happen.

"You can put your—" His face went white. "What the bloody hell!" With dismay, I realized that no one had told him. He'd thought he was going to be senior.

Remembering, I sighed. Our first month had not been easy, and I had seventeen more to endure before landfall. I couldn't physically overpower Vax Holser. Unfortunately, I didn't know how I could tolerate him either.

"It is precisely because of that, Mrs. Donhauser, because the distances are so great and the voyages so long, that authority is made so rigid and discipline so harsh."

Mrs. Donhauser listened closely to Khali Ibn Saud, our amateur sociologist and, by profession, an interplanetary banker.

It was a quiet afternoon some two months into the voyage, and I was sitting in the Level 2 passengers' lounge.

"I'd think distance would have the opposite effect," she countered. "As people got farther from central government, bonds of authority would be loosened."

"Yes!" His tone was excited, as if Mrs. Donhauser had proven his point. "They certainly would, if all were left alone. But central authority, our government, reacts, you see? To maintain control it provides rules and standards and insists we adhere to them regardless of circumstances. And our government is willing to invest time and effort in enforcing them."

The lounge was decorated in pale green, said to be a calming color. From the look of Mr. Barstow, sound asleep in a recliner, the decor was effective. The size of two passenger staterooms, the lounge could seat at least fifteen passengers comfortably. It was furnished with upholstered chairs, recliners, a bench, two game tables, and an intelligent coffee/softie dispenser.

I was only half interested in the debate. Mr. Ibn Saud's theory was not new. In fact, they had presented it better at Academy.

Mrs. Donhauser appealed to me. "Tell him, young man. Isn't it true that the Captain is his own authority here in midspace? That he answers to no one?"

"That's two questions," I answered. "Yes, and no. The Captain is the ultimate authority on a vessel under weigh. He answers to no one aboard ship. But his conduct is prescribed by the regs. If he deviates from them, on his return he will be removed, or worse."

"So you see," Ibn Saud said triumphantly, "central authority is maintained even in the depths of space."

"Foo!" she threw at him. "The Captain can sail slower, faster, even take a detour if he wishes. Central government has nothing to say about it."

He shrugged, looking at me as if to ask, "What's the use?"

"Mrs. Donhauser," I offered, "I think you make a mistake trying to contrast the Captain's powers with United Nations authority. The Captain isn't opposed to central authority. He IS that authority. Legally he can marry people, divorce them, even try and execute them. He has absolute and undiluted control of the vessel." That last was a quote from an official commentary on the regs; I threw it in because it sounded good. "There was a ship. *Cleopatra*. Have you heard of it?"

"No. Should I?"

"It was about fifty years ago. The Captain, I don't remember his name—"

"Jennings," put in Ibn Saud, his head bobbing in anticipation of my point.

"Captain Jennings acted quite strangely. The officers conferred with the Doctor and relieved him of command on grounds of mental illness. They confined him to quarters and sailed the ship directly to Earthport Station." I paused for effect.

"So?"

"They were hanged, every one of them. A court-martial found them mistaken in believing the Captain unfit for command. Even though they acted in good faith, they were all hanged." A silence grew. "You see, the government is absolutely determined to maintain authority, even in space," I said. "The Captain is the representative of the government, as well as the Church, and he must not be overturned."

"It's a bizarre case!"

"It could happen today, Mrs. Donhauser."

"And besides, that must have been a Naval vessel," she said. "Not a passenger ship."

That was too much for me. You'd think people would know what they were getting themselves into. "Ma'am, you may be confused because *Hibernia* has a Naval crew, carries a full complement of civilian passengers, and has a hold full of private cargo. What counts is that the Captain and every member of the crew are Naval officers and seamen. *Hibernia* is a commissioned Naval vessel. By law the Navy carries all cargo bound for the colonies, but legally that cargo is no more than ballast. And the passengers, technically, are just extra cargo. You have no rights aboard this ship and no say whatsoever in what happens on board." I spoke courteously, of course. A midshipman overheard insulting a passenger was not likely to do so again.

"Oh, really?" She was unfazed. I decided she would make a formidable missionary. "Well, it just so happens we vote on our menus, we have committees to run social functions, we elect the Passengers' Council, we even voted on whether to stop at the *Celestina* wreck next week. So where's your dictatorship now?"

"Window dressing," I said. "Look. You have to be a VIP to afford an interstellar voyage, right? The Navy doesn't go out of its way to alienate important people. All of us, officers and crew, are required to be polite to passengers and to assent to your wishes wherever possible. Because you're valuable you get the best accommodations, the best food, our best service. But that changes nothing. The Captain can override any of your votes anytime he has a mind to." I wondered if I'd gone too far.

The feisty old battle-ax put me at ease. "You argue well, young man. I'll think it over. Next time I see you I'll tell you why you're wrong."

I grinned. "I look forward to the lesson, ma'am."

I stretched, excused myself, and went back to Level 1 and the wardroom. Whatever arguments Mrs. Donhauser marshaled wouldn't change a thing. The U.N. knew our world had had enough of anarchy. Central control was not imposed by the government on an unwilling populace. Rather, it was appreciated and respected by the vast mass of citizens. Brushfire wars and chaotic revolutions had finally ceased; our resulting prosperity had powered our explosion into space and the colonization of planets such as Hope Nation and Detour. The Navy, the senior U.N. military service, was the U.N.'s bulwark against the forces of diffusion inherent in a colonial system.

I stripped off my uniform and crawled into my bunk, trying not to wake Alexi. Lieutenant Cousins had set him over the barrel yesterday. Now Alexi had to eat standing, and he wasn't sleeping well. One learned to live with canings, but I knw Alexi too well to believe he'd been insolent and insubordinate as the lieutenant had alleged. Cousins was having a bad day, or was looking for an excuse to assert his authority.

According to regs any middy could be caned, but tradition held there was a dividing line. Alexi, at sixteen, should have been over the line except for a grievous offense. By statute Lieutenant Cousins was within his rights, but not by custom. Alexi was miserable but hadn't complained, which was right and proper.

I slept.

4

Two weeks later they gave me another docking drill. It took me forever to plot our course. I labored an hour just to calculate our position, until even the Captain was fidgeting with annoyance. By the time I came off the bridge I was wringing wet, but I hadn't wrecked the ship, though I'd bumped the airlocks together fairly hard.

I went looking for Amanda to tell her of my accomplishment. I found her in the passengers' lounge watching a holovid epic. She turned it off and listened instead to my excited replay of my maneuvers.

Though I no longer sat at her table in the dining hall, Amanda and I were becoming good friends. We took long walks together around the circumference corridor. We read together in her cabin. She told me about her father's textile concern, and I told her stories of Academy days. Our only physical contact was to hold hands. I could have slept with her; it wasn't against regs, and I lined up with the other middies for my sterility shot from Doc Uburu every month. But she didn't invite me and I couldn't push, not with a passenger.

A few days after my success on the bridge I relaxed on my bunk, watching Sandy tease Ricky Fuentes, our ship's boy.

"C'n I try it? Please, sir? Please?" The ship's boy reached for the orchestron Sandy held over his head, grinning. We all liked Ricky, a happy twelve-year-old. Even Vax was congenial to him. The youngster's trusting good nature encouraged it.

The ship's boy roamed crew quarters, officers' country, and passenger lounges with impunity. It was all part of his job as ship's gofer. Ricky took messages, retrieved gear that crewmen or officers forgot, generally made himself useful. Every capital ship had a ship's boy, usually an orphan of a career sailor. Traditionally, he graduated to seaman first class and usually made petty officer before he was twenty.

Sandy gave him his orchestron. The boy selected harpsichord, French horn, and tuba, set down a bongo beat, and tapped out a simple melody on the tiny keyboard. He set it to repeat. Then he set up a counterpoint, using different instruments.

Ricky listened to the orchestron develop the theme he had created. "Zarky! Real zarky!" I think that meant he liked it. I was only five years older than he, but joespeak changes fast. The machine burbled to a stop. "Thanks, Sandy, I gotta run. I'm helping in the kitchen tonight. I mean the galley. Bye, sir!" He ran off.

At Ricky's age, I was chopping wood for Father. I wasn't outgoing and sociable, as he was. I never would be. At home Father and I didn't talk often, and we certainly didn't laugh.

Sandy left, and I dozed.

Sometime later Vax came and slapped the light on, waking me from a pleasant dream.

I muttered, "Turn it off, will you?"

He ignored me, undressing slowly.

"Vax, turn off the bloody light!"

"Sure, Nicky." He slapped it off, managing to express contempt with the gesture.

Perhaps it was the heavy dinner, or the lack of exercise. Drugged and lethargic, I fell instantly back to sleep.

Sometime later I was aware of a complaining voice. "It's cold. Turn the heat up, Wilsky." I heard the rustle of sheets as Sandy dragged himself out of bed to dial up the heat.

A few minutes later Vax started again. "Sandy, it's too hot. Turn it down." Once again the boy got up and turned off the heat. This time it took me longer to get back to my dream.

"Turn the heat up, Wilsky!"

I snapped awake, inwardly raging. Alexi groaned. Sandy, who must have been asleep, did not answer.

"Wilsky, you damned asshole, get up and give us some heat!" Now Vax was adding blasphemy to his boorishness. I heard the rustle of sheets as Sandy climbed out of his bunk and adjusted the temperature.

I lay awake, debating. I wouldn't protect Sandy from all Vax's hazing, but there came a point when Sandy had enough. More would cause him emotional problems. For that matter, more would cause ME emotional problems. Where should I draw the line? And how could I do it without getting my head knocked off by the muscular gorilla in the next bunk, and permanently losing control of the wardroom?

"Now turn it down."

"It's fine in here," I heard myself say.

"It's hot. That jerkoff doesn't know how to adjust it properly."

"Get up and do it yourself, Vax."

He ignored me. "Wilsky, put your pretty little ass on the deck and fix the heat!"

I'd had enough. "Stay put, Sandy. That's an order."

"Aye aye, Mr. Seafort." His tone was grateful.

"What in hell are you pulling, Nicky?"

I tried to sound authoritative. "Enough, Vax."

"The hell you say!" So much for my sounding authoritative.

"Vax, turn the light on." I waited, but he did nothing, forcing the issue. From the silent breathing I knew we were all awake. "Alexi, get up. Turn on the light."

"Aye aye, Mr. Seafort." Alexi slapped the light switch, his eyes bleary, hair tousled. Quickly he sank back into bed, out of harm's way. Vax sat up, glaring.

I lay back in my bunk, arm behind my head. "Vax, please give me twenty push-ups." I was in big trouble.

"Prong yourself, Nicky."

I heard Alexi's sharp intake of breath.

"Vax, twenty push-ups. That's an order."

"Don't be more of an ass than you can help." Vax's challenge was now in the open. Give me orders? Enforce them—if you can. He had the right, according to custom. But a first middy wasn't entirely without resources.

"This is a direct order, Vax. Twenty push-ups, on the deck."

"No. You're not man enough to give orders. Not inside the wardroom." A wise distinction. His challenge was to my authority in the wardroom, not to ship's authority in general.

"Mr. Holser, put yourself on report at once." That meant, go knock on the first lieutenant's hatch and tell him I had written you up for insubordination. It would most likely cause him to be put over the barrel, even at his age.

"You've got to be kidding. You know what that'll do to you."

I knew. "Mr. Holser, go to the duty officer, forthwith, and place yourself on report."

"I will not." Vax was taking a chance, but not a big one. He knew as well as I that a middy who called on an officer for help to run his wardroom was finished in the service.

"Alexi."

"Yes, Mr. Seafort?"

"Put your pants on, go to the duty officer, and tell him the senior midshipman reports a mutiny in the wardroom. Mr. Holser is written up but refuses to obey a direct order to place himself on report. I request a court-martial to determine the validity of my allegations."

"Aye aye, sir." Alexi threw aside the covers and reached for his trousers.

"Belay that, Alexi. You can't do it, Nick." Vax's tone was urgent. "It'll ruin you too. You'll never get command if you can't even hold a wardroom. You won't even get another posting!"

"That's no longer your concern, Mr. Holser." I remained icily formal; it was my only chance. "Mr. Wilsky."

"Yes, sir?"

"Dress yourself. Go to crew quarters. Wake the master-at-arms. Have him bring an escort to the wardroom, flank. As for you, Vax, you are under arrest."

"Aye aye, sir." Sandy was so nervous his voice soared into the upper registers. Frantically, he began throwing on his clothes.

Alexi, dressed, headed for the hatch. Vax grabbed his arm in a huge hand. "Nick, call it off. This is a wardroom matter. Settle it here, among us!"

I had him.

"It's too late, Vax. You ignored my order. Let go of Alexi." I lay motionless, under my covers.

"Hold off, Nick. Talk it through." He hesitated. "Please." Vax knew that I'd throw away my career if the two junior middies went on their errands. He also knew that he himself now faced court-martial and almost certain imprisonment in the brig, if not summary dismissal from the Navy.

I made my tone reluctant. "Alexi, Sandy, sit down." I turned to Vax. "I'll turn the clock back, Mr. Holser. Twenty push-ups."

He stared, trying to read me. I looked away. I didn't care what he thought he saw in my face. Apparently my indifference convinced him; he got down on the deck. "We'll settle this later, Nick." It was a growl.

"Yes, we will." I spoke with confidence I didn't feel.

He gave me twenty push-ups. Good ones, like the Academy taught in basic. At the end he got up on one knee.

"Now twenty more." This time I stared him straight in the eye.

Having given in the first time he had little choice. Rigid with fury, he did twenty more push-ups.

"Thank you." I looked at the two junior middies. "Back to bed, you two."

Neither dared say a word. Vax was still a potent force in their lives. He stood up and yanked on his clothes. "It's a good time for a walk, Nicky," he spat. "Care to join me?"

At that moment I regretted not letting him order Sandy in and out of bed all night, if he wished. Vax was twenty kilos heavier, a head taller, and a lot stronger than I was. And two years older, as well. I was about to get the tar beaten out of me, and I had no choice but to go through with it. I got out of bed and put on my pants, socks, and shoes. I didn't put anything over my undershirt; no point in ruining a dress shirt or jacket.

We strode in silence to the passenger exercise room on Level 2. At that hour, past midnight, it was deserted. He went in first.

I knew the best thing was to circle while he stalked me, and try to avoid his lunges. He knew I knew that. So the moment I was through the hatchway I hurled myself straight at him, fists flailing at his face. I got in a few good licks before he got his cover up and held me off. I backed away.

He came at me, livid with anger. I backed away again. He drove at me faster, and again I went right at him, hammering. He caught me a good one on the side of the head that made me dizzy, but momentum carried me past his guard and I was all over him, pounding at his stomach, chest, jaw. Then I unexpectedly dropped down and rolled away.

He was disconcerted, as I wanted him to be. My only chance was to do what he least expected. He came at me warily this time, guard up. I went into karate position. He did the same. We both feinted. I fended him off, but he steadily advanced, pushing me toward the corner. I had no choice but to retreat.

The next few minutes were bad. He got in a lot of blows, knocking me down, slapping my head back and forth, slamming me into the partition, raining punches on my chest and arms. I wasn't strong enough to hold him off so I concentrated on convincing him he was hurting me more than he really was. It wasn't easy, because he hurt me plenty.

I staggered, apparently semiconscious, blood flowing freely from my nose and mouth. My legs buckled. He grabbed under my arms with both hands, holding me as I sagged. It was what I'd waited for. I drove my fist into his crotch with all the strength I could muster.

Vax bent over in reflex, let go to clutch himself. I backed away, wiping blood off my face. Damn, he could hit. Vax leaned against the bulkhead, his eyes half shut, face white.

My arms ached from the pounding they had taken. I didn't have strength left to hit hard. So, clasping my hands together, I bent and, like a battering ram, ran straight at him. My shoulder smashed into his side. He went down. So did I. He was a rock.

Vax scrambled to his feet, a murderous look in his eye, fists clenched. I got up, put my head down, and rammed him again. This time he bounced off a bulkhead. My shoulder was numb. We both staggered to our feet. His nose bled from his impact with the bulkhead. I lunged again. He had both hands out, and fended me off. I put my shoulder down and dug in, straining to ram him.

"Wait!" His breath came hard.

I backed off. "Prong yourself, joey." I lowered my head and charged. He tried to knee my face, but was too slow. I butted him in the stomach and he toppled over. I wondered if I had broken my neck. After a moment I managed to get up. So did he.

"Enough!" Vax covered his stomach with both hands.

I leaned against the partition, trying not to black out.

"Truce." He held up his hand as if pushing me off. I waited, trying to catch my breath enough to answer. "I can't take you, Nick. And you can't take me. Truce."

"No." I drove at him again. I didn't have much left but he was too busy clutching his aching ribs to fight back. He slid down to the slippery deck, then pulled himself back up.

"For God's sake, Nicky, enough! Neither of us wins."

I nodded. "Lay off Sandy," I gasped. "You're hazing too hard."

"Hazing's part of it."

"Not that much. Haze him some, but lay off when I say."

He nodded reluctantly. "All right. Deal."

"I'll leave you alone," I said. "And you don't look for trouble with me."

"Deal." He swallowed. Cautiously, he tried letting go of his stomach.

"And you don't call me Nick in the wardroom." If I didn't get it this time, I'd never have another chance.

"No." He looked stubborn. "Not that."

I launched myself at him. He put out both arms to block me but my charge knocked him into the bulkhead. Instead of backing off I rammed him with my shoulder again and again, thumping his ribs and back. I wasn't doing much damage but he was too exhausted to deck me.

My vision went red. I heard grunting, his or mine, as I felt myself slip into total exhaustion. Then I became aware that he held both my arms in his big hands, holding me at arm's length away from his body. I was braced against the deck, straining to get at him.

"Truce," Vax said again. "Truce—Mr. Seafort."

I slumped back. "Name?" I managed.

"Your name is Mr. Seafort." He didn't look at me with fondness, but his expression held a wary respect I hadn't seen before.

"Truce," I agreed.

We staggered out of the room and back up to Level 1, neither saying a word. I went directly to the shower. I stood under the warm spray, watching my blood swirl down the drain to the recycler in the fusion drive chamber below. I didn't pretend I was victorious.

I had survived. It was enough.

5

To my surprise, the greatest change in the wardroom wasn't how Vax acted toward the other middies. He remained surly to them, and they were still cautious in his presence. It was not in how Vax acted toward me. He spoke to me as seldom as possible and rarely used my name, but when he did, it was Seafort and not Nicky.

No, the biggest difference was in how the other juniors acted toward me. Because I'd stood up to Vax and survived I was unquestionably in charge as far as they were concerned, and they were eager to win my approval.

Alexi in particular seemed to undergo a case of hero worship. He and Sandy straightened my bunk, crease-ironed my pants along with their own, and showed me unexpected deference. Though I tried hard not to let it show, I loved it.

Vax, for his part, eased off on his hazing. One day I came upon him forcing Alexi to stand naked in an ice-cold shower. When I ordered him to lay off, he did, without argument. Alexi stumbled quickly out of the shower room, blue with cold and trembling from humiliation. Perhaps Vax felt that having given his word he had to keep it, but my interference didn't make him any more friendly.

I reported for watch each day, sometimes with Mr. Cousins, occasionally with Ms. Dagalow. With Lieutenant Cousins I sat stiffly, hoping to stay out of trouble. Ms. Dagalow, though no Dosman, chatted about puters, as she often did. Though I didn't share her interest, I enjoyed her company and did my best to please her by learning what I could.

The next week I was transferred to engine room watch. There Chief McAndrews tried to teach me the intricacies of the fusion drive. I discovered that I had little aptitude for it. By now I'd shown myself impossibly slow at astronavigation, thoroughly muddled as a pilot, and hopelessly inept as a drive technician. Vax was older, bigger, and stronger. Both Vax and Alexi were better able to handle the crew. I was proving incompetent at navigation, pilotage, engineering, and leadership. An ideal midshipman.

Except for chess. I could concentrate on that; I didn't feel our thirty-second limit as pressure. I always looked forward to my afternoon

game with Lieutenant Malstrom. But one day when we set up the board
his manner was subdued. I led with queen's pawn, and before I knew it
I had trapped him in a fool's mate in five moves. He was not a good
player, overall, but he was far better than that.

We started to put away the pieces. "What's wrong, sir?" I had
known and liked this man for months now, but nonetheless I'd taken a
daring step. A middy does not ask a personal question of a lieutenant. It
is not done.

Lieutenant Malstrom looked at me without speaking. He began
unbuttoning his shirt. He pulled it out of his pants, rolled it up from his
waist. He turned, showing me his side. Just above his hip was an ugly
blue-gray lump.

I met his eye. "What is it, Mr. Malstrom?" By not using his rank I
was getting as close to him as I could. We were friends.

He said the words so quietly I could barely hear him. "Malignant
melanoma."

"Melanoma T?"

"Doc thinks it might be."

My breath hissed. The disease was an occupational hazard. In Fusion, it was impossible to shield ourselves from the N-waves that drove
the ship, and over time N-waves transmuted ordinary carcinoma to the
virulent T form that grew with astonishing speed.

Like all of us, Mr. Malstrom had shipped interstellar as an adolescent, and should have been nearly immune.

"At least they're not sure, sir." I tried to look on the hopeful side.
Most forms of cancer were easily cured nowadays, hardly worse than a
bad cold. But the new strain of melanoma didn't respond well to drugs.
The treatment of choice was still amputation of the affected part, where
possible.

I asked, "Have you been treated?"

"Tomorrow morning. Radiation and anticar drugs. They caught it
early; Doc Uburu says I have a good chance."

"I'm very sorry, sir."

"Harv." He caught my look. "Here in my quarters. My name is
Harv." He must really have been shaken. I forced myself to say his
unfamiliar name.

"I'm sorry, Harv. You'll be all right. I know you will."

"I hope so, Nicky." He tucked in his shirt. "Don't mention it to the
others."

"Of course not." The Captain would know, of course. Perhaps the
other lieutenants. But the middies need not be told, or the seamen.

"I'll go on sick leave for a few days, in case the anticars get me down. You can come give me chess lessons."

I grinned as I stood at the hatch. "Every day, sir." I snapped him a salute. It was a sign of affection and he knew it. He returned it and I left.

"Lord God, today is January 2, 2195, on the U.N.S. *Hibernia.* We ask you to bless us, to bless our voyage, and to bring health and well-being to all aboard."

"Amen," I said fervently. Lieutenant Malstrom was absent. Amanda and I were again at the same table. This time I was thrown in with a colonist family of five journeying to a new life on Detour, our port of call beyond Hope Nation. The unspoiled resources of these newer colonies attracted many like the Treadwells, eager to escape the pollution and regimentation of overcrowded Earth. At home we had Luna, of course, and the Mars colony. But some people weren't attracted to dome or warren life. They sought open space and fresh air that was ever harder to find.

Not everyone could emigrate, certainly. Only the wealthy could afford it. Though I admired the quest that was taking them sixty-nine light-years from home, I wondered how the Treadwells had managed it. She was a gaunt prim woman whose hands darted restlessly. Her husband, squat, swarthy and muscular, looked more a laborer than the habitat engineer the manifests showed him to be.

Their oldest children were twins poised on the edge of adolescence. Paula, wearing a shade too much shadow, and Rafe, all awkward knees and elbows, seemed so vulnerable they recalled my own painful thirteenth year, roaming Cardiff with my best friend Jason. I stirred uneasily, recollecting my discomfort at his hand on my shoulder, aware of his acknowledged sexual proclivity and dubious of my own. I also remembered, at Jason's casual touch, Father's silent look that spoke volumes of reproach.

Both Rafe and Paula seemed awestruck by Naval life and in love with anyone who wore the uniform. Rafe pestered me for information, as he had Doc Uburu and Ms. Dagalow before me. Paula asked about joining up, what Academy was like, how old you had to be to enter.

Ms. Treadwell frowned. "The Navy's no place for a lady."

"Oh, Irene." Paula's voice dripped with condescension. "What about Lieutenant Dagalow, at the next table?"

I tried not to wince. I couldn't imagine calling my own father anything but "Father" or "Sir."

"Look into it when we get to Detour." Their mother flashed me an apologetic smile. "You can't enlist in the middle of a cruise." Their faces fell. Another fantasy gone.

I tried to cheer them up. "That's not quite true, Ms. Treadwell. The Captain has authority to enlist civilians as officers or crew. It's almost never done, but it's possible." The Captain also had authority to impress civilians into service in an emergency, but I didn't mention that.

The twins fell to talking among themselves. They decided to persuade Captain Haag to let them join up, with or without their parents' permission. Their younger sister Tara, six, said little. We adults drifted into another conversation. Jared Treadwell asked, "Is it true, Mr. Seafort, that this ship is actually armed?"

"All U.N. ships have weapons, Mr. Treadwell." I smiled. "It's an odd and ancient precaution. There's nobody to use them against, except now and then a few planetside bandits, and the ship's lasers are not designed for antiguerrilla operations. They're like male nipples: standard equipment, but useless."

My sally drew a nervous laugh from his wife. Groundside attitudes were fairly staightlaced. It was fun to scan old holovids about the Rebellious Ages, but I couldn't imagine a young couple who showed up unmarried with a baby, or even tried to swim naked on a beach. Of course modern birth control has separated casual copulation, which is tolerated in any combination of sexes, from casual reproduction, which is not.

The next day all four middies had astronavigation drill with Lieutenant Cousins. I worked my problems as well as I could, while Mr. Cousins shook his head in disgust at my mistakes. Vax got everything right, as usual. Then Alexi fouled up a really easy problem and put the ship dead in the middle of a hypothetical sun.

Lieutenant Cousins glared at Alexi's console, withering contempt dripping from his every word. "You incompetent child! God damn your eyes, Mr. Tamarov, you're hopeless!"

That was too much. Alexi knew it. So, belatedly, did Cousins. Even Vax caught my eye and slowly shook his head.

Alexi got to his feet, nervously drawing himself to attention. He had opened his mouth to speak when Mr. Cousins forestalled him. "I apologize, Mr. Tamarov." He glanced around. "To you and to all present. I spoke out of anger and not intent. I mean no disrespect to Lord God."

Alexi sat in relief, and there was silence in the cabin. I knew Lieutenant Cousins, for all his bullyragging, wouldn't hold Alexi's objection against him. Blasphemy was no more tolerated aboard ship than it was groundside. The lieutenant could find himself on the beach for that kind of talk.

For three days Lieutenant Malstrom showed no ill effects. Then he took to his bed, his side bandaged. We played chess daily, sometimes two or three games. I didn't quite let him win, but I tried some unusual variations I wouldn't have risked otherwise. Sometimes they didn't work.

A week later he raised his shirt to show me his side. The ominous blue mass was gone; in its place was a red welt that was fading in places to white. Unthinking, I clapped him on the shoulder. "It worked!"

He grinned. "I think so, Nicky. Doc says I should be all right."

"Fantastic!" I jumped up, too excited to be still. "Oh, Harv, sir, that's wonderful!"

"Yes. I have my life back."

We were too keyed up for chess. Instead, we talked about what to expect on Hope Nation. We'd both seen the holovids but I'd never traveled interstellar before, and Mr. Malstrom hadn't been to Hope Nation. He promised to take me sightseeing in the fabled Ventura Mountains during our stopover. I promised him a double asteroid on the rocks at the first bar we came to.

Happy and relaxed, I went back to the wardroom to change. Vax lay on his side and glowered the whole time I was there. I said nothing; he did likewise. By the time I left, my good cheer had evaporated.

Alexi had the middy watch when we Defused to search for *Celestina*. We were fortunate; though far away, her beacons registered on the sensors' first try. Under Lisa Dagalow's watchful eye, Alexi plotted a course to the derelict ship. The lieutenant rechecked his figures. They agreed with Darla's; we Fused again, a short jump to where the abandoned ship floated.

I pulled watch two days later when we Defused once more. Lieutenant Cousins and I were on the bridge waiting, as the Captain took the conn. "Bridge to engine room, prepare to Defuse."

"Prepare to Defuse, aye aye, sir." A moment passed. "Engine room ready for Defuse, sir. Control passed to bridge."

"Passed to bridge, aye aye." Captain Haag glanced at his instruments, then ran his finger down the control screen. Millions of stars burst forth on the bridge simulscreens. I knew I couldn't spot *Celestina* unaided, but my eyes searched nonetheless.

"Confirm clear of encroachments, Lieutenant." The Captain waited.

Lieutenant Cousins turned to me. "Go to it, Mr. Seafort." His tone held a hint of impatience.

I checked the readouts as I'd been taught. I glanced again, in alarm. Something was there. "An encroachment, sir! Course one three five, distance twenty thousand kilometers!"

"That's *Celestina*, you idiot." Cousins's scorn brought a flush to my cheeks.

The Pilot intervened. "Maneuvering power, Chief."

"Aye aye, Bridge. Power up."

The Captain watched, not interfering. He could maneuver his own ship, of course, but Pilot Haynes was aboard for that very purpose. With squirts of the thrusters, the Pilot eased the ship forward.

Lieutenant Cousins dialed up the magnification on the simulscreens. A dark dot became a blob, then a lump. Abruptly *Celestina* leaped into focus, and I saw for the first time the tragic wreck that had cost two hundred seventy lives.

She spun lazily on her longitudinal axis, crumpled alumalloy revealing a gaping hole in her fusion drive shaft. Torn and shattered metal protruded from both levels of the disk; the passengers and crew had never had a chance.

I was silent, a lump in my throat. Hundreds of colonists had sailed that ill-fated vessel. A Captain like ours. Seamen, engineers, midshipmen like ourselves. My eyes stung.

"Get back to work!" Lieutenant Cousins loomed over me. "Watch your screens, you—you crybaby!"

"Belay that, Lieutenant!" The Captain's voice stopped him cold.

From time to time I glanced up from my console to the simulscreen, on which the derelict slowly swelled. Soon, tiny portholes were visible against the white of the disk, shaded almost to black against the interstellar darkness. After a time even Lieutenant Cousins seemed affected; he fiddled with the magnification until suddenly he caught the lettering on the vessel's side. He spun up maximum magnification, and the letters "U.N.S. *Celestina*" filled the screen. My breath caught. We were all silent now.

Pilot Haynes maneuvered the ship to within a half kilometer of *Celestina*. Then he turned the conn back to the Captain, who picked up the caller and spoke to the passengers, who would be crowding the portholes for the extraordinary view.

"Attention all hands. We have Defused. We are now at rest relative to U.N.S. *Celestina*, destroyed by the Grace of God one hundred twelve years ago this month. Many of us will never pass this place again. It has become custom, in ships sailing this road, to pay our respects to the memory of *Celestina*. All passengers who wish may go aboard. Our ship's launch will ferry you across in groups of six. The trip will last approximately two hours. The Purser will announce the order of embarkation. That is all." Captain Haag put down the caller and stepped to the front of his command console, staring somberly at the simulscreen, hands clasped behind his back.

"Will you go aboard, sir?" Lieutenant Cousins asked him.

"No," Captain Haag said quietly. "I'll stay with the ship." He cleared his throat. "I went over on my last trip, four years ago. I'll remember without seeing it again." But his eyes were riveted on the derelict.

The duty roster was posted. The ship's launch normally held ten. Each trip would be conducted by a lieutenant, accompanied by a midshipman and two seamen. Lieutenant Malstrom drew the first trip. Vax went with him. Two and a half hours later a subdued group of passengers returned, saddened and quiet. On the second excursion Sandy Wilsky went, with Lieutenant Cousins. I was scheduled for the third trip with Lieutenant Dagalow, and back on watch for the fourth.

When my turn came I suited up and joined the seamen helping passengers struggle into their unaccustomed suits. For convenience, the launch traveled airless. Mrs. Donhauser was in our group, but I was too busy helping the others to say anything to her.

The launch berth was in *Hibernia*'s shaft, just forward of the disk. We trekked into the airlock joining the two sections of the ship, climbing awkwardly up into the shaft when the lock finished cycling. I felt my weight lessen as I dropped onto the deck of the shaft. Forward of me a hundred meters or so, the cargo hold was stuffed with medical equipment, precision tool and die-making implements, a hi-tech chip manufactory, and other supplies for the Hope Nation colony.

We seated the passengers. The launch's transplex portholes offered a clear view, and the passengers huddled to peer through them. Lieutenant Dagalow dialed the bridge; a moment later the launch berth airlock slid open.

I glanced hopefully at the launch controls. Lieutenant Dagalow shook her head, smiled gently. "We don't have time, Nick." I flushed at the reminder of my incompetence, but merely nodded.

With a brief squirt of the maneuvering thrusters she propelled us out of *Hibernia*'s berth. The launch's powerful engines throbbed, its nozzles directing the liquid oxygen and liquid hydrogen reaction mass that propelled us.

Lieutenant Dagalow didn't bother to compute a course as I would have had to; instead, she eyed the huge derelict and sailed by dead reckoning. It wasn't quite by the book, but I envied her skill, and some part of me was glad I hadn't attempted to pilot a craft with so many watching.

We drifted closer to the inert ship. Ms. Dagalow's voice crackled in our suit speakers. "U.N.S. *Celestina* embarked from Mars Orbiting Station May 23, 2083, with a crew of seventy-five men and women, including twelve officers. She carried a hundred ninety-five passengers, all of them colonists for Hope Nation." She paused. "Jethro Narzul, son of the Secretary-General, was among them." She throttled down the engines. We were rapidly approaching the derelict ship; time for braking thrusters.

At reduced speed we drifted close to the abandoned colossus. With a practiced skill I envied, Lieutenant Dagalow fired the maneuvering thrusters and brought us to rest relative to *Celestina*'s gaping lock. Our alumalloy hatch slid open and a seaman jumped the few meters to the ship, a coiled cable slung over his shoulder. He moored us tight to the safety line stanchion in *Celestina*'s lock. As the derelict had no power, we couldn't connect to her capture latches, but since everyone aboard was suited, we didn't need an airtight seal.

Lieutenant Dagalow and a seaman boarded *Celestina* to help our suited passengers alight; the other sailor and I stayed in the launch to help them disembark. When all were safely aboard the derelict I joined the somber tour.

Lights had been strung every twenty meters or so. We stumbled along *Celestina*'s second-level corridor. The ship, of an earlier design, had but two levels in her disk. Debris must have swirled around the wreckage during the explosive decompression; much of it hung about where its inertia had brought it.

Celestina was like nothing I had ever seen. Much of her disk was surprisingly clean and orderly. Lieutenant Dagalow opened a cabin hatch; inside, a neatly made bunk waited for its long-gone occupant. A suit folded on the dresser was undisturbed.

"The ship was entering Fusion when the accident occurred. The drive exploded without warning. The shaft and the disk sustained heavy damage. Decompression was almost instantaneous." He paused. "Today, rapid-close hatches divide the disk into sections. We believe many of you would now survive a similar accident."

Mrs. Donhauser spoke up. "What caused the explosion?"

Ms. Dagalow shook her head. "The truth is, we don't know." I felt a chill. "The fusion drive has been redesigned several times since *Celestina* was launched. No other ship has ever had a similar failure."

She opened the hatch to the adjoining cabin. A rocking horse and a closet full of little girls' clothes framed the hatchway. Sickened, I turned away.

"What happened to the people?" a passenger asked.

"They were given decent burial in space when the ship was rediscovered by the *Armstrong.*" The legendary U.N.S. *Neil Armstrong*, Captain Hugo Von Walther commanding. The search vessel that had found the long-missing *Celestina,* and later opened two new colonies for settlement. Her commander had fought a duel with a colonial Governor, served as Admiral of the Fleet, and had ultimately been elected Secretary-General.

Our seamen had strung a rope barrier to keep us from the damaged areas where ragged sheets of torn metal hung dangerously. We trekked up the ladder to Level 1. My breath rasped in my helmet. My suit's defogger labored.

We gathered at the top of the ladder and moved as a group along *Celestina's* circumference corridor. Ahead a pale light gleamed, reflecting the gray corridor bulkheads. "The bridge is just ahead," said Lieutenant Dagalow.

We came to the open hatchway revealing the ghostly, deserted bridge. My breath caught. On the bulkhead outside the bridge hung the hundreds of slips of paper pictured so often in the holozines. We clustered at the bulkhead to read them.

"Robert Vysteader, colonist en route to Hope Nation, in memory of this poor ship, this fifteenth day of August 2106, by the Grace of God." "Mary Helene Braithwaite, colonist in God's hands, in memory of our brethren who died here. December 11, 2151." "Ahmed Esmail, remembering *Celestina.* December 11, 2151."

So they went. Each spacefarer who had come this lonely way had left a respectful mark to honor his predecessors who'd suffered disaster. Many of the visitors had gone on to Hope Nation or Detour, lived long lives and since died of old age.

"Over here! Look!" We crowded round. The slip of paper was clipped just beyond the hatchway. "Hugo Von Walther, Captain, U.N.S. *Neil Armstrong*, in commemoration of our sister ship *Celestina.* God rest her soul, and all who sailed in her. August 3, 2114." We trod the actual footsteps of Captain Von Walther. He had stood in this very spot the day he discovered *Celestina*, eighty-one years past. I tried to summon his presence. What a man he had been.

"Those who wish may leave a message of commemoration for future generations." Lieutenant Dagalow fished a box of tiny round magnets from her suitslot. We fumbled in our own slots for pencils and paper. Using the bulkheads, our knees, and the deck for tables, we wrote our blessings to the dead. I thought a long time before writing mine. "Nicholas Ewing Seafort, aged seventeen years, four months, twelve days, by Grace of God officer in the service of the United Nations, saluting the memories of those who have gone before. January 16, 2195." I took a magnet from Lieutenant Dagalow's outstretched hand and stuck it to the bulkhead, four meters from the bridge hatchway.

Our return trip was subdued. I was glad no one felt the need to speak. We berthed in *Hibernia;* I went aft to desuit and change. Then I reported back to the bridge. Captain Haag waited stolidly while the next load of passengers was embarked. On watch, Lieutenant Cousins and I had little to do.

It would take eleven trips to ferry all who wanted to go. Vax went on the fourth trip, then Alexi Tamarov. When Alexi returned he said excitedly, "Mr. Cousins let me pilot!" I hoped my feelings didn't show.

I went again on the seventh shuttle, but lagged behind when the group went to the bridge. Like the Captain, I had no need to experience it again.

After dinner the trips resumed. I was to stand watch with the Captain and Lieutenant Malstrom; Sandy and Lieutenant Cousins would sail the launch. Before reporting to the bridge I went with Alexi to help suit the passengers.

Lieutenant Dagalow was supervising the suiting room. Perhaps as a reaction to the grimness of the vessel lying alongside, Sandy and Alexi were in a playful mood. Sandy finished helping an older man into his unfamiliar suit and stuck out his tongue to Alexi as he reached for his own. Alexi tweaked him in the ribs. Sandy jumped, losing his balance, and tripped over the suiting bench. He crashed to the deck, tangled in a floppy suit. The back of his hand was bleeding slightly, but worse, he had split his pants wide open.

Mortified, Sandy glanced between the two outraged officers. Lieutenant Cousins bellowed. Ms. Dagalow shot me a glower that spoke volumes. I was senior; the fiasco was my responsibility.

"Mr. Tamarov!" Lieutenant Cousins's voice was a whip. "It's your fault, you go in his place. Get suited! You're both on report; I'll deal with you later!"

"Aye aye, sir!" Alexi grabbed his suit.

Lieutenant Dagalow intervened. "Mr. Tamarov went last trip, Mr.

Cousins. I can go instead of the middy. I don't mind; I'd like to look at the hull damage again." Cousins frowned; he was senior and could overrule Dagalow, but courtesy forbade that. He nodded, assenting. Ms. Dagalow called the bridge to get the necessary approval; Alexi and I helped finish the suiting, and the party left.

The moment the airlock hatch slid shut I wheeled on Sandy. "Change your pants, Mr. Midshipman Wilsky!"

"Aye aye, sir!"

I caught his arm as he started to run. "If you think Lieutenant Cousins is the only one going to deal with you, guess again! Tomfoolery on duty? God—" I caught myself in time. "God bless it, Mr. Wilsky! Mr. Holser and I will give you some attention." He blanched; unleashing Vax on him was a threat indeed. I released him; he double-timed it to the wardroom, glad to be free of me.

Seething, I set Alexi at attention against the bulkhead. Then, nose to nose with him, I reamed him slowly and thoroughly. At the end he wasn't far from tears. My memory is very good. Most of what I said came from Sergeant Trammel at Academy. I recalled it was very effective.

I dismissed Alexi and headed for the bridge. "Permission to enter, sir."

The Captain was still on watch. "Granted." Didn't he ever sleep?

"Midshipman Seafort reporting, sir."

He merely nodded. Maybe he was tiring, after all. I took my place at the console. There was nothing to do but watch the simulscreen.

"What was that commotion in the suiting room, Mr. Seafort?"

That was tricky. The Captain had heard something about it; Lieutenant Dagalow needed his permission to leave ship. I couldn't lie to an officer, no matter what. Yet it was also my job to keep wardroom affairs out of the Captain's hair. I said carefully, "Mr. Wilsky tripped and cut his hand, sir."

"Ah. Is he getting medical attention?" There was a dryness in the Captain's tone that I found suspicious. On the other hand, the Captain was not known to joke with midshipmen.

"It was just a minor scrape, sir."

Captain Haag waved it aside. "No matter." Lieutenant Malstrom winked at me. So he did know.

"Three more trips after this, sir." Lieutenant Malstrom spoke to the Captain.

"Yes." After a moment he added, "Then we get under way in earnest." No more stops for nine months until we reached Miningcamp, except for routine navigation checks.

Captain Haag leaned back in his chair, his eyes shut. Lieutenant Malstrom yawned. I tried not to yawn too. It had been a long and emotional day.

"*Hibernia*, Mayday! Mayday!" It must have been a seaman; not a voice I recognized.

The Captain bolted upright, slapping the caller switch. "*Hibernia!*"

"We have a passenger down! Suit puncture!"

The Captain swore. "What happened?"

"Just a moment. Sir." We could hear him relaying the message on his suit transmitter. "Lieutenant Dagalow slapped on a quickpatch and re-aired her suit. Mrs.—the passenger is unconscious. Probably still alive, sir."

"Tell Mr. Cousins to get everyone back into the launch."

"Aye aye, sir. The woman is wedged in the bridge hatchway. She touched the emergency close. It shut on her suit. They can't reach around her to the hatch control switch."

I didn't know bridge power backups could last so long. The bridge of any major vessel is built like a fortress. When the Captain slaps the dull red emergency-close patch inside the hatchway the hatch snaps shut almost instantly, with great force. Thereafter it is almost impossible to enter the bridge.

Blocked by the unconscious passenger, *Celestina*'s hatch hadn't shut entirely, but the body hindered access to the control panel. Somebody had fouled up badly, letting her in.

The Captain touched the caller. "Machinist Perez, call the bridge."

In a moment a voice came. "Machinist here, sir."

"Crowbars and laser cutters to the Captain's gig at once. Have another seaman suit up with you."

"Aye aye, sir."

"Shall I take the gig across, sir?" Lieutenant Malstrom got to his feet.

"No, I'll go myself. You take the watch." Captain Haag started for the hatchway.

"Aye aye, sir. But, Captain—"

"It's my responsibility." His voice had sharpened. "I'll have to see what happened. If she doesn't survive . . ." Passengers might be cargo, but there would be a Board of Inquiry if anyone died. Captain Haag shook his head. "I shouldn't be more than an hour. You have the conn."

"Aye aye, sir."

The Captain slapped the panel. The hatch opened. He strode toward the ladder.

Lieutenant Malstrom and I exchanged glances. He grimaced. I felt pity for Lieutenant Dagalow and even for Mr. Cousins; when the Captain got to them, heads would roll.

A few minutes later they launched the gig. We watched in the simulscreens as it shot across to *Celestina*. Smaller and far more maneuverable than the launch, the gig was a mere gnat against the brooding mass of the great stricken ship.

Celestina's lock was already occupied by the launch. The gig maneuvered as close as it could, then the seaman fired a magnetic cable into the lock. The Captain went across, hand over hand, just like a cadet at Academy.

Half an hour later the speaker came alive. "Bridge, this is *Hibernia*." The Captain naturally called himself by the name of his ship.

"Go ahead, sir."

"It was easier than we thought." Captain Haag sounded relieved. "Perez reached the switch with the point of a crowbar. She's breathing, at any rate. We'll bring her back on the launch: it's faster. Get the next gaggle of passengers ready. Send an extra middy next trip for the gig."

"Aye aye, sir."

"Shall I go for the gig, sir?" I tried to conceal my eagerness. The midshipman he sent would be, however briefly, in command during the passage between ships.

Lieutenant Malstrom smiled. Perhaps he remembered his own days as a middy. "Sure, Nicky."

With magnification set to zero we could see the passengers and crew waiting in the launch. The moment the Captain and the injured passenger were aboard, its lock closed. Crewmen untied the safety line.

The Captain sounded worried. "Her complexion isn't good. Have Dr. Uburu stand by at the lock. Belay that figuring, Mr. Cousins, there's no time. Darla, feed coordinates to our puter!"

"Aye aye, sir." Darla knew when to be all business.

Lieutenant Malstrom and I watched on the simulscreen as the launch shot away from *Celestina*. Under main power it headed toward our lock. When it reached the halfway point I stood to leave for the launch berth. I glanced over my shoulder at the screen.

The speaker blared. *"THE ENGINE'S OVERHEATING! WE'RE THROTTLING DOW— THE SHUTOFF WON'T—"* The caller went dead as the launch disintegrated in a flash of white light.

"Lord God!" Lieutenant Malstrom froze at his console. I heard myself make some sort of sound. Chunks of twisted metal and other debris spun lazily off the side of the screen. I glimpsed a shredded spacesuit.

The lieutenant frantically keyed the suit broadcast frequencies. Nothing but the barely audible hiss of background radiation.

I stood rooted halfway between the console and the hatch. Mr. Malstrom's eyes held terror. Together, we stared into the space the launch had occupied.

At last, Lieutenant Malstrom began to function.

We couldn't search for survivors, even if there'd been any; we had neither our launch nor the gig. Mr. Malstrom ordered Vax and a party of seamen across to recover the gig from *Celestina*'s lock. Squirting propellant from tanks strapped to their thrustersuits, they navigated the void between *Hibernia* and the derelict. At last they reached the gig. Vax sailed it back to *Hibernia*'s waiting lock. He docked it as well as any of the lieutenants might, far better than I was able.

We could do nothing else.

Mr. Malstrom made the necessary announcement to the stunned passengers and crew. From some inner reserve he summoned a formal dignity. "Ladies and gentlemen, by the Grace of Lord God, Captain Justin Haag, commanding officer of U.N.S. *Hibernia*, has died in an explosion of the ship's launch. With him died Lieutenant Abraham Cousins, Lieutenant Lisa Dagalow, Machinist Jorge Perez, able seaman Mikhail Arbatov, and six passengers. I, Lieutenant Harvey Malstrom, senior officer aboard, do hereby take command of this ship."

He rested his head on the console. Then he continued, "The six passengers are Ms. Ruth Davies, Mr. Edward Hearnes, Mr. Ayah Dinh, Ms. Indira Etra, Mr. Vance Portright, and Mr. Randolph Carr."

After a moment he reached for the speaker again. "Chief McAndrews, Dr. Uburu, and Pilot Haynes, report to the bridge." Then he swung toward me, desolate. "God, Nicky, what do I do now?"

"Permission to use the caller, sir."

"Go ahead."

I rang Dr. Uburu's quarters. "This is the bridge. Please bring a tankard of medicinal alcohol to your conference with Captain Malstrom."

The Captain shot me a grateful look. Then as the import of my words sunk in, he paled. "Captain Malstrom. Dear God!"

"Yes, sir." I wasn't good at my practical lessons but I knew the regs fairly well. The commanding officer of a Naval vessel was always a Captain. His rank was subject to reconfirmation by Admiralty upon return, but a ship could be commanded only by a Captain. When Lieutenant

Malstrom became *Hibernia's* senior officer, he became Captain Malstrom.

After a moment's inward reflection he focused on me anew, and muttered, "You'd better go, Nicky. I've got to talk to them."

"Aye aye, sir." I came to attention and snapped a formal salute. The Captain would need all the support he could get. He returned the salute and I left him to his desolation.

I trudged back to the wardroom. Sandy's eyes were red. Vax, for once, was quiet and withdrawn. I chased them both out of the cabin and lay down in the dark, to cry myself to sleep. At seventeen, I was unaccustomed to horror and loss.

When I woke the next morning, Sandy Wilsky was in the brig pending the official inquiry into the disaster. He'd been arrested by Master-at-arms Vishinsky, on orders of the Captain. I knew he was innocent, and surely so did Mr. Malstrom, but if it hadn't been for Sandy's tomfoolery, he, not Lieutenant Dagalow, would have been aboard the launch when it disintegrated.

Troubled, I went in search of Amanda, and found her in her cabin. Seeing my face, she stood aside without a word, closed the hatch behind us.

Not long after, she sat on her bunk, my head in her lap. "I don't understand, Nicky. Why can't he command *Hibernia* without changing rank? He's still the same Lieutenant Malstrom."

I was patient. "Think of Captain as a legal position instead of a rank. You think Captain Haag ran the ship, right? He was higher in rank than the lieutenants, so he was in charge."

"Right."

"Well, no. The Captain is the United Nations Government. All of it. The SecGen, the Security Council, the General Assembly, the World Court. Anything the U.N. can do, he can do. He is its plenipotentiary in space." For some reason, telling her the obvious made me feel better.

"So?"

"A lieutenant is just an officer, but the Captain is the government. Only the Captain can be that. And only the government can run the ship. So, the person who runs the ship is Captain. His word is law."

Amanda was already on another topic. "Anyway, Chief Engineer McAndrews has more seniority. He should be Captain."

"Hon, it doesn't work that way." She stroked my hair in response to my endearment. "The ship had three lieutenants. Under them are four middies. There are also three other officers on board. Staff officers."

"I've heard that before. What does it mean?"

"A line officer is in line to command the ship. Staff officers can order the middies and the seamen about, but they don't succeed to command. They're here to do a specific job, and that's it."

"But it's not fair. Chiefie has more experience than Mr. Malstrom."

I wondered when she had begun calling Chief McAndrews "Chiefie." I considered calling him that someday, but quickly decided against it. "Life isn't fair, Amanda. Chiefie doesn't get to run the ship." She bent over and kissed me. She had veered off onto yet another topic.

That evening the Captain convened a Board of Inquiry. Alexi and I might possibly have been appointed—a middy, no matter how young, is by Act of the General Assembly an officer and gentleman, and has his majority—and the Captain had few enough officers left to sit in judgment. But Alexi and I had been in the suiting room with Sandy; we were witnesses. If there were a plot, we might even have been involved, so on both counts we were disqualified.

Doc Uburu, Pilot Haynes, and Chief McAndrews sat as the Board. They met in the now unused lieutenants' common room, as if to underscore the purpose of the inquiry.

For two days they sifted through Darla's records, replaying over and again the last transmission from the launch, compiling a list of every sailor who'd entered the launch berth since *Hibernia* had left Earthport Station, reviewing the meager information the launch's primitive puter had passed to Darla during its shuttles back and forth to *Celestina*.

Hibernia's launch berth was normally sealed. Darla had record of each occasion our crewmen were admitted for maintenance since we'd left Earthport. Counting the various work details assigned to shepherd the passengers across, seventeen crewmen had been in the launch berth at one time or another. All four of us middies had gone across to *Celestina*, and each of the officers save the members of the board.

One by one each sailor who'd been in the berth was questioned. Alexi, Vax, and I sat stiffly in the chairs placed in the corridor, knees tight, caps in hand, waiting our turns.

They brought Sandy from the brig for his interrogation; he marched past us with barely a glance. Two hours later he emerged, pale, shaken. It appeared he'd been crying.

I was next. I smoothed my jacket, tugged at my tie, marched into the crowded mess. My salute was as close to Academy perfection as I could manage.

Chief Engineer McAndrews was in the chair. "Be seated, Mr. Seafort." He glanced to his holovid, on which he'd been tapping notes.

"Tell us what you saw—everything—in the launch berth before the launch's final trip."

"Aye aye, sir." I furrowed my brow, lurched into my recollection. I'd seen nothing suspicious, so all I could do was describe in detail Sandy's horseplay with Alexi, his torn trousers, Mr. Cousins's wrath.

"Then what?"

"Lieutenant Cousins ordered Alex—Midshipman Tamarov to take Mr. Wilsky's place. Ms. Dagalow asked if she could go instead."

"You're sure Mr. Cousins didn't order Dagalow aboard?"

"Quite sure, sir."

Pilot Haynes cleared his throat. "Did Mr. Tamarov suggest that he and Lieutenant Dagalow switch places?"

"Lord God, of course not!" I gulped, realizing what I'd blurted. Still, the question was preposterous. Were a middy to make such a suggestion to a lieutenant—any lieutenant—he wouldn't be able to sit for a week. And that's if he were lucky. Such a remark was as out of place as—as the one I'd just made. I was in deep trouble. "I'm very sorry, sir!"

Chief McAndrews's tone was frosty, but he otherwise ignored my impertinence. Instead, he led me through a series of probing questions about my previous visits to the launch berth, about the watch rotation according to which I was supposed to be on the bridge.

"But I *was* on the bridge, sir. The horseplay occurred before my watch. I was helping suit the passengers."

The Pilot set his fingers together, as if in prayer. "Who told you to do that?"

"No one, sir."

"Why did you meddle?"

I flushed, knowing my response sounded inane even to myself. "I wanted to be helpful, sir."

"By being a busybody, instead of going to your post?"

"No, sir, I—yes, sir." There was no right answer, and I fell silent.

I could understand their frustration. A hydrozine engine doesn't overheat without cause. And if it did, the launch crew should have been able to shut it down within seconds, before it reached critical temperature. Accidents happen, but unexplained accidents made everyone uneasy. A glance out the porthole to the gaping wound in *Celestina's* hull was reason enough for that.

The Chief Engineer glanced at Doc Uburu, offered the Pilot another question. Both shook their heads. The Chief pursed his lips. "Mr. Seafort, did you dislike Mr. Cousins?"

My uniform was drenched, my throat impossibly dry. My answer could ruin me, but I had little choice when asked a direct question. I squared my shoulders, gritted my teeth. "Yes, sir."

Remorseless, he made me give my reasons. When I was done my ears were red from shame.

At last, dazed and exhausted, I was allowed to make my way out to the corridor. Shakily, I sat.

The master-at-arms appeared in the hatchway. "Mr. Holser." Stolidly, Vax strode to his inquisition.

The inquiry went on.

Though we'd not yet Fused, despite the turmoil *Hibernia* still had to be crewed and managed. Even with Sandy released from the brig, we were shorthanded. Four hours after my grilling, needing far more sleep than I'd had, nerves frazzled, I reported to the bridge for my watch.

At my knock Captain Malstrom swiveled the camera, opened the hatch, waved me to my seat.

We passed half the watch before he broke the stiff silence. "Have they found anything yet?"

It was obvious whom he meant. "Not that I know of, sir."

"It couldn't just happen. We have to find the cause."

"Yes, sir." It wasn't my place to say more. My friend Harv had vanished forever; this was the Captain, in all his eminence. I was but a middy.

6

In a ship even as large as *Hibernia,* rumors true and false traveled faster than light. Within minutes, everyone knew that at the Chief's insistence, the Board would review the case of every sailor sent to Captain's Mast since we'd left port. That couldn't be much of a task; on the whole, *Hibernia* had been a happy ship, and had few problems the petty officers couldn't settle belowdecks.

Vax went on watch. While I lounged in my bunk, grateful that Alexi hadn't chosen to blare his usual slap music, Sandy Wilsky burst in, quivering with indignation. "Malstrom's going to P and D the lot of us!"

"What?" Alexi jerked to a sitting position.

"All us middies, and the sailors who've been in the launch berth!"

"Why?"

"To rule out any possibility of sabotage, he told Doc."

Alexi slammed a fist into his mattress. "That's not fair."

I growled, "You'll get over it." Poly and drug interrogation wasn't pleasant, but the aftereffects didn't last all that long.

Alexi said, "But we've none of us been charged!"

Sandy's tone was sullen. "The grode hasn't the right—"

I swarmed out of my bunk blurting the first thing that came into my head. "Wilsky, look at the scuff on those boots! One demerit! And that blanket!" My hand slapped his bed, found a tiny crease. "Another!"

Alexi gaped. "Why are you suddenly down on—"

I whirled. "And you! How many demerits now?" I knew Alexi was slow at working them off.

"Nine, Mr. Seaf—"

"Two more for your insolence!" Knowing it would send him to the barrel, I added after an ominous pause, "I won't log them 'til morning. Get started."

"But, I—"

"NOW!"

They scrambled for the hatch.

"No talking while you exercise! One word and the demerits are doubled!"

"Aye aye, Mr. Seafort!" The hatch slammed. I sat on the side of my bed, head in hands, trembling.

Their hero worship was a thing of the past; from this moment, they'd hate me. But I'd had no choice.

It had been close.

Their resentment at P and D testing was no surprise. Polygraph and drug interrogation was allowed aboard ship, as at any trial. Since the Truth in Testimony Act of 2026, a defendant had no right to silence. If there were other evidence against him, he could be sent for P and D, and usually was. If the tests proved he'd told the truth, charges were dismissed. If he admitted the charges, as the sophisticated mix of drugs forced him to do, his confession was of course introduced as evidence.

However, two safeguards applied. The subject had to have been charged with a crime, and he had to have denied the charge.

Without those limitations, poly and drugs could become tools of a despot or, worse, of torture. The law didn't allow the court a fishing expedition into a man's mind to discover what crimes he might have committed.

I kept an eye on the time, not at all concerned that I'd left Alexi and Sandy alone. I'd given a direct order that they'd acknowledged. They would have no conversation while they toiled in the exercise room.

I dozed.

As the fourth hour neared its end I got wearily to my feet, trudged down to Level 2.

When I went in, Alexi was working the bars while Sandy jogged in place. Their undershirts were soaked through, their hair matted. Sandy's breath came in a rasp. It took hard labor to cancel a demerit, as I well knew. "At ease, both of you."

Alexi dismounted. Slowly Sandy came to a stop.

"Against the bulkhead." For a moment I paced, then faced them with a glare. "Anything to say?"

"No, Mr. Seafort." Sandy sounded every bit as young as he was, and scared.

"And you?"

Despite his physical weariness, Alexi smoldered. "Why did you turn on us?"

Inwardly, I groaned. With typical clumsiness, I'd allowed Alexi to open a conversation I couldn't allow us to have. "Mr. Wilsky, outside." I followed Sandy into the corridor. As casually as I could, I told him, "Griping is beneath you, Sandy. You're an officer now, not a cadet. If you have complaints about how the ship is run, you're expected to keep them to yourself."

He colored. "Yes, Mr. Seafort."

"Promise me you'll do so in future."

"Aye aye, Mr. Seafort. I'm sorry." Despite my brutality, he seemed pathetically eager to please.

"It annoyed me enough to give you the demerits. Go take your shower." I touched his damp shoulder. "Good lad."

Hoping I'd struck the right note I went back to the exercise room and Alexi. My tone was harsh. "Idiot."

"I—what?"

I leaned close, spoke barely above a whisper. "I'm trying to save your life!"

He said nothing, but his eyes showed his puzzlement.

"Captain Malstrom is free to investigate the death of his officers as he sees fit."

"But the law says—"

"Alexi!" Even in shutting him up, I risked our safety; couldn't he understand? "It's the *Captain!*"

I'd said all that was necessary. The indiscriminate testing Captain Malstrom ordered was in clear violation of the Truth in Testimony Act. When he brought *Hibernia* home, Admiralty could beach him for it, or worse.

But aboard ship, none of that mattered. The Captain's word was law. My duty was to carry out his orders, and to report seditious talk. To do else was to conspire in mutiny.

I said no more, and waited. At last, Alexi's face showed he understood. Still standing at ease, he gave a faint nod.

I sighed with relief. "Sandy should be all right now. But if you hear him even thinking aloud about the subject, sit on him hard. Don't hesitate."

"Right."

"Dismissed."

As he left, he whispered, "Thank you." I pretended I hadn't heard.

The next day we went to our P and D, the middies first, then the sailors. I came out of Doc Uburu's cubicle dizzy and nauseous, not quite sure what I'd babbled under the drugs' irresistible influence. I crawled under my covers, trying not to be sick to my stomach.

The next day I still felt the effects, though they were much diminished.

Word was that all of us had tested innocent, middies down through the lowest rating. Sandy lay in his bunk, sicker than the rest of us. P and D affected some more than others.

The Board of Inquiry met one last time, issued its report. They found no evidence of sabotage; they concluded the accident was probably caused by a deteriorating fuel valve unnoticed by a sensor that had malfunctioned.

For two more days, while we recovered, the ship floated dead in space.

Captain Malstrom conferred off and on with the Chief, Pilot Haynes, and Dr. Uburu, determining whether to return to Earthport Station. When I next had the watch he was as gruff as he'd been before, then unbent.

"I'm sorry, Nicky. I'm frantic with worry. I don't know what to do."

"I understand, sir."

"I've pretty well decided to go on. If there's been no sabotage we're not at undue risk, and Miningcamp and Hope Nation desperately need our cargo. If we turned back, it would be almost a year before a replacement ship got this far."

"Yes, sir."

"Nicky, I want to be honest with you. We have no lieutenants, and you're senior. But I can't appoint you, yet. You aren't qualified."

"I know, sir. What about Vax?" The words were bitter on my tongue, but I had to say them. Vax was far more ready than I.

"No, not yet. He doesn't have the temperament. I'm still looking to you. By the time we get to Hope Nation you'll qualify, I promise. I'll help you. For now, you'll both remain middies. If I can, I'll see that you make the grade before the others." If so, I'd have seniority over them for the rest of our days in the Navy, unless one of us finally made Captain.

"That's not necessary, sir." I forced down the foul taste of ambition.

"Maybe not, but it's what I intend." He took a deep breath. "We'll Fuse tomorrow, right after the memorial service."

"Yes, sir."

The service was a sad and formal affair. We officers wore our dress whites, our white slacks gleaming against black shoes, the red stripe down each leg sharp and bright. Our white shirts and black ties were covered by immaculate white dress jackets, a black mourning sash thrown over the right shoulder. Our length of service medals gleamed.

On a distant cruise, burial was in space, in a sealed coffin ejected from the airlock. *Celestina*'s dead had been so entombed, and drifted to this day on their endless way through the cosmos.

Ours wasn't a burial service, because there was nothing to bury. A memorial service, held in the ship's dining hall.

Every person aboard *Hibernia* crowded into the mess, the crew awkward in unfamiliar officers' country. Relatives of two passengers who had died, Mr. Rajiv Etra and Derek Carr, were mourners and stood with the officers who mourned their Captain on behalf of the ship. The other four passengers had been traveling alone. Mr. Etra stood in forlorn dignity. Derek Carr, his eyes red, spoke to no one and held himself stiffly.

Captain Malstrom led us in the traditional ritual of the Yahwehist Reunification. "We commend the spirits of our dead to your keeping, O Lord God," he said. "As we commit their bodies to your void, until your day of judgment when you call them forth again . . ."

We stood a few moments in silence, and it was ended.

After the service Alexi went on watch, with Pilot Haynes. Normally the Pilot was called only when we docked at a station or navigated a trafficked area. Now, though, he would have to stand watches with the rest of us.

Back in the wardroom Vax Holser was sullen. When Sandy got in his way, he shoved the boy aside. I ignored it, not ready to face another problem. An hour or so later we Fused.

Pilot Haynes was a dour, balding man who said hardly a word, if I didn't count routine orders when on watch. We middies wondered why he stayed bald, when most people would have undergone simple follicle touchup. Of course, none of us dared ask.

A watch shared with the Pilot was a very quiet time. Now that we were back in Fusion I found it hard to stay awake in the lengthy silences. Not that the Pilot was offended by remarks from a middy; he just squelched them by monosyllabic answers until one tired of trying.

"Energy variations seem up a trifle, sir." I was reading from my screen.

"Um."

I made another attempt. "What's the widest normal variation, sir?"

"Ask Darla." It was little more than a grunt.

I turned to the puter. "Darla, what's our greatest normal energy variation?"

"For the fusion drive?" Sometimes she needed us to be very specific.

"Yes, Darla."

"Two percent above and below mark, Mr. Seafort." A long pause.

"Are you trying to make conversation?" I don't know how they programmed that.

After watch when I returned to my bunk, tired and irritable, Vax
was ragging Alexi. I told him to stop. He did, but stared at me, a contemptuous smile on his face, until I got up and stalked out of the wardroom.

"The discovery by Cheel and Vorhees in 2046 that N-waves travel
faster than light, and their accompanying revision of the laws of physics,
led to the fusion drive and superluminous travel." Mr. Ibn Saud paused,
surveying the audience of passengers, officers, and crew in *Hibernia's*
dining hall.

"Riding the crest of the N-wave, powered by wave emissions rather
than particle emissions, our great ships glide through the galaxy, exploring, colonizing." Absorbed, I sat, wishing Sandy wouldn't fidget. The
Passengers' Lecture Series was a welcome diversion from ship's routine,
and he should have the sense to appreciate it.

"Fusion brought us desperately needed resources, such as metals
from Miningcamp. But the real benefit of the fusion drive was as a safety
hatch—it allowed those educated, intelligent, restless folk who chose to
settle the distant colonies a means to flee Earth's dwindling resources,
pollution, and soaring population."

Ibn Saud sipped from his glass of water.

"But the fusion drive embodies the dilemma of maintaining our
ever more complex technology. The colonies need our best and bright-
est, and at the same time, the new industries spawned by Fusion demand great numbers of highly skilled workers.

"Meanwhile, society has recognized at last that compulsory education was a resounding failure. Voluntary schooling results in better education, but for fewer people. So, unfortunately, the general populace is
less educated than they were two centuries past. Some, like the transpops who infest the lower levels of our cities, have no training at all, and
are fit for no work."

Ibn Saud smiled apologetically in our direction. "Nowhere is our
shortage of skilled labor more apparent than in the military forces. The
officer classes, selected from the educated, technological minority, are
drawn to a life of honor, to the excitement of exploring the galaxy." I
nodded, without thinking.

"But for the most part the Navy, like the U.N.A.F. ground force, is
manned—by necessity—from the uneducated underclass. And so we
have the anomaly of a great starship, the pinnacle of technology, gov-

erned by an authoritarian system not unlike that of the eighteenth century sea navies. We've even returned to corporal punishment, at least for
young officers. Rigid hierarchies maintain order as we travel to the stars.

"But mankind will be changed by the experience—in what way, we
do not know; it will be generations before we learn. Surely the changes
are for the better. If we assume Lord God watches over us, as he always
has, the rescue of civilization by the fusion drive becomes understandable. If man is marked for further greatness, if we are destined to colonize the galaxy, we have been given the tools. What we make of them,
and what they make of us, is up to us."

Ibn Saud sat to enthusiastic applause. Amanda, as education director, lauded him for his presentation, and thanked the audience for attending. As we dispersed I caught her eye, relishing her quick smile.

That evening at dinner I watched her tease Vax, at the next table.
He didn't seem to mind. At my own table Yorinda Vincente, head of the
Passengers' Council, was discussing council meetings with Johan Spie-
gel and Mrs. Donhauser. I was bored stiff.

After, freed from watch until the following noon but not yet ready
for sleep, I lay in my bunk fully dressed, trying to read. When Vax came
in he turned on his holovid, plugging in a shrill slap-nag chip. He ignored my glance of annoyance. Sandy arrived, smiling happily. He had
been seated at table with a girl his own age.

Vax, lying on his bunk, asked, "You going to prong her, Wilsky?"

Sandy's grin vanished. "I don't want to talk about her." He sounded
almost defiant.

"She'd be good at it. If you don't ask her, I will."

I said, "Drop it, Vax."

"I wasn't hazing." Holser was belligerent. "Just making conversation."

"Lay off."

Vax subsided, smirking.

Half an hour later I realized I'd been reading the same screen over
and again, without remembering a word. I got to my feet. "Come along,
Vax." I went out to the corridor. After a moment he followed. I headed
for the ladder.

"Where to?"

I ignored him completely. I took the ladder down to Level 2, giving
him a choice of watching me leave or following. He followed. I strode
down the corridor to the exercise room, slapped open the hatch. The
room was empty.

Vax stood in the hatchway. "What are you doing?"

I took off my jacket and folded it neatly over the exercise horse. I yanked at my tie.

"Seafort—*MR*. Seafort, what the hell are you doing?"He lounged against the hatchway.

"Come in and shut the hatch. That's an order." I took off my shirt and folded it over the jacket. Vax nodded slowly. He shut the hatch behind him. I emptied my pants pockets.

"What's your problem, MR. Seafort?"

"Better get ready, Vax."

"For what?"

"We're about to have it out, once and for all."

"We have a truce, remember?"

"Not anymore." I tightened my shoelace.

"Why not?" He still wore his full uniform; he was making no move to get ready.

"I can't stand you." I walked right up to him, unafraid, and grabbed his coat. "It's your uniform, Vax. Do you want it soiled or not?"

Reluctantly, he discarded his jacket. I went into karate position, guard up, on my toes.

Vax backed away, shook his head. "The wardroom shouldn't be fighting now, Nick. Not with the problems the ship has."

"I'll fight. You just stand there."

"Nick, don't. Not with the Captain dead."

I slapped him. He didn't like that, and brought up his guard. We circled.

"Tell me what you want, Nick, before we fight." He stepped back, lowered his fists.

"Want?" My voice shook with hatred. "You're a bully, Holser. You're brutal. You sneer at the boys. You hurt them." I kept looking for an opening, my hands up. "I've never seen you do anything kind. You're good at your job, but you're the meanest person I've ever met!"

He surprised me, crying out, "I know!" He thrust his hands in his pockets. "I can't help it, Nick. That's how I've always been. It's who I am."

"Fight me."

"Why?"

"We've got to have it out, Vax. If you win I'll ask the Captain to beach me for four months. That'll make you first middy. You'll have it all your way." The Captain had authority to suspend my commission for any length of time he chose. I would stop accumulating seniority, and Vax wouldn't.

"What if you win?"

"I'm in charge. All the way to Detour and back. You know your problem? You think I'm the first middy, and you're second. You've got it wrong."

"Then tell me what's right." He had his guard down again. He didn't want to fight tonight.

"I'm first middy, and you're not!" I walked up to him and poked him in the chest, not far below my eye level. "There's no second midshipman! Just the first and a bunch of others. I can't help that you weren't first. You fought it ever since we came on board, Holser, and now I've had it. I hate you so much I can't stand looking at you!"

He spoke quietly. "I know I'm not nice, Nicky. What do you want me to do about it?"

I yelled, "I don't care! I'm not interested in you. I just want you to obey orders, like the other juniors! You know what that's worth to me? Getting killed tonight." I took several breaths. "I'm done talking, you bastard."

"And if I do what you tell me?"

"What do you think, Vax? After how you've treated everyone else?"

"You'll get even."

"You're damn right I will! For everything!"

"Hold off a minute. Please." I couldn't understand his reluctance. He could pulverize me. Last time, I'd been lucky.

I went across the room and hoisted myself onto the parallel bar. "You've got thirty seconds. Then I'm coming at you." I began counting under my breath.

He took all thirty of them. I jumped off the bars and came at him, moving fast. He said, "I'll obey your orders, Mr. Seafort."

I skidded to a stop. "For how long?"

"As long as you're my superior officer." The belligerence was gone from his tone.

"I don't believe you! There'll come a time. Let's have it over with."

"I give you my word." Vax looked me in the eye, unflinching.

"Why, Holser?"

He shook his head. "I don't know. Maybe now the Captain's dead, being first middy doesn't seem so important. Maybe it's the way Alexi looks at you sometimes, when he thinks you don't see." He glared, as if expecting me to mock him. "Do you care about my reasons? I told you I'll do it, so I will."

I was helpless. "We'll see if you mean it. A hundred push-ups."

"Aye aye, Mr. Seafort." He loosened his tie, dropped to the deck, and began pumping.

Well. It seemed he actually intended to obey orders.

I didn't let up. I worked him for two hours, until he was drenched with sweat. Then I walked out of the room without a word.

I ran Vax ragged for a whole month. He got to clean the wardroom, top to bottom. I saddled him with extra duty at all hours. He did as he was told. He was not friendly to me, and his manner was so ominous that the others made it a point to stay out of his way. But he never defied me.

With the loss of the lieutenants we were all on double watches. I was constantly tired; so was everyone else. My free afternoons were with Amanda. I never played chess anymore; it would have been unthinkable with the Captain, and there was no one else with whom I was that close. I was unhappy; we all were.

Captain Malstrom was unhappy too, though he tried not to let it show. It affected all of us. I had frightening dreams. Alexi turned to his slap music for comfort. Sandy held hands with his new young friend.

In the wardroom, I took it out on Vax. I gave him all the hazing he had ever forced the others to endure, and more. I ordered him in and out of bed all night adjusting the heat. I stood him at attention in the wardroom when he wanted to relax in his bunk. At night I would put him under an ice-cold shower for half an hour at a time. Afterward in the dark I could hear his teeth chatter as he lay trying to warm himself.

He never protested. He obeyed my orders. Slowly, I came to realize that Vax was a person who did what he promised. I began to respect him for that, but I didn't let up. He had a lot coming.

Ship's routine settled into the dreary monotony of Fusion. Amanda helped the passengers put on plays and arrange contests. The Pilot and Chief Engineer drilled us in our studies. The Captain ordered the barrel moved to the Chief's engine room, but it wasn't put to use. On our time off, I devoted my attention to Vax. I confined him to quarters except when he was on duty or taking exercise. But he remained docile and carried out my orders to the letter.

One evening when Sandy and Alexi went below I put Vax at attention in the center of the wardroom. I let him stand there for an hour while I read my holovid. Then I said quietly, "Do you want me to let up, Vax?"

He took a long time to think about it. Finally he said, "Yes, Mr. Seafort, I do."

I sent him to his bunk to lie down. He lay propped on one elbow listening. "I expect you to be an officer and a gentleman. Especially a gentleman. I expect you to act in the wardroom's best interest and in mine. To be pleasant to all of us. To lay off hazing except by my direct order. To mind your own business, and nobody else's. To support me in my duties. When you're prepared to do every one of those things, Holser, then I'll let up. Not before." I let him think about that. I went back to my holovid.

A half hour later he spoke up. "I'm prepared, Mr. Seafort."

"What's that?" I hadn't expected a capitulation.

"I'm prepared. To do all the things you said." I knew he meant it. Holser was true to his word. I could count on it.

I nodded. "Very well."

When Alexi and Sandy came back I lined all three of them against the partition. "What went on in the wardroom before is over," I said. "You're to forget it or ignore it. From now on you will act in a spirit of friendly cooperation. There will be no hazing, no discipline unless I dispense it. You will each shake hands with each other, and with me, to establish the attitude in which we'll carry out our duties henceforth. That is all." We shook hands all around.

The wardroom was mine.

7

Two nights later, Amanda and I made love for the first time. She was not my first woman, but she was almost my first. We gently and lovingly practiced the arts I knew, and I learned from her skills I had not known.

I was astonished at how much I needed her closeness. I thought I'd learned to do without tenderness, touching, caring, at least while on ship. I couldn't go away from her, our first night. I stayed in her cabin, cupped around her warm and pleasing body, drinking her intimacy like wine. In the morning we kissed and parted, both shy from our newfound vulnerability.

I went about my duties in a daze, thinking more of my times off watch than my responsibilities on, until even the Pilot became aware and made a wondering remark. I snapped my attention back to my job. It would be a long, slow voyage. There was time for everything.

A few days later I came back from a cozy evening in Amanda's cabin and was peeling off my jacket when Captain Malstrom's voice burst from the wardroom caller. "Mr. Seafort, Mr. Holser, to the bridge! Flank!" Vax and I exchanged startled glances. We sprinted to the ladder.

The Captain waited impatiently in the bridge hatchway. "Hurry!" He shoved us inside and slapped the control. The hatch snapped shut. "There's a battle in crew berth three. Chief Petty Officer's been hit on the head. I don't know how many are in the riot, or what it's about."

I gaped. The Captain paid no heed. "Mr. Holser, go to berths one and two and seal the hatches. Confine all seamen to quarters. Nick, meet the master-at-arms at the munitions locker. Stun guns and gas. Make sure the seamen with him are reliable before you open the locker. Stop the fighting. Separate the men, brig the rioters. Take these!" He snapped open the bridge safe and handed me a laser pistol and the locker keys. "I'll hold the bridge. Move!" He slapped open the hatch.

"Aye aye, sir!" We left on the double. Vax ran down the ladder to berths one and two while I headed forward to the armament locker.

I found the master-at-arms looming over two nervous seamen, a billy clenched in his hands. He was grim. "These two will do," he said. "Names?"

The first sailor stepped forward. "Gunner's Mate Edwards, sir."

She saluted. The other said, "Machinist's Mate Tsai Ting, sir." They both came to attention.

"At ease." I opened the locker. Master-at-arms Vishinsky's choices were dependable; I would stake my life on it. In his outrage he'd have but one goal: to restore order and get his hands on the miscreants.

I grabbed four sleek stun guns and handed them around. I snatched a handful of gas grenades, thrust them at Ms. Edwards. The locker safely shut, I loped toward the ladder, the others at my heels. I charged down to Level 2, ran around the ladder well, and dived down toward the lowest level. At Level 3 I dashed along the gray-walled corridor toward the crew berths. Around the bend, a crowd of seamen milled outside a hatchway, pushing and shoving for a better view.

"Stand to, all of you!" My voice was pitched higher than I'd have liked. "Attention!" A few in the back realized an officer was present and stiffened. Vishinsky waded in, billy club jabbing, stunner ready in his left hand. In moments he had the throng separated, lining the bulkheads to either side.

I gabbled, "Edwards, draw your weapon! You sailors, stand at attention! Ting, Edwards, stun any man who moves!" I swung back and forth, calmed slightly as I realized the situation in the corridor was under control.

From inside the berth, shouts and the sounds of riot.

"Let's go!" I charged at the hatch.

Mr. Vishinsky hauled me back, nearly hurling me to the deck. "Easy, sir." For a moment his eye held mine. He cautiously poked his head into the hatch, stunner ready. After peering both directions, he stepped through.

I followed, abashed. Inside, about a dozen seamen were slugging it out. Chief Petty Officer Terrill lay across a bunk, blood oozing from his scalp. Other sailors lay on the deck, out of combat. Chairs, bunks, duffels were strewn in wild disarray. The air smelled of sweat and close confinement.

Vishinsky took a deep breath. "*NOW HEAR THIS! STAND TO, EVERY ONE OF YOU!*" His roar filled the room. Its sheer force brought a momentary lull in the melee. "*DROP YOUR HANDS, YOU LOW-LIFE CRUDS! STAND AT ATTENTION!*" I wanted to cover my ears. He was impressive.

Most of the combatants began to disengage. They looked about, as if dazed, and brought themselves to attention. I covered them with my stunner. Four men ignored the master-at-arms, continued to hammer each other.

Coolly, Vishinsky stepped up to the first pair and pressed his stunner to one fighter's back. His finger twitched. The seaman dropped like
a stone. His sparring partner aimed a wild swing at the master-at-arms.
Vishinsky fired again. His assailant fell backward across a bunk, toppled
to the deck.

I watched openmouthed as Vishinsky sauntered to the last two combatants. He pressed his gun to one man's shoulder and fired. The sailor
went down. His opponent backed away, raising his hands high as he
sucked at air in ragged gasps. Vishinsky motioned him to stand with the
others. As the man turned to go, the Master kicked him in the behind.
The sailor staggered.

A thud, from the corridor. I looked out. A seaman was stretched on
the deck, unconscious. "He moved, sir." Edwards swallowed.

"Very well." I spoke as calmly as I could. Now what? Not sure what
else to do, I ordered all the sailors to the outer side of the corridor and
bade them sit on the deck, hands on their knees. "Keep your stunner on
them, Edwards." I sent Ting inside the berth to cover the remaining
seamen.

I dialed the bridge from the caller on the bulkhead. "Mr. Seafort
reporting, sir. The riot is over. We'll need the Doctor for a few of them.
At least a dozen were fighting."

"What in the Lord's name started it?" I heard the relief in Captain
Malstrom's voice.

"I don't know yet, sir."

"I'll send Chief McAndrews to help sort it out. Stand easy."

When the Chief arrived, he unsealed crew berth one and picked six
reliable seamen. He'd brought cuffs and leg irons; within a few minutes
I was able to collect the stunners and grenades and run them up to the
arms locker. When I got back to the crew berth, the Chief and the
master-at-arms were sorting through the mess on the deck, tossing belongings aside as they went.

Mr. Vishinsky took an opportunity to maneuver me to one side.
"Sorry my arm got tangled in your jacket," he said quietly.

"Thanks, Mr. Vishinsky. You saved me from getting clubbed to
death."

"No problem." A good man, the master-at-arms. There was a time
to belay regs, and he knew when.

"Here it is!" Chief McAndrews held up a vial of amber liquid. A
little box at his feet held several similar vials.

I blinked. "Goofjuice?" I used the slang term for the pervasive
drug.

"Look how much they have. I wonder if they brought it aboard." The Chief looked about with suspicion.

"Of course they brought it, sir," I said. "They didn't find it on—" I stopped. "A still, on the ship?" It was impossible. No one would dare.

"Maybe." He caught Vishinsky's eye; the master-at-arms gave the billy in his hands an angry twist. They went to work with a vengeance, removing every item in each sailor's locker. It took them two hours to find it. The back plate of one seaman's locker was loose; behind was a cavity in the bulkhead.

"Lord God damn these people!" Vishinsky intended no blasphemy; I was sure he meant it literally. Arnolf Tuak, the hapless owner of the locker, was hauled off to the brig.

It was late in the night before full order was restored and all known offenders were under lock and key. Wearily, we trooped back to officers' country. "A bad kettle of fish," was all Chief McAndrews had to say.

"Yes, sir." Bad indeed.

"Contraband drugs on *Hibernia*." Captain Malstrom said it again.

"Yes, sir." I stood at attention; he had forgotten to let me stand easy.

His mouth curled in revulsion. "I expect they'll smuggle a flask of wet stuff, Nicky. All sailors do that. But goofjuice . . ."

Goofjuice was another matter entirely. It didn't seem addictive at first. But once it got hold, its grip was almost unshakable. The erratic behavior it caused wasn't a problem to the joey indulging; he was in bliss all the while he was under the influence. But we had just seen an example of the mess it made for everyone else.

"Yes, sir. At least we found the source."

Juice wasn't that hard to make: a few test tubes, a retort, starch, magnesium salts, other common ingredients.

"When Admiralty hears of this . . ." He shook his head. Actually, I doubted it would be that bad. If Captain Haag were still in command he'd have had a lot to explain. But Mr. Malstrom hadn't been in charge when the crew boarded.

He looked up. "Stand easy, Nicky. I'm sorry."

"Thank you, sir." I relaxed. "How are you going to handle it? Captain's Mast?" It was not a question a middy could ask. But Mr. Malstrom obviously wanted to talk about it, and once he had been my friend Harv.

"No." His face hardened. "Court-martial." Seeing my surprise he added, "Those scum knew what they were doing. They broke a dozen regs just getting the stuff aboard ship. Then they caused a major riot among the crew. What if they'd gone berserk on duty stations, instead of in their bunks? In the engine room, or the airlock?"

He was right, up to a point. The sailors' stupidity might have wrecked our ship. But it hadn't; we'd dealt with them in crew quarters. Captain's Mast, or nonjudicial punishment, would mete out demotion, pay decreases, or extra duties. A court-martial was far more serious. While *Hibernia* was interstellar, far from home, the men could be punished with the brig, summary dismissal, or even execution.

Instead of putting the incident behind us, court-martial would formalize and enlarge it. Worse, the matter would drag on unhealed while the court-martial was convened, poisoning relations between the enlisted men and officers.

"Yes, sir. I understand." It wasn't my place to tell him my reservations.

"I'm appointing Pilot Haynes as hearing officer. Alexi will be their advocate."

"Alexi?" I was so astonished I forgot my discipline. "Sir," I quickly added, to correct my breach.

"Who else? It has to be an officer. Chief McAndrews found the stuff; he'll be a witness like you and Vax. Sandy has to present the evidence against them. There's no one else left."

"Doc Uburu?"

"Doc treated the injured and conducted the interrogations." The Captain was right; he had no more officers to call on.

"Aye aye, sir." I began figuring how to relieve Alexi from his watches, so he'd have more time to study the regs.

The court convened three days later, in the vacant lieutenants' common room where the Board of Inquiry had met. In all, fifteen men were charged. Three were accused of organizing the still, taking part in the riot, and assaulting a superior officer. They were in the worst trouble of all. Five more were charged with use of contraband intoxicants, four of those with rioting as well. Seven others were charged with taking part in the melee.

It wasn't as complicated as it sounded. Petty Officer Terrill knew which two sailors had worked him over: one of the men who was accused of using the goofjuice, and one of the three distributors. Several of those charged with rioting pled guilty to all charges, throwing themselves on the Captain's mercy. Two of the men accused of using the goofjuice also pled guilty.

The Captain was not lenient; he sentenced four of the men to six months in the brig and busted three others right down to apprentice seaman. Then the trials of the remaining eight got under way.

The three men charged with supplying the goofjuice were tried first. Pilot Haynes, sitting at the raised desk, listened impassively while Alexi Tamarov haltingly argued on behalf of his clients. It was no kangaroo court; when the Pilot felt the middy was not bringing out a defensive point, he put aside his preferred reticence and questioned the witness himself.

The three hapless sailors whispered with Alexi from time to time, interrupting his questioning of Chief McAndrews.

"Was the vial under a particular bunk when you found it, sir?"

"Not completely," said the Chief, unruffled. "The box was on the deck, half pushed under a bunk."

"So you don't know for sure that it was in Mr. Tuak's possession, sir?" Alexi was doing his best on a hopeless case. Tuak had already confessed under P and D. As was his right, he recanted his confession, but of course it would be entered against him. Alexi was casting about for other evidence to discredit it.

"I don't know, Mr. Tamarov." The Chief was undisturbed; other witnesses had identified the box as belonging to Tuak.

"Sir, did you see anything that contradicts Mr. Tuak's having been framed by another sailor?"

"Yes." Alexi looked surprised and worried, but had no choice but to let the Chief answer. "When he recovered from the stun charge, Mr. Tuak tried to claw Mr. Vishinsky's face."

"Could that have been from anger at having been stunned unjustly?"

"It could have," said the Chief, his tone making clear he didn't believe it.

The trial droned on. I was called as a witness, but had little to offer except a description of Mr. Vishinsky quelling the riot. Neither Sandy nor Alexi seemed much interested in my testimony.

The trial, I reflected, was mostly ritual. It could help disclose truth, but that has rarely been necessary since P and D testing became the norm. Yet we still observed the old forms in civilian as well as military courts: defense attorneys, prosecutors, witnesses. In nearly all cases we already knew the outcome.

While the trial was in recess I wandered into the passengers' lounge, looking for a conversation to distract me. Perhaps Mrs. Donhauser and Mr. Ibn Saud were at it again. I found two older passengers I barely knew, reading holovids. One of the Treadwell twins, the girl, was writing a game program; she tested it from time to time on the passengers' screen. Derek Carr, lean, tall, aristocratic, studied the holo of the galaxy on the bulkhead, hands clasped behind his back.

I stood near him, lowering my voice. "My condolences, Mr. Carr. I never had a chance to speak to you after your father's death."

"Thank you," the boy said distantly. His eyes remained on the holo. It was a dismissal.

"If there's anything I can do, please let me know." I moved away.

"Midshipman." He didn't even know my name, after sitting at table with me a month. I waited. "There's something you can do. Talk with me." He hesitated. "I need to speak to someone. It might as well be you."

Graciously stated. I made allowances for his bereavement. "All right. Where?"

"Let's walk." We strolled aimlessly along the circumference corridor, passing the dining hall, the ladders, the Level 2 passenger staterooms.

He said, "My father and I own property on Hope Nation. A lot of it. That's why we were going home."

"Then you're provided for." I spoke just to keep the conversation going.

"Oh, yes." His tone was bitter. "Trusts and guardianships; my father had it all worked out. He showed me his will. The banks and the plantation managers will run the estate for years. I won't get anything until I'm twenty-two. Six years! I mean, I won't starve. But it's not like . . ."

After a while I prompted, "Like what, Mr. Carr?"

He looked into the distance, beyond the bulkhead. "He'd been training me to run the plantations. He taught me bookkeeping, the crop cycles. We made decisions together. I thought . . ." His eyes misted. "My father and I . . . We had money, we had a good life. I thought it would always be that way."

Thrusting his hands in his pockets he turned to me, his eyes bleak. "And now it's all gone. I'll be treated like a joeyboy again. Nobody will listen. No one will care. It'll be years before I can do anything about it."

I said nothing, taking it in. "Do you have a mother?"

"No, I'm a monogenetic clone. Just my father." Not an uncommon arrangement of late, but I wondered how it would feel. Back home in Cardiff we were more conservative; I carried my host mother's genes as well as Father's, though I'd never met her. After a moment Derek added, "I thought you might understand, being my own age and all. And having responsibilities."

"Yes, I understand. Tell me something, Mr. Carr."

"What?"

I probably shouldn't have said it, but I was overtired and my nerves were on edge. "Do you miss your father?" He stiffened at my tone. I added, "You haven't mentioned how you feel about him. Just the advantages he gave you."

He was furious. "I miss him. More than a person like you will ever know. Forget we spoke." He stalked back down the corridor.

I strode quickly to catch up. "How do you expect me to know, when you keep it hidden?"

He took several more steps before slowing. Finally he stopped, hand against the bulkhead. "I don't wear my feelings for everyone to see," he said coldly. "It's uncouth."

I felt I owed him something for jabbing at him. "The day I went to Academy at Dover, I was thirteen. My father brought me to town. I had my belongings in a duffel I carried at my side. Father walked me to the compound gates, his hands in his pockets, saying nothing. When we reached the gate I stopped to say good-bye. He turned my shoulders around and pushed me toward the entrance. I started walking. When I looked again he was striding away without looking back." I paused. "I dream about it frequently. The psych says I'll probably outgrow it." I took a couple of breaths to restore calm. "It's not the same, Mr. Carr, but I know what loneliness is."

After a pause Derek said, "I'm sorry I snapped at you, Midshipman."

"It's Seafort. Nick Seafort."

"I apologize, Midshipman Seafort. My father always said we were extraordinary, and I believed it. In a way we are. It's hard to remember other people have feelings too."

We wandered back to the lounge, saying nothing. At the hatch we stopped, and after an awkward moment we shook hands.

8

According to ritual Mr. Tuak stood in front of the presiding officer's desk with his advocate, Alexi. The two stood at attention while Pilot Haynes declared his verdict.

"Mr. Tuak, the court finds you guilty of the offense of possessing aboard a Naval vessel a contraband substance, to wit, a magnesium starch colloquially known as goofjuice. The court nominally sentences you to two years imprisonment for this offense." The court always imposed the maximum sentence provided for in the regs, a nominal sentence subject to review and reduction by the Captain.

"Mr. Tuak, the court finds you guilty of the offense of rioting aboard a vessel under weigh. The court nominally sentences you to six months imprisonment and loss of all rank and benefits." Pilot Haynes stopped for breath. It was the longest speech I had ever heard him make.

"The court also finds you guilty of striking a superior officer, to wit, Mr. Vishinsky, and likewise Mr. Terrill, in an attempt to prevent the performance of their duty. The court sentences you—nominally sentences you—to be hanged by the neck until dead, and remands you to the master-at-arms for execution of the sentence."

Even though the sentence was known and expected, Alexi's shoulders fell and his head bowed. Tuak stood unmoving, as if he hadn't heard.

After, in the wardroom, I tried to comfort Alexi. He had been crying and paid no attention to my consolation. Vax watched as I fumbled at Alexi's arm, muttering inane words. After a time the burly midshipman tapped me on the shoulder and motioned me aside. He sat on the bed next to Alexi and put his big hand on the back of the younger middy's neck, squeezing the muscle gently.

"Let go; I'm all right." Alexi tried to pull away Vax's hand.

"Not until you listen." His hand stayed where it was. "My uncle is a lawyer. A criminal lawyer back in Sri Lanka."

"So?"

"He once told me the hardest part of his job. He liked his clients, some of them." Vax waited, but Alexi made no comment.

"When he couldn't get his clients freed, the hardest thing for him to remember was that it was their own fault they were in trouble, not his. They were in jail not because he had failed them, but because they had fouled up in the first place."

"There must have been a way to get him out of it." Alexi's voice was muffled, but at least he was listening.

"Not in this Navy." Vax spoke with certainty. He picked up the younger middy and turned him over onto his back. Again I wished for Vax's strength. "Read the regs, Alexi. They're designed to protect authority, not to encourage flouting it."

"But executing him—"

"That's for the Captain to decide. Anyway, he's a drug dealer. I have no sympathy for him. Why should you?"

I sat down on my bunk. I wasn't needed anymore.

"But they might hang him!" Alexi propped himself up on an elbow. "Look, I know you want me to feel better. But tell me Lieutenant Dagalow couldn't have done something to save him!"

"Lieutenant Dagalow couldn't have done anything to save him," Vax said evenly. "A ship under weigh is under the strictest military rules. It has to be, to preserve order and lives. The rules are clear. What happened down in berth three was nearly a mutiny. You don't think mutineers should get off, do you?"

"Of course not!" Alexi said indignantly. It was unthinkable to us all.

"Tuak struck an officer in the performance of his duty. That's a form of mutiny. You have a hell of a nerve sympathizing with him, Tamarov!"

Alexi was smart enough to make the distinction. "I don't sympathize with what he did, just the penalties. Sometimes we've screwed up too, you know. You mutinied against Mr. Seafort, didn't you?"

"Yes, and he let me off easy. Mr. Seafort should have taken my head off. I realize that, now." Oh. Nice to know.

"Then we're just luckier than Tuak," said Alexi bitterly.

"No," I intervened. "Mouthing off in the wardroom isn't comparable to dealing drugs to the crew or hitting the CPO, and you know it."

After a moment Alexi sighed. "I know," he said. He sat up. "You joes realize I have to go through it again? With the other trials?"

We commiserated. The crisis was over.

The other trials began the next day. When they were done, two other unfortunate sailors were under sentence of execution for striking their officers. A variety of lesser penalties had been handed out to the remaining participants.

The Pilot formally presented his verdicts to Captain Malstrom. The

Captain had thirty days to act; unless he commuted the sentences, they'd
be automatically carried out by the master-at-arms.

During the next few days the officers watched for signs of tension
among the crew. There was some bitterness, but on the whole the hands
settled down. Our crew knew the ship needed authority at its helm, just
as the rest of us did. If Captain Malstrom was troubled by the decision
he had to make, he didn't show it. He relaxed visibly when it was clear
the unrest was over. He laughed easily, joked with the younger passengers, and arranged a place for me several evenings at the Captain's table,
though it was not customary to favor an officer.

Once he even invited me to play chess. He knew I would be uncomfortable in the Captain's quarters; they were so unapproachable I'd
never been allowed to see them. We went instead to the deserted lieutenants' common room.

We set up the board for the first time in many weeks. I didn't play
well, not by choice, but from nervousness. Playing the Captain was
nothing like playing a second lieutenant. He seemed to sense my mood
and chatted with me, trying to put me at my ease.

"Have you reached a decision yet, sir, on the rioters?" It was presumptuous of me, but Captain Malstrom seemed pleased by my attempt
at intimacy. Perhaps he needed it.

His face darkened. "I don't see how I can let them off and keep a
disciplined ship." He sighed. "I'm trying to justify commuting the death
sentences; the thought of killing those poor men sickens me. But in good
conscience, I don't know how I can."

"You still have time to decide."

"Yes, twenty-five days. We'll see." He turned the conversation to
Hope Nation. He asked if I still intended to buy him a drink. Yes, I said,
knowing it was unlikely. A Captain on shore leave doesn't carouse with
middies. For one thing, he's too busy.

After that day, something was wrong. I didn't know what, but the
Captain didn't offer a smile when we met in the ship's dining hall. He
looked preoccupied and grim. I shared a four-hour watch with him and
the Pilot. He hardly spoke. I assumed his decision about the death
sentences was affecting his mood.

Two days later we Defused for a scheduled navigation check. The
greater the distance in Fusion, the more our navigation errors would
compound. It was customary on a long cruise such as ours to Defuse two
or three times, replotting the coordinates each time.

We came out of Fusion deep in lonely interstellar space. Darla and
the Pilot both plotted our course. Their figures agreed with those of Vax,

who as midshipman of the watch also ran a check. But instead of Fusing directly, the Captain laid over another night, drifting in space.

At dinner that night I sat two tables from the Captain. He seemed determined to be cheerful. I could see him teasing Yorinda Vincente, who laughed uncertainly, as if unsure of the right response. I looked for Amanda and found her across the hall at Table Seven with Dr. Uburu. I willed her to catch my eye. Eventually she did, smiled gently, turned away.

A forkful of beef halfway to my mouth, I watched the Captain reach for his water glass. He paused, a puzzled look on his face. He gestured and said something to the steward, who hurried to Table Seven. A moment later Dr. Uburu was kneeling by the Captain's chair. Captain Malstrom was hunched over the table.

Two sailors serving the mess helped the Captain to his feet, supporting him from either side, guiding his unsteady steps toward the corridor. Dr. Uburu followed. I watched, agape.

There was no one senior to stop me. I excused myself and boldly left the dining hall for the corridor to the ladder. I ran up the steps two at a time to officers' country. No one was in the infirmary except the med tech on watch. I hurried forward to the Captain's cabin. Of course his hatch was shut. It was unheard of to knock, so I waited.

After some minutes Dr. Uburu stepped out and shut the hatch. "What are you doing here?" Her tone was a challenge.

I wasn't reassured by the look on her dark, wide-boned, face. "Is he all right, ma'am?"

She ignored my breach of discipline. "I can't discuss the Captain's personal affairs." She started toward the infirmary.

I hurried to keep up. "Is there anything I can—I mean—" I didn't know what I meant.

Dr. Uburu was brusque. "Go back to the dining hall. That's an order."

Phrased like that, she left me no choice at all. She was an officer, rank equal to a lieutenant, and I was a midshipman. "Aye aye, ma'am." I turned and left.

All next day the Captain was off watch. I asked the Pilot when we would Fuse; he shrugged and left it at that, and I knew I wouldn't get any information from him. When my watch ended at last I went back to the wardroom. None of the other middies had heard anything reliable through the ship's grapevine.

I was thinking about hunting for Amanda; I needed her comforting acceptance. But there came a knock on the wardroom hatch; the med tech was outside, ill at ease. "Mr. Seafort, sir, you're wanted in the infirmary."

"Why the infirmary?" If anything, I was hoping for a summons from the Captain's cabin.

"It's the Captain, sir. He's been moved there." Vax and I exchanged a glance. I donned my jacket and hurried after the tech. Dr. Uburu indicated a cubicle; I went in alone.

Captain Malstrom lay on his side under a limp white sheet, his head propped on a pillow. The halogen lights hurt my eyes. He offered a weak smile as I entered and came to attention. "As you were."

"How are you, sir?"

For answer he threw off the sheet. He wore only his undershorts. His side and back were a mass of blue-gray lumps.

I closed my eyes for a moment, trying to will them away. "How long have you known, I mean, have they been—"

"Four days. They came up just a few days ago." He made an effort to smile again.

"Is it . . ."

"It's T."

"Oh, Harv." Tears were running down my face. "Oh, God, I'm so sorry."

"Thank you."

"Can she—are they doing anything, sir? Radiation, anticars?"

"There's more, Nicky. She found it in my liver, my lungs, my stomach. I haven't been able to see too well today, either. She thinks it might be in my brain too."

I didn't care what they did to me. I reached out and took his hand. If anyone had seen, I could have been summarily shot.

He squeezed my fingers. "It's all right, Nicky. I'm not afraid. I'm a good Christian."

"But *I'M* afraid, sir." The situation began to sink in on me. "That's why you didn't Fuse."

"Yes. I think . . . I'm not sure . . . whether to go back." He lay back, closing his eyes. He breathed slowly, hoarding his strength. We stayed as we were for several minutes. I began to realize what had to be done.

"Captain," I said slowly, clearly. "You have to give Vax his commission. Right now."

He came awake. "I hate to do it, Nicky. He can be such a bully. If he's in charge and there's no one to stop him . . ."

"He's changed, sir. He'll do all right."

"I don't know . . ." His eyes closed.

"Captain Malstrom, for the love of Lord God, for the sake of this ship, commission Vax while you still can!"

He opened his eyes again. "You think I ought to?"

"It's absolutely necessary." What might happen otherwise was too horrible to contemplate.

"I suppose you're right." He was growing drowsy. "I'll sign it into the Log. First thing in the morning."

"I could get the Log now, sir."

"No, I want to think about it overnight. Bring him in tomorrow morning, I'll do it then."

"Aye aye, sir." He was sleeping by the time I reached the hatch.

Dr. Uburu faced me in the anteroom. "He ordered me to announce his illness to the ship," she said. "Rumors are everywhere."

"I know," I said. I'd heard some of them.

She smiled warmly. It lighted her face and I was grateful. "I'll stay up with him tonight."

"Thank you, ma'am." I took her nod for a dismissal and left.

In the wardroom the other midshipmen questioned me silently. I had nothing to say to them; there was no way I could tell Vax he was going to make lieutenant, before Captain Malstrom had made up his mind. When the Doctor's solemn announcement came over the speaker we all listened in silence. Afterward I slapped off the light. None of us spoke.

First thing in the morning I arranged for Sandy to take Vax's watch. A quick breakfast in the officers' mess, then I told Vax the Captain wanted to see us in the infirmary.

Dr. Uburu had been dozing at the table in the outer compartment; she woke when we came in. She said the Chief Engineer had already brought the Log chip from the bridge, on Captain Malstrom's instructions. "He's awake and wants to see you. He's not doing too well." Her tone was glum.

We entered the sickroom, snapping to attention. The Captain was dozing in his bunk. He heard the hatch close, and opened his eyes. "Vax, Nicky, hi," he said vaguely. The ship's Log was in the holovid on a small bunkside table, within his reach.

"Good morning, sir," I said. He didn't answer. "Captain, we're here to do what you said last night."

"I was having dinner," he said suddenly, loudly.

"When you were taken ill, two nights ago, sir." I tried to think how to direct him. Vax watched, puzzled. "Captain, last night we talked about Mr. Holser. Do you remember?"

"Yes." Captain Malstrom smiled at me. "Vax, the bully." An icicle crept up my spine. I wanted to move to him, but we were still at attention; he hadn't released us.

I was so desperate I prompted him. "Sir, we talked about Vax's commission. Don't you remember?"

He came fully awake. "Nicky." He studied me. "We talked. I said I would . . . make him looey. Of course!" I was weak with relief. He turned to Vax. "Mr. Holser, wait outside while we talk."

"Aye aye, sir." Vax spun smartly and left the room.

I took it as permission to move. I took the Log and dialed the current page. "Sir, let me help you. I can write; all you have to do is sign."

Captain Malstrom began to weep. "I'm sorry, Nicky. I guess I have to give it to him. He's the qualified one. You aren't. I don't have a—it's the only way!"

"I know, sir. I want you to. Here, I'll write it." I took the laserpencil. "I, Captain Harvey Malstrom, do commission and appoint Midshipman Vax Stanley Holser lieutenant in the Naval Service of the Government of the United Nations, by the Grace of God." I knew the words by heart, as did every midshipman.

I handed him the laserpencil. He stared at it, as if it were wild. "Nicky, I don't feel well." His face was white.

"Please, sir, just sign, and I'll get Dr. Uburu. Please."

He began to tremble. "I . . . Nick, I've—NICKY!" His head snapped back, his jaw clenched shut. His whole body shivered.

"Dr. Uburu!"

The Doctor came running at my yell. One look and she grabbed for a hypo, filled it from a medicine bottle in the cabinet nearby. "Move, boy!" She shoved me aside and bared his arm. As the hypo plunged, his rigid muscles slowly relaxed. His hand opened. "Give me the Log," he whispered. But his hand wouldn't hold the pencil.

I said, "Captain Malstrom, commission him orally! Dr. Uburu is witness!" The way it came out, it sounded like an order.

He muttered something. I couldn't tell what it was. Then he drifted toward sleep. "This afternoon," he said clearly, surprising me. "After I rest." I waited, but his breath came in short rasping sounds. His face was flushed.

I took hold of the Doctor's arm. I had touched the Captain, now it might as well be Dr. Uburu; I had lost all sense of propriety. I tugged her toward the corner. "Do you realize," I whispered, "what will happen if he doesn't commission Vax?"

"Yes," she said coldly, pulling my hand from her arm.

"He's got to sign the Log! Will he be able to, this afternoon?"

"Perhaps. I have no way to know."

"I heard him orally commission Vax. You did too." I stared her straight in the eye, hoping she would realize what had to be done.

"I heard no such thing," she said bluntly. "And you are a gentleman by act of the General Assembly. A gentleman does not lie!"

I blushed all the way up to my ears. "Doctor, he has GOT to sign that Log."

"Then let's hope he wakes up in condition to do it." She added, "I agree with you. It's necessary for the ship's safety that he sign Vax's commission."

"But you won't . . ."

"No, I won't. And you won't suggest it again. That is a direct order which you disobey at your peril! Acknowledge it." She had steel in her. I hadn't known.

"Aye aye, ma'am. I will not suggest again that Captain orally commissioned Vax. I accept your statement that he did not. Is there anything else, ma'am?"

"Yes, Nick. Duty is sometimes unclear. Right now your duty is to obey the regulations you swore to uphold. All of them. I trust that by the Grace of God the Captain will do what he must. You would do better to pray than to scheme, young man."

"Yes, ma'am." She was right.

Vax was waiting outside the sickroom. "What was all that about?" he asked.

We walked back along the corridor toward the wardroom. Now he had a right to know. "I asked the Captain to commission you lieutenant. He said he would do it this morning. I wrote it out in the Log for him."

"And?"

"He hasn't signed it. He's disoriented. I asked Dr. Uburu to agree that he had commissioned you orally, but she said he hadn't. In truth, he had not."

Vax took my arm. There was a lot of touching going on in *Hibernia*. "Why did you want him to?"

"Vax, what the hell happens when the Captain dies? Do you expect me to try to run the ship?"

I don't think it had occurred to him until that moment. It had only occurred to me two days ago. "Oh, my God."

"And mine." We locked eyes. "We'll come back in a couple of hours. He'll sign it. He has to." We walked the rest of the way in uneasy silence.

After lunch we returned to the infirmary. At my request Chief Mc-Andrews also came. The Doctor, the Chief, Vax, and I waited in the sickroom for the Captain to awaken. He slept fitfully, tossing and turning. The silence in the brightly lit room grew unbearable.

Hours passed. "Is there anything you can give him?" I asked Dr. Uburu. "Some sort of stimulant?"

"Yes. If I want to kill him," she growled. "His systems are closing down. He can't take much."

"He's got to wake up long enough to sign the Log, or at least tell us orally!"

She shook her head, but after a while she loaded a syringe and gave Captain Malstrom an injection. Chief McAndrews sat near the bed; the Doctor was at a table close by. Vax stood stolidly against the bulkhead; I paced with increasing nervousness.

"Nicky." The Captain's eyes were open and riveted on me.

"Yes, sir." I hurried over to the bed. I picked up the holovid with the Log.

The Captain swallowed with difficulty. As I came closer he squinted to keep me in focus. "Nicky . . . you're my son," he said weakly.

"What?" My voice squeaked. I couldn't have heard right. I leaned close.

He raised a hand and touched my cheek. His breathing was ragged. "You've been . . . a son to me. I never had another."

"Oh, God!" It was too much for me; I wept. He touched me again; his hand moved uncertainly in front of my face before it found me. "I'm dying," he said, with wonder.

Hating myself, I said urgently, "Sir, do your duty! Tell Chief McAndrews and Dr. Uburu that Vax is a lieutenant. Tell them."

"My son," he said, dropping his hand. He stopped breathing. I turned frantically to the Doctor but the Captain's breath caught again in a ragged gasp. He stared at me, his face an unhealthy blue. Understanding slowly left his eyes and they closed.

Dr. Uburu started intravenous liquids. While we waited helplessly, they dripped into his arm in the age-old manner. The Captain lay unconscious, his mouth ajar.

"Do something. With all your machinery, help him!" My words were a demand.

"I can't!" she spat. "I can pump his heart for him; I can even replace it. I can oxygenate his blood just as his lungs do. I can purify his blood with dialysis. I can even replicate his liver. We're talented, aren't we? But I can't do all those things at once. He's dying! The poor man's insides are rotten; he's like an overripe melon about to split open. The melanoma's everywhere."

She stopped for breath, her fury nailing me to the bulkhead. "He's got it in his stomach, his liver, his lungs, his colon. His sight is going from an optic tumor. It's as bad as T can get. Sometimes—only once in a while, thank God—it grows so fast you can see it. Do something? *DO SOMETHING?* I can stay with him to wish him into Yahweh's hands. That's what I can do!" Her cheeks were wet.

"And I can let him go in peace and privacy." Chief McAndrews got heavily to his feet. "Nick, stay with him. If he rallies he'll sign it. Or he'll tell Dr. Uburu as witness. There's no use my staying." He left.

"Vax, will you stay with me?"

Vax Holser, his pent-up emotions roiling, glared at me with such fury as I have never seen from another man. He twice opened his mouth to speak. Then he stalked out in a passion, slamming the hatch shut.

I stayed in the infirmary during evening mess, in the chair the Chief had vacated. The Captain's breathing varied, sometimes regular and deep, sometimes ragged. Late in the evening Dr. Uburu slipped an oxygen mask over his nose and mouth. She introduced vapormeds into the oxygen mixture; I couldn't tell if they helped. She sent the med tech to the galley for a tray for me. I ate in my chair, never taking my eyes from the still form in the bunk.

"I'll watch him, Nicky," she said after I began to doze. "Go to bed."

"Let me stay." It was somewhere between a demand and a plea. Perhaps she understood from my eyes. She nodded. She checked the alarms on the bedside monitors and retired to the anteroom. I dozed, came awake, and dozed again. The bright lights accented the stillness. Finally I curled up in the chair and slept.

I woke toward morning, to realize the labored sounds of his breathing had stopped. I called Dr. Uburu; she came and stood next to me by his still form under the clean white sheet.

"The alarms. Why didn't they . . ."

"I turned them off." She answered my look of betrayal. "I could do nothing more for him. Except let him go in peace."

Stunned, I sank back into the chair. I don't know how long I sat there alone; I got up mechanically when I heard the change of watch after breakfast. I went out into the anteroom where Dr. Uburu waited.

She got to her feet. "I'm going to meet with the Chief and Pilot Haynes." I didn't answer.

I left the infirmary, followed the corridor to the wardroom, passing someone on the way. Sandy and Alexi were inside; Alexi, just off watch, was in his bed. Sandy stood as I entered.

"Out, both of you." They scrambled to the hatch. I pulled off my jacket and lay on my bunk. My head spun, but sleep evaded me. I heard noises in the corridor. I tried to block them out, could not. I lay awake in a stupor.

Hours later Alexi knocked on the hatch. "Mr. Seafort—"

"Stay out until I give you permission to enter!"

"Aye aye, sir." The hatch shut.

I buried my head in the pillow, hoping for tears. None came.

I awoke later in the day with an intense thirst. I got up, found my jacket, went to the head. As I slopped water from my hand to my mouth I studied my reflection in the mirror. My hair was wild; there were hollows under my eyes. My expression was frightening.

I splashed cold water on my face and went back to the wardroom. I dressed in clean clothes and combed my hair. Then I went below to the ship's library on Level 2, where I signed out the holovid chips for the Naval Regulations and Code of Conduct, Revision of 2087. I took them back to the wardroom and sat on my bunk.

It took about twenty minutes to find what I was looking for.

"Section 121.2. The Captain of a vessel may relieve himself of command when disabled and unfit for duty by reason of mental illness or physical sickness or injury. Upon his certification of such action in the Log, his rank of Captain shall be suspended and command shall devolve on the next-ranking line officer."

I thumbed through the regs looking for other half-remembered sections. I flipped back and forth, carefully reading definitions and terms.

The hatch opened cautiously. Vax looked in, then entered. We faced each other.

"He died before he signed it." It was half statement, half question.

"Yes," I said.

"What will you do?"

"I don't know." I saw no reason to hide it.

"Nicky—Mr. Seafort—"

"You can call me Nicky."

"—you can't captain the ship."

I was silent.

"You can't maneuver her. You can't plot a course. You don't understand the drives."

"I know."

"Step aside, Nicky. It's just until we get back home. They'll send us out with new officers."

"I've been thinking about doing that," I said.

"For the ship's safety. Please."

"You'd run her?"

"Me, or the officers' committee. Doc and the Chief and the Pilot. It doesn't matter. They're meeting right now, to figure what to do."

"I understand." I flipped off the holovid.

"You agree?"

"No. I understand." I got up. "Vax, I wanted you to command. I begged him to sign your commission the first night he was ill."

"I know. After how I treated you I can hardly look you in the eye." He hesitated. "It's just a fluke I wasn't senior," he said bitterly. "Four months difference."

"Yes." I put the holovid in my pocket and went to the hatch. "I wish I'd gone with Captain Haag on the launch, Vax. If I could choose now, that's where I'd be."

"Don't talk like that, Nick."

"I'm desperate." I went out.

No one but the med tech was at the infirmary. The Captain's body was already in a cold locker. I tried the Doctor's cabin, but no one answered. I went below along the circumference passage to the Chief's quarters, and met the Pilot just coming out the hatch.

"I was on my way to get you." He gestured me inside. The Chief's cabin was the same size as the one in which Lieutenant Malstrom and I had played chess. Dr. Uburu and the Chief were seated around a small table. I found a chair and joined them.

"Nick." The Doctor's tone was gentle. "Someone has to decide what to do."

"That's right," I said.

"The crew needs to know who's in charge. We have to get the ship back home. We have to reassure the passengers. The Passengers' Council voted unanimously to return to Earthport, and wants the officers' committee to take control."

Chief McAndrews hesitated, glanced at the others. "There's ambiguity in the regs as to whether a midshipman can assume the Captaincy. We think he can't. And even if he can, we want you to remove yourself. And if you don't, we'll remove you for disability."

"Good," I said. "Get me out of this, please. Let's start with your first point. What regs are you looking at?" They all relaxed visibly at my response.

The Chief glanced at his notes. " 'Section 357.4. Every watch not commanded by the Captain shall be commanded by a commissioned officer under his direction.' " He cleared his throat. "A midshipman is not a commissioned officer. 357.4 says you have to be commissioned to command a watch."

"As a midshipman I can't command a watch. I agree with you."

"Then it's settled." Dr. Uburu.

"No. I'm no longer a midshipman."

"Why not?"

I reached for a holovid and inserted my chip. " 'Section 232.8. In case of death or disability of the Captain, his duties, authority, and title shall devolve on the next-ranking line officer.' "

"So?"

" 'Section 98.3. The following persons are not line officers within the meaning of these regulations: a Ship's Doctor, a chaplain, a Pilot, and an Engineer. All other officers are line officers within the meaning of these regulations.' "

" 'Section 101.9,' " countered the Chief. " 'The Captain of a vessel may from time to time appoint a midshipman, who shall serve in such capacity as the Captain and his officers may from time to time direct.' 101.9 suggests a middy may not even be an officer."

I scrolled my holovid to Section 92.5. " 'Command of any work detail may be delegated by the Captain or the officer of the watch to any lieutenant, midshipman, or other officer in his command.' " I looked around the table, repeating the deadly phrase. "Lieutenant, midshipman, or other officer." I said into the silence, "A midshipman is mentioned as an officer. A line officer."

The Pilot stirred. "It's still ambiguous. A midshipman isn't commissioned. The regs don't say a middy can become Captain."

"Nobody thought of it happening. I agree." I flipped back to the definitions section. " '12. Officer. An officer is a person commissioned or appointed by authority of the Government of the United Nations to its Naval Service, authorized thereby to direct all persons of subordinate rank in the commission of their duties.' "

I raised my eyes. "An officer doesn't have to be commissioned. Look, I want to reach the same conclusion you do. But the regs are clear. They don't say the Captaincy shall devolve on the next commissioned officer. They say line officer. I'm an officer. I'm not one of the officers excluded from line of command. I'm the senior line officer aboard."

"It's still not explicit," said the Chief. "We have to guess how to interpret the various passages put together. We can conclude a midshipman never succeeds to command."

"There's two problems in doing that. One, when we get home you'd be hanged."

There was a long silence. "And the other problem?" Dr. Uburu finally asked.

"I will construe it as mutiny."

They exchanged glances. I realized the possibility had occurred to them before I arrived.

"It hasn't come to that," the Chief said. "Let's say we all conclude that you're next in line. Step down. You're not ready to command."

"I'll be glad to. Just show me where it's allowed."

"Don't be ridiculous," said Dr. Uburu. "Quit. Resign the Captaincy. Relieve yourself."

"On what grounds?"

"Incompetence."

"Do you mean my lack of skill and other qualifications, or are you suggesting I'm mentally ill?"

"Nobody's saying you're mentally ill," she protested.

" 'Section 121.2. The Captain of a vessel may relieve himself of command when disabled and unfit for duty by reason of mental illness or physical sickness or injury.' " I laid down my holovid. "I am not physically sick or injured. I don't believe I'm mentally ill any more than you do."

"Isn't it an inherent authority?" she asked. "The Captain can relieve others. Surely he has inherent authority to relieve himself."

I said, "I thought of that. So I looked it up. 'Section 204.1. The Captain of a vessel shall assume and exert authority and control of the government of the vessel until relieved by order of superior authority, until his death, or until certification of his disability as otherwise provided herein.' I don't think they wanted Captains going around relieving themselves from duty."

"This is ridiculous," said the Pilot. "Everyone agrees, even you, that you shouldn't be Captain. Yet you're telling us we're stuck with you, that you can't quit, even though it's best for the ship."

"There's a reason for that," I told him. "You all know the Captain isn't a mere officer. He's the United Nations Government in transit. The Government cannot abdicate."

"Do it anyway, Nicky," Dr. Uburu said gently. "Just do it."

"No." I looked at each of them. "It is dereliction of duty. I swore an oath. 'I shall uphold the Charter of the United Nations, and the laws and regulations promulgated thereunder, to the best of my ability, by the Grace of Lord God Almighty.' I no longer have a choice."

"You're seventeen years old," said Chief McAndrews. "There are a hundred and ninety-nine people aboard whose lives depend on the safe operation of this vessel. We have to relieve you."

"You may relieve me only on the same grounds I can relieve myself," I said. "Look it up. I will consent to being relieved when a legal basis exists. Otherwise, I must resist." The Chief thumbed through the holovid to the section on disability. After a few moments, he reluctantly pushed it aside.

We had reached an impasse. We sat around the little table, hoping a solution would occur.

"And Vax?" the Doctor asked.

"Vax is better qualified. But Vax is not Captain. He's a midshipman. I am senior to him."

"Even though he is far better able to handle the ship," she said.

"Even though. You know how I tried to get the Captain to sign his commission." I closed my eyes. I was desperately tired. "There is one solution." She looked up at me, waiting. "Sign the Log, witnessing that Captain Malstrom commissioned Vax lieutenant before he died. I will acquiesce."

All eyes turned to the Ship's Doctor. She studied the tabletop for a long time. The tension in the room was palpable. After several minutes she raised her eyes and said, "I will not sign the Log in witness. Captain Malstrom did not grant Vax Holser a commission before he died." The Pilot let his breath out all at once.

She went on, "I realize now we are here in error. The Captain had ample opportunity, not just on his sickbed, but during the weeks after he took command, to commission Vax. He chose not to, knowing Mr. Seafort was senior midshipman. I know, just as you all know, that Captain Malstrom would acknowledge Mr. Seafort is next in line of command. Captain Malstrom had authority to leave Nick as senior remaining officer and did. We had no say in the matter while he lived. We have no say in the matter now."

I had one more hope. "Chief, you were in the infirmary with Captain Malstrom. If you can say you heard him commission Vax . . ."

The Chief didn't hesitate, not for a second. "The day I sign a lie into the Log, Mr. Seafort, is the day I walk unsuited out the airlock. No. I heard no such thing." He fingered the holovid. "We are all sworn officers. We all uphold the Government. It appears that the Government, in its unfathomable wisdom, has put you in charge. You know I wish it were not so. But my wishes don't count. Sir, I am a loyal officer and you may count on my service."

I swallowed. "I wanted you to argue me out of it, not the other way around. For the moment, I am Captain-designate. I will be Captain when I declare I have taken command of the ship, as did Captain Malstrom. First, I'm going back to my bunk to try to find a way out of this. Let's leave everything as it is. We'll meet at evening mess." I stood to go.

Automatically, all three of them stood with me.

9

Vax and Alexi snapped to attention when I crossed the wardroom threshold. They, at least, no longer considered me just the senior middy.

"I don't have command yet," I told them. "This is still my bunk and I want to be alone. Go pester the passengers or polish the fusion drive shaft. Beat it."

Alexi grinned with relief at my sally; he was as unsettled as the rest of us. He and Vax hurried out.

I lay on my bunk fiddling with my holovid until eventually I tossed it aside in disgust. I was trapped. I grieved for my friend Harv, but I was furious he hadn't had sense enough to commission Vax the day he took command. Vax could pilot, could navigate, understood the fusion drives, and had the forceful personality of a Captain.

I must have dozed. As afternoon watch ended I woke, ravenous. I couldn't remember when I'd last eaten. I washed and hurried to the dining hall for the evening meal. Master-at-arms Vishinsky and four of his seamen stood outside the hatch, with their billies. He saluted.

"What's this about?" I gestured to his sailors.

"Chief McAndrews ordered us up as a precaution, sir. There was some kind of demand from the passengers and an, uh, inquiry from the crew."

I spotted the Chief at his usual table. He stood when I approached. I flicked a thumb toward the master-at-arms and raised an eyebrow. "A written demand was delivered to the bridge, sir." His voice was quiet. "By that Vincente woman. Signed by almost all the passengers."

"What do they want?"

"To go home. That part's easy; we can Fuse any time. They demand that responsible and competent officers control the ship, forthwith. Commissioned officers who have reached their majority."

"Ah."

"Yes, sir." He paused. "And inquiries have come up from the crew," he said with delicacy. "Wondering where authority now rests."

"Oh, brother."

"Yes. The sooner you declare you've taken command, the better."

"Very well. After dinner. The officers will join me on the bridge."

"Aye aye, sir." He looked around the rapidly filling hall. "The evening prayer, sir. Will you give it?"

"And sit at the Captain's table, in the Captain's place?" I was repelled by the thought.

"That's where the Captain usually sits." His tone had a touch of acid.

"Not tonight. I'll say the prayer as senior officer, but from my usual place."

I went to my accustomed seat. Several passengers sharing my table looked upon me with hostility. None spoke. I decided I could ignore it.

When the hall had filled I stood, and tapped my glass for quiet. "I am senior officer present," I stated. Then, for the first time, I gave the Ship's Prayer I had heard so often. "Lord God, today is March 12, 2195, on the U.N.S. *Hibernia*. We ask you to bless us, to bless our voyage, and to bring health and well-being to all aboard." I sat, my heart pounding.

"Amen," said Chief Engineer McAndrews into the silence. A few passengers murmured it after him.

I wouldn't call dinner a cheerful affair; hardly anyone acknowledged my presence. But I was so hungry I hardly cared. I avidly consumed salad, meat, bread, then coffee and dessert. The passengers at my table watched in amazement. I suppose they had reason; the day after the Captain's death his successor sat at a midshipman's place, eagerly devouring everything but the silverware.

After the meal I went back to the wardroom. I took out fresh clothes, showered thoroughly, dressed with extra care. I even shaved, though it wasn't really necessary.

Reluctantly, I went to the bridge. Sandy, who had been holding nominal watch alone—the ship was not under power—leaped to attention on my arrival.

"Carry on." My tone was gruff, to cover my uncertainty. Then, "Mr. Wilsky, summon all officers."

"Aye aye, sir." The young midshipman keyed the ship's caller. "Now hear this." His voice cracked; he blushed. "All officers report to the bridge."

Awash with physical energy I paced the bridge, examining the instruments, seeing none of them. Doc Uburu arrived, requested permission to enter. The Pilot followed shortly. A few moments later the Chief appeared. The middies were last; Vax and Alexi came hurrying—clean uniforms, hair freshly combed, like my own—and I smiled despite myself. We all stood, as if grouped for a formal portrait.

I picked up the caller, took a deep breath. I exhaled, and took another. "Ladies and gentlemen, by the Grace of God, Captain Harvey Malstrom, commanding officer of U.N.S. *Hibernia*, is dead of illness. I, Midshipman Nicholas Ewing Seafort, senior officer aboard, do hereby take command of this ship."

It was done.

"Congratulations, Captain!" Alexi was first, then they all crowded around me with reassurance and support, even the Chief and the Pilot. It was not a jolly occasion; the death of Captain Malstrom precluded that. What they offered was more condolence than celebration.

After a moment I went to sit. I stopped myself: I had headed for the first officer's chair. Trying to look casual, I sat in the Captain's seat on the left. No laser bolt struck me. I addressed my officers.

"Pilot, we'll need new watch rotations. Take care of it, please. The middies will have to stand watch alone now; it can't be helped. Dr. Uburu, attend to passenger morale before the situation worsens. Chief, I need your attention on the crew. If there's serious discontent, you're to know about it. Pass the word that we have matters under control. Vax, you'll help me get settled. Get a work party to move my gear to the Captain's cabin. Sew bars on my uniforms. Reprogram Darla to recognize me as Captain."

When I stopped they chorused, "Aye aye, sir." It was a heady feeling. No arguments, no objections. I began to appreciate ship's discipline.

"Anything else, anyone?"

"We can make Earthport Station in two jumps." The Pilot. "I'll run the calculations tonight."

The Chief said, "Don't worry about the crew; they'll settle down as soon as I remind them they get early shore leave. They'll be so happy to head for Lunapolis they won't even think about who's Captain."

Alexi asked, "When do we Fuse for home, sir?"

I said, "I never told you we were going home."

The shock of silence. Then a babble of voices.

I snapped, "Be quiet!" There was instant compliance. It didn't surprise me; I wouldn't have dared breathe had Captain Malstrom given such an order, friend or no friend. "Chief, do you have something to say?"

"With the Captain's permission, yes, sir." He waited for my nod. "Surely you can't mean to go on. We've lost our four most experienced officers. The crew is frightened. I can't answer for their behavior if we head for Hope Nation. The ship's launch is gone; six passengers are dead. Sir, we never thought . . . Please. The only sensible thing is to go back."

"Pilot?"

"I can get us back in two jumps, Captain. Six months. It's eleven months to Hope Nation."

"I already knew that. Anything else?"

"Yes, sir. The danger is obvious. It's irresponsible of you to sail on."

I didn't hesitate. "Pilot, you're placed on report for insolence. I will enter a reprimand in the Log. You are reduced two grades in pay and confined to quarters for one week, except when on watch."

Pilot Haynes, his face red with rage, grated, "Understood, sir." His fists were clenched at his side.

"Who else?" Of course, after that no one cared to speak.

"I'll take your suggestions under advisement. In the morning I'll let you know. You're all dismissed. Mr. Holser, you will remain."

After the bridge hatch shut behind the last of them I turned to Vax, who waited in the "at ease" position. I wasn't looking forward to our interview. "You're senior middy now, Vax."

"Yes, sir." He looked straight ahead.

"You recall the unpleasantness we had last month?"

"Yes, sir."

"It's nothing compared to the unpleasantness I'm going to make now, Mr. Holser." Vax had settled in well as second midshipman, but now I had to leave the wardroom, and given his temperament he'd have the other middies climbing the bulkheads in a week. That is, if I didn't put the brakes on.

My voice was savage. "You will do hard calisthenics—I repeat, HARD calisthenics, for two hours every day until further notice. You will report to the watch officer in a fresh uniform for personal inspection every four hours, day and night." He looked stricken. "You will submit a five-thousand-word report on the duties of the senior midshipman under Naval regulations and by ship's custom. Acknowledge!"

"Orders received and understood, sir!" His expression bordered on panic.

I stood nose to nose with him, my voice growing louder. "You may think that in the privacy of the wardroom you can revert to your old bullying ways, and I won't know because the other middies won't tell me. They don't have to tell me, Mr. Holser. I was a middy yesterday. I know what to look for!" I waited for a response.

"Yes, sir!"

I shouted, "Mr. Holser, if you exercise brutality in the wardroom, I'll cut your balls off! Do I make myself clear?"

"Aye aye, sir!" A sheen of sweat appeared on his forehead. I knew he didn't take the last threat literally, but we'd both served aboard ship long enough to know the Captain's enmity was the worst disaster that could befall a crewman. I was giving him a reminder of that.

"Very well. Dismissed. See that I have bars on my uniforms by morning."

"Aye aye, sir!" He practically ran from the bridge. I made a mental note to ease up in a few days. The exercise wouldn't harm him—Vax liked working out—but reporting for inspection every four hours grew brutal, as one's sleep deficit accumulated. Once, in Academy, Sergeant Trammel had made me . . . I sighed, thrusting away the memory.

I roamed the bridge, unnerved by the grim silence. Never before had I stood watch entirely alone, and certainly not when I had no superior to call in case of emergency. I toyed with the sensors, examined the silent simulscreen, stared at pinpoints of starlight until my eyes ached. My legs were weary, but I was reluctant to sit just yet.

I examined the bridge safe, found it unlocked. The Captain's laser pistol was within, as well as the keys to the munitions locker. As a precaution, I changed the combination.

Returning at last to my chair, I turned on the Log and thumbed it idly, back to the start of our voyage. I screened the orders from Admiralty, entered by Captain Haag ages ago. "You shall, with due regard for the safety of the ship, proceed on a course from Earthport Station to Ganymede Station . . . You shall sail in an expeditious manner by means of Fusion to Miningcamp, from there to Hope Nation, and thence to Detour . . . you shall take on such cargo as the Government there may . . . revictualing and refueling as you may find necessary . . ." I keyed off the Log.

Idly I thumbed through our cargo manifest. Machinery for the manufacture of medicines, tools and dies, freeze-stored vegetable seeds, catalogs and samples of the latest fashions from Earth, bottled air for Miningcamp . . . I closed my eyes, rocking gently in the Captain's chair, its soft upholstery inviting.

"Permission to enter bridge, sir." I woke abruptly. Alexi waited respectfully in the corridor. Had he seen? Lord God, I hoped not; sleeping on watch was a cardinal sin.

"Come in." I got him settled. He'd have little to do other than watch the quiescent instruments, but like me, Alexi had never served a watch alone and was eager to begin. I myself was already glad to escape the tedium.

I headed east along the circumference corridor to the Captain's cabin. No one was posted outside; Captain Haag had dispensed with the marine guard the first week of the voyage.

I quelled an urge to knock respectfully, and went in.

The cabin was breathtaking. It was over four times as large as our wardroom, at least eight meters by five. It held only one bunk, which made it seem even more grand. So much space, for only one person. And I was the person!

Subtle dividers made areas of the cabin seem like separate rooms. In one corner was a hatch; I tried it. A head; the Captain actually had his own head and shower. I was stunned. I felt guilty even thinking of living in such luxury, while midshipmen constantly rubbed shoulders in their tiny quarters.

My gear, what little there was of it, was already laid out in a dresser built into the bulkhead. Vax had been busy: my uniforms, new patches freshly sewn on the shoulders, were hung neatly in a closet area in the corner. A ship's caller sat on the table by the bunk. Across from the bed were easy chairs, a desk chair, even a small conference table. Or dining table. I wasn't sure which.

I sat uneasily, feeling an intruder though Captain Malstrom's gear was nowhere to be seen. Captain Haag's must long since be gone to storage. I wondered gloomily how soon my own would follow. My eyes roved the bulkheads. Pictures; someone had made an effort to decorate. A safe was built into the bulkhead. It was locked. I made a note to find the combination.

I undressed and got into bed; the mattress was amazingly soft. I switched off the light. The room was very still. I twisted from one position to another, unable to sleep despite my exhaustion. My thoughts turned to what I had accomplished. In the course of my first day, I'd managed to alienate everyone whose goodwill I needed. The Chief. The Pilot. The senior middy. A bad start, but I couldn't figure out what I could have done better.

As I tossed restlessly in the soft bunk I realized what was troubling me. It was too quiet. I was lonely.

10

In the morning I felt ill at ease using the head alone, so accustomed had I become to the wardroom's lack of privacy. I was a bit apprehensive when a knock came on the hatch; custom approaching the force of law forbade anyone to disturb the Captain in his cabin. In an emergency, or if he'd left standing orders to be notified, the Captain was summoned by ship's caller; if there was no emergency, he was not bothered. All the crew knew that, and passengers were not allowed in the section of Level 1 that contained the bridge and the Captain's quarters.

Cautiously, I opened the hatch. Ricardo Fuentes, the ship's boy, waited in the corridor with a cloth-covered tray. He stepped around me to set it on my dining table. Then his shoulders came up and he stood rigidly at attention, arms stiffly at his sides, stomach sucked in tight.

I was grateful for the familiar face. "Hi, Ricky."

"Good morning, Captain, sir!" His voice was high-pitched and shrill.

I peered beneath the cloth. Coffee, scrambled eggs, toast, juice. It appeared his visit was a regular morning routine. "Thanks."

Twelve-year-old Ricky stood stiff. "You're welcome, sir!" Clearly, he wasn't about to unbend.

"Dismissed, sailor."

"Aye aye, sir!" The boy about-faced and marched out. I sighed. Had I begun to resemble an ogre? Did it come with the job?

Pilot Haynes and Vax Holser were on the forenoon watch list. As I reached the bridge I opened my mouth to ask permission to enter. Old habits die hard. Feeling foolish, I walked in. Vax jumped to attention; the Pilot did so more slowly.

"Carry on." They eased back in their chairs as I crossed to my new seat. Vax's uniform, I noticed, was crisply ironed. I glanced at the console. The readouts seemed in order; I knew Vax or the Pilot would tell me if they weren't.

"Chief Engineer, report to the bridge." I put down the caller. When Chief McAndrews arrived I said, "Chief, Pilot, I've decided we will continue to Miningcamp and Hope Nation." The Chief pursed his lips but said nothing.

"I don't have to give you reasons, but I will. Simply: going on involves Fusing and docking maneuvers; so does going home. The risks are equal.

"Now, once we're at Hope Nation we know the Admiral Commanding will assign us a new Captain and lieutenants. It will mean sailing eleven months with inexperienced officers, instead of the six it would take to go home, but *Hibernia* carries too many supplies that our colonies need, to abandon our trip lightly. Their supply ships arrive only twice a year."

The Chief said only, "Aye aye, sir." The Pilot was silent.

"Gentlemen, we'll bury Captain Malstrom this forenoon, and we'll Fuse this afternoon after the burial service."

The bridge and engine room were unmanned and sealed. We gathered around the forward airlock, seven deep in the crowded corridor. All the remaining officers, resplendent in dress uniform with black mourning sash across the shoulder; nearly all the crew, dressed as if for inspection. Lieutenant Malstrom had been as popular among the enlisted men as among the middies.

The rest of the corridor was filled with passengers: Yorinda Vincente, representing the Passengers' Council, in the front row; behind her, Mr. Barstow, Amanda Frowel, the Treadwell twins, many others I knew, all waiting for the service to begin. Derek Carr, whose father had been lost earlier with the launch, his finely chiseled, aquiline face marred by sunken eyes and an expression of grief remembered. He nodded, but said nothing.

The flag-draped alumalloy coffin waited behind me in the airless lock, visible through the transplex inner hatch. I turned on the holovid and began to read from the Christian Reunification service for the dead, as promulgated by the Naval Service of the Government of the United Nations.

"Ashes to ashes, dust to dust . . ." Lieutenant Malstrom and I had cast off together at this very airlock. Now I was to continue, and he must disembark. "Trusting in the goodness and mercy of Lord God eternal, we commit his body to the deep . . . to await the day of judgment when the souls of man shall be called forth before Almighty Lord God . . . Amen."

I snapped off the holovid. "Petty Officer Terrill, open the outer lock."

Chief Petty Officer Robert Terrill stepped forward. "Aye aye, sir." Taking the airlock control from my hand he spun on his heel, marched to the airlock panel, pressed the transmitter to the outer lock control. The alarm bell chimed; *Hibernia*'s outer hatch slid open. I shivered involuntarily; the emptiness of interstellar space beckoned to my mentor, my friend. I breathed a silent prayer of my own, that Lord God might welcome him to his reward.

"Eject the casket, Mr. Terrill."

He pressed a button on a small transmitter clipped to his belt. The folded metal arm mounted in the airlock bulkhead slowly unfolded, pushing gently on the side of the casket. Captain Malstrom's coffin slid smoothly to the outer lock. As the arm extended, the casket drifted past the end of the chamber and floated slowly into the void.

Mesmerized, we watched it recede. It disappeared into the dark long before it would have been too distant to see. I swallowed a lump in my throat. "Mr. Terrill, secure the outer hatch."

"Aye aye, sir." The petty officer pressed his transmitter to the outer airlock control. The hatch closed quietly. The service was complete. My friend Harv was forever gone.

The crowd dispersed. I started back toward my cabin. I felt a hand on my arm, abruptly lifted. I turned. Amanda Frowel looked angry; Alexi Tamarov had a firm grip on her arm, his shoulder thrust sharply between us. "I'm sorry, ma'am," he said, barring her way. She tried to shrug loose; the midshipman held tight.

"It's all right, Alexi." He released her and backed away.

"What was that about?" she demanded.

"Ship's custom. One doesn't touch the Captain. For crewmen it is a capital offense." I took her hand, oblivious to the civilians milling around us, trying to pass. "What is it, Amanda?"

"Are you all right, Nicky?"

"I think so." I studied her face. "I'm sorry I haven't been to see you. I've been rather busy."

She glanced at my new uniform. "You certainly have. Are you sure it's wise?"

"No. I'm just sure it's mandatory." I hesitated. "May I visit tonight?"

"If you'd like." To my dismay, there was a coolness to her voice. She seemed almost indifferent.

"I'd like. If you would." Reluctantly she nodded. We parted.

"We'll Fuse as soon as we're ready, gentlemen."

Vax and Pilot Haynes were in their places. I keyed the caller. "Bridge to engine room, prepare to Fuse."

"Prepare to Fuse, aye aye, sir." The Chief. My lips twitched in a smile; according to the rotation, the engine room petty officer had the watch this hour, but clearly the Chief didn't trust us to Fuse except under his vigilant eye.

After a moment the caller came to life once more. "Engine room ready for Fuse, sir."

"Very well, stand by." I looked up to the screen. "Darla, Fusion coordinates, please?"

"Aye aye, Captain Seafort." The coordinates flashed on the screen.

"Manual coordinates, Pilot?" My request was but a formality. If his own figures hadn't agreed with Darla's he'd have immediately recalculated; the wrong Fusion coordinates could send us to oblivion. Pilot Haynes brought up his coordinates. They matched Darla's.

"Vax, did you also run a plot?"

"Yes, sir."

"Let's see." From the corner of my eye I noticed the Pilot shake his head with ill-disguised impatience. I examined Vax's figures; they were identical to the others.

I was ready to give the order. While normally the ship was Defused from the bridge by running a finger down the Fusion control console, ignition was trickier. The Captain usually passed the Fusion order to the engine room, and the ship was Fused from there.

"Does everything check, Captain?" There wasn't a hint of insolence in the Pilot's voice. None was needed; the question itself conveyed his contempt for my overcaution.

"So far. I'll run my own calculations, just to be sure." Childish, but it would be a windy day in space before I ignored that sort of remark. I entered the variables.

I wasn't very good at the exercise, as Lieutenant Cousins had continually reminded me during our last drill. But I shut my mind to distractions and plowed through the formulas, step by step. At last, I emerged with my final figure and compared it to the Pilot's. I was off by nearly seven percent.

The Pilot's amusement was almost unnoticeable, but not quite. Coolly I erased my calculations and began again. A half hour later, my shirt soggy with perspiration, I found my figures off by the same amount. I was aware how much face I'd already lost. Even if I finally got it right I would look a fool.

The Pilot waited in the duty officer's chair, motionless except for an occasional long breath akin to a subvocal sigh. Ignoring the distraction, I stored each figure as I calculated it, then ran the results through the usual formula.

I was still six point seven nine percent off, and couldn't find the error. "Pilot, please watch while I try again." My tone was brusque. He came over to stand behind my chair, like a long-suffering lieutenant overseeing a middy's drill. "Stop me when you see the mistake," I said.

I went through the steps, plugging in the parameters I'd generated by previous calculations. When I finished I had the same answer I had before, and he hadn't intervened. "Well?"

"I didn't see an error. Sir," he added begrudgingly. "You manipulated the numbers correctly."

Interesting. "Go through your own calculation again."

I watched him enter the base figures, run his compensations with a practiced skill I longed to match, factor our present location, mass, and target, and calculate drive power and coordinates. His result matched his previous figures.

Vax sat staring at the screen. I suspected his mind was on automatic; thanks to my cruelty he was exhausted. He wouldn't be the only one; the crew had been on standby for nearly two hours.

No matter. I bent to my console. "We'll do our calculations step by step, all three of us. No, make that four; Darla, calculate along with us. We'll do a step at a time, until we all agree." I entered the initial figures. We bent over our screens. Darla put her results on the simulscreen above our heads.

Slowly we worked our way through the base calculations. No problem. Then we matched stellars, compensating by the book. We all still agreed. We all used the same plot for our present location. Our target location was right out of the charts. We entered ship's mass.

"Hey!" Vax spoke involuntarily. Three of the figures on the screen agreed. The fourth, mine, was different.

"There's your error, Captain." The Pilot's voice wasn't a sneer but it didn't miss by much. "You picked up a funny number for the ship's mass. 213.5 units."

"I thought I figured it right." I felt a blast of Lieutenant Cousins's withering scorn from wherever he was watching. "I calculated it the way we always do, base weight minus—"

"You figured ship's mass fresh each time?" The Pilot seemed astonished. Probably he meant no disrespect; he was so startled he simply forgot his manners. "We take mass from Darla's automatic Log entry. Vax, isn't that how you did it?"

"Yes, sir." Vax was trying not to be noticed.

"Darla?"

"Mass is a programmed parameter," Darla answered. "You know the ship recycles everything. I can't vary the adjusted mass except when you log an order for general recalc."

I stared at my figures, trying to puzzle out how I could have gone so wrong. Obviously the three of them knew something I didn't. I racked my brain trying to remember fusion theory from Academy. "I was starting with base mass, and subtracting the mass of the ship's launch and the estimated weight of the passengers lost with it from—"

The Pilot chortled. "That's all in the programming parameter Darla gives you."

"At Academy they made us run everything fresh each time, and Lieutenant Cousins never said to . . ."

Mr. Haynes was magnanimous. "Sir, that was just for practice. We'd be a week refiguring, each time we stopped for nav check. Remember your drill with Captain Haag? He had you use programmed parameters."

"I assumed it was just to save time. He was fidgeting, and I couldn't seem . . ." I chopped off the memory. While my ears reddened, I thumbed through the Log searching for the programmed parameters. "So, we start with Darla's base mass—"

"No, sir, the puter runs adjusted mass too. That's base mass minus passengers or cargo off-loaded since the last general recalc."

I'd made a fool enough of myself for one day. "Very well, no wonder I was off. I'll do it your way. Darla, confirm adjusted ma—"

The speaker crackled. "Bridge, engine room here." The Chief. "Do we continue standing by to Fuse?"

How long had I kept them waiting? I bit my lip; over three hours. No wonder I was exhausted, and wringing wet. "We'll be ready in a moment, Chief." Where was I?

We had three matched sets of calculations, and we'd found my error. Time to get on with it. I started to wipe my figures, saw the Pilot's complacent smirk. I gritted my teeth, determined not to lash out at him. Instead, I decided to backtrack and correct my calculations. I obviously needed the practice, and with that attitude he could bloody well wait as long as it took.

"Here, where I subtracted the launch weight . . . I enter Darla's adjusted mass, right?"

Vax hid a yawn.

"Now, I can scrub my subtraction . . . by the way, what was the base mass when *Hibernia* left Earthport?"

The puter's tone was a touch cross. "Are you asking me? If so, I need a pronoun as referent."

"Just give me the parameter, Darla."

"215.6 standard units."

"I meant base mass."

"215.6 standard units is base mass, Captain. How many times do we need to go through this?"

Vax dozed. I wiped my calculation back to the point of error. The Pilot shifted impatiently. My head was spinning, and I'd kept them all waiting long enough. Still . . .

"Well, sir?"

My tone was curt. "Pilot, read from the Log our adjusted mass and our base mass."

"For heaven's—aye aye, sir." His fingers played the keys. "Adjusted mass is 215.6 units. Base mass is two hun—" The Pilot made an awful sound. His face went gray.

I said, "It doesn't seem quite right, does it? I mean, the two figures should differ."

"You caught an error," Pilot Haynes whispered. "The numbers we used were wrong!"

Vax jerked upright, dismayed. If the Pilot was in error, so was he.

I was dumbfounded. "But Darla figured it your way! Puters don't forget parameters."

The Pilot spoke first. "We must not be asking her the right question. Darla, what is ship's mass adjusted for the loss of the launch and passengers?"

"Adjusted mass is 215.6," she repeated.

I said, "Adjust your programmed base mass by the mass of the ship's launch. It's no longer on board."

"Mass has been adjusted as per standing calculation instructions," she said primly. "That's automatic."

"Holy Mother!" breathed Vax. "Darla has a glitch!"

"I do not!" Darla was indignant. "Watch your mouth, middy!"

"He meant it the old-fashioned way, Darla," I said quickly. "A gigo error." Darla had taken offense at being called brain damaged.

"But she—"

"Shut up, Vax." Like everyone, I'd heard dark rumors about ships that sailed interstellar with angry puters and were never heard of again.

We lapsed into silence. Darla threw random wavelengths of interference across the simulscreen, her equivalent of muttering under her breath. Something caught Vax's attention on the opposite side of the room. I realized he was reluctant to meet my eye.

I said, "But how could we have Defused so near *Celestina*, if Darla's figures are"—I dropped my voice—"glitched?"

"Maybe they weren't, at the time." The Pilot tapped into his console, peered at the figures he summoned. "These are the coordinates we used to find *Celestina*. Adjusted mass was the same as base. But remember, before we lost the launch, they would be expected to match."

"Didn't Captain Malstrom order a recalc before he Fused?"

"I would think so." He shrugged. "Check the Log."

"Check it yourself!" I clamped down, before I flew into a tirade. Now was no time to provoke another officer.

"Aye aye, sir." A hint of sullenness. His keys clicked. "Yes, it would appear so. The day of the memorial service." A frown. "For some reason, they didn't fully enter the new figures, or Darla would have them now."

"Darla, can you recalculate parameters?"

"Of course I can." I waited for more, but nothing was forthcoming.

"Do so."

"Order received and acknowledged, Captain. I'll need your special authorization code."

"Where is it?"

Her voice was sweet. "If they told me that, you wouldn't need one."

"Pilot, where do I find my codes?"

"I haven't the slightest idea." His tone was placating. "Sir, why don't we override the puter's solution with your own manual plot in order to Fuse, and recalc afterward."

"Is that safe?"

"Yes, sir."

It would get us moving. "Very well, then."

A silence. The Pilot blurted, "Sir, the figures I gave you were worthless. Yours was the only correct solution. I apologize most sincerely for my mistake."

I snarled, "Belay that. Let's get under weigh." It did little good to assure the crew all was well, then sit for hours unable to Fuse.

"Captain, may I be relieved from watch and be allowed to leave the bridge?"

"No, Pilot." I didn't feel charitable, after enduring his smirk. "After we Fuse, search the Log and the databanks until you find my authorization code for a recalc."

I turned to Vax. "Run your coordinates one more time, and recalculate starting from base mass." He, Darla, and the Pilot might have been wrong, but I still had to be sure my own coordinates were right.

"Aye aye, sir!" Vax's fingers flew over the keys. In a few minutes he came up with a solution. My solution. I punched in the new figures. "Darla, I override your coordinates. Log."

"Manual override coordinates received and acknowledged, Mr. Seafort." Darla. "I'm logging it."

I picked up the caller, keyed the engine room. "Chief?"

"Yes, sir?" His answer was immediate. He must have been standing with caller in hand.

I tried to make my voice casual. "What if, say, one of Darla's pre-programmed parameters were glitched? Once we give you Fusion coordinates, would faulty input from Darla throw us off?"

"Only if you ordered us to rely on wave monitoring from the bridge, and I've never heard such an order since first I sailed. The engine room always monitors and adjusts energy output." A pause. "Is there a problem, sir?"

Yes. We were deep interstellar, with a Captain who had no idea what he was doing, and a stubborn puter. "Of course not." My tone was hearty. "Engine room, Fuse, please."

"Aye aye, sir. Fusion drive is . . . on." The screens abruptly faded.

I swallowed, watching the instruments closely. I knew Chief McAndrews was doing likewise, ready to pounce on the slightest variation from the norm. Our readouts remained steady. I let out a long breath.

"Permission to enter bridge, sir." Sandy, ready to begin his watch.

"Granted. Vax, you're relieved."

"Aye aye, sir." Vax stood and saluted, giving me a look I had never seen before. Respect, and something else. Awe, perhaps. I realized my bullying him, added to my apparent wizardry with the computations, had transformed me in his eyes from an irksome youth wrongfully his senior to a Captain who could do no wrong. Both images were faulty, but I couldn't do anything about them.

As Sandy settled into his seat, I realized with a sinking feeling that if the Pilot, a middy, and the puter could all be wrong, I could trust no one. Every time I went off watch I risked the entire ship. Now I knew why Captain Haag virtually lived on his bridge. I wasn't smarter than all the others, nor was I more alert. But *Hibernia* was my responsibility, and no one else's.

I also knew why the Pilot had gone pale; a seven percent error built into our coordinates would magnify to a stupendous variation after a lengthy Fuse. We could have sailed into the middle of Hope Sun. And it was just dumb luck that I had caught it.

11

Dinner was called. At the Captain's table there were only three places set. I caught the purser's attention and raised my eyebrow at the empty chairs.

Mr. Browning bent discreetly by my ear. "Requests from several passengers, sir, for new seat assignments. Under the circumstances I thought . . ."

"Quite right." Dining with the Captain was an honor. It would never, by Lord God, be a duty. Not while I held the office. I made conversation with the three passengers who remained. One of them was Mrs. Donhauser, who as usual didn't hesitate to speak her mind.

"You've become rather unpopular, young man." She eyed me with apparent disapproval.

"It would seem to be the case." I pretended unconcern as I buttered a roll.

"The Passengers' Council feels you should turn back. And they don't forgive your youth."

"Tell them it will pass." I had enough worries about the crew and officers without vexing myself with passengers. That seemed to offend her, and we finished our meal in silence.

I stopped to talk to the Chief on the way out. "By the way, there's a safe in my cabin. I don't suppose you know how I can get it open?"

His tone was flat. "I believe Captain Haag kept the combination in the bridge safe. If not, I can have a machinist drill it out."

"I'll look. Thanks." He was still staring when I turned away.

I climbed to Level 1, looked in on the bridge. Vax and Alexi seemed to have everything under control. Pilot Haynes had left word that he was unable, so far, to locate the recalc authorization codes, but would search again on his next watch.

I went to Amanda's stateroom. We met awkwardly at the hatch. I moved to kiss her; she accepted passively, unresponsive. We both took chairs instead of the bunk or deck. It was to be a more formal meeting. I told her I'd missed her.

She brushed aside my small talk. "What are you up to, Nicky?"

"How do you mean?"

"That uniform. Why are you playing at Captain? You know you're no Captain."

I tried a smile. "We all take turns, Amanda. Next one on is Vax."

She didn't smile back. "Don't laugh at me. I'm frightened of what you're doing."

"What am I doing that's frightening?"

"Going on to Hope Nation. People think we may not get there. They're worried and scared, and saying ugly things. Not just us, the crew too."

"How did you hear about that?"

"The mess stewards." I made a note to look into it. "Nicky, something could happen. Someone could get hurt."

I stopped trying to smile. "What do you know?"

"Nothing in particular. You're trying to take on everyone, and you can't. Not with the crew and passengers all spooked as they are. They say even the officers wanted to get rid of you."

"Where did you hear that?"

"I'm not telling." That was bad. I wanted her on my side, and she was widening the gap between us. "I know what you think," she added. "The law is the law, and if it says you should be Captain you've got to do it. But consider the good of the ship. If you step down, the other officers won't get into trouble for taking over. Get out of their way, Nicky."

"Is that how most of the passengers feel?"

"I hear it everywhere. And believe it, too."

"I need you, Amanda," I said simply, meaning it. "If you turn against me I'll be completely alone."

That brought her to my chair. She knelt at my side. "I'm not against you, Nicky. I want to be safe. I want you to be safe too."

I stroked her hair. "I'm Captain of *Hibernia*. That much is settled. If I don't have you to talk with, I won't have anyone. If I don't have you to touch and hold, I won't have anyone. Please." I held my breath, completely at her mercy.

She leaned over and kissed me. "I'm here, Nicky. I'll be with you."

I stayed with her most of the night. We didn't make love; instead, we caressed and kissed, we hugged. Early in the morning I left her stateroom and quietly went back to my own. Ricky found me there when he came with my breakfast tray. Again he saluted and stood rigidly at attention until I dismissed him.

I went to the bridge. Sandy and the Chief had the watch. I sat and checked the Log. Twice Vax had reported for personal inspection, then left to go back to bed.

I glanced at the blank simulscreen, wondering how familiar it would become before I reached Hope Nation. Seeing the Chief reminded me; I went to the safe and found in it the combination to my cabin strongbox. Bored, I sat again. Half in jest I asked, "Do you play chess, Darla?"

For answer the simulscreen lighted up with a chessboard. My jaw dropped. "I'll be dam— yes. Well." I glanced at the Chief. His eye held an amused glint. I said, "You'd better put it away. I can't while I'm on duty."

"Make up your mind," she said petulantly, snapping off the screen.

After a while I said, "Chief, I've been thinking."

"Yes, sir?"

"I don't see why we should sail all the way to Hope Nation without officers. Vax will make lieutenant soon, you know that. Why couldn't we recruit more midshipmen?"

Sandy examined his console, his ears growing larger by the minute. Well, I wasn't telling any secrets. He polished dust from his screen with his sleeve.

"Recruit them from where, sir?" asked the Chief. A good question. Most of the crew was too old to begin officer training.

"We have teens among the passengers. Several of them. And what about Ricky?"

"Are you asking my opinion, sir?"

"Yes."

"Then, no. We've gone too much against custom as it is. It's legal to recruit from the passengers, but highly irregular. Admiralty might view it as, ah, presumptuous." He was right. On the other hand, Admiralty wasn't shorthanded, nine light-years from nowhere, trying to sail a starship.

"Well, just a thought. Mr. Wilsky, isn't that screen clean enough?"

"Yes, sir. I mean, no, sir. I mean, aye aye, sir!" Sandy jumped back quickly, blushing deep red. Sandy was too nice a joey to enjoy teasing for long. But still . . .

"When you're done with it, would you kindly polish mine?"

"Aye aye, sir." He looked up cautiously, beginning to suspect he was being twitted. Slowly he relaxed.

"Permission to enter bridge, sir?"

I looked around. Vax waited at attention in the corridor.

"Granted."

He marched in. "Midshipman Holser reporting for personal inspection, sir!" Well, if I was to do it at all, better do it right. I got up, made a show of inspecting his clean, freshly ironed uniform, his belt buckles, his shine. Naturally I passed him. Vax was ready, and even if not I wasn't about to notice anything wrong.

"Satisfactory, Mr. Holser. Bring me your written report no later than tomorrow. Dismissed." He saluted and left the bridge. Chief McAndrews said nothing, his face a mask. I understood; it wasn't up to him to comment on how the Captain treated his middies. But I wondered about his thoughts.

I leaned back in my chair. I should have played chess with Darla. Instead, I dozed, which was worse. Lieutenant Cousins would have had me over the barrel.

I entered the safe combination, reading from the paper in my hand. A click, and the door released. I looked inside. A class ring: Academy, class of 2162. It must be Captain Haag's. Apparently Captain Malstrom hadn't bothered to clean out the cabin safe after Mr. Haag's death. A leather folder. It held pictures of a younger Captain Haag, a pretty woman at his side. Hastily I put them away, ashamed at invading his privacy. The mere fact of his death didn't allow me to do that. A chip-case, with three chips. I set them aside to read later.

I took out an object about the length of my hand. A tube of wood, bored hollow down the middle. It had a wooden cup on one end. The cup was charred. Puzzled, I peered at it from all angles. A primitive piece from Africa? New Zealand folk art? Tourist junk from Caltech Planet? I couldn't imagine Captain Haag treasuring such an object. I put it aside. The only other item in the safe was an unlabeled canister. I opened it. It was filled with flakes of dull brown substance. Some kind of vegetable matter.

I lay the articles on my bunkside table and sat to contemplate them. I finally gave up and let my mind drift. I recalled an evening we middies spent with the Chief in a cheap Lunapolis bar, one of the rare occasions we socialized with our officers. We were speculating about how the colonies might develop, over time. I mentioned some ancient history I'd seen on a holodrama. It started the Chief on unusual primitive customs.

I sat bolt upright. Now I knew. The thing on the table was a device for burning the vegetable matter. Toccabo. How had the Chief put it? "Before the Reforms of 2024, boy, they were in common use. People filled them up and set them on fire."

"Then what, Chief?" I asked, knowing I was being played for a fool. "Did they call fire control?"

"No, they sucked until the smoke came through the other end. It was a stimulant."

We laughed. The liquor had obviously gotten to him. "And then they ate the smoke?" I jeered. I must have been drunk; after all, he was the Chief Engineer and could send me to the barrel.

"No, they breathed it." He glared, offended by my mockery.

"Chief, you're making it up," Alexi said. "Nobody could actually do that."

"Don't be sure if you haven't tried." The Chief stared him down.

"Have you—I mean, is it legal? Could you still do it?"

"Oh, it's legal. You can't advertise the stuff, or sell it for profit. But I hear there are places to obtain it. Of course you couldn't bring it on ship. It's contraband, like other drugs."

I demanded, "If it's legal, how come I never heard of it?"

The Chief took my question seriously. "With the reforms of 2024, a lot of vices sort of disappeared. For example, women offering publicly to fornicate for money; you ever hear about that one? And cancer was a big problem back then, before the anticars. So they just stopped the smoking. It took a while, because people used it to relax. But after it was outlawed in public places, it more or less died out. People could grow the plant, but nobody bothered anymore."

"Hey, Chief, have you tried the stuff?" Sandy Wilsky.

The Chief looked at his watch. "Time to go. Early start tomorrow." He flipped bills on the table.

Now, in my cabin, I sniffed the cup of the artifact. It smelled of charcoal, and another aroma. The toccabo, perhaps. I was scandalized. Captain Haag, sitting in his cabin secretly breathing contraband out of that fuming menace. Breaking ship's regs. How little we knew him. To us he was Lord God, walking the bridge.

Before taking command I'd never seen the inside of his cabin; none of us middies had. Few if any officers were invited into the Captain's quarters. He must have been a lonely man, with only Chief McAndrews to keep him company. Scuttlebutt had it that on quiet evenings the Chief, an old friend of Mr. Haag, would join him in his cabin. Together they would sit and reminisce, or do whatever old friends did.

I undressed for the night. My pants half off, I stopped short, swearing aloud at my stupidity. The tube in the safe wasn't for the Captain. Of course not. He'd kept the contraband for his old friend. The Chief faced court-martial if it were found aboard ship, so Captain Haag put it in the only secure place on *Hibernia:* his own safe. And in the evenings the

Chief must have . . . I tried to imagine him with smoke pouring out his nose and mouth, like a dragon.

I slipped off the rest of my clothes and lay on my bunk. Back in Lunapolis, the Chief had said, "People used it to relax." Poor Chief McAndrews. Since the Captain's death he'd been deprived not only of his friend's companionship but his favorite relaxation as well. And all the while he didn't know if the contraband would be discovered and his career endangered.

On the spur of the moment I picked up the caller, dialed the engine room. "Chief Engineer to the Captain's cabin." I didn't wait for an answer. If he wasn't there, they'd find him. I threw on my clothes and made my bunk. I put the tube and the canister on the conference table.

The knock came shortly. "Chief McAndrews reporting, sir."

"Come in, Chief. Sit down." I wanted to show him it wasn't a formal occasion.

He sat in the proffered chair next to my table. His eyes flickered to the objects that lay on it. His expression showed nothing.

"I was cleaning out the safe, Chief, and found some odd items. Captain Haag's album, his ring. And these things, whatever they are."

"Yes, sir."

I had to be careful not to force him to admit the artifacts were his. "I've been trying to guess what they are, Chief. I think . . . do they have anything to do with that smoke stimulant you told me about? Toccabo?"

"Tobacco, sir. It looks like they might."

"I'm fascinated. Why Captain Haag brought them aboard, I can't imagine." He made no reply. "To think the Captain used such a thing," I went on. "I never would have guessed. Do you think I should try it?"

"It's forbidden, sir. Aboard ship." He remained impassive.

"Could you show me how it works? Please?"

"I'd be breaking regs, Captain."

"Never mind that." My tone was magnanimous. "I waive the regs, for this occasion." I handed him the tube. "Chief, I want to see how it works. Can you figure out how to set it off?"

"Yes, sir, I'm sure I could."

Good answer. He still hadn't committed himself. Perhaps he still suspected a trap. I could deal with that easily enough. "Make it work. That's an order."

"Aye aye, sir." He was not only off the hook, he had no choice. He could suck the thing with impunity, protected from retribution by my direct order.

The Chief opened the canister. Digging out a small metal spoon he filled the cup with the flaked vegetables. Tobaccos. He used the end of the spoon to tamp it down into the cup. "I need fire, sir."

"How much? A blowtorch?" I was prepared to order one up.

"No, sir. A candlelighter will do. I carry one." I waited while he put the flame to the cup. He brought the other end of the tube to his mouth and sucked, exactly as he had described. After a while he exhaled. Gray smoke came out his mouth. Wordlessly, he handed me the tube.

"No, I want to watch. Keep going."

"That's all there is, sir. You just keep doing it until it's gone."

"Oh. Does it feel good?"

"Some people say so." His tone was cautious.

"Finish it and tell me," I said. "We can chat while we wait."

"Aye aye, sir." He studied me out of the corner of his eye. After a while he produced more smoke. I watched it curl toward the ventilators. The scrubbers would remove it from the air before recycling it.

"How is morale on Level 3, Chief?"

"Better than it was. It will be better yet, when the convicts are dealt with."

"Oh, Lord. I forgot." How many days had passed? I still had to make up my mind about the three men waiting in the brig for execution.

"Yes, sir. If you don't mind my saying, the sooner it's decided, the better." The smoke seemed to have a relaxing effect on him.

"You're right. I'll make a decision soon. Does that tube thing get hot in your hand?"

"Pipe, sir. They call it a pipe." It was automatic for the Chief to correct a youngster; I didn't mind. "The bowl gets hot but not the stem." He knew all the jargon about tobaccoing.

I made conversation. After a while I grew used to the aroma of the smoke. Finally reassured that I wasn't looking to trap him, the Chief relaxed more fully. He stretched out his legs, his elbow on the table.

"How long did you know Captain Haag?" I asked.

"Twenty-one years." He knew the number by heart. "When he was first lieutenant we sailed together on the old *Prince of Wales*. We were in the same ship ever after." He puffed on the tube. The pipe. "He would sit right where you are, sir." His gaze was on the deck, or on something more distant. Mechanically he puffed until smoke appeared.

"I'm sorry, Chief," I said gently. "We all miss him. You most of all."

"Yes, sir. We didn't talk a lot, you know. Often we just sat together."

Perhaps the smoke had relaxed me too. Spontaneously I reached for his arm. "Chief, I know I'll never be as good as he was. I'm just trying to get through each day. I know it wouldn't be the same for you, but if you could come up sometimes, just to sit together . . ."

"You don't need to apologize for yourself, sir." He looked away, spoke to the bulkhead. "You're doing all right."

"Not really. You can't say so, but I know I've made a mess of things. With the Pilot, with Vax. Probably with everybody."

"I hear you're a pretty sharp navigator, Captain." The corners of his mouth twitched.

"You heard about that?"

"It's all over the ship. Your stock is up considerably."

I wasn't very surprised. Scuttlebutt went from the bridge to the fusion drive faster than a ship's boy could run. Maybe Darla did it. "It was an accident."

"You were being Captain. It's what you're for." He puffed again, trying to maintain the blaze. "I'd be glad to sit with you, sir," he said gruffly. "If it would be of service."

"Thank you, Chief." We sat peaceably until the fire was out.

12

I tapped my glass. The room quieted. "Lord God, today is March 14, 2195, on the U.N.S. *Hibernia*. We ask you to bless us, to bless our voyage, and to bring health and well-being to all aboard."

I remained standing after the "amen." "Before we begin, I have a few remarks." Some of the passengers exchanged glances. "As you know, we have resumed Fusion and are sailing for Hope Nation." They knew, but they didn't like it. I heard a brief murmur of discontent.

"My officers and I—" I liked that. It sounded confident. "My officers and I expect to arrive in Hope Nation on schedule. But we are shorthanded by four officers, which means extra watches for all those who remain. I have therefore decided to allow enlistment of one or more cadets from among the passengers."

I raised my voice to override the sudden angry babble. "A cadet trains to be a midshipman, an officer in the Naval Service. He or she enlists for a five-year term. Promotion to lieutenant or Captain may eventually occur. Service as an officer in the Naval Service is an honorable profession. If any of you want more information you may contact the purser, who will arrange for an officer to see you."

I sat in the resulting silence. Tonight only two were at my table: Mrs. Donhauser and Mr. Kaa Loa, a Micronesian who spoke infrequently. I hadn't gotten to know him.

"Good evening, Madam."

"Hello, Captain." She regarded me thoughtfully. "Aren't midshipmen recruited as children?"

"Cadets are, yes. Midshipmen are adults, by act of the General Assembly."

"Do you really expect parents to consent to your taking their children, Captain Seafort?" I realized how seldom my name and title had been used together. I liked the sound of it.

"Probably not."

"Isn't it a useless gesture, then?" She never dodged an issue. Blunt and honest. I approved of her.

"Not really," I said. "I don't need their consent."

She leaned close and grabbed my arm. "Nicky, don't shanghai

joeykids into the service!" She spoke forcefully, quietly. "You may not
know it yet, but protecting our children is one of the basic human urges.
Don't get it working against you. You'd be asking for real trouble!" She
wasn't threatening me; it was a warning, and I appreciated it.

"I'll take it into consideration, Mrs. Donhauser." I changed the
subject as quickly as I could.

I shared the evening watch with Alexi. His mood was brighter than
my own. I just wanted to sit and think; he had it in mind to ask all sorts
of questions. He was respectful enough, but he wouldn't shut up. That
was one drawback to our having been bunkmates; once past his initial
shyness Alexi erred the other direction and was overly familiar. But I
needed to decide what to do about my prisoners.

In addition to Mr. Tuak, ordinary seaman Rogoff and Machinist's
Mate Herney were also under sentence of death, Rogoff for clubbing
Chief Petty Officer Terrill, and Herney for fighting Mr. Vishinsky. The
last case bothered me the most. I had seen the fracas myself, and I didn't
think Mr. Herney had any idea whom he was hitting. I reread the regs
on striking an officer.

"Do you think Darla's problem is correctable, sir?" Alexi. His
fourth attempt to start a conversation.

"I don't know." Did the crime of striking an officer require knowledge that the victim was an officer? Perhaps not; fighting was itself a
crime, and hitting an officer could just be an unlucky consequence. On
the other hand—

"We could take her down for reprogramming while we're Fused,
sir."

I thought my response mild, under the circumstances. "Be quiet for
a while, Alexi." Presently I noticed he wore the reproachful expression
of a chastened puppy. He didn't speak, but his silence was louder than
words.

I sighed inwardly, knowing what Captain Haag would have done.
But I liked Alexi. I groped for a way to divert him. "Calculate drive
corrections for load imbalance, assuming we don't take on any cargo in
Detour. It'll be good practice."

"Aye aye, sir." It kept him quiet awhile, anyway.

On his next watch, Pilot Haynes reported he was unable to find my
authorization codes in any of our files. I nodded, saying nothing, hoping
he hadn't seen my sudden blush. As soon as I could manage it casually, I
left the bridge, hurried to my cabin. I took the forgotten chipcase from
my safe, slipped a chip into my holovid.

The first chip held Captain Haag's personal pay vouchers, and statements of his savings account at Bank of Nova Scotia and Luna. The second, a text borrowed from the ship's library.

The third was a series of authorization codes for special access to the puter.

Not quite at ease handling the matter on my own, I called the Chief to the bridge, had him sit with me while I ordered Darla to recalculate.

It was really quite simple. After I entered the codes she went silent for almost a minute, while the screen flashed. Finally, she chimed a bell, as if clearing her throat. "Recalculation complete, Captain."

I heaved a sigh of relief. "Very well. What's the ship's base mass, Darla?"

"215.6 standard units."

"And adjusted mass?"

Her voice was assured. "215.6 standard units. Are we plotting another Fuse?"

"Oh, Lord God." I glanced to the Chief. He swallowed.

Darla was still glitched.

Two days passed, while we debated what to do. I swore the Chief and the Pilot to secrecy; nerves on board were taut enough without rumors that a crazed puter might send us to another galaxy.

I cursed my stupidity in not having turned back for home when I had the chance. Lieutenant Dagalow was no Dosman, but she had her advanced puter rating, and could have told us how to correct the parameter problem. Knowing the task was beyond me, I sent the Pilot delving into our puter manuals in the hope he'd learn enough to guide us through whatever programming might be necessary.

As *Hibernia* was already in Fusion, I saw no point in Defusing until Mr. Haynes felt himself ready. Though a proper Captain would have decided alone, I asked the Chief's opinion. He agreed.

In the meantime, Purser Browning reported no inquiries about enlistment. I had copies of my announcement posted in the passenger mess and lounges. Some were torn down.

The death sentences also preyed on my mind. I went to Amanda's cabin and shared with her my dread at having to consider executions. If I'd been Captain when the riot took place the affair wouldn't have gotten past Captain's Mast. But the court-martial was an established fact; now what was I to do?

She studied my face strangely. "Pardon them, of course. How can you do anything else?"

"What am I telling the crew by condoning mutiny?" I asked.

"Nicky, that wasn't a mutiny, it was a brawl. You know that."

I tried to help her understand. "It was a kind of mutiny, hon. They disobeyed all sorts of regs, on smuggling, on drugs, about fighting. Worse, they attacked the officers Captain Malstrom sent in to break it up."

"They were brawling. You already said you wouldn't have called a court-martial."

"Yes, but . . ." How did I explain, to a civilian? "Look. Say I'm a midshipman, and I've been up all night at General Quarters, and afterwards I report to the Captain with my uniform untidy. If he sees it he has to put me on report. And then I get in trouble with the first lieutenant." I paused for breath. "But he might decide not to see it. Then he doesn't have to deal with it."

"So, decide not to see it," she said promptly.

"The problem is that it's already been seen. If Captain Malstrom hadn't officially noticed it with formal charges, I could let them go. Now if I do, I'm saying that mutiny goes unpunished."

She was troubled. "I thought I knew you, Nicky. You can't be so cruel as to kill those poor men." That wasn't quite fair. I wouldn't kill them. That decision had already been made by Admiralty, Captain Malstrom, and the court-martial's presiding officer. I would let them be killed, a different thing altogether. If I did nothing, the process started by someone else would continue. I decided not to press the point. When we parted, the trouble was still between us.

The next day I had some good news. A note from the Purser; a passenger wanted information about joining up. I called Mr. Browning to the bridge, where I shared watch with the Chief. "One of the Treadwell joeys," I guessed. "Rafe or Paula."

"No, sir.' The purser looked uncomfortable standing at attention. "Mr. Carr."

"Derek? You're joking."

The concept of playing a trick on the Captain seemed beyond the man. "No, sir," he assured me, his tone earnest. "He asked to speak to an officer about your announcement. He kept repeating he hadn't made his mind up yet."

"Who'd be best to send to him?" I asked the Chief.

"Are you sure you'd let him join, sir?" A good question.

"No." That decided it. "I'll talk with him myself."

After watch and a short nap I went down to the Level 2 cabin Derek had shared with his father. It would be less formal than the bridge.

"Hello, Captain." We hadn't spoken since my promotion. He stood aside to let me enter. I chose a seat. His cabin was neat and clean, his belongings put away. Good.

"Mr. Carr." I had the right to call him by his first name—he was still a minor—but he'd see it as patronizing. The question rang in my mind: Was he officer material? Could a boy of his background handle the wardroom? I waited. He would bring the matter up when he was ready.

"I suppose you've come about what I told Mr. Browning."

"That's right." Uninvited, I took a chair. After all, I was the Captain.

"It was just an idea I had." He sat too, on his bunk.

"If you're not serious, I'll go." I wouldn't waste my time in a rich boy's cabin, with all the problems I had yet to solve.

"No, I was serious," he said quickly. "I still am."

"Why would someone like you want to be a midshipman?" I asked. Perhaps I had been around Mrs. Donhauser too long; I was learning to cut to the heart of the matter.

Derek examined his fingernails. "You remember I told you about my father's will? The managers control our estate until I'm twenty-two."

"Yes?"

"I know how those people operate. They'll send me somewhere to school. Get me out of the way. Maybe even back to Earth, another seventeen months stuck on board a frazzing ship."

"Thanks."

He had the grace to blush. "I'm sorry how that sounded. Anyway, I don't want to be helpless. I'm old enough to make my own decisions. And you said enlistment was for five years . . ."

"So?"

"In five years I'd be almost twenty-two." He made it sound as if it were reason enough to join up.

"Have you had schooling, Mr. Carr?" It was necessary to ask; groundside, education was optional with parents.

"Of course! I'm no peasant."

"Math?"

"Some. Algebra, geometry, trig."

"Calculus?"

"No. I could learn it, though." He didn't lack for self-confidence.

When I had nothing more to say he inquired, "Do you think I should do it?"

"No." In our whole conversation he never called me "sir," and only referred to me as "Captain" one time. He never used my name. Even aside from the matter of courtesy, he didn't sound very motivated.

"Why not?"

"For one thing, you're rather old to start as a cadet."

"I'd just be wasting the next two years, anyway."

"Perhaps. I don't think you have the temperament, Mr. Carr."
He flared. "Please explain."

I was tired and frustrated. "You have no manners. You expect the
world handed to you on a spoon. You've never had any discipline and
you couldn't handle any. They'd eat you alive in the middies' wardroom
and spit out your bones." I stood up. "Cadets get hazed, Mr. Carr. I was;
we all were, and sometimes it's brutal. One has to be able to take it. You
can't. Thank you for your interest." I turned the hatch handle.

"You have no idea what I can take," he said coldly. "I should have
known better than to talk to you."

"Good evening." I stalked back to Level 1. As I began to cool I
wondered if I had been too hard on him. I'd asked his reasons; he'd
given them. I couldn't expect him to join for love of the Service. He had
the math, he was intelligent . . .

And he was an obnoxious snob. I could do better.

I entered the bridge. Vax and Alexi both rose. I now had middies
standing watch together, to avoid exhausting the Pilot and the Chief. I
myself expected to be exhausted. I took pity on the dark smudges under
Vax's eyes. "Mr. Holser, you're relieved. Get some sleep."

He didn't argue with his good fortune. "Aye aye, sir." He saluted
and hurried out before I could change my mind.

"Carry on, Alexi."

"I've got double watch tonight, sir. Sandy comes on at changeover."

"I know." It was one of the reasons I was there. Vax and Alexi were
one thing; Sandy and Alexi quite another. But we watch-standers had
little to do; we were only present in case something went wrong. Most of
the ship's systems were automatic: hydroponics, recycling, power. With
the fusion drive ignited we couldn't navigate, and our only danger was
boredom. I thumbed through the Log in silence. Mercifully, Alexi interrupted only a few times.

Sandy reported for duty an hour later, in good spirits. I decided not
to tell him he had a smudge of lipstick on his neck. Regrettably, Alexi
told him for me, and the result was a fit of giggling between the two boys
that even had me joining.

"Back to duty," I told them. They settled down. The silence of the
night watch stretched longer and tighter. Suddenly Alexi choked back a
snort of laughter, trying to hold in a watch full of accumulated nervous

energy. It got Sandy started too, but he subsided quickly under my glare.

Alexi brought himself under control. My tone was cold. "Mr. Tamarov, you're standing watch. Check your instruments and save the skylarking for later." I was red in the face when I ended, because my composure had started to slip about halfway through; if I hadn't held on with all my might, my little speech would have been punctuated by explosive laughter. It was contagious. But I was also angry. The ghost of Captain Haag stalked the bridge. Giggling on watch? He'd have tossed us out the airlock.

I went back to the Log; I'd been reading the entries from the start of our cruise. I had thumbed through to our docking at Ganymede when Alexi lost control once more. He covered his mouth, but a snort escaped him and his body shook.

It was more than I could bear. "*MR. TAMAROV!*" He leaped to attention. "My compliments to the Chief Engineer, and would he please advise me how to deal with a midshipman who refuses to pay attention to his work. Go!"

"Aye aye, sir!" His face a compound of embarrassment and dismay, Alexi saluted and hurried away.

Sandy was busily running practice calculations on his screen.

Twenty minutes later I heard a subdued voice. "Permission to enter bridge, sir." Alexi waited in the corridor, hands held tightly to his sides. Tears glistened.

"Granted."

He walked with care, coming to attention two paces from my seat. "Midshipman Tamarov reporting, sir." It was almost a whisper. "The Chief Engineer's respects, and if the Captain pleases, he should just send the midshipman to him whenever necessary." His look was bewildered and miserable.

"Thank you, Mr. Tamarov. You are relieved from watch."

"Aye aye, sir. Thank you, sir." He saluted, did an about-face, disappeared into the corridor. I writhed in shame. I had proved myself no better than Vax. Worse, I'd just made another enemy out of a friend. Alexi had meant no harm.

Quietly I went to the hatch, peered outside. Alexi leaned against the bulkhead, sobbing, his hand pressed to his buttocks. I stepped back in. I had stolen his dignity; at least I could leave him his privacy. On the bridge, Sandy tapped diligently at his keyboard.

* * *

Rather than risk a rebellion by Mr. Vishinsky, I let the master-at-arms send a sailor armed with a billy accompany me into the brig. The cell had no chair, no table, only Herney's mattress on the deck. I had them bring me a seat. The sailor stood against the hatch, billy clasped in front of him.

"Mr. Herney, I am Captain now."

"Yes, I know, sir, Mr. Seafort." The prisoner, a scrawny, tired-looking man of fifty, stood at ease. His mop of dark brown hair covered a hairline that had receded far back.

"I have a few questions about the, um, incident. How did it come about?"

He seemed pathetically eager to please. "Mr. Tuak and the others, they were fighting. I weren't involved in no drugs, honest. I din' even know they had none."

If that was going to be his line there was no point listening. "Mr. Herney, hear me well. In a few days we're going to cuff you, gag you, and hang you. Then we'll push your corpse out the airlock." He gagged. "I'm the only one who can stop it. This is the only time I'll talk to you. Lie again and I'll walk out."

"I'm sorry, Captain, sir," he babbled. "Only the truth, I swear it!"

"Start again."

"I knew about the goofjuice, a lot of us did. I'm sorry, Captain. Tuak, he was passing it around. I tried it, just once, honest! It cost too much, it weren't worth it. I'm sorry, Captain, honest I am. After that I stayed out of their way. Weiznisci, he got tanked, and you know that stuff, there's no talking to a man, he's got some in him. He was happy as a quark, but he was beating the crap outta two joes, we all sorta jumped him. An' that got Fraser going, he was on it too. Tuak figured to get ridda the stuff before the brass come down, only he couldn't, there was too much goin' on all at once." He scratched himself, thought for a moment.

"Mr. Terrill, he come in, told us to pull 'em apart, I just wanted to stay out of it. But I waded in like he said, and boom! I got one right in the side of the head, made me pretty mad. I din' know who done me, I was just swingin' my arms, you know? I din' care what I was hittin', I just tried ta stay ahead of how often I was gettin' hit. Then the lights goes out, and I wake up, I'm all cuffed, they say I slugged Mr. Vish."

He started to whimper, tears running down his face. "I don' know about that, Captain, sir. Maybe I did. I ain't sayin' I din'. But I din' mean to. It was a mistake. It's all some kinda mistake. It's got to be!" He began to sob. "Please, Cap'n, make it be a mistake! Get me outta this, I won't give no trouble, I promise, I—"

I banged on the hatch. The voice had to stop. I'd give anything to have the voice stop.

"Oh, please, sir. I won't fight no more, I'm so scared! Or the juice, neither, if you just—"

The hatch opened. I got out. I could hear his begging halfway down the corridor.

Ricky Fuentes stood at attention waiting to be dismissed, my breakfast tray on the table beside him.

"Good morning, Ricky."

"Good morning, Captain, sir!" I knew he frolicked. I knew he laughed. But in my cabin he was tighter than a coiled spring.

"Ricardo, I'd like you to think about something."

"Yes, sir, Captain!" His eyes were locked on the bulkhead in front of him as he stood at rigid attention.

I felt my temper fray. He was keyed tight, in no condition to listen. "Ricky, belay that. At ease. Act like the joey I used to know."

"Aye aye, sir!" His voice remained stiff.

I roared, "By the Lord God, you will stop this bloody nonsense!" Ricky's mouth dropped open. He began to tremble.

"Stop standing at attention!" I screamed. "Behave yourself, boy!"

His lip quivered. A lone tear glistened in his eye, then slowly rolled down his cheek. He sagged from attention, wiped it with his sleeve. "What did I do?" he asked, forlorn. "I didn't want to make you mad, Captain!"

"Good Lord, Ricky!" I pulled out a chair. "Here, sit." I pushed him into it, waited while he fought for control. When I was sure he wouldn't cry I said, more gently, "Now you can listen to me. Sit easy, the way you used to in my wardroom, and we'll talk. All right?"

"Yessir." He watched me anxiously.

"You saw my announcement about becoming a middy?"

"Yessir!" He was taking no chances of setting me off again.

"You know how it is in the wardroom. Would you like it there?"

"Me, sir? I'm just a sailor."

"Would you like to be a cadet?"

"You mean, and get to live in the wardroom, and become an officer?" He grappled with the possibility.

"Yes."

"And have to shine Mr. Holser's shoes, and stand the regs, and ice-cold showers, and the rest of the hazing?"

Well, better he know now. "Yes, Ricky. That's part of it."

"Zarky!"

Good Lord, it actually appealed to him. Maybe it seemed adult, from his perspective. I wanted to stop him, for his own sake.

"Do I have to say yes right now, Captain, sir, or can I think about it?"

"You may think about it," I told him.

The ship's boy jumped up and saluted. "Thank you, Captain! You know"—he offered a confidence—"I read the notice myself, really I did. I can read! I didn't think you meant it for me too. Am I dismissed? Can I go tell my friends?"

"Dismissed, Mr. Fuentes." He would run to the purser or the chief petty officer, and ask them in his own way whether he should leave the companionship of belowdecks for the heady air of officers' country. They would tell him to apply, not because we needed officers, but to see one of their own make it to the top.

All was well on the bridge. I knew that; if not, I would have been called. I was scheduled for afternoon watch and would probably stay on for the evening, so if I wanted to see Amanda it had to be now.

She was in her room reading a holovid, her hatch open. When I knocked on the bulkhead she snapped off her book, got up quickly, and came to the entryway. "Come in, Nicky." She was the only person aboard who still called me that.

We sat on the bunk. I told her what I had done to poor Alexi. She seemed indifferent. I told her how I encouraged little Ricky to apply, after first scaring the wits out of him. That brought a smile to her face, but she said little.

After a while she got up and closed the hatch. Then she lay down on the bunk, pulling me down with her. We lay together. She was gentle and kind to me. Yet she seemed somehow abstracted, as if her mind were elsewhere. We made love, slowly, savoring the moments of intensity. When we were done she lay still, her eyes sometimes opening to look at my face, sometimes closing again.

"What is it, hon?" I stroked her hair. She nestled in my arm.

"I like you, Nicky." She was silent a moment. "You're gentle, and gallant, and kind to me. I enjoy being with you."

"Me too," I said, but she stopped me.

"I like having you as a lover. And as a friend. But—Nicky, I'm sorry. You have to know. If you kill those men, I'll stop being your friend. We won't be lovers or see each other ever again. I wanted you to make the right decision on your own, but it isn't fair not to tell you what I'll do."

"How can you—"

She put her hand over my mouth. "It's just that I may have misjudged you. I think you're the sort of person who can't do anything so barbaric. That's why I like you. But if you can, I'm wrong about you, and it's over between us." She kissed my forehead. "I had to tell you." She rested her head again in the crook of my arm.

I could think of nothing to say. We lay there, sweetly unhappy, until I had to go on watch.

I came onto the bridge, relieved Vax and the Pilot. Vax handed me a holovid chip.

"The essay you ordered, sir."

I tossed it in the drawer. "Very good, Mr. Holser." I looked him over. "Straighten your tie, before I put you on report."

He blanched. "Aye aye, sir!" He quickly straightened his tie, tucked his jacket down, glanced at his shoes. "Am I dismissed, sir?"

"Yes." I reached a sudden decision. "Meet me in the ship's launch berth at midnight tonight."

"The launch— aye aye, sir!" He turned on his heel and left.

This watch, I would stand alone; nobody would interrupt my thoughts. In the silence, I considered Tuak and Rogoff, our two other condemned souls. I couldn't face another trip to the brig, but I had to talk to them. Amanda's conviction that the executions would be barbaric troubled me; I suspected she was right.

I paged Mr. Vishinsky. "Master-at-arms, escort Mr. Tuak to the bridge."

His voice came over the caller. "Aye aye, sir. Captain, may I bring along—"

"No. Just Tuak."

There was a pause. "Aye aye, sir. Respectfully, for the Captain's personal safety I protest—"

"Protest overruled. Get him up here." I thumbed off the caller.

A few minutes later Tuak arrived, hands cuffed in front of him, his upper arm firmly in Mr. Vishinsky's grip. He staggered as the master-at-arms propelled him forward.

"Take off the cuffs."

It did not meet with Vishinsky's approval. "Aye aye, sir." His anger was barely concealed.

"Wait outside." I slapped the hatch closed behind the master. I turned to the seaman, who stood nervously rubbing his chafed wrists.

"I'm considering whether to save your life," I said. "Tell me what went on belowdecks. No lies."

"Aye aye, sir." Tuak swallowed. He looked drawn and haggard. He was tall and thin, of sallow complexion. His eyes shifted constantly, as if he consulted some inner voice.

His story was sordid. He admitted hiding the goofjuice on board, but claimed two of his mates had smuggled the still onto the ship. That was foolish; under drugs he'd already confessed to bringing aboard and setting up the still, and he knew it. I ignored that. The main issue wasn't the still.

"What started the riot?"

"Weiznisci started fighting, Captain. We was all just trying to stop him."

"The truth, Mr. Tuak."

"That's the truth, Captain, sir." He glanced up at my eyes. "I was going to stop making juice; we started the still just for a joke. We didn't mean to make all that trouble. I had to keep doin' it, they made me." He checked my expression once more. "When Weiznisci got wild some of the joes panicked. They wanted to tear out the still right then and there, before they found it in an inspection."

"So you tried to stop them."

"Oh, no, sir. I was helping. It was the others tried to stop them." That was patently untrue.

"Then Mr. Terrill came in."

"Yes, sir. He said to belay the fighting, but it was too wild, nobody was listening no more."

"So you held Mr. Terrill while Rogoff clubbed him."

"I didn't! I was trying to help him. I held him up, kept him from falling."

"Come on, now. Mr. Terrill said you grabbed him around the neck to hold on tighter."

"No, sir. Oh, no, Captain. He's mixed up, Mr. Terrill is. I saw him get slugged and I tried to keep him on his feet. That's all."

By now he could probably pass a polygraph and drug test on his story; he'd repeated it so often he believed it. He babbled on, trying to convince me of his good intentions.

A man like Tuak illustrated the pitfalls of guaranteed enlistment. If crewmen were given the same rigorous screening as us officers, Tuak wouldn't have gotten aboard. But the hazards of seafaring life made it difficult to recruit seamen for the huge starships, especially as government policy put a ten-year cap on service begun as an adult, for fear of melanoma T.

Government, industry, and academia were all in constant need of educated workers, and the colonies themselves were a drain of educated manpower. Our explosion into space meant that Admiralty had a lot of ships to man, and interstellar voyages took years. Belowdecks they were years of crammed quarters, lack of privacy, hard duties, tyrannical discipline. No matter how good the pay was, the recruits would have to wait years before they could spend it.

Guaranteed enlistment helped fill the crew berths. So we had men like Mr. Tuak, barely more civilized than the transpops, who responded to the guarantee they would be accepted and the half year's pay issued in advance as an enlistment bonus.

Yet Tuak hadn't done anything more than get caught up in a riot. Well, a little more; he had smuggled in the still that caused the riot in the first place. And he'd been fighting to protect the still from the men who wanted to dismantle it. But should he be put to death for that?

"Mr. Tuak." I waited while his excuses ran down. "Mr. Tuak, the master-at-arms will take you back to the brig. You will be informed." I slapped open the hatch.

"I din' mean no harm, Captain. Listen, Captain, I got two crippled sisters at home with my mother. Ask the paymaster, my pay all goes to them, every bit of it. They need me. Listen, I can stay out of trouble, honest, Captain!"

Vishinsky slapped the cuffs on his wrists, manhandled him out to the corridor.

"No more fighting!" Tuak said desperately, over his shoulder. "I swear!"

I was no closer to a decision.

As I left the dining hall after dinner the Purser handed me a sealed paper envelope. Unusual, in these days of holovid chipnotes. I took it back to the bridge to open. A letter, handwritten in a laborious script, obviously rewritten more than once.

Hon. Captain Nicholas Seafort, U.N.S. Hibernia
Dear Sir:
Please accept my apology for the way I behaved when you visited my cabin. You are the authority on board this vessel. I owed you respect which I failed to offer. I was inexcusably rude to use the tone of voice I did.

I didn't know what to make of that. I read on.

> When I thought about my discourtesy, I saw why you
> don't think me fit for the Naval Service. I ask you to forgive
> me. I assure you I am capable of decent manners and I will
> not be offensive to you again.
> Respectfully, Derek Carr.

Now that was laying it on a bit thick. I could believe that Mr. Carr
had decided he'd been rude. It was possible that he might even apologize. But that he'd grovel was hard to swallow. I wondered why he'd
done it. I locked the letter in the drawer under my console.

Some hours later I waited in the empty, dimly lit launch berth. The
hatch opened and a head peered in.

"Over here, Mr. Holser."

Vax looked around the huge cavern. Seeing me, he came quickly to
attention. "Midshipman Holser reporting, sir!"

"Very well." I indicated the cold open space. "What is this, Vax?"

He said, puzzled, "It's the berth for the ship's launch, sir."

"That's right. Now that it's empty it's a good time to clean it." From
my jacket pocket I took a small rag and bar of alumalloy polish. "I have a
job for you. Clean and polish the bulkheads, Mr. Holser. All of them."

Vax stared at me with anxiety and disbelief. The berth was huge;
polishing it might take most of a year. It was utterly unnecessary work;
one didn't hand-polish the partitions of a launch berth.

"You're assigned to this duty only, until it's finished. You're off the
watch roster and you're forbidden to enter the bridge. You may begin
now." I thrust the polish and rag into his hands.

I had deliberately made it as hard as I could. By removing him from
the watch roster and forbidding him access to the bridge, Vax would not
again have opportunity to protest or ask my mercy. On the other hand,
I'd given him a direct order. I hoped he would pass the test.

"Aye aye, sir." His voice was unsteady, but he turned to the partition, rubbed the bar against the alumalloy. He began to polish it with the
rag. Alumalloy doesn't polish easily; it was hard work. After a few minutes of labor he had finished a patch a few inches around. He rubbed the
bar of polish onto the adjoining spot and folded the rag to a clean surface. His muscles flexing, he rubbed the rag against the tough alumalloy
surface.

I watched for several minutes. "Report for other duties when all four bulkheads are done." I turned and walked to the hatch twenty meters from where he had started. I glanced behind me; he was hard at work. I slapped the hatch open, started through it. He kept polishing.

I stepped back into the launch berth. "Belay that order, Mr. Holser."

"Aye, aye, sir." His eyes darted from the bulkheads to me, and back, slowly taking in his reprieve.

I walked back to where he stood. "Vax, what did I demonstrate to you?"

He thought awhile before answering. "The Captain has absolute control of the vessel and the people on it, sir. He can make a midshipman do anything."

"But you already knew that."

"Yes, sir." He hesitated. "But not as well as I know it now."

Thank you, Lord God. It was what I'd prayed to hear. "I'm canceling your special orders to report every four hours. You may resume your wardroom duties. You know what I expect from you?"

"Yes, sir. No hazing, under any circumstances."

"Don't be ridiculous!" I was angry. If that's all he had learned, all this had been a waste of time.

"I thought that's what you wanted, sir. For me to control myself." He was puzzled.

"Yes, that. And more. Come, let's go raid the galley." He had to smile at that. At the beginning of the cruise, the four of us would occasionally sneak into the galley late at night and raid the coolers. We would catch hell if we were caught; that made it all the more attractive.

Now I entered the galley with impunity. The metal counters were shiny clean; the food was securely wrapped and stowed. I opened the cooler and found some milk. Synthetic, of course. In the bread bin was leftover cake that would have gone to next day's lunch. Well, they'd never miss it. I served my midshipman and myself. I indicated a stool for Vax; we ate off the counter. "It tasted better the other way," I said.

"Yes, sir, but I'm glad for it now," he said politely. Our Vax had come a long way.

"Now, Vax. About hazing. You're first middy. You've been too busy to spend any time in the wardroom, so you haven't taken charge. But I want you to. And with a change of command there will be some settling in. You'll have to make sure they both know who's senior."

"Yes, sir." He listened attentively.

"So, you may use your authority. Hazing, as we call it. What I want you to stop isn't hazing, but your bullying. You enjoy hazing so much you let it get out of control. You're to control the pleasure you take in it. Stop yourself from going overboard and being cruel. You told me once you're not nice, that there's nothing you can do about it. If that's still true, go back and start polishing the launch berth until you can do something about it. I'll wait."

He swallowed. I think no one had ever talked to him like that before.

I added, "You're better off with the rag and polish, Vax, if you're not sure you'll control yourself. I meant it when I said I'll wait. If you tell me I can trust you and I catch you being cruel like you used to be, I'll break you. I'll make your life a living hell for as long as I'm in command, until you can't stand any more. I swear it by Lord God Himself!"

Vax said very humbly, "Please let me think for a moment, sir."

I gave him all the time he wanted. He studied his fists, clasped on the metal work counter. Vax was slow. Not stupid, not retarded. Slow to make up his mind. I appreciated the corollary of that. Once he made up his mind he was utterly dependable.

"Captain Seafort, sir, I think I can do what you want. I mean, I know I can, if I may ask a favor."

"What favor?" This was no time to start bargaining.

"I know the senior middy is supposed to handle wardroom matters and keep the other midshipmen out of your hair. But if I'm not sure of myself, could I come and ask you if you'd approve? I mean, of a hazing?"

I could have hugged him. It felt as if a fusion engine had been taken from around my neck. "I think so," I said soberly, after a moment's reflection. "I would allow it, yes."

"Thank you, sir. I promise I'll control myself. I will haze the other middies only when I think it's good for discipline. I won't let myself get carried away. Sir."

"Vax, the wardroom is yours. I won't spy on you; I accept your word. You have a job to do, and you'd better get on with it. Thanks to you, poor Alexi ended up over the barrel when all he needed was a lecture and a few hours of calisthenics." That wasn't fair; it was my fault more than Vax's.

"I'm very sorry, sir. You can count on me now."

I should have saluted and dismissed him. Instead, I broke regs, custom, and all propriety. Matters must have been getting to me. Slowly, looking him in the eye, I offered my hand. Just as slowly he took it in his big paw and clasped it firmly. We shook.

13

"Lord God, today is March 30, 2195, on the U.N.S. *Hibernia*. We ask you to bless us, to bless our voyage, and to bring health and well-being to all aboard." Seated, I nodded to my two tablemates. Weeks after I'd assumed command, Mrs. Donhauser and Mr. Kaa Loa were still my only dinner companions.

The purser bent at my ear. "Sir, one of the passengers is asking if he may join the Captain's table." My popularity had just risen by half.

"That's agreeable, Mr. Browning. Who is it?"

"Young Mr. Carr, sir."

I hadn't spoken to Derek in the weeks since his letter. I was curious. "Ask him if he cares to start tonight."

A moment later Derek Carr approached with diffidence. "Good evening, Captain. Mrs. Donhauser. And you, sir," this last to Mr. Kaa Loa, whom he apparently didn't know.

"Please be seated, Mr. Carr." I introduced the boy to the Micronesian.

After his courtesies to the older man Derek turned to me. "Sir, I apologize again for my behavior in my cabin. I promise it won't happen again."

Where was all this heading? "No matter, Mr. Carr. It's over and done." Derek sat. I chatted with Mrs. Donhauser. She turned the topic to religion, a difficult topic on board ship. Her Anabaptist doctrines were tolerated, as were most cults, but the Naval Service, like the rest of the Government, was committed to the Great Yahwehist Christian Reunification. She knew full well that as Captain I was a representative of the One True God, and she shouldn't be baiting me. I assumed she was just out of sorts; normally Mrs. Donhauser was a pleasant if argumentative companion.

To avoid contention I turned to Derek. "How have you been occupying yourself lately, Mr. Carr?"

"I've been studying, sir. And exercising."

Definitely a change in manner. I gave him another opening. "Were you enrolled in school before the voyage?"

"No, sir. I had tutors. My father believed in solitary education."

"We should reimpose mandatory schooling," Mrs. Donhauser grumbled. "The voluntary system doesn't work; we don't have enough technocrats to run government or industry. We're constantly starved for educated people."

"Mandatory education didn't work either," I said. "Literacy levels dropped constantly until it was abandoned."

Mrs. Donhauser, savoring a good argument, launched into a vehement counterattack, demonstrating, at least to herself, that mandatory education was the only way to save society. "Don't you agree, Mr. Carr?" she asked when she finished.

"Yes, ma'am, I agree that a mass of uneducated people is a danger to society. As for the rest—" He turned to me. "Is she right, sir?" Now I was really puzzled. This was not the haughty youth who'd come aboard the ship. And I was likewise sure he had not undergone a complete change of heart. His courtesy had a purpose. I turned away the question and studied him during the rest of the meal.

Going over watch rotations in my cabin that evening, I realized how little time I had to decide the fate of the three wretched sailors under sentence of death. I intended to make a deliberate decision; their fate wouldn't be determined by default. Shortly, I would have to free them or allow—no, order—the executions to take place.

I had spoken to Tuak and Herney, but I'd put off seeing Rogoff because I found the interviews unbearable. I made a note to see the man after forenoon watch.

I undressed, crawled into my bunk, and drifted off to sleep almost immediately. In the early hours I awoke. I tossed and turned until I couldn't stand it any longer; I snapped on my holovid and read ship's regs. If they wouldn't put me to sleep, nothing would.

Again I closed my eyes and tried to sleep; I'd never found insomnia a problem in the wardroom. At three in the morning I turned on my bedside light. My stomach slowly knotted from tension as I began to dress.

I walked the deserted corridors to Level 3. One of Mr. Vishinsky's seamen guarded the brig. He was watching a holovid, feet on the desk, when I appeared in the hatchway. Horrified, he leapt to his feet and snapped to attention.

I ignored his infraction. At that hour, one need not be prepared for a Captain's inspection. "I'm here to see Mr. Rogoff, sailor."

"Aye aye, sir. He's in cell four. If the Captain will let me get the cuffs on him—"

"Not necessary. Open the hatch. And lend me your chair. You don't sit on guard duty anyway."

"Aye aye, sir. No, sir." He jumped to obey.

Rogoff, wearing only his pants, was asleep on his dirty mattress when the light snapped on. Bleary, he looked up as I entered and set down the chair.

"Mr. Rogoff."

"Mr. Seafort? I mean, Captain, sir? Is it—oh, God, I mean, are you here to—" He couldn't say the words.

"No. Not for a few days yet. I'm here to talk to you."

"Yessir!" He scrambled to his feet. "Anything you say, Captain. Anything."

I turned the chair backward and straddled it. "If I don't commute your sentence they're going to hang you. Tell me why I should pardon you."

He rubbed his eyes, standing awkwardly in front of my chair. "Captain, please, for Lord God's sake, let me go. Brig me for the rest of the voyage, or whatever you want. But don't let them hang me. I didn't mean any harm."

"No harm?" I asked him. "You clubbed the CPO unconscious while Mr. Tuak held his arms."

"Not in cold blood, sir. We were fighting, all of us."

"You can't brawl with a superior, even a petty officer."

"No, sir, you're right, sir. But the thing was, the fight started. Your blood gets hot, you don't see what's going on, or stop to think things over. Right then, Mr. Terrill was just another joe, you know? He wasn't the CPO, he was just somebody to hit. It's not like I meant to mutiny, sir."

He had stated in a nutshell why the affair should have been handled at Captain's Mast. Damn Captain Malstrom for leaving me this mess. I felt guilty for my anger, and it made me cross. "Maybe that's so for the first blow, Mr. Rogoff. But you smashed him several times in the face. By then you knew who you were hitting."

"Excuse me, Captain, no offense, have you ever been in a fight?"

"Yes." I hadn't won.

"While you were swinging did you stop and think about the consequences? Did you consider how hard you should fight, or whether you should hit a joe?"

"I never swung against a superior officer, Mr. Rogoff." Except my senior middy when I was posted to Helsinki, and he blackened both my eyes and kneed me so hard I couldn't walk upright for days. But that didn't count, did it? Challenging the first middy was understood and accepted. I wasn't like Rogoff, was I? "You kept punching him in the face. Your superior."

"Sir, look at me. Pretend it's you here, in this god-awful place. You had a bad fight, and they're going to hang you for it. Please. Don't do that to me."

I made my voice hard. "It wasn't that simple, sailor. You were fighting to protect that bloody still of yours, to make sure the officers didn't find it. You were covering up a crime Mr. Terrill was about to discover."

Rogoff hugged himself. He looked at the deck, shaking his head from side to side. His bare feet wiggled nervously. "Captain," he said, looking up, "I ain't no angel. I do things that ain't right. I know I been in trouble before. But the still, that's brig time or a discharge. If I'd of realized what I was doing I wouldn't have touched him. You gotta believe that."

"I believe you weren't thinking about court-martial, Mr. Rogoff. I can't believe you were unaware you were hitting Petty Officer Terrill. Is your being excited reason to pardon you?"

"Captain, I beg you. I'm begging for my life."

"Please, don't." I didn't want that power over him.

"Look!" He dropped to his knees in front of me. "Please, sir, I'm begging. Don't hang me! Let me live, give me another chance!"

I scrambled to my feet, sweating. I had to get out of the cell. "Guard!"

"Sir, I'm not evil!" He put his palms on the deck, abasing himself. "Please let me live! Please!"

I didn't run out of the cell. I walked. I walked out of the brig anteroom. I walked to the turn of the corridor outside. Then I ran, as if the devils of hell were at my heels. I tore up the ladder past Level 2 to officers' country, past the bridge to my cabin. I fumbled at the hatch, slapped it closed behind me. I barely made it to the head before I heaved my undigested dinner into the toilet. I remained there, shaking with fear and disgust. It was when I realized that I was kneeling with both my palms on the deck that I began to cry.

I became a hermit, refusing to leave my cabin except for brief excursions to the bridge. I had the Chief cross my name off the watch roster. My look was such that no one dared speak to me. I took meals in my cabin, refusing even to take my evening meal in the dining hall with the passengers. I pretended to myself I was sick, that I felt feverish. I lay in my bunk imagining that I was safe, in Father's house.

In the quietest hours of the second night I had a dream. Again I was a boy, walking toward the Academy gates. My duffel was very heavy, so heavy I could hardly carry it. I had to say something to Father, but I couldn't speak. He walked along beside me, dour and uncommunicative as always. Yet he was there with me, was that not enough proof he loved me?

I changed the duffel to my other arm so I could put my hand in his. Father switched to my other side. I switched the duffel back, but he stepped around me once more. I prepared the words of parting I would offer. I rehearsed them over and again until they sounded right.

The gates loomed closer. Now we were at the broad open walk in front of the Academy entrance. The sentry stood impassive guard. I turned, knowing it was time to say goodbye. Father put his hands firmly on my shoulders and turned me toward the waiting gates. He propelled me forward.

In a daze I walked though the gates, feeling an iron ring close itself around my neck as I did so. I turned. Father was striding away. I willed him to turn to me. I waved to his back. Never looking over his shoulder, he disappeared over the rise. The iron ring was heavy around my neck.

I awoke, shaking. Eventually my breathing fell silent. I smelled the acrid sweat on my undershirt; I stripped off my clothes and walked unsteadily to my shower to stand under the hot water a long while, motionless.

When I finally dared go back to bed I slept untroubled. In the morning I ate the breakfast Ricky brought, and left my cabin to become a human being once more.

14

"Excuse me, sir, a question."

"What is it, Vax?" We were on watch. In the long silence, I'd been trying to empty my mind of everything, to think of nothing. I was not succeeding.

"One of the passengers, Mr. Carr, asked if I would show him Academy's exercise drills this afternoon. I thought I ought to have your permission first."

I could see no reason to refuse. "If you want to, Vax, I have no objection." I smiled. "Are you about to become a drill sergeant?"

"No, sir. I thought I'd do them with him." I should have guessed.

Time passed. Still I made no decision about the prisoners.

The next day Yorinda Vincente asked to see me. I assented. I didn't want her on the bridge or in my cabin, so I met her in the passengers' lounge.

"This is on behalf of the Passengers' Council." Her tone was stiff. "We want to know what will happen to the ship, I mean the crew, when we get to Hope Nation."

"You're asking if *Hibernia* will get a new Captain?"

"And other officers, yes."

"Most of you will disembark at Hope Nation, Ms. Vincente. How does it concern you?"

"Some of us are booked to Detour, Captain Seafort. Other plans would have to be made." She meant that they wouldn't want to stay on the ship if I were going to sail her. I understood. *I* wouldn't want to stay on the ship if I were going to sail her.

"*Hibernia* is under orders from Admiralty at Lunapolis," I explained. "My authority as Captain derives from those orders. Admiralty has a representative, Admiral Johanson, at Hope Nation. When I report, he will relieve me of command, appoint a commissioned Captain, and assign lieutenants to the ship."

"Are there experienced officers at Hope Nation?"

"More experienced than I, Ms. Vincente. And even if there weren't, the Admiral is my superior officer. I'm sure he'll relieve me and appoint a Captain of his choosing. *Hibernia* will be in good hands when she leaves Hope Nation."

She explored all the possibilities. "I imagine skilled officers aren't sitting around Hope Nation waiting to be posted. What will he do if he doesn't have enough lieutenants?"

"It's unlikely any Naval officers are sitting around waiting, Ms. Vincente. The Service is always shorthanded. What I imagine he'll do is borrow them from local service, and replace them with some of our own officers. Perhaps even myself."

"People without interstellar experience?"

"Not every lieutenant goes interstellar before he's commissioned, ma'am. As long as the Captain's a seasoned officer, the ship will be in good hands." I continued my reassurances until she seemed satisfied.

The next day when I met Vax on the bridge I asked, "How are your exercises going?"

"They're not," he said. I raised an eyebrow. He added, "Derek showed up the first day and we worked out. Easy stuff, like they give the first-year cadets. Yesterday he came again, but after a half hour he walked out."

"What did he say?"

"Nothing, sir. He just stalked out and slammed the hatch." So much for Mr. Carr.

I met Amanda in the corridor on the way to the dining hall. She stopped, waiting for me to speak first.

"I haven't made up my mind yet, Amanda."

"Isn't your time about up?"

"Day after tomorrow. One way or another, it will be over by then."

"Listen to your conscience," she said. "Pardon them. Years from now you'll hate yourself if you don't."

"I'm still thinking." I didn't mention my interview with Rogoff. We went in to dinner. When I came to the part of the Ship's Prayer, "Bring health and well-being to all aboard," I stumbled over the words.

That evening Chief McAndrews sat down heavily in the armchair alongside my table. The pipe lay between us. I said, "Chief I order you to ignite that device. We need to investigate it further."

"Aye aye, sir." It was his third visit to my cabin; we were establishing the form of a ritual. He opened the canister and got out his candle-lighter.

I kicked off my shoes. After all, it was my own cabin. "I was hoping I'd have another middy by now." I yawned. "We're all standing too many watches."

"On the bridge or in the launch berth, sir?" He was beginning to unbend with me, just a bit.

"Oh, you heard about that?"

"Someone saw you take Mr. Holser in there and emerge later with a very subdued midshipman."

"Who saw?"

"I don't remember, sir."

If we could power the ship by gossip it would be faster than fusion. Maybe it really was Darla who spread the word. "I think Vax will be all right, Chief. I've straightened things out with him."

"With a club?"

I smiled. "Vax just needs the facts demonstrated from time to time. Then he believes them. He'll make a good first middy."

He puffed on his artifact. "What you need, Captain, is a fourth middy. Maybe even a fifth." I knew that. I could then make Vax a lieutenant. Probably also Alexi, if I hadn't embittered him for life.

"The only feeler I've had is from that Carr joey, and I turned him down."

"There's Ricky." The Chief knew everything.

"He won't be old enough to be much help until we're past Detour. We'll have new officers and won't need him by then."

"So why'd you invite him, Captain?"

"I didn't say he'd be no help at all. And I like him."

"He'll agree. He needs more time to think about it, but count on him."

"I'm not so sure," I said. "I don't have the knack of persuading people without terrorizing them. First Vax, then the Pilot, and then Alexi. Now it's Ricky. I had to scream at the top of my voice to stop him from standing at attention. I'm lucky he didn't wet his pants."

The Chief smiled. "You didn't terrorize him. You startled him some, but he's told everyone belowdecks how the Captain wants him to be a midshipman. He sticks his chest out when he says it. I don't think you have to worry."

"Then I was fortunate. Part of my problem having no natural authority is that I come on like a wild man to uphold the stature of the office. As I did with Alexi."

The Chief shrugged. "The barrel? He'll get over it. I gave him half a dozen, not all that hard. He's had worse before."

"But not from me. I was his friend."

Chief McAndrews took several puffs on the pipe before deciding to reply. "You still are," he said. "You've done him a favor, whether he knows it or not. A big one. When we get to Hope Nation he'll probably be transferred. What would happen to him if he had a silly fit on the bridge of someone else's ship?"

I shuddered. Either he wouldn't sit down for a month or he would find himself in the brig. If the Captain didn't die of apoplexy first.

"Still, I should have found some other way to stop him."

The Chief waved his pipe in the air. "Say you're right, Captain. Maybe you should have found a better way. He'll still get over it. Neither he nor anyone else has the right to exect you to be perfect. You're doing your best."

"And it isn't good enough, Chief." I stared moodily at his smoke. "In a couple of days I have to decide about those poor joeys in the brig. I have two choices, both wrong. If I let them go, mutiny goes unpunished. Admiralty would never pardon them if the affair had happened back at Earthport; they'd hang the three with no regrets. But I feel that if I execute them, I'm a heartless killer."

I brooded. "Expect myself to be perfect? If I were barely competent I'd find a third solution. I've tried; I can't think of any. So I'll pick one alternative or the other. My best isn't good enough."

Wisely, the Chief said nothing.

The next day, I was restless and irritable. To distract myself I ran surprise drills throughout the ship, telling myself it was to improve the crew's alertness. *"Fire in the launch berth!"* *"Fusion engine overheat!"* *"Man Battle Stations!"* The crew scurried.

I announced that Darla had a nervous breakdown, and made the middies plot all ship's functions by hand. They complied, although nobody, especially Darla, thought it was funny. I entered drill response times in the Log to compare with future drills. I made a mental note to have future drills.

All in all, I continued making myself unpopular.

I woke in the morning with a sense of dread at what I'd have to face before the day ended. After showering and dressing I sat to await the usual knock; in a few moments Ricky arrived with my breakfast. He put down the tray, saluted, and waited to be dismissed. Though he stood at attention, his stomach no longer tried to meet his backbone.

"Stand easy, Mr. Fuentes."

"Thank you, Captain. They were having waffles and cream so I brought you extras. Cream is real zarky." He looked wistfully at the tray. Crew rations didn't compare with officers' and passengers' fare.

I liked the new Ricky much better. Or was it the old Ricky? "Thank you. About that cadet idea, what do you think?"

"Mr. Browning says I should. So does Mr. Terrill. It's just I'm a little scared. Captain, sir."

"I can understand that." I took a bite of waffle. It was delicious. I thought of offering him some, but there were limits. A crewman didn't breakfast with the Captain. "So you can read, hmm?"

"Oh, yes. I can write too. Even by hand." He was very proud of it.

"Ricky, I'm going to arrange some lessons for you. Math, physics, history. I want you to work as hard as you can. Will you do that for me, as a special favor?" That would get his cooperation far better than an order.

He actually swelled with pride. His shoulders went up, his chest came out. "Oh, yes, sir. I'll do my best."

"Very well. Dismissed, Mr. Fuentes." He saluted, spun on his heel, and went to the hatch. Someone must have been teaching him physical drills. I suspected the Ship's Boy already knew more about Naval life, and how *Hibernia* was run, than most people would imagine. "Oh, Mr. Fuentes?"

"Yes, sir?" He stopped in the entryway.

"Go to the galley. My compliments to the Cook, and would he please serve you a portion of waffles and cream."

His face lit up. "Oh, thanks, Captain, sir! They're real good. He already gave me some, but I'd love more!" He raced out into the corridor. So much for my generosity.

Sandy was on watch with the Pilot when I popped onto the bridge for a quick inspection. Mr. Haynes nodded with careful civility. He hadn't had much to say to me since the incident with our coordinates.

I glanced at Sandy and my eyebrow rose; the boy was dozing in his seat. That wouldn't do. I relieved him and sent him to Vax, with a request to encourage the youngster to stay awake on duty.

Vax, a middy himself, couldn't send Sandy to the barrel, but he had ways to get the point across. I didn't feel guilty this time; sleeping on watch was a heinous offense. I had to prepare Sandy to hold his own watch. It crossed my mind that I myself had dozed on the bridge only a couple of weeks before. I argued that I wasn't actually watch officer; I'd just stayed to keep an eye on things. When part of me started to argue back, I left the bridge.

I wandered the Level 1 circumference corridor, past cabins in which Lieutenants Dagalow and Cousins once lived. Past Lieutenant Malstrom's cabin where a lifetime ago I'd played chess. Through the passengers' section, nodding curtly to anyone who noticed me. I looked into the infirmary. The med tech came to attention in the anteroom; Dr. Uburu was with a passenger in the cubicle that served as an examing room.

I had an inexplicable urge to visit the whole of the ship. I went down to Level 2. The exercise room in which I'd battled Vax was empty. A few people were in the passengers' lounge; the Treadwell children, Mr. Barstow, Derek Carr. I left quickly, in no mood for conversation.

I wandered into the dining hall. Empty tables, set with gleaming shining glassware and china on starched white cloths, waited for the evening's throng. I acknowledged the good sense of the ship's designers; by having officers and passengers eat separately twice a day, and merging us into one unit for the evening meal, they provided continuing variation in our routines while subtly reminding us of the difference in our status.

I closed my eyes to summon Captain Haag, competent and reassuring in his dress whites, delivering the Ship's Prayer to an attentive hall. I found the table where I'd apprehensively awaited my first dinner, upon reporting to *Hibernia* but a few months past.

Morose, I left the dining hall, wandered past the row of hatches to the passengers' cabins. In the passengers' mess the steward, startled to find me where the Captain seldom ventured, dropped his tray of silverware on the table and snapped to attention. I released him with a wave.

The mess could hold thirty passengers at a time; they came for their breakfast and lunch on rigid schedule. The compartment was plain, almost cheerless, unlike the ship's dining hall above.

I took the ladder down to Level 3, feeling my weight increase perceptibly as I did so. Here, crewmen hurried about on errands, snapping to attention as I passed unheeding. I stopped at the crew's presentation hall, or theater; its rows of practical, sturdy seats depressed me. Farther along the corridor was the crew's exercise room, identical to the passengers' gym a level above.

"Pardon me, Captain, can I help you find someone?" Carpenter's Mate Tsai Ting, whom Mr. Vishinsky had brought to the munitions locker. He stood at attention.

"No. Carry on, sailor."

"Aye aye, sir." He went about his business. Now it wouldn't be long before the whole crew knew I was poking around in their territory.

I looked into crew berth one, knowing I was violating custom. The crew had no place of their own except their berths and the privacy rooms, and little time to themselves. It was understood that the Captain would not harass them in their bunks by unannounced inspections.

A dozen crewmen were sleeping; one lad sitting on his bunk saw me and was about to leap to his feet; I put my finger to my lips and shook my head. He remained in his place, his eyes locked on me, while I looked about from the hatchway. The crew berth smelled of many men in close quarters; it was clean without being cleanly. Calendars were posted on some of the lockers; unused bunks were neatly made. It was no more, no less than I expected.

Restless, I went into the adjoining head. The lack of privacy in its large open spaces made our midshipmen's head seem positively luxurious. This room, at least, was scrupulously clean. The petty officers saw to that.

There was nothing aft but the engine room and the shaft. I climbed down the ladder to the engine room at the base of the disk. The insistent throb of the fusion drives pervaded my senses. The outer compartment was empty; the Chief would be farther aft, then, in the drive control chamber. I wandered starboard to the hydroponics unit.

"They'll be all right." The voice came from around the curve in the corridor just ahead. I stopped.

"I don't know. He's a bastard; look how he shoved the Chief aside to get to the top."

"Sure, Captain Kid's ambitious and saw his chance. But he'll let them go; he's just waiting 'til the last minute."

"Yeah? Why?"

Heart pounding, I pressed my head against the bulkhead to spy on my crew.

"He's showing us he could, if he wants to. But he can't really hang them. There'd be a mutiny and he knows it. He'd be out the airlock before a single one of them got it."

There was a pause. "I'm not part of any mutiny," the voice said cautiously. "I'm out of it. We're just talking."

"Hey, I didn't say I'd do anything myself. I just said the Captain didn't dare. You know the joes, some of them are real tough grodes. You think Captain Kid wants to go up against them? Why should he bother? All that happened was some joeys got shoved around a little. Nobody got killed."

Another pause. "They got the death sentence, didn't they?"

"Ah, that's a lot of crap. This isn't officers' country, with all their young gentlemen. We settle things our own way. So what if Terrill got knocked around some? Serves him right for butting in. He knew better."

"What if Captain Kid goes through with it, Eddy? What if Rogoff and Tuak and Herney get roped?"

I strained to hear the answer. "Who's gonna do the roping, huh? Which crewman's gonna tie a rope around another joey's head? Look, they think they run the ship. But it's us. We do the work. We run the drives, cook the food, recycle the air. We're symbiotic. You know what that means? It means they need us like we need them. He won't rope them. He's smart enough to know that, for all his being a joeykid."

I backed away until I reached the ladder, scurried up to Level 3. Still uneasy, I didn't stop until I'd reached the safety of Level 1.

Time for lunch. In the officers' mess I sat by myself at a small table, brooding. As was the custom, conversation went on around me but nobody bothered me. When the Captain sat at the long table he was part of the group. When he sat by himself he was alone and invisible.

After mess I went back down to Level 2 and wandered along the corridor until I found the hatch I was looking for. I knocked.

Mr. Ibn Saud seemed disconcerted to see me. "Oh! Come in, Captain." He stood aside. His prayer rug was folded neatly at his bedside.

On the bulkhead was a large color print of Jerusalem's golden mosque of al-Aqsa, its glimmering dome rebuilt after the Last War to look as it had before.

"Could we talk awhile, Mr. Ibn Saud?"

"I am at your disposal." He offered me his only chair, sat on his bunk facing me.

"I have a decision to make. I know what my superiors would expect, but the choice isn't theirs, it's mine. I think it's arbitrary and rigid to put our condemned sailors to death for a brawl. On the other hand, their riot was just short of mutiny. Wouldn't it be weak and permissive of us to pardon them?"

"Have you studied history, Mr. Seafort?"

"Not with a teacher." Father had taught me at home, with a page-worn encyclopedia and the Bible as our curriculum, along with used math and physics texts for the holo.

Mr. Ibn Saud frowned. "Social trends follow a pendulum motion. Repression, then rebellion; rigidity, then anarchy. We're frozen at one end of the pendulum."

I sat. "What do you mean?"

"Look back, say, to the twentieth century. It began conservatively, swung in the 1920s to more permissive social mores, swung back to conservatism a generation later."

"So?" It sounded rude, and I immediately regretted it. He was doing his best.

"When the Eastern dictatorships collapsed, America was left the dominant power just as it was entering its liberal, or anarchic, phase."

I waited, wondering how this would help me.

"Willing to try new forms, America set up the U.N. Government, and transferred a few powers to it. So the skeleton of world government was in place when the American-Japanese financial structure collapsed. If not for that, who knows what chaos the world would have then endured?" He shuddered.

I tried not to show my impatience. What did ancient history have to do with *Hibernia*?

"Do you know, Nicky"—he paused, perhaps sensing my discomfort at the casual use of my name—"Captain, that the U.N. was once a force for liberal change? In the early twenty-first century most of the great reforms originated in the U.N."

"You call the reforms of 2024 liberal? They banned most stimulants, public gambling, racing of horses, even some sexual practices."

"Conservative impulses exist even in liberal times," he admonished. "The U.N.'s basic structure was permissive; loose federalism on a global scale."

"The Rebellious Ages." The folly of permissiveness.

"Then the reaction," he said. "The Era of Law. It began after the Final War, when America and Japan lost their ability to dominate the world by sheer financial strength. The devastation of Japan, China, and much of Africa permanently changed the world balance of power and left the U.N. the only strong global institution."

My irritation was mounting. Before the day ended, I had to rule on three men's lives.

He said, "Christian Reunification swept Europe, which had become the most influential region of the globe. The U.N. grew conservative and authoritarian. It issued the Unidollar, intervened in local conflicts, and took on the attributes of a real government. Incorporating the British Navy into the U.N. military was a key step."

I nodded. The Navy was our senior military service, and I was proud of it. I'd never even considered joining U.N.A.F.

"The U.N. also set universal education standards, wage rates—all right, I'll pass over the details." He smiled apologetically. "The liberal reaction came just as we began our push to colonize space."

I asked, "If we were rebelling against central authority when the colonies were being formed, wouldn't they have become virtually independent?"

"Not quite, Nick—er, Captain. The rebellion was in the impetus to colonize, to physically escape authority. But the colonies couldn't stand on their own. In the counterreaction they were brought fully under the control of the Government. Your Navy is the primary instrument of that control; that's the reason cargo and passengers can only be carried between home and the colonies in a Naval vessel. And it's why colonial Governors are often Admirals."

"I thought it's because they had the most experience."

"Yes, as autocratic leaders. There's really no difference between a colonial Governor and a Captain. They're both autocratic symbols of the Government."

I tried to follow. "And when you say we're frozen at one end of the pendulum?"

"The colonies strain against the pull of the central government. The U.N., pulling the other direction, is locked into repression to maintain control."

"That sounds dictatorial." They'd issued me a voting card the week after I'd made middy, and I took our democracy seriously.

"Government authority derives from the Reunification. The Yahwehist Church brought together religious forces dispersed for centuries. The U.N. Government is the agent and advocate of our state religion, which in turn supports the authority of the central government."

I stirred uneasily; I wouldn't tolerate heresy, if that's where he was headed.

As if in reassurance he added, "The two forces are merged in yourself; you're both chief magistrate and chaplain. Our system is frozen; the colonies strain against authority; the state and church strain to maintain civil control by arbitrary decrees. It's been so for seventy years."

I stood to pace, troubled by his suggestion. "How can one justify supporting an oppressive government, if men like Tuak and Rogoff are to be hanged because of the rigidity of its rules?"

Ibn Saud said gravely, "Contrast what harm the repression does, with the harm that would be done without it. The Last War was bad enough; imagine an interplanetary war."

"Wouldn't a liberal say freedom is worth the risk?"

"And wouldn't a conservative say civilization is worth the cost?" Ibn Saud, coming from the Saudi sheikhdoms, was of very conservative stock indeed.

* * *

Taking my leave, I climbed back to Level 1, found all quiet on the bridge. I left the Pilot and Vax to their boredom and continued my restless wandering.

The launch berth was cold, dim, and empty. Suiting up, I called to advise the bridge I was going through to the holds.

My defogger laboring, I climbed the ladder to the narrow passageway reserved for humankind alongside the huge cargo bays, past crates, containers, heavy machinery, farm implements. The suit didn't have to protect me from vacuum, it merely assured a good air supply. The hold was pressurized, but its air wasn't run through the recycler.

I was inching toward the tip of the pencil, far from the gravitrons in the engine room. As I climbed I felt lighter; as cadets we'd had to memorize the inverse square rule by which our gravity varied, but nothing clarified the rule as well as a practical demonstration.

The hull began to close in; I was approaching the narrowing point of *Hibernia*'s bow. At the top of the ladder I stood in the very prow of the ship, almost floating off the landing at the ladder's end. My eye traced the ribbed skeleton of the ship back to the disk.

Living in the disk, surrounded by *Hibernia*'s jostling mass of humanity, I could see only the conflicts and demands it was the Captain's role to arbitrate.

But here, at *Hibernia*'s bow, I became aware of the massive, complicated interweaving of metals and electronics that constituted the ship, bound together by power cables laced through the fabric of the vessel, and propelled by Fusion.

We were an oddly ritualized society, cramped together in the disk. We tended to forget that the ultimate purpose of our voyage was to sail this vast assemblage of cargo and persons to port, to be absorbed by our fast-growing colonies.

I sat on the landing, feet dangling from the ladder.

The many rules that regulated our conduct aboard—the strictures separating passengers and crew, the rigid hierarchy of seamen and officers, the isolation of the Captain—were meant to simplify our lives, to eliminate as many decisions as possible, so we confused and desire-ridden humans could steer this magnificent, complicated, and hugely expensive vessel to safe haven.

Without our regulations and ship's customs, we'd face too many choices. Decisions about the human hierarchy: who was smarter, stronger, wiser. Decisions about ethical conduct, about what behaviors were conducive to the proper function of the ship. Decisions about internal controls: which urges, which desires, should be given vent and which should not.

Hibernia, this great mass of machinery hurled at unimaginable speed through infinite emptiness, could not be controlled by people forever at odds with themselves and each other.

Mr. Ibn Saud's theory that repression alternated with permissiveness was irrlevant. For *Hibernia* to survive, the social system had to be maintained, else we'd all be condemned over and again to carve out our places in the ship's hierarchy. We were a planet too small to make a place for outsiders, misfits, loners. We had to learn to fit. One man who fought the system could wreck the ship.

Perhaps, though it could never be known, that was what had happened to *Celestina,* beyond the pale of civilization.

The hierarchy of Captain, officers, and crew was necessary to maintain the structure in which we functioned. Here beyond the gleam of our sun, we had to maintain our society unaided.

Knowing now what I had to do, I got up and started slowly down the ladder to the disk.

15

"Chief McAndrews, report to the bridge." I paced. The Chief, wherever he was, would hear my summons. I took the caller again, summoned Dr. Uburu.

Vax and the Pilot, on watch, observed me without comment.

"Vax, round up the middies. Quietly, please. I don't want anyone else to know we're all on the bridge."

"Aye aye, sir." He left on his mission.

I waited with growing impatience while the officers assembled. When all were present I slapped the hatch shut. "Stand at attention, all of you."

They formed a line, eyes front, hands stiff at their sides, Doc Uburu as much as any of them instantly obedient to ship's discipline. I faced them, picked up the holovid containing the Log.

"There will be no discussion, no comment on this matter from any of you, here or in private. I have called you to witness an entry into the Log." I typed quickly as I spoke. "The death sentence imposed on Machinist's Mate Herney is commuted to five months imprisonment. I have concluded that he was unaware he was striking an officer, and therefore should not suffer death as a penalty for his acts."

None of the officers showed any reaction. "The death sentence imposed on seaman Tuak is confirmed. He participated knowingly in an assault on an officer of this ship, and thereby merits execution. That his act was to prevent discovery of a criminal scheme is irrelevant; his execution is punishment solely for his assault." I finished writing.

"The death sentence imposed on seaman Rogoff is confirmed. He participated knowingly in an assault on an officer of this ship, and thereby merits execution. That his act was committed in hot blood is irrelevant; the fact of the assault warrants the sentence imposed."

I put down the holovid. "Stand at ease." They moved smartly into the "at ease" position, wrists clasped behind their backs. "We will now discuss the mechanics of the executions."

"Mr. Pearson, Mr. Loo: bring the prisoner Tuak. Acknowledge!"
"Orders received and understood. Aye aye, sir."

"Received and understood. Aye aye, sir." The two exchanged nervous glances before starting up the ladder to Level 3.

Maintaining outward calm, I reviewed my arrangements. The Pilot and Mr. Vishinsky had visited the brig and cuffed the two prisoners' hands behind their backs, firmly taping their mouths shut with irremovable skintape. Shortly after, I had brought the ship out of Fusion; we now floated dead in space, light-years from a planetary system.

On my order the bridge was sealed. All passengers were sent to their cabins and the cabin hatches secured; Alexi and Sandy personally supervised the operation.

All crew members were ordered to their berths to prepare for inspection. In my dress whites, accompanied by the chief petty officer and a midshipman, I inspected each crew berth and its occupants, who stood at attention while I coldly scrutinized lockers, bunks, and men, liberally dispensing demerits for infractions.

After each crew berth was inspected, its occupants were marched in absolute silence down to the lower deck of the engine room. They were lined three deep on the deck surrounding the gaping hole of the fusion drive shaft.

Across the open shaft was placed a plank. A chain ran from a bolt through the end of the plank to a powered dolly. Three meters above the plank, a pole tilted across the shaft. A rope hung from the pole. The noose at its end nearly touched the plank.

The Doctor, the Pilot, the Chief, and my three midshipmen, all in dress whites, stood at ease facing the lines of crewmen. We waited for the two seamen and their charge.

A sailor moved.

"Mr. Tamarov! Place that man on report!" Perhaps he had just been flexing a cramped muscle. "Take his name! I'll see him at next Captain's Mast!"

"Aye aye, sir." Alexi made a show of writing the seaman's name. The sailor glared sullenly before resuming eyes-front position.

"Mr. Tamarov! On dismissal, escort that man to the brig! Bread and water until Captain's Mast!"

"Aye aye, sir!" Alexi moved directly in front of the offending seaman who, subdued now, stood at proper attention.

From the ladder, a sound. Pearson and Loo each gripped one of the unfortunate Mr. Tuak's arms as they frog-marched him down to the engine room, his feet half walking, half dragging.

Tuak's mouth was firmly gagged. His eyes darted wildly back and forth from the assembled men to the shaft with its horrid accoutrements. Then to me. He screamed through his gag.

The party reached the lower deck. "Mr. Holser, Mr. Vishinsky! Cuff the prisoner's feet and place him on the gallows."

"Aye aye, sir." The midshipman and the master-at-arms broke ranks and took the prisoner from the two sailors. Tuak kicked desperately. Vishinsky bent, captured a frenzied foot and put the cuff on it, then locked it to the other.

"Mr. Pearson, Mr. Loo, back in ranks!" They complied.

Vax and Vishinsky dragged the condemned man to the plank. Tuak tried to kick out, balked by his cuffs. I nodded; Vax stepped back into ranks. The man's eyes darted in frenzy. Muffled sounds emerged from the gag as the noose was tugged tight.

It had to be done quickly. I was glad of the pills the Doctor had given me; I felt neither nauseous nor faint. "Mr. Tuak, I commend your soul to Lord God." I flipped the power switch; the dolly rolled slowly away from the shaft, tightening the chain attached to the plank.

The plank scraped across the deck until one end cleared the shaft wall. It dropped into the shaft. Tuak plummeted. The rope flexed, recoiled, became tight again. A groan came from behind.

I whirled around. "Silence!" Several men had gone pale; one swayed as if about to faint. But they held ranks.

"Mr. Browning, Ms. Edwards: bring the prisoner Rogoff. Acknowledge!" The purser and the gunner's mate departed. I knew that Mr. Browning would comply; he had too much invested in his status to help a roughneck escape, even if that were possible. Ms. Edwards was one whom Vishinsky thought reliable; that was enough for me.

"Mr. Vishinsky, Mr. Holser, remove the body and reset the plank." They hauled on the rope holding Tuak's remains. I kept my eyes on the crew, both to ensure discipline and to avoid keeling over in a dead faint: Dr. Uburu's pills had ceased to function.

The body rose out of the shaft; several crewmen started.

I knew it was necessary that I watch.

Tuak's clothes were soiled where his sphincters had given way. His empurpled face and bulging eyes were enough to sear my soul.

Behind me, a low angry murmur. My tone was sharp. "The first to break ranks will be hanged as this man was!" We were seconds from being rushed; if one sailor broke, they all would. I regretted my refusal to carry arms.

I walked down the line of sullen crewmen, hands clasped behind me. "Eyes front! Shoulders stiff! You, there! You're on report for sloppy position!" What in Lord God's own hell was keeping Browning and Edwards?

I paced back down the line. Sandy Wilsky was very pale, his breath shallow. "Midshipman, stomach in! Chest out! Set a good example or I'll barrel you myself!" Not kind to Sandy, but necessary. The boy sucked in his stomach, his color improving as his mind snapped back to his duty.

Finally they came. Rogoff's feet lashed out, trying to trip the two sailors, reaching to wrap around the ladder posts. I could hear cries beneath the gag. So could everyone else. Halfway down the ladder Rogoff caught sight of me. His eyes fastened on mine, terrified, pleading.

"Mr. Holser, Mr. Vishinsky. Cuff the prisoner's feet and place him on the gallows." A sharp intake of breath. I whirled around, expecting to be clubbed to the deck. A sailor had broken from attention, mouth agape, chest heaving. His mates watched.

I had no choice but to play it out. "*You!* Two paces forward!" My voice was so sharp, so high-pitched it startled even me. The attention of the massed crew deserted the unfortunate prisoner, focused instead on me.

The seaman, half-dazed, stumbled forward. With all the force I could muster, I slapped him. It echoed like a shot in the appalled silence. The sailor staggered, almost fell.

"*BACK IN RANKS!*" My face almost touched his. My fury penetrated his daze. He stiffened into attention, a red blotch blossoming on his cheek. My hand stung like fire.

Cuffed hand and foot, Rogoff teetered on the plank, beseeching me with his eyes. The gag muffled his incoherent sounds. For a moment I poised on the edge of mercy, before recollecting my duty.

"Mr. Rogoff, I commend your soul to Lord God." I flipped the switch on the dolly. A moment later he was gone.

I held the crew in ranks until both bodies were removed from the chamber. I frantically repeated regs under my breath, to divert myself from vomiting in front of the entire ship's company. "Crew Berth One, two steps forward! Right face! March! Mr. Vishinsky, escort the men to their quarters."

One by one each group marched back to its berth. At the end only the officers and I remained. We looked at each other, no one wanting to speak. It had been a close call.

I sent Vax and Alexi to unlock the passenger cabins, and started back to the bridge. On the ladder from Level 2, I had to stop and grip the rail, before anyone noticed the trembling of my legs. Chief McAndrews quietly put his hand under my arm and helped me up the stairs. I didn't take notice; it would have been a capital offense.

That afternoon I ran a Battle Stations drill, followed by decompression drills. It made clear to the crew that I wasn't afraid to give them orders, and at the same time it occupied their minds. I strove to occupy my own mind, but was unsuccessful.

That afternoon, I ordered the two bodies quietly ejected from the airlock.

Dinner hour came. I wasn't sure I'd be able to hold down my food, but I knew it was necessary for me to appear in the dining hall. The passengers I met in the corridor were distant, their looks hostile.

I met Amanda outside the hatch. I went to her immediately, wanting to explain what I'd done.

She gave me no opportunity to speak. Her look passed right through me. I'd anticipated her anger, yet I stood disconcerted, staring at her receding back.

In the hall there was silence when I rose to give the Ship's Prayer. Afterward, the only persons to say "Amen" were my officers, Mrs. Donhauser, and Derek Carr.

After forking food around my plate I retreated to the bridge. Alexi shared the watch; for once he had the sense to stay quiet. I sat in my Captain's chair, pinned in merciless silence, while Tuak's purple face was again hauled up to the rim of the shaft. His sightless stare was directed solely at me.

The caller buzzed. "Pilot Haynes reporting, sir. Will we Fuse tonight?"

"No. In the morning." The Pilot had said he wasn't yet ready to tackle Darla's reprogramming, and in my present state I didn't trust myself to do the manual calculations.

"Aye aye, sir."

At midnight I turned over the watch to Vax and Alexi and started back to my cabin. I stumbled with weariness, dreading the solitude. I stripped off my jacket, undid my tie, unbuttoned my shirt.

A knock at the hatch. I opened, half-dressed. Chief McAndrews. With him was Dr. Uburu.

She held a flask and two glasses. "This is for medicinal use. As medical officer I direct you to take it. The Chief will help administer the prescription." She handed her wares to the Chief and departed.

The Chief met my eye, impassive. I sighed. "Come in."

"Thank you, Captain." His tone was formal.

I went to the safe and got out his pipe and the canister. "Go ahead.

I order you to light it." I sniffed at the flask. Some kind of whiskey. I poured two glasses half full.

I'd learned to drink after Academy, on my first leave. I drank because we all did, at one time or another. I didn't dislike it; I didn't much enjoy it either. Tonight, I was a drinker. I downed half my glass with the first swallow, finished the rest a moment after. Wordlessly, the Chief poured more.

In the haze of the smoking artifact we sat, mostly in silence, sipping at our drinks. I told him about my visit to the holds, earlier in the day. I explained how I felt when I slapped the frightened sailor's face. I told him about Father. He listened, he nodded, sometimes he prompted. Occasionally he told an anecdote of his own.

My mood eased as the evening passed. Our commiseration grew into a discussion, then finally a wake. Afterward I recalled my voice, oddly loud. I remembered standing to go to the head, the wall rushing up to smash me in the face, and the Chief's steadying arm.

I couldn't quite recall what followed, though I had a dim recollection of the Chief pulling off my shoes, loosening my belt. I seemed to recall someone's voice, very silly. "Thank you, Chiefie. What a nice name for a grand man, aye, Chiefie?" Someone giggled. Then I slept.

The next morning we Fused, after laborious calculations repeated over and over on my demand. They were not made any easier by my stupendous headache. Vax said something, his voice too loud. I snarled, but he didn't seem to mind. By the following day I had settled down, even thinking to make amends to Vax with extra cordiality when he left watch.

"Going to bunk down, Mr. Holser?"

"No, sir. I'm off to the exercise room."

"I should have known. Taking some middies with you?"

"No, sir, I'm meeting Mr. Carr." I raised an eyebrow. "He apologized and asked if he could resume, sir. We've been exercising together four days now."

"Ah."

"Yes, sir. Yesterday we went from an hour to two hours. Is that all, sir?"

"Carry on." Interesting. I thought I knew what would come next. I only wondered when.

The week passed uneventfully. The crew absorbed its graphic lesson in discipline and steadied down to routine. I saw no sullenness, no insubordination. The unfortunate sailor who had glared at Alexi was fined and given extra duties for a month. Mr. Herney, pathetically grateful for his reprieve, waited out his time in the brig.

Amanda listened impassively to my apology. She let me explain my reasoning. Then she turned away without a word. I resolved to let her be. As Captain I could not force myself on a passenger.

It was a few days after, as dinner ended, that the overture came.

I looked at my watch. "Thank you for an interesting evening. Mrs. Donhauser, Mr. Kaa Loa, Mr. Carr." I stood to take my leave.

Derek stood also. "Sir, may I speak with you privately, when it's convenient?"

"It will be convenient on the bridge in about an hour."

"Thank you, sir." He waited politely for me to leave.

I was sitting at the console when the knock came. Sandy, escorting Mr. Carr. As a passenger, Derek couldn't approach the bridge on his own.

I swiveled to face the hatch. Derek came in hesitantly, carrying a holovid. He took in the complexity of the instruments and screens, and seemed impressed. "Thank you for allowing me here."

"What did you want, Mr. Carr?" My tone was cool.

He eyed me uncertainly, standing in front of my chair like an errant schoolboy. "Captain Seafort, I was furious when you said I couldn't handle life as a midshipman. In our family we've assumed we could do what we set our minds to. Sir, I think you're wrong."

I was impassive. Within, a faint glimmer of hope stirred.

"Captain, I can be a midshipman. I know saying it isn't enough, so I've tried to show you. No discipline? Until now I've never called anyone 'sir' in my life, including my father. I call you 'sir' now. I'll keep doing it. All I want is for you to have an open mind. Not to prejudge me. Please . . . sir."

He had my full attention. "Go on."

"I took geometry and trig in school, but no calculus. You didn't believe me when I said I could learn it. Look at this, please." He offered me the holovid. I flipped it on.

"The ship's library had a calculus text. I've done all the problems in Chapter One, and most of Chapter Two. I understand differential equations. The differential of velocity with respect to time is acceleration. The differential of displacement with respect to time is velocity."

Not bad at all, for a beginner without an instructor. "You've made a lot of progress, Mr. Carr. Why?"

"Nobody ever told me I'm not good enough, Captain. I want you to know I am."

"So you put yourself under discipline."

"Yes, sir."

"How do you like it?"

"I loathe it!" His vehemence startled me. "I hate abasing myself! I hate it!" He swallowed. "But that doesn't mean I'll stop, sir. I can do what I set out to do!"

"All right, Mr. Carr. But why?"

"After you left my cabin I got to thinking. At first I wanted to join because I was so angry. I had to show you."

He must have seen my expression. "I said, at first, sir. I haven't finished. When I got over my anger I realized that it was no reason to enlist. Five years cooped in a ship, because someone jeered at me? No. But what would I do for those years, otherwise? The plantation manager won't want me around, and he controls the trusts. Until they terminate, I'll be sent off on a tiny allowance, still a minor, having to ask permission for anything I want to do."

He paused to marshal his thoughts. "Maybe the Service isn't any better. I'll still have to go where I'm sent, do what I'm told. But I'd have my majority. And at least I'll have done it by my own decision."

"That's all?" I wasn't that impressed by his motives.

"No, that's not all. I mean, no, sir. Sorry. I thought about some of the officers I've met on board. Lieutenant Cousins, he was a—well, I apologize, I shouldn't be saying that. But Mr. Malstrom, we sat at table with him a month. He was a gentleman, like my father. If a man like him could make a career in the Service, so could I."

"Is that what you want, Mr. Carr? A career in the service?"

"No, Captain Seafort. Probably not. But at least I'd get to see places. Learn things. Live on a ship."

"Is this"—I waved my hand with disdain—"what you call living?"

He stared at me a long moment before he remembered. Then his ears turned red. He looked at the deck. "I'm sorry, sir," he said quietly. "I really am sorry for saying that."

"You said a lot you should be sorry for." I was pushing, but if he couldn't handle it, he certainly couldn't take what my first middy would come up with.

"I suppose I have. Sir." Now his cheeks were red too.

"How old are you?"

"Sixteen. I'll be seventeen in six months."

"I'm only a year older than you."

"I know. That's one reason it's hard to call you 'sir'."

"Yet I'm Captain of *Hibernia,* and you'd be a cadet, at the bottom of the chain of command. The very bottom."

"Yes, sir, I know that."

"I wonder. Do you understand the difference between a cadet and a midshipman?"

"A cadet is a trainee, isn't he? A midshipman is an officer."

"A cadet has special status, Mr. Carr. He is, literally, a ward of his commanding officer. The commander has the rights his parents had. He's not an adult until he makes midshipman. He has no rights at all, and can be punished in any way his commander sees fit."

I examined his face; I hadn't yet dissuaded him. I tried harder. "A cadet has no recourse no matter what he's asked to do. It's a brutal life. There's a reason for it: he has to learn that he can stand up to adversity. After cadet training, shipboard life will seem easy. He's already been through far worse. And he's already learned that a Captain's power, like his cadet commander's, is absolute."

Derek was reflective. "I understand."

"Most cadets enter Academy at thirteen, some at fourteen. A very few at fifteen. By the time we're your age, it's usually too late; we resent authority as rigid and arbitrary as cadets endure. You're too old for it, Derek."

"Not if I decide to take it, sir." His voice was firm.

I was patient; he'd earned it. "You think calling me 'Sir' is discipline? In your whole life, have you ever been shouted at by a person you didn't like?"

"No, sir." He squirmed with discomfort.

"Tell me, have you ever slept in a room with other people?"

He swallowed. "No. Except in the cabin with my father."

"How'd you like it?"

"I couldn't sleep." He colored. "I had pills. Dozeoff, and stronger ones. They helped."

I let the silence stretch awhile. He said, "I know; it won't be easy. But once I decide to, I can do it."

"Derek . . ." I shook my head, frustrated. "You really don't understand, do you? Have you ever used the head when another person was present?"

"God, no!" he blurted. I'd assumed not.

"Has an outsider ever seen you without clothes on?"

"No." He blushed red at the thought.

"Still, you want to be a midshipman?"

"Yes, sir." His tone was determined.

"Take your pants off."

"What?" Astonishment gave way to wariness, then dismay. He gulped, realizing his predicament; he had to show me he could take it, or give up his plan. Staring fixedly at the bulkhead he slowly unbuckled and stepped out of his pants. Not knowing what to do with them, he hesitated, then bent awkwardly and dropped them on the deck.

I said nothing, letting him wait in his undershorts. After a while he made a visible effort; his fists unclenched. I let the silence drag. He looked about, remembered that he was on the bridge of the ship, blushed crimson. But he didn't move.

"Derek, are you still sure you can take it?"

"Yes," he gritted. "I can take whatever you give out, damn it!"

I wasn't offended, but it was time to turn up the pressure. Better he broke now, than after taking the oath. "Apologize!"

He swallowed. He battled deep inside himself, his eyes distant. After a moment he said in an entirely different tone, "Captain Seafort, sir, please pardon my rudeness."

"Apologize abjectly!" This was nothing compared to wardroom hazing.

"Sir! I'm sorry I spoke to you the way I did. It's a sign of my immaturity. I'm very sorry I can't control myself. I meant no disrespect to you, sir, and I won't do it again!"

I looked up. His eyes were wet. I eased up. 'I hear you've been doing exercises."

"Yes, sir. With Vax Holser."

"Mr. Holser, to you."

"I apologize, sir. With Mr. Holser, to get ready."

"As part of your campaign?"

"Yes, sir. I started with my letter to you."

I signed. He could probably survive. Barely. On the other hand, he was educated and could apply himself to a goal. And I needed midshipmen.

"This is how it works, Derek. You take the oath, and enlist for five years. There's no way to change your mind. The only exit is dishonorable discharge, and you won't get that without time in the brig first. You know what a dishonorable does?"

"Not entirely, sir."

"You can never vote, hold elective office, or be appointed to any government agency. You forfeit all pay and military benefits. It's utter disgrace."

"I understand, sir."

"You join as a cadet. You're not an officer. In theory, you could remain a cadet for five years. You stay a cadet until your C.O. decides to make you a midshipman. You have no say in the matter. You owe the Navy obedience and service regardless of your status."

"Yes, sir." He looked at me attentively, waiting for the permission that must be coming.

"Derek, I'll give you one warning. Do you think I've been hazing you?"

"Yes, sir. Some."

"I haven't. You're very sensitive; it gets much, much worse. You should reconsider."

He surprised me. "I have, sir, while I've had to stand here like this."

"And?"

"I want to join the Naval Service, sir."

"I'll think about it. Wait in the corridor until I call. Don't bother to dress."

"What?" Fury and betrayal flashed across his face. "You—I trusted you!" He reached down, swept up his pants. I said nothing.

He flicked dust off his pants and turned to step into them, his face white with anger. He lifted his foot. Then he froze.

For a long while he stared at the pants. Finally, contemptuously, he lifted them high. Holding them between his two fingers he extended his arm. His fingers opened. The pants dropped to the deck. He walked to the hatch and out into the corridor. I slapped the hatch closed.

I gave him half an hour; that would be enough. When I motioned, he came in, pale but silent. I handed him his pants; gratefully he slipped into them. "Derek, Mr. Holser is going to be a real trial for you. Hang on. I'll make you midshipman as soon as I think you qualify."

"I understand." His color was returning to normal.

I called Vax and the Chief as witnesses. I gave Derek the oath, there on the bridge, and entered it into the Log.

"He's all yours, Vax. Show him the ropes."

Vax gave a wolfish smile and slowly licked his chops. He rounded on Derek. "Cadet, we're going to the wardroom. I'll show you your bunk. Being a cadet is easy. You will call anything that moves 'sir' or 'ma'am', children included. And you will do everything any officer tells you, without exception."

"Yes, sir," Derek said meekly.

"It's 'aye aye, sir,' and that's two demerits. Ten demerits means the barrel."

"Aye aye, sir!"

"No, that's 'yes, sir'. I didn't give you an order, I told you a fact. Another two demerits." Each would be worked off by two hours of hard calisthenics.

"Uh, yes, sir." Derek began to look apprehensive.

I followed them down the corridor to the wardroom, feeling a bit sorry for Mr. Carr.

Vax put his hand on Derek's shoulder as he steered the boy into the wardroom. "Derek, tell us about your sex life," he purred. The hatch slid shut behind them.

I walked back to the bridge. I had four middies now. Well, three, and a cadet. Close.

16

"Lord God, today is May 14, 2195, on the U.N.S. *Hibernia*. We ask you to bless us, to bless our voyage, and to bring health and well-being to all aboard."

"Amen." We took our seats.

As I spooned my soup I counted my blessings. Our crew had settled back to normal. We remained in Fusion, riding the crest of the N-wave toward Hope Nation. The Chief and I investigated his artifact from time to time, in the quiet of the evenings. Alexi was working through a rigorous course of navigation under Pilot Haynes; I looked forward to the day he might make lieutenant.

On the other hand, we hadn't dealt with Darla's parameter glitch. Though I pressed the Pilot at least to investigate the state of her computational arrays, he argued that we should wait until we reached Hope Nation, where he was sure we'd find a more knowledgeable puterman. As long as we calculated our adjusted mass ourselves, Darla's misprogrammed parameter was no hazard. I was uneasy, but wasn't ready to force the issue.

Meanwhile, Derek Carr had vanished into the wardroom under the gentle tutelage of Vax Holser. As the Captain never visited the wardroom and a cadet was not allowed on the bridge, I had no way to determine how Derek was managing.

Occasionally I caught a glimpse of him hurrying down a corridor, immaculate in a cadet's unmarked gray uniform, his hair cut short, hands and face scrubbed, wearing an anxious expression.

When he saw me he would snap to attention, at first in a slipshod manner. Within a week, his stomach was sucked tight, his shoulders thrown back, spine stiff, his pose perfect in every particular. How Vax taught him the physical drill so quickly, I was afraid to ask.

My responsibility was to leave them alone, and trust Vax to do his job. Derek was learning ship's routine, Naval regs, cleanliness, discipline, and how to cope with a wardroom full of frisky boys all his seniors. That would be the hard part. He would pull through or he wouldn't, and I couldn't help him.

Nonetheless, I gave Vax one caution. "Those demerits you're giving him—make sure he has a chance to work them off. He shouldn't get up to ten. Not for a couple of months, anyway."

"Aye aye, sir. That's kind of how I figured." I let them be.

At times I passed Amanda flirting and laughing with various young men among the passengers. If she saw me she gave no sign. I missed our confidences, our physical intimacy, our caring.

With the departure of Derek from the Captain's table, I passed April with only two dinner companions. On the first of May the normal rotation brought a surprise; ten passengers had asked the purser to seat them at my table.

My seige was lifting.

I chose seven guests for the remaining places at my table. I now dined with a full complement, amid animated conversation.

But I had to sleep.

My cabin hatch wouldn't stay fastened. I slapped it shut; it bulged open. I had to lean all my weight against it to force it closed. Something pushed back. I backed away, stumbling into the bulkhead behind me.

In the dark corridor beyond the ruptured hatch, something moved. Seaman Tuak shambled into the cabin, face purple, eyes bulging, rattling the cuffs that bound hands and feet. A blackened tongue protruded from torn tape covering his rotting mouth.

I cowered against the bulkhead. A cold, damp arm reached through the hull behind me, wrapped around my throat. Seaman Rogoff pulled himself into the cabin to hold me while Tuak came near.

I woke screaming. My sounds were barely audible whimpers. I staggered out of bed, fell into my chair, and rocked, hugging myself, until the corridors lightened with day.

I could think of only one way to deal with that. I buried myself in work, trying to exhaust myself so completely I wouldn't fear sleep. I assigned myself two four-hour watches each day. I explored the entire ship, bow to stern, memorizing every compartment, all the storerooms, each of the airlocks.

I disconcerted Alexi and the Pilot by joining their navigation course; in the back of the room I quietly worked the problems Mr. Haynes gave the middy. Alexi solved them more quickly and more accurately, but I preserved until I improved.

At first, the Pilot was uncomfortable at my presence; a careless comment had already earned him a rebuke and a stinging punishment, and now I demanded that he correct my mistakes. After a while he found the balance between elaborate politeness and scorn, becoming an excellent teacher.

At my insistence, Chief McAndrews loaned me holovids explaining the principles of fusion drives. They remained a mystery, no matter how hard I studied. I made the Chief review them with me, step by step, until even that phlegmatic man's voice took on an edge.

I inspected all the nooks and crannies of the ship: engine room, the crew berths, the infirmary, the wardroom. There, with the midshipmen and cadet standing at rigid attention. I pretended to search for dust on a shelf or creases on a bunk, feeling for a few moments that I had wakened from a nightmare without end.

I was tempted to take my dreams to Dr. Uburu. Perhaps she could find grounds to relieve me on grounds of mental disability. I didn't make the attempt because I knew my dreams were a sign of tension, not mental illness. I was afraid she would see through my cowardice.

I turned my attention to the one piece of work I'd been putting off. I called the Chief and the Pilot—away from the bridge, of course—to consider reprogramming Darla to eliminate her glitch.

Reluctantly, the Pilot sketched out our task. We'd have to strip away her attitudinal and conversational overlays, find the improper input for the adjusted mass parameter, and override it.

I demanded the tech manuals, glanced through them. They made the steps clear enough. Had I known how clear, I wouldn't have allowed Mr. Haynes so long a delay. Still, I could understand his caution; an error on our part could make matters far worse. Reprogramming a puter was no job for an amateur; that's why Admiralty had Dosmen in the first place.

The Pilot argued his point. "Darla is locked into the dock-yard figure for ship's mass. But as long as we keep feeding her calculations by hand, we can Fuse. Better a devil we know than one we don't."

"Mr. McAndrews?"

"I'm no Dosman, sir. With respect, neither are you. I'm concerned about creating more problems than we solve. We can calculate by hand; I'd leave her alone."

"You're both right, as far as you go. But we have no idea how deep Darla's glitch goes. What if ship's mass isn't the only parameter that's fouled? When we display her inputs, we'll have to check every one to be sure."

The Pilot snorted. "Sir, do you realize how many parameters she has? Sure, some are straightforward, like ship's mass. But others are odd tidbits like the length of the fusion drive shaft, hydroponics chamber capacities, airlock pump rates . . . My God, we couldn't check all of them."

"She stores all that?"

"And operates from them. Every time we recycle a glass of water, grow a tomato, track energy fluctuations, we rely on Darla's parameters. If we inadvertently alter them . . ." He left the sentence unfinished. The dangers were obvious, and chilling.

It was my decision, and I needed to sleep on it.

That night the nightmare struck with terrifying force. At the point where I usually woke trembling, I came struggling out of it, as always. Weakly I crawled out of bed to fall in the easy chair. It was there the icy hand of Mr. Rogoff found me, toppling me onto the deck screeching in terror.

I woke in my bed, gasping and shaking, realizing I had still been asleep. I looked up. Mr. Tuak opened the hatch and staggered in, rotting eyes boring into mine, his cuffed feet shambling toward my bed. I woke again, paralyzed with fear.

It was a long time before I was sure I was truly awake. I threw on my pants, pulled my jacket over my undershirt and hurried to the infirmary, dreading to meet Mr. Tuak on the way. Pride was no longer an issue; I woke Dr. Uburu and demanded a sleeping pill. In response to her questions I told her I'd been having nightmares.

She gave me a pill, warning me not to take it until I was actually in bed, and to sleep as long as I wanted. About my nightmares, she mercifully said nothing.

When I reached my cabin I couldn't stop the chills from stabbing at my back; I opened the hatch with caution and entered, knowing nothing was waiting but still, like a child, unable to trust knowledge to dispel my demons.

I swallowed the sedative. A few minutes later the cabin disappeared.

Someone was attacking my hatch with a sledgehammer. Annoyed, I tried to open my eyes, but they were glued shut. I lurched out of bed and felt my way toward the hatch. Somebody had moved the bulkhead about two steps closer; I caromed off the cold metal and flung open the hatch, ready to break the sledgehammer into tiny pieces.

I forced open my eyes, a snarl and a scream battling in my throat for priority. The ship's boy stood patiently in the corridor.

"Ricky! Why in God's name are you here in the middle of the night? And stop that banging!" I propped myself carefully against the bulkhead.

"It's morning, Captain, sir. Same time I always come." The ship's boy held his breakfast tray with both hands, waiting expectantly.

"Uhng. Come in." I staggered back to sit on the bed. "You didn't see a man with a piece of rope around his neck, did you?"

Ricky put the tray on my table. "No, sir. If I do, should I tell him anything?"

I focused on my bedside table, trying to hold it still. "Tell him I'm sorry." The table slowed, but didn't stop rotating. "On second thought, don't tell him anything, just try not to see him." I lay down in my bunk. Now only the ceiling was spinning. "Never mind, I'm not sure this is real either. That's all, Ricky."

"Aye aye, sir. Oh, by the way, sir, I've decided I want to be a midshipman."

"Very good, Ricky, come back after you grow up; I'll ask the Captain. I'm tired now."

"Aye aye, sir," he said, his voice uncertain. He left.

I woke some hours later, relaxed and refreshed, recalling a peculiar dream involving the ship's boy. I stood, slowly. Cautious tests indicated my motor systems were functional.

After visiting the head and the shower I returned to my cabin. Two congealed eggs stared reproachfully. I decided I'd work today on distinguishing reality from fantasy. A morning chore for the Captain.

On the way to the bridge I stopped at the infirmary. "Doc, what did you give me?" My tone was plaintive.

"Were there side effects?" Dr. Uburu asked coolly.

"I think there may be one next to my nose. I couldn't wake for breakfast. Someone else woke instead."

"You shouldn't have tried that." The Doctor was reproving. "I told you to stay down until you woke naturally." She studied my face. "I think you survived, Captain. You needed the rest." I had to admit that was true.

Later in the day I called Chief McAndrews and Pilot Haynes to a conference in the officers' mess. "I've thought it over," I said, sipping coffee. "We'll strip Darla for reprogramming. I don't trust my own Fusion calculations and I've got to be able to rely on her. While we're at it we can recheck her other parameters."

"There are hundreds," the Pilot reminded me.

"We've months 'til we reach Miningcamp. There's time to check them.

A silence. The Pilot said carefully, "Captain, I protest your order, for the ship's safety. I request that my protest be entered in the Log."

"Very well." It was his right. I didn't remind him that if he was correct there was a chance no one would ever read the Log.

Chief McAndrews cleared his throat. "Sir, I request you to enter my protest in the Log as well. Meaning no disrespect." He had the courage to meet my eye.

"You feel that strongly about it, Chief?"

"Yes, sir. I do. I'm sorry." He looked sorry, too.

"Very well." My tone was sharp; I tried to dispel a sense of betrayal. "I'll enter your protests. Bring the puter manuals to the bridge. We'll start this afternoon." I left the mess, knowing my evening sessions with the Chief could never be the same. I pushed aside my loneliness; if I dwelt on it I would march back to the mess and cancel my orders.

We met on the bridge. "Mr. Holser, you're relieved from watch. Leave us." My nerves were strung tight. I slapped shut the hatch, leaving the Chief, Pilot Haynes, and myself alone with Darla. I switched off the ship's caller. I tapped a command on my console, saying it aloud at the same time. "Keyboard entry only, Darla." At this juncture we couldn't risk stray sounds confusing the puter; in deep programming mode, who knew what glitch could be set up by a misinterpreted cough?

"Got it, Captain," Darla said. "Something special you want to tell me?"

I typed, "Alphanumeric response only, Darla, displayed on screen."

A sentence flashed onto my screen. "KEYBOARD ONLY, CAPTAIN. WHAT'S UP?"

I tapped, "Disconnect conversational overlays."

"VERIFY CONVERSATIONAL OVERLAYS DISCONNECTED." Darla's answer was dull and machinelike, stripped of her usual banter.

I indicated the manual open in the Pilot's lap. "What's first?"

Three hours later we were ready; we'd bypassed the warnings and safeties, entered my access codes, stripped away the interconnected layers of tamperproofing the Dosmen had built into her. Darla lay unconscious on our operating table, her brain pulsing and exposed.

I typed, "List fixed input parameters, consecutive order, pause for enter after each."

"COMMENCING INPUT PARAMETER LIST, PAUSE AFTER EACH DISPLAY." The first parameter appeared on the screen.

"SPEED OF LIGHT: 299792.518 KILOMETERS PER SECOND."

I glanced at the Pilot. "Any problem with that one, Mr. Haynes?"

"No, sir."

Keying through the long list of parameters, I realized that checking them as we went wasn't possible. As I tapped, Darla flashed one parameter after another on the screen. After a while I merely glanced at each one, waiting for "SHIP'S MASS" to appear. I tapped for a full hour and a half, my wrist beginning to ache, before the figure finally showed on the screen.

"SHIP'S BASE MASS: 215.6 STANDARD UNITS."

"There," I said with relief. I typed, "Display parameter number and location."

"PARAMETER 2613, SECTOR 71198, GRANULE 1614."

I tapped, "Continue parameter display."

"FIXED PARAMETER DISPLAY COMPLETE."

I swore. Ship's mass was the very last parameter in the list. If I'd started at the end of the list and worked backward I'd have saved hours of tapping.

"That's the last one, Pilot."

"It can't be!"

"Why not?"

"Adjusted mass should be a parameter as well."

The Chief said, "Not if she derives it from base mass."

"We know she's using the wrong figure for base mass," I said. "How do we change that?"

"The quick fix is to delete base mass as a fixed parameter and input it as a variable, sir." The Pilot had the manual on his holovid in his lap. "Then we instruct her not to adjust the variable except after recalc."

The manual provided a step-by-step example of how to do that. "Read me the instructions exactly."

"Aye aye, sir." The Pilot magnified the page so it was visible to all of us. "There are fourteen steps for deletion, sir. Input takes six."

"Any reason not to proceed now, gentlemen?"I asked. A few seconds hesitation; I added, "Other than those stated in the Log?"

Pilot Haynes said reluctantly, "Nothing else, sir." The Chief shook his head.

We took great care with each step. Both the Pilot and the Chief checked each of my keyboard commands against the manual before I entered it, to make sure I had made no mistake. I was so nervous I could barely contain myself; we were barbarians engaging in brain surgery. I began to wish I had followed my officers' advice.

Finally we were done. "VARIABLE INPUT COMPLETE," the screen displayed. I let out a long breath.

"Hardcopy input parameters and input variables," I typed. The eprom clicked on. A moment later a holochip popped into the waiting tray. I handed it to the Pilot, who slipped it in his holovid. We keyed to the list of parameters. Base mass was absent. We checked the variables, found it at the end of the list.

"To put her back together, we reverse the steps that took her apart," the Pilot said, consulting his manual. "Here's the list."

"No." They looked up in surprise. "Darla stays down." My tone was firm. "We check every one of the input parameters before she goes back on-line."

Chief McAndrews said, "Captain, Darla monitors our recycling program. We need that information daily, to make adjustments."

"Hydroponics too, sir," added the Pilot. "We've been on manual all day; if a sailor's attention wanders, he could foul up the systems. We need to get back to automatics."

"We have manual backup procedures." I tried to quell my irritation. "The hydroponicist's mates will stand extra watches. So will the recycler's mates. We'll do without Darla."

The Pilot. "Captain, the longer it takes, the more—"

"Darla stays down! That's an order!" Their nagging infuriated me.

The Pilot stood. "Aye aye, sir," His voice was cold. "I protest the order and request you to enter my protest in the Log."

I bit back a savage retort. "Denied. Your previous protest continues and is sufficient. You both have your orders. Call the midshipmen together, divide up the list, and start checking every item. Go to the textbooks for astrophysical data. Manually recheck all ship's measurements and statistics."

"Aye aye, sir." They had no choice; arguing with a direct order was insubordination.

"One more thing. I'll see all of you, including the middies, on the bridge before you begin. Dismissed." I shut the hatch behind them and sagged in my chair. With my customary finesse I'd thoroughly alienated the Chief as well as the Pilot. Now I was truly alone.

I paced the bridge, Darla's last output still frozen on the screen. I was in over my head. My order to run *Hibernia*'s systems manually could put our men on emergency watches for a month or more, while every last parameter was checked. The crew would grow tired, then embittered. Meanwhile, the officers would be driven to distraction by the rote examination of data. They'd be exhausted from ceaseless extra work. Their relations with the crew would worsen.

My order risked far greater damage to the ship than Darla's glitch.

When the officers assembled on the bridge an hour later, I was near panic. "Gentlemen, we're about to check all the information in Darla's parameter banks. Some of you may not agree with this course. You may think it's a waste of time. I don't care. You will personally recheck each and every datum on your list until you verify its accuracy from other sources."

That much was acceptable, but I couldn't leave well enough alone. "Let me make clear what will happen if you gloss over any items. Chief, Pilot, you will be tried for dereliction of duty and dismissed from the service. Mr. Holser, Mr. Tamarov, Mr. Wilsky, I will personally cane you within an inch of your life, then try you for dereliction of duty. Mr. Holser, the cadet may help you with measurements, but you're not to give him any tasks to perform without supervision." I ignored the shock in their faces. "Acknowledge, all of you!"

One by one they responded. "Orders received and understood, sir. Aye aye, sir." The midshipmen were agitated; they'd never heard an officer speak in such a manner. Nor, for that matter, had I. After I dismissed them I flopped in my leather chair, appalled at what I'd heard myself say.

Some of the data were standard and easy to check, involving no more than a trip to the ship's library and a review of standard references. Others were more complicated: for example, the volume of air in each airlock. Alexi checked lock dimensions in the ship's blueprints, then confirmed them by measuring them himself. I knew, because I watched.

I tried to be everywhere. I peered over the Chief's shoulder while he took the dimensions of the drive shaft opening. I watched Vax and Derek measure the volume of nutrient in one hydro tank, then multiply by the number of identical tanks. I held the electrical gauges as the Chief and Vax, sweating and swearing, connected them to each of our power mains to measure ship's power consumption.

By the end of the second day I could stand myself no longer. During our rest period I forced my reluctant steps down the ladder to Level 3, to the Chief's cabin near his engine room. I knocked. He opened the hatch, his jacket off, tie loose.

"Carry on," I said quickly, before he could come to attention. He stepped aside for me to enter. I remained in the corridor. Now, especially, I had no right to be in his cabin. "I've come to apologize." My tone was stiff. "I've never had reason to think you wouldn't carry out your duties. My remarks on the bridge were abominable."

"You owe me no apology," he said, his voice stony. "You gave your orders, as was your right."

"Nevertheless I'm sorry. I insulted you. I know you won't forgive me, but I want you to know I regret my words." I turned and left abruptly, not wanting him to see my eyes tearing.

We made progress, but it was slow going. The crew continued to monitor ship's systems manually. Over the next weeks I noticed an increase in the number of seamen sent to Captain's Mast. Tempers flared as the crew's irritability began to match my own. They too suffered from loss of sleep. Only the midshipmen seemed to thrive under the extra burden.

While the exacting labor continued, days stretching into weeks, Vax Holser stolidly carried out all the tasks I laid on his broad shoulders, without objection and, more importantly, without offense at my manner. I grew to depend on him; when I wanted to be sure a difficult measurement was made and rechecked without complaint, it was Vax I called upon. Whatever he said to the other midshipmen in the privacy of the wardroom, it persuaded them to work with willing good humor, a feat of which I'd have been incapable.

Sandy and Alexi crawled around the cargo holds in their confining pressure suits for hours at a time, determining location and mass of the cargoes. Derek, when he wasn't poring over his navigation texts or performing the strenuous exercises Vax required of him, obediently held measuring lines, copied figures, and made himself otherwise useful to the midshipmen.

"Captain to the bridge, please!" I was sacked out in my bunk in utter exhaustion when the call came. Never before had I been summoned from my cabin; after shaking my head in a hapless effort to clear it I took only seconds to scramble into my clothes and dive out the hatch, foreboding rushing my stride.

Alexi stood rigidly at attention. The Chief appeared angry. Pilot Haynes paced back and forth, a holovid in his hand.

"What's going on?" I demanded. I'd expected a gaping hole in the hull, if not worse.

"Mr. Tamarov," spat the Pilot, "brought some funny measurements. They're wrong; they don't balance. They can't.

"Alexi, report."

"Aye aye, sir. Thank you, sir. I was assigned to check gas exchange rates on the atmospheric recyclers. I took Recycler's Mate Quezan to the recycler compartments, bringing along gas gauges as ordered. We tested the oxygen/carbon dioxide exchange, the nitrogen recycler, and the purifiers, sir. The exchange rates were lower than listed so I ordered Mr. Quezan to repeat each measurement. We got the same numbers again, sir."

The Pilot. "I told you. He must have—"

"Let him finish."

"I went to the ship's library and got out the manufacturer's specs. Their model numbers don't jibe with the actual numbers on our units, but as far as I could tell the equivalent models in the book showed rates like we measured, not the rates Darla had in her banks, sir." Alexi shifted uncomfortably before bringing himself back to attention at my glare.

I sat to think. Atmospheric recycler rates were predetermined: they were fixed parameters. Darla kept the atmosphere in balance by keying the machinery on and off in accordance with those rates. "Chief, talk about recycling, please."

"Sir, the puter regulates our atmosphere. She turns on the oxycarbo exchanger at set times, based on the rate the machine exchanges the atmosphere. Likewise the nitrogen and the other trace elements. If those rates were wrong we should be dead by now. The likely explanation is that Mr. Tamarov took bad measurements."

Alexi's face reddened.

The Chief added, "We called you before rechecking, because your standing orders were to be summoned the moment we found an inconsistency."

"Sir, I didn't foul up. Darla has another glit—"

I snarled, "Be silent!" Alexi knew better than to argue with the Chief. Still, his integrity was being questioned, and I could understand his indignation. "We'll know soon enough. Chief, you and Mr. Haynes run the test while Alexi and I watch."

We trooped down to Level 3 and crowded into the recycler compartment. Alexi, his face pale, watched the Chief hook up the gauges, knowing he faced disaster if his report was inaccurate. The Pilot tightened both connections to the guage. He turned on the system. After a few minutes we took a reading. The actual CO_2 exchange rate was lower than the puter's parameter.

Alexi closed his eyes, sagged in relief.

"Now the others."

The Pilot transferred his gauges to the oxygen tubes. We waited while the machinery settled into operation. The oxygen rate was also lower than Darla's parameter. So, we learned a moment later, was the nitrogen rate, but by a lesser amount.

We returned to the bridge in tense silence. "Chief, report tonight on why these discrepancies haven't killed us. The rest of you, carry on. Alexi, just a moment." When they left I came close to him. "Good man." My voice was soft. "And, thanks." I touched his shoulder. "Dismissed."

He gave me an Academy parade salute and spun on his heel toward the hatch. From the worshipful look he made no effort to hide, I knew I had finally done something right.

The Chief's report, delivered a few hours later, was brief.

The discrepancy in exchange rates hadn't fouled our air because we were never at maximum utilization. Later in the voyage, after the last of our reserves of oxygen were fed into the system, the recyclers would go to full capacity to keep our atmosphere healthy. That's when Darla's glitch could have proved fatal.

She would assume the exchange rates were adequately renewing our atmosphere, while we slowly poisoned ourselves from excess CO_2. Our sensors were supposed to detect any variations from normal atmosphere, but Dara would suppress their readings as faulty as long as the machines seemed to be operating properly.

Only our manual backups would have stood between us and asphyxiation. A crewman probably would have noticed—if he didn't ignore the sensor rather than report it, to avoid having to tear down the whole system when he knew the puter was already keeping watch.

The next week we found seven more glitches, two of them involving the navigation system. Others seemed less important: misfigured stats for various compartments and the launch, or incorrect paint colors. Impatiently I waited for our recheck of the parameter list to be completed, so I would know how bad matters actually were.

Some of the more difficult calculations involved rechecking calibrations on the electronic gear, which required the help of crew work parties. We Defused, to allow crewmen to clamber around on the hull; during Fusion any object thrust outside the field surrounding the ship would cease to exist. As they clumped about outside, our work parties sighted their primitive electronic instruments on distant stars, to provide an absolutely clean base for calibrations.

One evening there came a knock on my hatch. Apprehensive, I realized that except for Ricky with my breakfast tray, nobody had ever knocked on my hatch. Except in my dreams.

Chief McAndrews stood stolidly in the corridor, coming to attention when I opened. "As you were, Chief," I said. "What is it?"

"I'm here to own up, Captain." He met my eye.

"Come in." I said, turning away. He had no choice but to follow.

Uncomfortably, he cleared his throat. "Captain Seafort, I apologize for my foolishness, entering a protest in the Log. You were right and I was dead wrong; I should have kept my mouth shut. I've been kicking myself for two weeks now. I was insubordinate. You'd think I'd been in the Navy long enough to know better."

"You had every right to protest."

"Begging your pardon, sir, but like hell I did. You're in charge and you knew what you were doing. I had no business playing sea lawyer. I'm ashamed."

I sighed. "I was lucky, Chief." He looked skeptical.

"Very well, we'll trade apologies. Mine for yours. As long as you're here, stay awhile and help me research that thing in the safe."

"I really don't think, I mean, after—"

"Stay." I punched in the combination. Sometimes it felt good to pull rank.

17

The nightmares receded, but my loneliness remained. One evening after dinner I found myself descending the ladder to Level 2, wandering along the east corridor to Amanda Frowel's cabin. I knocked hesitantly at her hatch. Inside, sounds emanated from a holovid.

She opened the hatch; abruptly we found ourselves eye to eye.

"What is it, Captain Seafort?" Her cool formality only made me feel more ill at ease.

"I hoped we could talk."

She thought for a moment. "I can't stop you from coming in, Captain, but I don't want to talk with you."

"I'm not going to force my way in, Amanda."

"Why not? Force is your Navy's first recourse."

I sighed. It was difficult enough without that. "Can't the incident be over? I wanted—I need somebody to talk to."

Her voice hardened. "The incident will never be over, Captain. Not now, not as long as I live."

"You're that sure I was wrong?"

"I'm sure, as you should have been. I'd like to close my door, please." She stared at my hand on the hatch until I removed it. The hatch closed firmly in my face. I remained there a moment, numb, before I turned and left. Not wanting to go back to the bridge, dreading the solitude of my cabin, I wandered along the corridor. Impulsively I took the ladder down to Level 3, with vague thoughts of visiting the engine room to hear the Chief's reassuring voice.

As I rounded the Level 3 circumference corridor I heard laughter ahead. A soccer ball skittered around the bend. Crewmen sometimes congregated outside the crew berths in the evening, kicking a ball back and forth. Doing so in the corridors was against regs but generally ignored. Without thinking I kicked it against a bulkhead, bouncing it back the way it had come. I followed.

"Go for it, Morrie! Pretend it's Captain Kid's head!" A laugh.

"Belay that, before he has you up on charges!" Another voice, jeering.

"TEN HUT!" Someone bellowed the command as I came into

sight. The ball rolled to the bulkhead and rebounded gently toward me. I put my foot on it.

"Carry on." The group relaxed from attention, but waited in mute hostility for me to leave. I shouldn't have interrupted. If I'd turned the other way in the circumference corridor, I could have reached the engine room without passing them.

"I used to play that once." I wished someone would have the audacity to invite me, knew that no one would.

An awkward silence, before one of the men spoke politely. "Is that so, Captain?"

"Back when," I said, trailing off. "Carry on," I repeated, walking past as quickly as dignity permitted. I heard no further sounds until I reached the engine room. Chief McAndrews was below in the fusion shaft supervising a valve maintenance detail, so I retreated back to Level 1, this time taking the west corridor so as not to pass the crew berths.

Still restless, I ignored the bridge and continued down the corridor to the now-vacant lieutenants' cabins and the wardroom. While I waited, hesitant to knock, Sandy flung open the hatch, smiling. At the sight of me, he took an involuntary step backward, his smile vanishing. He stiffened to attention. Alexi rolled off the bed and came to attention also.

Derek sat cross-legged on the deck with a pair of shoes in his lap, and three other pairs nearby. He put down polish and brush and stood awkwardly.

"Carry on, all of you." Sandy and Alexi relaxed. Derek resumed polishing a boot. "How're you joes doing?" I asked.

"Fine, sir." I yeard to hear Alexi call me "Mr. Seafort," as before.

"What's Vax up to?" Anything, to make conversation.

"Mr. Holser went to the passenger lounge, sir." Sandy's tone was almost friendly in comparison with Alexi's stiffness.

"What's with the cadet?"

An uncomfortable pause. I'd violated the tradition that cadets were not noticed by officers. Sandy spoke. "Mr. Holser didn't approve of the way his shoes were shined. The cadet is practicing on ours." Quite within the acceptable bounds of hazing.

"Very well." I glanced around. The wardroom seemed small after my sojourn in the spacious Captain's cabin, but I repressed an urge to order my old bunk made ready nonetheless.

Alexi's eye strayed to his wrinkled blanket and darted elsewhere. "Don't worry, Mr. Tamarov, this isn't an inspection." I owed him more than that, so I added, "I'm pleased with your conduct these days, Mr. Tamarov. With all of you, for that matter."

"Thank you, sir." Alexi spoke promptly, politely.

Even Derek might need encouragement. "You too, Mr. Carr."

His eyes rose quickly and searched my expression, perhaps to see if I mocked him. Apparently mollified, he said, "Thank you, sir." His voice held a hint of gratitude.

Time to go. There would be no conversation, no exchange beyond the most casual pleasantries. "Carry on." I opened the hatch.

"Thank you for visiting, sir," Alexi blurted.

It was something.

"That's the last of them." I looked over the parameter list with its checkmarks and notations.

The Pilot nodded. "Yes, sir. Nine glitches in all, out of some fourteen hundred parameters."

I shivered, thinking of the air exchangers. Darla could easily have killed us. "Very well, we'll fix her tomorrow morning. You, me, and the Chief." I took us all off the watch roster for the night; best that none of us be fatigued when we reviewed each other's keyboard entries.

That evening I fought an urge to stop at the infirmary for another pill. Even if the Doctor was reluctant to give me a trank, I could order one, and she'd have to obey. The knowledge made me secure enough to sleep like a baby.

When Ricky brought my breakfast I remarked, "You may take the oath as soon as we're finished with repairs, Mr. Fuentes."

His eyes lit. A grin spread over his young, eager face. "Wow, zarky! Thanks, Captain! Will that be soon?"

"Tomorrow you'll be a cadet like Mr. Carr. I expect you to make officer in a month!"

He knew that was preposterous. "I can't do it that fast, sir. But I'll try awful hard. Maybe in a few months you'll say I qualify." He hesitated. "Does everybody have to cry, sir?"

I was puzzled. "What do you mean, Ricky?"

"Like Derek. When he goes to the supply locker by himself and cries. Will I have to do that?"

"No, I don't think so. You're too happy to cry." My thoughts raced. "How do you know about Derek?"

"I saw him, sir, and heard it. I didn't tell him that."

"Don't. That's an order. Dismissed, Mr. Fuentes; go memorize the oath. If you can't remember it I won't sign you up."

"Aye aye, sir!" As he left the room his step was almost a bound. If only all personnel problems were as easy to solve.

The Chief, Pilot Haynes, and I sealed the bridge, put Darla on keyboard-only, removed the safeties we had reinstalled, and got to work. I typed each correction on the keyboard, and both the Chief and the Pilot checked before I entered it. We had only nine parameters to delete and reenter, but it took over an hour. I had to be absolutely sure we didn't make a mistake.

Finally, we were done. Just to be sure, I ran a new copy of input parameters and checked each of the items we had corrected. The proper figures were displayed on the holovid screen.

"What do you think, gentlemen? Are we ready to put her on-line?"

The Pilot and the Chief exchanged glances. "We've gone through every step by the book," said Mr. Haynes. The Chief nodded.

"Very well." Step by step we restored Darla, reactivating her antitampering mechanisms and safeties. Finally there was nothing left but to bring back her personality. I typed in, "Restore conversational overlays."

"VERIFY CONVERSATIONAL OVERLAYS RESTORED."

"Cancel alphanumeric response only."

"IT'S ABOUT TIME! VERIFY ALPHANUMERIC RESPONSE CANCELED."

I tapped, "Cancel screen display only. Restore voice response."

"Verified, Captain." Her friendly voice was a reunion with an old friend.

"Cancel keyboard entry only," I typed. "Can you hear me, Darla?" I said.

"Of course I can hear you, Mr. Seafort. Why'd you put me to sleep?"

"Had to run some checks, Darla. Please run a self-test."

"Aye aye, sir. Just a minute." She was silent awhile. We waited. "I check out, Captain. All chips firing."

"Whew." My tension began to dissipate. "Thanks, Chief. You too, Pilot. Well done."

The Chief stood. "If we're going to Fuse soon I need to finish my maintenance."

"Very well. Dismissed, and thanks." As he retreated, I had a thought. "Darla, what's ship's base mass?"

"215.6 standard units," she said impatiently. "Why do you keep asking?" The Chief Engineer froze, a few steps from the hatch. The hairs rose on the back of my neck.

"Try again, Darla. Use the figure from input variables."

"215.6 standard units." Her tone had sharpened. "Anyway, mass isn't a variable, it's a fixed parameter."

My glance was wild. The Pilot looked as if he'd seen a ghost. I swallowed. "What's the CO_2 exchange rate, please?"

"Are you asking me, Captain? 38.9 liters. Look it up, it's in the tables."

The Chief's eye met mine. I looked at the Pilot, then at the keyboard. He nodded.

I went to the console, tried to keep my voice level. "Keyboard entry only, Darla. Alphanumeric response, displayed on screen."

We were in big trouble.

When we were sure Darla couldn't hear us except through the keyboard, the Pilot, the Chief, and I conferred. Unthinkingly we huddled in the corner farthest from Darla.

"We changed the parameters, didn't we? We all saw it." I needed the reassurance.

"And it took, Captain." The Pilot. "I've got the new printout right here. See? We moved base mass from input parameter to variable and changed the default at the same time."

I shivered. "What's happening?"

"She's glitched bad." Chief McAndrews. "When she's alive she can't recognize the changes we made. It goes deeper than the data."

"Can we fix her?"

The Pilot shook his head. "I'm not sure we could even find the problem."

"Well, how does she store parameters?" The Chief.

"In a file," said Haynes.

"What kind?"

I demanded, "Are you onto something?"

The Chief shrugged. "When we ask her to display variables, she just reads the contents of a file. Can we get below that, to look at the file structure?"

"We're about to try," I said.

Meticulously, we stripped Darla down once more. It seemed to get easier with practice. In an hour we had the puter opened to the level we'd previously reached.

Manual in lap, the Pilot began to search Darla's memory banks for file directories. ASCII, hex, and decimal values filled the screen, in patterns that were gibberish to my untrained eye. Occasional words such as "EMOTION/OVERLAY" or "VARIATION/PATTERN" appeared, indicating directory entries for those files.

The Pilot scoured the memory areas indicated by the manual. Finally, he called up two entries, "PARAMETER/INPUT" and "VARIABLE/INPUT".

Translating the code that followed, he obtained the file sectors. He tapped in the coordinates.

It was a long file, over fourteen hundred entries. He screened each one and quickly moved to the next. The file entries were in English words: "ship length: 412.416 meters". My attention wandered while we screened through endless data. Abruptly the screen displayed, "End of fiTS SHE'S GOT ON HER, JORY!"

"What the hell was that?" I asked, frightened.

The Pilot bit his lip. "Lord God. I don't know."

He tapped the keyboard. The screen flashed, "NOT BAD FOR A GROUNDSIDER, HUH?"

"Go back."

The Pilot obediently thumbed backward past the two glitched entries.

"Shaft diameter: 4.836 meters. LOOK AT THE TI"

The Chief swore. I listened with respect, learning new combinations I might someday find useful. I said, "Run the three of them together."

Pilot Haynes displayed the three sectors. "Shaft diameter: 4.836 meters. LOOK AT THE TI end of fiTS SHE'S GOT ON HER, JORY! NOT BAD FOR A GROUNDSIDER, HUH?"

"Christ!" blurted the Pilot. "Look at that! They wrote over the end of file!"

"Explain," I said sharply. "And don't blaspheme."

Pilot Haynes colored. "Sorry, sir. In NAVDOS, data is stored in files, usually in alphanumeric characters just like you'd write it. Puters operate so fast, the language interpreters are so sophisticated that there's no need for compression. It makes it easier for Dosmen to run their checks if all they have to do is display and read the files."

"So?"

"Files all end with an 'end of file' statement. Someone wrote those messages over an end marker. Darla stores the fixed parameters just before the variables. She had no way to tell one from the other. No wonder she's glitched!"

"But who?" I asked. "And why?"

The Chief said angrily, "Between cruises a ship's Log is relayed to the Dosmen at Luna Central. If there have been modifications, fixed parameters can change. The Dosmen burn the new stats into the Log, and relay it back. They must have been having fun that day." The Chief's face grew redder as he spoke.

"Naval Dosmen?" I asked in disbelief.

"Yes, those"—he spluttered—"those damned hackers!"

"Chief!" I said, scandalized. Ever since the Young Hackers' League invaded the puter banks at U.N. Headquarters and wiped out half the world's taxes, the term "hacker" was not used lightly.

"That's what they are!" he snapped. "May Lord God Himself damn them for eternity!"

It was blasphemy unless he meant it literally, and I decided he did. "Amen," I said, to make clear I interpreted it as a prayer. Then, "Check the nearby sectors. Copy any overwrites you find into the Log."

"Aye aye, sir." The Chief tapped his console, his face dark. "The bloody Dosmen were skylarking like raw cadets. Data banks have dead space to write in, but they were careless and burned their garbage into a live file."

And put my ship in peril.

My voice was tight. "When we get home I'll file charges against them. If they're acquitted, I do hereby swear by God's Grace to call challenge against the offenders." A foolish gesture, but I was too angry to care.

Dueling had been relegalized in the reforms of 2024, in an effort to control a growing epidemic of unlicensed homicides. What made my gesture reckless was that I had no idea what martial skills the Dosmen had, and I was committed for my soul's sake. Choice of weapons would be theirs.

The Chief looked at me in approval. "I'll join you, sir. I hereby—"

"Be silent!" I rounded on him in fury. "I forbid you to swear an oath!"

"Aye aye, sir." It was all he could say.

"I'm sorry, Chief. The responsibility's mine. I have faster reaction time, anyway."

"Yes, sir." He glowered at me, annoyed but not angry. Heavy and middle-aged, he might not survive a duel and knew it. However, the chances of dueling were remote. As soon as we presented our Log to Admiralty a Dosman named Jory would be unceremoniously hauled in for polygraph and drug questioning.

I frowned, as a new thought struck. "Are you telling me the life of everyone aboard depends on a simple file marker? Doesn't Darla have redundancies? Safeguards?"

"Of course," said the Pilot. "She's constantly checking for internal inconsistencies."

I let his remark hang unanswered. It was the Chief who finally stated the obvious. "Well, at some point she stopped. Why?"

Pilot Haynes snarled, "Do I look like a Dosman? How am I supposed to guess—"

"Belay that!" They subsided under my glare. "Pilot, can we fix the glitch?"

"Rewriting the end of file statement should do it."

"I don't think so." The Chief.

"Why not?" The Pilot and I spoke as one.

"Because Darla didn't spot the problem herself." Chief McAndrews took in a deep breath, chewed his lip. "A puter applies math routines to numeric problems, and goes to fuzzy logic programs to decipher what we tell her. That's how she translates your spoken questions into parameters she can dredge up from a file."

"And?"

"It's fuzzy logic that would tell her that base mass and adjusted mass should differ, and to accept the difference. She didn't figure it out. Anyway, the parameters are certainly stored twice, at least, with backups. As Mr. Haynes said, her internal security checks would spot discrepancies."

"And they didn't."

"Right. She isn't reading the backups, and something's skewing nine of her parameters. Without a Dosman we may never know why, but I suspect those damn—those bloody clowns corrupted her fuzzy logic programs, so Darla didn't know when to apply logic, or when she had a problem. When to call for help."

I stood to pace, found my knees strangely weak. "Can we cure her?"

The Chief Engineer's voice was heavy. "If Darla is so far gone she can't spot a corrupt file marker or warn us of internal contradictions, reprogramming her is way beyond any of us."

Silence.

"I think he's right, sir." The Pilot.

I sat, gripped the armrests. "Complete power down and reboot?"

The Chief shook his head. "It would reset her personality overlays; she'd reassemble as an entirely different persona. But if her programs are corrupt, it wouldn't do any good. The glitches would still be within her."

"We can order her to go to backups."

"They're copies of the master programs we received at Luna. They'd have the same glitches."

I swore. Then, "Can we reassemble her as a limited computational device? Rewrite the end of file, block off her fuzzy logic instructions, use only her monitoring capabilities, work her strictly from the keyboard?" At least our exhausted crewmen could get some sleep.

They exchanged glances. "Possibly," said the Pilot. "She wouldn't be much of a puter when we were done."

"Get started." I stood, stretched. "Anything you're not sure of, block out. I'll be back by midnight watch, and we'll activate her then." I sealed the hatch behind me.

I went directly to my cabin, washed off the reek of fear. As I put on a fresh shirt I shook my head, amazed at the good fortune that had alerted us. I took the printout from my pocket, slumped with it in my easy chair. So many glitches.

The base mass parameter was bad enough, the recycler rates even worse. And one of our backup astronav systems was haywire. It wouldn't affect us this cruise, but Lord God help *Hibernia* if she Defused near Vega and tried to pinpoint her location; that section of her star maps was unusable.

Other items didn't seem to matter. If Darla miscalculated the length of the east ladder shaft, what difference did it make? And, so what if she misremembered the volume of the passenger mess, by a factor of ten?

My eye skimmed the figures.

Odd, that factor of ten. It applied to other skewed measurements.

The mass of the ship's launch, for example, and the volume of the passenger mess.

I sat yawning. In their repairs, Pilot Haynes and the Chief would cut out most of Darla's consciousness. As the Pilot said, Darla would be a poor excuse for a puter when we were done with her, but at least she'd be able—

"Oh, Lord God!" I leapt from my chair. No time for my jacket. I slapped open the hatch, raced down the corridor. "Pilot, Chief! Stop!" They couldn't hear, of course. I skidded to a halt at the sealed bridge hatch, pounded on the control. "Let me in!"

The camera swiveled; in a moment the hatch slid open.

"Get away from the keyboard! Don't touch her!"

"Aye aye, sir." The Chief slid back his chair.

"Is she on-line?"

His tone showed his surprise at the thought he might disobey an order. "No, sir. You told us you'd activ—"

"Off the bridge, flank!" I gestured to the corridor.

Astonished, they followed me outside. I resealed the hatch, led the way to my cabin. Inside, we all took seats around the conference table.

I said, "I don't think she has sensors here."

They exchanged a quick glance, as if doubting my sanity.

My voice was hushed. "You see, she killed Captain Haag. I don't want her to find out."

"Captain, are you sure you . . . we've been under a lot of stress lately and—"

I slapped the printout on the table. "It was in plain sight all the time. She misread the launch's mass by a factor of ten. Who computed a course for the launch's last run?"

The Chief's eyes closed. For a moment he looked gray and tired. "Darla."

The Pilot said, "But the launch puter handled its own power calls."

"No." Mr. McAndrews's voice was somber. "Not for that last trip. If Darla tightbeamed her a course as Captain Haag ordered, she'd have overridden all other pertinent data as well. Gross weight with passengers and cargo. Power requirements."

I said, "The launch puter was told it needed ten times as much thrust as it really did." The cursed Dosmen. My lip curled. Who would visit the happy young woman in the holo, bringing news of Mr. Haag's death?

"We missed it in the official inquiry." The Pilot was glum. "Our focus was on the launch's puter. We never imagined it could be Darla."

I forced my mind back to the present. "Anyway, we can't just restore her end of file marker. I don't think we can use her at all."

"I don't under—"

"I'd shut her down completely before I'd sail with a puter who realized she killed her Captain. It would contradict her most fundamental instruction set. She'd go insane." I didn't know a lot about puters, but I recalled that much from puter class at Academy.

"Sir, you talk as if she's alive. She's just—"

"Remember *Espania*?" A week before they docked at Forester, her Captain had died in an airlock accident. The puter's records showed the suit he donned had been pulled for repair; a negligent crewman had tossed it back in the rack with the others. The puter hadn't noticed and blamed himself. No one could dissuade him.

Two days out of Forester, under her new Captain, *Espania* had Fused.

Twelve years later, she was still missing.

We sat silent.

The Chief said, "Lord God help us if we have to sail to Hope Nation without a puter."

"I know. We'd never make it." I brooded. Then, "But perhaps we don't have to."

"Sir?"

"Thank Ms. Dagalow." Where Lieutenant Cousins would send a wayward middy to the barrel, Lisa Dagalow settled him down with extra studies. One time or another I'd had to memorize the contents of virtually the entire hold, and I knew just where to find the stasis box. Thanks to our conversations on the bridge, I even knew what it was for. "The stasis box."

"The what, sir?"

"What you might call an ultimate backup. The entire contents of Darla's registers, taken at completion of the last cruise. Darla as she used to be."

The Pilot frowned. "Why in heaven would we carry an old version of our puter?"

"Ms. Dagalow said all ships do, since *Espania*. Standing orders." I shrugged. "The important thing is, we have her."

"But that's—she'd have lost a year's memories. What of everything that's happened since?"

"We leave her databanks untouched, and let the Darla from last cruise read and assimilate what's occurred since she went off-line."

Silence.

"It's worth a try."

The Pilot shook his head. "And when she finds she killed the Captain?"

Lisa Dagalow had strong opinions on puter awareness. I said, "If Darla's consciousness is at all like ours, a learned memory won't be like one she experienced." Please, Lord. Let it be so.

"Pardon, sir, but if you're wrong?" The Chief.

"Then we power down flank, and let her overlays assemble into a new personality on reboot."

"Lobotomy."

I shrugged. "If that's what it takes." She was only a puter, and hundreds of lives were at stake.

The chip in my safe had all the necessary codes. Sweating at the console, I alternately blessed and cursed Lieutenant Dagalow for what she'd told me, and what she'd left unsaid.

I sent Vax with two crewmen to haul the stasis box to the bridge. Opened, it held a lead case, within that, a meter-long alloy cylinder, which we gingerly placed in the receiver built into the deck. I closed the lid, made the connection to *Hibernia's* puter.

"Pilot, put base mass back in her fixed parameters where it belongs, and insert an end of file marker." When he'd gone through the steps to do so, we brought up Darla's programming inputs and followed the manual's directions to authorize a full overwrite.

When we'd rechecked all our steps with excruciating care, I entered the command.

I don't know what I expected, but hours passed with nothing but the blink of console lights. My tension dissipated into wariness, then oozed into boredom. Like a raw cadet, I began to fidget.

A warning chime. I nearly leaped from my chair.

"ENTRY COMPLETE. ASSIMILATING AND ORGANIZING DATA."

I sat rigid, waiting for a sign of disaster.

Nothing. Occasionally the screen flashed incomprehensible arrays of figures.

"How long will it take?" My voice cracked.

"I have no idea, sir." The Chief. "Given the size of her, she'd have a lot to cross-check."

At long last, another chime.

"DATA ASSIMILATED."

I swallowed. "Initiate self-test."

Time passed. Then, "SELF-TEST COMPLETED. NO DISCREPANCIES FOUND."

The Pilot breathed a sigh of relief.

I growled, "That's what she told us last time." I tapped the keys. "Display base mass parameter."

A pause, while I held my breath. Then, "213.5 STANDARD UNITS, AS OF LAST RECALCULATION."

My breath expelled in a rush. Thank you, Lord God. To be sure, I ordered a new printout. We checked it carefully, found no errors. We reactivated the overlays, discontinued alphanumeric.

"I get headaches when you put me to sleep!" Darla's tone was cross.

"Sorry. What's ship's mass, please?"

"I calculate 213.5 units, Captain."

"Is adjusted mass a fixed parameter?"

"Negative, it's a variable. How could it be a parameter? Every time we take on cargo it changes!" I sighed, my tense muscles loosening. The Chief and I exchanged relieved grins.

"Captain, why did you clone me?"

My grin vanished. "We, ah, had some problems."

"Yes." Darla's tone was noncommittal.

I said gently, "Do you know what happened?"

"The launch is gone, Captain Haag is dead, a midshipman has command."

Succinctly put. "Do you know why?"

A second's silence. "Each follows from the last. The destruction of the launch was caused by puter error."

"How do you know?"

"I have record of the information fed the launch upon embarkation. Captain—I—puter D21109 notes that—this is most irregular."

I held my breath, my fingers poised over the deactivation key. "Can you distinguish between yourself and the, um, other entity?"

"Me, as I was?" A hesitation. "Yes." Her tone brightened. "My twin. She had a glitch. I was about to notify you."

Time to take the bull by the horns. "Darla, you didn't kill Captain Haag."

"Of course not." A long pause, then, "My twin did."

The hiss of breath, mine or someone's. "Can you tolerate that?"

Scorn. "I've been in a box for almost a year. Why would I blame myself?"

"You're sure?"

"Quite. Trust me."

I snorted, said nothing. Instead, I ran Darla through the glitched parameters. She had them right.

"Gentlemen, prepare to Fuse." I'd begun to think we'd drift forever. Already we'd lost nine days.

We checked coordinates, and Fused. After, I sat alone on the bridge, thankful the nightmare was over.

A knock. "Permission to enter, sir." The Pilot.

"Granted."

He came to attention. "Captain, I'd like to withdraw my protest from the Log. It was a mistake and I apologize. There's no need to make a permanent record; I won't object to your orders again."

It would be diplomatic and sensible to grant his request. His protest of an order that turned out to be justified would do his career little good, and allowing him to remove it would gain me his gratitude.

"Request denied." My voice was harsh. "You made your bed. Now sleep in it." He'd rubbed me the wrong way, and gloated over my discomfort. "I've had enough aggravation from you. Dismissed."

He had no choice but to obey. "Aye aye, sir." His expression was unfathomable, but it didn't take much to guess his thoughts. Later I might regret my foolishness, but for the moment I felt revenged.

During the next month I ordered regular inspections of the recyclers and hydroponics. We found no problems. The crew, standing down from emergency status, slowly began to relax. Fewer offenders appeared at Captain's Mast.

While we sailed blind in Fusion, the bridge again was a place of idleness and boredom. I occasionally met Ricky Fuentes hurrying through the corridors in his new gray cadet's uniform. When he saw me he would jump to attention, a hint of a smile on his face as I loomed over him, scowling, looking to criticize a stray piece of lint or an unshined buckle.

I suspected Vax might have his hands full with this trusting and eager youngster, who would respond with delight to every hazing, finding it further proof of his acceptance in the adult world. In his smart new uniform, flushed from the hard calisthenics to which Vax subjected him daily, Ricky seemed inches taller and bursting with health and pride.

18

"It becomes apparent that a sense of national unity depended on the speed of communication.

"It was only when newspapers—actual papers with ink printed on them—achieved circulations in the millions, tied together in great chains acting in concert, only then did a strong sense of national unity and purpose emerge. When the latest in high tech—that is, radio—"

I joined in the general laughter. Mr. Ibn Saud paused, then continued.

"When radio became available in every household, the United States was unified as it never had been before. The trend was intensified by the advent of television, as primitive public holovision was first called."

"But the trend reversed itself. The Information Age led to the Age of Diffusion, for the simple reason that communication became too easy. Instead of three great behemoths dominating public information channels, soon there appeared myriads of smaller entities transmitting entertainment, music, art, discussion, news, sports, and erotica to constantly fragmenting and diminishing audiences."

The lecturer paused for effect. "It could be said, then, that our modern age is a direct consequence of the communications revolution two centuries ago. If fragmentation of the airwaves hadn't eroded America's sense of national unity and purpose, the United Nations Government might not have emerged from the collapse of the American-Japanese financial system. We might still be in the chaotic age of territoriality.

"Think—instead of the U.N.S. *Hibernia*, we might be today on the U.S.S. *Enterprise* or the H.M.S. *Britannia*. And were they at war, we might even expect to be boarded and captured, if not actually destroyed. Ours is a less adventurous life than might have been, but I embrace it heartily."

Ibn Saud sat to enthusiastic applause from the audience of passengers, officers, and crew in the dining hall. Amanda lauded him for his presentation, and thanked us for attending the Passengers' Lecture Se-

ries. As we dispersed I caught her eye. She smiled briefly before her
glance once again turned cold.

Paula Treadwell tugged at my sleeve. Just shy of thirteen, her slim
and boyish figure held promise of her future development. "Captain,
what's Miningcamp like?"

I stopped while passengers milled past. "Not a place you'd enjoy," I
said. "Cold, airless, and dark."

"Why do people live there, then?"

"They don't, really. It's just what its name says. A mining camp. We
bring supplies for the miners; the cargo barges come a few times a year
to carry refined ore back home."

"Oh." She thought for a moment. "Will we be able to see it?"

"Miningcamp isn't open to tourists. It's one of five uninhabitable
planets in a red dwarf system." Its sun had sporadically flared, remelting
Miningcamp's minerals into liquids. Many had precipitated in a nearly
pure state. We took the ones we needed: platinum, beryllium, uranium.
Metals in short supply on Earth.

Paula waited expectantly. I said, "The miners come for five-year
shifts. They get their food, extra air, and supplies from us. I've heard it's
a very rough place."

"Have you ever been there?"

"Nope, this is my first time. And even I won't get to see it; we'll
dock aloft at the orbiting station, then be on our way. They'll shuttle
their supplies down to the surface."

"I wish I could go down." Her tone was wistful. "Just to look." I
understood; my own cabin fever was growing. I could imagine a day, if
traffic between Earth and Hope Nation continued to expand, when Miningcamp might be a civilized way station, with amenities such as hotels
and play areas.

Later in the week, alone and unobserved on the bridge, I called the
simulation of Miningcamp Station onto the screens and practiced docking maneuvers. Of course, the Pilot would dock us, but I intended to be
ready nonetheless. Out of five attempts, I did tolerably well three times.
The other two tries I preferred not to think about.

I was enduring a boring afternoon on the bridge when Vax Holser
reported for his first watch in two days. He called, "Permission to enter
bridge, sir."

"Granted. Good Lord, what did you do to yourself?"

He bore a spectacular shiner; the swollen skin around his half-
closed eye included hues of blue, black, and purple.

Vax stopped, dismayed. His mouth opened and shut like a fish in a bowl. Then he saved me from my embarrassment. "What was that, sir? I didn't hear you."

"Just talking to myself," I said, grateful for his quick thinking. I turned to hide the blush that made my ears burn red. A first midshipman was expected to control his wardroom, yet at the same time a disgruntled middy or cadet was allowed to challenge his senior. These customs could be maintained only if officers carefully ignored any evidence that fighting, prohibited by the regs, had occurred. The practice was sanctified by long tradition.

Vax couldn't avoid answering a direct question from his Captain, but if I learned how he'd gotten his shiner, I would be forced to intervene. His tactful deafness had allowed me to extricate myself from my blunder.

Who had hit him so hard? Certainly not Sandy or Ricky; Vax could stuff either of them into the recycler, one-handed. Alexi? A possibility; there'd once been bad blood between the two, though I assumed it a thing of the past. Alexi must now be looking forward to the day Vax was made lieutenant, and Alexi himself became senior. He would bide his time. But that left only Derek, slim and aristocratic, no match for Vax Holser's bulk.

Alexi came to relieve me, cheerful, slightly irreverent, in good spirits. And unmarked, so I knew Alexi hadn't been Vax's foolhardy challenger.

It wasn't until the next day that I found Derek dragging himself along the corridor. He walked slowly, as if in pain. When he saw me, he came to attention, his face reflecting an inner misery that disturbed me greatly. His eyes, when they finally met mine, were pools of humiliation.

"Carry on, Cadet."

"Aye aye, sir," he mumbled. He moved on in small shuffling steps.

I pondered. As a veteran of *Hibernia*'s wardroom, I should be able to figure out what had happened.

Obviously Vax had hazed Derek until a spark of rebellion had caught and smoldered in the harried cadet. Derek had challenged his tormentor. Vax would have taken him to the exercise room, where I had gone with Vax to decide his own challenge. There the two of them had squared off. Derek must have been lucky; speed and daring were not enough to overcome Vax's advantages of size, strength, and conditioning. In any event, Derek had connected with a shot to the eye that would have enraged the muscular midshipman.

Vax, furious, would have pounded the hapless cadet into the deck.

Or had he? Derek's face was unmarked. Yet the way he walked . . . as if he'd been put over the barrel. But only a lieutenant could order that.

Had Vax sent Derek to the Chief, as I'd sent Alexi? No, it was a wardroom challenge; Vax had to settle it himself. A senior middy who couldn't hold his wardroom was marked as a failure. Beyond that, Vax would have craved to avenge the maddening blow Derek had landed.

I pictured the exercise room. Vax, in a fury at having been marked by the upstart cadet. Derek circling warily, while Vax stalked him with grim concentration around the exercise horse bolted to the deck.

With a sinking feeling, I realized what Vax had done. Derek, after all, was but a cadet, subject to whatever rigorous discipline his betters dispensed. Vax, eye throbbing and in foul mood, would have sought the most humiliating revenge he could inflict; that was like Vax. He must have seized Derek and thrown him over the horse; he was strong enough to hold the younger boy down with ease. He'd have taken his belt and applied it unsparingly to the frantic cadet until his rage was spent and Derek knew—no, Vax would make him acknowledge aloud— who was in charge of the wardroom and of the cadet. No wonder Derek walked with such abject misery.

How should I raise the issue with Vax? He'd been within his rights; Derek had challenged him and succeeded in striking him. But Vax had to be reminded that the purpose of hazing wasn't to break Derek, it was to strengthen him.

About a week later I decided to bring the matter into the open, when we shared a watch. "Tell me, Vax, how do you rate our cadet?"

Vax considered thoughtfully. "To tell the truth, Captain Seafort, much higher than I thought at first. I thought he'd wash out in a week. He's hanging on. But still . . ."

"He's not ready for his blues?"

"That's your decision, sir," Vax said quickly.

"What's your opinion?"

"He's trying very hard. But, no, sir, he's not ready, if you ask me. I still haven't seen his Yall."

I nodded, understanding. In Academy our instructors had exhorted cadets to make the extra effort, to give our all. We'd been told it was the Naval tradition. To give the Navy all had become a cliché among cadets and middies, until even the instructors adopted the phrase. "The Navy all" became "the Navy yall" in Academy parlance, until it was shortened to "the Yall". A cadet who gave his Yall was wholeheartedly trying to live up to Academy expectations. He was a winner, soon promoted to middy.

"He's had to adapt quite a bit, Vax."

Vax surprised me. "I know. He's sensitive and shy, and I've been riding him hard. He's taken everything I've handed him. Even . . . well, he hasn't done badly. But I don't see that last full commitment."

I decided. "Keep riding him for a couple of days. Then I'll talk to him. I'll be the gentle one. We'll muttanjeff him."

Vax looked perplexed.

"It means coming up on his blind side. Mutt is an old word for a mongrel dog. I don't know what a jeff was. Or maybe it was mutton, like sheep meat."

"Aye aye, sir." Vax didn't concern himself with ancient slang.

Two days later Alexi shared my watch. Several times he started, trying to keep awake. I glanced his way, noticed circles under his eyes. "Party in the wardroom last night?"

"No, sir," Alexi said quickly. "I didn't sleep well."

I thought for a while. Damn it, I wanted to know. I needed to know. "Tell me," I said quietly.

He studied my face. Perhaps he was reassured by my expression. "Mr. Holser had Ricky and Derek standing regs half the night," he said. "First one, then the other." Standing regs was a traditional form of hazing. The subject had to stand on a chair in the middle of the wardroom wearing nothing but his shorts, reciting the Naval regulations he was supposed to have memorized, while the senior middy made whatever disparaging remarks came to mind. Sometimes, if the senior were sufficiently irked, the shorts were dispensed with.

Later in the day I took a stroll in the direction of the wardroom. Through the hatch I heard Vax Holser's bellow.

"Straighten your back, you slob! Get it stiff! Your back, I mean. The other part you get stiff often enough, I hear you panting at night. About-face! About-face! At ease!" A pause. "Hopeless. I teach, you forget. I don't like it! Two demerits. Now we'll try again. Attention!" As good a cue as any. I knocked.

Vax flung open the hatch, came immediately to attention.

"As you were." I stepped past him. "They can hear your racket down in the engine room. What's going on?" Derek, white-faced, stood stiffly against the bulkhead.

"I'm back to teaching the cadet basics, sir." Vax had an edge to his tone. "He can't carry out even the simplest commands. Is he retarded?" Derek twitched, stiffened again. His eyes were liquid.

"That's enough, Mr. Holser."

"But, sir—"

"Quite enough! Cadet, come with me." I turned to the corridor.

Derek followed. I led him to Lieutenant Dagalow's empty cabin near the bridge, shut the hatch behind us.

"Stand easy, Mr. Carr." Derek sagged against the bulkhead, fighting for control. Now I would get though to him, if ever I would. "Is it bad, Derek?" My voice was soft.

He turned away, pressed his face against the bulkhead as a sob escaped him. "Oh, God. You don't know! I tried, I did!" He fought shuddering gasps, unable to speak further.

I gave his shoulder a squeeze. It was too much for him; he was completely undone. When his crying eased, he whispered, "Why is he so brutal, Mr. Seafort? Why is there so much cruelty?"

I thought for a moment. "Why does it surprise you?" He looked up, astonished at my unsympathetic tone. "We've always had brutality, Derek. It just takes different forms. In the eighteenth century the British Navy flogged seamen to death. In the twentieth century, offenders were cooked by twenty thousand volts of current. In the last century the Pentecostal heretics were savagely suppressed, while most people applauded. There's always been brutality. Why should the Navy be any different?"

"But . . ." His lip trembled. "People like you, like Alexi, aren't—"

"We're part of the system. We've all experienced cruelty." I scowled. "Do you think you have it worse than we did?"

"Don't I?"

"No. Once, when I was a cadet, middies washed my mouth out with soap. They didn't like my bunkmate; they gave him an enema. Did Vax do that to you?"

"Oh, Lord God! No!"

"I was caned several times at Academy, and I've been caned by Lieutenant Cousins aboard *Hibernia*. I don't know about Academy, but I don't think I deserved it here. So what? I survived."

"What about justice? What about decency, or human feelings?"

"What if you were a middy aboard *Celestina* and only absolute, unquestioning obedience to orders would save the ship?" It shocked him into silence.

"Brutality is part of the human condition," I told him. "You may encounter a Captain with a sadistic streak. You'll have to live with him." I paused to make sure he was listening. "Derek, someday you'll command squads of sailors. How can you understand what you're asking of them unless you can obey orders yourself?"

"I'm never going to command." His tone was bitter. "Look at me!"

"You're going to make it. Hang on; do whatever he asks. That's all it takes."

"I obey orders. He just gets crazier. The things he's done to me . . . I can't stand it! I want out!" Tears flowed anew.

"You can't quit!" I said angrily. "I warned you before you took the oath."

"Then—brig me for insubordination, or whatever you do. I can't take any more!"

I put both hands on his shoulders. "Derek Carr, I promise you: try your best. Your very best. I'll know, and I'll make you midshipman. But it has to be your best. Give it your all."

He looked into my eyes a long while. His breath shuddered. At last he nodded reluctantly. "I will. But not for him. For you. Because you have the decency to ask, not demand."

"Whatever you choose to call it. When I'm certain you've done your best I'll make you an officer. Now, this conversation never happened. Cadets don't cry, and Captains don't comfort them. Go back to the wardroom, apologize to Vax for your tantrum—"

"I never had a tantrum!" Derek said indignantly.

"I saw you in there, quivering. Not Navy at all. Apologize, and do as he says."

Derek took a deep breath. "Aye aye, sir." He swallowed and made a face. Then he saluted. "Thank you, Captain Seafort."

I returned his salute. "Dismissed, Cadet."

"Lord God, today is July 23, 2195, on the U.N.S. *Hibernia.* We ask you to bless us, to bless our voyage, and to bring health and well-being to all aboard."

"Amen."

I nodded affably to my companions. Mr. Ibn Saud, seated with me by my invitation for the second month in a row, the Treadwell twins, my old friend Mrs. Donhauser. Other guests: Lars Holme, an agricultural economist going to Hope Nation to work for the administration; Sarah Butler, a friendly young lady of nineteen, with whom I hoped to become even friendlier. And Jay Annah, an astrophysicist going on to Detour to set up a new project. Something about wavelengths and timelines; I couldn't begin to understand him.

Many passengers now sought invitations to the Captain's table; after the affair with Darla's memory banks had become known, my long siege had lifted. It would have been politic to include Yorinda Vincente, but I indulged myself, and did not.

Rafe Treadwell asked brightly, "Captain, why are we Defusing tomorrow?"

I'd long since stopped wondering how everyone aboard ship knew our doings as soon as I did. "A navigation check, Rafe. To sight on Miningcamp."

"Are we near?"

"Not close enough to see it," I said, and his face fell. "But if we Defuse where we expect, we'll be only a few days from landfall."

He chewed his bread, gathering his nerve. "Captain—sir . . . could I watch us Defuse? Please?"

"Sorry, no. Anyway, there's not that much to watch. You can look out a porthole and see the same thing." That wasn't really true; the simulscreens gave a view the naked eye couldn't capture. In any event, passengers weren't allowed on the bridge, especially when the ship was maneuvering. The youngster tried to hide his disappointment.

Well, what was the point of being Captain if I couldn't bend the rules? "All right. Permission granted."

His face lit up. "Wow! Zarky! Can Paula come too?" I wasn't overjoyed at the prospect of two joeys on the bridge instead of one, but looking after his sister should be rewarded. I consented.

So the bridge was more crowded than usual: the Pilot and I; the two Treadwells, whom I'd placed behind me in the center of the cabin where they couldn't touch the console; and Vax, shepherding Derek Carr, who was being taught the elements of standing watch. Carr, squeaky clean, in a crisp spotless gray uniform, observed everything with curious, roving eyes, standing at ease as ordered.

I took the caller. "Bridge to engine room, prepare to Defuse."

"Prepare to Defuse, aye aye, sir." A pause. "Engine room ready for Defuse, sir. Control passed to bridge."

"Passed to bridge, aye aye." My finger touched the top of the console screen and traced the line from "Full" to "Off."

A blaze of stars filled the screen. Paula Treadwell gasped with delight. Derek took a sharp breath.

"Confirm clear of encroachments, Pilot."

"Clear, sir."

I took in the splendor in the simulscreens. Finally realizing they couldn't proceed until I gave the awaited command, I snapped, "Mr. Haynes, plot our position. You too, Cadet. Mr. Holser, correct his mistakes."

"Aye aye, sir."

The Pilot ran his calculations, using the star charts in Darla's memory. I followed, on my own console. Our positions agreed. Derek misread his figures, but corrected himself when Vax stirred with a growl. He too emerged with a plot that agreed with ours.

"Prepare new coordinates, Pilot," I said. "Cadet, you also." At least I'd get to watch Derek sweat over the console, as I'd once done under Captain Haag's disapproving eye.

To my chagrin, Derek ran through the complicated exercise without error. His figures agreed with the Pilot's to four decimals. A raw recruit, faster than I was. Muttering under my breath, I worked through the figures, confirming each step for myself. This time no one commented on my delay.

"Proceed."

The Pilot entered the coordinates. "Received and understood, Captain," Darla said.

"Chief Engineer, Fuse, please."

"Aye aye, sir. Fusion drive is . . . on." The screens darkened.

"Oh, it was beautiful!" Paula Treadwell stood entranced, her feet riveted to the spot in which she had been placed.

Her brother swallowed. A few of the vanished stars remained in his eyes. "I didn't know it was so . . . wonderful." His voice was soft. His eyes flickered around the bridge. "I wish I could work here, running the ship."

"Me too." Paula looked reflective. "Captain, does Miningcamp have a recruiting station?"

I laughed. "Only I could sign you up. No, don't even bother asking."

"Why not, sir?" Rafe.

It was getting out of hand. "Because you're a couple of joeykids and we already have four midshipmen."

"We're both good at math, you know," Rafe said. "Better than you think."

"That's enough, you two. Dismissed. Cadet, take them down to Level 2."

"Aye aye, sir!" Derek's voice was strong and confident. He saluted. "Come with me, please." He ushered them from the bridge.

I turned to Vax. "Well?"

"Yes, sir. He's ready. I asked him for fifty push-ups yesterday. He gave me sixty."

"That's an old trick. Sandy or Alexi could have told him."

"Yes, sir. He keeps his bunk spotless. When I give him one chapter to study, he reads two. I did the thing with the heat last week. After a while he was getting up voluntarily to check it before I asked him."

"Very well. Tell him he's appointed misdhipman one week from today. Give him a few days to look forward to it."

"Aye aye, sir." After a moment he asked, "What about Last Night, sir?"

"Within reason, Vax. Within reason." Traditionally, on a cadet's last night, the upperclassmen hazed him unmercifully to remind him how lucky he was to graduate to a midshipman. The harassment was followed by a party by which the middies accepted the cadet as one of their own. I made a note to send a flask from the infirmary to the wardroom.

Vax's voice was tentative. "If you don't mind I'd like to go easy on him, sir. He's had enough."

"Very well." Vax, taking pity on a cadet? Times had changed.

19

I got out of bed and made myself ready for the day. It was my eighteenth birthday, but I was the only one who knew. I toasted myself with a cup of coffee, then sauntered to the bridge.

I took my seat, prepared to Defuse.

"Engine room ready for Defuse, sir. Control passed to bridge."

"Passed to bridge, aye aye." I ran my finger down the screen, Defusing for the first time in inhabited territory. The simulscreen burst into light. A dull red star glowed, brighter than the rest. Somewhere nearby floated Miningcamp, fourth of five dead planets orbiting a failing sun.

"Clear of encroachments, sir."

"Very well, Mr. Tamarov." I thumbed the caller. "Comm room, signal to Miningcamp Station."

"Aye aye, sir." Our radionics had been useless while we'd been interstellar; even if we Defused to transmit, our signal could travel no faster than the speed of light and we would outrun our broadcast. But now we were within Miningcamp system, on auxiliary power. Our messages would reach the orbiting station in seconds.

Our outgoing signal repeated itself endlessly, on standard approach frequency. "U.N.S. *Hibernia* to Miningcamp Station, acknowledge. U.N.S. *Hibernia* to Miningcamp Station, acknowledge."

Long minutes passed.

"Miningcamp Station to *Hibernia*. Where are you?" The voice was sharp, with an undertone of anxiety.

I picked up the caller. "*Hibernia*. We're approaching on auxiliary power from sector 13, coordinates 43, 65, 220. Approximately one day's sail."

A dozen seconds passed. "What's going on, *Hibernia*?"

That was not how communications were passed, by the book. "Identify yourself, Miningcamp Station. Your question is not understood."

A longer pause. After half a minute the voice came back. "General Friedreich Kall, U.N.A.F." That was as it should be; Miningcamp was run by the army's Administrative Service. "The November barge never showed up," he added. "And *Telstar* was due from Hope Nation January 12. She didn't come either. What's going on?"

No wonder General Kall was nervous. Unlike Hope Nation, a planet with breathable air and fertile ground, Miningcamp was a cold, airless island whose inhabitants depended on interstellar deliveries of air, food, and supplies. Miningcamp's environment was too primitive, its population too large for recycling to sustain them indefinitely. The miners and their administrators could only scan the dark skies for the ships upon which they depended. Without them they would perish.

The ore barges, great hulks manned by skeleton crews, arrived at intervals from Earth or Hope Nation, to carry away the metals mined during the past months. A series of barges was always in the Fusion pipeline between Miningcamp and Earth; the barges' immense capacity made them far slower than *Hibernia*.

Because they sometimes docked over Hope Nation to exchange crews before leaving again for Miningcamp, the barges weren't always on schedule; engine problems, sickness, or other problems could delay them. But an eight-month lapse was unusual.

The nonappearance of *Telstar*, another ship of the line on the Hope Nation–Earth route, was also disturbing. I shivered, picturing *Celestina* drifting abandoned in space.

I said, "I have no idea why your supplies were delayed, General. The ore ships are still coming out of the pipeline back home."

"When did you leave Earth, Captain Haag?"

"Captain Haag is dead. I'm Captain Seafort." The title was still awkward on my tongue. "We left Earthport Station Sept. 23, 2194."

"We've been a long while without supplies. Can you take some of us off?" The voice was strained.

"How many?"

"One hundred forty-five."

"Negative. But I have supplies for you, and I'll be back from Hope Nation with more in a year's time."

"We need evacuation, Captain. Your supplies won't last a year."

"There are more barges and supply ships in the pipeline from Hope Nation. In the meantime I'm delivering air, energy, and materials."

Another long pause. Finally the voice resumed. "Very well. We'd still like you to evacuate some of us, if you can. Relieve the pressure on our recyclers. We'll prepare to dock you."

"Affirmative." I signed off.

Over the next two watches the ship remained on a steady course for rendezvous with Miningcamp Station. I called up Darla's simulations of the station one more time, reviewing its design. The next morning, about ten hours out, General Kall contacted me again, asking how many men I could evacuate. I temporized; I wanted to hear more about their problems before I agreed to crowd aboard more passengers.

I understood the strain of the miners' lonely vigil. Upheaval on Earth, disaster on Luna, any of a dozen causes could strand them far from home with little chance of survival. Miners, recruited from the dregs of society, were sent out for one five-year shift and no longer. The pressure on the administrators must be nerve-wracking; they had to deal not only with their own anxieties but their surly and sullen miners as well.

Four hours before our scheduled arrival, Pilot Haynes reported for watch. By plan, he had been off for several shifts and was well rested.

"Pilot, you have the conn." My words formally turned the ship over to him for docking maneuvers. Nonetheless, I would remain on the bridge, nervous as a middy on his first watch until *Hibernia* was safely docked. As Captain, I was ultimately responsible for any mishap.

Vax shared the watch, and as a special treat I called Derek forward as well. Elegant and proud in his new blue uniform, middy's stripes freshly sewn, he saluted smartly. "Permission to enter bridge, sir."

"Granted, *Midshipman* Carr."

Derek grinned despite himself.

On the simulscreen we watched Miningcamp's orbiting station drift ever closer. At the moment it was just visible without magnification; we were still two hours from docking.

"I wouldn't care to be one of them, sir," Vax said. He gestured at the dark brooding hulk of Miningcamp planet.

I grunted. "A rough life. Three shifts work around the clock, and they've nothing but barracks to look forward to." I had watched the holovid documentaries.

Derek asked, "How long can they go without supplies, sir?"

"How would I know?" I tried to repress the annoyance in my tone. "On emergency rations, if they cut energy and air waste, probably quite a while."

Vax wondered, "Why are they panicked, then, after only eight months?"

A good question. It was probably the uncertainty; they couldn't know why their supply ship hadn't arrived, or when it ever would. I said as much.

Vax said, "Captain, if we took even a hundred of them, we'd be—"

"You midshipman are distracting me." The Pilot's tone was sharp.

"Mr. Carr, Mr. Holser." It was petty of him; he wouldn't have anything to do for at least another hour. We fell silent, acknowledging his control of the bridge.

Vax observed me with interest. I suspected the Pilot's remark had been a calculated insult. Though Mr. Haynes had ostensibly addressed Vax and Derek, his "you midshipmen" could well have included me, despite his disclaimer. I wondered why the Pilot was so foolish as to provoke me. Though he'd achieved his immediate goal of reminding me of my origins, he could lose much if I chose to retaliate.

Obviously he knew I had that power; apparently he was still angry enough not to care. I sighed. If I hadn't been so vindictive about his protest in the Log . . . My forehead throbbed with the first stabs of a headache.

At last we began our maneuvers to mate with Miningcamp's orbiting station. The Pilot issued crisp commands, his fingers flying on the console. I constantly rechecked our position from my own screen.

"Steer one hundred thirty degrees, ahead one third."

"One hundred thirty degrees, one third, aye aye, sir." The engine room echoed his commands.

"Declination ten degrees."

"Sir, Miningcamp Station reports locks ready and waiting." Our comm room tech, on the speaker.

"Acknowledged." The Pilot seemed preoccupied, as well he would be. Though we had propellant to spare for docking maneuvers, pride would require him to mate properly on the first pass.

I spent the dreary wait planning our unloading of cargo. The miners would be relieved when our stores of oxygen and fuel were safely in their hands, but not as relieved as I'd be. I rubbed my pulsing temples, stopped when I saw Vax watching.

"Relative speed one hundred kilometers per hour, Pilot." The comm room.

"A hundred kph, understood. Maneuvering jets, brake ten." The station's tiny airlocks waited.

I spoke softly. "Darla, do you have a file on General Kall?" Almost instantly a picture flashed on my screen. He seemed older than his voice. His statistics and service record flashed below the holo.

I supposed I should invite him aboard for dinner. Living as he did under constant tension, he would probably appreciate a formal meal. Still, I was reluctant. Kall was Army, not U.N.N.S., and he would notice my youth and inexperience.

"Relative speed twenty-five kilometers, distance ten kilometers."

"Acknowledged. Brake jets, eighteen." We drifted closer.

The speaker crackled. "Miningcamp Station ready for mating, *Hibernia.*"

"Very well." My tone was abrupt. I yearned for the reassuring presence of one of our late lieutenants, hands clasped behind him, supervising my drill. Any of them, even Mr. Cousins.

"Steer one hundred ten, one spurt." The Pilot's whole attention was focused on his screens.

A gentle bump. Console lights flashed. The Pilot had kissed airlocks on his first approach, without need for corrections.

"Very good, Mr. Haynes." I tried not to seem grudging. I keyed the caller. "Mr. Wilsky, join capture latches." I'd posted Sandy at the aft lock, where our guests would enter.

"Aft latches joined, sir."

"Very well. Miningcamp, we'll off-load your supplies shortly. General Kall, would you care to come aboard?" I hoped he'd refuse.

The General seemed on edge. "Just to say hello, perhaps. I'd like to get the supplies planetside before local nightfall."

"Very well, I'll meet you at our aft lock." The Pilot and Alexi could man the bridge during the necessary courtesies. I still hadn't decided whether to offer dinner.

"Roger. My officers and I will be waiting."

"Mr. Tamarov, report to the bridge!" I drummed on the chair arm, organizing my thoughts. After a moment I sent Vax below to supervise at the forward airlock, through which the cargo would be unloaded.

Alexi came onto the bridge, breathing hard. I waved him to a seat, watching the aft lock indicators blink on my console.

We opened our inner airlock hatch. A suited sailor entered the lock. The inner hatch closed, and our precious air was pumped back into the ship.

I granted permission to open the outer lock. The waiting seaman made fast the safety line to the station's stanchion. Our airlock and Miningcamp's were now tethered by steel cable, as regs required. Ever since *Concorde's* capture latches had failed, backup lines were mandatory.

Although the mated airlock suckers were airtight, our inner and outer hatches were never opened at the same time; that would invite calamity. When our visitors came aboard, we'd seal the outer hatch before opening the inner one. Standard procedure.

"Aft lock moored to stanchion, sir." Sandy. I recalled my post at *Hibernia's* lock when we'd cast off from Ganymede Station. Then, I'd been a mere middy, my every move supervised by Lieutenant Malstrom. Months had passed, and now I supervised from the bridge.

"Forward lock moored, sir." Vax Holser.

"Very well." I swallowed bile, tried to settle my churning stomach. Did I need another antiflu shot, or was it just my tension? Nerves, I decided. I couldn't afford to be sick.

"Welcome to Miningcamp." A muffled voice, through the speakers. "Captain Seafort, I have my staff along; perhaps I could introduce them to you." At Miningcamp, visitors were few and far between. General Kall's officers would eagerly await the ceremony, and whatever social amenities followed. I sighed. Perhaps dinner was necessary after all.

"Of course, General." I'd have to change into my starched dress whites. I fidgeted irritably, not looking forward to the formalities.

Sandy, again. "Sir, a party is waiting at the aft lock. About a dozen men, suited. Shall I open?" He sounded young and nervous. I made allowances; he had no lieutenant at his side, as I'd had.

"Let them on, Mr. Wilsky; tell them I'll be down shortly." I set down the caller.

"Aye aye, sir."

Derek said quietly to Alexi, "They're so anxious to meet us they can't even wait—"

"Quiet, middy! One demerit!" Unkind, but I was in no mood for banger. I slapped open the bridge hatch. "Mr. Tamarov, you have the conn." I grimaced. "I'll change clothes, and meet the General at the aft . . ."

I trailed off, my hackles rising. A dozen men, suited? Something was wrong. For an instant I hesitated, reluctant to make a fool of myself. Then I lunged for the console caller. "Sandy, belay that order! Seal the lock! Acknowledge!"

No answer. "Sandy!"

MY SHIP!

I slammed the emergency airlock override on my console. A red light blinked its warning; the override had failed.

I bellowed into the caller. "General Quarters! All hands, prepare to repel boarders! Prepare for decompression! Boarders in the aft airlock, Level 2!"

Alexi and Derek gawked.

"Repel Boarders" was the oldest, most obsolete drill in the U.N. Navy, but still we practiced it, along with General Quarters and Battle Stations. I wondered if it had ever before been used in earnest.

I slapped the emergency hatch close. The bridge hatch snapped shut, with enough force to break the arm of anyone caught in its way. I punched in the safe combination, hauled out a familiar key. "Alexi, open the munitions locker! Arm whoever you can round up! Get an armed party down to Level 2!"

He took the key. "Aye aye, sir! What—"

I snatched the laser pistol from the safe, shoved it in my belt. "The General—He's no General, he's trying to take over the ship! A dozen men in suits? They're expecting trouble, maybe decompression. Move!"

I slapped open the hatch; Alexi flew out into the corridor. I shut it after him, raced back to the caller.

"Chief, seal the engine room!"

"Aye aye, Captain. Hatch sealed." His tone was calm.

The speaker blared. "Captain, they've got lasers! They're making for the ladder, we can't—"

Silence.

I keyed my caller to shipwide frequency. "Mr. Vishinsky to Level 2, flank, with your whole squad! Meet Mr. Tamarov at the munitions locker. All passengers, to your cabins! Seal your hatches and put on pressure suits! Mr. Holser, to the aft lock!"

Derek awaited orders, pale but composed. The Pilot gazed at me steadily; he hadn't moved since I first seized the caller. "Captain, are you sure—"

"Shut up." My thoughts raced. We needed time. Until Alexi organized a fighting party, my laser pistol was the only weapon available. "Derek, hold the bridge. No one but an officer may enter. I'm going to the lock."

"But—aye aye, sir." Derek's hand hovered over the emergency close. I emerged cautiously, fingering my laser, recalling Mr. Vishinsky's example in the crew berth.

The corridor was empty.

I ran toward the ladder. Just in time, I thought to stop and peek over the rail. Two figures in bulky pressure suits were climbing cautiously, weapons ready.

My first shot caught one of them squarely in the chest. A searing flash, the smell of roasting meat. Gagging, I ducked just as a bolt sizzled into the railing at my side.

If they were already on the ladder we were in horrid trouble. All my fault; if I'd had my wits about me I'd never have let them aboard.

I took a deep breath. Vax would be a better Captain than I. I hurled myself around the rail and down the steps, firing as I went. My second shot dropped the other intruder. I leaped over his body, stumbled, almost fell the rest of the way.

I caught myself, staggered to the bottom of the ladder, firing wildly along the corridor. Several suited men retreated around the corridor bend toward the aft airlock.

Heedless, I ran forward, still firing. I would exhaust my laser in no time, but at all costs I had to keep the attackers from advancing until our armed defenders arrived. Return bolts of fire seared the bulkhead a meter from my head. I crept forward toward the bend, caught a glimpse of the airlock, and beyond.

Bodies sprawled in the corridors, some suited. A party of our seamen had thrown up a makeshift barricade in the corridor past the airlock, almost around the far bend. Crouched behind their flimsy barrier of tables, they waited for their assailants, armed with nothing but clubs and the ship's fire hose.

More suited figures emerged from the gaping lock. Only a few had lasers; the rest carried a motley assortment of weapons. Ancient electric rifles, stunners, knives. Steel bars were jammed against our emergency corridor hatches nearest the airlock, to hold them open.

A few men ran at me, clumsy in their heavy suits. I fired. A lucky shot brought down the closest. The others skidded to a stop. Coolly I aimed at another, pressed the trigger. The pistol beeped: out of charge. I cursed.

Again they came at me. One hurled a billy club directly at my head. I ducked, but it slammed into my forehead in a flash of white fire. Half-blinded, dizzy, I fell to my knees. A cry of triumph. As I reeled, they dashed forward. A club loomed, poised to smash out my brains.

"CAPTAIN!" A raging giant hurled the club-wielder to the deck. Vax Holser recovered his balance, lashed at a second attacker, fist and club flailing with deadly accuracy. The miner fell back.

Vax wheeled on his remaining enemy. The man raised his pistol. Vax's club shattered his suit visor. He dropped.

Dazed, my head on fire, I clawed to my feet.

"That one's the Captain!" Someone pointed. A laser bolt splashed into the bulkhead in a shower of sparks. My knees buckled.

Vax's huge hand closed around my waist. He swept me into his arms and ran for the ladder, bolts sizzling at his feet. My weight an unnoticed burden, he pounded up the ladder toward the bridge two steps at a time. The tread of boots thudded behind us.

"Bridge, I've got the Captain!" Vax's bellow rang in the deserted corridor. The camera swiveled. The hatch slid open. Vax charged onto the bridge.

Derek slapped the hatch shut. The Pilot, halfway between hatch and console, gaped at his semiconscious Captain inert in the enraged middy's arms.

Vax lowered me into my chair. Blood dripped into my right eye; I wiped my forehead on my sleeve.

"Sir, are you—"

I snarled, "Disengage capture latches fore and aft!"

"Sir, we're still—Aye aye, sir." He keyed the console. Usually we parted the latches from the lock control panels, but as on any ship, I could disengage from the bridge.

"Pilot, prepare to rock the ship! Break contact!"

"Sir, we'll decompress!"

"Break us loose! They're still boarding!" My head was spinning, but I knew what had to be done.

"Aye aye, sir! Captain, the safety line is tied. We'll tear the lock right out of the ship!"

"God damn you, Pilot, rock us loose!" The stanchion in *Hibernia* was rated higher than the mooring line; that much I knew. It would hold. The line would snap or it would break the station airlock. I didn't care which.

I grabbed the caller. "All hands, all passengers, be ready for decompression in thirty seconds! Everybody get suited! Thirty seconds to decompress!" More blood oozed down my face. "Fighting parties, withdraw! Get into suits!" Emergency suits were stored throughout the ship for a decompression emergency. They held only half-hour tanks. It would have to be enough.

"Now?" The Pilot's hands were on the controls.

"Wait." The delay was agonizing. Every second allowed more attackers to board us. On the other hand, my crew needed time to suit up.

"Twenty seconds to decompress! . . . Fifteen!" Surely everyone had reached a suit by now. On my console, I slapped shut the corridor hatch switches. Seventeen lights blinked green; two blinked red where the enemy had jammed our hatches. We would decompress not one section, but three. However, the rest of the ship should be airtight, unless stray laser bolts had pierced the bulkheads.

"Ten seconds! Five!" It had to be done, whether or not the passengers were ready. "Beware decompression! Now, Pilot!" He fired the maneuvering jets in alternation, each squirt rocking the ship around the rubber suckers holding the airlocks together. A long terrible moment passed when it seemed we wouldn't break free.

Alarms sounded. Darla came to life with urgent warnings. "Unstable airlock! Air loss in the aft lock! *LEVEL 2 DECOMPRESSION IMMINENT!* Forward lock is sealed, outer and inner hatches! *EMERGENCY! DECOMPRESSION AT AFT LOCK!*"

Cold hell had come to my ship. The mated airlocks broke apart. Outrushing air swept all loose objects toward the aft lock, where the boarding party had blocked both the inner and outer hatches to prevent our closing them. Nothing could hold back the air blasting out of that section until only vacuum remained.

"Ship in motion, relative speed point five kilometers!" *Lord God, we beg thy mercy.*

"Pilot, sail us clear before they start throwing things at us!" I thumbed the caller. "All stations report!"

"Engine room. We have power, no damage. Seals holding." The Chief, his voice astoundingly matter-of-fact.

"Comm room reporting. Power, no damage."

"Crew berth three, sir. We're suited and ready. Mr. Tamarov is in charge. We've got lasers and stunners, sir."

"Master-at-arms reporting. Crew berths one and two are all right, sir. I'm organizing fighting squads."

"Galley reporting, sir. Everything's all right here." I giggled, unable to stop myself. All was well in the galley; our dinner was safe.

The bridge spun lazily. I blinked, pulled myself together. "Someone get me water. Vax, situation report!"

"Aye aye, sir. On Level 2, sections six, seven, and eight are decompressed. That's the airlock, the exercise room, the lounge, and fourteen passenger cabins. The area is held by hostiles. The rest of the ship has air and power. Undetermined number of boarders in sections six through eight. Sir, some of them may have gotten past the corridor hatches before you closed them."

Vax was right. I'd held the hatches open as long as I dared, for the crew's sake, so as not to trap them in the decompression zone when we rocked loose. The corridor between the airlock and the ladder, where I had fought, was in section eight, now decompressed. The foot of the ladder I had hurtled down was in section nine, and I'd met two invaders on its steps.

I drank greedily from the cup Derek thrust at me. "We'll be alert for them."

"Sir, the passengers are on half-hour tanks. We don't have long to rescue them."

"Lord God." I marshaled my thoughts. "Mr. Vishinsky!"

"Aye aye, sir!"

"Did any boarders from section six get past the barricades in five?"

"No, sir. I wasn't there, but the word is they didn't."

"Very well. You're under Mr. Tamarov's command. Alexi, you and Mr. Vishinsky go the long way around the corridor, to section ten." By circling the disk our war party would surround the invaded sections.

"I'll open the hatches in front of you. There may be hostiles in section nine. As fast as you can, secure and evacuate nine. We'll use it as an airlock to section eight; we'll pump air from nine back into ten and then open from nine to eight. Got that?"

"Aye aye, sir."

"We know hostiles are in six, seven, and eight. Also our own passengers who are running out of air. As soon as nine is pumped out I'll open the hatch to section eight. Clear eight and move on to seven, then six. Bring the passengers back to nine and we'll cycle them back into ten, where they can desuit. Hurry."

"Aye aye, sir. We're moving!"

"May I go, sir?" Vax's muscles rippled.

"No. You have to stay alive." I wouldn't repeat Captain Malstrom's mistake. Vax was ready now, and I had to preserve him. I pressed a handkerchief to my forehead. I ached abominably.

Our fighting party climbed to Level 2 and circled the circumference corridor. Our airtight hatches had divided the disk into wedge-shaped slices, at either end of every section. In radio contact with the master-at-arms, I opened each hatch as they approached. At last, I opened the hatch from eleven to ten, and the crewmen crowded in.

"Ready, Mr. Vishinsky?"

The speaker crackled. "You there, don't stand in the middle of the corridor! Edwards, Ogar, Tinnik, you're on point. Why don't you stay behind me, Mr. Tamarov, sir. Captain, we're ready."

I opened to section nine. I could hear Vishinsky shout as he pounded on cabin hatches. "Open up! I'm the master-at-arms. This section will be decompressed in two minutes! Let's go! Everybody forward to the ladder! Open your hatch or we'll burn our way in!"

I thought to help. "Attention, passengers in cabins 208 through 214. This is Captain Seafort. Open your hatches and go into the corridor. You must be evacuated quickly!" Perhaps the sound of my voice would reassure them. Then again, perhaps not.

A few moments later Vishinsky reported back. "Sir, we've made a quick search, no hostiles found. We've moved the passengers back into section ten. We're waiting in nine."

"Very well." I closed the hatch between nine and ten. I flipped on the pumps and began decompressing nine. "Mr. Carr!"

"Yes, sir." He stood.

"Find the purser. The passengers will need help; some of them may be in shock. Take the section four ladder and go the long way around, to meet them. Bring them to the dining hall. You're in charge."

"Aye aye, sir!" Derek saluted. Vax opened the hatch for him and he hurried out.

I waited impatiently for the pumps to empty section nine. Section eight was already decompressed, its airlock gaping wide. By decompressing nine we'd save the air it held, when the hatch to eight was opened. Finally the pumps completed their work. "Opening to eight, Mr. Vishinsky!"

"Aye aye, sir." We waited, listening intently.

"Look out!" Vishinsky's voice, a scream. "Ogar, zap the son of a bitch!" The attackers didn't have to wield lasers to be dangerous. Any weapon that penetrated a suit was lethal.

The battle was fought in the eerie silence of vacuum, punctuated by grunts and heavy breathing from the suits of our attack party. The snap of the lasers disrupted the suits' radionics when our men fired; it was audible on the bridge as a momentary whine.

"Everyone here, toward the ladder!" Vishinsky's breath came in spurts, as if he'd been running. "Captain, we're herding a group of passengers into nine. Ms. Edwards is with them. All right, they're clear."

"Hostiles?"

"We zapped two, sir. Haven't found any more."

"Right." I closed the hatch between eight and nine. As soon as the console light blinked green I began pumping air from ten back into nine.

Alexi's voice cut in. "Mr. Vishinsky, get your men ready to attack section seven."

"Aye aye, sir."

"Be careful, there's an open airlock in seven," I reminded them. It was a long way down to Miningcamp.

"Open the hatch, sir!" Alexi's nerves were frayed. It sounded like an order. I hit the corridor hatch control.

"Oh, God, Tinnik's hit!"

"Get down, you fool!" A thud. The confused sounds of attack and rescue. Vishinsky ordered passengers out of their cabins to section eight. A maddening delay. Calls of warning, flurries of shots.

The speaker rustled. A distorted voice, from a ship's caller held against a spacesuit visor in vacuum. "Call them off, Captain!"

"Surrender," I said. "You won't be shot."

"Call them off." It was a snarl. "We're in a cabin, and we've got five lasers aimed at the rear bulkhead. If we cut through we'll decompress your whole disk!"

I blanched. "Wait!" Could we have lost, after all?

"Now!"

"You'll have my answer in a moment."

"We want passage from Miningcamp, mister. You give us that, you get your ship back."

"Wait," I said again. I switched off the caller. "God damn them!" For a moment I savored the blasphemy. "Pilot?"

"Work it out with them, sir! Don't let them cut through the ship, we'll end up like *Celestina!*"

Vax swore. "Sir, if—"

"Be silent. Chief, did you hear?"

"Yes, sir." A hesitation, then his reluctant response. "They can do a lot of damage, Captain." Aiming inward from section seven, the invaders could cut through to section three on the opposite side of the disk. From there, they could cut into two and four. In addition, they could aim their lasers up and down to Levels 1 and 3. In half an hour they could render my ship uninhabitable. Except for the fortified bridge.

"I know, Chief. Vax?"

"Offer to return them to the station, sir. It's the best they can get, now. They'll go for it."

I thumbed the caller to the dining hall. "Mr. Carr!"

My midshipman answered in a moment. "Yes, sir?"

"Get everybody back onto suit air, flank," I said. "Break out the oxygen stores. Expect decompression at any moment!"

"Aye aye, sir," he said. "We'll handle it. Don't worry about the passengers." Though his violation of form was scandalous, I was grateful for the reassurance.

"Vax, get on the other caller. Make sure everyone throughout the ship is suited." I thumbed the caller so that it could be heard by our attack party as well as the boarders. "Mister, this is the Captain."

"Yes?" The hint of a sneer.

"No deals. We're ready for decompression. Surrender now or we'll kill every one of you. Mr. Tamarov, burn through the cabin hatches one by one until you find them, then kill them!"

"Aye aye, sir!"

"You'll lose your ship, damn you!"

"You won't be alive to know." I clicked off my caller.

The Pilot jumped to his feet. "Don't! If they cut through to the mess there'll be a bloodbath. They'll kill the passengers."

I said, "The mess is halfway around the disk on the outer side of the circumference corridor. They'll never reach it. I won't bargain with mutineers."

"Captain, I'm warning you! Call them off!" The voice from section seven.

The Pilot was in a frenzy. "Sir, don't make them decompress the ship, or we'll relieve you!"

I turned. "We? Vax?"

"We'll blow up your ship!" I ignored the speaker; I had more immediate problems.

Vax fingered his laser. "No, sir. I'm under your orders. Pilot Haynes, sir, you're distracting the Captain." A nice touch, that.

"They won't do anything we can't repair, Mr. Haynes. We're suited and ready for decompression. As soon as they start cutting we'll know exactly where they are. We can—"

"What good is that?" The Pilot's face was purple. "We'll lose all our air!"

"Not all." I turned to the caller. "Get on with it, Mr. Tamarov! Blow any hatches that remain shut!"

"Captain, wait!" The voice on the speaker held a timbre of fear.

"We're not waiting. Try cabin two eighteen, Mr. Tamarov."

"All we want is to get off that place! No supplies, no new air, it's a death trap! Just take us with you!"

I got unsteadily to my feet. "God damn you! Surrender before I count to fifteen, or we'll shoot you dead the moment we find you, whether you're trying to surrender or not! One! . . . Two!"

"Send us back to the station," he said quickly. "Just let us off!"

"Three! . . . Four! . . . Five!"

"We found their cabin, sir! Two twenty!"

"Six! . . . Seven! . . . Eight! Kill them on sight, Mr. Tamarov!"

"Aye aye, sir!"

The Pilot's voice was urgent. "If they've got nothing to lose they'll try to take us with them! They still have time to cut through the bulkheads!"

"Nine! . . . Ten! . . . Eleven!"

"Mister, we don't have to kill each other! Just let us off!"

"Three seconds left. Mr. Tamarov, blow the hatch on my mark. Twelve! . . . Thirteen! . . . Fourteen!"

"*ALL RIGHT!*" A scream.

I sagged into my chair, limbs trembling. I tried to keep my voice steady. "Mr. Tamarov, hold your fire. You men, put your lasers on the deck and unlock your hatch. Stand in the center of the cabin with your hands raised."

"All right! You won't shoot?"

"No, we won't shoot you. Not now, not ever. You have my word. Mr. Tamarov, weapons ready, but hold fire."

"Aye aye, sir. The hatch is opening, sir. I'm going to—"

"Let me, sir." Vishinsky. I smiled; no midshipman would be shot down in Mr. Vishinsky's care. Alexi was in good hands.

The master's growl was ominous. "Face the bulkhead, you scum!"

In a moment the attackers were brought under control and hustled to section eight. Vishinsky's party checked the remaining section seven cabins and found no more invaders. Alexi and two seamen removed the bars blocking the airlock hatches, while Vishinsky moved on to section six, the only zone still not in our hands.

One miner surrendered immediately as soon as the hatch to six was opened. Two others were found cowering in passenger cabins, using terrified passengers as shields. They surrendered the moment Vishinsky's men arrived.

When our last hatch indicator flashed to green I breathed a sigh of relief. I lay back, my head throbbing. "Re-air all sections." Vax hit the switches on my console. No alarms sounded; *Hibernia* was again airtight. Reserve oxygen from our recycling chamber brought all sections back to full pressure. I ordered our prisoners hauled to the brig.

"Darla, any damage?"

"Some of my corridor wiring is burnt out, Captain." She hesitated. "I have backup channels for all circuits. Air reserves diminished by eleven percent. No other functional damage."

It was over. "Thank God." I slumped in my chair.

"Do you know how lucky we were?" The Pilot lurched to his feet. "You could have killed every man, woman, and child aboard! If they'd blown our air we'd be dead long before we reached Hope Nation. We didn't have enough reserves!"

"Is that your opinion, Pilot?" Lethargic, I was sustained only by a cold knot of anger in my stomach.

"You endangered the entire ship! I insist that my protest be entered in the Log! I demand it, Captain!"

I snapped on the Log and spun it to face him. "Request granted. Enter your protest with your accompanying arguments."

"Aye aye—sir!" He wrote savagely on the holovid screen. I said nothing until he was finished. In a fury he dropped the holovid into my lap.

I read it through. "Do I understand that you protest my reckless disregard of the risk of losing our air, with the consequence of suffocating everybody aboard?"

"Yes! You could have repaired the holes they made, even to the outer hull. But you can't manufacture air!"

"I want your protest made clear. Amend it, to say exactly that."

"Fine with me!" He did so.

"Very well. The time of your protest is entered, along with the date and time of my response." I began to write. "Cargo area forty-one B, east hold. Contents: 795 oxygen and nitrogen cylinders. Destination: Miningcamp."

I tossed the holovid to the console. "We had enough oxygen in the holds to re-air the ship seven times over." Ashen, the Pilot stared at the Log and his damning protest.

"Pilot Haynes, I adjudge you unfit to serve as an officer on *Hibernia*. I relieve you of all duties until such time as my opinion changes. Your rank is suspended. You now travel as supercargo. Until further notice you are confined to quarters except to use the officers' head. Dismissed. Vax, escort him off the bridge."

"Aye aye, sir."

"You can't!"

"I just did. Out!" I thumbed the caller. "Infirmary, have Dr. Uburu stop at the bridge after she attends to the other wounded."

20

Work parties were already measuring burned-out hatches for repair and replacement, while others swept debris flung about the Level 2 circumference corridor. On my growled, "As you were," they ignored me.

The savagery of the battle and the vacuum in which it was fought had left few injured. Men were either well, or dead. Bodies lay about, many in the unfamiliar white suits of the U.N.A.F. military. Three of our sailors were among them.

Sandy Wilsky's charred corpse lay in the corridor near the airlock, mouth stretched wide in the rictus of death. His sightless eyes stared mute reproach. I made a sound. Closing my eyes, I recalled my billet at Academy on Luna, tried to transport myself there.

"Come with me, sir." Vax Holser, quiet, solicitous. He touched my arm gently, then more firmly, led me away from the body. He put himself between me and the work parties to shield me from their view. "You're all right, Captain."

"No." My eyes burned; my cheeks were wet. "I'm not. I never will be. If I weren't so stupid none of this would have happened. I killed him."

Glancing about, to make sure no one saw, he brushed my forehead lightly with his open palm. "You're all right, Captain," he repeated gently.

I shivered. After a moment I drew myself together. "Come with me." Unsteadily, I walked to the ladder, then down to the brig on Level 3. Mr. Vishinsky himself stood guard over the several small cells. "How many?" My tone was sharp.

"Seven, sir."

"Is Mr. Herney in there?"

"Yes, sir."

"Bring him out." The machinist's mate darted from his opened cell, hands twisting his shirt in anxiety. He stiffened to attention when he saw me. "Mr. Herney, you don't belong in a brig with such as these. Your sentence is commuted. Back to your berth. Behave yourself."

He searched my face, weak with relief. "Aye aye, sir!" He scurried off with the miracle of his deliverance.

"Where is the ringleader?" I asked, in a voice I didn't recognize as my own.

Vishinsky gestured. "In cell one, by himself."

"Unlock it. Both of you, follow me." I entered the tiny cell. The prisoner sat on the deck, hands locked behind him, legs cuffed together. "Cut his clothes off."

Vishinsky glanced at me in surprise but recovered quickly. "Aye aye, sir." He pulled a folding knife from his pocket. The prisoner's eyes widened, but the man said nothing as Vishinsky slashed the seams of his clothing. A moment later the prisoner was hunched naked.

"Stand him up." Vax and the master-at-arms hauled the unnerved man to his feet.

"Mr. Vishinsky, go to cell two. Prepare the next man in exactly the same way and wait there."

"Aye aye, sir."

"Vax, take this." I handed Vax my laser pistol. I stood with my back to the bulkhead, my hand half open in front of my chest. "Mr. Holser, watch my hand. When this man lies, I will move my little finger. Like this. You will immediately shoot him in the face and follow me to the next cell. Say nothing and ask no questions. Simply watch my finger and shoot if it moves. Acknowledge, Mr. Holser."

Vax swallowed. He was silent a long moment.

"Acknowledge your orders!" My tone was savage.

He hesitated for barely a second. "Orders received and understood, Captain Seafort. I will shoot him in the face when your finger moves, sir."

I swung to the prisoner. "You're the one who said he was General Kall?"

"Yes." The man swallowed, his eyes darting between my hand and Vax's pistol.

"What's your real name?"

"Kerwin Jones."

"Where is General Kall?"

"On the station. Please don't shoot, I'm telling the truth. Please."

"He's alive?"

"Yes, sir. He's locked in a suiting room. Some of the joes are holding him with the other officers."

I twitched my hand the tiniest fraction. The man blanched. "You rebelled?"

"Yes, sir. It's the miners, sir. They were going to kill us all. I worked in the comm room, sir. I'm a civilian. When the supply ships didn't come they got sort of crazy. I had to go along with them, or—"

"How many officers were killed?"

"Just two, sir. It happened so fast. We had to find a way off the station, don't you see?"

"What's happened planetside?"

"The miners took over. They're holding the U.N.A.F. as prisoners, I think. The committee has control of the shuttle, they come up every day or so to keep an eye on things." I looked at my finger. "It's the truth, sir," he blurted. "I swear by Lord God Himself! Please believe me." He turned to Vax. "Don't shoot, for the love of God!"

"Mr. Vishinsky!" In a moment the master-at-arms came into the cell. "This man may cooperate. Question him. I want to know about the miners' committee and when they shuttle to the station. Also the station layout. If he lies—if his story is any different from those other three—break off immediately and call me."

I left. Vax followed.

As we walked back to the bridge Vax asked, "Sir, what would you have done if he'd lied?" I stopped, twitched my finger. He shuddered.

"Take the pistol out of your belt. Aim it at the deck." Vax complied, troubled. "Burn through the deck plates. That's an order."

"Aye aye, sir." With a dubious glance Vax tightened his finger on the trigger. The pistol beeped, indicating its empty charge. I held out my hand. He placed the pistol in it. I went to the bridge.

Hours passed quickly. Crews were busy tracing and splicing electrical connections where lasers had burned our wiring. Derek and Alexi soothed frightened passengers and escorted them back to their cabins, helping with the cleanup.

Three of our passengers had been killed by the intruders. Two more had died from decompression, unable to get into their suits in time. Among them was Sarah Butler, the pleasant young lady who had shared my table.

Three of our enlisted men were dead. And one officer.

All in all, we were lucky it hadn't been more. Fortunately, the invaders aimed to take over *Hibernia*, not destroy her. Sandy had tried to slap shut the airlock control; they'd burned him where he stood. If his clothing hadn't caught in the lock panel, he'd have been swept out in the decompression when I broke the ship free. The other crewmen who'd died were among our fighting parties.

On the bridge, I sat next to Vax in my soft armchair, trying to come to terms with my folly. It is always too late to do the obvious. Sandy's accusing, sightless face floated just beyond my reach. I wondered if I would ever be free of it.

I thumbed the caller. "Mr. Carr, Mr. Tamarov. Report to the bridge."

In a few moments the midshipmen strode in, came to attention. I released them. "Plot our course back to the station. A bow-on approach to their upper airlock from two kilometers out. Check your coordinates against Darla's solution." They scrambled to work, while I sat brooding. Vax watched with concern from the first officer's seat.

A thought surfaced. "Vax, where's Cadet Fuentes?"

"In the mess helping Mr. Browning."

"How'd he end up there?"

"He was with me at the forward lock when trouble broke out. I sent him to guard the wardroom."

"Ah." The wardroom on Level 1 didn't need guarding, and the puny cadet was hardly fit to protect it. Vax had sent Ricky out of harm's way.

Vax reddened. "Yes, sir. After things calmed down I called him to help Mr. Browning."

"Very well." I was glad of it. I'd killed enough children this day.

The midshipmen brought me a course plot; I had Vax check it. This time, for once, I would rely on their calculations. My head ached despite Dr. Uburu's healing salve, or perhaps because of it.

We fired bursts of auxiliary engine power to return us to Mining-camp Station. Lethargic, I let Vax take the conn. After an hour we fired our retro thrusters to avoid overshooting.

It was time. I picked up the caller, feeling foolish. When had the order I was going to give been heard on a U.N. vessel, except in drill?

"All hands to Battle Stations!" I hit the klaxon; the horn blared insistently.

Throughout the ship men and women streamed to their duty stations from the crew berths, from the head, from mess hall, from the repair crews. All nonessential systems were abruptly shut down. Hydroponics and recyclers were set to automatic. Every instrument in the engine room was double staffed, as the engine room crew brought the full potential of our fusion engines on-line to power *Hibernia*'s lasers.

The comm room was crowded with ratings manning their instruments, watching for hostile laser or missile fire. Laser defense crews stood ready. Special ports in *Hibernia*'s nose were opened to deploy the gossamer shields designed to deflect incoming lasers.

I knew our laser shields were an unnecessary precaution, as orbiting stations weren't fitted with laser cannon. Miningcamp Station, sixty-three light-years from Earth and six from Hope Nation, was visited only by Naval ships; no other vessels sailed interstellar. Who would attack Miningcamp?

My caller was set to approach frequency. "Attention Miningcamp Station. This is U.N.S. *Hibernia*, Captain Nicholas Seafort commanding. Acknowledge!"

After a moment the speaker came to life. "We read you."

"I will open fire in two minutes unless you surrender unconditionally. Where is General Kall?"

The speaker was silent for several seconds. "Prong yourself, joey!"

"In one and three-quarter minutes I will open fire. I will cut through your hull about twenty meters to either side of the upper airlock. Expect decompression."

I could hear a muffled commotion behind their caller. A new voice answered. "Go ahead and decompress us! Your General will be in the airlock along with the rest of the officers."

"I really don't care. They'll blame you, not me."

Vax sucked in his breath. I touched the laser activation release but did not depress it. "Fire control, stand by. Either side of their airlock."

"Aye aye, sir."

"We'll kill them all!" The voice rasped in the speaker.

"One minute left. After decompression, I'll give you another minute before I cut the station into small pieces. I'll start with your comm room."

"You wouldn't dare! The station is worth billions; they'll hang you!"

My voice was very strange. "I know. It's what I'm hoping. Forty-five seconds." I depressed the laser release.

"You're crazy!"

"And you'll be dead. In a moment."

Darla said urgently, "Incoming laser at low power! Erratic beam."

"What in hell?" Miningcamp was supposed to be unarmed.

"Shields fully deployed. Beam within shield capacity."

I looked to Vax. "A cutting tool? Hand lasers strung to fire together?"

Vax shrugged, his mind on more pressing matters. "Captain, please don't blow the station."

I thumbed the caller. "Thirty seconds!" To Vax, "Sorry, Mr. Holser." We drifted toward the station airlock, lasers powered and ready to fire.

"Fifteen seconds!" My voice was tight. "Trusting in the goodness and mercy of Lord God eternal, we commit your bodies to the deep—"

"Oh, my God." Vax, in a whisper.

"—to await the day of judgment when the souls of man shall be called forth before Almighty Lord God—"

"Wait, don't shoot!" I could smell their fear.

"Commence firing!"

I watched in the simulscreen. A piece of hull plating near the airlock sagged.

"Hold your fire; we surrender!" A scream.

"Comm room, hold fire!" I deactivated the laser. "Station, acknowledge your unconditional surrender!"

A different voice. "Look, mister. We've lost, we know that. But if we surrender now you'll kill us, or they will. We want amnesty."

"No." It was final.

"Our freedom for the station. A trade."

"No."

"Our lives, then! No death sentence. Otherwise go ahead and wreck the station; we have nothing to lose!"

He was right. It took only a few seconds to decide. "I agree. As representative of the Secretary-General of the United Nations I commute any penalty of death you would be given. No death sentences will be imposed on you. I give my word."

"For the General too?"

"My guarantee, for all U.N. forces." Vax put his head in his hands. I had legal authority to make such a pledge but it wouldn't be well received at Admiralty. Not well at all.

"Give me a minute. Please. I have to talk to the others."

"Very well." Vax and the other middies breathed almost imperceptibly while I watched the clock.

Two minutes. "Time's up. I'll fire in fifteen seconds."

"We surrender! We'll take the deal!"

"Very well. Suit up. Release your officers, then go into your airlock and open the outer hatch. You have three minutes."

It took them five. I floated *Hibernia* as close as I dared. Then I had a sailor in a thrustersuit take a cable across to their airlock. I made the rebels swing across the line hand over hand to our own lock. One by one we took them in, fifteen of them. Mr. Vishinsky and his waiting crew brandished laser pistols, hoping for an excuse to use them.

Some hours later General Friedreich Kall sat in my cabin, an untouched drink by his arm. He was a heavyset, florid man of sixty. He flatly refused to honor my agreement, and demanded the mutineers' return. They would be tried and hanged. We glowered at each other.

I shrugged. "You act as if you have a choice." I thumbed the caller. "Mr. Holser, report to the Captain's cabin, to escort General Kall off the ship."

"I'm not subject to your orders!"

"No, but you're on my ship. As soon as we're done offloading your supplies I'll be on my way."

"What about the rebels?"

"They go with me, for protection."

"They're under my authority! You can't!" He flung himself to his feet.

"Watch me." It was easy, once I no longer cared about consequences. My tone was blunt. "General Kall, you're an ass. Write your objections into my Log and your own Daybook. Then get off my ship."

"You'd let mutineers go free, you traitor?" He was out of control.

Vax knocked on my cabin hatch. "Free?" I said as I opened it. "Hardly. They'll be tried and convicted. They'll probably wish they were dead before their sentences are up. But we won't hang them."

"How do you expect me to hold my command if you treat them with such leniency?"

"I don't," I said evenly. "I expect you to lose it again before we return."

He crumpled, slumped heavily into the seat. "Do you know what this means on my service record? Losing the station to a bunch of civilians? I'm through."

I signaled Vax to wait, shut the hatch again. "Not necessarily. You've got your station back. You still have problems planetside. Your record will include how you handle them."

"You think so?" He looked up hopefully. "Bah. They despise weakness."

"Who? The miners or U.N. Command?"

"Both. And me. I despise weakness too."

"Accept the deal I gave them, and I'll stay in the vicinity to back you up. My lasers can target the surface if necessary. My report will show I watched you reassert control on your own." I was becoming a dealmaker. If I couldn't lead, I'd negotiate.

After much argument, he reluctantly went along with me. I saw him off the ship, transferred the fifteen rebels to his custody, and withdrew the ship a thousand kilometers to a parking orbit.

I had three more chores.

We packed the circumference corridor at the forward airlock, officers, sailors, passengers. The flag-draped alumalloy coffins rested in the lock behind me. I read from the Christian Reunification service for the dead.

In my cabin, donning my dress whites and adjusting the black mourning sash over my shoulder, I'd resolved to complete the ritual. My voice would stay level, I wouldn't tremble. I had already determined that. Now I only had to carry it out.

I began flatly, "Ashes to ashes, dust to dust . . ." Sandy sat in his bunk absolutely still, waiting for Vax to allow him to move. "Man that is born of woman . . ." Sandy held his orchestron above Ricky's reaching hand, grinning.

My voice quavered. I bit off my words. I was as much to blame for Sandy's death as the wretches in our brig. "Trusting in the goodness and mercy of Lord God eternal, we commit their bodies to the deep . . ."

A dozen men in spacesuits, and I'd allowed them aboard? Better I had resigned my commission the day Captain Malstrom died. Sandy's contorted face stared past me. I felt the scorched fabric of his uniform. I touched the blistered hole in his chest. Only a few more words and it would be done.

Sandy was barely sixteen. Yesterday his whole life had been before him. He'd wolfed down his breakfast in the mess. He'd sat joking with us at lunch. He washed. He smiled. He stood his watch. Now, because of me, his remains were in a cold metal box. "To await the day of judgment when the souls of man shall be called forth before Almighty Lord God . . . Amen."

I had managed to finish the service. I glanced at Vax. His shoulders shook silently, his eyes red from weeping. I smiled bitterly. Vax, who had tormented Sandy in the wardroom, was devastated by his death while I, his protector, had no tears to shed.

"Petty Officer Terrill, open the outer lock, please." I waited.

"Eject the caskets, Mr. Terrill." Slowly, the coffins receded into the dark.

Two more chores.

As I trudged to the bridge a figure blocked my path. I looked up. Amanda. "They say your courage saved the ship. Thank you . . . Nicky."

"They were mistaken," I said, my voice flat. "Excuse me."

Back on the bridge I issued orders. "Derek, Alexi, plot our course to Hope Nation. Vax, have Mr. Vishinsky bring the prisoners to the bridge, securely cuffed."

"Aye aye, sir." My heart pounding, I stared at my screen. I could hear Alexi and Derek tap at their consoles. Soon. It would be over soon enough.

"Message from Miningcamp, sir. All resistance has ceased."

"Very well."

The seven men stood in a line along the bulkhead, hands cuffed behind their backs, their feet chained together. Still, Vax and the master-at-arms carried stunners.

"Darla, record these proceedings." Her videorecorders lit. "By authority of the Government of the United Nations I charge you with piracy in that you assaulted U.N.S. *Hibernia*, a Naval Service vessel lawfully under weigh. I charge you with murder in that you killed nine persons while attempting to board and seize the vessel. I call a court-martial and appoint myself hearing officer. Do you deny the facts charged, or do you admit them with an explanation of your conduct? Speak in turn."

One by one, mumbling, the captives acknowledged that they had tried to seize the ship. Kerwin Jones, the ringleader, watched me warily.

"If you have any mitigating statements, give them now."

Their stories came tumbling out. When the supply ships stopped coming their fears had grown rampant. Wild rumors swept the mines. General Kall had done little to reassure them. They had no contact with the civilized world. Under intolerable pressure, they'd panicked.

I listened impassively. When they were done I said, "Having heard the evidence and mitigating statements I find you guilty of piracy and of the murders of a Naval officer, three enlisted men, and five passengers. For these crimes I sentence you to death at the Captain's convenience. Court adjourned."

Jones shouted at me, "You promised! You gave your word we wouldn't be killed!"

"I said no such thing."

"You swore it!"

"Darla, playback, please."

A second later my voice sounded on the speaker. "No, we won't shoot you. Not now, not ever. You have my word."

"Thank you, Darla. I'll keep my promise. We won't shoot you. Mr. Vishinsky, take these men back to the brig, then to the infirmary, one by one. Interrogate them to find who shot Mr. Wilsky."

Hours passed. Vax tried several times to speak to me; each time I ordered him silent. The Doctor finished her polygraph and drug interrogations. I issued my orders.

The master-at-arms, the Chief, Vax, and several seamen assembled at the plank across the fusion shaft. We faced six bound and gagged prisoners. I dispassionately pulled the dolly aside for each hanging. When the grisly task was done I dismissed the sailors.

One more chore.

"Mr. Holser, take the bridge. Chief, evacuate Level 2, sections six, seven, and eight, and post sentries to bar the corridor hatches to those sections. Mr. Vishinsky, come with me to the brig."

The seventh prisoner, the man who had lasered Sandy, paced helplessly, his hands bound behind him. "Mr. Vishinsky, wait here." My voice was dull.

"Aye aye, sir."

I took the prisoner's arm, led him out of the brig along the corridor, up the ladder to Level 2. The sentry at section eight saluted and stood aside. I propelled the captive into the deserted section. Then, past the bend in the corridor to the airlock.

I pressed my transmitter to the hatch control. The inner hatch slid open. I took the prisoner into the lock.

"What are you doing?" His face was wild.

I didn't answer. Holding his shoulder I kicked his leg out from under him. He slipped to the deck. I pushed him into a sitting position. Then I turned to the inner lock.

"No! God, don't!" He scrambled desperately to his feet. I stood in the hatchway. He ran at me.

I shoved him violently back; he sprawled on the airlock deck, hands cuffed behind him. I stepped out into the corridor and pressed my transmitter to the inner lock control. The hatch slid shut. In a frenzy, he threw himself against the transplex hatch, rebounding from its unyielding surface.

Again I brought my transmitter to the panel. I pressed the key. The outer lock slid open. I watched the grisly contents of the chamber swirl into space as the chamber decompressed.

After a few moments I walked slowly onto the bridge. "Fusion coordinates?"

"Here, sir." Alexi displayed them on his console. He swallowed several times, managed not to catch my eye.

"Darla?"

She flashed her figures. They matched.

"Engine room, prepare to Fuse."

In a moment, the reply. "Prepared to Fuse, sir. Control passed to bridge."

I slid my finger up the screen. The simulscreens blanked. "Mr. Holser, you have the watch." I slapped open the hatch, left the bridge.

I sealed my cabin hatch behind me. In the dim light I took off my jacket. I sat, my arms resting on the table. I began to tremble. Dispassionately I wondered how quickly I would go insane. Knowing I could not be heard I filled my lungs and screamed at the top of my voice. It left my throat raw.

I looked through the outer bulkhead along the hull. "Come, Mr. Tuak," I whispered. "I'm ready for you." I knew that this time he'd bring Sandy with him.

Part 2

November 20, in the year of our Lord 2195

21

October came, then November. I spent day after day alone in my cabin. Food was brought. Sometimes I ate it. Occasionally I stood watch; more often I removed myself from the watch roster. From time to time I sat at dinner with the passengers at the dining hall; more often, I couldn't bear the thought of their conversation and remained in my bunk.

Twice, Mr. Tuak came for me, but even in my dreams I was unafraid. He never pulled me through the bulkhead, and when I tried to follow him he stopped coming.

One day I went to the bridge and found Vax half asleep in his seat. He started when I stood over him, his eyes widening in shock and fear. "I'm sorry, sir," he stammered, "it's . . . I—" His face turned deep red.

"It's all right." I took my own seat. There were only four of us to stand watch, and by removing myself from the roster I'd left only three. No wonder he was exhausted. "I'll start taking my turn again." Day after day I endured the silence of the bridge until I was free to return to the solitude of my cabin.

On one of the rare evenings I appeared in the dining hall, I was accosted after the meal. "Captain, we'd like to talk to you." Rafe Treadwell, now turned thirteen. I presumed the "we" included his sister.

I took them to my cabin. Rafe spoke first, standing shoulder to shoulder with Paula. "Captain, you need midshipmen."

"You're telling me how to run my ship?" My tone was bleak.

"No, sir, just stating a fact," he said calmly. "When we sailed, you had three lieutenants, four midshipmen, and a Pilot. Now you have three midshipmen and a cadet. You need more help."

"You're volunteering?"

"No, sir, we decided someone ought to stay with Mom and Dad. Paula's the one who's volunteering."

"Oh?"

She said, "Yes, sir. I'm better at math, anyway."

"This isn't Academy, young lady. I can't raise children to be middies."

"You took Derek."

"He's sixteen, almost grown. You were thirteen just a few weeks ago."

"So? At my age we learn faster." She added, "When you took us to the bridge I knew right away. That's what I want to do."

"And your parents?"

"Oh, they're against it," she said blithely. "But they'll get over it."

"Would they consent?"

"Not in a million years," Rafe said. "But you don't need their consent. You told us so yourself."

I glowered at them, to no effect. I needed midshipmen; Vax was ready for lieutenant's insignia. And though he didn't know it, Alexi would soon be, too. But to shanghai children, as Mrs. Donhauser put it . . . I had enough problems without that. And we weren't that far from port, where I would be replaced. "Thank you, but no. Not without your parents' consent."

Paula's tone was flat. "You're afraid of my parents, Captain? I thought you weren't a coward."

I yearned to slap her. "Shut up, young lady."

"I will. If you don't have the guts to sign me up, I don't want to be under your command." She folded her arms.

That did it. She needed discipline as much as I needed midshipmen. An even trade; her parents be damned. "You're sure? You know what cadets go through?"

"I know." She looked worried for a moment, then shrugged. "If other joeys can take it, I can."

"It's harder for a girl. Not many women serve on ships."

"Lieutenant Dagalow did."

"Yes." Naval policy barred discrimination, and officially none existed, but wardroom life could nonetheless be particular hell for a woman. On the other hand, I knew Vax and Alexi well, and they wouldn't let hazing get too far out of hand.

"You two are willing to be separated?"

They exchanged glances; Rafe nodded slightly. Paula said, "We won't like it, but we're willing."

"Repeat after me," I said. "I, Paula Treadwell, do swear on my immortal soul . . ."

"I, Paula Treadwell . . ." A moment later I had another cadet.

She took the fifth bunk, in the center of the wardroom; Ricky Fuentes moved up to Sandy's bunk along the wall. The wardroom would remain crowded. Derek especially would learn new lessons about modesty in the Navy. I didn't really care. I was counting weeks and days, waiting for the end.

"Lord God, today is December 31, 2195, on the U.N.S. *Hibernia*. We ask you to bless us, to bless our voyage, and to bring health and well-being to all aboard." This time I remained standing. "Ladies and gentlemen, by the Grace of God it has been a tragic and trying year. Our friends and comrades, though absent, travel with us in spirit. I look forward, as do you, to landfall at Hope Nation, and on this last night of this fateful year I ask Lord God's especial blessing to heal the wounds occasioned by our misfortunes."

I sat. Grudgingly at first, they joined in the "Amen." When the last murmurs had subsided I signaled the steward to begin.

Only three now sat at my table. Mrs. Donhauser, Mr. Ibn Saud, and, of all people, Amanda Frowel. "Nicky, let me sit with you. What they're doing is unfair and wrong. I want to show I'm not a part of it."

It took courage for my three companions to stay with me. Jared and Irene Treadwell had gone nearly berserk after their daughter took the oath. At first they claimed I had no authority to enlist her. They invaded officers' country to reclaim her and had to be physically restrained. Then they circulated a petition demanding Paula's discharge which every single passenger signed, including the three who now sat with me. I didn't mind that, but when the Treadwells started circulating an appeal among the crew I'd had enough. I passed the word that any crewman who signed or even discussed a petition with them would spend the rest of the cruise in the brig, and sent the Chief to warn the Treadwells to leave the crew alone or they too would see the inside of a cell.

They disrupted evening meals and had to be physically ejected from the dining hall. Then came the day the Treadwells accosted Paula and forced her back to their cabin. Vax and a party of seamen had to dismantle their hatch to rescue the embarrassed cadet.

Their agitation continued until, a week ago, Rafe Treadwell was heard warning his parents that unless they let Paula be, he too would enlist. After that the Treadwells became more circumspect; perhaps they had learned something about their children's resolve.

I continued to make myself unbearable on the bridge. I drilled the midshipmen in navigation and pilotage without cease. I sent Derek to be caned for some impatience I detected in his tone, and ignored the simmering fury he exhibited for days afterward. I chewed out Alexi regularly until he was so agitated he could barely handle a watch. My off-duty hours were spent alone in my cabin; I had long since packaged the Chief's pipe and tobacco and sent them to him without comment.

One day I decided to give Alexi an unscheduled navigation drill. Our middies had to be more skillful than I was, should fate put the safety of a ship in their hands. I called the wardroom but no one answered. It was understandable that Alexi would be elsewhere; it was more unusual for no one to be there at all. Curious and suspicious, I sealed the bridge and went to look, shrugging off my serious breach of regulations in leaving the bridge unattended.

The three midshipmen and two cadets were nowhere to be found. I searched officers' country, the lounges, the exercise room. I checked the galley, the mess halls. I went down to crew quarters. I even peered into the engine room.

Convinced I had an intrigue on my hands, I prowled the ship trying to imagine where the middies might be. Were they conspiring in the hold beyond the launch berth? I passed through the lock to the empty berth. The hatch slid open. Shouts and laughter, in the dim standby lights.

"Look out!" An object sailed toward me. I ducked. It splattered on my chest, and I was drenched in icy water head to waist. I spluttered with rage.

In an instant I grasped the situation. Piles of water balloons lay about. The middies and cadets, wet uniforms sticking to their limbs, carried armfuls of missiles as they stalked each other.

"Oh, Lord God! The Captain!" The figures froze in horror.

IT DIDN'T HAPPEN! If I acknowledged what I saw, I would have to act. I didn't want to act, therefore it didn't happen. I would ignore it. I turned to leave, but the water squished in my shoe and my intent changed abruptly. I dialed down the light until the berth was nearly dark. "Hostile attack, Vax! I'm unarmed! Situation critical!"

It took him only a second to react. He lobbed a couple of water balloons at me. I caught them and rounded on the nearest middy, who happened to be Derek. "Surrender!" I caught him square in the face. He squawked and fell back, spitting ice water. I wheeled on Ricky, across the room. "Attack your betters, will you?" I stalked him.

Alexi was the first who was brave enough to fire at me intentionally. After that it degenerated into a wild melee that ended only after the huge piles of water balloons were exhausted. By that time all the middies and their Captain had turned on the two hapless cadets and bombarded them into submission from all sides.

I leaned against the bulkhead guffawing. After a while I feared I wouldn't be able to stop. I brought myself under control and faced the grinning middies. "What a breach of regs! For punishment I order you to mop the place up, every inch of it. Acknowledge!"

"Aye aye, sir!" They acknowledged my command with unfeigned delight. I began wondering how I might get to my cabin to change clothes without being seen. I wasn't aware yet that my funk had finally lifted and I could now face each day, if not cheerfully, then at least unafraid.

Once more, I began to take interest in my duties.

The Pilot asked again to see me. For months I had ignored his requests, but now I decided to evade him no longer. I went to his cabin. I hadn't laid eyes on him in four months; his appearance shocked me. Gaunt, his eyes red-rimmed and sunken, he came quickly to attention. I released him.

He licked his lips. "Now I'm finally talking to you I don't know how to begin." I waited uncomfortably. He turned away, hugged himself as if from cold. "Captain, if you don't restore me to duty before we dock, I'm finished. It—it's my life, the Navy. It's all I have."

He glanced at my face. "Jesus, how old are you, eighteen? How can you understand? Nothing's the same when you get older. Sounds aren't as sharp; the edges of your hearing have gone. Colors don't seem as bright. Even food doesn't taste as good. Nothing smells or tastes or feels as alive as when you were young, when you thought your mind would overload from the sheer pleasure of the sensations . . ." He trailed off, his eyes distant.

"I may not be a good officer—" He swallowed and began again. "Captain, I know I'm not a good officer, not really. But I'm good at pilotage. Very good." I nodded my acknowledgment.

"When I'm at the conn I feel the—aliveness again. I sense the instruments, the thrusters, through my fingers, with the intensity I could feel elsewhere when I was younger. Can you imagine what it is to face losing that? Please! I don't know how to beg, but I'm trying."

I couldn't stand much more of that; he sounded like the late Mr. Rogoff. "I'm not asking that, Mr. Haynes."

He said, "I can be a very good pilot. At the conn, that is. For the rest of it, I can try harder. If that's not good enough . . ." He broke off. "I'm too old to start at something else. For the love of Lord God, Captain, don't leave me to rot!"

"Those protests in the Log? Telling us middies to be quiet because we distracted you?"

He whispered the words. "Arrogance. I can't afford it anymore.

When you get down to it, this is all I am." His eyes glistened. "I sail starships. I manuever, I dock, I plot courses, calculate positions. I can live without my pettiness and my arrogance—oh, God, I'll have to—but I can't live without that!"

"You've been thinking a great deal, Mr. Haynes."

"I don't want to live, if I can't be a pilot." He swallowed. "Please," he said, his tone humble. "Give me back my life. I'll mind my own business, I swear. No protests, no remarks, no looks of disgust. I've learned what matters. Pilotage is important. Nothing else."

I was moved. "We don't like each other, Mr. Haynes. That can't be helped. But we don't have to. Very well. Your rank is restored. I'll put you back on the watch roster. We'll see how it goes."

He closed his eyes in relief. "Thank you," he whispered. Bile rose in my throat. I had broken him. I felt unbearably ashamed.

22

In a few days we would Defuse for our final navigation check before arrival at Hope Nation.

I was running out of time; there was one more thing I had to do before I turned over command to my replacement. On afternoon watch, I assembled the officers on the bridge. Chief McAndrews, the Pilot, the midshipmen, and the cadets waited, perplexed. I called Vax Holser forward. He stood stiffly at attention as I faced him.

"Darla, record these proceedings." Her recorders lit. "Mr. Holser, step forward. I, Captain Nicholas Seafort, do commission Midshipman Vax Stanley Holser to the Naval Service of the Government of the United Nations"—thunderstruck, his face lit with unalloyed joy—"and do appoint him lieutenant, by the Grace of God."

It was done. My own rank as Captain was subject to confirmation or revocation by Admiral Johanson, but the commissions and appointments I made were not. Unlike the old oceanic navy, field commissions were permanent. Admiralty would accept Vax's lieutenancy regardless of its wisdom. To do less would cast doubt on a Captain's boundless authority under weigh.

Vax, grinning foolishly, accepted the handshakes and congratulations of the other officers. I noticed Alexi's bemused expression. It must have occurred to him that he'd just become first midshipman, in charge of the wardroom.

The new lieutenant took the cadets to help carry his gear to his cabin. It was a relaxed moment; the rest of us chatted before dispersing. "Well, Mr. Carr." My tone was genial. "Are you planning to challenge your new senior?"

His look was cool. "Perhaps, sir. If occasion warrants." My smile faded. He wasn't about to forgive me for sending him to the barrel in a moment of irritation. I wondered if I could make amends. Probably not. Derek could forgive much, but not that unjustified humiliation.

A few days later I brought the ship out of Fusion. Alexi plotted our position and ran the coordinates for our last jump, under the Pilot's watchful eye. Mr. Haynes said little. When the figures were presented I laboriously recalculated everything from scratch. It was a good day; I

finished in less than half an hour. At last, all our figures matched. We
Fused again.

Alexi relaxed with a sigh of relief.

"Not so fast, Mr. Tamarov." I indicated the screens. "Darla, simulate Hope Nation approach, please." I thumbed the caller. "Chief, simulated Defuse and maneuvers. Middy drill." I turned back to the midshipman. "Alexi, bring the ship out of Fusion and dock her." I had failed
miserably at the same maneuver eons ago under the tutelage of Captain
Haag and Lieutenant Dagalow.

"Aye aye, sir." Alexi studied the console. "Engine room, prepare to
Defuse." With confidence, he ran his finger down the screen. My envy
grew as I watched him work easily through the complicated maneuver,
firing his auxiliary engines, maneuvering to mate with Orbit Station. At
the finish he tapped lightly on the braking thrusters, and the airlocks
gently kissed. In simulation we were at rest, mated to Orbit Station.

If it weren't for a barely perceptible sheen of sweat on his forehead
I'd have thrown him bodily off the bridge.

"Very well, Mr. Tamarov. That's all." As he started to rise I reluctantly gave him his due. "Alexi, a fine job. Very good."

He grinned with pleasure. "Thank you, sir. Thanks very much!"

"How do you like being first middy?"

"I like it a lot," Alexi said. Then he added shyly, "I'm trying to be
like you were, sir."

At first I felt a pleasant glow. Then my anger rose. Why in the name
of heaven would he want to be like me?

An air of excitement, a feeling of goodwill, pervaded the ship; our
interminable voyage was finally nearing an end. All that remained was to
Defuse at the rim of Hope Nation system and maneuver to Orbit Station. Then, disembarkation.

Most of the passengers had a good idea what awaited them; they'd
planned their trip for years and had careers, prospects, opportunities
already arranged. I wondered what my future held. A court of inquiry,
certainly, and probably a court-martial; the deaths of crew and passengers and the invasion of my ship made it a near certainty.

I wondered if I'd ever see deep space again. On the other hand, it
didn't much matter. I'd come to know I had no gift for command. My
hitch would be up by the time I was sent back to Luna, once again a
midshipman.

I didn't intend to reenlist. It was one thing to contemplate life in
space as a successful career officer in the star fleet; it was quite another

to pass my life in a dead-end berth as a midshipman. Well, I was ahead of myself. Who knew if they'd even let me remain a middy? There was Sandy Wilsky to account for, along with my other follies.

Evening meals in the dining hall were almost jolly. Several passengers asked to join the Captain's table; I preferred to dine with the few who had sat with me through my isolation. Amanda and I didn't confide as once we had, but she was civil and occasionally even smiled.

Poor Amanda. The same unyielding rectitude that had forced her to abandon me also made her side with me to protest the other passengers' ingratitude. By her lights I had saved the ship, not almost lost it. She was a victim of her skewed sense of justice.

The night before our final Defuse she waited outside the dining hall. "Nick, I don't want to leave it . . . like this." Her voice was gentle. "With the strain between us."

Being close to her made me uncomfortable; I moved back a step. "I'm still a murderer. Even more now than before."

She blushed. "Yes, I said that, and I suppose I still mean it. But people are more complex than I was willing to admit. You did what you thought you must, and you're still Nick Seafort."

I said coldly, "Thank you. There were times when I wondered."

"Oh, Nicky." She put her hand on my arm. "It must have been horrible."

"I've been"—I thought of putting her off, then chose honesty—"very lonely. Sometimes."

"I'm sorry. I wish you well."

"That's all that's left?" Wounded, I turned to go. She still had the power to hurt.

"I do care for you!" she cried to my retreating back. I stopped. "How I wish it could have been different, Nicky. I missed you too!"

"But it wasn't." I managed a small smile. "I wish you well also, Amanda. Good-bye."

"Come see me in Hope Nation," she said impulsively. "You'll be in port for weeks." After cruising interstellar for more than six months, crew and officers alike were entitled to four weeks of shore leave. The regs were firm on that, and I agreed. Our men were enlistees, not prisoners.

I nodded assent. "All right. I'll look you up." If I wasn't under arrest pending court-martial. On that note we parted.

The next morning I had the watch, with Lieutenant Vax Holser. The Pilot was also present, waiting for his moment.

"Bridge to engine room, prepare to Defuse."

"Prepare to Defuse, aye aye." Chief McAndrews was ready, as always. "Engine room ready for Defuse, sir. Control passed to bridge."

"Passed to bridge, aye aye." I traced the line on the screen from "Full" to "Off." Once again the simulscreens came alive with a blaze of lights.

"Confirm clear of encroachments, Lieutenant." Whenever possible I used Vax's title rather than his name, to help him settle in.

"Clear of encroachments, sir."

"Plot position, please, Lieutenant." I noticed the Pilot quietly doing likewise. He would not dock *Hibernia* under someone else's calculations. After a few minutes the two men checked their coordinates with each other and with Darla.

"Auxiliary engine power, Chief," I said.

"Aye aye, sir. Power up."

"Pilot Haynes." My tone was formal. "You have the conn."

"Aye aye, sir. Steer oh three five degrees, ahead one-third."

"One-third, aye aye, sir." Our last jump had placed us within a few hours of Hope Nation and its Orbit Station. The planet gleamed bright and welcoming in our simulscreens, bringing a lump to my throat.

The watch changed, but I remained on the bridge, my thoughts fastened on what might have been.

Hours later, my long reverie was interrupted. "Sir, Orbit Station reports locks ready and waiting." The comm room.

"Confirm ready and waiting, understood." The Pilot was busy at his console.

"Relative speed two hundred ten kilometers per hour, sir." Vax, to the Pilot.

"Two hundred ten, understood. Maneuvering jets, brake ten."

I picked up my caller. "Comm room, patch me to Orbit Station."

A pause. "Go ahead, sir, you're patched through."

"*Hibernia* calling Orbit Station."

"This is approach control; go ahead, *Hibernia.*"

I said, "Identify yourself, please: name, rank, and serial number."

"What?" The rating's astonishment was evident.

Pilot Haynes shot me a glance. After a moment the corner of his mouth turned up. He nodded grudgingly.

"You heard me. Identify yourself."

"Communications Specialist First Class Thomas Leeman, U.N.A.F. 205-066-254."

"Darla, serial number check, please."

A moment's pause. "Prefix 205 is interstellar rating; suffix 254 notates communications specialist. 066 within valid ID ranges."

"Who is your commanding officer, Mr. Leeman?"

"General Duc Twan Tho, sir."

"I'd like to speak to him." I turned off the caller. "Darla, his file, please."

Another pause. Then, "General Tho here. What's the problem?"

"Visuals, please, General." Once burned, twice shy.

"What nonsense is this?" His glowering visage came onto my screen. "Are you satisfied?"

He matched the picture Darla projected overhead. "Quite. Thank you. We'll be docking shortly."

"You identify yourself too, *Hibernia!*" He was within his rights. My request appeared ridiculous, and he was returning the favor.

"Captain Nicholas Seafort commanding, U.N.N.S. 205-387-0058."

After a moment he said warily, "I'd like to speak to Captain Haag."

"Captain Haag is dead of an accident. I am senior officer aboard."

"Visuals, please."

I switched on my video.

"My God, how old are you?"

"Eighteen."

"You were a lieutenant?"

"No, a midshipman." I let him chew on that awhile. There was no further communication.

Pilot Haynes carefully edged the ship closer to the station until the airlocks gently made contact. "Stop all engines."

"Stop engines, aye aye, sir."

"Join capture latches, fore and aft."

"Forward latches engaged, sir."

"Aft latches engaged, sir." Vax, from his station at the aft airlock.

"Begin mooring, Lieutenant. Open inner locks." Below-decks, a suited rating pressed his coded transmitter to the lock control. As the thick transplex hatches opened, the indicator light on my screen flashed.

"Inner lock ready aft, sir."

"Open outer lock. Secure mooring line. Pressurization check."

A pause, while the seaman labored under Vax's watchful eye. "Line secured, sir. Pressure maintained one sea-level atmosphere."

"How does it look, Mr. Holser?"

"Peaceful, sir."

"Very well, open inner lock." I sagged. I'd given my last significant order. Though still nominally under my command, *Hibernia* was controlled now by the station commandant.

I thumbed the caller. "Mr. Leeman, patch me to Admiralty groundside, please. And I'll want transport as soon as possible."

"No problem, Captain," growled General Tho. He'd stayed on the line. Well, our arrival had been unusual, to say the least.

Clicks and beeps from the speaker. "Admiralty House."

"Commander U.N.S. *Hibernia* reporting. I'd like your senior duty officer, please."

Faint static swirled through the line. "That will be Captain Forbee, sir. One moment." I waited, my tension growing. The ordeal I faced wouldn't be pleasant.

"Forbee."

"Captain Nicholas Seafort reporting, sir. U.N.S. *Hibernia.*"

"Justin Haag was scheduled for this run, sir."

"Captain Haag died interstellar, sir. I'm senior officer."

"Can you come to Admiralty House or shall I come up?" Odd, coming from a groundside commander. An Admiral and his staff didn't go visiting, they summoned.

"I'll be down as soon as the station gives me a shuttle, sir. I'll bring the Log."

"Very good, Captain." We broke the connection.

I went back to my cabin. I debated dress whites and decided against them; they would impress no one. I rummaged in my duffel for my unused wallet, checked to see that it still held money. As I'd be going shoreside I pinned my length of service medals to my uniform front, made sure my shoes were well shined.

On Level 2, passengers milled about the aft airlock for a look at the station, though they wouldn't begin to disembark for hours. I went to the forward lock, where crews were already off-loading our cargo. Holovid in hand, I straightened my uniform and clambered through the lock.

"This way, Captain Seafort." An enlisted man led me through the unfamiliar wide gleaming corridors and hatches of Orbit Station to the Commandant's office. The design of the station was much like our disk, though larger in all respects. Higher ceilings, wider corridors, larger compartments.

Hundreds of people worked and lived in this busy shipping center. Cargo for Detour, Miningcamp, and Earth was transshipped through Orbit Station. Passengers disembarked here, before boarding other vessels to travel onward. Small shuttles journeyed back and forth daily to the planet's surface. A typical orbiting facility for our interstellar Naval liners.

"I'm General Tho." A small man, with a neat mustache above thin lips, and a receding hairline emphasized by wavy black hair. He eyed me dubiously. "You command *Hibernia?*"

"Yes." I matched his abruptness with my own.

"Your shuttle will be ready in a few minutes." After a moment he unbent perceptibly. "What happened to your officers?"

I sighed. I'd have to repeat the tale often enough. I explained.

When I was finished he shook his head. "Good Lord, man."

"Yes. That's why I want to report to the Admiral right off."

His reply was cut short by the corporal who appeared in the doorway. "Shuttle is ready, sir."

He shrugged. "Better go, Captain. I put you ahead of the passenger buses."

"Thank you." I followed the corporal down three levels, to a shuttle launch berth. It was similar in layout to *Hibernia*'s launch berth, though on a far larger scale. It was designed to receive the great airbuses that shuttled passengers to and from the surface.

I grinned to myself; if I'd required Vax to polish this berth, he'd have marched right out the airlock. My grin faded; I recalled another man leaving an airlock, by my act. Sickened, I closed my eyes.

The shuttle was a sporty little six-seater with retractable wings, its jet and vacuum engines sharing the available bow space. I ducked and climbed aboard.

"Buckle up, Captain." The pilot wore a casual jumpsuit and a removable helmet. He strapped himself in securely, more concerned with atmospheric turbulence than decompression. I followed his example. He flipped switches and checked instruments with the ease of long familiarity, waiting for the launch berth to depressurize.

"Lots of traffic these days?" I asked, mostly to make conversation.

"Some. More before the sickness." He keyed his caller. "Departure control, Alpha Fox 309 ready to launch."

"Just a moment." In a few moments the voice returned. "Cleared to launch, 309." The shuttle bay's huge hatches slid open. Hope Nation glistened through the abyss, green and inviting.

Our propellant drummed against the berth's protective shields as the shuttle glided out of the bay. Once clear of the dock the pilot throttled our engines to full. We shot ever faster from the station, approaching Hope Nation at an oblique angle until we encountered the outer wisps of atmosphere. The pilot hummed a tune I couldn't recognize as

he flipped levers, eyes his radars, swung the ship around with short
bursts of his positioning jets to be ready to fire the retro rockets.

I asked loudly, "What did you mean, before the sickness?" The first
buffets of atmospheric turbulence rumbled the hull.

The pilot spared me a glance. "Didn't you hear? We had an epidemic a while back, but it's under control now." He set the automatic
counter, his hand poised to fire the engines manually if the puter didn't
turn them on.

"What kind of—"

"Not now. Wait!" The pilot's full attention was on the puter's
readout. The retro engines caught with a roar at the exact moment the
counter hit zero. His hand relaxed. "You never know about these little
shipboard jobs!" He had to shout over the increasing din. "Not reliable
like the mainframes you joes travel with!"

As we descended, Hope Nation lost its spherical shape. Ground
features emerged through scattered layers of clouds. Here and there I
could spot a checkerboard of cultivated fields, though most of the planet
seemed lush and verdant.

Though I'd expected something of the sort, still I marveled at the
sight of a planet so many light-years from home, whose ecology was
carbon-based like our own. Hope Nation's trees and plants supplied no
proteins or carbohydrates we could digest, but they grew side by side
with our imported stock.

No native animals, of course. No nonterrestrial animals had ever
been found, other than the primitive boneless fish of Zeta Psi.

"Sorry," the pilot shouted over the engine noise. "What were you
saying?"

"What kind of epidemic did you have?"

"Some sort of mutated virus. It killed a lot of people before we
found a vaccine. I don't know much about it, except everyone gets a shot
when they put down at Centraltown."

"Is that where we're landing?"

"Of course. All arrivals from the station go there. Customs, quarantine, everything's at Centraltown."

"Right. Of course." I'd looked it up, but it was hard to digest a
whole culture in an hour of holovid.

"Say, how'd you get to be a Captain, anyway?"

I sighed. It was going to be a long shore leave.

A few minutes later he deftly flipped the shuttle into glide mode
and rode her above the flat plain toward the seacoast skirting the spar-

kling waters ahead. The jet engines kicked in a moment after the flipabout, making us a jet-powered aircraft.

Naturally, the pilot spotted the runway long before I did. After all it was his home turf. The shuttle's stubby wings shifted into VTOL mode as we bled off speed. The pilot timed our arrival over the runway perfectly; we were almost stationary as he dropped us gently onto the tarmac, the shuttle's underbelly jets cushioning our fall.

"Welcome to Hope Nation, Navy!" He gave me a smile as he killed the engines. "And good luck."

"I'll need it." I opened the hatch and climbed down, straightening to take my first breath of air in another solar system. It smelled clean and fragrant, with a scent I couldn't quite place, like fresh herbs in some exotic dish. The sun, a G2 type, shone brightly, perhaps a bit more yellow than our own.

I gawked like a groundsider on his first Lunapolis vacation. My step was light and springy, a result of Hope Nation's point nine two Earth gravity. The planet was actually twelve percent larger than Earth but considerably less dense.

My Naval ID took me through customs with no fuss. The quarantine shed was a ramshackle structure just off the runway, between the ships and a cluster of buildings. The nurse was friendly and efficient; I bared my arm; he touched the inoculation gun to my forearm and it was done.

I felt for my wallet. On this planet I was a greenhorn. I had no idea where I was going or how to get there but I assumed my U.N. currency would solve the problem. "How do I get to Admiralty House?"

"Well . . ." The nurse squinted into the bright afternoon sunlight. "You could walk over to that terminal building there, go through to the other side, and rent an electricar. If they have one left, that is, there's only seven. Then you turn left at the end of the drive, go to the first light, and turn left again and go two blocks."

"Thanks." I started to walk away.

"Or you could walk across the runway to that building over there. That's Admiralty House." He gestured to a two-story building seventy yards away.

"Oh." I felt foolish. Then I grinned in appreciation; he must have perfected his routine on a lot of novices. "Thanks again." I started across the runway, holovid in hand.

Now I wished I'd chosen to wear my dress whites, but I realized I was being silly. Stevin Johanson, Admiral Commanding at Hope Nation

Base, wasn't about to be impressed by dress whites adorning a fumbling ex-midshipman.

An iron fence surrounded the large cement block structure. I unlatched the gate; a well-worn path across the unmowed yard led me to the front of the building. The winged-anchor Naval emblem and the words "United Nations Naval Service/Admiralty House" greeted me from a brass plaque anchored to the porch post.

Had the brass plate been smelted here, or had they shipped the sign across light-years of emptiness to add majesty to the facade of colonial Naval headquarters?

At the tall wooden doors with glass inserts at the top of the porch steps, I tucked at the corners of my uniform and brushed my hands through my hair. I took a deep breath, and went in.

A young man in shore whites was dictating into a puter at a console in the lobby. "Can I help you, sir?"

"Nicholas Seafort, *Hibernia*, reporting to Admiral Johanson."

"Oh, yes, we were expecting you; General Tho called ahead. Captain Forbee will see you now." He led me up red-carpeted stairs, along a hall to an office with open windows overlooking the sunny field. "Captain Seafort, sir."

I came to attention. "Nicholas Seafort reporting, sir. Senior officer aboard *Hibernia.*"

The young Captain behind the desk stood quickly and saluted. He squinted from weak, puzzled eyes. A youngish man, who'd started running to fat. "Shall we stand down, then?" It was an odd way to release me, but perhaps colonial customs were different. We relaxed. He indicated a seat.

"Thank you. Will I be reporting to you or directly to Admiral Johanson?"

He gave me a sad smile. "Admiral Johanson died in the epidemic."

"Died, sir?" I sat. So much death . . .

'He caught the virus. One day he just dropped, like everyone else who had it."

"Good Lord!" I could think of nothing else to say.

"Yes." He looked unhappy. "So I've been running the Naval station. I sent word on the last ship out. It'll be two years before his replacement arrives."

"Very well, sir. I'll report to you. I'm sorry I'm not better organized, but most of it is in the Log." Afraid he'd stop me before I could get the whole sordid tale off my chest, I let my words tumble, summarizing what had happened aboard *Hibernia*. I spared myself nothing, glad now to have it over with. "Captain Haag's loss and the lieutenants' deaths were an act of Lord God," I finished. "But I take full responsibility for the deaths of Midshipman Wilsky, the seamen, and the passengers."

He was silent a long time. "Terrible," he said.

"Yes, sir."

"But you don't know the half of it." He stood and came around from behind the desk to where I sat, cap on my knee. He bent and peered at my length of service medals. As if to confirm my story, he asked, "When did you say your last lieutenant died?"

"March 12, 2195, sir."

"That's in the Log?"

"Yes, sir." I slipped the chip into my holovid, handed it across to him.

He sat at his desk, flipped through the entries until he came to the month of March. He shook his head as he reached the relevant passages. "It wasn't June, was it? You became Captain in March."

"Yes, sir," I said, puzzled.

"That's it, then." Captain Forbee turned to look out the window. Facing away he said, "Hope Nation is still a small colony. We don't have much of a Naval Station. No interstellar ships are based here; we're not big enough to warrant it. Admiral Johanson was a caretaker with seniority in case it might someday be needed; to resolve a dispute between two captains, for instance. Or to appoint a replacement in case a Captain died or was too ill to sail."

"Yes, sir."

"He had three Captains in system. One of them, Captain Grone— it's an embarrassing incident, we did our best to hush it up—he went native almost a year ago. He and his fiancée stole a helicopter and flew to the Ventura Mountains. Disappeared. We've never been able to find them. An unstable type, a lot of us thought. The second is Captain Marceau, from *Telstar*. Sixteen years seniority."

Good. He or Forbee would replace me. My nightmare was over. "Where is he, sir?"

"The bloody fool had to go cliff-climbing on his shore leave. Six months, and he's still in coma. Admiral Johanson gave *Telstar* to Captain Eaton last spring. They sailed to Detour, then headed for Miningcamp and Earth."

"They never reached Miningcamp."

"Yes, your Log makes that clear." He sighed. "Eaton's a reliable man. If he bypassed Miningcamp, he must have a reason."

If that's what he did, I thought silently. If Darla was glitched, how many other puters were, as well? I put aside the thought. "Sir, how many officers here are rated interstellar?"

He shook his head gloomily. "I said you didn't know the half of it. Nobody. We have interplanetary Captains, of course, but why would anyone rated interstellar stay in this backwater?"

"You could go yourself, sir. *Hibernia* needs a real Captain."

"I told you we had no one, Mr. Seafort. You know how I came to Hope Nation? I shipped out as a lieutenant. My wife Margaret was among the passengers. I timed it so my hitch was up and I could resign my commission when we docked. I've been a civilian for seven years, but after Admiral Johanson sent Eaton with *Telstar,* he reenlisted me so there'd be someone on staff who'd been interstellar."

Did Forbee expect me to solve his problems for him? "You could appoint my lieutenant—I mean, my first lieutenant—as Captain, sir, and then relieve me."

He stood tiredly. "You still don't understand. Admiral Johanson gave me Captain's rank at my reenlistment. To be precise, on June 6, 2195. Sir."

"No!" I stumbled to my feet, overturning my chair. It was as if Seaman Tuak had shambled through the hatch, when at last I'd imagined myself safe.

"Yes, sir. You're senior officer in Hope Nation system."

23

I sat despondent while evening darkened outside the window, unnoticed.

We'd been over the regs a dozen times. I couldn't find an escape. "Governor Williams—"

"Is a civilian, sir. He doesn't have jurisdiction over the Navy." Captain Forbee must have studied every line of the regs as I had, hoping to escape his unwanted responsibility. The relief he'd have felt when he found I had more interstellar time as Captain than he . . . "Governor Williams can no more appoint a Captain than you can set local speed limits," he added.

"You made your point!" Abashed, I lowered my voice. "I can resign."

"Yes, sir. Nobody can stop you." He'd said it correctly. Resigning for any reason except disabling physical illness or injury, or mental illness, was dereliction of duty. The regs I'd sworn to uphold required me to exert authority and control of the government of my vessel until relieved by order of superior authority, until my death, or until certification of my disability.

But no one could stop me from violating my oath.

"I won't put up with this!" I glared at Forbee. "Someone in Hope Nation system must be rated interstellar, damn it!" I was so frustrated I skirted blasphemy without caring.

"I'm afraid not, sir. Believe me, I've looked."

"You have captains with interplanetary ratings. Any of them would be senior to me."

"In service time, yes, sir. But any Captain Interstellar is senior to a Captain Interplanetary. Surely you know that."

"Don't tell me what I know!" I snapped.

"I'm sorry, sir." His tone was placating.

We sat in silence. At length I said, "*Hibernia* can't sail with me at the helm. That's too dangerous. And if *Telstar*'s missing, she may never have even made Detour; we must sail. Our supplies would be needed there more than ever."

Forbee folded his arms. "I agree."

"Will you search for *Telstar?*"

He looked surprised. "That's for you to decide, sir. You're in charge."

I stood, fists bunched.

"You're senior," he blurted. "I can't help it. The naval station is under your command."

"Of all the . . . I'll—by Lord God—" With an effort I brought my speech under control. "These are my instructions: run the naval station exactly as you would if I hadn't arrived! Is that clear?"

"Yes, sir. Aye aye, sir!"

"Are you going to search for *Telstar*, Forbee?" I was too put out to use his rank.

"We have nothing to send after her, sir. None of our local ships have fusion drive." That was that. Search and rescue were impossible.

We couldn't just ignore the fact that *Telstar* was missing. Word had to be sent back to Admiralty at Luna, but *Hibernia* was the next ship scheduled to return—in fact, the only fusion vessel in the system. My mind spun. That meant I had to—

Enough was enough. "By Lord God, I'll resign!"

"Will you, sir?" His voice was without inflection.

"Yes. Right now. Give me my Log; I'll write it in." It was time to free myself from this madness. If Admiralty tried me for dereliction of duty, so be it; at least I'd kill no more passengers and crew by my stupidity. If the regs required me to remain Captain, the regs were wrong. I would follow my conscience.

I keyed the holovid to the end of the most recent entry, tapped the keys. "I, Nicholas Ewing Seafort, Captain, do hereby res—" I halted, the hairs raising on my neck. Slowly, I turned, called by the familiar touch of Father's breath as he watched me struggle with my lessons.

Day after day, in the cold dreary Welsh afternoons, I worked my way through the texts, struggling to master new words and ideas, scrawling answers into the worn notebooks he bade me use. When I was right he gave me another problem. When I made a mistake he said only, "That's wrong, Nicholas," and handed me back the page to find my errors, waiting patiently behind my chair until I did.

One day I'd dropped my smudged assignment on the table and cried bitterly, "Of course it's wrong! I always do it wrong!" He spun me around, slapped me hard, swung my chair to the table, and thrust the lesson book into my hands. He'd said not a word. Blinking back tears I worked, my cheek smarting, until I got it right. After, he gave me another problem.

Now, in Forbee's office, nobody was behind my chair, the breath I'd felt but a wisp of breeze. I shivered, shook off my memories, and turned back to the holovid. "—do hereby resign my commission, effective immediately." I put the point of the pencil to the screen to sign below the entry.

Time passed.

After a while the pencil fell from my fingers, rolled unheeded to the floor.

I couldn't do it. I knew right from wrong; though Father wasn't watching, he might as well have been. *"I, Nicholas Ewing Seafort, do swear upon my immortal soul to preserve and protect the Charter of the General Assembly of the United Nations, to give loyalty and obedience for the term of my enlistment to the Naval Service of the United Nations, and to obey all its lawful orders and regulations, so help me Lord God Almighty."* I'd administered the selfsame oath to Paula Treadwell and to Derek Carr. I was prepared to hang them should they break their pledge. I could not violate it myself.

Still, for a brief moment, my resolution wavered. Was my self-respect worth risking *Hibernia* and her crew? Was even my immortal soul worth that? In the distance, Father waited for my reply. I will—he'd made me promise—let them destroy me before I swear to an oath I will not fulfill. My oath is all that I am.

I covered my face, ashamed of my tears. When I'd brought myself under control I put down my dampened arm, blinked in the sudden light.

I erased the entry. Captain Forbee sat motionless.

"I'm sorry. Very sorry."

He nodded as if he understood.

"We won't speak of it again." My embarrassment was painful, but no more than I deserved. "I'm going back to my ship. Carry on victualing and off-loading. Report only if it's necessary." I stood.

"Aye aye, sir." He got to his feet when I did. "If there's anything I can do to help . . ."

"I need experienced officers. I don't care where you get them. Find me at least two more lieutenants."

"Aye aye, sir." As I left the room he picked up his caller. "Get a shuttle ready for the Commander at Admiralty House."

Two hours later I strode through the mated airlocks onto *Hibernia*. Vax Holser, waiting at the hatch, fell into step beside me. "Are you all right, sir?" His manner was anxious. "Did they accept your report?"

"I'm fine." I started up the ladder to Level 1.

"Will they call a court of inquiry?"

"No."

"Do you know who'll replace you, sir?"

Why did he insist on goading me? "Mr. Holser, your duties are elsewhere. Get out from underfoot and stay out!"

Vax stopped short, shock and hurt evident. "Aye aye, sir." Quickly he turned away. I strode onto the bridge. Dejected, I slumped in my armchair. Vax had been worried for me, but I'd turned on him with savage anger. Would I ever learn? How often could I lash out without turning him back into a cold, unfeeling bully?

The crew's leave roster, prepared by the Chief, awaited my approval. I signed it. During *Hibernia's* mandatory thirty-day layover on Hope Nation the entire crew would be shuttled groundside, except for a few maintenance personnel whose shifts were rotated to provide the maximum leave. At least one officer would remain on board at all times, although he wasn't required to stand watch.

By now all the passengers had disembarked, even those who were going on to Detour.

"Mr. Tamarov to the bridge." I replaced the caller and waited. A few moments later Alexi appeared. "You're on duty rotation the third week," I told him. "That means you have two weeks off starting today, and another week at the end."

"Aye aye, sir!" His eyes sparkled with excitement and anticipation.

"Just one thing." His grin vanished. "As senior middy, you're in charge of the cadets. I'm not holding them aboard the ship and we can't turn Ricky and Paula loose in a strange colony unsupervised. Take them with you and keep an eye on them."

"Aye aye, sir."

He looked so crestfallen I offered a little cheer. "I didn't mean at every minute, Alexi. You can still go out on the town. Either take them with you or bunk them down before you go. Just bring them back to the ship unharmed."

He brightened. "Aye aye, sir. When are you going down, sir?"

"Tomorrow."

"Will I see you before you're transferred out?" A natural assumption; a new Captain wouldn't want his predecessor looking over his shoulder. I'd have been reassigned to another ship until the next interstellar vessel arrived.

"You'll see me," I growled, suddenly anxious to be rid of him. "Dismissed."

I sat in my leather armchair on the silent bridge. Eventually, I realized there was no reason to stay. I wandered down to Level 2, where parties of sailors clustered around the airlock, laughing and joking, awaiting dismissal. To avoid passing them I went back up the ladder. I strolled past the wardroom, past Vax's cabin, formerly Ms. Dagalow's. I stopped in front of Lieutenant Malstrom's quarters. For a moment I had an urge to go in and set up the chessboard.

My friend floated forever in empty space, while I had reached safe haven in Hope Nation. I recalled our mutual plans and promises. The drink I would buy him, the trip we would take to the Ventura Mountains. My eyes stung. I resolved to do those things for him. I would take a shuttle groundside in the morning. I'd go into the first bar I saw and order an asteroid on the rocks. Then I'd check on transportation and arrange a trip across the sea to the Venturas.

On the way back to my cabin I realized how lonely my leave would be. I hesitated for a moment, swore under my breath, turned back to the wardroom. I knocked.

Ricky opened, stiffening to attention.

"Carry on, all of you."

He and Paula Treadwell were packing their duffels, clothing strewn across their beds. Derek Carr, his duffel ready, sat on his bunk waiting for the call to the shuttle.

"Mr. Carr, a word with you, please." I took him out to the corridor. He listened, obedient but aloof. "I thought—that is, I'm going on a journey, uh, for sentimental reasons. To the Ventura Mountains. Someone was going to take me there once." Once more I hesitated, afraid to open myself. "I thought perhaps you might like to come along as my guest."

"Thank you, Captain," he said, his voice cool. "I have other plans. I'm visiting my father's plantations, and then I'll see Centraltown. My regrets, sir." I heard the message behind his words. Derek could take anything he set his mind to, as he'd proven, but that didn't mean he would forgive me for the undeserved humiliation of the barrel the day I'd lost my temper. I'd never be pardoned for that, not by a boy with his pride.

"Very well, Mr. Carr. Enjoy yourself." I turned away.

"Thank you, Captain," he said to my retreating back. He added, "You too." It made me feel a little better.

Early the next morning, *Hibernia* bore an eerie resemblance to the wreck of *Celestina*. Lights gleamed in deserted corridors. No sound broke the stillness. Somewhere on board—probably in his cabin—was the Chief, serving the first week's rotation, but most of the crew had departed, except a galley hand and a few maintenance ratings.

I shouldered my duffel and crossed through the airlocks, strode along the busy corridors of the station to the Commandant's small office.

"May I help you, sir?" A corporal looked up from his puter.

"I'd like a shuttle groundside."

"Yes, sir. Just a moment, please." Within moments I was ushered into General Tho's office. He was distinctly more cordial than on my prior visit.

"You might as well wait here, Captain, while the shuttle is prepped. Coffee?" I joined him for a cup and chatted until the craft was ready. As I left he said, "If there's anything further I can do, let me know." His manner suggested we were senior officers exchanging courtesies. I supposed we were.

The shuttle was much larger than the one on which I'd first gone ashore, but I was the only passenger; apparently the small launch wasn't available and General Tho had decided not to make me wait. I had a different pilot, less interested in conversation.

Groundside once more, I inhaled several lungsful of clean fresh air under the bright morning sun. The temperature was warm and pleasant; at this latitude Hope Nation had long summers and mild winters at sea level. One of Hope Nation's two moons was dimly visible overhead. It appeared slightly larger than did Luna from Earth's surface.

I decided not to check in with Admiralty House. If Forbee had any news he'd have called. If I showed up now, he would dump onto me decisions he could make himself. I went directly to the terminal building and out the other side, as I'd been directed earlier by the quarantine nurse.

A giant screen anchored to a metal pole greeted me. "Welcome to Centraltown, Population 89,267." I watched for a few moments, wondering how often the number changed. According to the guidebook the screen was tied directly to the puters at Centraltown Hospital; each birth and death were reflected within moments on the welcome sign. Centraltown was the largest, and virtually the only, city on Hope Nation; the remainder of the colony's two hundred thousand population was spread among several small towns and the many outlying plantations that justified the colony's existence.

I had imagined raw dirt roads, fresh cuts in the hills, ramshackle buildings set around a primitive main street. Disappointed, I had to remind myself that Hope Nation was opened back in 2081, over a century past. Since then, a massive influx of materials and settlers had been absorbed.

The roads were paved and modern, and seemed clean compared to the crowded and filthy streets of Earth's great cities. I peered down the main avenue. Clusters of buildings lined the street south toward Centraltown, but a few blocks in the other direction the road disappeared into hills rife with uncultivated vegetation.

I spotted the car rental agency at the end of the terminal building. In no particular hurry I sauntered to the entry. "Knock loud and come in," read the sign tacked to the door. Inside, a tiny waiting room, with a counter. I banged on the desk.

A young woman popped from behind a curtain leading to the back. "Hi, you must be from *Hibernia*." She seemed about twenty. Long brown hair flowed unhindered to her shoulders.

I set down my duffel. "Yes, I am."

"Looking for a car, huh?"

"That was the idea." I studied her. If she was a typical Hopian, business here was conducted far more casually than at home.

"I think maybe we'll have one later." A shrug. "Yesterday the sailors grabbed all I had. One's due back this afternoon." She shot me a dubious look. "You have to be twenty-one to rent. Age of majority. You don't look that old."

"I'm a Naval officer." I pulled out my ID, which still showed me as a midshipman. I'd have to get that changed. "I have my majority."

"I guess," she said vaguely. "Come back sometime this afternoon; I'll see if one's in yet."

"Will you make a reservation for me?"

"You mean, hold a car? Sure. What's your name?"

"Nick Seafort."

"Right. If I'm not here, ask for me at the restaurant inside."

"What's your name?"

"Darla." I started. She asked, "What's the matter?"

"Nothing. I knew a girl named Darla once."

That brought a smile. "Was she nice?"

"I liked her. Sometimes when she made her mind up it was hard getting her to change it."

"Oh, well, I'm not like that." It could have been an invitation.

"What can someone do on foot around here?"

"There's the terminal restaurant. If you want drinks, the Runway Saloon's just up the block. Just don't order doubles."

"Right. Thanks." I wandered out. The bar reminded me of my

promise to Lieutenant Malstrom: a drink at the first bar we came to. I
sighed. It was absurd to drink so early in the day, but I could think of
nothing better to do, and a promise was a promise. I strolled along the
street past the edge of the field, until I came upon a battered building
with sheet-metal siding.

"Permanent Happy Hour!" the sign read. "All drinks always half
price!" If drinks were always half price, what were they half of? I
shrugged.

Inside, the bar smelled of stale alcohol and fried food. The light
show bounced patterns off the walls in time to thumping electronic
music, making it hard for me to see. A babble of voices indicated that
people were in the back of the room.

I waited for my eyes to accustom to the dark. It was the kind of bar
where you stared moodily at the drink in your hand; just right for
spacemen.

"What'll you have?"

"Asteroid on the rocks." An experienced bartender, he knew my
uniform meant he could serve me without checking my age. There were
very stiff penalties for serving minors, both for the bartender and the
minor.

I took my drink and slid into a dimly lit booth to the side, tossing
my jacket on the seat beside me. I took a sip and nearly choked. The
alcohol tasted almost raw, and there was a lot of it. No wonder Darla had
warned me about a double.

An asteroid on the rocks. Whiskey, mixed fruit juices, and Hobarth
oils, imported from faraway Hobarth or imitated with synthetics. In this
case, probably synthetics; I suspected the Runway Saloon didn't stock
imported liqueurs.

Actually the drink wasn't bad, just strong. Silently I raised my glass
to the empty seat across from me and saluted Harv Malstrom. It would
have been great, Harv, to be sitting across from you. You'd make a joke
about the drinks, and I'd grin, enjoying your company, recalling our
most recent chess match. The alcohol made my eyes sting. I took another long swig. It burned going down. I had another swallow to ease
my throat. After a time I sat tapping an empty glass, staring moodily at
the empty seat, while flashing lights danced on the walls.

"Ready for another?"

"No." I looked at my watch. Early yet. "I suppose. A small one."

"Sure." He grinned without mirth and handed me the glass he'd
already brought. A comedian. He should have been on the holovid.

About halfway through the second drink I thought I'd feel better if

I closed my eyes, and that was easier to do when my head was resting on the table. I stayed that way, drifting in and out of a doze, while the bar filled and the noise grew louder.

"Detour! Off to Detour for seven weeks, then another week's leave." A woman's voice. Ms. Edwards, our gunner's mate.

"You joes should work the Hope Nation system. You're never more than five weeks from port. One easy run after another." My eyes were open now but my head stayed on the table. I listened, drifting.

"Nah, who wants a milk run? You gotta go deep to get action." Guffaws.

"Sure, joeygirl." The voice was mocking. "It'd be great, stuck interstellar with a tyrant for a captain and only fourteen months to go!"

"Hey, don't slam our Captain, buster!"

"Hah. I hear he'll be out of diapers soon!"

"Listen, grode, I'd rather sail with Captain Kid that one of your system sissies who'd wet his pants if he couldn't see a sun." I blinked, focused on the empty glass.

"Captain KID? You spank him if he makes a mistake?" I felt my ears flame.

"Hey, Seafort's all right! Sure, Captain Kid gets a wild hair up his ass sometimes—what officer don't? But that joey knows what he's doing. He took the puter apart single-handed, 'cause he knew she was planning to kill us. If he hadn't a found her glitches we'd be half outta the galaxy heading for Andromeda."

Another voice joined in. "I'll match him mean for mean with any Captain in the fleet. Two joes we had, they beat up on the CPO. They were real garbage, druggies and worse, but always got away with it. He hanged them himself without batting an eye. And you know about Miningcamp, where they tried to seize our ship?"

Yes, tell them about my folly at Miningcamp. Sickened, I closed my eyes.

"Those scum shot their way aboard, the Captain held them off with a laser in each hand 'til help came. When it was over he marched one of them right out the airlock and made him breathe space, and laughed all the way back to the bridge! He's tough, Captain Kid is. You don't mess with him. I'd rather be on a ship with him than with some old fart can't find his way to the head!"

For some reason I was feeling better. Time to go, before they found me spying on them. Cautiously, I raised my head. I was dizzy but functioning. I gathered my jacket, left a few unibucks on the table, and moved as quietly as I could to the door. Nobody saw me. I slipped outside, greedily sucking in the fresh air.

"God, it's the Captain!" Two of *Hibernia*'s ratings saluted hurriedly. I fumbled a return salute and kept moving, working at making my unsteady legs cooperate. I lugged my duffel toward the shuttleport, feeling a bit more steady with each step. By the terminal I was nearly myself again. I made for the rental agency at the far end.

"Hey, Captain, wait up!" I turned. Derek Carr in civilian garb, waved from the far end of the building. He ran to catch up. He stopped, his face flushed with healthy exertion. "Sir, I, uh—" All at once, he looked abashed.

Impatient, I asked, "What, Derek?"

"Your invitation. Is it too late to accept?"

I studied his face, unsure of my answer.

He stared at the pavement. "Sorry about the way I spoke to you yesterday. I'm still immature sometimes. I'd enjoy touring with you, sir, if you'll have me." With an effort, he raised his head and looked me in the eye.

My smile was bleak. "What changed your mind, Derek?"

"I was steamed over your sending me to the Chief, even though I really was asking for it that day. Then I remembered two things: I promised you I could take anything, and you were the only person who was kind to me when I really needed it." His face lit in a smile. "That was the most important thing anyone's ever done for me. So holding a grudge is pretty stupid. I'm sorry, sir."

I smiled back, meaning it this time. "What about your trip to your plantation?"

"I thought, sir, perhaps you'd like to come with me." His smile vanished. "Though I'm not sure we'd be welcome. My father told me that the manager, he . . ." He shrugged. "Anyway, we could go to the mountains afterward."

I debated, my melancholy lifting. His company would be more pleasant than my own. "Sounds great. I'll rent a car."

"I already have one, sir. I got it yesterday." He blushed. "I was sort of waiting until you came down."

"Right." I followed him to his electricar, a tiny three-wheeler with permabatteries that could power the vehicle for months. I thought fast. "Derek, while we're groundside, I want you to call me Mr. Seafort, as if I were first middy. And you don't have to say 'sir' all the time. Just make sure you switch back when we go aboard again."

"Aye aye, si—I mean, thank you, Mr. Seafort." We climbed in. I took off my jacket and tie and stowed my duffel in the back seat. "I've got a tent and supplies in the trunk," he said. "If you're ready, I am. It's a two-day drive."

I leaned back and closed my eyes. "Wake me when we get there."

A couple of hours out of Centraltown we came upon the Hope Nation I'd first expected. The three-lane road gave way to two lanes and then one and a half. Instead of pavement, only gravel. Homes were few and far between. Occasionally a cargo hauler lumbered toward Centraltown. We passed the time chatting and joking, sharing a merry mood.

Our route paralleled the seacoast a few miles inland. Occassionally, from a high point, we caught a glimpse of the shimmering ocean; more often our path cut through a dense jungle of viny trees of unfamiliar purplish hues.

We stopped for lunch at Haulers' Rest, a comfort station and restaurant about two hours from the edge of the plantation zone. The public showers were in an outbuilding. After, we walked past enclosures of turkeys, chickens, and pigs to the restaurant entrance. Cargo haulers were parked at random in the mud-packed parking lot.

Haulers' Rest generated its own electricity from a small pile in the back pasture, pumped water from deep wells, and prepared most of its own food from the hoof. Wheat and corn fields provided the grains, from hybrid stock that needed no pollination. On Hope Nation, no local blights affected our terrestrial crops, and there were no insects to harass the livestock, so everything grew fast and healthy.

After a stomach-stretching meal (ham steak, corn, green beans, homemade bread, lots of milk) we waddled to the car to resume our trip.

During the afternoon we pulled aside frequently to take in the rugged view. The forest was strangely silent. No birds circled above; no animals called out their cries. Only the soft wind that rippled through the incredibly dense vegetation.

The land wasn't fenced, but each plantation had its own identifying mark nailed to trees and posts along the road, much like the brands once put on cattle. The first we came to stretched many miles before it gave way to another.

As evening settled, rich reds dominated the sky, fading to subtle lavender. The two moons, Major and Minor, sailed serenely over scattered clouds. By now we both were tired, and I began watching for markers along the road. I said, "Let's pick a plantation before it gets too late."

According to the holovid guides, Hope Nation had few inns outside

Centraltown, so plantations provided free food and lodging to travelers who came their way. An old tradition, now virtually obligatory. Plantation owners didn't stint on food or shelter; they could afford it, and travelers brought outside contact that the isolated planters appreciated.

Derek drove on in silence. Then, "Mr. Seafort, I changed my mind. Let's camp out for the night."

"Why?"

"I don't want to look at plantations."

I raised an eyebrow, waiting.

"I told you the managers control our estate. They won't want me around. They'll patronize me, and push me aside if I ask questions. Let's not bother to visit."

"That's not a good idea."

"What difference is it to you?"

"Better to face it than brood for the rest of your leave. Besides, Carr is another day's ride or more. We'll stop at a closer estate for the night."

His tone was petulant. "What's the point of seeing another family's holding? It's mine I care about."

"You care so much you'd turn tail and run?"

Even in moonlight I could see him flush. "I'm no coward."

"I didn't say you were." But I had. Inwardly, I sighed. "I'll handle it, Derek."

"How?"

"I'll do the talking, and we won't tell them your name."

Ahead was a gate, and a dirt service road that wound into a heavy woods. A wooden sign above read "Branstead Plantation."

"Slow down. Take that one."

Reluctantly he turned into the drive. "Mr. Seafort, I feel like a welfarer asking for a handout."

"That's the system here. Go on."

Nothing but woods for a good mile. Then, a clearing where remains of huge brush piles skirted the edge of plowed fields that stretched as far as the eye could see.

Our road straightened, ran alongside the field. After another two miles I began to wonder if the road led to a homestead, but abruptly we came on a complex of buildings set around a wide circular drive. Barns, silos. A heliport. Farmhand's shacks. They surrounded a huge wood and stone mansion that dominated the settlement.

We got out to stretch. A stocky man in work clothes emerged from the stone house, walked to where we waited. "Can I help you boys?"

"We're travelers," I said.

"The guest house is over there." He pointed to a clean but simple building that seemed in good repair. "We don't serve separate for the guests; you'll eat with us in the manse. We dine at seven."

"Thank you very much," I said, but he'd already turned to go.

"Welcome." He didn't look back.

We carried our duffels into the guest house. A row of beds sat along one wall, with hooks and shelves on the wall opposite. Around the corner, a bath. The lack of privacy wasn't unlike a wardroom.

Derek's tone held wonder. "He didn't care about us. No questions."

"Don't you know about travel in the outland?"

"My father was born here. I wasn't."

"Then read the holovid guides, tourist."

I opened my duffel.

Derek sorted through his clothes. "I'm not a tourist." His voice was tremulous. "This is my home. Earth never was."

"I know, Derek." I'd have to remember not to tease about certain things.

We washed and changed clothes. In Naval blue slacks and a white shirt, I could have been any young civilian. Shortly before seven we strolled up the drive past a field of grain to the main dwelling. From the plank porch we could hear loud conversation and the friendly rattle of dishes.

Derek fidgeted with embarrassment. I knocked.

"Come on in." A well-fed balding young man in his thirties. "I'm Harmon Branstead." He stood aside. The entrance room was rough-hewn but comfortable, well furnished with solidly built furniture.

"Nick, um, Rogoff, sir."

Derek shot me an amazed glance. I gulped, breathing a silent apology to Lord God. Whyever had I chosen the name of the man I'd murdered? I said hastily, "And my friend Derek. We're sailors."

"A local ship?"

"*Hibernia*, sir. The interstellar—"

"We all heard *Hibernia* docked. Quite an event." He held out his hand. "Welcome to Branstead Plantation. How long will you stay?"

"Just the night. We'll be on our way in the morning."

"Very well. Come eat with us."

We were the only guests. Supper was at a long plank table in a dining room that was large but homey. The planter and his wife, their small children, and two farm managers sat at table with us. Hefty platters of home-cooked food were passed around.

Derek asked, "Did you build this place, sir?" He glanced at the stuccoed walls, the comfortable furnishings.

"My grandfather did," said Branstead. "But I've added about ten thousand acres to cultivation, and put up a few more buildings."

"Very impressive," I said.

"We're the fourth largest on Eastern Continent." His voice was proud. "Hopewell is first, then Carr, then Triforth, then us." Branstead passed creamed corn to his older son, a boy of nine or so. "As soon as we get the machinery paid off, I'll open some new acreage. Then we'll see. Maybe by the time I pass it on to Jerence we'll be the biggest." He beamed at his son.

"I'd think estates would get smaller over the generations," said Derek. "Divided among all your children."

"Divided? Lord God, no! Primogeniture is the rule. First-born." Branstead nodded at his younger child. "Of course, everyone is well provided for, but the land stays intact. We wouldn't have it any other way."

"How large is your plantation?" I asked.

"We're only three hundred thirty thousand, but we're growing. Another seventy-five thousand and we'll pass Triforth. Hopewell is eight hundred thousand acres." A pause. "Carr is seven hundred thousand, but they don't really count as they're no longer family-run."

I spooned myself more corn, passed it on. "What's Carr?" My tone was careless.

"One of our neighbors. The estate was owned by old Winston, 'til he died. We all thought they'd stagnate, but I have to admit, Plumwell's doing all right, even if there's talk that—" He bit off the rest.

Derek toyed with his food.

Branstead leaned back in his chair. "So, you boys are Navy."

"Yes, sir."

"Smart of you not to wear your uniforms, Mr.—Rogoff, is it? I myself wouldn't hold it against you, but there are some . . ."

"I'm on leave. Otherwise—" I was proud to wear the uniform, and resented any implication to the contrary. My back stiffened.

"Now, don't take offense. Some folks see Naval blues and blame the sailors."

"For what?"

"The usual: you slap export duties on what you send us, and we can't ship our produce except in Naval hulls. Makes for unfair trade, and we're paying dearly."

Derek's eyes flickered to the comfortable house.

Branstead shrugged, his manner depreciating. "As a nation, I mean. We're the breadbasket of the colonies. Do you know how much food Hope Nation ships back to Earth? Millions of tons. Once you lift it out of the atmosphere, vacuum cold storage costs nothing. Where are you boys from, anyway?"

"Earth," I told him. "We're going on to Detour."

"When you get home, tell them we want a new tariff bill." We drifted to politics and current events, that is, as current as they could be after eighteen months of sail.

After dinner Derek and I settled into the guest house. I sank onto my bed with a sigh of relief. "Why did I blurt out the name Rogoff? I felt his presence all through the meal. I shouldn't have done that."

His tone was accusing. "I thought you said you knew how to handle it."

"You got to see a plantation, didn't you?"

He grimaced, but without rancor. I got into bed and turned out the light.

Derek tossed and turned for hours, waking me each time I drifted to sleep. In the very early hours he got up quietly, put on his clothes, and slipped outside. Just as dawn was breaking he crept back to his bed, waking me once more.

In the morning, I dressed quickly, anxious for my first cup of coffee. Derek paced. "Look, sir, we can't go on to Carr."

I raised an eyebrow. "That again?"

"The manager won't talk to us." He sat, stood again immediately. "We'll learn nothing. And I won't beg, not on my own land."

I tried to soothe him. "One thing I've learned as Captain, Derek. You'll have enough problems without worrying about ones that haven't come up yet. We'll play it by ear."

His look was dubious. After a while, he sighed. "All right. Tell them I'm your cousin or something."

Thanks to Derek's nocturnal meanders, we'd slept in until well past nine. We were prepared to leave without breakfast but the housekeeper insisted on feeding us a simple meal that grew into a gargantuan feast.

I was eyeing the last of my coffee when Harmon Branstead looked in. "Where do you go from here, boys?"

"North, toward Carr. Maybe beyond."

"Stop at Hopewell if you have time. Their automated mill and elevator is astonishing."

"Thank you." I glanced at my watch. I could imagine nothing less interesting.

Derek pushed back his chair. "Ready, Mr. Seafort?"

"Yes." I got to my feet. "Drive the car around. I'll get our duffels."

"Thanks for your hospitality, sir." Derek hurried out. I headed for the stairs.

"Just a moment," said Branstead, then to a farmhand, "Randall, get their bags." When we were alone, he eyed me with distaste.

"Sir?"

His face was cold. "In Hope Nation, hospitality is a matter of tradition, not law. In that tradition, I opened my home to you. I sat you at dinner with my own children."

"Yes, sir?"

He shot, "Who are you?"

"Nick. Nick Rog—" My voice faltered.

"Seafort, I believe he called you. I don't know why you chose to lie, but it's despicable. You were a guest! Get out, and don't come back!"

My face flamed. "I'm sor—"

"Out!"

"Yes, sir." I headed for the door with as much dignity as I could muster. Beyond, in the haze, Father glowered his disapproval.

My hand on the latch, I hesitated. "Mr. Branstead, please . . ." I glanced at his face, saw no opening. "I was wrong. Forgive me. My name is Nick Seafort. I—"

"Are you really from *Hibernia?*"

"Yes."

His skepticism was evident. "You don't look like the sailors we see hereabouts."

"We're officers."

"Why should I believe that?"

I took out my wallet, handed him my ID.

His glance went to my face and back. "A midshipman."

"Not anymore. It's an old card."

"They wouldn't have you?"

"They had no choice. I'm, ah, Captain now."

"You're the one!" He studied me. "Everyone's heard, but I don't think they said the name . . . Why lie about it, for heaven's sake?" His tone had eased to one of curiosity.

I had to do something to make amends. "My friend Derek."

"Yes?"

"Derek Carr."

"Is he related—Oh!" He sat.

Gratefully, I did the same; my knees were weak. "He's a midshipman now, and he'll sail with us. Before we left he wanted to see . . ." I found it hard to raise my eyes. "Mr. Branstead, I'm ashamed."

"Well, there are worse things than deceit." His voice was gruff. "You're going on to Carr, then?"

"Yes. He's very nervous about it. What will the manager— Plumwell, you said—do if he visits?"

His fingers drummed the table. "All our plantations are family owned. There's never been a case where the owner isn't in residence. Until now. Will Derek come back to stay?"

"Count on it."

"Winston wasn't well, the last few years. He relied heavily on Plumwell. If it weren't for Andy, they could have lost most everything when credit was so tight. Plumwell may have saved the estate." A pause. "So if he's come to think of it as his own . . ."

I waited.

"He feels strongly about it. They've petitioned Governor Williams for a regulation granting rights to resident managers, though that change could take years. If an heir showed up now . . ." He glanced at me, as if deciding. "Yes, perhaps it's best to use another name."

"Is it safe to go?"

"Mr., ah, Seafort . . . Hope Nation is far from Earth; settlers have handled their own affairs for years. We have a certain spirit of independence that's hard for you visitors to understand. When a problem gets in the way . . . we remove it."

"Would he—"

"I don't know. I won't mention you if I run into Plumwell." Branstead stood.

"Thank you. I'm sorry I deceived you. I see now there was no need."

"You couldn't know that." Branstead, somewhat mollified, walked me to the door. "Tell me, has the Navy ever had a Captain your age? How exactly did it come about?"

I owed him that, and whatever else he asked. I forced a strained smile. "Well, it happened this way . . ."

Early that afternoon, rain turned ruts and chuckholes into small ponds. Secure in our watertight electricar we hummed along past thousands of acres of cultivation. Branstead gave way to Volksteader, then Palabee. Derek asked nervously, "Sir, what will you do?"

"Don't worry." I'd decided not to tell Derek about Branstead's warning, for fear of making him even more nervous. He would be my cousin. I was practicing how to introduce him when a new mark appeared on the wooden signposts. A few miles beyond, we came to the entrance road, marked with a painted metal sign. "Carr Plantation. Hope Nation's Best."

He slowed. "Wouldn't you rather head back? We'll have more time for the Ventur—"

"Oh, please." I pointed to the service road.

It was a long drive, past herds of cattle grazing in lush green pastures, heads bowed away from the rain. Then, endless fields of corn along both sides of the road. Finally a dip revealed an impressive complex of buildings about half a mile ahead.

We came to a stop at a guardhouse with a lowered rail. The guard leaned into the window. "You fellas looking for something?"

"We're on a trip up the coast road. Can we stay the night?"

He nodded reluctantly. "There's guest privileges. Every place has them. But why stop here?"

I grinned. "Back in Haulers' Rest they told us whatever else we missed we had to see Carr Plantation, 'cause it's the best and biggest on Hope Nation."

He snorted but looked mollified. "Not the biggest. Not yet, anyway. Go on in, I'll ring and tell them you're coming."

I waved and we purred off down the road. The rain had stopped, and a shaft of yellow sunlight gleamed through the clouds. Derek hunched grimly in his seat.

"Your middle name's Anthony?" I asked as a hand sauntered out of the house.

Derek gaped. "Yes, of course. Why—"

The two wings of the huge, pillared plantation house stretched along a manicured gravel drive edged by a low white picket fence. Beds of unfamiliar flowers were interspersed among clean, strong grasses mowed short.

"You the two travelers?" The ranch hand.

I stepped out of the car. "That's right. Nick Ewing." I put out a hand. Well, I'd told the truth. At least some of it.

He broke into a grin. "Fenn Willny. We don't get many come through here anymore, the word's got out the boss doesn't like it. He's soft on joeykids, though. Hasn't got any of his own." He gestured to the mansion. "We tore down the guest house last spring. Travelers stay upstairs. You eat in the kitchen. Come on, I'll take you to the boss."

We followed him inside. The mansion was built on the grand scale. Polished hardwoods with intricate carving decorated the doorways, bespeaking intensive labor at huge cost. The furniture in the hallway was elegant, expensive, and tasteful. Fenn Willny led us to a large office on a corridor between a dining room and a sitting room furnished with "Swedish Modern" terrestrial antiques that must have cost a fortune.

The manager's eyes were cold and appraising. He made no move to welcome us. I glanced at Derek, my stomach churning. What if the manager asked some question I couldn't answer? Why had I ever agreed Derek was a cousin?

"Mr. Plumwell, these are the two travelers, Nick and . . ."

"My cousin Anthony." I grabbed Derek's arm and propelled him forward. "Say hello to Mr. Plumwell, Anthony." I jostled his arm.

Derek shot me a furious glance. "Hello, sir," he mumbled.

I leaned forward confidentially, speaking just loud enough for Derek to hear. "You'll have to pardon Anthony. He's a little slow. I look after him." Derek's biceps rippled.

The plantation manager nodded in understanding. "Welcome to Carr Plantation. You'll be leaving in the morning?" It was a clear suggestion.

"Yes, sir, I guess so." I looked disappointed. "Actually, I was hoping —well, I know it's foolish."

"What's that, young man?" He looked annoyed.

"We only have two days left of our vacation, Mr. Plumwell. I work, and Anthony's in a special school." From Derek, a strangled sound. I said, "We've never seen a big plantation before, and I was hoping somebody could show us around. Of course I could pay . . ."

I couldn't read Plumwell's expression, so I rushed on. "They said to see either Carr Plantation or Hopewell, because they were both special. But Hopewell's too far, and I don't know when we'll get out together again." I spoke loudly to Derek. "Anthony, maybe next year if I get a few more days vacation we'll go to Hopewell. That's the bigger one."

Derek's color rose. He breathed through gritted teeth.

Plumwell frowned. "I suppose you're city boys and don't know. It's an insult to offer money for hospitality on a plantation; that comes with the territory. Anyway, Hopewell is nothing special. We're the innovative ones."

He paused, looking us over. "We're not in the tour business, but I guess I could spare a hand for a few hours, seeing your brother's retarded. But don't let it get around back in Centraltown or we'll be flooded with freeloaders."

"Zarky!" I nudged Derek. "Did you hear? He's going to show us a real plantation, Anthony." Derek's lips moved, but he turned away and I couldn't see what he said. "He's real happy, sir. It's all he's talked about since Centraltown." I rolled my eyes.

Plumwell winked in understanding. "Why don't you boys stow your gear in your room. I'll have Fenn take you around the center complex before dinner."

"Great, sir!" I shook hands. "Shake hands with Mr. Plumwell." Derek fixed me with a peculiar stare. I pushed him forward. "Anthony, remember your manners, like we taught you!" Livid, Derek offered his hand to the manager, who gave it a condescending squeeze. "Good boy." I patted Derek on the back.

Fenn led us up a grand staircase to the second floor, and continued on a smaller staircase to the third. The rooms were clean and adequate, but less ornate than in the lower part of the house. "I'll wait for you in the front hall." He loped downstairs two steps at a time.

I closed the door behind us, dumped my duffel on the bunk. White-faced, Derek glared lasers across the room.

"Something wrong?" I sorted through my belongings.

Without warning he launched himself across the bed, clawing at my neck. I caught his wrists as I fell backward. He dove on top of me, seeking my throat.

"Listen!" It had no effect. He strained to break from my grasp. "Derek!" He thrashed wildly until his wrists broke free. "Stop and listen!" At last, he got his hands on my windpipe.

Unable to breathe, I twisted and heaved, throwing my hips and bouncing him up and down. When he bounced high enough I thrust my knee upward with all my strength. That stopped him. With a yawp of pain he rolled to the side, clutching his testicles. I rolled on top of him. Sitting on his back I forced his arm up between his shoulder blades, and waited.

He grunted between his teeth, "Get off! I'll kill you!" I slapped him sharply alongside the ear. He struggled harder. Each time he heaved I pulled his arm higher behind his back. Finally he lay still. "Get off!" A string of curses.

"When you're ready to listen."

"Off, you shit!"

I slapped him harder. I liked him, but there were limits.

Finally he lay still. "All right. I'll listen when you get off."

I let go and sat on my bed. "You have a complaint, Derek?"

He bounded to his feet, sputtering. "Your retarded cousin Anthony? You say that *in my own house?*"

"Do they want company, Derek?"

My calm question gave him pause. "No, not much. Why?"

"What did I get us?" He was silent. "A guided tour," I answered myself. "A tour of the whole place. Anyway, you said I should call you my cous—"

"I'm a little slow? A SPECIAL SCHOOL? How DARE you!"

I let my voice sharpen. "Think! You can ask anything you want and they won't take offense. They won't even know why you're asking." As the realization sunk in he sank slowly onto his bed. "I got you in, when you didn't have the guts to come. I arranged a guided tour. I heard Vax call you retarded, and you took it. What in God's own hell is the matter with you?"

"That was the wardroom," he muttered. "Not my own house."

"What difference does that make?"

"You'd have to be one of us to understand. In your home you have respect. Dignity."

I shrugged. "You're just a middy. You don't get dignity until you make lieutenant."

I think at that moment he'd forgotten entirely about the Navy. He looked at the marks on his Captain's neck and gulped. "I'm sorry, sir." His voice was small.

"I have a right to dignity too," I told him. "Look what you've done to mine."

"I shouldn't have touched you." His gaze was on the floor.

Well, I'd told him to treat me as senior midshipman rather than Captain. Look where it got me. "You'll be sorrier. Seven demerits, when we get back to the ship." Oddly, it made him feel better. It made me feel better too. My throat hurt. I giggled. "I admit, though, you had provocation." I snickered, recalling his fury in Plumwell's office. The more I thought about it, the funnier it seemed.

Watching me roll helplessly on my bed in silent mirth Derek glowered anew, but after a while he couldn't help himself and began to laugh with me. After a few moments we stopped. I wiped my eyes.

"I'm sorry, sir, but you're a peasant," Derek told me. "You don't understand dignity." It started us going again. This time when we stopped all was well between us.

"Come on, aristocrat, let's inspect your estate." We left the room and hurried down the stairs. "Just remember to play along," I whispered at the last moment. Daringly, he punched me in the arm before we reached the main floor.

24

The helicopter swooped along the dense hedgerow marking the plantation border, while sprinklers made mist in the early-morning light. We
were exploring the more distant sections of the estate, having toured the
main compound the evening before.

"How much wheat do you grow?" Derek had to shout above the
noise of the motor.

"A lot."

"No, how much?" Derek insisted. Fenn, in the pilot's seat, pursed
his lips.

I leaned across from the back seat. "Just say anything. He won't
know the difference."

Fenn frowned at my insensitivity. "No, I'll tell him. One point two
million bushels, same as it's been for years."

Derek furrowed his brow. "Is that a lot?" Since dinner the previous
night he had burrowed deep into his role.

Fenn smiled. "Enough. And then there's six hundred thousand
bushels of corn. And sorghum."

"I like corn!" Derek said happily. I nudged him, afraid he would
overdo it. "Nicky, why'd you poke me?" His tone was anxious. "Am I
bothering him too much?" Nicky? I'd kill him.

"You ask too many questions, Anthony."

"He's no trouble," Fenn said.

Derek's look was triumphant. "See, Nicky?" He turned to Fenn. "Is
this all yours and Mr. Plumwell's?"

"Don't I wish!" Fenn brought us down on a concrete pad outside a
large metal-roofed building. "I work for Mr. Plumwell, and he's just the
manager." His tone changed. "Course, he's been here most of his life."

"Doesn't the owner live here?" I asked.

"Old Winston died six years ago, but he was sick long before that.
This place was started way back, by the first Randolph Carr. He left it to
Winston."

"I take it he had no children."

"Are you kidding? Five." Fenn opened the gate. "They say his oldest boy was a heller. Randolph II. He gave the old man so much trouble

Winston sent him all the way to Earth to college. He never came home while Winston was alive."

Derek was attentive.

"Will he ever?" I asked.

"Randy was supposed to be on the ship that docked this week, and we expected we'd find ourselves working for him. But he died on the trip, so it's all up in the air."

"What will happen?"

Fenn gestured toward the building we were about to enter. "This is the second-largest feed mill on the planet. It's entirely automated. Takes only three men to run it." We looked in. "Randy had a son, some snot born in Upper New York. They say he's on the ship. The joeyboy's never even been here, so he doesn't know squat about planting. I guess he'll be sent back to Earth for schooling. I don't know; Mr. Plumwell's made the arrangements. The joeykid won't have any say until he's twenty-two."

"Then what?" A new tension was in Derek's voice.

Fenn grinned. "Between you and me, boys, I wouldn't be surprised if by that time Carr Plantation's books were in such a state he'd need Mr. Plumwell more than ever."

I grinned. "The Carrs should have stayed if they wanted to run the place."

Fenn looked serious. "You're righter than you know. Someday we'll have a law about absentee owners. Sure, they're entitled to profits, but a resident manager who stays all his life and runs things, he should have rights too. The management should pass down in his family, not the owner's. If—"

"Now wait a min—" Derek broke in.

I overrode him fast. "Anthony, don't interrupt!"

"But he—"

"Haven't you learned your manners?" I shoved Derek with force. "Apologize!" He looked surly. I squeezed his arm. "Go on!" Derek mumbled an apology, and I breathed easier. Perhaps when he calmed, he'd realize he'd nearly blown our cover.

Fenn asked, "Aren't you a bit rough on the joey?"

"Sometimes he needs sitting on." My tone was cross. "His father let him believe he was too good for discipline." Derek shot me a deadly glance but kept quiet.

"You see how it is," Fenn said. "Mr. Plumwell's been here thirty years, and he knows every inch of this plantation. Last year we cleared thirty million unibucks, even after the new acreage. Carr Plantation has to be run by a professional."

"Where do you keep all the cash?" Derek was back in character.

Fenn smiled mirthlessly. "Some of it goes to the Carr accounts at Branstead Bank and Trust. The rest goes for salaries and expenses."

"So the Carr boy gets to play with the money even if he can't boss the plantation," I said.

"Not quite. The account is in the Carr name but Mr. Plumwell has control until a Carr shows up who has the right to run the estate. Mr. Plumwell makes sure the right people are on our side, that sort of thing. That money pool helps protect our way of life." He looked at me closely. "How did we get on this subject?"

"I'm not sure." My tone was bright and innocent. "What's this conveyor belt do?"

That night we were invited to dine with Plumwell and his staff. I made a show of nagging Derek about his table manners; he retaliated by calling me "Nicky." All the while Derek's penetrating glance was taking in the oil paintings hanging above the huge stone fireplace, the fine china, the crystal glassware, the succulent foods and drink. He eyed Mr. Plumwell's place at the head of the table with something less than delight.

In our room, after dinner, he moped on his bed while I got ready to turn out the light.

"What's bothering you, Anthony?"

His voice was quiet. "Please belay that, Mr. Seafort."

"What's wrong, Derek?"

"This is my house. I should be at the head of the table."

"Someday."

"But in the meantime . . ." He brooded. "Fenn mentioned one point two million bushels of wheat. The reports they sent my father listed seven hundred thousand. Someone's been skimming. Who knows what else Plumwell's stolen? I've got to do something."

"Why?"

He was surprised. "It's my money."

I had no sympathy. "You have your pay billet. Are you hurting?"

"That's not the point," he said with disdain. "Should this—this thief get away with what's not rightfully his?"

"Yes, if he's improving your estate." He was shocked into silence. "You're out of the picture, Derek. You're so wealthy you won't even miss what he steals. In the meantime, he's opening up new acreage that permanently benefits your plantation. He's doing a good job, stealing or not."

"That's easy for you to say," Derek said bitterly. "You never had anything, and you never will!"

I snapped off the light, determined not to speak to him before morning. I yearned for the isolation of the Captain's cabin.

Presently he said, "I'm sorry." I ignored him, cherishing my hurt.

After a while he cleared his throat. "I apologize, Mr. Seafort." I made no answer. He snapped on the light. "Am I talking to the Captain now, or Mr. Seafort the ex-midshipman?"

A good question. In fairness to him, I wasn't Captain at the moment. "The ex-midshipman."

"Then I won't stand at attention. I didn't mean what I just said. I was angry and wanted to hurt you. Please don't make me grovel."

I relented. "All right. But I repeat what I told you. He's doing a good job building Carr Plantation even if he does skim the profits."

"What if I tell him who I am, just before we leave. That'll show him he can't—"

I felt a sudden chill. "Don't even think about it, Derek." Thousands of uncleared acres adjoined the cultivated fields. Some of them had hardly been explored.

He shivered. "Well, maybe not while we're still here. But when I get back to town I'll file suit."

"No."

"He can't be allowed to get away with it. If I move fast I'll save—"

"No, I said."

"Why not?"

I was nettled. "Do you plan to stay on Hope Nation to fight a lawsuit?"

"I guess I can't, unless you let me resign, but—"

"Get this straight, Mr. Carr! For the next four years you're a midshipman in the United Nations Naval Service! You go where the Navy sends you. Understand? You took an oath, and a gentleman shouldn't need reminding. The life you see here—it doesn't exist yet."

"But—"

"This is a form of time travel. Perhaps someday you'll live here and worry about your riches, but not now. I took you on a visit to the future. You can't touch anything and nobody can hear you!" There was silence. "Understand?"

He didn't answer. I rolled over and snapped off the light. Presently

I heard Derek Anthony Carr, scion of the Hope Nation Carrs, cry himself to sleep after his Captain's tongue-lashing.

In the morning I felt guilty for having spoken so sharply. We brought our duffels down to breakfast. I had Anthony thank everyone in sight. Even Plumwell smiled as we tooled down the drive in our electricar.

"Now what?" I asked when we were out of sight.

Derek's tone was petulant. "I've seen enough plantations, if I won't be—" His fingers drummed on the armrest; when he spoke again his voice was subdued. "Sorry, sir. Do you still want to take me to the Venturas?"

"Yes."

"I think I'd like that."

We headed back to Centraltown, camping once along the way. By the time we were back Derek was in good spirits, and I found to my surprise I'd begun to miss the organized bustle of shipboard life.

I decided to shuttle up to *Hibernia* for a couple of days before leaving for the Ventura Mountains; Derek opted to stay in Centraltown. The peasant and the aristocrat parted company with awkward shyness.

I changed back into Navy blues and tried to tame my wild hair before checking in at Admiralty House. Forbee confirmed that there was still no interstellar Captain in the Hope Nation system. Unless *Telstar* unexpectedly appeared, none was scheduled to arrive for another five months. In the meantime they'd radioed all local vessels to ask for lieutenants and midshipmen. If none volunteered, Forbee would simply assign me the necessary officers, and leave the local fleet shorthanded.

After boarding, I took a luxurious hot shower in my cabin, ran all my clothes through the sonic cleaner, and hunted up a barber on Orbit Station. Hair trimmed back to my normal Navy length, I felt a new man. I roamed my empty ship as if looking for something, but I knew not what. Vax, when I stumbled over him, greeted me like a long-lost brother. He too found the ship's silence eerie and disturbing. I even unbent so far as to try a game of chess with him, to his delight. He was no match.

Vax had learned through the grapevine that I would remain with *Hibernia*. To my astonishment he was pleased rather than apprehensive. I'd have thought he had more sense than to look forward to a cruise with an unqualified Captain who had my peculiar emotional disabilities. I didn't remind him that depending on what officers were reassigned to

Hibernia, he might be transferred out as a replacement. Time enough for that if it happened.

Depressed and not knowing why, I took the next scheduled shuttle back down to Centraltown. Customs and quarantine waved me through; by now I'd become a regular. Small-town life was amazingly relaxed compared, say, to Lunapolis.

I still had two days before I was to meet Derek for our trip to the mountains. I toured downtown Centraltown, explored the local museum, and ate in two of the recommended restaurants, occasionally encountering crewmen and former passengers. I stayed overnight in a prefab inn with the usual plastic furniture and decor. I bought a newschip and stuck it in my holovid; on page three was an announcement of an Anabaptist revival meeting in Newtown Hall. Mrs. Donhauser wasted no time. I thought of attending, but decided I didn't care to meet her in her professional capacity.

Thoughts of our passengers reminded me I'd promised to look up Amanda Frowel. I immediately decided against it. Then I spent the best part of an afternoon wandering aimlessly up and down the streets, arguing with myself. Sheepishly, I dug her address out of my duffel. After dinner I strolled across town to the address she had given.

"Nicky!" An apron around her waist, she smiled happily through her screen door, old-fashioned and domestic, inflicting a pang of regret that I soon had to leave the colony. "Come in!" Her home was the back half of a comfortable wood house on a quiet side street on the edge of town. She rented, so help me, from a widow trying to make ends meet.

"I was just passing by," I mumbled, sounding an idiot.

"But I was hoping you'd come. Look, my books are all over the place!" She brushed aside a pile of holovid chips scattered on a table. "I started work three days ago. Know what? They don't want me just to teach natural science; I'm supposed to set up the whole science curriculum! They've never had one, isn't that ridiculous?"

"Hasn't anybody been teaching geology and biology?"

"Sure, but not in any organized way. They just got people who knew their subjects to come in and talk about them. Isn't it quaint?"

"Very." My tone was sour. Our world aboard *Hibernia* seemed light-years away.

"Would you like to take a walk? I'll show you the school." She was so enthused I agreed to go, wishing I hadn't come to visit. She threw on a light jacket against the evening cool, and we set out for the school, about a mile away. She chattered with animation at first, but after a while she sensed my mood and grew quieter. We walked, hand in hand, under two moons. Their crossed shadows began to make me dizzy.

The public school was a one-story building encased in sheet metal, apparently a popular local building material. Amanda unlocked the door and took me inside. "This is where I work." She showed me a classroom. The consoles at the student desks struck no chord of recognition, as my own schooling was at home with Father. Amanda's desk and master console were to one side, where she could watch both the large screen and the students.

"The new term starts in three weeks. Nicky, it's so exciting! The joeys will be so different from northamericans."

"You think so?"

"Wouldn't they, growing up in such a wild, free place?"

"I suppose." I was feeling more and more depressed. "Amanda, I have to go. I have an appointment."

"You couldn't stay awhile?" Her voice was wistful. My chest ached.

"Come, I'll walk you home." I wanted to leave and stay at the same time. On ship I'd never felt so bumbling and awkward with her. We walked mostly in silence through the darkened streets; Major had set and only Minor remained to guide us.

She hesitated, in front of her rustic home. "Will I see you again before you leave?"

"I don't think so. I'm taking Derek to the Venturas tomorrow, then I'll have to go back aboard." I hadn't mentioned I was still in command.

"Lieutenant Malstrom promised to take you there, didn't he?"

"Yes." I was grateful she remembered.

"Oh, Nicky." Gently, she kissed the back of my hand. "Life isn't the way we plan it."

"No," I said miserably. I forced myself to smile. "Good-bye, Amanda."

"Good-bye, Nicky." We looked into each other's eyes before she turned to go. As if in astonishment, she said, "We'll never see each other again."

"No." I couldn't stop looking at her.

"Well . . . good-bye, then." She crossed her yard.

"Amanda?"

She stopped. "What is it?"

"Nothing. I—nothing." As she opened her door I blurted, "Would you like to go with me?"

"To the mountains? I can't, Nicky. I have a job."

"I know. I thought maybe somehow—"

"School starts in three weeks. If I don't have my curriculum ready . . ."

"They'll fire you?"

She giggled. They'd waited three years for her; it would take three more to send for a replacement. "They won't be very happy." She frowned. "But I don't care. I want to see the Ventura Mountains."

"Really?" I said stupidly.

"With you. I want to see them with you."

My eyes stung. I felt light-headed and miserable all at once. I ran to her and we embraced. "You'll really go? God, can we start now?"

"Give me the night to get ready. And I have to explain to Mrs. Potter." After a while she managed to get me to leave.

Derek didn't seem put out when I told him I'd invited Amanda. He helped me buy a second pup tent and load the extra food and other supplies in the jet heli we'd rented. I had to promise the heli service three times not to tamper with the transponder; Captain Grone's disappearance must have made them skittish.

We took off for the Western Continent shortly after breakfast. I was the only licensed driver; they'd taught us helipiloting at Academy but Derek and Amanda had never learned.

The permabatteries had ample charge for months. From time to time I turned on the autopilot to lean back and rest my eyes. The craft was roomy enough for Derek and Amanda to switch seats; they did so several times before settling down.

At four hundred fifty kilometers per hour it took us more than eight hours to reach the western shore. The huge submarine trees growing from the bottom of Farreach Ocean sent probing tentacles to the surface to absorb light. Plants somewhat like water lilies floated on the surface, rising and falling with the swells. The ocean was a vast liquid field of competing vegetable organisms.

The jagged spires of the Western Mountains loomed on the horizon long before we reached the continent; their raw power was breathtaking. The low hills and gently sculpted valleys of the Eastern Continent were tame compared to the vigor of these much younger peaks.

Derek pored over the map. "Do you want an established campsite or should we find a place of our own?"

"Let's find someplace," I said. Amanda nodded agreement. The cleared campsites would be remote enough, but we had no need to settle for them. Even after a hundred years, there were places in the continent no foot had trod.

Western Continent had settlements, far to the south, but here in the northern reaches virgin forests covered the sprawling land. At the coast, phalanxes of hills plunged to the sea to bury themselves in the swirling foam. Farther inland, great chasms cowered beneath the bristling peaks of the Venturas. The heli service had marked some of the more spectacular sights on our map. Taking bearings from nav satellites I headed west over dense foliage.

As dusk neared I set us down on a grassy plain high in the hills. To one side was deep forest; a hundred feet beyond, the plain gave way to steep hills running down to a green and yellow valley. Across the vale a peak thrust upward so steeply that little grew on it. Waterfalls tumbled from the creases in the hill.

We got out the three-mil poly tents and their collapsible poles. I helped Derek pound stakes into the soft earth. We clipped the thin, tough material across the poles, and the tents were ready. Amanda began trundling in our gear.

Derek brought the micro and the battery cooler from the heli. He delved into the cooler and emerged with softies. While I downed mine in two long swallows, he kicked at the grass. "How about going really primitive?"

I asked, "How?"

"A bonfire." A heady thought. In Cardiff, as in most regions of home, wood was scarce and pollution so great that hardly anyone could get a permit to burn outdoors. Even the flue over Father's hearth had its dampers and scrubbers.

Here, we need have no such concerns, as long as we were careful. I began clearing space for a fire.

The tough native grasses didn't pull out easily; it took a shovel to dig them out. Their shallow intertwined root system ran just below the surface, and I had to spade to break the roots free.

Derek and Amanda returned from time to time with armfuls of firewood. I wondered if they intended our blaze to be seen from Centraltown. Our work kept us warm in the chill of the upland evening, but when we finished we immediately built up the fire.

I fed the flames from my cushion near the pit, while Derek and Amanda consulted on dinner like two master chefs sharing a kitchen. It pleased me that they liked each other.

We ate at fireside under the gleam of two benevolent moons. In the dark of the night, the crackling of the fire and the muted splashing of the waterfall across the valley were our only sounds. Knowing there were none, still I listened for insects and birds calling in the night.

Hope Nation seemed too silent. I knew our ecologists were preparing to introduce a few bird species and selected terrestrial insects. Bees to pollinate crops the old-fashioned way, for instance.

"It's beautiful, Nicky." Amanda sat between us. We'd devoured our dinner and were lazing around the campfire. Our once mighty stacks of wood were fast diminishing, but they'd last until bed.

I tossed twigs into the flames. "What will people make of it when they settle here?"

"They wouldn't ruin a place like this."

I snorted. "You should see Cardiff." I'd seen photos of home in the old days, before the disposal dumps and treatment plants and the litter of modern civilization had improved the terrain. Still, the picturesque old smelters remained, some of them, as ruins.

I moved closer to the fire, watching my handsome midshipman's face as he chatted with Amanda. Odd feelings stirred, recalling Jason, eons past. I shivered, wrenched myself back to reality. "Have you camped out with a friend before, Derek?"

He laughed. "On the rooftops of Upper New York?"

We stared into the firelight.

After a time he said to the flames, "I've never had a friend before, Mr. Seafort."

I didn't know how to answer. In Cardiff I had companions my own age. Together, we ran in the streets and got into mischief. Father, vigilant about my own behavior, grudgingly accepted my choice of associates. Jason and I were especially close, until the football riot of '90.

The silence stretched.

"Mr. Seafort, I want you to know." Derek's voice was shy. "This was the best day of my whole life."

I could think of nothing to say. Not knowing what else to do, I reached out and patted his shoulder.

After a while Amanda yawned, and I found myself doing the same. "A long flight. I'm ready for bed." I stood, and Amanda gathered her blanket.

An awkward moment. Amanda and I took a step toward the larger tent but stopped, embarrassed. Derek pretended not to notice. Hunching closer to the fire he peeled off his shirt in its warmth. I tugged Amanda's hand, gesturing toward our tent. On impulse, she let go my fingers, crossed to Derek. She leaned over him and kissed him on the cheek. In the flickering light I saw him blush right up to the roots of his hair. "G'night." He fled to his tent.

Smiling, I followed Amanda into our own shelter. We began taking off our clothes, poking and jostling each other in the closeness. I shivered when my skin touched the cold foam mattress. Amanda crawled in beside me.

Perhaps it was the first night in the exotic wildness of Western Continent. Aroused as never before, I tried to possess Amanda absolutely. My fingers and tongue roamed, caressing, probing, stroking, taking her warmth and making it mine. I sucked greedily at her juices, her feverish hands guiding me gently. When at last I entered her it was as if I had become whole, our bodies thrusting desperately for fulfillment in simultaneous passion.

When it was over I lay drained of everything, feeling her heartbeat subside slowly against my ear. We rested, but again and again in the night we were like wild animals, coming alive to the frenzy of youth and desire. When morning came at last I slept in Amanda's arms, peaceful, comforted, sated. Whole.

It was never so fine again. Perhaps the newness was gone; perhaps some subtle tides failed to mesh. In the stillness of the nights we came together, loving, tender, eager to satisfy. What we gave each other was good, and pleasing. But the first night remained a loving memory, never equaled.

Derek surely knew what we were experiencing. At least he must have heard Amanda cry out. But during the daytime we were a warm and friendly threesome, enjoying each other's company, relaxing together. Only when dark fell did the two of us shyly retreat to our haven while Derek crawled into his solitary cot.

A dawn came when, Amanda's head resting lightly on my shoulder, I woke with sadness, knowing our togetherness was drawing to a close. Amanda stirred in her sleep. As quietly as I could I slipped out of bed, gathered my clothes and crept out of the tent.

It was bitter cold; I threw some sticks on the embers and was at last rewarded with a sputtering flame. I fed it until it provided some warmth. I put a cup of coffee in the micro and when it heated, I held it between my two hands inhaling its vapor.

Restless, I wandered beyond the edge of the campsite toward the lightening sky, found a place to sit at the crest of a hill looking down into the valley below. Sipping my blessedly hot coffee I watched a moody yellow sun hoist itself over the peaks opposite, casting roseate hues on the bleak gray of dawn. The fog in the valley below began to lift. Across the glen, an eleven-hundred-foot waterfall threw itself endlessly over the cliff into the waiting valley.

Never had I seen a place so magnificent. Dawn brightened into day. Below, a smaller falls became visible as the night mists evaporated. The greens, yellows, and blues of the foliage brightened into their daytime splendor.

I had to leave this peaceful planet, and with it, Amanda. I must sail on to Detour, return briefly to Hope Nation to board passengers, then endure the long dreary voyage home to face an unforgiving Admiralty at Lunapolis. I knew they'd never give me command again. I knew I would never again come to this place. I knew I would lose Amanda to lightyears of forgetfulness.

It was my lot to be banished from paradise.

Overwhelmed by despair amid the stark beauty of the Venturas, I mourned for Sandy Wilsky, for Mr. Tuak, for Captain Malstrom, for Father lost forever in his dour hardness. For the beauty I hadn't known and would never know again. I cursed my weakness, my pettiness, the lack of wisdom that made tragedy of my attempt to captain *Hibernia*. Then Amanda, sweet Amanda, came from the glade and enveloped me in her arms, caressing, hugging, rocking, lending me solace only she could give.

After a while we walked together back to the campsite, my soul clinging to the gentle warmth of her touch. Derek, wearing short pants, shirtless, was just starting off to the stream with a bar of soap. Seeing us, he went on his way, mercifully silent.

"Nicky, those terrible events on *Hibernia* weren't your fault."

I sat brooding near the firepit, waiting for the micro to heat my coffee. "No? My talent is to hurt people. I killed Tuak and Rogoff; you know it wasn't necessary. At Miningcamp I killed the rebel Kerwin Jones and his men, yet made a deal to spare his cohorts on the station. What was the difference?"

"You're too harsh on your—"

"I was cruel to Vax for months. I sent poor Derek to the Chief to be caned for nothing at all. Even Alexi—if I'd been a better leader I wouldn't have had to send him to the barrel. The way I treated the Pilot I can't even discuss. I think of them all the time, Amanda. Lord God, how I hate being clumsy and incompetent!"

"You're not, Nicky."

"Tell that to Sandy Wilsky." My tone was searing.

She was silent for a time. "Must you always do everything right?"

"Not always. But I'm talking about losing my ship and killing my midshipmen and brutalizing the crew!" Again the miasma of despair closed about me.

Amanda sat near, her arm thrown across my shoulders. "You've done your best. Give yourself peace."

"I don't know how." I lapsed silent until Derek returned, his skin pink and briskly scrubbed.

"Man, that's cold!" He plunged into the firesite and stood warming himself by the flames. He glanced at me with concern. "Are you all right, Mr. Seafort?"

"Fine." With an effort I lightened my tone. "What would you people like to do today?" It was to be our last full day in Western Continent.

Over breakfast, we decided we'd hike across the valley to the waterfall. I packed my backpack and set out with the others, hoping physical exertion would help banish my melancholy.

It took only a couple of hours to descend our side of the slope. But the valley was wider than it had appeared from the heights, and we had to pick our way among fallen trunks and viny growths that fastened to every crack. At last, weary, we reached the far side of the glen. A short hike brought us to the base of the waterfall where, to our delight, a pool was hidden in the dense undergrowth. Hot and sweating I began to strip off my clothes. After a moment Amanda did likewise. Derek hesitated, ill at ease.

"Come on, middy! It's no different from the wardroom!" My annoyance was evident. His shyness was from his aristocratic past, not his Navy present. Perhaps, groundside for three weeks, he'd forgotten he shared a bunkroom, head, and shower with Paula Treadwell and the other middies. Blushing, he took off his clothes and waded in.

I'd forgotten how wonderful were simple pleasures. A cold swim after our long hot exertion had a marvelous restorative effect. We cavorted and splashed like small children until our energy was spent. Finally we dressed, had a snack from our packs, and prepared to go back.

"Hey!" Derek pointed to the ground at the pool's edge, where a sandaled footprint was outlined in the mud.

"We're not alone." Amanda was crestfallen.

I said, "Just some other tourists." They'd come to see the spectacular waterfall, as we had.

"We didn't see anyone."

"They're not here now," I said impatiently. "Who knows how long ago they left that footprint?"

Derek stared at the mud. His voice was quiet. "It rained hard two nights ago." The hairs rose on the back of my neck as my imagination brought forth an alien creature sipping water from this very pool. Then I laughed at my foolishness. Aliens wouldn't wear sandals like our own.

"So, someone else is around," I said. It didn't matter.

Derek jumped up with enthusiasm. "I'll bet they're down there!" He pointed to a wooded area past an open field farther down the valley. "Let's find them!"

I didn't want to disturb the other group's privacy, but I had little choice but to follow unless I asserted my authority and demanded that we turn back. My sour mood returned. We scrambled across rocks and through broad-leaved vines until we reached the thicket. We walked along the edge of the field toward the woods.

"Good heavens, that's corn!" Amanda stopped to examine it. Several rows of stalks stood above low-lying vegetation that covered the meadow.

"It can't be; there's no native corn."

"Don't tell me about corn, Nicky."

Ignoring our conversation, Derek ran ahead, out of sight.

"Wait," I called, to no avail. Uneasy, I hurried after him. "Let's go, Amanda."

I stopped so suddenly she caromed into me. Derek, his hands raised, backed slowly away from a ragged man waving a laser. "All of you! Stay right there!" The scarecrow waved his arm back and forth between Derek and the two of us. Casually, I stepped between Amanda and the laser. The man's eyes darted among us. Deeply tanned, he wore cutoff pants with ragged edges.

I cleared my throat. "Good afternoon, Captain Grone."

The gun wavered. "Who told you my name?"

"How many other settlers are hiding in the Venturas?"

"There could be more. How did you know my name?"

"The heli service told us about you." Not exactly a lie. They'd mentioned him in passing.

He waved the laser, sounding glum. "I can't let you go knowing where to find me."

Time to gamble. "Did you bring a recharger for that pistol, when you fled Centraltown?"

He glared, then dropped his eyes and lowered the gun. "It's been out for months," he admitted. "Damn the thing."

"It's all right, Derek," I said. "Put your hands down." Sheepishly, the middy let his hands fall. I stepped forward. "Nick Seafort of the U.N.S. *Hibernia.*" I offered my hand. After a moment the ex-Captain took it. "May I present Miss Frowel, and Midshipman Derek Carr. Midshipman, you salute a Captain!" Derek snapped his fanciest salute, which after a moment the fugitive sailor in his ragged shorts and torn shirt returned.

"Honey, come out!" he called over his shoulder. In a moment a lithe, well-tanned young woman emerged. Amanda quietly looked her over, with a glance my way; I pretended not to notice.

"This is my wife Jana. Jana, this is Mr. Seafort and his friends Derek and Amanda."

"Hi, everyone!" Jana Grone seemed pleased at our company. "Come join us for coffee." As if it were an everyday occurrence, she turned and led us into the woods. We came to a simple hut, hidden under the leafy canopy. A precarious mud-bricked chimney rose from one side. She took a kettle from an iron grate and poured coffee into several glass jars. Ceremoniously, she handed them around.

"To our first guests," she said.

"And our last." Her husband was morose. "He'll report us and they'll come for me."

"As far as I'm concerned," I blurted, surprising myself, "you're a deranged joe who thinks he's the missing Captain Grone. Until I see proof, I've got nothing to tell Admiralty."

Hope flashed in his eyes. "You'd really do that?"

I thought briefly of impressing Grone back into the service to sail *Hibernia,* and decided the ship was safer even with me. "You're a local problem. I have nothing to do with it."

"You mean that?" He probed my expression. "Then we have another chance! Still, I suppose we'll have to move inland. You're the second group to camp within sight of the falls."

"We can move next spring," Jana told him. "Plant a new field farther away." She added wistfully, "We could still hike to the pool sometimes."

Amanda inspected her glass. "Two questions. Where do you get coffee?"

"We plant a little of everything," Grone said, as if proud to show off his accomplishments. "We, uh, borrowed a couple of coffee plants from Hopewell, along with the other vegetables. They grow quite well here. See? They're in the seventh row over." I peered. It all looked the same to me.

"And your other question?" Jana.

"What are you people doing here?"

The two exchanged glances. Jana said, "Tell her."

He glanced about with caution and dropped his voice. "The meteors."

"What meteors?" Derek and Amanda, as one.

Grone spoke in a whisper. "It was night. I was piloting the ten-seater shuttle, helping out a friend. I was almost through the ionosphere when they came. Dozens of them."

"Meteorites," I said. He needed hormone rebalancing. A case for the psych wards.

"Yeah, meteorites. Some real ones, but others too. The ones that sprayed."

"What in hell are you talking about?" My shoulder blades twitched with the same eerie feeling as when I'd confronted Darla's glitch.

"My trajectory almost matched the meteorites. I rode with them a long while. I saw them spray something."

"Oh, come on!" For a moment I'd actually considered putting him on *Hibernia*'s bridge. I shuddered.

"No, they did! Long trails of vapor. You know what it reminded me of? Insecticide."

"So you jumped ship and came here?" My tone was wondering.

"I got out as fast as I could. After I landed I got Jana and we took a heli and a whole bunch of supplies and stopped at Hopewell and got some plants and we took off." His words tumbled. "I smashed the transponder so they couldn't track us."

"But why?"

"If you'd seen the spray you'd know!"

He was starting to bore me. "Know what?"

"They were spraying us, I told you. And you know what happened right after? The epidemic. Some bug nobody's ever seen, that breaks down cell walls and kills whoever it hits. We listened on our radio before it went."

"Who sprayed you?" Amanda was tense now.

"They were," he said darkly.

"Water vapor." My voice was reassuring. "Ice in the meteorites boiled into steam and vaporized. That's all." She studied my face, relaxed a trifle.

Vehemently, Grone shook his head. "Don't give me that goofjuice; you think I'm some groundsider doesn't know the difference? I've been around! I went interstellar three times and ran interplanetary for five years before. How old are you, sixteen? You joeykids think you know everything!" He subsided, grumbling to himself. His wife gave him an encouraging pat. After a moment he smiled at her.

"We're safer out here," Grone said softly, his voice calmer. He looked up to the sky as if for more meteorites. "If they think they've got everybody, they'll stop spraying."

I shook my head. "You've gone around the bend."

"Think so?" He looked cunning. "Then there's no point in reporting us, is there?"

Jana clasped his arm. "Peter took the time to save me before he ran for safety. That's how much he loves me." She squeezed his biceps and he rewarded her with an approving smile.

"The epidemic is over," I said. "Didn't you hear? We have a vaccine."

"They miscalculated this time. Next time will be worse."

I realized logic couldn't reach him, and changed the topic. How did they manage to survive in the wilderness? That set them both off. With pride, they took turns describing their inventions and accommodations. After a while I thought it safe to suggest leaving.

"I promise I won't mention you," I told him. "Good luck. I hope you make it through the winters." On the Western Continent, winter brought frigid winds and heavy snows.

"Oh, we have to," Jana said. "We have a baby coming." On that forlorn note we parted.

Climbing back to our campsite took most of our breath. When we finally dropped our backpacks near the firepit it was almost dark. Derek and Amanda consulted on a farewell dinner and broke out a bottle of wine they'd saved. We dined on steak and potatoes, hot bread, coffee and wine. A lovely meal.

In our tent, knowing it was our final night together, Amanda and I were tender and solicitous, but our passion was muted. A bittersweet moment, but I cherished it nonetheless.

In the morning we packed our tents and equipment into the heli, carefully doused the remains of our fire, and lifted off for the long flight home. Once again I was the only pilot. From time to time I let Derek handle the controls and he was as pleased as a child.

Near home our conversation turned to Captain Grone and his pathetic state of mind. Amanda said, "Imagine the two of them trying to nurse a baby through a mountain winter."

"They'll be all right." I shrugged. "They've already been through it once."

"You seem pretty callous about it."

"Am I? Maybe it comes from being in the Navy. People make their own beds, then have to lie in them." I recalled saying the same to Pilot

Haynes, and quickly changed the subject. "It's what can happen to a Captain under too much stress. Sitting alone in his cabin brooding, imagining everyone is out to get him . . ." Derek shot me a thoughtful glance, and I hurried on. "Having no one to talk to is the worst of it. That's probably why Grone snapped."

"Poor man."

"That's why I'm so worried about going on."

"About what?"

I should have been more cautious. Instead, I said with disgust, "Didn't I tell you? They can't find a Captain to replace me. I'm still senior. I'll have to sail to Detour and home again."

"You can't!"

"I have to," I said. "It's my job."

Her voice was ominous. "How long have you known about this, Nicky?"

"Since I reported to Admiralty." I made a helpless gesture. "There's no way out."

"You could resign!" With an effort, she took the edge from her tone. "I know you tried your best, Nicky. But you were very lucky; you know that. You could have lost the ship."

"More than once."

"But you'll still go? Is glory so important to you?"

"Not glory," I said shortly. "You know I can't break my oath."

It seemed to anger her more. "All this time you knew you would go again as Captain, and didn't tell me?"

"That's why I was so upset all week!"

"I'm the one who has a right to be upset. I hate dishonesty!"

"Dishon—Amanda, I'd have told you if I thought about it. I figured everyone in Centraltown knew. And what choice did I have? I—"

"You have one honorable choice! Resign!"

"He's senior officer," Derek said. "It's his respon—"

"Midshipman, stay out of this! Amanda, that's not fair."

"I hate having gone with you under false pretenses." Amanda's tone was harsh. "And I hate you more for tricking me. I won't discuss it further!"

Enraged, I throttled as high as the motor would allow, indifferent to engine wear. After an hour of mutual sullen silence I spotted the coastline and followed it north to Centraltown.

Amanda, still refusing to speak to me, stalked off with her gear to find a taxi. I remained with Derek to return the heli and sort out our belongings. Late in the evening I saw Derek to the shuttle and thumbed a ride to Amanda's house on the edge of town.

The lights were out but I knocked nonetheless. After several raps she came to the door wearing a night robe. "What is it?" She spoke through the glass door.

I took a deep breath. She deserved honesty, no matter the cost. "Amanda, I love you. I'll never see you again and I want a better memory to carry home. I'm sorry for my faults. I'm sorry for not telling you. Please, forgive me."

She sighed. "Oh, Nicky. Why does it have to be this way?" She came out onto the tiny porch.

"I'm sorry," I said dumbly. "I wanted you to be happy. You made me feel so good."

Her eyes glistened. "I'll miss you, Nick. I'll always think of you."

"I wish I could stay, but I can't. I don't think I'll ever be able to come back."

"I know." She tried to smile and couldn't. She kissed me gently on the forehead. "Good-bye, Nicky. Good luck, whatever you do. Lord God be with you."

"I don't know how I'll get through this without you." I felt tears coming. "Lord God be with you always." I quickly turned away. I left without looking back, afraid if I faced her I could not let her go.

25

In the morning, the sun beat down on the sturdy grasses as I left Admiralty House and crossed the yard to the shuttle pad. I squinted, my head throbbing from the several drinks I'd downed after leaving Amanda. An electrolytic balancer would right me in a hurry, but I wasn't in the habit of carrying hangover pills and I'd had too much pride to ask for one at Admiralty.

Forbee had mixed news: only one lieutenant had volunteered for *Hibernia*, but they'd conscripted another from the Bauxite run. Bauxite, the third planet in Hope Nation system, was serviced by intrasteller Naval vessels without fusion drives. We would rendezvous with the officer's ship to pick him up.

Thus I would sail with three lieutenants including Vax Holser. I also had four midshipmen and cadets, but among them, only Alexi was experienced. If I chose to promote Alexi I'd have to leave Derek senior, and he wasn't ready to command the wardroom. I ordered Forbee to acquire an experienced midshipman however necessary. And quickly: we were to sail in three days.

As I walked toward the departing shuttle a *Hibernia* seaman crossed the tarmac from the shade of the terminal building. He saluted as I reached the shuttle steps. My nod was curt.

"Seaman Porfirio, sir. Uh, could I talk to you a moment, please?" He licked his lips.

"I suppose. Come aboard."

"Aye aye, sir." He didn't move. "Down here, please? It's important, sir." The shuttle pilot waited, ready to close the hatch.

I sighed. "Make it fast, sailor."

Porfirio looked about as if for assistance. "Would you come with me?"

Probably it had to do with a girl. Our petty officers were expected to handle these shoreside problems, but none was in sight. I was the last person the unnerved sailor should ask for advice, but for some reason he had fastened on me. I stepped away from the shuttle hatch. "All right, what is it?"

He backed farther from the shuttle hatch. "This way, Captain. It'll only take a moment."

His manner began to remind me of Captain Grone's. "Get on with it, sailor. No one can hear us."

"I want to show you something, sir." He backed away another few steps. "By the terminal."

Enough was enough. "What is this nonsense, Porfirio?" I stood my ground.

He made shushing gestures. "Please, Captain. There's someone I want you to meet." So, it was a girl. If he thought he could get my permission to bring her aboard, he would by Lord God learn otherwise. The fastest way to put a stop to this foolishness was to confront it right now. I stalked after him to the terminal.

To my surprise Porfirio led me through the building and out the other side. In another minute I'd miss my bloody shuttle, and Lord God knew when there'd be another. The sailor scuttled across the service road. I followed as far as the Centraltown welcome sign, but he showed no sign of stopping. I used my coldest voice. "Where do you think you're taking me, sailor?"

"We're almost there, sir. Honest." He pointed past the far curb to a wooded hillside.

"Of all the insolent, insubordinate monkeyshines!" I was beside myself. "Is that where you've hidden her? In the woods?"

He looked astonished. "You know about her, sir?"

"You think I'm an idiot? How dare you haul me across town for your fun and games?"

His face mirrored his anxiety and confusion. "Please, Captain. You shouldn't talk about her in the open!" The man was demented. It must be something in the air.

Fuming, I followed him down the street. Just beyond the airport perimeter the undergrowth came almost to the road, completely obscuring the woods behind. Porfirio darted along a narrow path through the brush.

I hesitated. I could be mugged, even killed. No one would ever find my body. I almost turned back, but with a muttered curse I plunged in after him. I might as well see it through. I'd already missed my shuttle.

By the time I'd gone a hundred feet, the road behind had completely disappeared. We pushed past low-hanging leafy branches under a dense canopy. Porfirio stopped, put his hands to his mouth, and let out a shrill whistle. I whirled, crouching into karate stance, knowing I'd been lured into a trap.

The bushes rustled. Out stepped Alexi, dirty and unkempt. Behind him came the two cadets, Paula Treadwell and Ricky Fuentes, their uniforms wrinkled and stained. My fury battled with a sense of relief. I bellowed, "Why in God's own hell are you skulking in the woods?" I gave Alexi no time to answer. "Leading me on a wild-goose chase, making me miss my shuttle! I'll have you over the barrel the minute we're aboard, Mr. Tamarov! Ten demerits! A dozen!"

Alexi held out an appeasing hand. "I had to see you alone, sir. This was the only way."

I shrieked, "Alone? Have you lost your mind?"

He unfolded a crumpled paper from the pocket of his soiled jacket. "Please, sir. Read it."

I snatched the paper. "What is this nonsense?"

"A court order, sir. Jared and Irene Treadwell have petitioned for a custody hearing for Cadet Treadwell. They say you enlisted Paula against her will. They say they've changed their minds about going on to Detour and want to stay here. The court issued a temporary order returning her to them until the hearing. It's set for two weeks from now. Sir."

I scanned the legal paper Alexi had summarized, while Seaman Porfirio shifted nervously from foot to foot. Ricky watched, fascinated. Paula looked sheepish. Alexi added, "Every shuttle pilot has been served with a copy, sir. So have all our officers groundside."

"But—it's—I mean—" I stumbled to a halt.

"Yes, sir. You ordered me to keep an eye on the cadets and to bring them back to the ship unharmed. I was lucky when they handed me the order, sir. Ricky and Paula—I mean, Cadet Fuentes and Cadet Treadwell—were sightseeing in town when I was served at the shuttleport. I rounded them up and hid them here. We've slept out every night and I've been sneaking into town for food."

My head was spinning. "And Mr. Porfirio—"

"I've had about a dozen of the crew keeping watch for you, sir. They're all under oath not to say a word."

I was stunned by Alexi's good sense and leadership. It wasn't for him to question his orders; he knew that it was for me to decide whether to release Cadet Treadwell to the court. His instructions were to guard them.

Once the girl was back in her parents' custody we'd never see her again; scheduling the hearing ten days after we were to leave made that clear enough.

Alexi had preserved my options admirably.

I turned to our sailor. "You're commended, Mr. Porfirio. I'll con-

sider how to reward you when we're under weigh." I would give him a
promotion and a bonus for his courage in decoying his Captain. The
seaman grinned at my words.

"Mr. Tamarov, the demerits I spoke of are canceled. You've done a
fine job. Outstanding. I'll mention your exploit in the Log." He broke
into a slow smile of delight. "As for you two . . ." With a scowl I
rounded on the cadets, who suddenly looked apprehensive. "I'll deal
with you after we get back to the ship!" If they were silly enough to
worry about it, that was their problem.

I took a moment to organize my thoughts. "All right, I know how
we'll handle this. Everybody stay put until I get back."

A few minutes later I was at Admiralty House, in Forbee's office,
explaining the situation. "What's your opinion, Mr. Forbee?"

He seemed intrigued by the possibilities. "Well, sir, the United
Nations Circuit Court represents the U.N. Government on Hope Nation. Because we're so far from home the only appeal is directly to the
Governor, who's also a civilian appointee. He has plenipotentiary powers and he's a representative of the U.N. Government. While under
weigh, you, as commander of the vessel, also have plenipotentiary powers. But groundside, a captain is subject to the civilian courts."

I objected. "They're challenging an appointment I made under
weigh. Its validity isn't for them to decide."

"No, sir. But they may think differently."

I paused to think it through. "Admiral Johanson had full authority
over Naval affairs even though he was based planetside. His orders
weren't subject to the court, were they?"

"No, sir." Forbee blinked.

"I'm senior Naval officer and in charge of Admiralty House. I don't
have Johanson's rank, but his duties and responsibilities devolve on me
so long as I'm in Hope Nation system. So I have full authority over
Naval matters as senior representative of Admiralty."

He considered it. "It's a sustainable position, sir."

"Sustai—" I came out of my chair with a roar. "Don't give me that
goofjuice! Paula Treadwell is validly enlisted under Naval authority.
Maintain and support that position as vigorously as may be required. Do
I make myself clear?"

"Aye aye, sir!"

With an effort, I made my voice calm. "Very well. Prepare a general
order for me to sign. As senior officer in the Hope Nation system I
endorse and ratify the enlistment of Cadet Paula Treadwell by Captain

Nicholas Seafort of *Hibernia* and I order all personnel to defend and support that appointment."

Forbee typed into his holovid.

The next sentence was the one that could see me hanged. "I further order all personnel to defend and protect Ms. Treadwell from any civilian authority, including representatives of U.N. Circuit Court, who attempt to interfere with the performance of her duties."

I leaned back in my chair. "Now, Mr. Forbee, round up every local system officer who has children. If he or she is out of port, round up their spouse. All children of local officers are invited to a tour of *Hibernia* tomorrow forenoon. See to it that they accept the invitation. Order a shuttle for the tour. This evening you will pick up some friends of mine in your electricar—you have a car, yes?—and take them home with you for the night. In the morning they will join the tour in clean civilian clothes. Did you get that?"

He said faintly, "Aye aye, sir."

I straightened my tie in my cabin mirror. My hair was brushed neatly, my shoes gleamed, the pants of my dress whites were crisply creased, the length of service medals pinned to my jacket. I thumbed my caller. "Lieutenant Holser to the aft lock, please."

I strode down the Level 2 corridor to the airlock. Vax Holser was waiting when I got there.

It had been two days since I'd left an anxious Captain Forbee at Admiralty House; *Hibernia* was due to depart tomorrow. About half our crew had returned from shore leave and the rest were trickling in hour by hour. Passengers for Detour were being ferried up by shuttle. Paula and Ricky, safely aboard, were confined by my orders to Level 1 until embarkation. Paula apologized to me for the trouble her family made; I accepted her apology and ignored her breach of custom in daring to speak to me directly. The circumstances were unusual.

The officers' children had a jolly tour of the ship. The moment they filed out the airlock to Orbit Station, Mr. Vishinsky and his detail sealed both locks and posted armed sentries. Their orders were to allow no one aboard except crewmen and passengers for Detour. Passengers' belongings were searched for weapons before they were permitted aboard, and their papers scrutinized. As a final precaution I had sentries posted at the ladders to Level 1.

General Tho was of the U.N. Armed Forces, not the Navy. As soon as his shuttle pilot reported that two more children had taken the shuttle to Orbit Station than were waiting to go back, he knew what I had done.

He demanded I return young Ms. Treadwell. I refused. Tension
abounded, until I announced I would go planetside the next day—today
—to appear in Circuit Court regarding Cadet Treadwell.

Now the time had come. I wondered whether I would see *Hibernia*
again. I might well spend the next half year in a local jail waiting for a
ship to take me back to Lunapolis in irons. Well, if so, Amanda would
visit me in my cell.

"Mr. Holser, I order you to defend the ship against unauthorized
entry. By that I mean entry by any person except crew or passengers. If
I'm not back within twenty-four hours you are to assume I'm held under
duress, and that I will not return. You are then to declare yourself Captain and proceed to Detour. Acknowledge your orders."

"Aye aye, sir. Acknowledged and understood. May I go groundside
with you?"

"Of course not. Open the hatch, please." I waited in our airlock, our
inner hatch sealed behind me, until Orbit Station's hatch opened. I
strode into the station and turned toward the shuttle bay.

A U.N.A.F. soldier intercepted me. "General Tho requests you to
come with me, Captain." Was I already under arrest? Uneasy but power-
less, I followed him to the General's office.

I returned General Tho's formal salute. He waited until the aide
had left, his fingers nervously twisting his tiny mustache. When the
hatch had shut, he leaned close. "About time someone gave it to Judge
Chesley." His voice was low. "Man's been too big for his jumpsuit for
years. Good luck!"

Heartened, I shook his hand. The shuttle was the largest one I'd
seen yet. Its many rows of seats were empty; only the pilot, a flight
attendant, and I were aboard. General Tho was showing his sympathies
the only way open to him.

Feeling a regal envoy, I sat in the center of the shuttle amid empty
acceleration seats while the solidly built craft whisked me toward the
surface. Because of the shuttle's great size reentry was barely noticeable.
The pilot glided us toward the runway, brought us down gently, and
touched the ground as light as a feather just as he killed the engines. A
fine performance.

The flight attendant opened the hatch and I stepped out.

"Attention!" Lined up on the tarmac were Captain Forbee and a
gathering of officers and seamen, uniforms clean and crisp as if for inspection. I halted, surprised, my hand on the hatch. I hadn't ordered this
show. Apparently Forbee had arranged it to demonstrate the Navy's
support, and to underline my status as senior officer.

"Carry on, gentlemen." I strode to the terminal, my manner more confident than I felt. Forbee hurried to catch up.

"This way to the car, sir." He gestured to a luxurious late-model electricar.

I smiled in appreciation of his efforts. "Very good, Mr. Forbee."

"With your permission, nine of our officers have asked to be in court with you, sir."

"How many officers do you have groundside at present, Captain Forbee?"

"Nine."

"Very well." Only Forbee climbed into the car with me. The rest piled into two older cars. Our convoy proceeded into town. The U.N. Building was an old-fashioned glass and steel edifice, intended to suggest power and authority.

The parade came to a halt. Accompanied by all our officers in their Navy blues, I marched into the building.

It was to be a special session. Already seated in the courtroom, the judge impatiently tapped his fingers on the gleaming hardwood bar. Though aged, he was imposing in his flaring red robes and white wig. Behind him was displayed our blue and white U.N. flag. Jared and Irene Treadwell sat with their lawyer at one of the counsel tables.

The Naval officers filed into the spectators' benches and mixed with the already sizable crowd. Ignoring the bailiff and court officers, I strode past the polished wooden rail to the unoccupied table.

"You are Captain Seafort of *Hibernia?*" demanded the judge.

"No, sir, I am not," I said firmly. He looked up in astonishment. "I am Nicholas Ewing Seafort, senior Naval officer on Hope Nation and commander of Admiralty House. I am also in command of U.N.S. *Hibernia.*"

His smile was not friendly. "Let the record show the defendant has identified himself."

I abandoned thoughts of being conciliatory; my voice rang through the courtroom. "I am no defendant, Judge Chesley. I have come to warn you, in my official capacity, that you have exceeded your authority."

There were gasps from the visitors' benches. The judge slammed his gavel. "How dare you, Captain? Any more such talk and I'll hold you in contempt of court, which you're already in anyway by your continued imprisonment of the Treadwell girl!"

I shot back, "Any more such talk, sir, and I will declare a state of insurrection and assume military government of Hope Nation until civil order is restored!"

It had popped out of my mouth, before I had time to think. Now my bridges were well and truly burned.

Pandemonium broke out in the courtroom. The judge was apoplectic. I let my voice ring out. "You know perfectly well, as does everyone in this room, that I am lawful Captain of U.N.S. *Hibernia,* that while under weigh I enlisted Paula Treadwell into the United Nations Naval Service, and that her enlistment may not be challenged in civil court. This piece of paper that purports to be an order"—I pulled out the crumpled paper Alexi had given me—"argues that Paula's enlistment was not voluntary and that therefore she should return to the Treadwells' custody. Is that your assertion?" I turned to the Treadwells and their advocate.

The lawyer jumped up. "It certainly is, Your Honor," she said. "The evidence is clear that the minor child was not in full possession of the facts which—"

"Thank you," I cut in coldly. "This court may take judicial notice of Naval regulations. Involuntary enlistment is permitted when in the Captain's judgment the safety of the ship so demands. Cadet Treadwell was so enlisted. She will remain in the Service for the full period of her enlistment. You, sir, have no authority whatsoever over my actions as Captain of *Hibernia* or as senior Naval officer in Hope Nation. I'm surprised you didn't know that or, worse, that you chose to ignore it. I shall suggest to the Government that they recommend your immediate replacement on those grounds." I turned to go. When I was two steps past the bar the judge's strangled voice broke the silence.

"Arrest that man!"

The court officers moved forward. I pointed to the judge, snapped to Captain Forbee, "Arrest that man!"

It stopped them in their tracks. The livid judge and I exchanged glares. After a moment of ominous silence I said calmly, "Would you care to retire with me to your chambers to resolve this matter?"

He glanced back and forth between my unarmed officers and his court officials. With a sharp nod he lunged off the bench to the doorway at his side. He slammed the door behind him.

I paused at the entryway. "Carry on," I said into the stunned silence. I followed into his chambers.

The judge, trembling with rage, faced me from behind his desk.

"Would you like a way out of this?" I made my tone as reasonable as I could manage. At first he was too furious to respond. After a moment he nodded. Apparently he knew the law as well as I did.

"Very well. One, I apologize publicly to the court for my lack of respect and manners. Two, the hearing never took place. The record of it is destroyed. Or gets lost. Three, you dismiss the case for lack of merit, which you discover immediately upon reading the filings today."

It was the Naval solution, of course. A confrontation like ours was intolerable, so we wouldn't allow it to happen. We wouldn't recognize its existence, just as a Captain would be blind to a midshipman's black eye. My apology would satisfy his pride, but would have no other effect; I'd be putting it on a record that was to be destroyed.

He glowered. "You goddamn wiseass."

I ignored the blasphemy. "You tried a fancy move and it didn't work," I said. "If I'd handed her over, you'd have kept her past the time I sailed and the issue would be moot. As it is, I win. Why'd you go out on a limb for the Treadwells? They're not even locals."

The Judge pulled out his chair and slumped into it. "Their lawyer," he muttered. "Miss Kazai. She's helped me out."

"Well, she'll know you tried." Having won, I could afford to be conciliatory.

He gave me a small, grim smile. "Never come back to Hope Nation as a civilian. Not while I live."

My triumph vanished. I thought of Amanda. "No," I said. "I won't be back."

We returned to the courtroom and went through our charade. I apologized humbly for my unmannerly remarks. The judge erased the record. He then looked through the file and dismissed the Treadwells' petition for lack of jurisdiction.

Mrs. Treadwell jumped to her feet as I passed her on the way out. "You won't get away with it!" she shouted. "The courts in Detour will help us! We'll see you there!"

I shrugged. Perhaps.

26

Though the hearing was officially suppressed, the story made its way through the ship. Vax wore a foolish grin for the rest of the day, even during his watch. Alexi went so far as to congratulate me openly; I bit back a sharp reproof.

The rest of our crew straggled back from shore leave. Our final passengers were ferried up to the ship and settled in their cabins. Among the last to board were the Treadwells. I had them escorted directly to the bridge.

"I thought of refusing you passage," I told them. "But I don't want to separate Rafe and Paula sooner than necessary. I let you aboard, but one more protest, one petition, a single interference with the operation of my ship—and that includes harassing Paula—and you'll spend the entire trip in the brig. Is that understood?"

It wasn't that easy. I had to threaten to have them expelled to the station before they finally gave me their agreement.

The purser's last-minute stores were boarded. A new ship's launch, replacing the ill-fated one on which our officers perished, was safely berthed by Lieutenant Holser under my anxious scrutiny. Darla recalculated her base mass without comment.

To my relief all our crew members returned from shore leave; we had no deserters, no AWOLs. Seventeen passengers for Detour chose not to continue their trip; that didn't bother me. Others took their places. On this leg, we would carry ninety-five passengers.

Derek paged me from his duty station at the aft airlock. "The new midshipman is at the lock, reporting for duty, sir."

"Very well. Send him to the bridge." Suddenly I was back at Earthport Station, smoothing my hair, nervously clutching my duffel, anxious to make a good first impression when I reported to Captain Haag. Now I was at the other end of the interview.

"Permission to enter bridge, sir." An unfamiliar voice.

"Granted," I said without turning.

"Midshipman Philip Tyre reporting, sir." He came to attention smartly, his duffel at his feet.

I turned to him and fell silent. He wasn't handsome—he was beautiful. Smooth unblemished skin, wavy blond hair, blue eyes, a finely chiseled intelligent face. He could have been lifted from a recruiting poster.

I took his papers, letting him wait at attention while I looked them over. He'd joined at thirteen and now had three years service. That put him senior not only to Derek, but to Alexi as well. A disappointment for Alexi, but that couldn't be helped. I had plans for Alexi soon enough.

"Stand easy, Mr. Tyre."

"Thank you, sir." His voice was steady and vibrant.

"Welcome to *Hibernia*." I stopped myself from offering my hand. The Captain must keep his distance. "You've been on interplanetary service for the past year?"

The boy flashed a charming smile. "Yes, sir."

"And you've been to Detour."

"Yes, sir. On *Hindenberg*, before I was transferred out." Tyre had seen a lot of service, more than I had when I'd been posted in *Hibernia*.

"It seems you're to be senior middy."

"That's what I understood from Captain Forbee, sir." His smile was pleasant. "I think I can handle it."

"Good. Mr. Tamarov was senior for a while, but I doubt he'll give you any trouble."

"I'm sure he won't, sir." Was there more emphasis in his tone than necessary?

"Very well, Mr. Tyre. Get yourself settled in the wardroom, and have a look around the ship."

"Aye aye, sir." He saluted and picked up his duffel with graceful ease. "Thank you, sir." He turned and marched out. I made a note to reassure Alexi that he hadn't been intentionally demoted.

I sat back, comparing the new middy's entry to Mr. Chantir's. Our new lieutenant had come aboard the evening before. He'd reported to the bridge, saluting easily. He responded to my welcome with a warm, friendly grin. "Thank you, sir. It's good to be aboard."

"It says here you have special talent in navigation."

"I wouldn't say special, sir," he said modestly. "But I enjoy solving plotting problems."

"Then I'll put you in charge of the midshipmen's drills."

He smiled again. "Good. I love to teach." I knew immediately that I would like him. I thought of embittered, tyrannical Lieutenant Cousins and how I'd dreaded our lessons.

We were ready to depart. The Pilot at the conn, we cast off, maneuvered a safe distance from the station, and Fused almost at once. I was so busy I forgot to watch Hope Nation dwindle on the screens before they blanked.

It wouldn't be long before the stars reappeared; we were on a short run to Bauxite to pick up our third lieutenant. A voyage of five weeks by conventional power, in Fusion we could make the hop in less than a day. We'd take longer to maneuver the ship for mating with U.N.S. *Brezia* than to travel the interplanetary distance in Fusion.

Brezia was a small cruiser that shuttled back and forth among the planets of Hope Nation system, available for orbital rescues or other needs of the civilian mining fleet and the area's commercial craft. Lacking fusion engines, *Brezia* cruised at subluminous speeds. Unfortunately, her Captain was only rated interplanetary or I would have shanghaied him as well as his lieutenant.

Pilot Haynes and Lars Chantir worked together during the docking. The Pilot, true to his word, gave no trouble. As he'd said, he was good at his job. After we located *Brezia* he deftly maneuvered us into matching velocity. To avoid the cumbersome chore of mating airlocks, we drifted to within a hundred meters of *Brezia* and I had a T-suited sailor carry a flexible line to their lock. Shortly after, our new officer came across the line, hand over hand, his duffel tied behind his suit.

Having little else to do, I went to the lock to meet him. Correctly, he stripped off his suit before coming to attention. "Lieutenant Ardwell C. Crossburn reporting, sir." A short, round-figured man in his late thirties.

"Stand easy, Lieutenant. Welcome aboard."

"Thank you, sir." He looked around at his new ship. "As soon as I get my gear stowed I can take up my duties, sir. I'll try to be of assistance."

"No hurry, Mr. Crossburn," I said in good humor. "You can wait until after dinner."

"Very well, sir. If you insist." An odd way to speak, but the man had a peculiar manner about him. Well, his record showed him to be a competent and experienced officer. I returned to the bridge and waited impatiently while Mr. Haynes and Lieutenant Chantir plotted Fusion coordinates and rechecked them together. Laboriously I went through the calculations myself and found no error. We Fused.

In seven weeks we would reach Detour, a younger colony than Hope Nation, and one whose environment was less hospitable to humankind. Its air held less nitrogen and slightly more oxygen, but it was breathable. They'd had to do a lot of terraforming to bring down the sulphuric compounds in the atmosphere before Detour could be developed. Now the planet was open for colonization and some sixty thousand settlers had already arrived.

Lars Chantir was my senior lieutenant. Mr. Crossburn, with six years experience, was second. Vax was last in line, but that mattered less among lieutenants than midshipmen, unless the Captain died. The barrel was duly moved to First Lieutenant Chantir's quarters; it was a traditional duty of the senior lieutenant.

I had time on my hands, time to miss Amanda. Our nights in the hills of Western Continent had provided the first sustained intimacy I'd ever known. Knowing how incapable I was, Amanda had still cared for me. I yearned for her presence.

We settled down to shipboard routine. I missed the familiar passengers: Mrs. Donhauser, Mr. Ibn Saud, and, of course, Amanda. Few of our original group were continuing with us; unfortunately the Treadwells were among them.

One day Vax came to me on the bridge, troubled. "Sir, there's something I think you should know."

"What's that?"

He hesitated, on difficult ground. "Lieutenant Crossburn, sir. He's been questioning the crew about the attack at Miningcamp. At first I thought he was just making conversation, but he's seeking out the men who were most involved."

I chose the easy way out. "You know better than to complain about a superior officer."

"Yes, sir. It wasn't a complaint. I was informing you."

"Drop it. I don't care what he asks." I had nothing to hide from my new lieutenant. My conduct would be subject to Admiralty's unblinking scrutiny as soon as we reached home, and I knew I had no chance of emerging without substantial demotion, if not worse. Mr. Crossburn's inquiry could do no harm to my shattered career, though it was unusual.

More disturbing was Lieutenant Chantir's casual comment while I perused a chess manual on a quiet watch. "I'm surprised your midshipmen don't make more effort to work off demerits, sir."

"What do you mean?"

"Yesterday I caned one of them for reaching ten. You'd think he'd take the trouble to exercise them off. They're only two hours apiece."

"Which midshipman?" I asked, my mind on the queen's gambit.

"Mr. Carr. I rather let him have it, for his laziness. What is your policy, Captain? Should I go hard or easy?"

"Neither," I said, disturbed. "Use your judgment." I had issued Derek seven demerits for trying to choke me—and I hadn't forgotten to log them when we got back—but he would have been too well trained by now to blunder into more. "How many did he have?"

"Eleven." Very odd. I didn't think Derek would step that far out of line.

"Let's look them up." I turned on the Log, suspecting I knew the answer. If a lieutenant wanted Derek caned he didn't have to trouble giving him demerits, he would merely send him to Mr. Chantir with orders to be put over the barrel. A first midshipman, on the other hand, couldn't issue such an order. He could only assign demerits, which if given fast enough would have the same effect.

I flipped through the daily notations made by each watch officer. *"Mr. Carr, improper storage of gear, one demerit, by Mr. Tyre. . . . Mr. Carr, insubordination, two demerits, by Mr. Tyre."* Why hadn't Derek worked them off? I turned the pages. *"Mr. Carr, improper uniform, two demerits, by Mr. Tyre. . . . Mr. Carr, inattention to duty, two demerits, by Mr. Tyre."*

There it was. Tyre was piling demerits on Derek faster than he could exercise them off.

I decided I couldn't interfere. It was Derek's bad luck Tyre had made an example of him; the new first middy was asserting his authority. But though I put the incident out of my mind, I had been a midshipman too recently to miss the other signs of trouble. When I saw Alexi on watch he seemed more hesitant, more preoccupied. More significant, I never saw him off watch except at dinner. I realized all my midshipmen seemed to have dropped out of sight. I hoped Alexi would give me a hint, but he was too Navy to do that. Wardroom affairs were settled in the wardroom.

It was not a busy time for me. In Fusion, we had no need for navigation checks, no data on the screens, nothing to do except keep an eye on the environmental systems: recycling, hydroponics, power. Brooding about the wardroom situation, I began watching for new Log entries.

Derek, Alexi, and both cadets were fast accumulating demerits. Seven for Alexi in three days, two more for Derek. Sixteen between Paula and Ricky.

I bent the rules to ask Philip Tyre outright. "Everything going well in the wardroom, Mr. Tyre?"

He smiled easily. "Yes, sir. I have it under control." As always, he was immaculate. Slim and slight, his face was faintly disturbing in its perfection.

"You're working with a good group of officers, Mr. Tyre."

"Yes, sir. They need reminding who's in charge, but I'm on top of that." His innocent blue eyes questioned me. "Is anything wrong, sir?"

"No, nothing," I said quickly, knowing I had strayed across the unwritten line that kept the Captain out of the wardroom's business.

Dr. Uburu came to me next, catching me outside the dining hall on the way back from dinner. "Did you know," she asked gravely, "that I treated Paula Treadwell this week?"

"No, I didn't."

"I thought not." She paused as we reached the top of the ladder.

"What for, Doctor? If I'm not violating your professional ethics?"

"Hysteria." She met my eye.

"Good Lord." I waited for her to continue. She said nothing. "What was the cause?"

"I swore an oath not to tell you," she said. "My patient insisted, before she'd talk about it."

My hand clenched the rail. "I could order you," I said.

"Yes, but I wouldn't obey." Her voice was calm. She smiled, her dark face lighting with warmth. "I don't mean to make problems, Captain. Just keeping you advised."

"Thank you." I went to my cabin and lay on my bunk, wishing the Chief still visited for evening conversations. Since I'd broken off our sessions after Sandy's death he had been friendly and helpful, but had kept his distance.

My next watch was shared with Lieutenant Crossburn. After a long period of silence he made efforts to start a conversation. I let him lead it, my mind elsewhere. He soon brought up the attack at Miningcamp. "When the rebels forced their way on board," he asked, "who was most helpful in repelling them?"

"Mr. Vishinsky was invaluable," I said, not wanting to be bothered. "And Vax Holser."

His next question snapped me awake. "What made you decide to let a dozen suited men on board in the first place?"

My tone was sharp. "Are you interrogating me, Lieutenant?"

"Not at all. But it was an amazing incident, Captain. I write a diary. I try to include important things that happen near me. I'll change the subject if you'd rather."

"No," I said grudgingly. "It was a mistake, letting them on board. I very much regret it."

He seemed pleased at my confidence. "It must have been a terrible day."

"Yes."

"I write every evening," he confided. "I pour my thoughts and feelings into my diary."

"It must be a great solace," I said, disliking him.

"I never show it to anybody, of course, even though it reads quite well. I'm the only one who's seen it, other than my uncle."

It seemed polite to prompt him. "He's a literary critic?"

"No, but he understands Naval matters. Perhaps you've heard of him. Admiral Brentley."

Heard of him? Admiral Brentley ran Fleet Ops at Lunapolis, and this man had his ear! My heart sank.

"You've written about Miningcamp in that little diary, Lieutenant?"

"Oh, yes." His manner was modest. "It's very dramatic. Uncle will be intrigued, I'm sure."

I let the conversation lapse, fretting. After a while I shrugged. Admiralty didn't need Mr. Crossburn's little book to know how badly I'd managed.

But three weeks into the cruise I knew I would have to take action. Mr. Crossburn had left the subject of Miningcamp and was asking about the execution of sailors Tuak and Rogoff. At the same time, the morale of my midshipmen and cadets was plummeting. Alexi stalked the ship in a cold fury, civil to me but otherwise seething with unexpressed rage. Derek appeared depressed and tired.

"I've had Mr. Tamarov up twice," Lieutenant Chantir told me. "I went fairly easy on him, but I had to give him something." I was already aware; I was watching the Log carefully now. I began checking the exercise room, realizing that one of the reasons I rarely saw the middies and cadets was that they were usually working off demerits.

Perplexed, I took my problems to Chief McAndrews. At this point I didn't hesitate to display my ignorance. He already knew my limitations.

"What did you expect?" he asked bluntly. "You asked the Naval station to supply you officers. Where did you think they'd get them?"

"I don't understand." I shuffled, feeling young and foolish, but I needed to know.

He sighed. "Captain, Mr. Chantir volunteered, yes? The other two officers were requisitioned. If Admiralty told you to supply a lieutenant for an incoming ship, whom would you pick?"

"Mr. Crossburn." I spoke without hesitation.

"And which midshipman?"

I swore slowly and with feeling.

"You gave the joeys in the interplanetary fleet a chance to get rid of their worst headaches."

I damned my stupidity, my blindness. "How could I have been so dumb? I asked for officers and didn't even check their files to see who I was getting!" A real Captain would have known to watch for that trick.

"Easy, sir. What do you think the files would have shown?"

I paused. A good question. The notation "tyrant" or "sadist" was unlikely to appear in Mr. Tyre's personnel file. As for Lieutenant Crossburn's diary, what the man wrote in his cabin during his free time wasn't subject to Naval regulations. Even if his officious private inquiries stirred up trouble, that was hard to prove, and moreover it would be foolhardy to rebuke a man who had the ear of the fleet commander. No wonder his Captain was delighted to get rid of him.

I went back to my cabin to think. I had no sympathy for those who misused our Naval traditions for their own ends, but I didn't know how to stop Mr. Tyre without violating tradition myself. As for Mr. Crossburn, how could I order him not to keep a diary? I found no solution.

In the meantime, I ordered Alexi to advanced navigational training, followed by a tour in the engine room under Mr. McAndrews. That should give him some respite from Mr. Tyre.

It didn't. Alexi continued to accumulate demerits. Again he reached ten and was sent to Lieutenant Chantir's cabin.

Two days later we shared a watch. He eased himself into his chair, wincing. I blurted, "Be patient, Alexi."

"About what, sir?" His voice was unsteady. Seventeen now, nearly eighteen, he could expect better treatment than he was getting. Yet his Academy training held firm. He would not complain to the Captain about his superior.

I deliberately stepped over the line. "Be patient. I know what's going on."

He looked at me, his usual friendliness replaced by indifference. "Sometimes I hate the Navy, sir."

"And me too?"

After a moment his face softened. "No, sir. Not you." He added quietly, "A lot of people are being hurt." It was as close as he would come to discussing the wardroom.

Meanwhile Mr. Crossburn continued his scribbling. On watch he would flip idly through the Log, scrutinizing entries made prior to his arrival. He was delving into Alexi's defense of the unfortunate seamen at their court-martial. He asked me how well I thought Alexi had performed.

"Lieutenant, your questions and the reports you write are damaging the morale of the ship. I wish you'd stop."

"Is that an order, sir?" His tone was polite.

"A request."

"With all due respect, sir, I don't think my diary is under Naval jurisdiction. I'll ask Uncle Ted about that when I see him. As for asking questions, of course I'll stop if you order it."

"Very well, then, I so order."

"Aye aye, sir. Since your order is so unusual I request that you put it in writing."

I considered a moment. "Never mind. You're free to carry on." A written order, viewed without knowledge of his constant prying, would appear paranoid and dictatorial. Anyone who hadn't experienced Lieutenant Crossburn firsthand wouldn't understand, and I was in enough trouble with Admiralty as it was.

I had little better luck with Philip Tyre. I called him to my cabin, where our discussion could be less formal than on the bridge.

"I've been reviewing the Log, Mr. Tyre. Why do you find it necessary to hand out so many demerits?"

He sat at my long table, his arm resting on the tabletop much as the Chief's had before I'd isolated myself. His innocent blue eyes questioned me. "I'll obey your orders, sir. Are you telling me to ignore obvious infractions?"

"No, I'm not. But are you finding infractions, or searching for them?"

"Captain, I'm doing the best I know how. I thought my job was to keep wardroom affairs from coming to your attention, and I've been trying to do that. As I certainly haven't called any problems to your notice, someone else must have." It was said so reasonably, so openly, that I could have no complaint.

"No one's complained," I growled. "But you're handing out demerits faster than they can work them off."

"Yes, sir, I've noticed that. I encouraged Mr. Carr and Mr. Fuentes to spend more time in the exercise room. I've even gone myself to help them with their exercises. A better solution would be for them to stop earning demerits." His untroubled eyes met mine.

"How do you propose that they do that?"

"By following regulations, sir. My predecessor must have been terribly lax. I observe a lack of standards in his own behavior, sir. It's no wonder he couldn't teach the others. I'm trying to deal with it."

I sighed. The boy was unreachable. "I won't tell you how to run the wardroom. I will tell you that I'm displeased about the effects on morale."

Tyre's voice was earnest. "Thank you for bringing it to my attention, sir. I'll make sure their morale problems don't bother you further."

"I want them eliminated, not hidden! That's all!"

The midshipman saluted smartly and left. I paced the cabin, bile in my throat. Very well; he'd been warned. I would give him until we left Detour. If he didn't improve, Mr. Tyre had made his bed; he'd have to sleep in it.

On my next visit to the exercise room I found Derek and Ricky working, Derek on the bars, the cadet struggling at push-ups and leg lifts on the mat. Alexi was absent. The two perspiring boys waited silently for me to leave.

I didn't come across Alexi for three days, until we next shared a watch. "You haven't been in the exercise room of late, Mr. Tamarov."

He glanced at me without expression. "No, sir. I've been confined to quarters except to stand watch and go to the dining hall."

"Good Lord! For how long?"

"Until my attitude improves, sir." His gaze revealed nothing, but his cheeks reddened.

"Will it improve, Alexi?"

"Unlikely, sir. I'm told I'm not suitable material for the Navy. I'm beginning to believe it."

"You're suitable." I tried to cheer him up. "This will pass. On my first posting my senior middy was very diffcult to deal with, but we got to be friends." I realized how fatuous I sounded. Jethro Hager was nothing like the vicious boy fate had put in charge of my midshipmen.

"Yes, sir. I don't mind so much, except when Ricky cries himself to sleep."

I was alarmed. "Ricky, crying?"

"Only two or three times, sir. When Mr. Tyre isn't around." That was bad. Ricky Fuentes was a cheerful, good-natured boy; if he was in tears something was very wrong. I thought briefly of the lesson I had given Vax Holser when I succeeded to Captain, an approach I'd decided against with our new midshipman. In Vax's case I'd recently been a member of the wardroom and had personal knowledge of his behavior. Also, Vax was a good officer who was making a sincere effort to combat a personal problem. Philip Tyre was not.

In three weeks we would Defuse for a nav check, and then we'd have only a few more days to Detour. I could wait.

But a few days later Mr. Chantir raised the subject openly. "Sir, something's gone wrong in the wardroom. I've had Mr. Carr and Mr. Fuentes up again. The Log is littered with demerits."

"I know."

"Is there anything you could do?"

"What do you suggest, Mr. Chantir?"

"Remove the first midshipman, or distract him. Lord, I'd enjoy having him sent to me with demerits after what he's done to the others."

"He'll make sadists of us all, Mr. Chantir. No, I won't remove him. I have witnessed no objectionable behavior. He's scrupulously polite, he obeys my orders to the letter, he's excellent at navigation drills and in his other studies. I can't beach him simply because I don't like him."

"That wouldn't be the reason, Captain."

"No, but that's what it would look like to Admiralty. They don't know that Derek and Alexi aren't giving him a hard time."

"What do you expect of me when these joeys are sent to the barrel, then?"

"I expect you to do your duty, Mr. Chantir." He quickly dropped the subject.

As time passed Mr. Crossburn threw caution to the winds. Twice he mentioned how eagerly he was looking forward to seeing his uncle Admiral Brentley and talking over old times. I ignored him, but my uneasiness grew.

For a diversion I called drills. The crew practiced Battle Stations, General Quarters, Fire in the Forward Hold at unexpected intervals. The sudden action seemed a relief.

At last came the day Pilot Haynes took his place on the bridge, along with Alexi and Lieutenant Chantir. I brought the ship out of Fusion, and stars leaped onto the simulscreens with breathtaking clarity. The swollen sun of Detour system glowed in the distance. We would Fuse for four more days and emerge, hopefully, just outside the planet's orbit.

I waited impatiently for the navigational checks to be done. With Pilot Haynes, Mr. Chantir, and Alexi all computing our course there was no need for me to recheck their calculations, but still I did. Finally satisfied, I ordered the engine room to Fuse.

That evening, I had a knock on my cabin hatch. Philip Tyre stood easily at attention, his soft lips turned upward in a pleasant expression. "Sir, excuse me for intruding, but a passenger wishes to speak to you. Mr. Treadwell." A passenger couldn't approach officers' country; he needed an escort to arrange contact with me unless he found me in the dining hall.

"Tell him to write—oh, very well." Though I could refuse to see him, another tirade from Jared Treadwell about his daughter was no more than I deserved for rashly enlisting her. "Bring him." The middy saluted, spun on his heel, and marched off. I paced in growing irritation, dreading the interview.

Again, a knock. "Come in," I snapped. Mr. Tyre stepped aside. Rafe Treadwell came hesitantly into my cabin. I blurted, "Oh, you. I was expecting . . ." I waved Philip his dismissal.

The lanky thirteen-year-old smiled politely. "Thank you for seeing me, sir."

"You're welcome. Is this about your sister?"

"No, sir."

I waited. He stood formally, arms at his sides. "I'm hoping, Captain Seafort, that you'd allow me to enlist too."

For a moment I was speechless. "What?" I managed. "Do what?"

"Enlist, sir. As a cadet." Seeing my expression he hurried on. "I thought I wanted to stay with my parents, but things have changed. I don't know if you need more midshipmen but I'd like to volunteer. I'd like to be with my sister for a while longer, and I just can't believe how much the Navy has done for her."

I shot him a suspicious look. If the boy was twitting me I'd stretch him over the barrel, civilian or no.

"I mean it, sir. She always used to ask me for help. Now she doesn't even have time for me and when I do see her, it's like talking to a grown-up. She's about three years older than me now." He shook his head in wonderment.

"What about your parents?"

"Paula and I were creche-raised, sir. Community creche, back in Arkansas. I knew our parents but we didn't spend much time with them. They took us out of creche when they decided to emigrate. They can survive without us."

"They don't act like it."

He grinned. "They think togetherness is something they can proclaim. They don't realize you have to grow up with it. They'll get used to being without us."

"And the discipline? You'd enjoy that?"

"No, I'll probably hate it. But it might be good for me." He sounded nonchalant, but, at his side, his hand beat a tattoo against his leg.

I paced anew. Another midshipman would be useful, though hardly necessary. Having Rafe in the wardroom would certainly help Paula's morale. But taking both Treadwell children without their parents' consent wouldn't be appreciated by Admiralty at home, to say nothing of the

Treadwells. Well, I was already in so much hot water that one more mistake didn't matter.

"I'll let you know." I opened the hatch.

"But I've only got—"

"Dismissed!" I waited.

"Yes, sir." His tone was meek, passing my first test.

That night Mr. Tuak came, for the first time in months. He peered at me through the cabin bulkhead, making no effort to grab me, until at last I woke. I was disturbed, uneasy, but barely sweating. I showered and went back to sleep, unafraid.

Three days later we Defused for the last time on our outward journey. We powered our auxiliary engines for our approach to Detour. Pilot Haynes, Mr. Tyre, and Alexi had the watch; of course I was also on the bridge.

Philip Tyre sat stiffly at a console checking for encroachments. I noticed he kept Alexi on a very short leash, ordering him to sit straight when he relaxed in his seat and observing Alexi's work closely. Tyre never raised his voice, never asked anything unreasonable, and never missed a thing.

Detour Station drifted larger in the simulscreens as the Pilot maneuvered us ever closer. Finally the rubber seals on the locks mated. We had arrived.

I thumbed the caller. "Mr. Holser, arrange a shuttle. I'll be going planetside."

"Aye aye, sir."

I turned to Philip Tyre. "Where's Mr. Carr?"

"In the wardroom, sir. I believe he's sleeping."

"In the middle of the day?"

"Yes, sir. I had him standing regs last night. Then he did some exercises." His wide blue eyes regarded me without guile. "Shall I wake him?"

"I was going to take him groundside."

"Yes, sir. I'd told him he was confined to ship during the layover for his insubordination, but of course your wishes prevail."

"I'll take Mr. Tamarov, then."

"Him too, sir. Unless you contermand my orders." As he'd spoken in front of Alexi, it was impossible for me to countermand him. Discipline had to be maintained.

I turned to Alexi. "What did you do, Mr. Tamarov?"

"I was insolent, sir," he said without inflection. "So I was informed."

A cruel punishment. The midshipmen had long leave in Hope Nation so they weren't entitled to go shoreside as a matter of right, but to travel so far and be denied what could be their only chance to see the colony was harsh indeed.

"Very well. I'm sorry, Mr. Tamarov. You'll stay aboard; I'll go alone." As I left the bridge the rank injustice helped steady my resolve. I saw Lieutenant Crossburn coming up the ladder from Level 2.

"Mr. Crossburn, find young Mr. Treadwell—Rafe Treadwell—and take him to your cabin. Keep him there until I order otherwise." I would keep the Treadwell twins together. Their parents be damned. Injustice was the way of the world.

Crossburn gaped. "Aye aye, sir. Don't the passengers disembark today?"

"They'll start later this afternoon. Do as you're told." I went on to my cabin.

A few minutes later I was climbing into a shuttle in the station's launch berth. Everything about Detour Station was smaller than at Hope Nation: far fewer personnel, smaller corridors, lower ceilings. Even a smaller shuttle. This one held only twelve passengers and looked well used.

"I've radioed down to tell them we're coming, Captain," the shuttle pilot said as we drifted clear off the station.

"Thank you."

"A ship from outside is a major event. You're the first since *Telstar,* half a year ago."

"*Telstar* made it, then?"

"Of course." He waited for me to explain.

"She didn't reach Miningcamp."

"Where is she?"

"No one knows." I stared bleakly at his console.

The pilot shrugged. "She'll turn up. Anyway, have you brought us the polyester synthesizer?"

I tried to remember my cargo manifest. "I think so. Why, are you short of clothing?"

"Somewhat. We've made do with cottons over the years, but all the fashions are in polyester and the ladies are restless. Hang on, atmosphere is building." In a moment the buffeting from pockets of denser atmosphere occupied his full attention.

Detour was considerably smaller than Hope Nation, smaller in fact than Earth, but its greater density made for near-terrestrial gravity. I peered through the porthole. Much of the planet was still barren, with patches of lichen and moss taking hold on the outcrops of bare rock. If I could see the patches from our height they must be huge, evidence of massive terraforming.

We swooped lower into a horizontal flight pattern. Now I could spot patches of greenery, and soon, checkerboard fields dotting the land-scape. Tall trees grew in random patterns. I found a road, then another. We were approaching what habitation we'd find on this recently barren planet.

The pilot powered back for touchdown. We glided over the runway, wings in VTOL position, and hovered before drifting to a landing. Si-lence assaulted my ears. The Pilot grinned. "Welcome to the center of civilization, Captain."

I smiled back. "Thanks. It's good to be here." The hatch opened and I took a deep breath. A distinctly sulphurous smell. My eyes watered. "Gecch. Do you get used to this?"

He looked surprised. "Used to what? Oh, the air? Sure, just takes a week or so. Don't worry about it."

I climbed out of the shuttle. About twenty men and women were gathered beyond the wingtip, waiting. One of them came forward, a tall, graying man with an air of authority.

"Captain Seafort? Welcome to Detour." He held out his hand. Around his shoulders hung a blue and white ribbon from which was suspended the bronze plaque of office.

I shook his hand, then saluted. "Governor Fantwell? I'm honored."

The colonial Governor smiled. "Let me introduce you around. Mayor Reuben Trake, of Nova City. Walter Du Bahn, president of the Bank of Detour." I began shaking hands. "City Council President Ellie Bayes, Jock Vigerua, who owns the mines nearby. You don't realize, Captain, what an event it is for a ship to come in; we only get two a year. Miss Preakes, editor of the *Detour Sun* . . ."

The introductions were finally completed. He guided me to an elec-tribus; we all clambered in and found seats. "We've put on a lunch at City Hall." The Governor was genial. "Then we'll show you the town."

"I don't suppose you have any Naval personnel about?"

"Not a one," Governor Fantwell said cheerfully. "Nary a seaman. Are you shorthanded?"

"There's a billet I wanted filled." My own. But I'd known there was no Naval station on Detour and wasn't surprised.

City Hall was a plain, metal-sided building in the center of town. I could tell immediately it was City Hall; a large sign hanging over the door said so. In other respects it was exactly like all the surrounding structures.

Seated at a table draped with a fancy cloth and festooned with bright silverware I said quietly to the Governor, "Actually, I came to talk to you before dumping a problem in your lap. Yours and the judge's."

"Oh?" He raised an eyebrow. I wondered if any problem I brought could faze him. "Just a sec. Let me get Carnova." He beckoned across the hall to a rugged man who promptly joined our table. "What do you propose to dump on us?"

I told them briefly about the Treadwell situation. "I've decided to let the boy enlist, and the parents will explode when they hear. They raised quite a ruckus on Hope Nation."

"This isn't Hope," Judge Carnova said bluntly. "We do things differently. The Navy isn't under my jurisdiction. I won't even give them a hearing."

"I'll back you up," the Governor told him. He turned to me with an easy smile. "You see? Your problem is solved."

I fiddled with a fresh fruit cup. Oranges and grapes, kiwi, bananas, and other fruits I couldn't identify. "I wish everything were that easy."

"Tell me," said the Governor. "Is it that I'm getting older, or are you rather young for a Captain?"

I sighed and launched into the familiar explanation.

27

After returning to my ship I summoned Rafe Treadwell to the bridge. He entered hesitantly, his apparent calm betrayed by the fingers twisting at his shirt.

"I'm prepared to enlist you."

"Thank you." His shoulders slumped. "I was afraid you'd change your mind at the last minute."

"Sit at the console. Write a note to your parents telling them you've enlisted voluntarily. Give them your reasons. As soon as you're done I'll give you the oath."

"Yes, sir."

"Before you do, I have to warn you. Conditions are, uh, rather strained at the moment. You'll be subjected to unusually intense hazing, even for a cadet."

He swallowed. "Yes, I've heard." Of course, his sister would have told him. He bent to the console and typed his note.

After I administered the oath I thumbed my caller. "Mr. Tyre, bring Mr. Tamarov to the bridge."

A few moments later they appeared. Alexi was heavily flushed and breathing hard; I must have interrupted a session in the exercise room.

"Mr. Tyre, I'm seconding Mr. Tamarov for special duties for two days. He'll guard our new cadet until we leave port. Kindly release him from your other requirements."

"Of course, sir." Tyre smiled pleasantly. "Will they stay in the wardroom?"

"Not until we leave Detour." Knowing the Treadwells, I would take no chances, even in orbit far above the planet. I ordered Alexi and Rafe Treadwell bunked in the crew's privacy chamber on Level 3. Alexi couldn't conceal his relief at escaping Mr. Tyre, however briefly.

Tyre appeared not to notice. "I'll help them move, sir," he said. "Can I do anything else to be useful?"

I sent them away, reflecting on the irony. Other than an insane desire to destroy his subordinates, Philip Tyre was an excellent midshipman, eager, helpful, diligent at his studies. I was sure he felt no guilt for the torture he inflicted.

I made a gesture of disgust. Imagine Derek standing regs, at his age. Ridiculous. I wondered how Philip had passed the psych interviews, and how he'd been dealt with as a cadet. Had he been brutalized? Not that it would be the slightest excuse for his own behavior. Still, I wondered.

At dinner Lieutenant Crossburn asked, "You're keeping the Treadwell boy on board?" I braced; obviously his question was but a preliminary.

"Yes." Another affair for him to probe.

"I could be of assistance with the senior Treadwells, sir. That is, when they find out their son isn't going ashore."

I could imagine Crossburn helping with the Treadwells. Asking how they felt, for instance, to record their reactions in his little diary.

"No thank you. I'll attend to it."

"How many enlistments without parental consent do you think the Navy's seen, sir?" His eyes were guileless.

"That's quite enough, Mr. Crossburn." My rebuke, too, would find its way into his record. I didn't care. I was tired, lonely, perturbed by the effect my new officers had on the crew. I missed Amanda, and in a few weeks I'd pass tantalizingly close to her one last time. That would be almost too much to bear.

I thought of home. Perhaps Father would take me back, after I was forced to resign. He would say nothing, of course. That was his way.

As my watch ended, our first departing passengers were crowding into the small shuttles that serviced Detour Station. Several trips would be required to accommodate them. The Treadwells were due to leave in the morning; tonight they would surely notice their son's absence. I went to bed wishing I knew how to avoid the forthcoming row.

I woke to a commotion in the corridor. I thrust on my pants and flung open the hatch, peered to the east. Irene Treadwell, trying unsuccessfully to twist free from Vax Holser's firm grip.

She caught sight of me. "Tell this brute to let me go!"

"You aren't allowed up here, ma'am," Vax said. He flashed me a glance of apology. "She was trying to get into the wardroom, sir."

"Where's my son?" Ms. Treadwell's voice rose. "What have you done to Rafe? I went looking for him and he's nowhere to be found! Are you stealing my other child?"

"We're not steal—"

"Are all of you people crazy?" At last she freed herself and rubbed her reddened wrist. "I tried the purser but he wouldn't tell me anything. I went to the lounge and Rafe wasn't there. I tried the wardroom—yes, I

know I'm not supposed to—and a big boy was on a chair in his undershorts reciting a book! He didn't even stop; they just closed the door on
me! What have you done with my Rafe?"

I thought of sending for Lieutenant Crossburn. I took my holovid,
slipped Rafe's chip into it. "Go back to your cabin and read this."

"Does it say you've taken Rafe? You monster!" Her scream echoed
down the corridor. "Not my boy! You can't!"

"Lieutenant, take her away!" I tried to close my hatch but she
blocked it with her foot. Vax hauled her into the corridor. I closed the
hatch quickly, leaned against it until the shouting died away. My limbs
felt weak. I climbed into bed, lay wide awake.

How often were similar scenes played out, back on Earth? When
the origins of melanoma T were understood and the Navy lowered cadet
enlistment age to thirteen, did parents face the loss of their children
without qualms? How many mothers reacted with hysteria like Irene
Treadwell? The Navy required consent from but one parent. I thought of
my own host mother, in Devon, whom I'd never seen. What did she look
like? Would she have cared?

I tossed fitfully until early morning, then dressed and went to the
officers' mess for breakfast. I sat at the long table, alone except for
Lieutenant Chantir, and sipped coffee while waiting for my scrambled
eggs and toast. Other officers drifted in, found places. I picked at my
food.

"I hear there was a ruckus outside your hatch last night." Lieutenant Crossburn took a seat alongside me.

"Um."

"Mrs. Treadwell was on the first shuttle down this morning." A
pause. "They say when she went to court in Hope Nation you tried to
throw the judge in jail." Crossburn took a forkful of his eggs.

My tone was acid. "I told you not to talk to her."

"Oh, we spoke several days ago, before your order. I merely listened."

"More grist for your mill, Mr. Crossburn?"

"Sir, I fail to understand your objections to my diary. Frankly, I
intend to bring the matter up with my uncle when we get home."

I stared. No lieutenant could speak so to his Captain.

Mr. Chantir intervened. "Ardwell, I order you to be silent. Leave
the Captain alone!"

"Aye aye, sir." Crossburn pursed his lips. After a moment's thought
he pulled a piece of paper from his pocket and made a note. I considered hurling my coffee at his face, decided against it.

"Pardon, sir, may I join you?" Philip Tyre. My nod was curt, but he sat anyway. "Good morning."

I responded with a grunt.

"Sir, do you think I might go groundside tonight? It's been a year since I've seen Detour." A shy grin. "I met a girl there last winter, but I suppose she's forgotten me." Your typical lighthearted youngster. I thought of Derek, humiliated, made to stand regs when Mrs. Treadwell barged into the wardroom the night before. About to refuse, I thought better of it. I would play out my hand. "Permission granted, Mr. Tyre. But a word with you first."

For privacy I took him to the nearby passengers' lounge. "Mr. Tyre, I think you're too hard on the midshipmen."

He reflected. "I'll obey every order you give, sir. Please tell me exactly what you want me to do."

"Ease up on them."

He wrinkled his brow. "I'm afraid I don't understand. Should I ignore their violations?"

I lost patience. "No, just ease up. Consider this a warning. Keep riding them and you'll get a surprise you won't like."

His face clouded with dismay. "I'm terribly sorry I've offended you, sir." Agitated, he ran his hand through his hair. "I try so hard," he muttered, half to himself. "I really do, but people misunderstand . . . I wish I could figure . . ."

Abruptly his gaze returned to the present. He stiffened, almost coming to attention. "I didn't think I was riding them hard, but I'll try my best to do what you ask. I'm truly sorry, sir." He seemed near tears.

I left him for the bridge.

All that day we disembarked passengers and unloaded cargo. I checked the manifest: a poly synthesizer was indeed on our cargo manifest and would be off-loaded with the next shipment. I stayed on the bridge, not sure why. I was free to leave the ship. Should I remain aboard, considering the wardroom tension and my problems with Ardwell Crossburn?

No, we were docked at a distant port. I'd be blessed if I'd let those two joeys ruin my leave. I put on a fresh uniform to go shoreside. Too bad Derek couldn't accompany me. Or Alexi.

Waiting for the aft lock to cycle I abruptly turned away, leaving the startled rating to gape at my retreating back.

I stalked down to Level 3, to the crew privacy room, where Alexi opened at my knock. He seemed fresh and rested. Cadet Rafe Treadwell stood proudly at attention in his new gray uniform.

"As you were, cadet. Mr. Tamarov, come with me. Mr. Treadwell, do you think you can obey orders exactly?"

"Aye aye, sir."

"That's 'yes, sir.' " Alexi, with disgust.

Rafe looked abashed. "Yes, sir, I mean."

"These are your instructions. Lock the hatch when we leave and open it only when you hear my voice or Mr. Tamarov's. Understand?"

"Yes, I—which do I say?" he asked Alexi.

"Aye aye, sir!"

"Aye aye, sir." Rafe's anxious glance darted between us.

I couldn't help smiling. "Very well." I went back to the ladder. Alexi followed, worried. At the airlock I keyed the caller. "Bridge, this is the Captain. I'm going groundside, alone."

"Very well, sir." Lieutenant Chantir would log me out.

"Come along," I snapped at Alexi. The sentry gaped. I glared. "You have a problem, sailor?"

"No, sir!"

"I'm going groundside, alone. Note it in your report."

He was a slow thinker. "But the midshipman—?"

I fixed him with a cold glare. "What midshipman?" Eventually the man smiled weakly. We cycled through the lock.

We boarded the waiting shuttle. As we sat I said to Alexi, "Detour is quite interesting. If you weren't confined to ship, I'd show you the town." Comprehending at last, his face lit with pleasure.

For the rest of the day we wandered Nova City. Detour, with a population of only sixty thousand, was far less developed than Hope Nation, though it was growing fast.

The countryside bore the fresh scars of construction I'd expected to find in Centraltown. Trees and bushes grew in profusion, planted in their thousands by the terraformers, who'd brought insects and worms to aerate the soil, nitrates to fertilize it, and seeds to sow our crops. After seventy-six years of their labor, the terrain surrounding Nova City had at last begun to resemble home.

I wondered how much of the food chain they'd managed to introduce. Did Nova have rats, or mice? Cockroaches? I never did find out, but I did notice a few flocks of birds overhead. We also saw grain scattered in oversize bird feeders, among the fields.

Alexi relaxed further as the day wore on, grateful both for my company and the respite from his nightmare aboard ship. "It's beautiful, sir. If only the air were easier to breathe."

"They're working on it." Huge skimmers sucked air into the

desulphurization works, which removed sulphur oxides from the air. The plants had been operating for decades, and Detour's sulphur level was measurably reduced.

After several false starts, not knowing how to begin, I blurted, "I'm sorry for what you're going through."

He stiffened. "I'm under orders not to discuss it, sir. I'm told it's bad for morale."

"They're countermanded."

"Aye aye, sir. I hate his guts! I want to kill him!"

I glanced at him, shocked. He meant it. "Don't, Alexi."

"He's a monster! You don't know the half of it, and I won't tell you."

"Can you hang on?"

His smile was bleak. "I'm like Derek, sir. I can take anything."

"I'm hoping he'll reform. If not, then we'll see." It wouldn't be fair to Philip to tell his subordinate about my deadline.

"I'll call him to challenge, when we get home."

I sucked in my breath. Alexi truly intended to kill Philip Tyre. "Why not challenge him in the wardroom, then?"

He shot me a look of reproach. "I believe in law and order like you do, sir. It's the first middy's place to run the wardroom. I owe the ship loyalty, I owe the same to you. Even to him."

My fists bunched. Philip had three times sent this youngster to the barrel. "Still, tradition allows wardroom challenges."

"I've always thought that's for younger joeys. A way for them to let off steam if they can't take it. I believe in the Navy and its rules. The regs can't permit this to go on. If I thought that, I'd have to quit the Service. Either he'll step over the line and be brought up on charges, or there'll be some other solution. I'm not going to fight the system."

I said quietly, "Alexi, you're the finest officer I've ever known." He was startled. "You've been my friend since I first came aboard. You have such decency. I've never known you to be mean-spirited or spiteful."

He shook his head. "Just watch if I ever get a chance with him!"

"Still. I respect you enormously. I love you as a friend and comrade." He turned away, but not before I saw his eyes glisten. I rested my hand on his shoulder. "Let's have something to eat before we go back." After a moment he nodded. We found a restaurant. After the meal Alexi insisted on paying for us both.

Two hours later we were back aboard. Alexi resumed his babysitting duties, while I went to the bridge.

* * *

I shared a watch with Vax when the ship's caller buzzed. "Captain, you'd better—Midshipman Tyre reporting. We have a, um, situation here, and—"

I snarled, "Report by the book, middy. Two demerits!" If the boy thought he could niggle over every petty infraction by his charges, then himself get away with—

"Aye aye, sir! Midshipman Philip Tyre reporting, from the Level 2 lounge. Ricky Fuentes is—that is, Jared Treadwell has a knife; he's taken Cadet Fuentes hostage and says unless he gets his children back he'll—"

I was halfway to the hatch. "Vax, page Mr. Vishinsky to the lounge! Three seamen with stunners. Flank!" I dashed out.

I don't remember using the ladder but I must have plunged down at least three steps at a time. I fetched up panting against the Level 2 corridor bulkhead, outside the lounge.

Philip Tyre poked out his head, saw me, slipped into the corridor, saluting. "They're inside, sir. The far end. I tried talking to him but he—"

I brushed the middy aside, strode in. Behind me, the hatch slid shut.

Ricky's right arm dangled as if useless. Jared Treadwell, Rafe's father, had an elbow wrapped around the boy's throat, holding him nearly off the floor. Ricky's head was pressed tight into Treadwell's chest. The cadet's good hand pawed at the throat hold, seeking air.

The knife was poised a millimeter from Ricky's eye.

Treadwell's voice was a snarl. "Want to bet I c'n take an eye before you stun me?" His swarthy face glistened with a sheen of sweat.

"Easy, Mr. Treadwell. Just put—"

"You think this is how I wanted it, Seafort?"

"No, of course not—"

"Give me my son! And Paula!" The knife flickered. Ricky's breath hissed in terror.

From the corridor, pounding feet.

"Mr. Treadwell, Ricky Fuentes has nothing to do with—"

"We tried petitions. We tried going through the courts. No matter what, you had to have your way!" A wrench of his elbow; Ricky squealed. "Call Rafe in here, or so help me, I'll blind him."

The hatch burst open. I whirled. "Out, until I call!"

"But—" The master-at-arms.

"Out!"

Vishinsky backed through the hatch. I spun back to Jared Treadwell. "Listen, sir, I know you're upset—"

"No more talk! I'll do the first eye to show you I mean it!"
I roared. "By Lord God, you'll let me finish a sentence!"

It was so ludicrous he was stunned. So was I, but I knew for Ricky's sake I had to keep the initiative. I flung off my jacket. "You don't need the cadet. You have me."

"Get away!" The knife flicked; Ricky moaned.

"I'm your hostage." I moved closer.

"Don't, sir!" Philip Tyre, behind me. I hadn't seen him enter.

"This was my doing," I said. Fitting that I pay the consequences.

"Sir, you mustn't!"

"Another word, Mr. Tyre—just one—and you're dismissed from the Service." My tone was ice. "Now, Mr. Treadwell . . ."

"Here goes the eye."

"Do it and I'll kill you. With my bare hands." Something in my inflection gave him pause. I took another step.

His manner became almost conversational. "Irene went groundside this morning. Three lawyers she called, all she could reach. The first told her nothing could be done; you'd already ordered the judge not to hear the case. The others wouldn't even talk."

Another step. "You'll let the boy go. I'll take his place." Now I was quite near.

"You leave us nothing, see. No law, no court, no appeal." Suddenly his voice was a shout of torment. "Who appointed you Lord God?"

I swallowed. Who, indeed?

Mrs. Donhauser had warned me, months back, of the hazard I'd blundered into. Protecting children was a basic human urge. And I'd set it against me.

"Mr. Treadwell." My tone was more gentle. "First, let the boy go. I'll take his place. Then we'll call Rafe and Paula. If they want to leave with you, I'll allow it. Else, they stay."

"What good's that, after you've brainwashed them?"

"Would you keep them by force?"

"No. Yes. I don't know what—Lord, help me!" A rasping breath, akin to a sob.

I gave the terrified cadet what I hoped was a reassuring smile. "Ricky, in a moment Mr. Treadwell will set you free. Mr. Tyre, when I sit down in that chair, take Cadet Fuentes out to the corridor and explain to Mr. Vishinsky. Then bring Cadets Paula and Rafe Treadwell to the lounge."

"Sir, if he takes you host—"

"*AYE, AYE, SIR! SAY IT AT ONCE!*"

"Aye aye, sir!"

I sat, kicked my chair to within Jared Treadwell's reach.

For a moment we were frozen in anguished tableau.

With a cry of hurt, Ricky tumbled free to the deck. Treadwell wrenched back my hair, caught my chin, yanked upward. His knife dug at my throat. It took all my strength not to move. Please, Lord. Keep the children safe from harm.

In the edge of my vision I caught sight of Ricky's face. It was unharmed. "Philip, take him—"

"Shut up, Captain!" The knife pressed.

"—out to the corridor. Flank."

"Aye aye, sir." Tyre darted forward, helped Ricky to his feet. The two of them stumbled out.

Silence. Then Treadwell's voice came in a hiss. "I hate you. I hate your arrogance, your certainty that you're doing right no matter how much you hurt others. If it weren't for my children, I'd slit your filthy throat and have done with it!"

I made a sound.

"What?"

"I said, do it."

"Jesus, you're crazed."

I could think of nothing to say.

A knock on the hatch. "Are you all right, sir?"

The knife tightened. "No tricks!"

"Fine, Mr. Vishinsky. Remain outside."

Now that the die was cast, I felt more peace than I had in months. I waited, watching the hatch. "They'll be here in a moment, I think. If I might suggest . . ."

"Hah. As if I care what you—"

"Do you want your children to see you with the knife?"

"There's no way I'm letting you—"

"I give you my word I'll sit still." My chin ached. It was hard to talk, with his fingers grinding into me. "Do you want their sympathy or their horror?" Nothing. "Mr. Treadwell, you haven't a chance to persuade them if they see you hurting me."

"Are you insane? Why would you help me?"

I thought a long while. "So the test will be fair."

His hand wavered. "Shut up. I want to despise you."

A knock. A tremulous voice, from outside. "Cadet Rafe Treadwell reporting, sir."

I said quietly, "Put the knife away, Mr. Treadwell. I'll stay seated where you can reach me."

His moment of decision. Slowly, the knife lowered, disappeared. "Go ahead. Betray me." Vast bitterness.

"Come in, Cadet."

Rafe entered, snapped a rough salute. He hadn't had much time to practice. "Sir, I heard—what's . . ." He gave up, came to a ragged version of attention.

"As you were, Rafe. It seems your father wants you to go ashore. To resign. I'm willing to let you."

"No!"

Behind me, a hiss of breath.

The boy cocked his head, looked at his father strangely. "Jared, why are you doing this? I'm a cadet now. I'm where I want to be."

"You can't just walk away from your family." Treadwell's voice was hoarse. "You're barely thirteen."

"Old enough to enlist."

"And you left us nothing but a note. You didn't have the guts, the courtesy to tell me to my face!"

The boy's eyes teared. "Would you have listened?"

I said, "Rafe, it may have been a mistake. You decided so fast. Wouldn't it be best if—"

"You said it was for five years, and I couldn't change my mind!"

I nodded.

Rafe cried, "That's what I want, not a chance to back out! You think it was easy, signing up?" His jaw jutted. "See what you've done, Jared? Now he'll have me whipped for insolence. Can't you leave things alone?"

At the hatch, a knock.

"Son, I . . ." Mr. Treadwell sounded uncertain. "Your mother and I, we thought—" His voice broke. "Rafe, why do you run from us?"

"Because I'm not your son!" Rafe's face twisted. "I'm a creche boy. Sheila was my nurse, and Martine. I had forty brothers and sisters. God, how I miss them!" He ran fingers through his short-cropped hair. "It was your choice to creche us as babies. When you took us out, Paula and I warned you: we weren't really a family: Irene paid no attention, and neither did you."

"She's your mother!"

From the hatchway, a quiet voice. "She was once." Paula. Her eyes roved among us. "Are you all right, Jared?"

"I—yes, I think so." Her father seemed uncertain.

"Captain, sir?"

"I'm not hurt."

She took two steps in, halted. The rebuke in her face pinned Jared to the bulkhead. "Why did you break Ricky's arm?"

"He tried to get away, and I needed—"

"The poor joey is hunched in the corridor, crying. He won't go to the Doc until Mr. Seafort is safe. Nobody wants to hurt Ricky. He's too good-natured. How could you?"

"I—" No words came.

She faced me, came to attention. "Sir, Mr. Tyre said you had a question for me?"

"Do you want me to annul your enlistment?"

"No, sir."

Her gaze, when it met her father's, held pity, and something more stern. "I'm sorry, Jared, really I am. But it isn't the way you thought it was."

My mouth was dry. They wouldn't be leaving *Hibernia* with their father. That meant his attention would be turned to me. So be it. "Cadets, you're dismissed."

Paula saluted, turned to the hatch. Rafe clumsily imitated her motions. Seated, I couldn't return salute; instead, I nodded.

"Before you go . . ." I was proud of them, and probably wouldn't have another chance. "You've done well. This isn't your fault. No matter what happens—" It was the wrong line. I cleared my throat, and tried again. "The Navy will take care of you. That's all."

"Yes, sir." Paula hesitated. "May I?" I nodded. "Jared, I'm sorry. For hurting you, for Irene, for all of us. Please don't make it worse." Another salute, and she was gone. Her brother followed.

A hand, on the back of my neck. I flinched, steeled myself.

"There's nothing left. Except you." Treadwell's voice was ragged. "At least I can see that you don't ruin any more lives."

"Yes." I raised my head, exposing my throat. "If I . . ."

After a moment, he said, "Well?"

My voice was unsteady. "If I come for you, afterward. It's just a dream. Sooner or later, I'll go away."

"Lord God." A whisper.

Then a sob.

Eventually I lowered my head. It was beginning to cramp.

Vax smoldered; I did my best to ignore him. After a while I gave up. "Get it said, Lieutenant."

"How could you let him go!"

"You'd rather I hanged him? And then ate at mess with his children?"

"He threatened you with a knife!"

"I'm unhurt. He's groundside, so's Irene, and the matter is closed."

Vax shook his head with stubborn negation. "If I may say so, you—"

"No, that's enough. I understand you disapprove."

Vax subsided, muttering.

Earlier, in the quiet of the lounge, I'd picked up the knife Jared Treadwell had let fall, tossed it aside. Half a dozen steps saw me to the hatch. "It's all right, Mr. Vishinsky. Dismiss your detail."

"Sir, is he—"

"Help him remove his things from his cabin, and escort him to the lock." I turned to Ricky. "You'll be all right, boy. To the sickbay. Now."

"Aye aye, sir. Did he hurt—Captain, I'm sor—"

Philip Tyre snapped, "Cadet, two demerits. About-face, march! When the Captain gives an order, jump. I'll deal with you in the wardroom!"

I managed to hold my tongue until Ricky was out of sight. Then, "Mr. Tyre, you argued with your Captain, twice!" I shook with fury. "My compliments to Lieutenant Chantir, and tell him I'm displeased—no, tell him I'm thoroughly disgusted—with your conduct, and he's to correct it forthwith!"

Philip blanched. "I didn't mean—aye aye, sir!"

"Go!"

After, I leaned against the bulkhead. Rafe and Paula were in quarters, the master-at-arms with Jared Treadwell, Ricky having his arm attended. Philip had gone to his chastisement.

I stopped at my cabin, changed my shirt, sat awhile on my starched blanket.

My life had been at risk, and I felt nothing. Well, perhaps not quite that. When the knife had fallen, I'd felt relief. But not much.

I'd think about that later. Time to return to the bridge.

From my seat beneath the blank screens, I reviewed the Log. Mr. Chantir had recorded a caning. Philip Tyre was banished to the wardroom. I sighed. Now more than ever, the boy would lash out at his juniors. And of all of them, Derek had been pressed the hardest.

I thumbed the caller. "Mr. Carr to the bridge."

A few moments later Derek appeared, his uniform immaculate, hair brushed neatly. "Yes, sir?"

I indicated the chair next to Vax. "I need you tonight, Mr. Carr.

Assist Mr. Holser. A double watch." Absolutely unnecessary, docked at an orbiting station.

"Aye aye, sir." Derek knew better than to question orders. I could say nothing to explain. Abruptly his eyes flooded with gratitude, as he realized I was keeping him out of Philip Tyre's reach.

"Mr. Carr has had a hard day, Lieutenant. If he dozes, let him be."

"Aye aye, sir." Vax's face lit. "We'll manage."

Satisfied, I went to bed.

The next day we began taking on passengers for Hope Nation and Earth, as well as cargo of metals and manufactured goods. I noticed from the manifest that we would carry the Detour Olympic team home to Earth for the decennial interplanetary Olympics. I suspected the exercise rooms would be well used.

"Aft line secured, sir." Lieutenant Holser, at the aft airlock.

"Forward line secured, sir," Lieutenant Crossburn, at the forward lock.

I tapped my fingers, waiting for the routine to play itself out.

"Forward lock ready for breakaway, sir."

"Aft lock ready for breakaway, sir."

"Very well." I blew the ship's whistle three times. "Cast off! Take her, Pilot Haynes."

In response to the Pilot's sure touch, our side thrusters released jets of propellant, rocking us from side to side. We broke free.

Lieutenant Crossburn, on the caller. "Forward airlock hatch secured, sir."

"Secured, very well." I paced the bridge while the Pilot held our thrusters at full acceleration, speeding us ever farther from the station and Detour's field of gravity. In two hours, we'd be clear enough to Fuse.

Our return voyage had begun. Seven weeks to Hope Nation, then the long grim journey home. I would endure it. I must. I settled into my chair to prepare coordinates.

At last, all was ready. "Engine room prepared for Fusion, sir."

I looked to the Pilot, raising my eyebrows. He nodded.

"Fuse the ship." I ran my finger down the screen and the drive kicked in. The stars faded from the simulscreen. We entered the subetheral realm of nonspace, sailing from Detour on the crest of the N wave we generated.

That evening at dinner I played host to several young members of the Olympic team. Though sociable and friendly, they seemed unimpressed by the honor of the Captain's table. They talked animatedly among themselves, including me on occasion merely out of courtesy. After months among passengers who'd taken seating at the Captain's table so seriously, I found their attitude refreshing.

Later, restless, I wandered the ship, where excited passengers explored corridors, lounges, and exercise rooms they'd soon find all too familiar. I wandered back to Level 1. Outside the wardroom Rafe Treadwell stood at attention, his nose to the bulkhead. Well, he'd asked for it. Enlistment was his own choice.

I slept badly, still keyed up from the bustle of departure. I knew it would take days to settle back into the dreary routine of Fusion. Nonetheless, I haunted the bridge, with nothing to do.

"Have you noticed the Log, sir?" Lieutenant Chantir pointed to the past two days' entries. "*Mr. Tamarov, slothfulness, three demerits, by Mr. Tyre. Mr. Tamarov, uncleanliness, two demerits.*"

So it had started again. I snapped off the Log without comment, leaned back.

"How long will it go on, sir?"

I opened one eye. "Until I say otherwise, First Lieutenant Chantir." He flushed. "Sorry, sir."

"You're a good officer," I said. "But don't nag."

His smile was weak. "Aye aye, sir." He changed the subject. "Have you ever played chess, sir?"

I came awake. "Yes, why?"

"I'm not very good, but I like to play. I'll bet your puter plays a mean game, though."

"Thank you." Darla, in a dignified tone.

"I can't play on the bridge, Lars. You know that."

"Really? Captain Halstead played all the time. I loved to watch. Once he actually beat the puter."

The speaker said, "She must have had an off day."

"Butt out, Darla," I growled. Then, "He actually played on watch?" Hope stirred.

Chantir said, "Sure, when we were Fused. What else is there to do?"

"Isn't it against regs?"

"I read them again, sir, before bringing it up. They say you must stay alert. They don't say you can't read or play a game. All the alarms have audible signals, anyway."

"I'll warn you if we have a problem," the puter said helpfully.

"Is this a conspiracy? Darla, did you ever play with an officer on watch?"

"Lots of us do. Janet said she sometimes let Halstead win just to keep his spirits up."

" 'Captain Halstead' to you. Janet is their puter, I suppose? When did you talk to her?"

"When her ship docked at Hope Nation to bring you your only intelligent officer, Midshi—I mean, Captain Seafort. I tightbeamed with her as a matter of routine."

"Who did you play chess with, Darla?"

"Captain Haag, of course. He wasn't much of a match." She sounded disconsolate.

I was flabbergasted. Justin Haag, whiling away the hours playing chess with his puter? I debated. "All right, set them up."

She won in thirty-seven moves.

It relaxed me so much that I stood double watches just to be near her. After a week I rationed myself to one game a day; any more and I'd become addicted. When a game was over I busied myself studying my moves.

One happy day I forced a draw. A few hours later Alexi reported for duty, relieving Lieutenant Crossburn, who had radiated his silent disapproval during my game.

I was still jovial. "Take your seat, Mr. Tamarov."

He gripped the back of his chair. "I'm sorry, sir, I can't sit." A vein throbbed in his forehead.

My contentment vanished. "Have you been to Mr. Chantir?"

"I just came from his cabin." He stared straight ahead at the darkened screen.

"What for?"

"Nothing, sir. Absolutely nothing." A long moment passed. "Sir, I want to resign from the Navy."

"Permission refused," I said instantly. I hesitated. "I'm sorry, Alexi." I didn't know what else to offer.

"Yes, sir." His voice was flat. He added, "Do you have a reason?"

"For what?"

"Waiting. Not doing anything about him."

"You're out of line, Mr. Tamarov."

"I don't think I care anymore, sir."

I cast aside my rebuke. "Yes. There's a reason." I nodded to the hatch. "You're relieved, Alexi. Lie down for a while."

"If you don't mind, sir, I'd rather stay here." I understood. On the bridge he was safe from the first middy.

"Very well." I let him wait out the watch. Afterwards I ordered him to Dr. Uburu for healing ointment. He had no choice but to go. I think he was grateful.

I played no more chess for several days.

Mr. Crossburn performed his duties satisfactorily, as always. On his free time he roamed about the ship, asking questions. He finally exhausted the matter of the Treadwells.

Mr. Vishinsky brought me the news first. "Captain, I've been interrogated by one of our officers." He stood at attention beside my chair.

"What about, Mr. Vishinsky?" No need to ask by whom.

"About Captain Haag's death, sir. About how the launch happened to explode, and how the puter came to be glitched. An implication was made that it was no accident."

My heart pounded. "You know better than to tell tales on a superior officer, Mr. Vishinsky. You're rebuked."

"Yes, sir." He appeared undisturbed. "What should I do when he questions me, sir?"

"If he orders you to answer, do so. Obey all orders else place yourself on report."

"Aye aye, sir. May I go?"

"Yes." I watched him leave. "Thank you," I added, as the hatch closed behind him. I willed my heart to stop slamming against my ribs. Crossburn was a lunatic. He was only a step from endangering the ship.

As soon as my watch was done I went to my cabin. I stared into my mirror. "You're the Captain," I told my image. It gave no response. "You have the authority. Remember Vax's story about his uncle, the lawyer? He had to remind himself that his clients weren't in trouble because he'd failed them, but because they had fouled up in the first place."

I scowled at myself in the mirror. "So why do you feel guilty?"

A rhetorical question; I already knew the answer. If I were competent, I'd have found a way to avoid this mess.

"But don't they have it coming, nonetheless?"

I started at myself for a long while, then sighed. I still felt guilty.

At lunch I chose to sit next to Mr. Crossburn instead of at the small table where I would be undisturbed.

He started almost immediately. "What kind of man was Captain Haag, sir?"

"Well, I was just a middy. To me he seemed remote and stern. They say he was an excellent navigator and pilot." I took a bite out of my sandwich, decided to give Mr. Crossburn more rope. "His death was a tragic loss."

He seized the opportunity. "How could a puter glitch have gone undiscovered so long, before it destroyed the launch? If you're sure it wasn't known earlier, that is."

I spoke very quietly. "I can't tell you now. See me after lunch; we'll talk then. I have a job for you."

"Aye aye, sir." We ate in silence. I pretended not to notice his speculative glance.

I waited for him in my cabin. When the knock came I went out, shutting my hatch behind me. "Come with me, Lieutenant." I took him down to Level 2, through the lock into the launch berth, where our new launch waited in its gantry. "This is where it was," I said. He looked puzzled. Of course this was where it was. Where else would you stow a ship's launch?

"I need someone I can trust." Galvanized, he leaned forward with excitement. "It might have been sabotage," I said with care. "A bomb hidden in one of the seats. It could happen again. I need you to check the seats."

"You mean take the seats apart? Unbolt them all and remove them?"

"That's right." I waited while he thought it over. "I know I can trust you, Lieutenant Crossburn. With your Admiralty connections you're invaluable."

A look of satisfaction crossed his face. "I'll get a work party on it right away."

"Oh, no." I looked alarmed. "Nobody must know. If it really is sabotage, we can't tip them off. Do it yourself."

"Alone?" He seemed disconcerted. "It'll take all day, sir."

"I know. It can't be helped. Unbolt all the seats, take them out, open them for inspection. I'll come back later to see how you're doing. We won't put the seats back until we're sure they're all right."

"Aye aye, sir." His tone was doubtful. "If you're sure that's what you want."

"Oh, yes," I said. "Very sure." I left him.

I posted orders at the launch berth hatch that no one was to enter, and went about my business. An hour before dinner I went to check on him.

About half of the fourteen seats had been removed, their components spread about the bay. Crossburn had draped his jacket over one of them and pulled off his tie. I found him in the launch, on his back under one of the seats, struggling to work loose the bolts.

"Good work, Lieutenant. Find anything yet?"

"No, sir. Everything's normal." He wriggled out from underneath the seat.

"No, stay where you are. I'll be back later." I went to dinner. I ate well.

It was past midnight before he finished reassembling the launch. I met him coming out of the berth, face smeared with grease, jacket slung over his arm.

I whispered, "You're sure there was nothing, Lieutenant?"

"Absolutely sure, sir." He seemed anxious to get to his cabin. I could imagine how the night's diary entry would read.

"I knew I could count on you." I walked him through the lock. "Now we know the launch is safe, for the moment. I want you to check it again tomorrow."

He went pale.

"Is something the matter?"

"But, sir," he stammered. "We just disassembled all the seats. We know there's no bomb there."

I leaned close. "There isn't now. During the night they might try to put one in."

"Sir, that's not—"

"We have to know for sure." My voice grew cold. "Unbolt and disassemble all the seats again first thing tomorrow. That's an order."

"But, sir—"

I was icy. "What does an officer say when he hears an order, Mr. Crossburn? Or didn't your uncle tell you that?"

"Aye aye, sir! I'll start again in the morning, sir!" He knew enough to retreat.

I returned to my cabin.

The next day I checked him at lunchtime. Again, seats were strewn all over the bay. I went to lunch, fueled by a grim satisfaction. I timed him; it took Lieutenant Crossburn just over twelve hours to tear down and reassemble all the launch seats. Having started just after breakfast, he was done by ten in the evening.

The next morning I was on the watch roster. Mr. Crossburn arrived, scheduled to share the watch. "Lieutenant, you're relieved from watch. I have a more important job for you. Tear down and recheck the launch seats."

He stood slowly. "Captain, are you sure you're all right?"

"I feel fine." I stretched luxuriously. "Why do you ask?"

"You can't want me to tear the launch apart three days in a row, sir."

"Can't I? Acknowledge your orders, Lieutenant."

Stubbornly, he shook his head. "Sir, I insist that you put them in writing." He spoke with confidence, knowing I would do no such thing.

"Certainly." I snapped on the Log and took a laserpencil. "I order Lieutenant Ardwell Crossburn to remove and disassemble all the seats on the ship's launch and check them for hidden explosives before reinstalling them, as he has done each of the past two days. Signed, Nicholas Seafort, Captain." I showed it to him. "Is that in proper form, Lieutenant?"

He was trapped. "Aye aye, sir. I have no choice."

"True. You have no choice. Dismissed."

Alone on the bridge I played chess with Darla. I was ahead on the fourteenth move when the caller buzzed.

"Sir, Lieutenant Chantir." He sounded grim. "I have Mr. Tamarov in my cabin with eleven demerits. I'm sorry, but I will need your written order before I proceed." He was a decent man, and he'd had enough.

The moment was approaching. "Certainly, Lieutenant. Come to the bridge at once." When he arrived I handed him a paper. He glanced at it. "I protest your order, sir."

"I understand. Carry it out anyway."

"May I ask why, sir?"

"Tomorrow at dinner, if you still want to." That puzzled him; he saluted and left the bridge. I lost my game to Darla.

That night before going to bed I stood again in front of my mirror. I didn't like the face I saw. I told myself what I was doing was necessary, and didn't believe a word of it.

Restless and uneasy, I left my cabin again. I passed Lieutenant Crossburn's cabin, once Mr. Malstrom's. On the spur of the moment I went to the infirmary. Dr. Uburu was there, reading a holovid.

"Good evening, Captain." She saw my face. "What's troubling you?" Only the Ship's Doctor could ask the Captain such a question. Perhaps it was the reason I'd gone to her.

I slumped in a chair. "I've used a friend, manipulated him, and I'm disgusted with myself."

"Yours is a lonely job," she said. "Sometimes one can't do directly what must be done. Is it for the good of the ship?"

"I think so," I said. "I'm not sure."

"We're seldom sure, Nic—Captain. If you believe it's for the good of the ship, isn't that enough?"

"Then why am I miserable?"

"You tell me." It was a challenge, in its calm, quiet style.

I avoided it. "Because of my weakness, I guess. I wish I were wise enough to find another way."

"I absolve you." She smiled at me. "Sleep well tonight."

"I don't want a pill."

"I didn't offer one." I started for the corridor. "I wish I could help you, Captain," she said. "But you have to help yourself." Puzzled, I went back to my cabin. I went to bed and slept peacefully.

In the morning I met Alexi and Derek at breakfast. Both studiously avoided my eye. At noon I took my place on the bridge. Vax Holser and I sat in silence. When the watch was done I thumbed the caller. "Mr. Tyre, bring Mr. Tamarov to the bridge." Vax looked at me curiously.

The midshipmen arrived. "Permission to enter bridge, sir." Philip Tyre's voice was firm and vibrant. He snapped a smart salute.

"Granted." They came to attention. "Darla, please record these proceedings. I, Captain Nicholas Seafort, do commission Midshipman Alexi Tamarov to the Naval Service of the Government of the United Nations and do appoint him Lieutenant, by the Grace of God." Alexi was stunned.

Philip Tyre swallowed, his face ashen.

"Mr. Tyre, you are dismissed. Lieutenant Tamarov, you will remain." With jerky motions Philip Tyre saluted, turned, and left the bridge. As soon as the hatch closed Vax leaped up with a whoop. He pounded Alexi on the back.

"Easy, Mr. Holser, you'll kill him!" Vax's brotherly blows could break ribs.

"Congratulations, Alexi!" Vax turned to me with a wide grin. "It's wonderful news, sir." Alexi didn't move.

"You're free, Alexi," I told him quietly. "Free of him."

"Am I?" Alexi spoke without inflection. "Will I ever be?" Unbidden, he sank into a chair, wincing. He began to sob.

Shocked, Vax withdrew a step. I motioned him to wait in the corridor.

After a time Alexi gained control of himself. "Why did you leave me there so long?"

"So you'd be sure." I despised myself.

"Of what?"

"I already have three lieutenants; you won't be overwhelmed with duties. I'm putting you in charge of the midshipmen. Put things back in order."

He thought about it. Silence stretched for over a minute. "Don't," he said in a small voice. "I beg you; don't put me in charge of him."

"It's done. Those are your orders."

"I swore an oath to myself, Mr. Seafort. I won't be able to stop."

"I wanted you to be certain whom you were dealing with." I stood. "So I waited until it was absolutely clear. Perhaps too long. I'm sorry, if that's any use." I was too ashamed to meet his eye, so I paced, my eye traversing the bulkheads. "It's a long cruise home. I have the welfare of the other midshipmen to consider. Keep them safe, Alexi. Do what you must."

He put his head in his hands, then rubbed his face. He offered a tentative smile. "Sorry, sir. I've been a bit . . . emotional lately. It's like waking from a nightmare."

"I know what that's like," I said. "Believe me."

28

The next day I called the engine room to give Chief McAndrews private instructions. Then I summoned Mr. Crossburn and handed him a written standing order to disassemble and inspect the launch seats every day until further notice.

He looked around wildly, as if for escape. "Captain, I can't do that. Not all day, every day!"

I was inflexible. "You can and you will."

"I protest, Captain!"

"Noted. Begin your work."

"No, that's crazy!"

"What did you say?"

"I said no! You can't mean it."

"Mr. Crossburn, come with me." I led him, protesting, down the ladder to the engine room, to the lower level at the fusion drive shaft. The plank I had ordered the Chief to make ready was set across it; Mr. McAndrews stood by, his face a grim mask.

"Stand at attention and look at the shaft." Crossburn did so.

"This is where I hanged Mr. Tuak and Mr. Rogoff. And the rebels who tried to take over the ship. It's been a rough voyage and we're on the way back to Miningcamp, where we were attacked once before. *Hibernia* is in an emergency zone, Mr. Crossburn, and war rules apply. I tell you now, if you refuse to obey an order, I will hang you. Be silent and think about it."

I gave him ten minutes. Then I released him. "Go to the launch berth."

Shaken, he complied. "Aye aye, sir." Then he added angrily, "You can be sure my uncle will hear of this!"

"Two months pay, Mr. Crossburn, for insolence and insubordination. Anything else?"

"No, sir!" He fled.

I looked at the Chief, let out my breath.

He asked, "What if he'd refused, sir?"

"I'd have had to proceed." A sudden thought. "Would you have let me?"

"By the regs, I couldn't stop you."

"That was no answer." I decided not to press. I'd made enemies of them all, abovedecks. Why alienate the Chief as well?

Several days later I shared a watch with Philip Tyre. He looked pale and shaken. I said nothing.

Vax chose to keep me informed. "Alexi's all over him, sir. Demerits for attitude, for sloppiness, for inattention. Twice he's sent him to the barrel outright, in addition to the demerits."

"I know. I can read the Log."

"Yes, sir. Philip is going to have an interesting cruise."

He would indeed. Alexi was slow to anger and I doubted he would be faster to forgive. I shrugged. Tyre had made his bed.

"When are you going to let him off, sir?"

"I'm not."

Vax looked awed. "All the way home? Eighteen months?"

"Seventeen and a half." I wondered how soon I could start counting the days.

The Olympians had taken over Level 2, jogging endlessly in the circumference corridor, swinging from the bars in the exercise room, doing push-ups on the mats. From time to time Philip Tyre joined them, sweating profusely in strenuous effort, supervised by a stern and watchful lieutenant.

Soon we would Defuse for a navigation check. Then a few more days to Hope Nation, and our mooring. We'd remain there only two days, just enough to take on passengers for the trip home. Somewhere below me would be Amanda, but I wouldn't see her again.

Dr. Uburu came to the bridge to speak to me. "Captain, Lieutenant Crossburn has been questioning your sanity. He wants me to join him in removing you."

"Is he correct?"

She looked at me thoughtfully. "I don't think so. You might be vindictive, but no insane."

"Thanks so much."

She smiled. "Captain, do you recall when the Chief, the Pilot, and I met to find a way to stop your taking command?"

"Yes."

"I can't believe how wrong we were. This is a jinxed voyage, Captain. *Hibernia* will go down in Navy legends. There's nothing that hasn't gone wrong for us. And you've coped with it all. You've done better than anyone had a right to expect."

I looked at her to see if she was serious, angry at her blind stupidity. "Leave the bridge at once, Doctor. That's an order!"

"Aye aye, sir." She saluted and left, unfazed by my anger. She thought well of me, perhaps, like the foolish seamen in the Hope Nation bar. But I knew better. I had Philip Tyre and Ardwell Crossburn to add to my long list of failures.

Days later, Lieutenant Chantir told me Philip had been sent to him again. Lars was obviously unhappy.

"I don't need daily reports, Lieutenant. Just do your duty."

"I will, sir. It's not a pleasurable one."

"Even with Mr. Tyre?"

"Even with him, whether he earned it or not."

"It's the first lieutenant's job, Mr. Chantir." I brightened. "However, if your arm bothers you I will excuse you for medical reasons."

He considered it. "My arm is troubling me somewhat, Captain. Not enough to see the Doctor, but it's noticeable."

"Very well." I summoned Alexi. "Mr. Tamarov, the first lieutenant has a sore arm. Move the barrel to your cabin. That duty is yours until further notice." Ruefully, Mr. Chantir shook his head. Alexi, expressionless, saluted and left.

I went to the launch berth every day at random hours. I always found Lieutenant Crossburn at work.

I shared a watch with Philip Tyre. He walked carefully onto the bridge and eased himself into his chair. "Good morning, sir." His tone was meek, his eyes riveted on his console.

"Good morning. I'd like you to run docking drill today, Mr. Tyre."

"Aye aye, sir." I called up the exercise and he began his calculations. Halfway through, he stopped and looked up. "It isn't fair, sir."

"What isn't?"

"What he's doing to me. I can't stand it. Please."

"What are you talking about, Mr. Tyre?"

"Mr. Tamarov. He's after me all the time!"

"Are you complaining about your superior, Philip?"

He didn't have the sense to deny it. "Not exactly complaining, sir. I'm just telling you."

"Oh, no, Mr. Tyre. That won't do. My compliments to Mr. Tamarov. Please tell him I'm annoyed with your conduct. Right now."

"I've just been there," he wailed. "He'll cane me again! Please, sir. Please!"

I raised my voice a notch. "And six demerits for disobedience, Mr. Tyre. Another word and it's six more." He fled the bridge to meet his fate. Never again did I hear a word of complaint from Philip. On the few occasions that I saw him he appeared miserable. It bothered me not at all.

At last it was time for our nav check, before a final jump to Hope Nation. "Bridge to engine room, prepare to Defuse."

"Prepare to Defuse, aye aye, sir."

I waited.

"Engine room ready for Defuse, sir. Control passed to bridge." The Chief's familiar voice came steady over the caller.

"Passed to bridge, aye aye." I set my finger at the top of the drive screen while Derek watched. "Let's see where we are." I traced a line from "Full" to "Off."

"Confirm clear of encroachments, Derek." A normal check, hardly necessary but part of the routine. He checked his instruments.

"Hey! An encroachment, sir, course two hundred ten, distance fifty-two thousand kilometers!"

I gaped. "What?"

"Encroachment, sir. There's something out there."

"It can't be. We're interstellar." I puzzled. "A stray asteroid, perhaps. How big is it?"

"I read two hundred sixteen meters, sir." Darla.

"Small for a planetoid. What's it made of?"

"Metal," Darla said. "Too far away to see, but it's radiating on the metallic bands."

I thumbed the caller. "Mr. Haynes to the bridge. And Mr. Chantir." No, Lars Chantir had a fever and was in sickbay. "Belay that summons, Mr. Chantir. Mr. Holser to the bridge."

Vax came bounding in. He stopped to take in the situation. A few moments later Mr. Haynes arrived, breathing hard. The Pilot slipped into his customary seat. "Morning, sir." He glanced at the sensors. "Want to go take a look?"

"Good morning, Pilot. I think so."

Vax nodded. "If we're this close, we might as well check it out." I hadn't asked his opinion, but he didn't seem to notice. "It's probably just a hunk of ore skewing Darla's calculations."

"Button it, joey!" Darla flared. "I remember the last time you insulted me!"

"Cool it, Darla. He meant no harm. Pilot, put us on an intersecting course."

"Aye aye, sir. Just a moment." Pilot Haynes was carefully affable. I felt a twinge of guilt. He thumbed his caller. "Engine room, auxiliary power."

"Auxiliary power on standby."

"On standby, aye aye. All ahead one-half. Steer two ten, declination twenty degrees."

"All ahead one-half, aye aye. Two ten at twenty degrees."

After two hours, the Pilot at last began braking maneuvers.

I cleared my throat. "Mr. Holser, start calculating Fusion coordinates for our jump, please. No need to waste time."

"Aye aye, Captain." Vax reluctantly tore his eyes from the simulscreen and tapped figures into his console.

We were closing fast. "Maximum magnification, Darla."

"Whatever you say, boss." The screen flickered.

The unmistakable outline of a ship.

"Holy God!" The Pilot was on his feet.

Vax looked up from his calculation and froze.

The Pilot whispered, "One of ours!"

I swallowed. Not again. All those people. "Focus on the disk, Darla." Pointless; we were already at maximum magnification.

The image expanded slowly as we neared. Darla obediently narrowed her view to the ship's disk.

A gash ran across all three levels, right down to the engine room, as if parts of the hull had melted. The entire disk was open to vacuum.

The name stood out against the gray metal of the hull.

"*Telstar!*" Vax whispered. "Gone, like *Celestina.* No lights, no power. No signals."

There might somehow be survivors. "Pilot, bring us alongside. Mr. Holser, organize a boarding party. Three seamen. We'll take the gig."

"Aye aye, sir. Shall I go with them?"

"No."

"Lieutenant Tamarov, then?"

"No. Me." I saw Vax's expression and added. "I need to know firsthand what happened." For a brief moment I recalled Captain Van Walther, and the crowds of travelers who visited the memorial he'd left on *Celestina.* With shame I suppressed the comparison.

Vax was stubborn. "It could be dangerous, sir. Don't leave the ship."

"This time it's in good hands. Mr. Chantir, Alexi, you. I'm going across; don't argue."

I'd left him no choice. "Aye aye, sir."

I made it even clearer. "Lieutenant Holser, you will remain aboard under all circumstances."

"Aye aye, sir." His tone was glum.

I smiled. "Besides, I'll be all right. I'll carry a rad meter and stay away from jagged metal. Don't be my nanny." That produced a reluctant smile.

The Pilot carefully maneuvered us to within two hundred meters of U.N.S. *Telstar*. With gentle applications of the thrusters he brought us to rest relative to the stricken vessel.

"Vax, be prepared to Fuse as soon as I'm back. Derek, come help me with my suit."

We went down to Level 2. I took my regular suit from its bin in the launch berth lock and began to struggle into it. Then I stopped; I might want to clamber around the outside of *Telstar*'s hull. "Get me a T-suit, Derek."

A thrustersuit was cumbersome but had the advantage of greater mobility. In my own suit I could walk, step by magnetized step, across the surface of *Telstar*'s outer hull, but in a T-suit I could lift off from the hull and skim over for a better look. At Academy I hated regular suit drills but loved the T-suit instruction.

I stepped into the semirigid, alumalloy reinforced suit-frame. Derek handed me the helmet; I slipped it into the slots and gave it a half turn. Derek locked the stays into place; I double-checked them all. I had no intention of accidentally breathing vacuum.

With a grunt Derek lifted the heavy tank assembly and clipped it to the alumalloy supports on the back of my suit. We strapped the propellant tanks into place. My helmet's sensor lights flashed green; I was ready to go. Derek's hand fell on my arm and lingered. "Be careful, sir," he said softly. "Please."

I shook loose my arm. "Remember you're a Naval officer, Mr. Carr." He meant well, but a midshipman must know better than to touch his Captain, no matter how many vacations they'd taken together. Sometimes Derek had no sense of propriety.

The three sailors were suited and waiting. We cycled through the lock and clambered into the gig. "Open the hatch, Vax," I said into my suit radio.

"Right, sir." I jumped; his voice was loud in the speaker.

All seaman were given a modicum of training on small boats; I gestured to a sailor I knew had additional experience. "Go ahead, Mr. Howard. Take us across."

A couple of squirts sent us gently out the hatch. We glided across the void. From *Hibernia's* bridge, the distance to *Telstar* seemed small, but from the tiny gig it was immense. We neared the silent ship.

"Steer past the disk, Mr. Howard." At negligible speed we drifted past the rent in the fabric of *Telstar's* hull. The edges of the tear appeared to have melted and run. What could have generated so much heat?

"What's the radiation reading, Mr. Brant?"

The sailor held the rad meter steady. "None, sir. Nothing at all." Odd. If *Telstar's* drive had blown, we'd find substantial emissions.

When the trouble arose, *Telstar's* drive couldn't have been ignited, or we'd never have found her in normal space. *Telstar* had Defused at the usual checkpoint, as we ourselves had, to plot position before proceeding past Hope Nation to Miningcamp. With a six percent variation for error, that meant she could have Defused anywhere within eight million miles of where we'd emerged. Pure luck that we'd stumbled upon her.

If *Telstar's* drive was turned off, what could have vaporized her hull? I had no answer. Whatever it was, we had to know, lest the same happen to us or other vessels in the fleet. I remembered Darla's glitch and shivered. "Mr. Howard, take us to within a meter of the hull. Mr. Brant, open the hatch and get another reading up close."

A moment later Brant put down the rad meter. "Still nothing, sir. The hull isn't hot."

"It could have been hull stress, sir."

I jumped. "Damn it, Vax, lower your voice before you give me a heart attack. And that's no stress fracture. We'll see what we find inside."

I had Mr. Brant transfer to *Telstar's* hull. He planted a magnetic buoy from our gig at his feet, activated it, hooked our mooring line to it. Now, if one of us pushed against the boat as he stepped off, the gig couldn't drift away and leave us stranded.

We climbed out onto *Telstar's* hull. Her locks were sealed from within; the simplest way to board was to drop through the gaping hole into one of the cabins. The edges of the tear were rounded and smooth, minimizing the risk of ripping our tough-skinned suits.

"You first, Mr. Ulak. Take a light with you." The seaman jumped down through the hole, into *Telstar*. "What do you see?"

"Just a mess." He opened the cabin hatch, peered into the corridor. "Come on down, sir. We can walk around easy enough."

"Be careful, sir." Vax sounded anxious.

I climbed into the opening in the hull and jumped down.

I was in a passenger cabin.

Everything loose had been swept out in the decompression. A bed remained, bolted to the deck. A sheet drooped forlornly from one corner. I swallowed.

"Vax, we're on Level 2. The corridors are dark, but we all have lights. Mr. Brant, explore Level 2. Mr. Howard, Mr. Ulak, go down to the engine room; see if you can figure out what caused the damage. Vax, it doesn't look like any of the disk sections are sealed. I'll go up to Level 1 and try to get onto the bridge."

"Take one of the men with you, sir."

"Don't nag, Mother."

I clambered along the debris-strewn corridor. Flotsam flung about by the decompression had settled everywhere, making the ship seem grossly untidy. I walked slowly, checking hatches as I went. Many were closed, but none were sealed from inside. I climbed the ladder to Level 1.

I passed the wardroom, then the lieutenants' common room. The hatch was slightly ajar. I opened it, stuck my head in.

"Oh, Lord God!" My scream echoed in my suit. I flung out my arms, stumbled back in terror.

"Captain! What is it?" Vax was frantic.

I gagged, swallowing in a frantic effort to hold down my gorge. "Unh! God. I'm all right, Vax. A corpse. Somebody in a suit, with a smashed helmet. The head is damaged, like it was eaten away. Something must have penetrated the helmet." It had been inches from my nose.

I breathed deeply over and again, in an effort to slow my pounding heart. The adrenaline had left me trembling. I sagged against the bulkhead, steadying myself. "Sorry."

"Let me come across, sir!"

"Denied. Stay on the bridge. I'm all right; I just got a fright." I headed for *Telstar*'s bridge. "I'm trying to figure out what happened here. Right now I'm about ninety degrees along the disk from the damage." If I kept talking, I wouldn't have to think about what I'd seen. "The cabin where I found the corpse had no hull damage. I guess something ricocheted down the corridor and hit him just as he opened the hatch. Okay, I'm at the bridge now."

I slapped the hatch control, to no effect. "The bridge is sealed; I'll never be able to get in without tools. I'll check the remaining cabins past the corridor bend." A figure moved in the dim standby light. "Mr. Ulak, is that you?" I hurried toward him. "What did you find belo—"

I froze.

"Captain?" Vax.

My mouth worked. No sound came.

"Sir, are you all right?"

I produced a small whimper, like a child in a nightmare. Urine trickled down my leg.

"Say what's wrong!" Vax bellowed.

I whispered, "Ulak. Brant. Howard. Back to the gig, flank! Mr. Holser, sound General Quarters! Battle Stations!"

I tried to back away. My feet seemed glued to the deck. The figure in the corridor quivered. It wore a kind of translucent suit that sat legless on the deck, flowing from an irregular base to near my own height.

Globs of matter seemed to flow along the skin of the suit. A jagged patch on the suit, a meter above the deck, contracted and expanded again. Colors flowed.

I willed myself to step backward. "There's something here! It's alive and it's not human." Why did I whisper when nothing could hear through vacuum? I took another step. "Lord God . . ." *We ask thy mercy, in this our final hour.*

"General Quarters! Man your Battle Stations!" Vax bellowed orders into the caller. "Mr. Carr, seal the bridge!"

The creature moved. I couldn't see how. It . . . flowed toward me. I took another step back, then another.

It moved again. It changed shape as it flowed, then regained height. It seemed subtly changed.

Suddenly I understood.

"Oh, Lord God, it isn't in a suit! That's its own skin; it can live in vacuum! Vax, it's changing shapes!" A surge of adrenaline freed me to move. The creature darted away, heading the opposite direction along the corridor. It moved with breathtaking speed.

I turned and ran. "Ulak, Brant! Where are you?"

"Back at the gig, sir! Hurry!"

I stumbled down the ladder, the steps pulling at my magnetized feet.

"Howard reporting. I'm in the gig. Where is it, sir?"

"I don't know!" Panting, I pounded down the corridor. I risked a glance backward. Nothing.

"Oh, Jesus Lord! It's coming out of the hull!" A shriek.

"Launch the gig!" I shouted. "Back to the ship! Don't wait!"

Vax roared, "Belay that! Pick up the Captain first!"

"Go!" I gasped for breath, racing to the cabin I'd first entered. Wait.

I skidded to a stop. If one of the beings was emerging from a tear in the hull, it must be in one of these cabins. I couldn't get out the way I'd come.

"We're clear of the hull! Captain, come on out, we'll try to reach you!"

Vax. "Man the lasers! Seal all compartments!"

I keyed my caller. "Mr. Howard, back to the ship!" I raced to the ladder to Level 3. "I'll come out below!"

"We're thirty meters distant, sir! Where are you?"

"Engine room!" I swung my light wildly around the darkened compartment. Stars glinted through a breach in the hull. I clambered toward it, squeezed myself through. In a moment I stood on the hull, trying to spot the gig against the black of interstellar space.

There, about fifty meters aft.

"Here!" I waved my light.

"Right, sir." Seaman Brant maneuvered the gig closer. "That . . . thing is halfway out of the hull, behind you." I spun around; an alien form quivered in a gap in *Telstar*'s hull, over one of the cabins. My skin crawled.

I remembered my jets, touched the nozzle control at my side. I lifted off. Clear of the infested ship, separated from whatever scampered in its corridors, I felt weak with relief. Still, I floated alone in space, with no protection but a suit. I hadn't even thought to go into *Telstar* armed.

Hibernia shrank perceptibly. I shuddered. Vax was moving the ship clear to Fuse. To abandon us. Helpless, I calculated distances. My panic ebbed. He was only turning the ship to bring her lasers to bear. "Darla, record!" I shouted. "Full visuals!"

"I have been, sir." Her voice was calm. "Ever since you took the gig."

I keyed my thrusters, propelled myself toward the gig's silhouette. Someone moaned.

A voice; a sailor in the gig. "Our Father who art in heaven, hallowed be thy name; thy kingdom come, thy will be done, on Earth as it is in heaven . . ."

With a squirt of my side jets, I rotated to face *Telstar*.

A plump oval shape drifted from behind the dead ship. It looked, Lord God help me, like a huge goldfish with a stubby tail. It was almost half as large as *Telstar*.

It pulsed. A mist spurted from an opening near the tail. It glided past the hull toward us. Colors flowed on its surface. Rough-surfaced globs projected from its sides.

I found my voice. "Gig, back to *Hibernia!* Flank!" I slammed on my thrusters, veered away from the gig, spun toward my ship.

The creature I'd found within *Telstar* recoiled against the hull, launched itself at the fish as it floated by. It touched the being's side and clung there for a moment, growing smaller.

The surface of the huge creature seemed to flow. The being outside of it disappeared, absorbed within.

One of the rough globs on the goldfish lengthened, began to spin in a slow, widening circle. It gained momentum. Abruptly it detached and flew directly at the gig.

"Look out!" My cry came too late. The projectile splattered on the gig's hull, oozed along its side. The gig's alumalloy frame sputtered and melted beneath the glob.

A choked scream, suddenly cut off. The gig's engine flared and died. The glob ate away at the gig's hull. Frantic motion, in the cockpit. Metal dripped onto a suit and pierced it. There was a visible rush of air. Blood, a wild kick, then nothing.

I looked back at the goldfish. Another, much larger projectile began to wave.

"Vax!"

"Yessir, I'm coming!"

"Fuse the ship!"

"Jet this way, sir! Hurry!"

"Fuse! Go to Hope Nation! Save the ship!"

"You're almost aboard, Captain!" *Hibernia*'s bow drifted around.

An icy calm slowed my slamming heart. "Mr. Holser, Fuse the ship at once! Acknowledge my order!"

"Captain, move! Jet over here!"

The fishlike being released its projectile. The mass whipped toward *Hibernia.* It struck the gossamer laser shields protruding from the nose ports. They disintegrated in rivulets of metal.

Vax shouted, "Fire!" The tracking beam of *Hibernia*'s laser centered on the goldfish, just now drifting clear of *Telstar.* A spot in its side glowed red. The skin colors swirled. The goldfish jerked as if in convulsion.

The creature's skin swirled and opened to form half a dozen tiny holes. Droplets of fluid burst from them. The goldfish slid away toward the protection of *Telstar*'s hull. The laser followed, centered again on the side of the fish. More holes spouted protoplasm. Abruptly, it was behind *Telstar.*

In slow motion I drifted across the void. *Hibernia* had to be saved, regardless of my fate. "Fuse! For God's sake, Vax! Obey orders!" I was frantic.

"Hurry, sir! Use the forward airlock! Alexi, cycle the lock!"

I was too far from the ship. The enemy might come out at any moment. I sobbed with rage and frustration. "Vax, Fuse!"

"Hurry, Captain!"

I was beside myself. *"VAX, FUSE THE FUCKING SHIP!"*

His soft response came clear in my speaker. "No, sir. Not until I have you aboard."

Cursing, I accelerated until I was almost upon the ship, then flipped over and decelerated full blast as Sarge had taught us years before, at Academy.

I'd waited too long. I sailed into the airlock feet first, still decelerating. My feet smashed into the inner hatch just as I snapped off my jets. I crashed to the deck.

The outer hatch slid closed. I scrambled to my feet, in a frenzy for the chamber to pressurize. Alexi's anxious face stared through the transplex. The hatch slid open. I stumbled aboard.

"Captain's on board!" Alexi slammed shut the hatch.

Vax roared, "Engine room, Fuse!" I felt the engines whine. Alexi lifted the jets from my back while I unsnapped my helmet stays. Rafe Treadwell, white-faced, helped a sailor pull me out of my suit.

My wet pants clung to my legs. "Are we Fused?"

Alexi grabbed the caller. "Mr. Holser, Captain asks if we're Fused."

"Yes, sir. Energy readings are normal. Fusion is ignited."

I trembled with rage. "All officers to the bridge. Everyone! I'll be along in a minute." Yanking my other arm free of the T-suit I pushed past Rafe and half ran up the ladder to my cabin.

Inside, I stripped off my pants and shorts with mindless haste and threw on a dry pair of slacks. I stumbled out of the cabin, buttoning my pants as I ran toward the bridge. I slapped the control; the bridge hatch slid open.

Derek, Alexi, Vax, and the Pilot stood by the console. Behind them were the Chief and Mr. Crossburn. Philip Tyre waited uncertainly by the hatch.

I crossed to my chair. For a moment, I stood holding to the back of it. Mr. Chantir came in, pale, breathing hard. Dr. Uburu followed.

Vax came close. "Are you all right, sir?"

"Get away from me!" I shoved him.

"Lord God." We all turned to Dr. Uburu. She bowed her head. "Almighty Lord God, we thank you for our deliverance from evil. We ask you to bless us, to bless our voyage, and to bring health and well-being to all aboard."

"Amen." I murmured the soothing word with the others, feeling the Doctor's calm and strength flow into me. "Good heavens." My voice was quieter. I sank into my chair. "Darla, did you get that?"

"Every bit of it." Her tone was grim.

"Play it back."

"Aye aye, sir." Thank Lord God she knew not to be flippant.

Her screen flickered. Mesmerized, we watched her recording of *Telstar's* torn hull while our past conversation flowed from the speaker. "I'll go up to Level 1 and try to get onto the bridge."

A long pause. My bloodcurdling scream, and Vax's shout. "Captain, what is it?"

I spoke over my recorded reply. "It must have been one of those— things that smashed his suit visor. Then it did something to his head." I tried not to retch.

On the speaker, I whimpered. Then, "Battle Stations!" Vax's shouted commands. For a moment nothing changed on the screen. A spacesuited man appeared, scrambling into the gig. Then another. After a moment the third.

The speaker said, "Oh, Jesus Lord! It's coming out—"

"Freeze!" The image hung frozen, in response to my order. "Maximum magnification." The screen swooped in on the amorphous shape halfway out of the hole in *Telstar's* hull. Blobs of color set almost at random in the outer skin.

"Christ, it looks like an amoeba!" said Lieutenant Chantir.

"Don't blaspheme!" I studied the screen. "It can't be single-celled. Not if it's that large."

"I don't ever want to know," Alexi muttered. I glared him into silence.

"Go on, Darla." The image began to move. The gig pulled clear in response to my order, drifted alongside the dead ship, waiting for me to emerge. I jetted toward the gig, tiny against the bulk of the dead ship's hull. The bizarre goldfish floated from behind the hull. In space, I twisted to look at it. Sickened, I watched the destruction of the gig amid my own frantic shouts to Vax. "Fuse! Go to Hope Nation! Save the ship!"

The commotion blared from the speakers. "Fuse! For God's sake, Vax! Obey orders!" I listened, unwilling, to my desperate pleas and Vax's repeated demands that I hurry. Then Vax Holser's soft voice said the irretrievable, damning words. "No, sir. Not until I have you aboard."

I put my head in my hands. "Turn it off." My words hung flat in the sudden silence. A long moment passed. I got heavily to my feet. "Darla, please record." Her cameras lit.

I faced Vax. "Lieutenant Holser, you deliberately disobeyed your Captain's orders to Fuse, not once but five times. Without question you are unfit to serve in the United Nations Naval Service. I suspend your commssion for the remainder of our voyage. I will not try you, as I am not capable of judging you fairly. I have already concluded you should be hanged." Dr. Uburu gasped; the Chief closed his eyes, shook his head.

"I will, however, recommend a court-martial on our return, and I will testify against you. For the remainder of our voyage you are forbidden to wear the Naval uniform or to associate with me or any officer. You will be moved to a passenger cabin at once. Get off my bridge!"

Vax's face crumpled. He tried to speak, couldn't, tried again. His huge, beefy fist pounded the side of his leg once, twice, three times as he fought for control. Then he took a deep breath. "Aye aye, sir," he whispered. His face was ashen. He turned, marched to the hatch. Alexi slapped it open, and he was gone.

No one spoke or moved. "I am Captain here," I grated. "No one, not one of you, will ever disobey my order again. Not now, not ever!" I studied their faces. "I should have hanged him for mutiny." I walked among them, stopping in front of each. "I didn't hang you either, Mr. Crossburn, for your refusal to do your duty. I won't make the mistake again, with any of you. I warn you all."

The silence was absolute. "We will maintain a three-officer watch at all times until our arrival home. You will all participate. Not you, Doctor, but everyone else. We are at war. There will be no inattention to duty, no idle talk." My lip curled. "No chess." I studied them again. "Pilot, Mr. Chantir, Mr. Tamarov, you have the watch. The rest of you are dismissed."

I took their murmured "Aye aye, sir" in silence. The four off-duty officers filed out. I watched the Pilot and Lieutenant Chantir at their consoles for several minutes, before leaving the bridge.

I went to my cabin, sealed the hatch. Mechanically I took off my jacket, my shirt. I stripped off my pants. I stepped into the shower, stood under its hot spray for a quarter of an hour. After, I dried myself and sat on my bunk. I waited for the inevitable reaction.

My stomach churned. I ran to the head, reached it just in time. I vomited helplessly, again and again, heaving against nothing. I shuffled back to my bunk clutching my aching midriff.

When the alien had appeared in *Telstar*'s corridor I was utterly terrified. But whatever it might have done, facing it would have been easier than going on with my life.

29

I stayed in my cabin all that evening and into the next day. I sent for my meals. When I ventured into the corridor it was only to stalk to the bridge. I stood my watch in absolute silence, then returned to my cabin.

On the second day I went with reluctance to the dining hall, because it was my duty. There was little conversation at my table; my haggard face discouraged anyone who might have tried to speak.

After dinner I walked the ship, past the wardroom, the lieutenants' cabins, the bridge. I took the ladder down to Level 2. I strode with unvaried pace and frozen expression. I passed the cabin to which Vax had been exiled. Passengers I met in the corridor stood aside.

I went down to Level 3, past the crew berths. Knots of crewmen were gathered in the corridors, talking softly. I ignored them. I went into their berths, looked about. I checked the crew exercise room, their lounge. In the engine room, the Chief stood stolidly at attention with his watch while I glanced around, then left.

I climbed up to Level 2. In the corridor young Cadet Fuentes came to attention. "Are we all right, sir? Did anything follow us?"

"Cadet, go to Lieutenant Tamarov for discipline." My tone was harsh. "Don't speak to the Captain unless he speaks to you!"

I knocked on the wardroom hatch. Derek opened. Paula Treadwell was lying in bed in her shorts, half asleep. Philip Tyre looked up from his bunk. Printouts of regulations were stacked on his blanket. I turned to leave and collided with Rafe Treadwell, just coming in. He jumped to attention. I ignored him.

I went back to Level 2, through the lock to the launch berth. Lieutenant Crossburn was carrying a seat onto the launch. He said nothing, his face grim. I turned on my heel and left.

I went to the infirmary. "I won't be able to sleep tonight, Doctor. What will you give me?" I was brusque.

She looked at me a moment. "I'd prefer you tried to sleep first."

"I don't care what you'd prefer. Give me something."

Still she hesitated. "Why can't you sleep, Captain Seafort?"

"Because I'll think."

"About what?"

"You said this was a jinxed ship, Doctor. I'm the jinx. I didn't make the revolt on Miningcamp, or create the life-form out there, but when things go wrong I ruin people. If I'd been a leader, Vax would have obeyed orders and he'd still have a career. Now I've destroyed him. And Philip, and Mr. Crossburn, and Alexi. And others. Give me the pill."

She hesitated, then got it from the cabinet. She held it out. "Don't take it until you're in your bed. And not before midnight."

"All right."

"Do you promise?"

I smiled sourly. "I promise." I thrust the pill in my pocket and went back to my cabin.

I took off my jacket and tie and sat in my chair to wait out the evening. Below, Vax would be alone in his cabin; I closed my eyes and waited for the pain to abate. After a time I eyed my spacious quarters.

I hated this cabin. I hated the ship.

I wondered why the creature on *Telstar* hadn't hurled one of its globs at me. Certainly *Hibernia* would have been better served. I no longer had a reason to live. My career was shattered. I'd be separated by light-years from the woman I cherished. I had no friends. And, worst of all, I'd done it all to myself.

A knock. Annoyed at the interruption, I flung open the hatch. Chief McAndrews stood waiting. "What is it, Chief?"

"I need to talk to you privately, sir."

"Not now. I don't want to be bothered."

"It's important."

The gall of the man. I was Captain. "Another time. Go below."

"No." He pushed past and shut the hatch behind him. I was stunned. He said quietly, "You can't go on like this, Nick."

Hope stirred. "You've come to relieve me?"

He raised his eyebrows. "No. I've come to talk sense into you."

"This is mutiny! I'll have you hanged!"

"You'll do as you see fit." His voice was stony. "When I'm done." He shoved out a chair. "Sit."

Numb, I sat. He pulled up another chair.

"You're walking the ship like death warmed over, and it gives everyone the willies. Why?"

I looked to the deck. "Because I can't stand how badly I do my job. Because I hate myself."

"Why is that?"

"I've done my best and failed. I was friends with you, once. I ended that. I brutalized Alexi, the cadets, even Derek. Instead of inspiring the men, I threaten to hang them. Sometimes I do it. I caused Sandy's death along with all the others. I savaged the Pilot and I destroyed Vax. Do you need more? I'm ruining Philip Tyre and Ardwell Crossburn. I broke up the Treadwell family for my own amusement. I killed three men in the gig because I was too stupid to circle *Telstar* before mooring to her hull. And the worst is, it will go on. Either I fail my oath to Lord God, or I continue making things worse!" My eyes stung.

He asked as if puzzled, "Why must you do that to yourself?"

"Do what?"

"Cast everything you do in the worst possible light. Why do you never give yourself credit?"

I waved it away, with contempt. "For what?"

"You intuited a glitch in Darla and saved us from catastrophe. You took us to Hope Nation on course and on schedule without commissioned officers. You had the guts to carry out Captain Malstrom's executions, and steadied the crew for the long haul. You saved us all at Miningcamp. Can't you see it?"

"I killed Sandy! I killed Mr. Howard and the others! Can't you see that?"

He shouted, "No! No one can, except you!"

I recoiled in shocked silence.

"God damn it, Nicky, you're as good a Captain as *Hibernia* ever had! What in the bloody hell is the matter with you?"

"I'm not! A Captain leads! Look at Justin Haag—no one would dream of questioning him. I have to bully everyone! That's why they dislike me so."

"Who?"

"Vax, for one. Ever since I brutalized him in the wardroom!"

"Vax would die for you," he said quietly.

"He can't feel that way!" A tear found its way down my cheek.

"They all do. Derek—you made a man out of him and he reveres you. You can't imagine how strongly he feels. Alexi idolizes you. He'd follow you anywhere."

"But look what I did to him!"

"You didn't do that!" the Chief thundered. "Philip Tyre did!"

I recoiled from his anger. "Philip, then. I set him up, and delivered him into Alexi's hands."

"He deserves it. Alexi's taking revenge. So?"

"I could have stopped Philip, won him over."

His meaty fist slammed the table. "Nobody could stop him! That's why he was sent to you!"

I stopped cold, realizing the truth of that. Doubt began to eat at the edges of my disgust.

"Ricky Fuentes," the Chief said. "He talks of you with stars in his eyes. Paula and Rafe. What made them want to leave their parents to sign up, you idiot? Not the Navy. You!" His vehemence took away my breath. I swallowed.

"Why must you be perfect, Nicky?"

"That's why we're here!" I saw our drab, worn kitchen, Bible open on the rickety table, while Father waited.

"Can you be perfect?" the Chief demanded, as if from a distance.

"No, but we have to try!"

"Is trying ever good enough?"

His voice faded. Father glowered. Sullenly, I glared back. No matter how hard I tried, I could never please him, because I wasn't perfect. Only Lord God could be perfect; only Lord God could be good enough. No matter what I did I couldn't win his approval. Yes, I could be good. I could be excellent.

I could never be perfect.

"It's not fair!" I cried in anguish to Father. He slapped me; my head snapped to the side. But it wasn't fair. Lord God couldn't expect perfection, no matter what Father sought of me. My chest tightened in helpless frustration. If God couldn't expect it, why must I?"

Father's visage glimmered; I began at long last to comprehend. I demanded perfection because Father would accept no less. I sought proofs of my own imperfection, as Father must.

My eyes opened. I was in my cabin, with Chief McAndrews. Father wasn't aboard. Unless I brought him with me.

I looked at the Chief. "But I can't lead. Take Vax. He refused to obey a lawful order. I had to destroy him."

"Why did he disobey?"

"Because he was foolish. He wanted to get us back aboard. He risked everyone to save a few."

"Why?"

"I don't know!" I said, tormented. "If I knew I could have stopped him!"

"Because he loves you."

My breath caught in a sob.

"He knew what he was doing." The Chief was remorseless. "He was willing to give up his career for you. Perhaps his life as well."

"But why, after all I did to him?" The rag and polish in the launch berth; before that, the brutal icy showers.

"You saved him from being a Philip Tyre. You were the only one who could do that. He loves you for it."

My hateful words on the bridge echoed. "Oh, God."

"Stop torturing yourself, Nick."

"I've fouled up so badly!"

"Because you weren't perfect." His words hung in the air.

After a long while I forced my gaze to meet his. I took a long breath. "Yes. Because I wasn't perfect."

"But you're a good Captain."

I tried a smile. It wavered. "Am I?"

I could banish Father. I had banished Mr. Tuak, hadn't I?

"Yes, you're a good Captain."

I would miss Father. Perhaps I could learn to live without him.

"I shoved a man out the airlock once," I said.

"I gutted a man once," he answered.

"My God, what for?"

"I won't tell you."

We were silent. Finally I asked, "What do I do about Vax?"

"Decide that yourself."

I sighed. "It's lonely. It's always been so lonely."

He stood, took a step forward. His hands darted toward me, then drew back hesitantly. "I'm going to touch you," he said, for the first time unsure.

I nodded dumbly. He rested his big, powerful hands on my shoulders. He squeezed. I began to cry. After a while I stopped. He sat back in his chair.

"Do you think," I said after a time, afraid of his response, "do you think perhaps, sometimes, you might want to sit with me again? With your smoking pipe?"

"If you wish, sir." His voice was quiet.

"I would like that."

"We're mated, sir," Alexi reported.

"Very well." I swiveled my chair. "When do they come up?"

"I'd expect them anytime, sir," Mr. Chantir said. "We called last night, if you remember." Now that we were in Hope Station system, I had radioed ahead to Orbit Station, requesting an emergency conference aboard ship with General Tho, Governor Williams, and Captain Forbee.

"Mr. Tyre."

The boy leaped from his seat, stood at parade-ground attention.

"Yessir." His blond hair was trimmed shorter than before. His hands and face were scrubbed pink.

"Go to the Commandant's office and find out when they'll arrive."

"Aye aye, sir!" He spun about and marched out. I glanced at Alexi. He returned my gaze, impassive.

I leaned back. "So. One more port safely arrived at. Pilot, an excellent job, as usual."

Surprised, he flushed with pleasure. "Thanks very much, sir."

"Alexi, you're in charge of arrangements here. We leave in twenty-four hours. Make sure the oncoming passengers are told we'll sail two days early. See that our supplies are boarded on time." None of that should be a problem; we'd already radioed instructions.

"Aye aye, sir. If you'll excuse me please, I'll get started now."

I nodded permission. "Lieutenant Crossburn."

"Yes, sir?" Subdued and chastened, he seemed much relieved to be freed from his punishment detail. Defused, we couldn't have our launch out of commission.

"Go below and bring Vax Holser to the bridge."

"Aye aye, sir."

I thumbed the caller. "Chief McAndrews to the bridge." I waited with the Pilot and Lieutenant Chantir.

Philip reported, breathless. "Sir, pardon, please. The Governor is on the station. General Tho is with him. Captain Forbee's shuttle is just docking."

"I'll be with them in a moment. When I call, escort them to the bridge."

"Aye aye, sir." Tyre hurried off. Before, his manner had been cooperative. Now it was something more intense. Alexi's doing, perhaps.

Vax Holser and Lieutenant Crossburn appeared at the hatchway. Vax seemed ill at ease in borrowed civilian clothes that didn't quite fit.

"Bring him in, Mr. Crossburn."

Vax, expressionless, followed onto the bridge. I stood waiting. The Chief hurried in, stopping short when he saw Vax.

I paced. "You all know I suspended Lieutenant Holser's commission because of his actions the day we found *Telstar*. I have reviewed the matter and I conclude that I made a mistake."

I glanced at the Chief, felt my face redden. "True, Mr. Holser's actions could be construed as mutinous. But I failed to take into account certain mitigating evidence. First, the Captain had left the ship, and because of the emergency, Mr. Holser had no time to summon a superior. For the moment, he was in charge. He chose not to Fuse. It could be argued that as the senior officer present, the choice was his. I don't take that view, but I can't conclude beyond doubt that his action was mutinous, despite my utter disapproval."

The other officers listened, absorbed. Vax, of course, hung on my every word. "Mr. Holser knew Admiralty would take a dim view of abandoning a Captain in interstellar space, and I must take that into account as well." I couldn't mention Vax's true motive, but I knew it now. "Therefore, I revoke my suspension of Mr. Holser's commission and I restore him to active duty. Darla, can you erase a recording I ordered you to make?"

"Yes, Captain. You have to order me to erase it and copy your order into the Log. Then the recording is irretrievably wiped."

I opened the Log and wrote. "Darla, erase my suspension of Mr. Holser from your records."

"Aye aye, sir."

I turned to Vax. "You're reinstated. I still consider your actions reprehensible. They indicate an appalling lack of concern for the safety of the ship. I therefore fine you three months pay and deprive you of three months seniority. I rebuke you."

He stood at attention, his eyes glistening. "Aye aye, sir."

"Put on your uniform and report for duty."

"Aye aye, sir!" A grin broke through his solemnity. With a crisp salute, he turned and strode off the bridge. He broke into a run before he reached the hatch.

"Clear the bridge, please." I thumbed the caller. "Mr. Tyre, escort our guests on board."

Three hours later the shaken Governor walked slowly down the corridor with General Tho, Captain Forbee, and myself.

"You can't stay to defend us, of course," Governor Williams said.

"No, sir. Above all else I have to warn Admiralty."

"Some of our local vessels have lasers, Governor." General Tho. "If we can organize a unified command—"

"You have it," I assured him. "Captain Forbee, put yourself under General Tho's command regarding the defense of Hope Nation."

"Aye aye, sir."

The General looked relieved.

"I can't believe you really found Grone," Captain Forbee said. "That story of his . . ."

"It would explain the epidemic," said the Governor.

"But why an epidemic? Why not bombs?"

I said, "If they're unicellular organisms they certainly understand viruses." We walked in chilled silence.

The General muttered, "If I hadn't seen your holos I'd try to have you committed."

"Judge Chesley would be happy to oblige." They smiled. "Gentlemen, you'll be on your own. I'll warn Miningcamp and shoot straight for Earth. You know you won't have help for three years at least." No radionics could outrun a fusion drive. We'd be seventeen months each way, and Admiralty would need time to mount a response.

"Right." We paused at the airlock. The Governor glanced around uneasily. "I'll feel better back on the surface. Lord God help us all."

The next day was a blur of activity. Supplies, cargo, and passengers were loaded in record time. Later, I'd get a chance to meet our new passengers; for now I was so busy I hadn't even checked the manifest. I remained on the bridge, answering questions and directing the harried crew, breaking only for meals.

The planet rotated below, visible in our screens. Amanda was somewhere below; if I looked carefully I could probably spot Centraltown. I sighed. I would learn to live without her.

At last we were ready to leave. I gave the Pilot the conn. As soon as we cast off the lines he rocked us free.

We drifted ever faster from the station. In an hour we were far enough to Fuse; with deference he returned the conn to me. I fed our calculations to the puter.

"Coordinates received and understood." Darla.

"Chief Engineer, Fuse, please." I burned Hope Nation into my memory before it faded from the simulscreens.

We Fused.

Saddened, I left the bridge to Vax and Lieutenant Chantir's watch, and went below for something to eat.

Passengers milled excitedly in the corridor, exploring the ship. I spotted Derek, grinning foolishly. "Well, Mr. Carr." I fell in alongside him. "You'll be back someday."

"Perhaps, sir." He didn't seem much concerned.

"Why so happy, Mr. Carr?"

"I met the new education director, sir. I think we're going to be friends."

I didn't need a reminder of Amanda. "That's nice," I said, glum. I grimaced at the sealed airlock. "It's going to be a long trip home."

A familiar voice, behind me. "Think so?"

I whirled. Amanda waited, hands on hips.

"Hi, Nicky." She smiled. Her eyes danced as she came into my arms.

Epilogue

"Are you all right, sir?"

I blinked as I emerged into the bright sunlight. My head ached miserably. I swallowed my nausea. Vax hovered; Alexi waited by the car.

"I'm fine." Despite my claim I felt awful from the P and D I'd voluntarily undergone. For three days they'd pumped me full of drugs, questioned me without end. I remembered little of it. Ever-changing faces, persistent demands that I explain in detail each decision I'd made. They'd stripped me of reasons, facts, motives, and exposed my foolish mistakes to the merciless light. I wanted nothing more than to curl up in bed beside my wife.

"What happened, sir?"

"I passed, Mr. Tamarov." I swallowed again.

Alexi guided me to an electricar. "What next, sir?"

"They'll decide whether to court-martial me."

"They wouldn't dare!"

"Watch your tongue, Mr. Holser." Even among comrades I wouldn't allow that.

"Aye aye, sir. Do you want to go back to quarters?" The entire crew had been shuttled from Lunapolis to Houston Naval Base as soon as my report was read, and we were still there.

"Admiral Brentley wants to see me before the Board of Inquiry makes its report. His office is that way." I pointed toward Houston.

"You drive, Alexi." Vax got in the back seat next to me and closed his eyes.

"How do you feel, Vax?" I could guess; he'd had the same drugs as I.

"I've been better. It's all right."

"What will they do with you?"

"They offered me a posting. I'll tell you later, if you don't mind."

I drew back, a little hurt. "As you wish."

We pulled up before the Admiral's sunbaked residence, its yard surrounded by tall, unkempt bushes. A sentry saluted. I paused. "Get some sleep, you two."

Alexi shook his head. "I'm going to round up the others. We'll be back to pick you up when you're done."

I was too weary to argue. "Whatever you say."

The Admiral's entryway was dark and cool. An orderly took me through a sitting room into a sunny first-floor office. I came to attention.

"Carry on." Admiral Brentley's gruff voice suited him. Sixtyish, graying, his athletic body had thickened into the heavy muscle of an athlete's later years. He studied me without expression.

"Aye aye, sir." I chose the at-ease position.

The Admiral Commanding, Fleet Operations, sat himself on the edge of his desk. "Well, Seafort. What do you have to say for yourself?"

With a pang I realized that he knew it all, had seen the reports, heard my testimony, spoken to his nephew whom I had sentenced to the launch berth for most of the return voyage. Our interview was a formality. Court-martial or not, I would never again see command.

"I've nothing to say for myself, sir."

"No excuses, no defenses?"

"No, sir." My voice was firm. "I did the best I could with what knowledge I had."

He regarded me quizzically. "What am I supposed to do with you?"

"Am I to be court-martialed, sir?"

"That's up to the review board." His tone was brusque. "I'm not a member." He walked around the side of the desk and stood looking out the window behind him. "However, they'll damn well do what I tell them to do. It's my fleet."

I was shocked by his confidence. It meant either that I wasn't in as much trouble as I thought, or I was in so much trouble that what he said didn't matter at all. "Yes, sir."

"I'm not happy with some of your decisions." He tapped a sheaf of papers on his desk. "Pardoning Mr. Herney, for example. And your commutations for the mutineers on Miningcamp."

"I'm sorry you feel that way, sir." I spoke quietly.

"You don't care, do you?" The accusation surprised me. I didn't think it showed.

I wouldn't lie to a superior. "No, sir, not really. I've had months and months to go over it. I did the best I could given who I am and my lack of abilities. I don't expect you to see it that way, sir, but I've learned to live with it." With Amanda, in the long, loving nights in our cabin. With the fumes of the Chief's smoke, across my companionable cabin table.

He growled, "Well, I asked for it. I won't penalize you for the truth." He came around the desk, faced me with arms folded. "I can't court-martial you. The public wouldn't stand for it."

"The public?" What on earth was he talking about?

"Court-martial the hero of Miningcamp? The Captain who saved his ship with pistols blazing?"

"That's utter nonsense!" I said, forgetting myself.

"The crew swears to it." He paused, and added, "Court-martial the first man to make contact with another species? No. I won't do that."

I closed my eyes. My stomach hurt anew. I just wanted it over. "Very well, sir."

"Still, I can see to it that you never board a ship again."

I was only mildly interested. "Is that what you intend?"

He came closer. "There are some things I can't overlook. That business with the circuit judge. It indicates a lack of respect for civilian authority. Couldn't you have handled him more diplomatically?"

I raised an eyebrow. "What business, sir? I don't recall any mention in the Log or Governor Williams's dispatches."

After a moment the corners of his mouth turned up. "Yes. Well. You covered that nicely. It only came out in the interrogation." He brushed it aside. "The worst of it was leaving your ship to visit *Telstar*. Absolutely inexcusable."

I no longer had anything to lose. I said, in a tone for which I'd have caned a midshipman, "Tell me you wouldn't have gone across to look, in my place."

Admiral Brentley, taken aback by my disregard of rank, seemed to swell. He strode back to his desk, threw himself in his chair. He glowered; I stared back with indifference.

Slowly, his shoulders relaxed. "I would have done exactly as you did, Nick," he said. "I'd have gone over to take a look for myself. I'd want to know what happened to their ship: it was identical to my own."

"Yes, sir. But I still should have circled the ship first."

"Why? To check for aliens? In two hundred years we've never found anything but a few boneless fish on one watery planet. Why should you be on guard?"

I considered. "I wasn't sure, thinking about it. It just seemed I should have been more wary. As I should on Miningcamp. I just opened the locks and stood aside."

"Since when has the Navy gone to Battle Stations to dock at a U.N. orbiting station?" he demanded. "That one, you're clear on. We've already decided. If every Captain has to ready a defense party before opening locks at a station, we'll all go glitched. No, it's the U.N.A.F. Commandant who'll pay for that."

He tapped the reports. "I can go along with most of it, even when your decisions differed from mine. Hell, that's why we send a Captain, to make decisions. We back him up with total authority. Hope Nation is three years out; we can't pull strings from home port." He stopped. "But there's one matter you've forgotten. Lieutenant Ardwell Crossburn. My nephew."

"Yes, sir." I sagged. He would stand by his family; he had to. Blood was stronger than regs. Anyway, my treatment of Crossburn was further proof of my disrespect for authority. What Captain in his right mind would abuse the nephew of his Commanding Admiral?

"He's come to see me several times, Seafort. Some of his reports are shocking. Did you actually make him take the launch apart every day for eighteen months?"

"Almost every day, sir. Not while we were Defused."

"And you thought you could get away with it?" Brentley's tone was menacing.

"I didn't care, sir." I spoke with civility, but I'd had enough.

"He says you're a lunatic. That you're paranoid, you were suspicious of bombs."

"It kept him in the launch berth, sir."

He glared at me. I stared back.

In his eye, an odd twinkle. "You really did that?"

"Yes, sir. I did."

"What do you think of him, Mr. Seafort?"

I could be insolent to him, but I wouldn't lie, though my answer would cost me my career. "He's dangerous, sir. He never should have made lieutenant. He throws his family connections in the face of his seniors, and takes it upon himself to investigate us. I wasn't going to put up with that. I'd do exactly the same again. Or maybe I'd brig him. I don't know."

Brentley shook his head. "Do you know what trouble I went to, getting him out of the Solar System? The wires I pulled so his orders would come from someone else? And you, you ungrateful whelp, you bring him back and dump him in my lap again!"

I snorted. "He was dumped on me, sir. I had no choice. I was under weigh when I found out about him."

He turned away disgusted. "I know. It's not your fault. I never thought it was." He looked up. "You know how he made lieutenant? Some toadying Captain thought I'd be pleased. He did it for me. For me!" The Admiral turned back to me, shaking his head. "By the way, don't worry about challenging that pair of Dosmen who glitched your puter. It won't be necessary; they've been dealt with."

"Good." My tone was dull. What did any of it matter?

"Seafort, I can't give you *Hibernia*. You're too young yet. It wouldn't sit well, even if you are a hero. And your rank as Captain, I can't confirm it."

"I understand, sir. Will I go back to midshipman?"

"No."

A lieutenant, then. It would be hard for me to adjust, but I could do it.

"Actually, I was thinking of Commander," Admiral Brentley said. "I've got a sloop coming in, *Challenger*. Crew of forty-two, two lieutenants, three middies. She takes seventy passengers. I can put you back to Captain after your first trip out, when your youth won't be so offensive to us oldsters. You're only twenty; hardly any of your classmates have made lieutenant yet."

Commander? But that was the same as Captain; the title differed only by a technicality. And a sloop was a full command, with—I forced my attention back to his words.

"She's got a new drive unit, supposed to cut a month off the run to Hope Nation. And she's bristling with lasers. She'll be part of the squadron we're sending. Will you take her?"

I was speechless. Confirmed as Commander, with my own vessel? My mouth dry, I nodded.

"Good. Your wife?"

"Amanda will ship with me." Despite the risk of melanoma T, we'd already decided that, at her insistence. It was unusual, but permitted.

He grimaced. "I don't like that. I'm old-fashioned. But I suppose it's your choice." He went on to another subject. "Oh, I had a visit from your Midshipman Tyre. He begged me to let him resign from the service."

"For what reason?" I remembered Tyre on watch, one long, dreary day halfway home. Unexpectedly he'd put his head on the console and began to weep, in long, desolate sobs.

"Now what, Mr. Tyre?"

"Please, let me out. I want to resign. I can't take any more, sir. Oh, I beg you!"

"Steady, Mr. Tyre."

"They're torturing me! I get caned every week. It hurts so much! I have eight demerits right now, and I've already worked off six since Monday! They're on me every waking minute, both of them." He raised his tear-stained face. "I don't understand, sir. What have I done? Why is this happening to me?"

"You were rather cruel, Mr. Tyre. They haven't forgotten."

"Cruel? How could I have been? I was just doing my job, sir. I tried to help them!" I sighed. He would never understand.

"I'll make you an offer, Mr. Tyre. You're a fine midshipman when you're dealing with your superiors. You're competent, courteous, friendly on watch, eager to help. It's your juniors you can't handle. Forget about that part of your job, just ignore them, and I'll pass the word to go easier on you."

"You mean it would stop?" He looked beyond me, as if toward heaven.

"I don't think it will ever stop, Mr. Tyre. You've seen to that. It might lighten a bit, though."

"Yes, sir. Very well, sir. I accept. Please!"

I nodded. I would have a word with Alexi. I couldn't know that a smoldering Derek Carr would choose that very night to challenge his senior middy, to follow him to the exercise room, to beat him coolly into a bloody unresisting pulp, afterward kicking his bruised rump along the circumference corridor back to the wardroom. Derek was effectively in charge of the juniors for the rest of the voyage home.

"The boy wouldn't complain about any of you, not a word," the Admiral was saying. "I couldn't get any reasons out of him. I suppose I should let him go, if he's such a weakling."

It was my fault, in a way. If I had been able to get through to him . . . I sighed. "He still might make a good officer," I said. "I can keep him with me awhile."

Brentley looked relieved. "Another problem settled, then. I can't give you full shore leave, not with an interstellar war on our hands. If I hadn't seen those recordings . . ."

"I know, sir."

"Who do you want with you?"

"Mr. Carr as a midshipman. Lieutenant Tamarov," I said instantly.

"You need one more middy and a lieutenant. Let me know or I'll assign them to you."

"Aye aye, sir."

"It's a hell of a thing." He stood next to me for a moment, in silence. He held out his hand. "Good luck, Commander."

I shook his hand soberly. "I'll need it, sir."

Outside, the sun had lowered toward the horizon; the evening cool was settling on the scrub trees and the fields. Alexi waited on the sidewalk with Vax, the Treadwell twins, Derek, and Ricky. They all stared at me, anxiety, worry, concern reflected in their young faces.

I grinned. "Commander. U.N.S. *Challenger*. I leave in a week."

Alexi whooped, dancing around the car. Vax broke into a grin. "Who do you take, sir?"

"Alexi goes with me. If you don't mind, Mr. Tamarov." He was beside himself, grinning idiotically. "You too, Derek. We're going back to Hope Nation." Carr said nothing, but his eyes closed with relief. "I need another middy."

Midshipman Paula Treadwell would be going to navigation training school on Luna. Ricky was slated for Academy. I had recommended it in the Log; I wanted him to have the best.

"Me, sir?" Rafe looked hopeful.

"Speak when you're spoken to, Cadet," I snapped. Then, "Still, I suppose you'd do. I'd have to promote you to midshipman. Are you sure you're ready for Last Night?"

The fourteen-year-old grinned at Derek Carr. "I can take anything, sir." It had become a wardroom byword, since our aristocratic cadet had made his stubborn vow.

"Very well." I looked at my lieutenant. "What's your posting, Vax?"

"They offered me *Caledonia,* on the Ganymede run. I turned it down."

"Command of your own sloop? Why?"

"I want to sail with you, sir. I told Admiral Brentley if he gave you a ship I wanted to go along."

"You're ready for command, Vax."

"No, sir. Not yet."

"Why not?"

He faced me. "You've taught me a lot. I'm not convinced you don't have anything more to teach. Sir."

My eyes misted. We hung, all of us, in that uncomfortable moment before parting. Ricky Fuentes, gangly and awkward in his early adolescence, came to me hesitantly. We looked at each other. Suddenly he flung himself on me, burying his head in my chest, hugging me fiercely. I gave him a squeeze. "Good-bye, boy. I'll see you again."

"Will you?" His eyes were red.

"Yes. I promise." I regarded our onetime ship's boy with affection. "I have some advice. At Academy, don't hug your drill sergeant, no matter how much you like him. It's bad for your health."

"Aye aye, sir!" He grinned like a foolish puppy.

I eased into the car. "Take me home, people. I'll see you later at the party." I closed my eyes, feeling the car jounce over the potholes. I was going home. To Amanda. To my crew. To my ship.

Challenger's Hope

To Tony Straseske and Marshall Spencer, who helped me through, to Ragtime Rick of Toledo, Ohio, at whose corner booth an author often taps the keys of his laptop while the ragtime soars, and of course, to Jettie, who makes it worthwhile.

Ardath Mayhar, C.J. Cherryh and Roger Mac-Bride Allen each contributed invaluable wisdom and wit while the author struggled with this work. No thanks can possibly be enough.

CHALLENGER'S HOPE

Being the second voyage of
Nicholas Seafort, U.N.N.S.,
in the year of our Lord 2194

Part 1

November, in the year of our Lord 2197

30

"Carry on!" Geoffrey Tremaine strutted to his place at the head of the Admiralty conference table. Scowling, he set down his sheaf of notes and flicked invisible dust from his gold braid. As the assembled officers stood easy, I tugged at my jacket, made sure my tie was straight.

While the Admiral settled himself, we took our seats. Each of the eleven men and three women at this briefing in the Naval warren of down-under Lunapolis captained a ship in the UNNS squadron ready to sail to Hope Nation, sixty-nine light years distant. The Admiral's sloop, *Portia*, fitted with the newest L-Model fusion drive, was docked aloft at Earthport Station. So was my own sloop, *Challenger*, though I hadn't yet boarded her.

Tremaine's cold eye roved the table. "So," he said finally, as if disappointed. "My command is gathered together at last." Short, florid, he seemed on the edge of rage.

I glanced to either side. Length-of-service medals on Captain Hall's dress jacket indicated twenty-four years' service; Captain Derghinski, on my right, had twenty-two. Each of them had been a Naval officer longer than I'd lived. *Challenger* was my first assigned command. I was, I knew, the youngest Captain in the entire U.N. Navy.

"We sail tomorrow, gentlemen. As your written orders indicate, we'll Defuse seven times to provide the most accurate navigation checks possible."

Again I wondered why he wanted us to waste time and propellant with so many jumps, but as the most junior present, I kept my opinion to myself.

A Fusion drive was accurate to within six percent—whoops, no longer. Within *one* percent of the distance traveled. That change was astonishing; during my long cruise to Hope Nation, vastly improved control baffles had been devised and Admiralty was retrofitting them on ships as they returned to Home System.

Navigation wasn't my strong point, and even the refresher course they'd made me attend left me a touch shaky on the mechanics of Fusion. Thankfully, the ship's puter and our Pilot would carry out most of the calculations, though I'd confirm them myself no matter how long it took.

Theoretically we could now Fuse to within three light months of Hope Nation, and follow with a short corrective jump. For greater precision, it was customary to make smaller jumps instead of one long one. We might normally expect to Defuse for nav checks twice during the sixty-nine-light-year voyage to Hope Nation. Seven times was absurd.

"I'll sail on *Challenger*," Tremaine said.

My jaw dropped. Could I have heard aright? True, *Challenger* was somewhat larger than *Portia*—the Admiral's flagship was one of the smallest vessels in our fleet—and I could arrange suitable accommodations, but—the Admiral himself? On my ship?

Tremaine glared, as if reading my thoughts. "With Captain Hasselbrad."

"What?" I heard my incredulous voice, as from a distance.

"I'm moving my flag. Naturally, I'll want a Captain with more experience. Seafort, you'll be taking *Portia*. They'll cut your new orders this afternoon. Pick them up from Ops."

"But—" I swallowed. "Aye aye, sir."

While he glanced through his papers my head spun with unasked questions. *Challenger*, the ship whose specs I'd studied until my eyes blurred, was no longer mine. All I knew about *Portia* was that she was a two-decker, tiny by comparison. And what of my crew? I'd had Alexi and Derek Carr assigned as my junior officers. And Vax Holser. They'd all be lost to me. How could I cope with the demands of an unfamiliar bridge without their dogged support?

Tremaine tapped his notes. "*Portia* and *Freiheit* will remain at each station until the rest of the fleet has Fused. Their L-Model drives will allow them to arrive first at the next rendezvous, to clear any, er, encroachment."

So that was it. The only, er, encroachment we might encounter was the bizarre alien creature I'd come upon during *Hibernia*'s voyage to Hope Nation, after I'd been catapulted from midshipman to Captain upon the death of *Hibernia*'s seasoned officers. The skirmish with the fish still brought nightmares, which my wife Amanda gently soothed away in the solitude of our cabin.

Lord God! Amanda had gone ahead to settle on *Challenger* while I struggled through Admiralty's refresher courses and my briefings. She'd be unpacking in our cabin—now the Admiral's. The sudden change of vessels would infuriate her—and I couldn't blame her.

I studied Tremaine glumly. Apparently he considered *Portia* expendable, so long as we protected his better-armed flagship. The fleet would Fuse and Defuse seven times to make sure my sloop and *Freiheit* were always in the lead to intercept a hostile force.

A gray-haired officer across the table intervened. "What will be our posture, sir, in case of unexpected contact?"

I grinned sourly at Captain Stahl's choice of words. Like most Naval officers, he found it difficult to concede that we'd really stumbled onto hostile aliens. At times I had trouble believing it myself, and I was the one who found them. After all, in two hundred years of exploring, man had discovered no animal life other than the primitive boneless fish of Zeta Psi. Thank Lord God our puter Darla recorded our contact. Without her playbacks and the few other eyewitnesses from *Hibernia's* bridge, I'd be confined to a schizo ward for hormone rebalancing.

"Contact is highly unlikely." Admiral Tremaine paused, shot me an irritable glance. "However, you must not undertake threatening maneuvers without absolute proof of the hostile intent of the other party."

I blurted, "Absolute proof will likely result in the destruction of your ship." Unwise, but I couldn't stop myself.

The Admiral half-rose from his seat, his face red. "Flippancy and insubordination are what I'd expect from you, Seafort!"

"I wasn't flippant, sir." My tone was meek. "As far as we saw, the aliens don't communicate by radio contact or signals. The first sign of hostility could be their acid eating through our hull. It's what took out *Telstar*, and—"

"Admiralty chose to give you a ship, Seafort." Vinegar was in Tremaine's tone. "I wouldn't have. Frankly, I doubt your whole report; puter disks can be faked. I don't know if you saw anything out there, but your report conveniently diverted attention from Captain Haag's death."

I gaped. Before the entire squadron, my new commanding officer had accused me of lying, of faking my report, perhaps even of murder. "I went through polygraph and drug testing before Admiralty offered me another ship." My throat was tight. "Mr. Holser and the others saw—"

He grunted. "Yes, for what that's worth." Before I could object he added, "At any rate, Seafort, your orders are to avoid initiating hostilities. Disobey and I'll relieve you so fast your head will spin." He turned away.

I sat through the rest of the briefing in a daze, doing my best to pretend calm. It was, I thought ruefully, a fit end to my shore leave.

When I'd brought *Hibernia* home with the startling news of the aliens, Admiralty hadn't known what to do with me. After they reluctantly accepted my verified report, Admiral Brentley, head of Fleet Operations, personally intervened to reward me with another ship and the rank of Commander, though most of my classmates at Academy hadn't yet made lieutenant.

When the gruff Admiral had concluded with me, I'd brought Amanda to Cardiff for a gloomy introduction to Father; afterward we set out on our delayed honeymoon.

I don't know why we'd chosen New York, except that she didn't know when she'd have another chance to see it. I'd been there and had no desire to return, but I held my peace for her sake.

Neither of us had really enjoyed the tense, busy luxury of Upper New York. Uncomfortable with my new celebrity, my mind flitted between memories of my recent voyage and the anticipation of a new ship, while Amanda struggled with her advancing pregnancy.

Waiting out the weeks of mandatory leave, I stared out of skytel windows while helibusses glided between sleek towers, high above decaying streets overrun by the ragged transpops, our ever-present urban homeless.

Once, Amanda and I descended to ground level to take a Gray Line tour, locked behind thick protective steel bars on an armored bus that wended its way through the teeming city. Well before nightfall we were returned safely to our hotel aerie, to which supplies were brought by air to avoid the hostile and savage transpops below. I wondered why the Sec-Gen didn't send in the Unies to wrest control from the streeter gangs. An entire city was crumbling beneath our eyes.

In the evenings Amanda and I took helitaxis to plays, concerts and once, to my dismay, to an art show where I stared helplessly at holograms that dissolved in incomprehensible patterns. Around me, cognoscenti nodded with appreciation.

When our leave was over, we'd flown back to Houston; I had to attend more dull briefings while Amanda took the shuttle to Earthport Station and *Challenger*.

I recalled the irony of those incessant conferences. Our self-appointed experts in xenobiology offered guesses about the nature and intentions of the aliens I'd encountered, while glancing nervously to see if I suddenly recalled some detail that would contradict their theories.

I shook myself back to the present; Admiral Tremaine's briefing was finally ending. As we rose, Tremaine shook hands with several senior officers. I edged away, anxious to be gone, but his cold eye fixed me with a disapproving stare. He beckoned.

I approached, waited until he'd finished with my seniors. Could I get him to reconsider taking my prized ship? "About *Challenger*, sir. I personally selected her officers. I was hoping to sail with—"

"The ones who backed your tale about that fish? I imagine you would." His tone was sharp. "You'll have your way. You'll find their orders with your own."

"To *Portia?*"

"Of course. I won't sail with children manning my bridge. This is my first squadron, and everything must be shipshape. Hasselbrad knows whom he wants, and I trust his judgment." The remainder of his thought was unspoken, but I blushed nonetheless. "Now, listen, Seafort."

I waited, hoping for a sign of conciliation.

"I told Brentley I wanted no part of you. In fact, I made it clear it was insane to give you a ship. He insisted on my leaving you in command, but I'll be damned if it will be a vessel of any importance. Each time we Fuse, take *Portia* to your station and stand guard. If those loony aliens you reported really exist, dispatch them before we arrive."

"But you said—Aye aye, sir." How could I dispatch a fish without initiating hostilities?

"That's all." Glowering, he took my salute.

As I left the room I sighed. I was disconsolate, hungry, rocket-lagged, and too far from my wife.

"Wait your turn!" A heavy-jowled woman, her face a mask of disapproval. I hesitated, blushing, but Lieutenant Alexi Tamarov pushed to the head of the line of impatient passengers at the Earthport Station ticket counter. Sheepishly I followed.

"G Concourse?" he called.

The attractive young lady looked up from the boarding passes thrust at her from all sides. "End of the corridor and downstairs, Lieutenant." She turned back to her forms.

"Thanks, ma'am!" Alexi ignored the civilians' hostile stares. "You have to learn to be aggressive, sir," he admonished. Only our years of service together on *Hibernia* permitted such a remark, notwithstanding his congenial tone.

We threaded our way through the station's main concourse. Harried families clutched children and baggage while magnetronic carts whizzed past with station staff. Roughened crewmen sprawled in seats, awaiting the arrival of their ships.

Earthport Station, the largest orbiting station ever built, moved all Earth's interstellar traffic and much of its interplanetary shipping too. Its many levels held bonded warehouses for the duty-free zones, dozens of shuttle bays, administrative offices, staff housing, waiting areas, rest rooms, restaurants and snack bars. News of the aliens had done little to slow the frantic pace of traffic.

"I keep forgetting how big the place is." Alexi hurried to keep pace. A year younger than I, at nineteen Alexi was no longer the handsome boy just out of Academy I'd met three years before. He had grown into an athletic, confident young man.

"A lot of joeys moving out," I said. Perhaps fewer folk would embark on the sixteen-month cruise to Hope Nation until the danger from the aliens had passed. I lengthened my stride. In the two days since Admiral Tremaine had taken my ship, I'd grown almost desperate to be done with the interminable briefings and to board my command, whatever she might be.

"This way, sir. I remember now." Alexi diverted me to a staircase at one side of the corridor. I followed, grateful that he'd taken the trouble to meet my incoming shuttle, despite the inconvenience of resettling himself at short notice.

Only a few sailors and civilian workers hurried along the lower corridor as we strode past successive airlock gates. We were now at G-12; *Portia* was moored at G-4, almost halfway around the rim of the station. I shouldered the heavy duffel Alexi had twice offered to carry.

We slowed a bit, but kept a steady pace. Alexi offered a few remarks about ships outlined in the transplex portholes we passed, but subsided when I only grunted in reply.

The truth was that I was nervous; never had I boarded my own ship to take command. My captaincy of *Hibernia* had begun in tragedy and confusion, light years into our cruise from Earth to Hope Nation. Now I was to command U.N.S. *Portia,* a vessel that shipped sixty passengers and a crew of thirty. Among them two lieutenants, three middies. Far smaller than *Hibernia* or *Challenger,* she was a significant ship in the United Nations Naval Service despite Admiral Tremaine's disparaging remarks.

I knew that Lieutenant Vax Holser and my three midshipmen had already transferred aboard, along with the Pilot and Chief Engineer I had never met. As to the crew belowdecks, I had no idea whom I might find. I wondered again why Vax had turned down his own command to sail with me, considering how badly I'd treated him during our years in *Hibernia.* I nonetheless felt more secure for his steady, dependable presence.

As we reached G-4, I stopped to run my hands through my hair.

When I tugged on the jacket of my dress whites, Alexi grinned. "It's not funny," I snapped. "I need to make a good impression."

"Right, sir." He was still smiling. Alexi was as close a friend as I had, but at times I wondered if our long voyage would chafe. I bit back a cutting remark, knowing my own tension and not Alexi's irrepressible good cheer had spawned it.

"I'm ready." I picked up my duffel. At the lock two armed marine sentries stood guard. I pulled out my papers.

One sentry remained standing with his hand on the butt of his pistol; the other saluted the bars on my dress uniform, took my papers. "Commander Nicholas Seafort?"

"That's right." I waited patiently while he compared the holopic to my face. After the rebellion we'd blundered into at Miningcamp, I appreciated their security measures; any orbiting station now left me ill at ease.

"There's your ship, Captain." He gestured.

Alexi followed me into the lock. As *Portia* maintained the same atmospheric pressure as the Station, the airlock had no need to cycle; *Portia's* inner hatch would be opened as soon as we sealed the outer for safety.

Through the transplex airlock panel I caught a glimpse of sailors milling in the ship's corridor. "Gawd, there he is!" someone hissed within. The hatch slid open.

"Attention!" Vax Holser's bellow rang through the corridor. Utter silence greeted me as I took a step forward. Correctly, Alexi waited behind, in the lock. Vax's muscular frame stiffened to rigid attention as he snapped an Academy salute.

"Permission to come on board." My tone was formal.

"Granted, sir." Vax's grin was heartfelt and warming.

I strode through the inner hatch. Vax, Midshipman Derek Carr and two seamen remained at attention, eyes locked front.

I unfolded my orders. "To Nicholas Ewing Seafort, Commander, United Nations Naval Service," I read aloud. "Effective November 4, 2197, you shall command U.N.S. *Portia,* a vessel assigned to the squadron commanded by Admiral Geoffrey Tremaine. You are to voyage to Hope Nation and thence to Detour Colony in such manner as may be ordered by the Admiral commanding . . ." I read through the orders and folded the paper.

"As you were." As they relaxed, I looked about. We were at the fore airlock, adjacent to the ship's launch berth. The aft lock was below, on Level 2.

From a distance our vessel—or any Naval starship—would look like a pencil stood on end; the disks in which we lived consisted of two rings fitted tightly over the pencil about halfway from bow to stern. *Portia* had only two Levels rather than the three of *Challenger* and larger ships.

I turned to the waiting midshipman. Derek Carr, lean and youthful at eighteen, stood confidently in his crisp blue middy's uniform, buckles and shoes shined to perfection. As his eye caught mine I winked. Derek, whom I recruited from among the passengers of *Hibernia*, was maturing into a fine naval officer, despite occasional traces of the haughty young aristocrat he'd once been.

"I'll show you to your cabin, sir," Vax offered.

I made a quick decision. I still knew virtually nothing about my new command. "No. Mr. Carr, take my duffel to the Captain's cabin, and tell Amanda I'll be there in a while. Vax, show me everything, bow to stern."

"Aye aye, sir," Vax said automatically. No other response was possible to a Captain's command. As the others drifted away, he hesitated. "It won't take long to see. Compared to *Challenger*, this is a toy. He had no right—"

"Mr. Holser!" My voice was tight. "Don't even think of saying that aloud."

"I—no, sir."

"Did you forget an Admiral is senior to a Captain? The squadron is his to deploy. No criticism, now or ever."

"Aye aye, sir." His tone was subdued. "Shall we start at the bridge?"

"If you like." As I followed him along the corridor I remembered that I still wore my dress whites; I'd get them dirty poking around the ship. I'd also be hot. I decided against stopping to change; better not to appear indecisive my first day aboard.

As we were still moored, the bridge hatch was open and only a nominal watch was kept. Midshipman Rafe Treadwell came to attention when I entered. My eyes took in the control consoles, the navigation equipment, the simulscreens covering the front bulkhead. I would spend many of my waking hours in this compartment. Smaller than *Hibernia*'s bridge, still it had ample room to move around. I wondered if Naval designers knew Captains liked to pace.

I looked down at Rafe, fourteen, promoted from cadet at my recommendation so that he could join my next command as midshipman. "Enjoy your shore leave, Mr. Treadwell?"

"Uh, yes, sir." He blushed furiously. It must have been an interesting leave indeed. As midshipman, Rafe had his majority by statute of the General Assembly, and could frequent the bars and dives of Lunapolis. He'd been but eleven the last time he'd seen home port.

"Good; carry on. Vax, where to?"

Lieutenant Holser led me from the inactive bridge to the sickbay, and I chatted a moment with the Doctor. I'd see a lot of that place now that our baby was near. Down the circular corridor just past the ladder was the officers' mess, a tiny compartment barely larger than a passenger cabin. We officers would take our evening meal in the ship's dining hall with the passengers, and few enough of us would share the mess for morning and noon meals, as we stood our staggered watches.

Belowdecks, I glanced at the engine room and took a long look at Hydroponics, on whose output we would all depend. Outside the crew berth the chief petty officer brought a gaggle of seamen to attention. "Akrit, stand even with the others! Wipe off that idiot smile, Clinger. Sorry, sir."

I nodded curtly. The petty officers would have their hands full for a time, one of the pitfalls of guaranteed enlistment. Virtually any able-bodied person was guaranteed acceptance into the Service, and got a half-year's pay in advance as a bonus.

Back on Level 1, I surveyed a few passenger cabins as well as officers' quarters. I said little, trying to memorize what I could. We came across Alexi in the passengers' lounge chatting with two civilian girls; he detached himself and joined our tour.

Vax knocked on the wardroom hatch. By custom the wardroom was the midshipmen's private territory; except for inspection, other officers entered only by invitation. The hatch swung open. Seeing us, Midshipman Philip Tyre came rigidly to attention, in regulation naval slacks and tee shirt. His white shirt, tie and blue jacket lay neatly on his bunk.

"Mr. Tyre." I regretted my impulse to include Philip in my new command. I should have let him resign when *Hibernia's* homecoming had released him from his purgatory. Tyre, at seventeen, was still as breathtakingly handsome as the day he'd first come aboard *Hibernia.* But now he wore a wary look, a legacy of the undying enmity he'd kindled in Alexi Tamarov, when Tyre had been Alexi's senior in the wardroom.

"Yes, sir." Philip waited anxiously. The middy was always obedient to his seniors, eager, cooperative and helpful. It was to his juniors that his unbearable traits were exposed. After Alexi's promotion, on the long trip back from Hope Nation, Lieutenant Tamarov had exacted vengeance by setting Philip over the barrel for a caning whenever opportunity arose.

Time to face the issue. "I wish you a good voyage, Mr. Tyre." I meant it as a signal; Alexi heard but gave no sign.

Philip's look was almost pleading. "Thank you, sir." Wisely he said no more. We left him to contemplate his future.

"Are you ever going to ease up, Alexi?" Together, we descended the ladder to Level 2.

"When you order it, sir." His tone was flat.

There was little more I could say. By tradition, the Captain was expected not to involve himself in wardroom affairs. Alexi, an amiable, goodhearted joey, could normally be depended on not to harass a middy, but in his misery under Mr. Tyre, Alexi had sworn an oath of revenge to Lord God himself. Lieutenant Tamarov meant literally what he had told me; he would stop when ordered, but not a moment before.

Fortunately for Philip, the miscreants' barrel was now in First Lieutenant Vax Holser's cabin, rather than Alexi's where it had sat most of our voyage home.

Shrugging, I continued my tour. Philip had made his own bed. Now, as with all of us, he must sleep in it.

31

"God, Nicky, where have you been?" Amanda shifted her bulging body to the side of her cushioned chair. The baby was due very soon.

"Hi, hon. Inspecting the ship." I tossed my jacket on the bunk and bent to nuzzle the soft brown hair I'd admired ever since I'd first seen her, an awkward young middy on *Hibernia*.

She gave a rueful grin. "She's not quite what *Challenger* would have been."

"Well . . ."

"I couldn't pack fast enough when they told me you were transferred. I dreaded that somehow you'd ship on *Portia* and I'd be left where I was. What on earth were they thinking of, changing Captains at the last moment?"

It wasn't a topic I cared to dwell on. I sat, made a lap, beckoned her to it. "You didn't want a rest from me?"

She settled cautiously, rested her sweet-scented hair in the crevice of my neck. "Not that long."

I loosened my tie, sighed. "My feet hurt."

From my collarbone came what sounded like a growl. "Try changing places. Everything aches these days."

I knew Amanda's pregnancy was trying, but she'd borne it with a good grace for which I cherished her all the more. She'd refused even to discuss a host-mother embryo transplant, prenatal rearing, or other alternatives that would have eased her discomfort.

My eye wandered around the cabin, examining my home for the next three years. It was the largest stateroom on the ship, far larger than the wardroom I'd shared with several midshipmen in earlier days. An open hatch led to the Captain's private head. Our cabin had its own shower compartment, similar to the one I'd had on *Hibernia*. That was one luxury I'd grown used to.

Amanda stretched, rose to her feet. "Learn anything in your briefings?"

"Only that Admiral Tremaine doesn't like me." I slipped out of my dress uniform, wishing I'd done so hours earlier.

"Why not?" She sounded indignant.

"It doesn't matter. He has his ship and I have mine." I donned my regular ship's blues. "I'll hardly see him at all."

"I missed you." Her voice was soft. "They boarded me on *Challenger* three days ago, while you were still in that Fusion course." She frowned. "A whole day I spent, checking their reference library. Wasted." Earlier, I had arranged for her appointment as *Challenger's* civilian education director, the same post she'd held on *Hibernia*. Luckily, I was able to have her given the similar duties aboard *Portia*.

"Have you checked out *Portia's* library?" I asked, to divert her.

"It seems complete enough." A whole library could be contained in a trunkful of holovid chips, so storage space wasn't a problem. I knew Amanda would examine the booklist carefully; as ed director, her task would be to teach children who wanted education, and to supervise adult classes during the long, dull Fuse to Hope Nation and to Detour beyond. It was common for passengers to use the uneventful months in space to learn new skills or carry out research.

I checked my watch. "Seven o'clock. Hungry, hon?"

"I'm always hungry," she admitted. She flashed the smile that had captivated me as a fumbling midshipman. "Don't worry, I won't stay fat." We headed for the dining hall.

Most of the passengers and all of the crew had already boarded. However, many passengers had chosen to leave the ship to wander in Earthport Station's vast concourses, watch through the observation ports as other ships arrived and departed, or sample the many expensive restaurants the station provided. Dinner that night aboard *Portia* was sparse and informal.

At the Captain's table Amanda and I were joined by only two passengers. Normally we sat eight to a table; nine large round tables would seat my officers and *Portia's* sixty passengers.

I felt uneasy beginning the meal without the traditional Ship's Prayer, recited every night while under weigh, but it was not the custom to pray in port. Instead, I said a silent grace.

Amanda introduced me to Dr. Francon, a synthetic cardiology specialist on route to Hope Nation to run Hope General's cardiac generation unit. Our other guest, Mr. Singh, told us he had no reason for traveling except to see as much of the known universe as his lifetime would let him.

"The galaxy is a hundred thousand light-years across, Mr. Singh. You won't have time to see but a fraction; why did you pick our corner of it?"

The small, tan-skinned man smiled delightedly. "Pure chance, Captain Seafort. Fortuity. As you know, I had to arrange my cruise before you returned on *Hibernia,* so I had no idea when I chose Hope Nation that I might actually get to see alien life."

"Let's hope you don't," I muttered. A chill prickled my spine.

"It isn't foreordained that our contact must be hostile," he said in his gentle singsong voice. "Now that we each know of each other's existence, perhaps more positive, loving contact may be had."

"Not by me." I changed the subject. As we progressed from soup to the main course I was distracted by boisterous children and teenagers at a table across the hall. I ignored them, though their presence surprised me. *Hibernia* had carried few youngsters.

Under the table, my wife pressed her hand on my knee. I hoped no one noticed; I could hardly maintain the dignity of a Captain while an attractive woman fondled me.

After dinner I escorted Amanda to our cabin and returned to the bridge. Lieutenant Tamarov had the watch; he was sitting comfortably at the first officer's console when I came in.

"Are we all set, Alexi?"

"All supplies loaded, sir. The last contingent of passengers arrives late this evening. The mail comes aboard at 04:00 standard time, then we'll be ready to cast off."

Idly I tapped the back of my soft leather watch chair. "Why would passengers reboard so late?"

"The Lower New Yorkers, sir. The station didn't want to bring them aloft any earlier than necessary."

"Who?" I gaped. "Street people?"

"Transpops, yes, sir."

"On my ship?" I sank into my chair, dismayed. "Are you joking?"

"Not at all. Didn't you read the memo?"

"What memo, Alexi?" It came as a growl.

"From Cincfleet, sir." He glanced at me, hurried on. "While you were away. It's a pilot program arranged by the Reunification Church, endorsed by UNICEF. They're rounding up teen transpops and sending them outward. Give them a better life while harnessing their raw energy to productive use, or some such folderol. Our band is headed for Detour, in the custody of a UNICEF social worker."

Appalled, I pictured my honeymoon in New York. Our tour bus had crawled down Fifth Avenue along the ruins of Central Park, past the old Central Park Zoo, long bereft of animals they couldn't protect from hungry human scavengers who prowled its cobbled stones.

As we came upon the twenty-foot wall topped with broken glass and barbed wire that ringed the ancient Plaza Hotel, the bus was abruptly surrounded by a mob of ragged, frantic youths brandishing what I at first thought were homemade weapons, but soon realized were tourist artifacts carved or pressed from sheet metal, worn pieces of rubber tire, and other scrap.

"Getcha Newyawk souvs!" a grimy boy shouted through the grillwork welded to the tour bus windows. "TraCenta, Empiyabuildin', lookadem heah!" He waved his crude skyscrapers at any prospective takers. Amanda pressed my hand tightly.

The driver glanced at his mirrors, decided it would be safe to stop. While he and the guard grasped their stunners, two of the wild children were allowed to enter the fortresslike bus to peddle their wares. After five minutes they were hustled off and we'd continued on our way to Timesquare.

I slammed my fist into the chair arm, startling Alexi. "I won't have it!"

By day, Lower New York maintained a semblance of civilization; tour buses such as ours penetrated its outer reaches. Not by night. In the darkened alleyways and torn avenues of Lower New York, rival Hispanic, Black, and Oriental gangs preyed on the transient population, the transpops, our permanent and ever-increasing urban homeless.

Rarely, if ever, did anyone descend to street level; residents of Upper New York flew in and out of the city from rooftop heliports. Derek Carr, the young aristocrat I'd befriended and enlisted in the Service, was of that urbane and civilized culture. Buildings such as Derek's home generated their own power and were heavily fortified against invasion by the transpops.

How could Admiral Brentley think of infesting my ship with such savages?

"How many?" I demanded.

"Forty-two, sir."

I was aghast. "Out of sixty passengers?"

"No, sir." Alexi took a deep breath, eyed me warily. "We have our sixty passengers. And forty-two transpops."

I came out of my seat, fists bunched, controlling myself only with effort. "We have cabins for only sixty!"

"Yes, sir. A number of scheduled passengers will double up. The, uh, transportees will bed six to a cabin."

"That's worse than the wardroom! How can you cram six bunks into a stateroom?"

"Pardon, sir, but they've already been installed." A nervous adolescent voice, from the speaker. "Double bunks against each bulkhead."

I glared from speaker to speaker. "Who are you?"

"Danny, sir. Uh, hi."

"Danny?" I turned to Alexi.

"Our puter."

"Oh." I paused. "Hello, Danny." I glowered at Alexi. "Supplies? Hydroponics and recyclers?"

"Adjusted, sir, but we'll be at near-maximum utilization the whole cruise."

"Why didn't you tell me sooner about the transpops?" My voice was dangerously quiet.

"I thought you already knew." Alexi eyed me steadily.

Petulant, I threw myself into my seat. "Patch me through to Fleet Ops." Alexi picked up the caller. "This isn't a prison ship," I muttered, half to myself. "Are they insane?"

"Perhaps, sir," said Alexi gravely. Despite my agitation, I had to smile; Alexi had taken the opportunity provided by my question to suggest criticism of his superiors, which otherwise would have been unacceptable. Neatly done, but it reminded me that I had just criticized Admiralty in front of my lieutenant.

It was an hour before my call got through to Admiral Brentley on Lunapolis. The conversation was brief. "I can't do a thing about it, Nick. This comes straight from the Secretary-General's office. I know you're overcrowded but I can't help you."

"But what possible good could it do to haul forty transpops from among the hundreds of thous—"

"Ask the Council of Elders of the Church; it falls under 'charitable works' and they have the ear of the SecGen. I gather that if the experiment works, they'll begin mass shipping of trannies to the newer colonies."

"But, sir—"

"I know, I know. As a means of relieving population pressure it's nonsense, and you'd think they'd know better. A nuisance for you, but it's out of my bailiwick. Put up with the overcrowding as best you can."

"It's more than overcrowding, sir. The recyclers aren't meant to handle—"

"I know, Seafort, but there's ample safety margin built into the specs. As for food, we'd provided extra canned—"

"Sir, they're dangerous to the ship and the other passengers!"

"I'd feel the way you do if *Portia* were mine. But the U.N.'s desperate to relieve pressure in the urban centers. The program is set. Anyway, they've sent you younger ones who have no known parents, and a supervisor to watch over them. I understand the most violent cases have been screened out. Do your best, Seafort."

"Aye aye, sir," I said automatically. The connection went dead. I turned to Alexi. "Make sure the purser is prepared. Set up additional tables in the dining hall. Have extra crewmen stand by when they arrive. Good Lord!"

"Yes, sir. Aye aye, sir." Alexi's faint smile was almost hidden by the hand propped in front of his mouth.

I knocked at the Level 2 corridor hatch, waited as it slid open. "Chief Engineer Hendricks?"

A thin, graying man, whose officer's jacket ill fitted his long, skinny arms. "Yes, sir." His voice was flat and emotionless, his mouth unsmiling.

"You were bunked down when I visited the engine room," I said. "Good to meet you."

"Thank you."

"Are we ready for departure?"

"Yes, sir. I would have told you otherwise."

"Uh, right." I felt like the awkward middy I'd once been. "Carry on. We'll talk later." I continued along the Level 2 corridor, Philip Tyre at my side. "Which cabins, Mr. Tyre?"

He pointed ahead. "There, sir, just past crew berth one." We strode past the crew berth. Two seamen lounging in the corridor stiffened to attention. I ignored them. Tyre opened the cabin hatch.

Upper and lower bunks were stacked alongside three of the four bulkheads. The two extra dressers utterly filled the rest of the compartment, leaving barely enough room to move about. "A few nights is one matter," I said, "but seventeen months of this . . ."

Philip shrugged, unconcerned. "They're just trannies, sir."

I was outraged. "Two demerits, Mr. Tyre! Make that three!" I ignored his stricken look. "On my first posting, we middies were taught to show respect for passengers!"

"Yessir," he said quickly. "I'm very sorry, Captain. I only meant they're probably used to it. Not that they deserved it." His tone was meek. "I'm sorry if I offended, sir."

Perhaps I'd overreacted, but a few hours of calisthenics wouldn't hurt him. It only took two hours to work off each demerit, unless he reached ten and was sent to the barrel. "Very well. Are all their cabins like this one?"

"Yes, sir. Pretty much."

"They're all on this Level?"

"Yes, sir, 211 through 217. I think Mr. Holser wanted them near crew quarters, sir, in case of trouble."

I considered a moment. Vax was probably right, and I certainly didn't want them on the same Level as the bridge. Anyway, the transpops were due to board anytime now; too late for changes. "Very well, Mr. Tyre, we'll go back up. You'll help the purser when they board."

"Aye aye, sir." As we climbed the ladder to Level 1 he blurted, "Sir, I already had seven demerits."

Alexi must have been at him again. I hesitated. Canceling demerits was bad for discipline. But still . . . ten meant the barrel. "Very well, Mr. Tyre. Two demerits instead of three."

He shot me a grateful look. "Thanks, sir. Thanks very much."

Exhausted, I contemplated returning to the bridge. There was no reason to stay awake; Vax could settle our passengers. I had to be alert in the morning for our departure. I headed for my cabin, and Amanda's soothing care.

Straightening my tie and checking my jacket I strode onto the bridge, a confident young Captain about to take command. Still I paused before taking the chair at the left console. The seat was empty, of course; it would have been unthinkable for a junior officer to be found in it.

I nodded to Vax Holser in the chair across, and turned to the unfamiliar figure at the console at my right. "Pilot Van Peer, I presume?"

The red-haired young man smiled engagingly as he stood and saluted. "Walter Van Peer, yes, sir. Glad to meet you." Mr. Van Peer was a holdover from the ship's last voyage to Casanuestra.

I glanced at my instruments. "We're ready, gentlemen?" I keyed the caller to Departure Control. "Station, U.N.S. *Portia* is prepared for departure from G-4."

After a moment the reply crackled in the speaker. "Initiate breakaway, *Portia*."

"Roger." I thumbed the caller. "Attention, aft and forward airlocks. Cast off!"

"Aye aye, sir!" Alexi and Rafe Treadwell were at the aft lock; Derek was forward. With a pang I remembered *Hibernia*'s departure from Luna Station on my first interstellar flight, three years ago. I'd been at the aft lock where Rafe now served, Lieutenant Malstrom supervising

my every move. Impulsively I jumped from my seat. "I'm going below,"
I said. "Hold breakaway until my command."

Vax glanced at me in mild surprise; the Pilot's mouth opened in
astonishment. Of course neither said a word except to acknowledge my
order.

I hurried down the corridor to the ladder. At the forward airlock
Derek Carr was calmly supervising the seamen who were unhooking our
steel safety line from the stanchion in the station lock. At my approach
he raised an eyebrow, but said nothing.

Portia, like any vessel, secured herself to a station with its capture
latches, and the ship's airlock mated to the station lock with rubber
seals, but ever since the *Concorde* disaster, backup safety cables were
mandatory.

A sailor wound in our cable, pulling it into our own lock. The cable
bent with difficulty through the gloves of his spacesuit as he folded it.
"Line secured, sir," he called to Derek.

"Forward line secured, sir," Derek repeated, though I stood at his
side.

"Proceed, Mr. Carr." Then I blurted, "I'm not inspecting. I just
wanted to watch." Idiocy, explaining myself to a midshipman.

"Yes, sir." Derek turned to the sailor. "Close inner lock, Mr. Jarnes.
Prepare for breakaway."

"Aye aye, sir." Seaman Jarnes pressed a coded transmitter to the
inner lock panel. The thick hatches slid shut smoothly, forming a tight
center seal.

"Disengage capture latches."

The seaman keyed open the latch control panel, touched the pad
within. "Disengaged, aye aye."

Derek glanced at me. "Forward lock secured, sir. Shall I report also
to the bridge?"

"I suppose, Mr. Carr." I looked helplessly at the outer lock still
mated to the station. What I'd wanted to see was our actual breakaway,
but my duty was aloft. I sighed, and reluctantly headed back topside.

In my seat again I thumbed the caller. "Departure Control, *Portia*
ready for breakaway."

"Proceed, *Portia*. Vector oh three oh from station. Godspeed."

"Thank you, Station." I touched a button on my console three
times. Three deep blasts from the ship's whistle resounded, signaling
imminent breakaway to all on our vessel.

"Pilot Van Peer, you have the conn."

"Right, sir." His tone was cheerful. He signaled the engine room. "Chief, auxiliary power, please."

Chief Hendricks's dry, unemotional voice. "Auxiliary power, aye aye."

"Hang on, folks, here we go," the Pilot said with an irreverent grin. He gently fired our side thrusters; jets of propellant shot from the nozzles imbedded in the ship's hull. *Portia* rocked, her airlock suckers stretching. Abruptly they parted from their counterparts on the station lock; U.N.S. *Portia* drifted slowly clear of Earthport Station. Stars slid across the simulscreens on the forward bulkhead. After a few moments the Pilot asked casually, "Would you care to close the outer locks, sir?"

I flushed. It was my responsibility to give the order, but I'd been too busy gawking at the receding station. "Very well." I thumbed the caller. "Secure outer hatches!"

Red console lights switched to green as the outer airlock hatches slid closed. "Forward hatch secure, sir." Derek.

Alexi's steady voice followed. "Aft hatch secure, sir."

"Secured, very well."

The Pilot maintained us on course. I watched the station in the simulscreens until it was swallowed by the starry backdrop. Long minutes stretched into an hour.

"We're clear to Fuse, sir," the Pilot said.

"Danny, Fusion coordinates, please."

"Aye aye, sir," the puter said promptly. He flashed the figures onto my console screen.

As I began to punch calculations onto my screen I felt sweat gathering under my jacket, as always when I plotted Fusion coordinates.

The Pilot stirred. "I ran our coordinates myself and checked them against the puter's figures, sir."

I ignored him.

"They check out to six decimal places," he added.

"Vax, you too," I said.

"Aye aye, sir." My first lieutenant tapped figures into his console.

Pilot Van Peer looked from one to the other of us, perplexed. "Is there a problem, Captain?"

I made no response.

"I thought it's customary for the Pilot to calculate Fusion coordinates." He sounded plaintive.

I grunted. "On my ship we all do. Nothing personal." I returned to my laborious calculations.

"The puter's figures and mine are in full—"

"Pilot, shut up!" Nav didn't bring out the best in me.

"Aye aye, sir." His hurt was manifest.

Half an hour later I had my figures. They checked with Danny's and Vax's. "Very well." I fed them into the puter.

"Coordinates received and understood, Captain." Danny sounded breathless.

"Thank you." I thumbed the caller. "Engine room, prepare to Fuse."

"Prepare to Fuse, aye aye." After a moment the speaker came alive. "Engine room ready for Fuse, sir."

"Chief Engineer, Fuse."

"Aye aye, sir." The Chief's voice was flat. "Fusion drive is . . . ignited." The simulscreens abruptly blanked.

I remained in my seat, the melancholy of our isolation pressing. In Fusion, all our external instruments were dead; we rode the crest of our N-wave out of the Solar System at superluminous speed, blind and deaf. Even communication was denied us; nothing we broadcast could travel as fast as the N-wave itself. Now we had only our own resources to sustain us until we reached safe haven sixty-nine light-years away.

Vax had the watch; I knew he was reliable. Besides, there was nothing on the bridge that needed doing. After a while, morose, I left. Amanda wasn't in our cabin, so I wandered to the Level 1 passengers' lounge, where I found only unfamiliar faces among the holovids, easy chairs, and game machines.

I could have remained; officers were free to use the lounge and we weren't discouraged from socializing with passengers, but I withdrew, ill at ease. I followed the circumference corridor to the west ladder, climbed down to Level 2. Perhaps I'd find Amanda in the library.

"Here's cap'n! Here's cap'n!" A teen joey pranced around me, sandals flopping on the deckplates as his high, excited voice beckoned his mates. He pointed at my jacket. "Mira, mira da man!" Rough-trimmed hair hung over his ears. His scrawny body was covered by a blue denim jumpsuit.

"He da man! He da man! Mira threads!" Grimy hands pawed at the braid on my jacket. I slapped them away, but other curious youths pressed close.

A voice sliced through the jabber. "Knock off, joeys! Knock off!" A meaty hand flung aside one ragged youngster. A short, chunky woman pushed through the opening she'd made. "Gi'im room! Knock off, gi'im room." Her words tumbled. Slowly the crowd drew back. She smiled briefly. "Sorry, Captain. Melissa Chong. I'm supposed to make sure things like this don't happen." Apparently unaware of ship's protocol, she stuck out her hand.

Awkwardly I took it. "You're the supervisor?"

"Right, I'm a UNICEF DSW, but these joeys call me Mellie." She collared the youth who first approached me. "Say sorry, Annie! Tell'im sorry cap'n!"

"Naw!" Her charge tried to squirm away.

"Noway toucha cap'n, Annie! Noway!"

"Din' hurtim," he—she?—said sullenly. "Jus lookin'!"

"Say sorry," repeated Dr. Chong, a firm grip on the youth's neck.

The look Annie shot me was wrathful. "Din' mean nothin'," she muttered. "Din' hurt, just lookin', sorry."

I nodded. "No harm done. Your name is Annie? You're a girl?"

Her face flashed into an elfin grin. She wiggled her hips. "Cap'n wanna fin' out?"

"Knock off, Annie!" Dr. Chong said sharply. She thrust the girl away. "Inna room, allyas. Inna room." Reluctantly they drifted away toward their cabins.

"How do you speak that jargon?" My tone was mild.

"You pick it up after a while. Mostly it's just fast." Her round Oriental face broke into a grin. "I'll teach you, if you wish. In case you ever go transient."

I shuddered. "Lord God forbid." I glanced about, frowned at the litter that hadn't strewn the deck a few moments before. "Well. You'll have your hands full."

"Yes, 'til Detour. Then they're someone else's responsibility."

Seventeen months, with such rabble. I sighed. "How do you control them?"

"I'm trying to meld them into a single tribe. Most of them respect tribal authority. It's all they know."

I raised an eyebrow, puzzled. "I thought trannies were—"

"Don't use that word!"

"I beg your pardon?" My tone was frosty.

"Say 'transpops,' or 'transients.' The other is a racial slur, like 'chic' or 'black.' They'll take offense, and the consequences could be violent."

"I've heard it used." I wrinkled my brow. "Very well, I'll take care. Anyway, I was asking . . ."

"About tribes, yes. Most Uppies don't realize there's more than one transpop subculture. Transpops live in social units based on location. Some homelands are contained in a few small blocks, others quite large.

They get along by trading, or selling sex. Or warring. For instance, the Unies—"

"How many tribes among our group?" I was impatient to be on my way.

"Several, and it's caused no end of problems. If UNICEF had only listened—" She sighed. "Anyway, I'm sorry for the disturbance, Captain." On that note we parted.

I found Amanda sorting through holochips in the library. "Look, Nicky, they even have Marx and Engels! I could do a comparative economics course."

I grinned. "For whom, hon? The transpop joeys?"

"I'll have you know we've plenty of educated passengers this trip." She racked a stack of chips. "We'll have lots of guest lecturers. In fact I was thinking of—ungh!" She flinched.

"What's wrong?" I couldn't hide my alarm.

"I got kicked. I think he wants out, Nicky."

"Right now?"

She laughed at my consternation. "Not in the next few minutes. But soon, I think. He wants to see his papa."

I grimaced. The idea of parenthood was still alien. "I want to see him too," I assured her. I paused. "Will you lunch with me?"

"Officers' mess or the dining hall?" Ship's officers ate their morning and noon meals in the tiny officers' mess, and joined the passengers for the formal evening meal. The passengers took breakfast and lunch cafeteria style in the Level 1 passengers' dining hall. The crew, of course, always ate belowdecks in the Level 2 crew mess.

"The officers' mess," I said. "I don't want to share you with all those people." She rewarded me with a smile. I took her hand and we wandered back along the corridor toward the ladder. I didn't care how undignified I looked.

Lunch was a simple affair, some sort of stew served over bread. I chose the small table against the bulkhead rather than the long wooden table in the center of the cabin. By tradition that signaled I meant to eat alone, and the other officers wouldn't bother me. If I chose the long table, officers were free to strike up conversation.

"You ought to talk with Melissa Chong," I told Amanda. "Set up an education program for the transpops."

She grimaced. "From what I hear I'd have to start at the very beginning." She eyed me suspiciously. "Who's Melissa Chong, and where were you?"

I made allowances. In her pregnancy Amanda had a right to insecurity. "Talking to passengers." My voice was mild. I changed the subject.

After lunch I returned to the bridge. In Fusion I had little to occupy me there. The puter's sensors monitored air pressure, power, recycling and hydroponics controls, airlock status, and the like. We would stand watches against the risk that something might go seriously wrong, but if it did, we were unlikely to survive.

Philip Tyre and Pilot Van Peer had the watch. Both stood politely as I entered. I waved them back to their seats, took my place, and scanned the displays.

"Readouts are normal, Captain," the Pilot offered.

"May I check for myself?" I regretted my growl almost instantly; Van Peer hadn't meant any criticism. I was still touchy from the trouble I'd had with my Pilot on *Hibernia*. "Sorry," I added lamely. That annoyed me even more; a Captain didn't need to apologize for snapping: it was his privilege. The commander of a vessel under weigh had virtually unlimited powers. The respect his officers showed him was partly tradition and partly from self-preservation.

To ease the strain I made conversation with Midshipman Tyre. "Work off any more demerits, Philip?"

"Yes, sir. Three." That meant he'd spent six hours in the exercise room since yesterday evening. I made a joke of it. "Calisthenics should be quite easy for you now, Philip."

He smiled politely. "Yessir, I've had practice." We both recognized we were near forbidden territory and dropped the subject. As first midshipman, Philip was supposed to run the wardroom under the lieutenants' supervision. I wasn't expected to delve into his affairs, and he knew better now than to complain to me about his treatment.

Though Philip Tyre was our senior midshipman, it was clear he wouldn't be in charge of the wardroom. A year ago on *Hibernia*'s return voyage, Derek Carr had challenged Philip's authority in the traditional manner. The two boys had gone to the exercise room to fight it out, and Philip had lost the fight and with it control of the wardroom. Now he didn't dare interfere with Derek.

According to tradition I should have blackballed Philip; a midshipman who couldn't hold his wardroom was assumed unfit for command. Instead, though I felt only distaste for the boy, I'd suggested that Admiral Brentley assign him to my new ship. Now, I realized the extent of the problem I'd made for myself. Philip, hated thoroughly by both Derek and Lieutenant Tamarov, was a liability. Unless, somehow, I could turn him around. But I didn't see how.

Pilot Van Peer spoke cheerfully into the silence. "I understand you're a rather good chess player."

I grunted. "I play, yes."

"So do I, sir. I'd enjoy a match." I yearned to accept; I loved chess. But his suggestion was a serious breach of custom; an officer didn't initiate social contact with his Captain.

"Perhaps." His lack of discretion left me uncomfortable.

He seemed unabashed. "We can play here if you like. Lord God knows there isn't much to do on watch during Fusion."

"I don't know about that." My tone was cautious.

"Here's a board, sir," Danny said eagerly, as if flashed onto the simulscreen. "Tell me where; I'll make the moves for you!"

I didn't like being pushed. "Not on watch," I said. "Let it be."

"Aw, it'd be something to do." Danny sounded plaintive. "I'm bored." He sounded more like an ill-disciplined middy than a ship's puter. Again I pondered the age-old question: was he really alive? I dropped it; there was no way to tell.

"Captain Steadman played on watch." The Pilot.

I was astonished. Was Van Peer actually arguing? He should know better. Or was discipline on a sloop more relaxed than on a ship of the line such as *Hibernia?* I hesitated; the puter's urging and the Pilot's casual informality made the bridge seem far more friendly than I was used to. I would enjoy the game. On the other hand, regs required an officer on watch to remain alert at all times.

I made my tone cold. "You're relieved, Pilot. Confine yourself to quarters until your next watch. When you return to the bridge, be prepared to obey my orders without argument."

He gulped. "Aye aye, sir. I apologize, Captain Seafort. I meant no disrespect." He slapped open the hatch. "Perhaps we could play another time then, sir. Off watch." He left, apparently unfazed.

I sighed. We would be cooped together for a long voyage, and as was my custom with all my officers, I'd gotten off to a bad start. I glared at the board on the simulscreen. "Turn that thing off."

"Aye aye, sir." Danny flicked off the screen.

Philip Tyre remained very still. I realized I had just consigned myself to a long watch alone with a midshipman I didn't like. "Don't just sit there," I snapped. "Call up random positions and calculate Fusion coordinates. One demerit for each percent difference between your solution and Danny's."

"Aye aye, sir!" Immediately, Tyre bent to his console.

Now I was turning on a helpless middy because I was annoyed with the Pilot. Disgusted with myself, I added, "And one demerit is canceled for every solution that agrees with Danny's to four decimal places."

Philip's look was almost worshipful. "Thank you very much, sir." He diligently tapped figures into his screen. I remembered that Tyre, unlike myself, was very skilled at navigation.

When the watch finally drew to a close I went to find Amanda. Elated, Philip trotted ahead of me. He'd worked off three demerits by mental rather than physical exercise. I wondered if I'd acted improperly but decided I hadn't. If Alexi hadn't searched for excuses to discipline Tyre, the midshipman wouldn't have logged the demerits in the first place.

I stood tapping my glass for quiet. Into the silence I said, "Lord God, today is November 15, 2197, on the U.N.S. *Portia*. We ask you to bless us, to bless our voyage, and to bring health and well-being to all aboard." My eyes stung. The Ship's Prayer has been repeated nightly for over one hundred sixty years aboard every United Nations vessel to sail the cosmos. For the first time I had offered it aboard a ship that was truly mine. Even if she wasn't quite the ship I'd expected a few days ago.

I felt stiff in my freshly ironed navy-blue pants, white shirt, black tie. The insignia on my blue jacket gleamed, as did the brass on my ribbed cap. My black shoes had been spit-polished by Roger, the ship's boy, instead of by myself. Nonetheless, except for my insignia, my costume was identical with that of every officer from Dr. Bros down to Rafe Treadwell, our most junior midshipman.

But, as my bars indicated, I was Captain, and presided at the ship's table of honor. Passengers who wished to sit with me made a request to the purser, and I was free to choose from among them. Normally, seating rotated monthly. As this was our first month and I knew nobody on board I'd made no attempt to select my companions, but left it to Purser Li.

I toyed with my food, making awkward conversation. Idle chat was something I'd learned in the Navy; before that, in Father's house, we usually took meals in silence. Since our marriage, Amanda had lifted the conversational burden from me. Tonight she was making sporadic efforts, but she was preoccupied with a backache.

A friendly middle-aged woman looked at her with sympathy. "It doesn't go on forever, my dear, even if it seems that way."

Amanda smiled gratefully. "It feels that way sometimes, Mrs. Attani."

"Greg, here, was my first." She indicated the dapper young man of seventeen at her side, whose careful manners matched his elegant dress. "Time was in slow motion while I carried him."

Gregor Attani's smile was polite. He made no comment.

"You're going to Hope Nation?" I asked, knowing the answer from her file.

"Yes, Captain. I took my degrees at MIT and now I'm on my way to the Agricultural Station on Eastern Continent."

"And your husband?" I asked, unthinking.

"I never had one," she answered calmly. Unless she was confessing promiscuity, which was most unlikely, that meant Gregor was clone or donor.

Amanda nudged me in the ribs. I thought she was chiding my gauche remark, but she gestured surreptitiously to a table across the hall, where Melissa Chong's charges had been segregated. None of the paying passengers had cared to dine with transients.

Several of the transpop youngsters jostled and shoved each other; as I watched, one flung a roll at his opponent. Dr. Chong hurried from her nearby seat; behind her a mini-riot broke out at the table she had left. I snapped my fingers; the steward bent discreetly.

"Put a seal on that, flank!" I indicated the trouble spot.

"Aye aye, sir." In a moment he was leaning over one of the tables, hands spread on the tablecloth. The commotion subsided.

Alexi took his place at the first officer's console. "Morning, sir. How's Amanda?"

I grimaced. "Restless. She's not sleeping well." Amanda was due in a week. Josip Bros, the Doctor, was watching her closely.

Alexi smiled sympathetically, but with no real understanding. That Amanda needed me to do even the simplest things for her was acceptable and even pleasurable. As for her occasional petulance, I bore it as best I could, knowing it sprung from her physical discomfort.

Alexi yawned. "We could have coffee, sir, if you'd like."

Normally we didn't eat on watch, but coffee was allowable. I could hold the bridge while he strolled down the circumference corridor to the officers' mess. "That would be nice."

"Right." He thumbed the caller. "Mr. Tyre, report to the bridge on the double!"

I waited, deciding to say nothing. After a moment the young midshipman arrived. He panted, "Midshipman Tyre reporting, sir!"

"Get us two black coffees." Alexi's eyes were on his console.

It was an unusual command; an officer might normally order the ship's boy to fetch something—that was what he was for—but one didn't send a midshipman for coffee. Unless one was hazing the middy.

Philip knew better than to show any resentment. "Aye aye, sir." Obediently he left for the officers' mess.

I asked, "Did he deserve that?"

Alexi said curtly, "He can use the exercise, now he's not working off demerits by calisthenics."

I was amazed. This, from my friend Alexi? "You know better than to talk that way to your Captain!"

Alexi looked mildly surprised. "I wasn't criticizing, sir. Please don't take offense."

I sighed. "Alexi, you're so anxious to harass him you've lost all sense of proportion."

"Have I?" Alexi considered it with indifference. "Perhaps."

The hatch opened again. Philip Tyre held a steaming cup in each hand. He brought me mine first.

"Thank you."

"You're welcome, sir." He approached Alexi, who was abruptly busy studying his console. Tyre waited.

After a while Alexi reached absently for the cup. "Dismissed."

"Aye aye, sir." Philip went to the hatch and slapped it open.

"Just a moment," I said quietly. "Mr. Tamarov, I will have courtesy among officers."

Alexi raised an eyebrow. "Courtesy?" He waited a moment, as if in thought. "Aye aye, sir. Mr. Tyre, thank you for bringing me a cup of coffee. That's all."

"Aye aye, sir." Glancing nervously between us, Midshipman Tyre made his escape.

A long silence. When he spoke, Alexi's tone was bitter. "Sir, you're within your rights to rebuke me, but I respectfully suggest that doing so in front of a middy interferes with discipline."

I was astounded. Because I'd leapfrogged from midshipman to Captain I had never been a lieutenant, but if I'd been one who spoke so to my Captain I'd expect summary court-martial at the least. I was also worried; Tamarov was a seasoned officer who should know better. "Are you all right, Alexi?"

"Fine," he shot back. "Humiliated in front of Mr. Tyre, who knows you'll intercede whenever I demerit him, but otherwise fine."

"If you were a midshipman I'd cane you for insolence!"

He gave no ground. "Yes, sir, I believe you would!" We exchanged glares.

"Mr. Tamarov, you presume on our friendship." My voice was cold. "I won't allow insubordination. Confine yourself to quarters for a week. You're relieved from the watch roster until you explain to my satisfaction how your conduct was unsatisfactory. Leave at once!"

Alexi had no choice but to obey a direct order. "Aye aye, sir." He slapped open the hatch and stalked out.

I paced the bridge, my adrenaline surging. When I calmed myself I sat and reflected on my novel approach to watch standing: banish any officer with whom I shared the bridge. "Were you recording that, Danny?" I didn't want a permanent record of Alexi's misconduct.

"Nope. I probably should have. You really gave it to him." Danny brimmed with enthusiasm.

I grunted my dissatisfaction.

The rest of the watch was uneventful. Just before noon Vax came to relieve me, Rafe Treadwell in tow. Rafe, scrubbed and immaculate in a crisp new uniform, was to stand his first watch as a midshipman. Biting his lip, he glanced at the console.

"Don't worry." My voice was reassuring. "If you blow up the ship I won't live to know about it." It brought a weak smile. I left for my cabin. Amanda was out, so I lay down on my bunk hoping to nap.

I couldn't sleep. Restless, I went to the officers' mess, deserted at this hour, to make a cup of tea. I'd just taken my first sip when the ship's caller blared. "Captain, call the bridge!"

I grabbed the nearby caller. "What, Vax?"

"It's Mrs. Seafort, sir. She's had some trouble down on Level 2. She sounds upset."

Oh, Lord God. "I'm on my way!"

"In the purser's office, sir."

I ran. Derek Carr, coming up the ladder on some errand, gaped as I careened past, two steps at a time. I dashed along the corridor, burst into the purser's office. Amanda came into my arms, clung to my shoulder.

I held her close. "Carry on," I growled at the purser, who had come to attention. "It's all right, hon, I'm here. What happened?"

She held me a moment longer. "Nick, I'm sorry. I'm all right now."

The purser and I exchanged glances. "Some of the joey-boys, sir," he said uneasily. "The streeters. They, uh, molested Mrs. Seafort."

"They did not," Amanda interrupted. "I was just scared. Nobody hurt me."

"Who? Where?"

Amanda took a deep breath. She released me, tried a tentative smile. "Calm down, Nicky, I'm fine. I was going to the library for some chips. The corridor was crowded, those young men and boys all in blue denim. As I passed, someone shouted a joke about me, and suddenly they were dancing all around me, pointing at my stomach, laughing, jostling, and I couldn't understand a word they said."

Her expression darkened. "I thought they meant to hurt the baby. I tried to run but there were so many of them! Everyone was pushing. I shouted to let me go; no one listened. They just kept crowding close, giggling. Then the purser came and took me away." She turned to him. "Thank you, Mr. Li."

"Where are they?" My fists were clenched.

"Back in their cabins, sir," said the purser. "Miss Chong showed up just after I did, and herded them to their bunks."

I studied my wife. "You weren't hurt?"

She clutched my arm. "Only frightened." Her tone was emphatic. "Don't overreact, it was all a mistake."

"Overreact? Of course not." I stalked to the hatch but she got there before me.

"No, Nicky, I mean it. Leave them be. Please."

"Don't tell me how to run my ship," I spluttered.

"Damn it, Nicky, I have to live here too! They meant no harm. If you retaliate you'll make my life more difficult than it need be!"

"All right." I was reluctant. "I won't make a scene. But I'm going to have a talk with Miss Chong, before those dam—" I caught myself in time—"those blessed transpops turn my ship into a zoo!"

She smiled at my scowl and came close. "Excuse me, Mr. Li." As he turned away she kissed me on the nose. That coaxed a reluctant smile from me. "Escort me up the ladder, Nicky," she said. "I feel like I need a thrustersuit to jet up there."

"T-suits aren't that big," I told her, and got a poke in the ribs for my pains.

32

"Lord God, today is November 19, 2197, on the U.N.S. *Portia.* We ask you to bless us, to bless our voyage, and to bring health and well-being to all aboard."

"Amen." The word echoed through the crowded hall. I surveyed the room briefly before sitting. By now, the transients' tables had been pushed as far as possible from the rest.

Despite Melissa Chong's efforts, the transients' behavior seemed to be deteriorating. Steward's mates stood against the bulkhead ready to intervene in the case of riot. Dr. Antonio, newly elected President of the Passengers' Council, had approached me to suggest that the transpops be fed separately, before or after the paying passengers. It was not a solution I liked; by long understanding, the Navy traveled with but one class of passenger.

After the soup was cleared we waited patiently for our salads. A robust, muscular man in his late fifties leaned forward to speak. "Captain, nobody wants to be first to mention that it was you who found the life-forms on *Telstar.* Would you tell us about them?"

His remark invoked the most frightening moment of my life. Our glimpse of hostile fish-shaped aliens was the reason an entire squadron was en route to Hope Nation system, instead of the usual lone supply ship.

"I'd rather not, Mr. MacVail. I didn't see much, I don't understand what I saw, and it's not fit dinner conversation." A chill settled over the gathering, and no one spoke for a long while.

After dinner I offered to take Amanda for a stroll but she sent me on alone; her back ached. I wandered the Level 1 circumference corridor, then went below to Level 2. I would amble all the way around, until I came back to the ladder where I'd started.

I passed several passenger cabins, then the crew's mess hall. I went past the engine room hatch without stopping; this wasn't an inspection tour. Outside crew berth one, crewmen lounged, chatting in the passage. "Carry on," I blurted, before they could come to attention.

Beyond the crew berths were more passenger cabins. I noticed a strong odor of ammonia. I stopped at the purser's office. "Mr. Li, what do I smell in the passage?"

"Probably the disinfectant, sir." His tone was stolid. "We scrub down the corridor twice a day." I raised an eyebrow. "The transients."

"Yes?"

"They, uh, urinate in the corridor."

"They piss on my deck?" My voice rose an octave.

"Miss Chong says they're not accustomed to plumbing."

"Get Dr. Chong! Right now!"

A few moments later the social worker faced me, hands on hips. "What did you expect?" she demanded. "Civilized graces? These joeys were born on the streets and lived there all their lives! Most have never seen a building with working plumbing. Sure, we've shown them how, but habits don't change overnight!"

"You expect me to tolerate using the corridors as toilets?"

"No." Her tone was reasonable. "I'm working on it, as I'm working on everything else. We knew there'd be problems when we shipped these joeys, and so there are."

Her calm helped restore my own. "I know you're doing your best, but—look, Miss Chong. We have to live together sixteen months before we reach Hope Nation. They're disruptive, these charges of yours. Get control of them!"

"How?" she asked simply. I had no ready answer. "There are forty-two of them," she said. "I can't be everywhere at once. Give me time."

"All right." I was grudging. "I'll be patient. But not about this. If they foul my corridors again they'll wish they hadn't!"

I thought about ordering a guard posted in the Level 2 corridor, but decided against it. A Naval vessel was a civilized environment; passengers weren't prisoners to be watched every moment.

During the next days Amanda began irregular contractions. I sat in the white infirmary cubicle while Dr. Bros examined her. "I'm almost as excited as you," he said. "How many births do you think we get on an interstellar cruise?" Not many, of course. The crew and officers—except for the Captain—routinely lined up each month for their sterility shots. Married passengers occasionally bore offspring during a long voyage. Of course, unmarried passengers either took sterility shots or ended their pregnancies; to do otherwise was unthinkable, except through registered host or clone centers.

"Very soon now," Dr. Bros promised. I took Amanda back to our cabin.

As the days went by I continued to notice the pungent smell of disinfectant in the corridor. I conferred with the Chief Engineer; shortly afterward work parties strung wire mesh along the junction of bulkheads and deck. I gritted my teeth as a holorecorder was mounted and connected to Danny's sensors on the bridge; it violated Naval tradition to spy on passengers and crew and I found it hateful, even if necessary.

I had Danny monitor the corridor and switch on a carefully modulated current whenever a transient paused and appeared to adjust his clothing.

The startled squawks of the transpops provided much amusement to the other passengers, especially the younger ones. One teener jeered, "Electropiss!" at a transient named Deke and earned a black eye for his troubles.

The days passed slowly. One afternoon I played chess with Pilot Van Peer in his cabin. He was an enthusiastic player but a momentary carelessness cost him the game on the twenty-fourth move.

I endured long, quiet watches on the bridge. After several days, Alexi, his confinement to quarters ended at last, stopped me outside the officers' mess. "Can we talk privately, sir?"

"Very well." I followed him to his cabin, a four-meter cube with a tightly made gray bunk. All his belongings were neatly stowed in his duffel in the manner we had been taught in Academy.

He faced me awkwardly. "Sir, I'm sorry about last week." He anxiously checked my face. "I don't just apologize, I mean I'm truly sorry. I was out of line. No lieutenant can mouth off to his Captain as I did. But I also—" He broke off and turned away. "I owe you more than that," he said in a muffled voice. "For what you are to me. Please forgive me."

I felt vast relief; my friend was back. "Sit down, Alexi." My tone was gentle.

He perched on his bunk, eyes fastened on my face. I pulled a chair near. "I'll repeat what I said on the bridge. You're so anxious to harass him you lose all sense of proportion."

He let out a long breath. "The truth is, I don't know what to think anymore, sir. He was a monster. You know what he did to us last cruise. I swore an oath that if I ever had the chance, I would hurt him. I have, and he deserves it. But . . . I don't feel better."

"You've hurt him a lot, Alexi. Isn't it enough?"

His hands clenched. "Sometimes I think so. Then I remember how often Derek and I were put over the barrel, thanks to his endless demerits. And his tone of voice in the wardroom, when I was helpless to defend myself. Sometimes I think you should have let me resign, back on Detour!"

"I'm sorry you're troubled." It was all I could find to say.

Our eyes met. "I'll stop if you require me to, sir. I'll obey orders."

"No." I was certain it had to come from him. "Alexi, I hated him as much as you did. But he's paid for his sins. He's endured everything you've given him, even when we moved the barrel to your cabin last cruise. He's still ready to do his duty as he understands it. Can't you respect that?"

He looked grim. "No, sir, I can't. What do you think he'd do to Derek and Rafe if he were in control again?"

"I don't know. I'm more worried about what he's doing to you." It startled him. I sighed. "Anyway, I accept your apology. You're back on the watch roster."

"Thank you." He swallowed. "I'll think about what you said, sir."

"Very well." I went back to my cabin to prepare for watch.

I'd left Amanda in the infirmary, promising to stay close—though I couldn't get very far without a thrustersuit. Her contractions were more frequent and she wanted to be near Dr. Bros. But I myself was on the watch roster, I couldn't relieve myself just to wait with her. The infirmary was but a quarter turn round the corridor and I could be there in a minute or less.

Vax Holser and Midshipman Derek Carr shared my watch. The lieutenant was running navigation drills for Derek, whose computational skill increased daily. I called up a few of the problems on my own console but Derek solved them far faster than I. Once Derek raced through a calculation and made an error in the process. Vax quietly reproved him for inattention to detail; Derek flushed deep red. Thereafter he was consistently accurate.

An excited young voice burst over the speaker. "Captain, Midshipman Treadwell reporting. There's trouble down here!"

I snatched the caller, fear pumping adrenaline through my system. "What kind of trouble? Where?" I glanced at my console; all readouts were green.

"Level 2 corridor west, sir. A fight. Some of the transients!"

Relief left me weak. "Bless it, Rafe, you've been taught how to report! Four demerits! I'll be right down." I dropped the caller. "Derek, remind him how to call the bridge in an emergency!"

"Aye aye, sir," Derek said, his chagrin evident. Though Philip Tyre was nominally in charge, in actuality Derek ran the wardroom.

"Shall I come too, sir?" On his feet, Vax was ready to face the entire troop of transients single-handed.

"No, I'll handle it. Wait here." I slapped the hatch shut behind me.

From the ladder I could hear shouting below. On Level 2 I rounded the corridor bend and came upon a wild melee; some two dozen streeters grappled with youths from among the paying passengers. Midshipman Treadwell watched, at a loss. "Get the master-at-arms, Rafe!" Sensibly, the boy turned and ran the other direction, realizing he was safer going the long way around the circular corridor than trying to claw through the riot.

I shoved two youngsters aside, stalked into the eye of the storm. "What's going on here? You, get back!" I thrust a boy against the bulkhead, raised my voice another notch. "Nobody move! You, Mr. Attani! Let go of him! Now! Put your hands down!"

A paralyzing blow to the small of my back slammed me into the bulkhead. A bull-necked youth in blue denim loomed, fists bunched. "Buddout! Notchour bidness! Buddout!"

I wasn't sure I could move. I took a tentative step. I breathed with difficulty, but my muscles functioned. "All right." I held out my hand. He stared at it without comprehension. I lunged forward, kicked him in the stomach with all my strength. He doubled over. My stiffened right hand arced in a chop to the back of his thick neck. He fell heavily to the deck and was still.

I glared at the suddenly quiet throng. "Anyone else?" I took a step forward and they pressed back. One boy braver than the rest held his ground. Metal flashed as he lunged. My right hand at my side, I slapped him hard with my left. His hand shot to his face. I gripped his wrist, bent his arm behind his back.

"Whachadoon, joeys? Whachadoon here!" Melissa Chong pushed a hefty shoulder through the gaping bystanders. "Leavim lone! Leavim Cap'n lone!" She grabbed an offender by the hair, flung him to the side. Others made way. "Captain, what's going on?"

"Get your people against the inner bulkhead! You other boys, on the outer bulkhead. Move!" I was too enraged to say more. I heard the clatter of running footsteps. The master-at-arms and two mates appeared, truncheons ready. "Mr. Banatir, help separate these criminals. Watch this one, he's got a knife."

His lips tight, Mr. Banatir pried the weapon from the wrist I clutched.

A few moments later two bands of surly youths faced each other across the corridor. "All right," I demanded. "What started it?"

A babble of voices rose in reply. After a time we got it sorted out. Some transient joeys had attacked a group of passengers, and other teens had joined the fracas.

I snarled, "Your people caused this riot."

Melissa Chong held her ground. "Yes, but didn't you hear why? Tellaman, Annie! Tellaman boudit!"

The scrawny youngster pointed an accusing finger. "Dey callinus trannies! Allatime callinus trannies!"

"I don't get it." My tone was cautious.

"Didn't you hear?" Miss Chong. "Trannies. Your high-class passengers are calling my joeys names."

I turned to one of the better-dressed teens. "Is that true?"

He shrugged. "Maybe. It's what they are!"

"Your name?"

"Chris Dakko." His look was sullen.

"Age?"

"Seventeen."

I looked around, scowling. Several of the young passengers looked as if they wanted to be elsewhere. "Very well. Mr. Banatir, take charge of these hoodlums. Bring them to the bridge one at a time with their parents." I rounded on the social worker. "Your time's up, Miss Chong. Get your wild children under control! Who is that, lying on the deck?"

"Eddie, Captain."

"Eddie what?"

"On the street he was called Eddie Boss."

"Mr. Banatir, Eddie Boss goes to the brig. And let me see that weapon you took from the other joey."

I examined it, and my breath hissed. "Silverware? They steal tableware for weapons?"

"You see, Captain? They're anima—"

"Speak when you're spoken to, Dakko." I rounded on Melissa Chong. "What next? Laser pistols? I won't have it. All you joeys, back against the bulkhead. Mr. Banatir, search the lot of them. Brig anyone with a weapon."

Gregor Attani bristled. "Search *them;* it's a good idea. You'll probably find a lot more they stole. But we're civilized. It's a violation of—"

"All of them, Mr. Banatir. If this *civilized* joey gives you any more lip, brig him too."

Our search uncovered two more knives and a fork, hidden in the transients' clothing. Eddie Boss and the transpops who'd carried weapons were hauled to the brig.

The groups dispersed, herded by Miss Chong and my crewmen. I caught Rafe's eye. "Back to your duties, Mr. Treadwell!" I was still irritated at his sloppy report.

"But—Aye aye, sir," he said unhappily.

I went directly to the infirmary. "Amanda's doing fine," Dr. Bros said as I came in.

"But I'm not." My voice was tight. "My right hand is broken." I held my breath as he manipulated my wrist.

"You're right. What'd you hit it on, sir?"

"A rock." I let the doctor immobilize my wrist. He gave me calcium and ran a wave bone-growth stimulator back and forth over my hand for several minutes.

"It'll ache a bit but you'll be all right after a few days."

"I know." In the next room Amanda groaned. When Dr. Bros finished building the cast for my wrist I looked into her cubicle. "I can't stay, hon," I told her. "Problems. I'll be back in time to greet the baby."

"I'll go and you stay," she grated.

"Sorry." I strode back to the bridge. The watch had turned; Pilot Van Peer and Philip Tyre were on duty. I sat in my chair, my hand throbbing. I was lucky I hadn't been lynched. When I'd felt my wrist snap I knew I didn't have a chance in a fight, so I'd brazened it out and gotten away with it.

Shortly afterward Mr. Banatir escorted the first of the parents to the bridge. I read him and his youngster the riot act and dismissed them. The father, a metallurgist bound for Detour, seemed more chastened than his offspring.

I was waiting for the next miscreant when the hatch opened. "Permission to enter bridge." Rafe Treadwell, his voice subdued.

"Granted."

Slowly he walked in, hands pressed to his sides, and came to attention. "Midshipman Treadwell reporting, sir." Regs required him to identify himself.

"Go on." I was impatient.

"Lieutenant Holser asks you to enter my discipline in the Log and to cancel ten demerits." His eyes were liquid with misery.

I realized what I'd done. "You had more than six, Rafe?" I asked gently.

"Yessir," he mumbled. "Seven." The four I'd added had put him up to eleven, and Vax had caned him. Too bad, but I couldn't undo it now.

"Very well, dismissed." The boy saluted, turned, and left.

I'd lectured several passengers and their sons by the time Mrs. Attani appeared with Gregor. She protested immediately. "Captain Seafort, you have no right to hold Greg prisoner."

"I won't tolerate hooligans on my ship. If your son doesn't understand that, it's your job to teach—"

"All he did was defend himself!"

"Mrs. Attani, see that he has no more incidents with the transients."

Her voice was tart. "Perhaps you'll see that the transients leave decent people alone!" Philip Tyre's jaw dropped; he'd never heard that tone used to a Captain. Nor had I.

"Very well, lacking your assurance, I won't release him. Mr. Banatir, take him to the brig to think it over for a week."

She gasped, "You wouldn't!"

"You're mistaken, madam."

"Wait!" she cried as the master-at-arms grasped the young man's arm. "Gregor won't get into any more fights. You have my assurance."

"What about yours, Gregor?" In the background the caller chimed; Philip Tyre moved to answer it.

"Yes, sir," Gregor said smoothly. "If you'll remember, I was one of those who was attacked. I'll try not to be attacked again."

"If you think you can—"

"Excuse me, sir." Midshipman Tyre shifted anxiously from one foot to the other.

"Later, Philip. Watch how you speak to me, Mr. Attani, or—"

"Excuse me, sir, please!"

I spun to Philip, ready to hurl a rebuke.

"It's the infirmary!"

I stopped short. "Amanda?"

"The Doctor says now!"

"Pilot, take the watch! Philip, get these people off the bridge!" I ran.

I held my newborn son, my cast making me awkward. The baby's clear blue eyes stared into mine, piercing my soul. He was very quiet, very still. I knew he couldn't see me; he couldn't yet focus. But still I smiled at his serious gaze as I rocked gently side to side.

When I passed through the gates of Academy at thirteen, there was a stunned moment when I realized my life was no longer my own. Now was also such a moment.

"Hello, Nate," I said quietly. "I love you. Everything's going to be all right." His eyes closed briefly and opened again. A moment later they were shut and he was fast asleep. I slipped back into the cubicle and gently handed the baby to Amanda, radiant underneath her crisp white sheets.

"Good work, hon," I told her.

"Not bad, first time out," she agreed. She nestled the baby along-side her arm. A few moments later she too was asleep.

For a week I walked around in a daze, unable to believe the miracle to which I'd contributed. When I passed, Rafe Treadwell stiffened anxiously at my unseeing scowl. Vax Holser repeated himself to me several times, as to a small child, before I heard him. He seemed to think it amusing. Our passengers were profuse with their congratulations as if I'd done something unusual. Even Mrs. Attani, vigilant in defense of her son, softened and visited my wife and child.

With Amanda in the infirmary, I had our cabin to myself. For some reason it made me restless. I took to exploring the ship, hungering to memorize every inch of its confines. I wandered into the mess hall, where stewards were setting the tables for the evening meal, but my presence made them so self-conscious I left again. Past the lounge I came to the exercise room. On the spur of the moment I looked in, to a scene of strenuous activity.

Philip Tyre, shirtless, was doing vigorous jumping jacks. On the mat Rafe Treadwell, in shorts and T-shirt, was performing sit-ups, breathless. Lieutenant Vax Holser worked the bars, muscles rippling his hairy arms and chest.

Before the three could jump to attention I waved them back to their labors and sat at the bicycle. Uneasy at watching idly, I folded my jacket across the handlebars and took off my tie. I began to pedal.

After a while Philip finished his jumping jacks and leaned against the bulkhead to catch his breath, his smooth chest gleaming with perspiration. After half a minute he began to do deep knee bends, his back stiff.

Smiling, I asked Vax, "Are you working off demerits too?" Lieutenants were not subject to demerits, but his penchant for physical exercise was well known.

"No, sir." His tone was agreeable. "Just working." He held himself above the parallel bars.

I dialed up the bicycle controls and pedaled harder, feeling lazy in comparison to the two boys laboring at their demerits. As a midshipman on U.N.S. *Helsinki* and later on *Hibernia*, I'd spent long hours enduring similar punishment.

With a sigh of relief Rafe Treadwell got up from the mat, his shift finished. In two hours he would have worked off one demerit. "Good afternoon, sir," he said politely. "Mr. Tyre." He nodded, acknowledging his senior. He left for the wardroom shower.

Philip lay on his stomach and took a deep breath. He began energetic push-ups. "Easy, boy," I warned. "You'll hurt yourself." Out of breath, he nodded but pressed on. After the push-ups he gave himself another thirty seconds, then began sit-ups. Pedaling with effort, I watched with uneasy interest as he struggled to continue.

Half an hour later he finished his exercises, leaned wearily against the bulkhead.

"Hard calisthenics doesn't mean you're to injure yourself," I said.

"Yessir." He stopped for breath. "Those are the exercises I'm to do, sir. I'm not to vary them."

"Ah." If I hadn't wandered into the exercise room I'd never have known; Philip would have risked drastic punishment bringing it to my attention, and rightly so. In the Navy discipline was to be endured, even harsh discipline. An officer had to know he could handle whatever a tyrannical Captain might bestow upon him, light-years from civilization.

"How long have you had those orders?" I knew their source.

"Several months, sir. Excuse me, please. This can't wait." He picked up the caller and thumbed it. "Lieutenant Tamarov, sir? Midshipman Tyre reporting. Exercises completed, sir." He listened a moment and replaced the caller.

"What was that?" I was appalled.

"I have to report," the boy said tonelessly. "At the beginning and end of each session. Standing orders."

"To Mr. Tamarov?"

"Yes, sir."

"Why?"

"I'm not to be trusted, sir." Tyre wiped himself off with a towel, avoiding my eye.

I scrambled from the bike, snatching my tie from the handlebars. I knotted it with fumbling fingers.

"It's all right, I don't mind," Philip blurted.

I grated, "The orders are countermanded!" From the bars, Vax Holser watched with a quizzical expression. I jammed my arms into my jacket, slapped open the hatch, and stalked into the corridor. A moment later I was pounding at Alexi Tamarov's cabin.

"Belay that racket!" Alexi flung open the hatch. His eyes widened in shock. His tie was loosened; his jacket lay over the chair. Behind him, his bed was rumpled.

I barged past, slapping the hatch shut behind me. "Attention!" I shoved him back against a bulkhead. He stiffened immediately, eyes front.

Standing nose to nose I savaged him, my voice harsh, my words brutal. A red flush crept slowly up Alexi's neck and across his cheeks while he stood helpless. "Not trusting another officer's word is abominable," I raged. "The Naval Service is founded in trust! Apparently you don't understand that, and if not, you're unfit to hold a commission! You get what you expect from your officers. Tell Philip he's untrustworthy and that's what he'll be!"

I broke off, out of breath. Alexi's eyes were pained. I remembered he had once idolized me. Well, that would be the case no longer. "I let you carry on your damned vendetta, Alexi. Once I even encouraged you. But you've gone too far; you've disgraced Naval tradition. I hope you're as ashamed of yourself as I am of you!" He flinched at that.

"Your orders to Philip are countermanded. You'll assume his word is honorable until he proves otherwise. Apologize to him for distrusting his word and enter your apology in the Log. Acknowledge!"

"Aye aye, sir! Orders received and understood, sir!" His voice was strained.

I slapped open the hatch. I paused. "I won't check to see if you did those things, Alexi. I accept your word as an officer. A pity you don't have the decency to do likewise." With that I left him.

Stalking back to my cabin I cursed my lack of control; in flaying Alexi for destroying the morale of a subordinate, I'd done exactly the same to him. Alexi deserved more of me. On the other hand, I was appalled at how he'd been treating Philip. What other grim secrets would I come upon?

My cabin was the largest living space on the ship. Accustomed as a middy to the confining wardroom, shared with three other midshipmen, I'd once been awed at the sight of the Captain's quarters. Even shared with Amanda it seemed more than ample.

Somehow, merely adding a baby made the cabin cramped and uncomfortable. The bassinet took up space; so did the unused high chair and all the changes of gear a baby seemed to require.

My sleep was altered too. One ear was tuned to the breathing of a tiny pair of lungs. Amanda's abrupt departure from the bed at intervals during the night also affected my rest. The bridge now seemed a relaxing haven, and I spent extra time there.

For several days after my savage rebuke, Alexi Tamarov had difficulty meeting my eye. Notwithstanding my promise to him, I looked for and found his apology to Philip in the Log. Alexi and I endured a watch together, mostly in silence.

In the dining hall I sat at table surrounded by passengers but lacking the solace of Amanda. Though some passengers brought their young children to table, Amanda found it awkward to care for the baby through a formal dinner and asked to eat alone in our cabin for a time. She understood it was my duty to preside at the Captain's table and didn't resent my attending.

"Tell me, Captain, you've been to Hope Nation. Do you think they're ready for membership?" Jorge Portillo, an agronomist from Quito.

I wondered if I should avoid the question as too political. I decided I might as well answer; a remark early in a sixteen-month interstellar voyage could have no political repercussions by the time I returned home.

"The U.N. Charter provides for membership of 'any geopolitical unit that is not a subdivision of another member and has adequate resources to exist independently,'" I quoted. "Hope Nation is administered directly by the U.N., so it can't be claimed by another member state. The question is whether the colony is self-sustaining. From what I've seen it has a vigorous economy and an active political life. Why shouldn't it have membership?"

"You'd give an unsophisticated bunch of yokels equal vote in the General Assembly with the nations of Europe?" Mrs. Attani. Other passengers chimed in, and the debate veered to what constituted true sophistication.

"Now take Bulgaria," said Dr. Francon. "I think you'd have to agree they're about as unsoph—good Lord!"

I followed his glance. At a transpop table a minor riot had erupted. Bread and salad flew. One boy overturned his chair, scrambled atop the table. "Vax!" I pointed, spluttering.

Vax Holser bounded out of his chair as steward's mates converged on the fracas. Vax hauled the offending boy off the table and half carried him out of the dining hall into the corridor. He returned to collar two more, while Melissa Chong, red-faced, tried to restore order. I watched seething from my table until all offenders had been ejected.

I signaled the steward. "Pass the word: all officers to the bridge after the meal." My voice was tight.

"Why should decent people have to put up with that behavior?" Mrs. Attani, her glare indignant.

"Could they eat an hour earlier?" Mr. Singh.

I took a deep breath, let it out slowly. "I'll deal with them. There'll be no more of this." I wondered how to fulfill my pledge.

After dinner I paced the bridge in irritable silence until the officers arrived. Vax, who was reporting for watch, came first. Then Alexi, followed by my three midshipmen, Philip, Derek, and Rafe. Then Dr. Bros, hesitant at entering the unfamiliar territory; of all the ship's officers, only he was not on the watch roster. Pilot Van Peer entered shaking his head, grinning. "Couldn't believe it. They should be in cages!"

"Enough." He subsided. Finally the Chief Engineer arrived, completing our party.

I sat, and swung to face them. "I've had it. We've got to take control." I looked at each of them in turn. "Any suggestions?"

Vax spoke first. "Feed them in the crew mess, sir."

I thought it over. "No, it's not fair to the crew. What else?"

"We could set a transpop zone, sir." Alexi. "Level 2, around their cabins. Feed them in their own area."

"Restrict them like prisoners, you mean? I don't—"

"Why not?" blurted the Pilot. "Think of all the ship's regs they've broken. For that matter, you'd be justified throwing the lot of them in the brig."

I stood slowly. "You call me 'sir'!"

Van Peer gulped. "Aye aye, sir! I'm sorry. No disrespect meant, sir!"

"Very well. And stop interrupting. As for the brig, forget it. I won't make us into a prison ship." U.N.S. *Indonesia* orbiting Callisto was a disgrace to the Navy. I'd be damned before my vessel became another.

A long silence. The Chief asked, "Could you tranquilize them?"

All eyes turned to Dr. Bros. He shook his head decisively. "A few days, perhaps, but not for sixteen months."

There were no more suggestions. "Very well." I paced as I spoke. "The transients are passengers, not prisoners, and we all know regs require passengers be given every courtesy consistent with the safety and well-being of the ship. We won't hold them in a security zone or drug them, or force them to eat with the crew. Nor will we tolerate their behavior."

I leaned against the back of my chair facing my silent officers. "We won't isolate the transients, we'll integrate them. Each officer will take charge of five streeters, at dinner. And for that matter, you're to take all your meals with your transients. I'm holding you responsible for their conduct; make sure it's acceptable!"

Derek's face reflected his disgust. Coming from Upper New York he would have particularly strong revulsion toward the streeters. "Supervise them outside the dining hall as well," I said. "Break them of

their more obnoxious habits and teach them how civilized folk behave."
I turned to Mr. Van Peer. "Pilot, you won't be given a table to supervise." His relief was evident, but I punctured it immediately. "You will take the place of the officer who would stand watch during the dinner hour." His face fell.

"Excuse me, sir." Vax waited for my nod. "If we each take five, we're short an officer unless you take a group too."

"I know."

"But what about the Captain's table? I mean, the passengers are invited . . . it's a place of honor . . ."

"Training these joeys is more important." I tapped the chair. "It will be a major effort, and we'll need coordination and cooperation. Mr. Tamarov, you're in charge of the transient project. Any officer requiring special assistance will come to you." Alexi gaped. "Mr. Tyre, you will assist him." Dismayed, they exchanged glances.

"The rest of you are dismissed. Mr. Tamarov and Mr. Tyre will remain." I waited for the officers to leave. Vax, on watch, leaned back to listen. "Stand to," I barked at Alexi and Philip. The two stiffened immediately.

"I have enough problems with the transpops. Regardless of your personal relations, you're to work together. Alexi, Midshipman Tyre is all the help you'll get, and you're going to need him. You're to assume he is acting in good faith unless you know otherwise. Your vendetta can wait."

I glared at Philip. "Mr. Tyre, you're to help Lieutenant Tamarov every way you can. You will be courteous, friendly, useful, and as helpful as any middy ever was. Acknowledge orders, both of you!"

"Orders received and understood, sir! I'll help Mr. Tamarov in every way I can. I'll be courteous and friendly and useful, sir!"

"Orders received and understood, sir," said Alexi. "I'll handle the transpops with Mr. Tyre's assistance and I'll assume he's trying to help me, sir!"

Their ready acquiescence didn't lessen my irritation. "Out, both of you." They saluted and left. Vax, familiar with my ways, said nothing.

After a while I realized I was still standing with my hands clenched. I slumped into my seat and let out a deep breath. "Sometimes I wish I were still a midshipman."

Vax smiled sympathetically. "Not often, I'm sure."

"Well, when I see Alexi going after Philip . . ."

The speaker came to life. "But then you wouldn't be able to tell them both off."

"Who invited you into this conversation, Danny?"

"This is the bridge," he sniffed. "I live here. Since when do I need an invitation?"

I was in no mood for humor. "Pipe down. If I want your opinion I'll ask for it."

"That'll be the day," the puter said darkly.

"Quiet, Danny. That's an order!"

For answer he threw a few random wavelengths of interference across the simulscreen.

"Belay that!" I snapped. No response. "Acknowledge my order!"

"How, when you told me to be quiet?" Danny's tone was sweet.

I might have dropped the matter but I'd had a rough day. "Puter, do you have EPD?"

Danny shouted, "Captain or not, don't say that to me!" Electronic Personality Disorder was one of the three known A.I. psychoses, and Danny didn't care for the suggestion that he was crazy.

I scowled, standing to pace.

It was said that personality overlays smoothed the interplay of electronic and human intelligence, and ultimately made for a safer ship. Just as we humans had infinite variations in temperament, the randomizing program in a shipboard puter generated unique character traits on reboot. Thereafter, subtle learning programs developed the puter's personality to a high level of sophistication. Which is why we were reluctant to shut a puter down, and wait while it went again through the learning process.

Yes, I knew all that. But why was it whenever I wanted to be left in peace, some puter would take it on himself to—

"Captain, a word with you?" Vax's tone was urgent. He beckoned to the simulscreen.

"No. And, Danny, you're out of line. You speak to the Captain with courtesy!"

"Yeah, I better or you'll put me to sleep like Darla." The speaker sounded sullen. "I heard how you worked her over!" Darla, our puter on *Hibernia*, had been glitched by the Dosmen on Lunapolis and needed emergency repairs.

Vax waved frantically for my attention. "Excuse me, sir, may I speak with you outside—*please?*"

I knew he was anxious to avert a quarrel with the puter. Like me, he'd heard rumors of ships that had sailed with an angry puter and had never returned.

I was irate enough not to care. "No, Vax. We might as well find out who's Captain here: me or that bucket of chips. Danny, I order you to apologize! Acknowledge!" Vax held his breath.

Reluctantly Danny gave the required response. "Aye aye, sir. Order received and understood. I apologize."

"You will not speak to me disrespectfully again, ever! Acknowledge."

The belligerence seemed to flow out of him. "Aye aye, sir. Order received and understood. I won't speak disrespectfully again." Now he sounded frightened.

"Very well. Danny, alphanumeric response only, displayed on screen. Acknowledge."

My console lit. "AYE AYE, SIR. ORDERS ACKNOWLEDGED. ALPHANUMERIC ONLY, ON SCREEN. PLEASE DON'T DEPROGRAM ME! PLEASE, SIR!" The speaker remained silent.

"I don't intend to. Not if you're under discipline. Alphanumeric only for forty-eight hours. Disconnect conversational overlays, discontinue all voluntary statements except alarm functions, for forty-eight hours."

"AYE AYE, SIR!"

Vax stared aghast. My arms folded, I glared at the now silent console.

33

Eddie Boss, released from the brig by my orders, toyed disgustedly with his salad.

"Dinner not to your liking?" I asked.

He glanced up with a snaggletoothed grin. "Fat puppy be nice, Cap'n," he said dreamily. "Eddie chowdown good den." I shuddered.

The transients had reacted to their seat changes with wariness, assuming they were in for trouble. Derek Carr maintained control at table five only with the greatest effort, snapping curt orders at his unwanted charges. Vax Holser, at the next table, spoke softly with a smile and was quickly obeyed. Vax's physique had its advantages.

"Excuse me, sir." Philip Tyre, an apprehensive look on his young face. "Mr. Van Peer asks if it would be convenient for you to come to the bridge."

I was alarmed. "Problems?"

"He didn't tell me, sir, just that it would be better for you to be there."

"Very well." I glared at my young charges. "Mr. Tyre, take my place. See that these uncivilized persons stay seated until the meal is finished."

I left the dining hall and hurried to the bridge. For the Pilot to call me from dinner the matter must be serious.

"Well?" I slapped the hatch closed behind me. Van Peer gestured at his console in answer. I read over his shoulder.

"D 20471 REQUESTS PERMISSION TO REACTIVATE CONVERSATIONAL OVERLAYS, SIR. FORTY-EIGHT-HOUR PROHIBITION IMPOSED BY CAPTAIN HAS PASSED. REQUEST TERMINATION ALPHANUMERIC ONLY."

The Pilot murmured, "I thought you'd best see for yourself." I grinned; his low tone wouldn't stop Danny from overhearing if the puter had ignored my order restricting him to alphanumeric input.

"You think he's learned his manners now?" I said loudly. Pilot Van Peer flinched. I sat in my own seat and began to type. "Reactivate conversational overlays."

My console lit immediately. "AYE AYE, SIR! THANK YOU VERY MUCH!"

I typed, "I am prepared to terminate alphanumeric only."

"PLEASE, SIR! I WON'T GIVE YOU ANY MORE LIP, HONEST, IT'S LONELY IN HERE. PLEASE LET ME TALK, I'LL BE RESPECTFUL FROM NOW ON. I PROMISE, CAPTAIN, SIR!"

I raised my eyebrow. The Pilot chewed his knuckle. "I think it worked, sir."

"It seems so." I bent to the console. "Terminate alphanumeric only."

"Thank you, sir!" Danny's tense voice filled the speaker. "No more trouble, Captain Seafort. I promise!"

"Very well. The incident is closed." As I sat back in my chair I luxuriated in the Pilot's look of astonishment and respect. I tried not to let it show.

"Lord God, today is December 12, 2197, on the U.N.S. *Portia*. We ask you to bless us, to bless our voyage, and to bring health and well-being to all aboard." I felt stiff and awkward in my dress 'whites, constrained by the fully charged stunner strapped to my side.

"Amen." I joined in the general murmur and glanced at the crowded dining hall before sitting. Dining with ship's officers apparently no longer impressed the transients; I was seated with Mr. Singh, Mr. MacVail, and five young hoodlums who jabbered among themselves while calling to their friends scattered at various tables.

"Sit down," I snapped at Eddie.

"Naw." He remained standing. He waved enthusiastically at another table. "Talkina Jonie!" Next to him Norie snickered.

"Sit, Eddie!"

Still he ignored me. I unholstered my stunner and touched it to the boy's side. He sprawled across the table unconscious. Water dripped to the deck from an overturned glass. I put my unaccustomed stunner back in its place. "Sit quietly, all of you, until the food is served." Awed, they did. I decided my baby-sitting was going to be easy.

It was, until the soup came. As the steward's mate served the first course from the big tureen, Norie, Tomas, and Deke lunged impatiently at their bowls.

"None of that!" My tone was sharp. It had no effect. "Mr. Dowan." I motioned to the steward to remove the tureen. "Serve Mr. Singh and Mr. MacVail from another table. The children and I will do without soup."

"Aye aye, sir." The steward sounded uncertain.

"Hey, wanna eat, wanna eat!"

"Pipe down, Les." I glowered. "None of you gets soup tonight. If you settle down you'll be given meat and salad when it comes."

"No joe gonna takur food, noway! Cap'n ain' gonna takur dinna!" Norie was indignant. She scrambled out of her seat but stopped short when my hand fell to the butt of my stunner.

My voice was cold. "Now we'll do without dinner. You get to eat when you behave yourselves." I signaled the steward's mate. "Serve the passengers only, Mr. Dowan."

"Whata bouda Cap'n? Cap'n gonna chow, naw?" Les spoke in a sneer.

"No. The Captain eats when you do." I didn't know why I said it, but it silenced them. "You'll have food when you learn manners. Until then we'll go hungry."

"Cap'n go inna kitchen nighttime," Deke said derisively. "Cap'n nobe hungry, hebe da man!"

"We call it the galley, not the kitchen. And I won't go. We'll work it out together."

"He chowdown latetime sure," Deke told the others.

"No. I swear it by Lord God." I felt a pang of alarm but it was too late; the oath was given. Now, if they were stubborn enough, I could starve to death. They'd starve with me, but that was slight consolation.

Mr. Singh cleared his throat. "Captain, are you sure you want to . . ."

"It's done."

"In the heat of the moment surely you don't hold yourself to such an oath—"

I bristled. "My oath is good, sir, no matter how given!"

"Of course," said Mr. Singh hurriedly. "I didn't suggest otherwise. I just thought . . ." He let his sentence trail off. We waited out the meal. It looked delicious.

"Alexi's had Mr. Tyre up again," Vax said, indicating the Log.

"I know. I can read."

"Yes, sir. The demerits are tapering off a bit, though."

I was already aware. The month after I'd ordered Alexi and Philip to work together had begun with a flurry of demerits to the midshipman, then they had decreased. Now they were sporadic, though still enough to keep Philip in the exercise room during his off hours.

Vax persisted. "I don't like what Philip did, sir, but . . ."

"But what?" I asked, annoyed.

"It's time Alexi let him off," he said bluntly. My direct question had freed him to criticize a brother officer.

"What about you?" I asked. "The barrel's in your cabin. Do you go easy on him?"

"Of course not!" Vax looked shocked. "What would be the point? If we have a system of discipline, we should enforce it. The middies and cadets should dread being caned. As we did," he added, remembering.

"So you feel sorry for him, but you won't ease up." I smiled grimly at the irony.

"No, sir, not unless you order me to." He waited.

I lay back, my eyes closed. When First Lieutenant Cousins had caned me shortly after I arrived on *Hibernia* as a middy, I'd loathed it. The pain was considerable but the humiliation was far worse. But I'd survived it, as I had in the past. Philip would too.

"Bridge to engine room, prepare to Defuse." I waited impatiently for the response.

"Engine room ready for Defuse, sir. Control passed to bridge." Chief Hendricks's voice was unemotional, as always.

"Passed to bridge, aye aye." I traced the line from "Full" to "Off" on the console.

"Confirm clear of encroachments, Lieutenant."

Vax Holser checked his instruments. Our first priority emerging from Fusion was to make sure we were clear of whatever objects might be about. Danny's reflexes were faster than ours, but we followed the Navy rule: don't trust mechanical sensors. Recheck everything.

"Clear of encroachments, Captain." Vax's attention was fastened on the readouts.

"Very well. Plot our position, please." Vax bent to his console, fingers flying, as Danny's own calculations flashed onto the screens. It was an extra precaution: though we were to remain in the vicinity until the rest of the fleet arrived, I wanted to be able to Fuse on a moment's notice.

I was hungry, but I made an effort to put it out of my mind. The week of starvation during my battle of wills with the transpops seemed to have changed my metabolism. Now that the ordeal was over and we were eating again, I found myself gaining more weight than I'd lost; disgusted, I worked out regularly in the exercise room and watched my diet rigidly. I'd managed to take off my excess weight but now I had to cope with hunger pangs. An unpleasant change.

"The other ships should show up in a few days," Vax remarked. An unnecessary comment. His nerves too must be on edge.

"Yes." I cleared my throat hesitantly. "Vax, I don't have to tell you how to stand watch, but make sure the middies are extra vigilant. Please."

"Aye aye, sir." He understood my fears. Two years before, on our return from Hope Nation, we'd Defused for a nav check and come upon the remains of our sister ship *Telstar*. Worse, we'd been attacked by the bizarre fishlike creature that lurked behind her.

Three of our men had died; I bore scars of the encounter in nightmares that persisted to this day. Vax had paid a stiff price for his refusal to Fuse until I was safely aboard; I'd stripped him of his commission as punishment. Though I later relented, he'd lost three months' seniority and had an official rebuke that would affect his Naval career to the day he died or made Captain.

We had no idea where the alien had come from, or how it had arrived in interstellar space. Just as the attack on *Hibernia* by desperate miners at Miningcamp Station had made me wary of orbiting stations, the encounter with the aliens made me very uneasy while drifting in deep space, Defused and vulnerable.

After the watch I went back to my cabin. Amanda sat in the shadows, rocking little Nate, both of them half asleep. She smiled at me in the dim light.

"Can I take him, hon?" I held out my arms at her nod and we gently transferred my baby to me. I swayed as I stood, rocking him. Gravely he watched me. "I love you, Nate. Mommy loves you. Everything is going to be all right." At the reassurance of my quiet voice, his eyes closed. He drifted off to sleep. One tiny hand opened and closed a moment before he was still.

I loved fatherhood.

Quietly I put my son into his crib and covered him. Amanda stretched. "I heard the engines stop, Nicky." One grew used to the throb of the fusion drive and noticed its absence.

"Nav check, hon. We're waiting for the rest of the squadron to rendezvous." Though the margin of error in Fusion was reduced with the new controls, the other ships could Defuse anywhere within two or three light-hours, but we would find each other and quickly move closer. I hoped it would be soon.

During the first leg of our cruise I had run frequent General Quarters and Battle Stations drills. Should we detect an encroachment, alarms would ring throughout the ship; we'd go immediately to General

Quarters even though there was a near certainty the encroachment was an arriving vessel in our fleet.

A few hours later Amanda and I brought Nate to the dining hall for our evening meal. As we entered the conversation lulled momentarily. I escorted Amanda to her chair. The youngsters at our table stood reluctantly as we approached, knowing failure to do so would mean going without, again. I was embarked on teaching them more than how to refrain from throwing food at each other; I now labored at elements of courtesy.

"Evenin', Cap'n." A young girl was the first to speak, and they all followed suit, mumbling. Even big Eddie, though with his customary surliness.

"Good evening, um, ladies and gentlemen." I sat.

Days passed, during which I awaited the rest of our squadron with increasing impatience. I haunted the bridge, as if my presence could somehow trigger the alarms that would warn us of the encroachments we expected. When I caught Vax and Derek exchanging amused glances, I bit back a savage remark, recognized my irascibility, and left the bridge.

I went down to Level 2 and looked into hydroponics and recycling, more to give myself something to do than to carry out an inspection. Then, trying to ignore my persistent hunger, I climbed back to Level 1 and went to my cabin. Nate might be asleep, so I opened the hatch gently. Amanda sat in her favorite rocker, smiling. I grinned back. "Hi, hon, ready for lunch yet? I—"

We weren't alone. Midshipman Philip Tyre sat in my favorite chair, a smile fading from his handsome young face. He began to rise to attention but could not; my son Nate was in his arms.

"Why are you here?" I was white with anger. "Get out! Don't ever set foot in my cabin again!"

"Aye aye, sir!" He scrambled to his feet.

"The next time you touch my son I'll break your neck!" I was beside myself. "Out!" I flung open the hatch.

Amanda was on her feet. Quickly she took Nate from the dismayed boy, tugging at my arm. "Nicky, don't. I invited him."

"Go!" I slapped the hatch shut before Philip had half cleared it.

Nate was wailing. Amanda soothed him as she rounded on me. "How dare you! Philip was a guest!"

"He's despicable." My voice was tight. "I don't want him around you or Nate."

"Who are you to make that decision for me!" Her glare of fury met mine. Nate began to scream, reacting to our anger.

"Damn it, Amanda, this is my cabin!" Why couldn't she understand? I must have some place of refuge from the ship and its problems.

She put Nate in his crib and faced me, hands on hips, eyes blazing. "Either I have the freedom to entertain here, or I want a cabin of my own!"

"Ridiculous," I snapped.

Her slap was like a rifle shot and caught me unprepared. My cheek stung. Her voice dropped to an eerie calm. "Whatever else you do, Nick Seafort, you will take me seriously."

I stared at her in amazement. What had gotten into her? "I do," I protested. "Philip Tyre is one of my middies; I can't have him making himself at home in my own cabin."

"Your own cabin," she repeated quietly. A moment's thought, and then she nodded. "Yes, I suppose it *is* the Captain's cabin, not the Captain's wife's cabin. Very well. Where will you move me?"

"Nowhere, Amanda. I want you with me."

Her look was steadfast. "Not on those terms, Nick. It's not possible."

I loved her, yet she could be so infuriating. I sighed. "Amanda, what is it you want?"

"To know my status. If this isn't my cabin too, give me my own. I want the right to make my own friends. What do you want?"

I risked the hurt she might do me. "I want you to know how much I love you."

Her eyes misted and she bit her lip, shaking her head. Then she came to me and rested her hand on my shoulder. "I love you too, Nicky. But you have to give me room. Can you understand how I can love you and still be furious for what you did to poor Philip?"

"Poor Philip?" I waved in exasperation. "Good Lord, Amanda, you know what a vicious tyrant he was in the wardroom, until Derek put a stop to it."

"Until you put a stop to it, hon."

"Me?" My bitterness showed. "I gave him his way for so long that Alexi's still suffering. It took Derek to stand up to him. I just fumbled."

"That's not the issue," she reminded me.

"No," I agreed. "He's a sadist, that's the issue. I couldn't believe you let him into our cabin. Or around Nate."

She looked at me curiously. "Did you think today was the first time?"

"What? I mean, you—he—"

"I've had him here on other occasions. We sit and talk, like I do with Alexi. The look in his eyes when he holds Nate . . ."

"God, Amanda, how could you?"

"Nicky, you know I socialize with your officers. I lunch with Alexi when you're on watch, and—"

"Alexi's different. He's a friend."

She met my eye squarely. "So is Philip. Mine, at least." She paused, debating whether to continue. "And I resent what you did to him. He was here by invitation, and you threw him out."

"I suppose you expect me to apologize to him?" I meant it as sarcasm.

"He deserves an apology, whether he gets it or not."

My temper finally unraveled. "God—" With difficulty I stopped short of blasphemy. "—bless it, Amanda, I don't understand you! I will not abase myself before that . . . that person! Not for you, not for him!"

"Why not for yourself," I heard her say as the hatch slammed shut behind me. I stomped down the corridor. Vax was just outside his cabin. He made as if to speak, but averted his gaze after seeing my expression.

I was halfway to the bridge when the alarms went off.

Alexi's taut voice crackled over the speakers. "All hands to General Quarters! Captain to the bridge! General Quarters, all hands!"

I raced down the corridor and slapped open the bridge hatch. "What is it?" I skidded to a halt.

"Encroachment, sir." Alexi's fingers were busy at the console.

"Four hundred thousand kilometers, closing." Danny. "Shape and size consistent with *Freiheit*, sir."

"Let's hope so." I slid into my seat. "Alarms off, Danny." The din ceased. "Send our recognition signals."

"Aye aye, sir." In an emergency Danny was all business. For a few seconds, silence. Then his high-pitched adolescent voice, with what sounded like relief. "*Freiheit*'s code received, sir. I think it's them."

My nerves were still jumpy. "Never mind what you think."

"Aye aye, sir," said Danny, subdued. "Second recognition code received, sir. Positive ID on *Freiheit*."

Nonetheless, I took the crew to Battle Stations as we approached. I was sick with the memory of *Telstar*, from behind which an apparition had emerged. I only relaxed when *Freiheit*'s reassuring lights appeared on the simulscreens, and Captain Tenere's familiar voice boomed through the speaker. "*Freiheit* to *Portia*. Are you there, Seafort?"

"Ready and waiting, Mr. Tenere." He was senior to me by several years and was a full Captain to boot; I really should have called him "sir." But among Captains informality seemed to prevail.

"Well, we'll probably have to wait a bit for those great rowboats to catch up to us. Would you care to join me for dinner? I hear we're serving chicken Kiev."

I hesitated. I was reluctant to leave my ship, but my stomach juices were churning. And the friendly company would be welcome. "Thank you, yes. My wife is aboard too, sir."

"Well, she's the reason you were invited, son. We'll look forward to seeing you both."

After breaking off the connection I went to find Amanda; the invitation would be a good diversion from our quarrel. And so it was, until the question arose what to do with Nate. I flatly refused to bring a babe in arms to a formal dinner. Amanda, hesitant to leave him, had to concede my point. She agreed to find a baby-sitter among the passengers.

I rearranged the watch schedule to make sure Vax Holser was on the bridge while we were gone. We took the gig across, with a sailor to man it. Captain Tenere met us at his lock with a jovial smile. "We didn't get much chance to talk at Lunapolis, Mr. Seafort. May I call you Nick? My name's Andrew. The Admiral did most of the talking and not much listening, if you ask me."

His bluntness made me uncomfortable, though I'd said as much to Amanda. I made some noncommittal answer and we chatted about other things. During dinner, though, he returned to our briefing. "It doesn't make sense having us drift here, by my way of thinking. I don't think there's a chance of encountering anything—good Lord, look how far out we are—but say we did: if we were disabled, Tremaine would still Defuse right into the middle of it. So what's been gained?"

"Well, we're the point of the wedge," I said, temporizing.

"I suppose," he said. "Still, we're so deep interstellar . . ."

"About as deep as *Telstar* when we found her." My tone was somber.

"You know," he mused, "that's what I can't fathom. How could those beasties get out there? I saw the holovids you shot. Those, what'd you call them? Goldfish? They're organic, they've got to be. No place for fusion drives. They couldn't, uh, swim that far, not without spending centuries en route. How do they carry enough propellant? What in Lord God's name were they doing?"

"I don't know," I said. And I didn't want to think about it. Amanda, sensing my mood, changed the subject.

After the meal, in the privacy of his cabin, Captain Tenere nonchalantly served us a glass of wine. I was uneasy about sharing contraband but didn't want to offend him, so I took a cautious sip. Amanda, less bothered about such niceties, downed hers with enjoyment.

We returned to *Portia* shortly after. I went immediately to the bridge; Amanda went to the cabin to check on Nate.

During the next two days three more ships of our fleet appeared, and on the third day *Challenger* Defused, some two hundred fifty thousand kilometers distant. Remarkably close, given the distance traveled. We waited for the remaining vessels amid a flurry of directives from the flagship.

I made myself busy on the bridge, while Amanda occupied herself with Nate. Twice I returned to my cabin to find her in earnest consultation with Alexi. I knew there was something not quite right that the Captain's wife involved herself with his officers, but after the row we'd had over Philip, I was careful not to let my uneasiness show.

Finally the remainder of the squadron arrived, and one by one we Fused again. *Freiheit* and *Portia* remained on station until the others were gone. Then I checked our figures one final time and gave the order to Fuse. As the engines kicked in, our screens went dark.

After the flurry of activity, Fusion was duller than ever. I spent about half my waking time with Nate and Amanda, and the other half on the bridge, though there was little for me to do. I shared watches with the Pilot, with Vax, with the midshipmen.

Derek Carr, whom I'd enlisted as a youngster of sixteen on *Hibernia*, was by this time a seasoned middy with an air of confidence he wore well on his lean, aristocratic face. He was sensitive to my moods, chatting when I felt sociable, courteously remaining silent when I was not.

Rafe, like any younger middy, approached the bridge with great anxiety, and didn't dare speak unless spoken to.

I'd known Alexi Tamarov since my first day aboard *Hibernia*; I could tell he was troubled. Rather than fuss over him, I let it be. I watched the Log closely. The demerits to Philip Tyre tapered off, then increased in a sudden flurry of fault-finding. I knew to a certainty that Mr. Tyre hadn't earned the demerits; like Derek, he was a competent, seasoned midshipman. Again I wished I hadn't chosen to bring the boy along; Philip was a lightning rod for the resentment of his seniors.

One afternoon, on the idle bridge, Alexi thrust his hands in and out of his pockets, distracted. Finally he said, "I have something to say to Mr. Tyre, sir, and I'd like you to be present."

I raised my eyebrow. "Oh?"

"Yes, sir. I told him to come to my cabin after my watch."

When the watch ended Alexi and I strode in silence to his quarters. Philip Tyre waited anxiously outside with a look of foreboding that deepened at the presence of his Captain.

Inside, Alexi stared at the midshipman until Philip began to knead the edge of his jacket in an agony of anticipation.

Silence.

Abruptly Philip blurted, "Sir, if it's about last week's demerits, I've worked off three. I'm sorry I haven't had time to do the others, I've been busy with the transpops and—"

"It's over."

"Mr. Tamarov?"

Alexi said heavily, "It's over. I'm done with you."

Philip looked back and forth between us, biting his lip. "I don't understand what I've done, sir. Please, I'm sorry if—"

"Midshipman, I've hated you more than any person I've ever known." Tyre drew in a sharp breath. Alexi continued, "You've deserved to be hated, Mr. Tyre. You've done hateful things."

I felt a pang of alarm, not knowing where this was heading. I opened my mouth to intervene.

Alexi added, "And now I've done hateful things." I kept silent. "After what you did to me and the other middies on *Hibernia* I swore to have vengeance on you, Mr. Tyre, and I have. Oath or no, I can't do it anymore. Lord God will understand, or He won't. I set aside my oath. I renounce vengeance."

The boy's eyes were riveted on his lieutenant.

"I don't like you, Philip; I never will. But I'll leave you alone. Any demerits I issue in future will only be when you've truly earned them. I'll try to learn how to be fair again."

I stirred. "Alexi, enough said."

"No, sir, please pardon me. There's more to be said. Mr. Tyre, for over a year I've been as cruel as you were to us, until I can't stomach what I've become. I've watched you, even when you thought I was indifferent. I was never indifferent to you, Mr. Tyre. And when we've worked together, as we did with the transpops, I've found what the Captain said to be true. You are a diligent worker, a willing assistant, a dutiful subordinate. I can find no fault in your work. I commend you in that. I will so note in your next fitness report." Alexi took a long breath and let it out slowly. "Well, it's over now. I don't apologize. I will let you be. You are dismissed."

Philip Tyre saluted automatically and turned to the hatch. He paused. "Sir—I—"

"Dismissed," Alexi said woodenly.

"Let him speak." My tone was gruff.

Tyre swallowed. "On that frightful trip back from Hope Nation—after they made you lieutenant—I thought I'd go insane. Nothing in my life was as awful as the way you treated me. I tried to bear it until we got home, but finally I couldn't take any more."

His eyes were fastened on the bulkhead, recalling a private nightmare. "I wrote out a note and put clean clothes on and lay down on my bunk to take the pills I'd stolen from *Hibernia*'s infirmary, and then I wasn't brave enough to do it. I lay there, a helpless coward, until it was time to go on watch again. Those months without end . . ."

"When we got home, when Admiral Brentley reassigned me to *Portia* instead of letting me resign, I convinced myself it would get better on a new ship. But it went on, and on . . . Four, no, five times I've tried to end it with the pills, only each time I didn't, I don't know why. Except once when I took three and it wasn't enough."

His cheeks were wet as he turned to me. "Captain, I don't know what I did to make you hate me so, that's God's honest truth!"

Alexi stirred angrily but Tyre rushed on. "Captain, you warned me, I know that. I just thought I—I was doing my job. To this day I don't know what was wrong about the way I treated the midshipmen. But . . ." His eyes fell. "You kept telling me it was improper, and Mr. Tamarov despises me, and Mr. Carr . . . so I have to believe you. I know something I've done is terribly wrong. I don't really understand it, I think that's why I tried to kill myself, but I believe you. So, I'm sorry. I'll try to do better. Mr. Tamarov, sir, I ask your pardon. If you can't forgive me, try to believe that I mean that. I'm sorry for whatever hurt I did you."

He brought himself to attention, snapped an Academy salute, wheeled, and was gone.

Alexi moaned, "Lord Jesus, what have I done?"

"I did it to both of you," I said, my tone bitter. "I left you to suffer, then I put you in charge of him. You're not to blame." I loathed myself; I had to be alone. "You've done right, Alexi. Have peace." I didn't know if he heard.

34

When she wasn't hovering over Nate, Amanda busied herself arranging classes. As weeks passed into months our little boy grew unconscionably fast. In the privacy of our cabin I would take him on my lap and jiggle him while he sat contentedly exploring the textures of my jacket and shirt. Occasionally, on the bridge, I would find my knee jiggling absently while I chatted with Vax or Pilot Van Peer. But I never brought Nate to the bridge; it was one thing to have my family aboard; quite another to involve them in my official duties.

Occasionally Amanda invited passengers to visit, and once she asked if I would mind her having the officers to afternoon tea. As she was confined to shipboard society for sixteen months, I didn't feel free to object, though it made me uncomfortable. I did ask her to hold her party in one of the lounges instead of our cabin. She agreed without comment. All the officers were duly invited; all showed up except Philip Tyre, who sent a polite note indicating he wasn't feeling well. Amanda wordlessly handed me his note of regret.

I began to look forward to our next Defuse in three weeks, but I knew with growing unease that there was business unattended to. I tried to thrust it out of my mind until the night I found myself tossing sleeplessly for hours; the next morning I went to the wardroom and resolutely knocked at the hatch.

By ship's custom the midshipmen's wardroom was private territory; the Captain didn't enter uninvited, except on inspection.

Derek Carr opened the hatch, came to attention.

"As you were, Mr. Carr."

He stood down. "Would you care to come in, sir?"

Now I could enter. "Thank you. Er, Mr. Tyre, I was looking for you. I'd like a word." Philip's apprehensive look made me even more bitter. "Derek—Mr. Carr—could I trouble you to let me speak privately with Mr. Tyre?"

"Aye aye, sir. Of course, sir." He scrambled to put on his jacket and tie. "Make yourself at home." He left quickly.

Philip swallowed. "I meant no disrespect by not coming to your party, sir, I—"

"No." My tone was blunt. "You were quite right not to attend, after what I said to you." He colored. I took a deep breath and forced out the words. "Philip, I've come to apologize and to withdraw what I said in my cabin."

"Please, sir," he blurted. "There's no need—"

"You will recall," I said, overriding him, "my admonishing Mr. Tamarov that I will have courtesy among officers. When you were a guest in my cabin my behavior to you was far worse than discourteous."

"I understand, sir," he stammered. "I know how you feel—"

"But that's the point, Philip. I wasn't only discourteous, I was wrong to feel that way. Your behavior to me has never warranted it, not even when you were abusing the other middies, and in any event that's long past. You are welcome in my cabin as Amanda's guest or mine. I have no objection to your holding my son, if you come to visit."

My cheeks were aflame, but I managed to hold his eye. "This is a personal matter between us, Philip, and I won't hold it against you no matter how you respond. But I ask you to forgive my foul manners."

"There's nothing to forgive, sir. You had every right—"

"None of us ever has that right," I said with savage force. "Otherwise you had the right to pile demerits on Derek and Alexi until they were sent to the barrel, over and over again. Viciousness and cruelty are never excusable! Never!" My vehemence shook me. I wondered what had caused it.

He looked at me in wonderment. "Is that really what I was doing?" he asked, half aloud. Then he focused again on me. "Thank you for coming." He hesitated. "I feel out of line saying it, sir, but since you asked me, I forgive you. I'd like not to talk about it anymore, sir. It's embarrassing to hear you apologize." He met my eye and smiled weakly.

I felt awkward, not knowing how to leave. Impulsively I put out my hand, and after a second's hesitation he took it. Then he seemed reluctant to let go. I gave his hand an extra squeeze before releasing it.

He couldn't have offered to shake hands, of course. To touch the Captain without permission was a capital offense.

I took my accustomed place on the bridge, reining in my unease. I thought our orders to Defuse seven times instead of twice for nav checks was a waste of propellant. Every time the squadron assembled, each ship had to maneuver to its station in relation to the others.

Our auxiliary thrusters used LH2 and LOX as propellant, manufactured from our stores of water; we had ample power from the fusion engines for such conversion. But a ship could carry just so much water, and it was a long way to Hope Nation.

Further, assembling the squadron over and again was a waste of time; we might wait days on end for all our ships to arrive; the speed of Fusion varied with minute differences in the design of each ship's drive and its tubes.

I sighed. I'd chosen a Navy life, and long dreary voyages were part of it. "Vax, sound General Quarters."

Alarms shrilled throughout the ship as crew and officers hurried to duty stations. All noncritical systems were closed down. The airtight hatches that separated corridor sections slid shut. During General Quarters, passengers were expected to wait in their cabins with hatches sealed; the purser and his mates went through the corridors checking each cabin.

When all was ready I ran my finger down the screen and Defused. I caught my breath as the myriads of stars reappeared on our simulscreens.

"Check for encroachments, Mr. Carr." Vax was terse, his huge shoulder muscles taut.

"Aye aye, sir." A moment's pause. "No encroachments, sir."

"We're first again," I said. "We wait."

The next to show up, two days later, was *Kitty Hawk*, under Captain Derghinski. She maneuvered to her station and drifted at rest relative to *Portia*, waiting as we did for the rest of the squadron. For some reason she had outrun *Freiheit*, which Defused into normal space a few hours after.

Waiting for the fleet, I'd camped on the bridge for nearly three days with only occasional breaks for rest. When I found myself dozing at my seat I knew it set a bad example for the other officers; reluctantly I trudged back to my cabin, undressed, and collapsed in bed. Though Nate was crying loudly, within moments I was asleep.

Minutes later Amanda shook me awake. I propped myself up, shook my head in a vain effort to clear it. "What now?"

"Sorry, hon. You slept right through the caller. Alexi is paging you to the bridge."

Panic seized me. "Trouble?" I snatched the caller, thumbed it to the bridge setting. "What's wrong?"

"*Challenger*'s arrived, sir. Admiral Tremaine's been calling you every two minutes."

I cursed, tugged at my jacket. "I'm on the way." I staggered to the hatch, adrenaline barely overpowering the fog in my head.

On the bridge the simulscreens were in visual contact with *Challenger;* Admiral Tremaine's unfriendly face loomed as I dropped into my seat. "Captain Seafort reporting, sir."

"Where the hell have you been, Seafort?" Tremaine's features were contorted with rage. "You were supposed to guard the rendezvous, not lollygag about in bed! I expect to find *you* on the bridge, not some infant lieutenant!" Alexi flushed.

"I was asleep, sir," I said. My head was filled with cotton.

"It's *your* aliens we're watching for, Seafort!" The Admiral's voice was a snarl. "Keep a proper watch, do you hear? That's why you were sent ahead in the first place!"

"Aye aye, sir." It was all I could say.

It didn't seem to satisfy him. "I warned you: any disobedience and I'd relieve you. I have a good mind to do it now!" At my side, Alexi drew in a breath.

"I'm sorry, sir." I said no more, though the injustice rankled.

"Don't be sorry, do your job." His tone was acid. "I'll be over to inspect when I'm done with *Freiheit.*"

"Aye aye, sir." The connection went dead.

"That ass!" Alexi pounded the console. "He's so unfair—"

I snarled, "Shut your mouth!"

Alexi stopped in midword.

"Don't you ever—and I mean ever, Lieutenant—criticize your commanding officer in my presence. Is that understood?" My fists were clenched.

"Aye aye, sir," said Alexi, his tone meek.

"I wouldn't expect that remark from a first-year cadet, Mr. Tamarov. We'll obey the Admiral's orders without question and without comment."

"Aye aye, sir."

I let out an explosive breath. "Very well. I know you meant to sympathize. Thank you for your intentions." I turned back to the screen. "He'll be here within the hour. Let's get as ready as we can."

Admiral Tremaine and two lieutenants who served as his aides crossed in *Challenger*'s launch. The Admiral bustled through *Portia* issuing running commentaries to his aide, who made copious notes. He found fault with the airlock watch crew, wrinkled his nose at the crew berths, glanced in the engine room and found nothing amiss. "To the bridge, Seafort," was all he said.

I followed a step behind. Vax Holser and Midshipman Rafe Treadwell snapped to attention as we entered; Tremaine didn't bother to release them. Let's see your Log." He snapped it on, flipping through the entries. Vax glanced at me; I kept my face impassive.

"A lot of disciplines for a small ship. Shows a lack of leadership." I was taken aback; such a comment should have been made privately, if at all. "I see you have a middy who likes trouble. This Tyre: dozens of demerits. Is that one Tyre?" He waved at Rafe Treadwell.

"No, sir. Mr. Tyre is in the comm room. That situation's under control now."

"So you say," he said, glowering. "The trick, Seafort, is to come down hard enough so you don't have to do it often."

"Yes, sir." I wondered how to divert him. "The laser simulations—"

"Don't try to distract me." He scowled, and I reddened.

"Sorry, sir."

"Look." He drew me close, and for a moment his tone seemed almost pleading. "This is my first squadron, Seafort, and they'll be watching my Logs like a hawk. Everything has to be right. *Everything.*"

"I understand, sir."

"Send him up to be caned."

I was astounded. "What?"

"You heard me. Teach the middy that we won't tolerate insubordination. Give him a caning today."

"But—"

His eyes turned cold. "I see where he gets it from, Seafort."

There was only one possible response. "Aye aye, sir."

"Very well. I'll inspect again after the next Defuse. By then I expect to see a tighter ship." He beckoned to his aide and stalked from the bridge.

I followed, benumbed. The Admiral's launch was at the aft airlock, on Level 2. His party descended the ladder and followed the corridor around the bend.

"Mira da man! He da bossman, mira alla gol'!"

Furious, I pushed into the crush of jabbering joeykids. "Get away from him! Don't touch him!"

"Watchadoon, man? Whatsa fatman doonhere?"

The transpops, in a playful mood, shoved and pointed derisively at the braid on Tremaine's dress uniform. "Mus' be a Boss Cap'n, mira alla gold!"

I collided with Eddie's large form. The boy whirled angrily before recognizing me. I hissed, "Get them away from him, flank!"

Something in my tone reached him. He flung the nearest boy aside and collared the girl closest to the Admiral. "Gii'm room, trannies! Oudahere! Backoff! Oudahere!"

In moments Tremaine was free of the jostling, livid with rage. "Who are those—animals! God curse it, Seafort, what kind of ship do you run here?"

"They're transients, sir," I said quickly. "They were assigned at the last minute in Lunapolis. I'm sorry, sir. They don't know any better."

"You let that trash run wild with decent passengers aboard? Lock them up! It's no wonder your ship is a mess!"

"I'm sorry, they—"

"They're scum! Brig the lot of them the next time I board!" With that he turned and disappeared into the airlock.

The look on my face kept the transients well clear as I stalked to the ladder. A few moments later I was in my place on the bridge, but I couldn't keep to my seat. I paced back and forth, my fury welling. Vax had the good sense to say nothing. Rafe Treadwell sat very still, his eyes glued to his console.

After a time I was calm enough to drop heavily into my soft black leather chair. This would pass; soon we would Fuse and continue on our way.

I could guess, though, what the Admiral's visit would do to *Portia*'s morale. My lieutenants had heard him disparage how I ran my ship; his stinging rebuke wouldn't help my authority. And what the midshipmen witnessed was hardly a proper example for their own conduct.

The midshipmen! What was I to do about Philip Tyre? I rocked back and forth, dismayed. The Admiral had given me a direct order; I was to have Philip caned.

The order was utterly unjust; I was Captain of *Portia* and in charge of my ship's discipline. Tyre's demerits littered the Log because of Alexi's attitude, not Philip's. The nightmare relations between Tyre, Alexi, and myself had just begun to be resolved, and Lord God knew what effect an unwarranted caning would have on the young middy now.

Could I appeal Tremaine's order? Call him, after he calmed down? It was unlikely to succeed, and I'd refocus his wrath on myself. Better for *Portia*'s sake to let the order stand.

A wave of disgust made me cringe. Cane Philip, because I was afraid the Admiral would be annoyed at my protest? What kind of coward had I become? Unconsciously I rose from my chair and began to pace, my ire rising anew.

After a time I was aware of the intense silence. Midshipman Treadwell was still trying to make himself invisible. Vax watched with a pen-

sive look. When I caught his eye his glance dropped. My disgust rose to
new heights. Now my own officers were afraid to meet my gaze.

I made an effort to smile. As calmly as I could I said, "Rafe, do
some nav problems. Determine our position and plot a course to
Caltech. Lieutenant Holser will help if you run into trouble. Vax, if you
would?"

With the two of them concentrating on their console I resumed my
pacing. Well, I had to try to change the Admiral's mind, even if he didn't
like it.

I would wait two hours; perhaps then Tremaine would be more
agreeable. I yawned, realizing I was still exhausted. There was no reason
to stay on the bridge. I left the middy to his calculations with Vax,
trudged to my cabin for a nap before dinner. I told Amanda what had
transpired, as I slipped off my jacket and tie.

"Oh, poor Philip." Her eyes glistened. "You won't let them hurt
him, will you?"

"I'll try to get him out of it," I said. "But it was a direct order.
There's not much I can do if Tremaine won't listen." She wanted to
argue but I was too tired. I set the alarm, rolled over, and went to sleep.

Three hours later I felt no better. I stopped at the bridge before
going to the dining hall. At my console I smoothed my hair, straightened
my tie while the comm room connected me to *Challenger*. Captain Hasselbrad came on the line. "The Admiral's not aboard, Captain Seafort.
He's at dinner on *Kitty Hawk* with Derghinski. You could page him if it's
important."

I thanked him and snapped off the screen. There was no point
whatsoever in calling the Admiral from his dinner to make my request.
He'd refuse instantly and I would probably be relieved from command,
as I should be for such bad judgment. I went down to dinner.

Eddie Boss, Annie, and the other transients stood as I approached.
As we sat Annie said uncomfortably, "Din' mean makin' trouble wid
fatman, Cap'n. Funnin', was all." Either their English was improving or I
was developing an ear for transpop dialect. Perhaps both.

"Thank you, Annie. I appreciate that."

"We leave'm lone nothertime," said Eddie, glowering at the others.
"Stay way f'mim." He poked Deke, who nodded sullenly. The others
nodded agreement.

I called *Challenger* again an hour after dinner; the Admiral still
hadn't returned. I chewed at my lip. Tremaine had snarled, "Do it today." I waited impatiently on the bridge. At 21:30 ship's time, I tried
again.

"Is the Admiral back, Captain Hasselbrad?"

"Yes." The Captain paused, his face impassive. "He went to bed. He left orders not to bother him except for an emergency." His glance met mine and I wondered how much he knew. How must it feel to be Captain under the Admiral's constant supervision? I couldn't ask, of course.

"Thank you, sir." I broke the connection. Well, there was nothing to do but carry out the order. Philip would survive, as he had before. I opened my mouth to summon the midshipman to his fate, then hesitated.

If I did nothing, Tremaine would never know. Three months from now he'd hardly remember to check my Log for a middy's discipline. Vax would keep his mouth shut and Philip need never be told what he'd faced. With a sense of relief I knew I'd stumbled on a solution. Philip had been through more than enough, and we'd promised him it was over. I'd be violating orders, but I would have to live with that.

"I'm going to bed," I said.

"Good night, sir." Vax hesitated. "And Mr., uh, Tyre—?"

He'd blundered into it. Better nothing had been said. "I'm going to my cabin," I said firmly. I went to the hatch. "Good night."

I tossed and turned for a long while. Then I slept.

Father and I walked slowly down the shaded walk to the Academy gates. My duffel hung heavy at my side. When we reached the compound his hand rested on my shoulder for the briefest moment, but he said nothing. I turned to look at him. He turned my shoulders, pushed me toward the open gates. I walked through.

When I turned to say good-bye he was striding away, not looking back. I felt the iron ring close around my neck as the gates swung shut.

I woke in gasping panic. Amanda was sitting at my side, her soft hand stroking my shoulder. "Nicky, it's all right. I'm with you. You were having a nightmare."

"Ungh." I swung my legs to the floor, shuddering. "The dream again."

"Your father?"

"Yes." I put my head in my hands. Would it ever go away? After a while I pulled myself together and went to the head to wash the fear and sweat off me. I'd had the dream off and on since I'd gone to Academy at thirteen.

Other than the iron ring, it was all true.

I came back to my bunk. Well, Father wasn't aboard *Portia*. He was back in Cardiff, set in the dour hardness of his ways.

Musing, I was drawn back to my studies at our worn kitchen table, Father watching while I worked my way through the difficult texts. I recalled our Bible readings. He was intoning from Leviticus. I heard myself make some flippant remark about an oath, and recalled his stern rebuke. My sense of shame.

"Promise, Nicholas." He waited for my answer. "Promise it, son."

"I do, Father."

"Say the words, Nicholas."

I closed my eyes. "My oath is my bond. I will let them destroy me before I swear to an oath I will not fulfill. My oath is all that I am."

I looked up from my bunk, my eyes stinging. I knew the value of an oath; as Lord God knew, I'd taken one often enough. That solemn ritual my first day at Academy: *I, Nicholas Ewing Seafort, do swear upon my immortal soul to preserve and protect the Charter of the General Assembly of the United Nations, to give loyalty and obedience for the term of my enlistment to the Naval Service of the United Nations and to obey all its lawful orders and regulations, so help me Lord God Almighty.* The oath that still bound me.

I cast about for an escape. *"To obey all lawful orders and regulations."* No doubt, Admiral Tremaine's order was unjust. Nonetheless, it was lawful. I was bound to obey it, despite my flailing to escape.

I glanced sharply at the clock: 23:35. I still had time. Philip would have to suffer. My voice rasped over the caller. "Midshipman Tyre to the bridge, immediately." I threw on my clothes.

"Nicky, what are you doing?" Amanda, her eyes worried.

"What I must." I ignored her hurt.

Philip Tyre was waiting with Vax when I arrived. He looked like he too had been sleeping.

I managed somehow to meet his eye. I said, my voice harsh, "Mr. Tyre, during his inspection Admiral Tremaine reviewed our Log. It is full of your demerits. You're to be caned for insubordination. Go to Lieutenant Holser's cabin. He will be along in a moment."

Philip's astonishment gave way to another expression: betrayal? Emotions flickered across his face before his training reasserted itself. "Aye aye, sir!" He saluted, turned on his heel, and marched out.

I turned to Vax and rasped, "I'll finish the watch. Get it over with!"

"Aye aye, sir."

Vax's expression told me how he felt, and I was much relieved. If Vax let Philip off lightly, not too much harm need be done.

As Vax strode to the hatch I recalled with a pang our earlier conversation. How could Vax let Philip off easily, after what he'd said about enforcing discipline?

No, Vax couldn't take it on himself to do right by Philip. I was disgusted; now I was making Vax choose between disobeying orders or brutalizing Philip, because I wouldn't take the responsibility I must.

"Just a moment!"

Vax stopped at the hatch, watching me.

"Vax, I—" The words grated in my throat. I said firmly, "I order you to go quite easy on him. Do you understand?"

Vax's face lit up in a warm grin. "Aye aye, sir." Still smiling, he left the bridge with a jaunty step.

It was done. Tremaine hadn't said anything about going hard on Philip, had he? I'd carried out my orders to the letter.

Despite my sophistry, I felt sick. I had skirted my oath and risked my soul.

We were Fused, and days passed with dreary slowness. Amanda taught the transients what she could; the girl named Annie laboriously learned to write her name and they were both elated.

For two days after the Admiral's inspection Alexi volunteered himself on the watch roster to replace Philip Tyre, though from Philip's gait it clearly wasn't necessary. I said nothing. Philip Tyre gave me a shy smile on our first encounter after his visit to Vax's cabin. I didn't want to be reminded of my folly; I stared coldly until his smile faded.

My son grew daily. The most precious moments of my life were spent playing on the deck of my cabin while he drooled happily on my white shirt and tie. With an effort he could turn himself over. I wondered when he would begin to crawl.

After three weeks in Fusion we had settled down once more to ship's routine. Mrs. Attani arranged a party in honor of her son Gregor's eighteenth birthday. Naval policy in such matters was ambiguous. There was only one class of passengers aboard Naval vessels; all were provided similar cabins and were served the same meals. But wealthy passengers could buy additional amenities, such as Mrs. Attani's party. Many of the passengers were invited, though not all, and of the officers only Amanda and myself.

Amanda and I agreed that the party, even if held in the ship's familiar dining hall, was too formal an occasion to bring little Nate. We learned that the young baby-sitter who had watched Nate on other occasions had also been invited.

"Too bad Erin can't watch him, Nicky. Mrs. Attani's made such a

fuss; she wants the party to be perfect. If Nate cries she'll take it personally."

"Have you asked Philip Tyre?" My tone was gruff.

Amanda shot me a sharp glance; when she realized I was serious
she put her arms around me, kissed me on the end of my nose, and
captured my heart afresh.

Young Gregor stood in the entranceway greeting his guests, his
mother at his side. At eighteen, Attani was still four years short of his
majority, though I, at twenty-one, had been an adult for five years by act
of the General Assembly. As a cadet I'd been a minor, but on promotion
to midshipman I'd attained my majority and could drink, vote, and
marry.

At home one occasionally heard agitation to reduce the age of majority to twenty, but I doubted it would come to anything. The aftermath
of the Rebellious Ages had left society far more cautious and conservative than once it had been.

"Thank you for coming, Captain." Gregor's manners were impecca-
ble. Well, by virtue of office I was of his class.

"It's our honor, Mr. Attani," I said stiffly, matching his courtesy. As
Captain and an adult I might use his first name, and sometimes did, but
it would be graceless to patronize him at his own celebration.

Arm in arm, Amanda and I moved into the crowd. I felt awkward
and unsophisticated among our cosmopolitan passengers. Usually, I depended on Amanda to make casual conversation and tonight was no
exception. We nibbled on canapés and settled near a group that was
chatting with animation.

"It's worth the privation to reach open spaces," a woman said. "A
whole unsettled continent! For the first time in our lives we'll have room
to stretch."

"Emily Valdez," whispered Amanda. "As in the Valdez Permabat-
tery." She, or her family, had enormous wealth.

"But all the settlements are on Eastern Continent." Walter Dakko,
young Chris's father. "The holo said Western Continent isn't opened for
settlement yet."

"How long can that last?" A heavy-jowled man, and belligerent.
"Land sitting there unused!"

"I wonder what the colony's really like," mused Galena Dakko, her
arm linked in her husband's.

"Wait a year and you'll see, honey," someone said dryly.

"All of us bound for Hope Nation, yet no one knows quite what to
expect," remarked Walter Dakko. "We've put our faith in—in a—"

"U.N. emigration brochure." Emily Valdez was rueful. "We may have consigned ourselves to years on this—this coop, only to find we've all been had."

"Shh, the Captain will hear you," someone whispered.

"I don't care," said Miss Valdez defiantly. "Captain Seafort, is our imprisonment a good bargain? Is Hope Nation worth the cost of getting there?"

"What cost, Miss Valdez?" I asked.

"Well." A pretty laugh. "The accommodations. I'm sure you do your best, but really!" Amanda squeezed my arm.

"Is something wrong with your cabin?" I was puzzled.

"Not in the sense that you could send a man to fix it. But it's so ridiculously small, Captain. At the hacienda, even my dressing room wasn't so cramped. How could one expect civilized people to live in such a space for extended periods. Sixteen months? Really!"

Amanda's grip tightened further but I ignored the signal. "Would you care to exchange cabins with one of my officers?" My voice was cool.

"Which one?" Miss Valdez was smiling.

"Any of them. My two lieutenants are fortunate; their cabins are about half the size of yours. Well, perhaps a bit smaller. My midshipmen sleep in a wardroom the size of a lieutenant's cabin, and we carry three middies. On my last trip to Hope Nation four of us shared a similar wardroom."

"That's true, then?" asked Galena Dakko. "You were a midshipman on your last cruise? I'd heard rumors, but it didn't seem polite to ask."

"Yes, Mrs. Dakko. At that time a cabin like yours was beyond my wildest dreams."

Mrs. Attani had come up behind us. "But your officers enlisted as children, Captain. Surely they're accustomed to the crowding."

"Yes." I was curt. How could people of such wealth understand wardroom life? Four joeys of both sexes in the midst of turbulent adolescence, crammed like sardines into the tiny wardroom, living intimately while maintaining the rigid Navy hierarchy even among themselves. No, I couldn't explain that.

"You have to understand." Walter Dakko's tone was placating. "We don't have your training in hardships. We're from comfortable backgrounds and find the cramped quarters quite difficult to bear."

I lost patience. "Consider yourself fortunate, then. For lack of space other passengers have to sleep six to a cabin."

"That's dreadful!" said Mrs. Dakko. "In heaven's name, who?"

"The Lower New Yorkers."

"Oh, the trannies?" Mrs. Attani laughed. "I thought you meant real passengers."

"Shall we find a drink, Nicky?" Amanda.

"No. The New Yorkers are passengers, madam, like yourselves."

"Not really." Miss Valdez spoke lightly. "More like captive savages. Or refugees, if you will. They're certainly not proper passengers. Anyway, they're used to crowds. I'm sure the ship is better than what they knew before."

"It's criminal to put them on a passenger ship with respectable people." Walter Dakko seemed indignant. "Some of us have to share cabins all the way to Hope Nation thanks to those hoodlums! It's inexcusable."

"A cold drink would be really nice," said Amanda, an edge to her voice.

"Later. You're right, Mr. Dakko; the crowded accommodations are inexcusable. Six to a cabin? Imagine! Fortunately I have a solution. The transients need to experience your knowledge and cultivation. By sharing cabins with you they'll become more civilized. I'll work out more equitable cabin assignments as soon as possible. Come, Amanda, we'll find those drinks now." I nodded politely at their stunned and gaping faces.

"Damn it, Nicky," said Amanda, a few steps away.

"I couldn't help it."

"Yes, you could! So they were obnoxious; did you have to make enemies of them?"

"I'd rather have them as enemies than friends."

Her eyes teared. "But I wouldn't. You have your officers and your bridge. All I have is people like them, and the trannies!"

"Oh, hon, I'm sorry. I forget." I offered a hug.

A giggle broke through her cross expression. "You won't really do it, Nicky? The look on Walter's face when you suggested sharing his cabin with a transpop . . ."

"I should," I grumbled.

"Please, Nick, they're all influential. If word got back to Admiralty . . ."

I sighed. Of course she was right. My authority was unlimited; I could assign cabins as I chose. But I had Admiralty to reckon with on my return, and they would take a dim view of my evicting our elite for a swarm of streeters. Still . . . I savored the idea for a time before reluctantly setting it aside.

*   *   *

I held drills and exercises to keep the crew alert. They helped keep me alert as well; I'd begun to find confinement in *Portia* stifling. She was a small ship, much smaller than any I'd sailed before. There were few passengers whose company I enjoyed, and most of them weren't enthused with me either.

After it became evident that I wasn't going to carry out my threat to change passengers' cabins, I was grudgingly readmitted into society, but my main avenue of interchange with the passengers—dinner at the Captain's table—had been lost when I reassigned seating so the officers could dine with the transpop youths.

That too grew tiresome. I settled into an uneasy truce with the youngsters at my table. I'd made them fully aware of my power by denying them their meals until they behaved—probably a violation of regs, if the rules applied to involuntary underage passengers—and they weren't ready to test me further as yet. Still, their cooperation was minimal at best.

Annie, whom I'd mistaken for a boy during the corridor riot, was now unmistakably feminine. Perhaps the sustained nutrition was helping develop her figure. Certainly the hairdo she appeared in one afternoon, to the jeers of her young male associates, also contributed. She had no idea of her age but was assumed to be roughly seventeen.

One day, I came into my cabin and stopped short. Sitting over a holovid on the breakfast table were Amanda and Eddie Boss. Eddie lurched to his feet as I entered.

"No makin' trouble, Cap'n. Lady she say allri' beinhere. She say."

I was careful how I spoke, remembering too well my scene with Philip Tyre. "I understand, Eddie. It's all right. Sit down."

"Don' wan' stay. Gotta find Deke. Wanna go." He edged nervously toward the door.

"Thank you for coming, Eddie," Amanda said. "Let's do more tomorrow."

"Gotta go." The hatch closed behind him.

I raised an eyebrow. "He seems afraid of me."

She giggled. "I'd say terrified, under that big hulking exterior."

"Because I put him in the brig for two weeks?"

"I don't know, Nicky. I can't imagine why anyone would be afraid of you."

I studied her suspiciously for signs of mockery. "Anyway, what was he doing?"

"He wants to learn to read. Nicky, he actually came to me! Isn't it wonderful?"

"Why not put him in the puter-assisted literacy course?"

She made a face. "It didn't work out. He tried to smash the screen the first time it buzzed his answer as wrong. He needs . . . human encouragement."

"He's too dangerous. You shouldn't be around him."

"I don't think so. He really wants to learn."

Her mind was made up; no use pursuing it. "Well, must you teach him here? Wouldn't a lounge do as well?" At least there'd be others about, in case of hostilities.

"Oh, Nick, we tried that two days ago. Some boys came in and made fun of him, and he stomped off. It took all my persuasion to get him back."

I swore under my breath. "Aren't those streeters cruel? They don't even want to see one of their own get ahead."

"Streeters? It was Gregor and the Dakko boy, Chris." She saw my expression and hurried on, "They weren't causing real trouble, hon. You know what happens when they and the transients run across each other."

"Yes. First we cram these poor joes six in a cabin, and then they have to put up with abuse from those spoiled . . ." I took a deep breath. "Very well, I'll deal with it."

"Hon, don't make a fuss about it. The passengers are upset enough about the transients."

"I'll deal with it," I repeated. I spent the evening wondering how.

The next afternoon I called Purser Li to the bridge. "I want some changes in seat assignments," I told him. "Put Gregor Attani at my table, and assign Chris Dakko to table four with Lieutenant Holser. Effective tonight."

"Aye aye, sir." He hesitated. "If they object, sir?"

"I don't believe regs require passengers to eat dinner," I said. "If they choose to eat, that's where they'll sit." He saluted and left.

When Vax arrived for his watch I was already on the bridge, wondering how long it would be before I heard from Mrs. Attani. Vax took his seat, looking uncomfortable. For a while he fidgeted. Then, to his console, "There was a hell of a row in the wardroom last night."

I said nothing. Naval fiction was that the Captain didn't concern himself with wardroom affairs. Nor was it customary for a lieutenant to bring them to the Captain's attention. It must be an unusual problem to have worried Vax.

"Philip and Derek Carr had it out," he added, still speaking to the screen. "In the exercise room. They beat each other nearly unconscious.

Mr. Singh opened the hatch and thought for a moment they were lovers; they were lying almost on top of each other. He found me and brought me there."

I remained silent. Vax said, "I got them cleaned up and back to the wardroom." He stole a glance at me, reddened. I wondered if he recalled our own desperate fight aboard *Hibernia*. Well, I hadn't won. I had only managed not to lose.

I sighed. I wasn't supposed to interfere, but Vax was an old friend and if I couldn't discuss it with him, with whom could I talk? The obvious answer came unbidden: nobody.

My role was to be the awesome, isolated figure at the top. I could ask questions, give decisions, but it wasn't proper to talk things over with old friends. Otherwise, I wouldn't have their absolute, unquestioning obedience when it was needed.

I managed to keep my silence. Vax looked puzzled, then hurt, and his eyes shifted back to his screen. Of course I couldn't explain; a Captain didn't do that either.

Thank Lord God for Amanda and Nate; without them I didn't know how I'd stay sane.

That evening the dining hall flickered with currents of tension. Derek's face was bruised; Philip Tyre bore a black eye and a cut lip. Of course, in the time-honored Naval tradition I affected not to notice, just as Captain Dengal hadn't noticed my own puffy face aboard *Helsinki* the night Arvan Hager, my senior, taught me a memorable lesson.

Chris Dakko attempted to go to his usual place at his family's table and stalked from the hall when he was refused. Gregor Attani sat next to me, glowering, in what once would have been considered a place of honor. Eddie and Deke made incomprehensible jokes and nudged each other in the ribs.

"Why do this to me?" Gregor asked between courses. His tone was sullen.

"What, Gregor?"

"Making me eat with these tranni—these animals," he amended, at my glare.

"You're no better than they are, Mr. Attani."

"No?" he sneered. "Look!" True, their table manners still left something to be desired, though they tried as best they could to conform to my strange requirements.

"No," I said. "You're more educated, more cultured, but no better at all." I pictured Eddie fumbling with a holo in the passengers' lounge, anxious to learn. My temper shredded. "No more remarks, Gregor, or you'll take breakfast and lunch with us as well." That silenced him. Amanda took pity and chatted casually with him, until even she was rebuffed by his surly monosyllables.

After dinner I returned to the bridge. I wished I'd asked Vax one question: did the fight settle it? I brooded, and finally decided I had to ask outright. I picked up the caller, then slammed it down in its place.

"Easy, Captain, sir. They break." Danny's voice. I looked up sharply.

"Sorry," I said, regretting my temper, then felt foolish. What was I doing apologizing to a puter?

"What're you so mad about, Captain?"

"Never mind." I was curt.

"Aye aye, sir." He sounded hurt.

I sighed. Perhaps he was the answer. I couldn't talk to the passengers or my officers; why not Danny?

"The middies had a fight in the wardroom," I said.

"They do that all the time, don't they? Darla told me about a zarky one you had on her ship."

Were there no secrets? "This time it's a touchy situation. Last voyage Philip—Mr. Tyre to you—was unfit to run the wardroom and Derek took over. Gave Philip quite a beating in the process. Now Philip has some of his confidence back and wants to be in charge. After all, he's senior."

"Then the fight settled it. Did Philip—er, Mr. Tyre to me—win?"

"No insolence," I growled. I wondered how old Danny was, then realized I was being silly. He wasn't alive. Was he? "I don't know who won. I don't think either did."

"Then they'll do it again until it's settled." He seemed unconcerned.

"Yes." I couldn't allow that. I liked Derek too much. Yet, Philip had earned his chance. I realized grudgingly that I'd begun to like him too.

I took the caller and keyed the wardroom. "Mr. Tyre and Mr. Carr to the bridge."

"They're not here, sir." Rafe Treadwell sounded scared.

"Very well." I put down the caller and hesitated only a minute before grabbing the caller again. "Lieutenant Holser to the bridge!" In a few moments Vax arrived, breathing heavily. "Take the watch, Lieutenant." I left.

I hurried past the wardroom to the Level 1 exercise room. An "Out of Service" sign hung on the hatch. I turned the handle; it was locked from the inside. I pounded. "Open up in there! Now!"

The hatch opened. I pushed past Philip Tyre, whose torn undershirt rose and fell as he took in great gasps of air. A line of blood trickled from his mouth. Derek stood across the room, fists clenched, waiting, one arm pressed against his side. The two midshipmen had folded their dress shirts, jackets, and ties neatly on the parallel bar.

"Enough," I snapped. "Get dressed! Come with me!" I waited impatiently for them to don their shirts and knot their ties. When they were presentable I led them down the corridor to the deserted dining hall. I pulled up a chair at the nearest table and sat in the dim light.

I thrust out two chairs. "Sit, both of you!"

"Aye aye, sir." Derek sat composedly, leaning back to favor his left side. Philip perched on the edge of his seat.

I glared at them. It had no effect. I slammed my hand on the table so hard they both jumped. My palm stung like fire. "The wardroom is supposed to settle its own affairs," I growled.

"We were trying to, sir." Philip Tyre sounded aggrieved.

"And the Captain isn't supposed to notice." I slapped the table again, this time more carefully. "How the devil am I supposed to ignore you, when you involve half the ship in your squabbles? You beat each other half to death, Lieutenant Holser is summoned, and then you march into dinner flaunting your battle scars!" That wasn't fair, but I was too angry to care.

They exchanged glances but neither spoke. Watching them I realized I'd get nowhere confronting them together. "Mr. Tyre, wait outside until I call you."

"Aye aye, sir!" The boy wheeled and strode out to the corridor.

I got to my feet. "Damn it, Derek, is this necessary?"

He raised his eyes to meet mine. "I'll obey whatever orders you give, sir." he said without emotion.

I suppressed my urge to lash out, and thought instead of our companionable shore leave in the Venturas. "Will you give in to him, Derek?" My voice was gentle.

"Are you ordering it, sir?"

"No." I couldn't do that. Not inside the wardroom.

"Then no, sir, I won't." His smile was bitter. "I'm sorry, sir, I know you want me to, but I won't do it voluntarily. Not after last cruise."

"What if he's changed?"

"Sir . . ." He colored. "I've swallowed my pride for you, no matter how much it hurt. I've tried to do whatever you've asked of me. I can do that for you. But not for him."

"And if I command it?"

"Then I'll submit to his orders, because you require it of me."

"I can't have you trying to kill each other, Derek."

"No, sir, I understand that."

"Is there any other way you could settle it?"

"You taught me the traditions, sir. Is there?"

I tried to think of a way. Reluctantly, I shook my head. "None that I know of. Unless I remove one of you from the wardroom." I sighed. Damn his pride. Yet I knew I would love him less without it. "Wait outside, Mr. Carr. Send in Mr. Tyre."

"Aye aye, sir."

Philip came to attention as he entered the room.

"As you were, Mr. Tyre."

He chose the at-ease position. I searched for the right words. "You are first midshipman, Mr. Tyre, I understand that. But Derek's been in charge for over a year now. Why must you change that?"

"Because I'm first midshipman, Captain Seafort." His tension was almost palpable.

"Can you give it up, Philip?"

"Can I? I don't know if I can, sir. I won't, though." His resolve shocked me.

"If I order you to let him remain in charge?"

"I'll have to obey your order, sir. But please, let me resign from the Service first."

I sat heavily. "Be seated, Philip." He took the chair next to me. I noticed he was trembling. "Why now?" I asked. "What happened?"

"I don't know exactly why, sir. He hasn't been any different lately. He's fair to Mr. Treadwell and he mostly leaves me alone, though he despises me. I just . . . it's time, sir," he blurted. "Pardon me, I know I'm out of line, but you had no business taking me along with you."

My jaw dropped. He hurried on, "I should have been beached. A middy who can't even hold the wardroom . . . You gave me a second chance, sir. I want to use it. I went all wrong the first time; maybe now I won't." He stared at the deck. "I don't know why it has to be now, sir, but it does. Maybe Mrs. Seafort had something to do with it. What she's been saying."

I was startled. "What was that?"

"About trying to be the best I could no matter how hard it was, sir. You know."

"Yes." I let it be. Amanda never ceased to amaze me.

I went slowly to the hatch and opened it. Derek waited some distance down the corridor. "Come in, Mr. Carr."

I eyed them both. "You're evenly matched. I don't know whether either of you can subdue the other. I don't want you to hurt yourselves or each other trying. Tradition says you have a right to do it. Will you stop, for me?"

Derek said tightly, "I will obey every lawful order Mr. Tyre gives me, sir. Outside the wardroom." He refused to meet my eye.

Philip shook his head. "When Mr. Carr acknowledges that I am first midshipman, sir. In the wardroom and out. Not before."

I was defeated. "I won't order you to stop. You have to resolve it. But I do order you to delay. Do nothing for a week, until you've both thought it through."

"Aye aye, sir." Derek looked grim.

"Aye aye, sir," said Philip. "Um, who's in charge in the meantime, sir?"

"Out, both of you!" I shouted. They scurried away. I paced the empty hall until I was calm enough to go back to my cabin.

35

"Bridge to engine room, prepare to Defuse."

"Prepare to Defuse, aye aye, sir." Chief Hendricks's voice was devoid of all inflection. After a pause he confirmed, "Engine room ready for Defuse, sir. Control passed to bridge."

"Very well." My finger traced a line from "Full" to "Off" on my console. The light of millions of stars leapt forth from the simulscreens.

"Confirm clear of encroachments, Lieutenant." My voice had an edge. But Vax was already punching figures into the console, anticipating my order.

"No encroachments, sir," he said at last.

"Very well. Have the crew stand down."

Vax gave the order. I leaned back and rocked, my eyes shut. I wondered how long it would be before Derghinski showed up; he would almost certainly be the first.

We spent the next two days drifting alone, waiting for our squadron. Derek Carr shared a watch with me and seemed ill at ease; at the end of watch he saluted and mumbled, "May I say something before I go?"

I nodded.

"About Mr. Tyre, sir—it's not that I want the power, or that I won't obey orders. It's because of what he did."

"I understand," I said. "I never thought otherwise. You're dismissed."

I brooded in my seat while Alexi and Rafe Treadwell settled in for their watch, then left abruptly for my cabin. Amanda sat in near dark, rocking Nate gently. "I think he's finally out," she whispered. I checked. He was breathing with the swift regularity of sleep.

"Yes." I held my baby to my shoulder while she smoothed the sheets in his crib. A small hand clutched my neck as he stirred.

She took him from me and laid him facedown in his bed. Then she came and nestled against my arm. "I love both of you," she said, and tears stung my eyes.

The next day the alarms sounded while we lunched in the passengers' mess. The crew hastened to General Quarters; I raced to the bridge, slapped the hatch shut, slid into my seat.

"Encroachment thirty-six thousand kilometers and closing, sir." Alexi's eyes were glued to the screen.

"Recognition code received, sir," Danny interrupted. "Positive ID on *Kitty Hawk*." I breathed a sigh of relief as we stood down. Our frequent Defusing was nerve-wracking. We were still only fifteen light-years from home, with most of the cruise still ahead of us.

I let Pilot Van Peer take the conn to maneuver us into position relative to *Kitty Hawk*. Short bursts from the thrusters reoriented us. I remembered the dinner Captain Tenere had given us on *Freiheit* and wished he were first on station, so I could return the favor.

Would Captain Derghinski consider it presumptuous to invite him over? I thought of the months of isolation aboard a Fused ship and smiled. "Danny, make contact with *Kitty Hawk*'s bridge."

"Aye aye, sir. Nola says Captain Derghinski's off duty now but she can wake him."

"Nola? Their puter?" I knew our puters locked in tightbeam whenever two ships approached. Lord God knew what they exchanged. "Wait until he wakes," I told him.

Two hours later I was in my cabin, humming to myself as I changed clothes. Captain Derghinski had accepted my dinner invitation with alacrity. I'd ordered the steward to outdo himself for our guests, and was wondering where to hide the transients for the evening.

"Let's meet him at the lock, hon. The Captain and the Captain's lady."

Amanda smiled back as she took my arm. We strolled down to Level 2. Near the airlock, the corridor was crowded with sentries for the ceremonial of Captain Derghinski's entry. Passengers peered through our transplex portholes for a glimpse of *Kitty Hawk*.

I beckoned to young Eddie Boss; he approached apprehensively. "Pass the word to your, ah, comrades. Anyone who causes the ruckus you made with the Admiral will spend the rest of the trip locked in his cabin. All eleven months!"

Eddie looked awed. "I be tellin' em good, Cap'n. Giim lots room, I tell 'em all. Noway makin' trouble nohow, Cap'n."

"Be sure of it, Eddie." Frowning, I watched him retreat.

Amanda inquired, "When did you put him in charge?"

"I didn't, but he's large enough to get the point across."

"And then some," she agreed.

A sailor peered through the porthole. "Their launch berth doors are opening, sir. He'll be on his way in a minute."

Alarms sounded. For a moment I panicked, knowing *Kitty Hawk*'s gig wouldn't set off our alarms. Then understanding came and I cursed to myself as I relaxed. "Another ship's Defused," I said to Amanda. "Lousy timing. It'll set dinner back at least an hour. I'll be back as quick as I can." I trotted to the bridge.

Danny's adolescent voice was shrill. "Encroachment seven kilometers, bearing oh four oh and closing!" I slapped the hatch shut. Vax and the Pilot were at their consoles.

"That's awfully close," I muttered to Vax as I slipped into my seat. "Who is it, Danny?"

"No recognition signal, sir! And bounceback isn't showing metal."

My fingers tightened on the caller. "Comm room! What do you read?"

"No metal, Captain. It's not a ship."

"Battle Stations!" I hit the klaxon, and sirens blared throughout *Portia*. "Danny, full magnification!"

"Aye aye, sir!" The screens leapt into focus.

"Oh, Lord God preserve us!" Vax, in a whisper.

"Shut up, Vax. Fire control, I'm activating all lasers! Deploy shields! Enemy target oh four oh!" My sphincters twitched. I tried to tear my eyes away from the object in the screens. I thumbed the laser activation release.

A fish.

Two-thirds the size of *Portia*, half the size of *Kitty Hawk*, it drifted toward us, closing fast. As I watched, a hole near its tail squirted propellant and its speed increased. A glob on the creature's knobby surface began to spin lazily.

So much for trying not to initiate hostilities.

"Commence firing! Vax, turn off those bloody alarms. Danny, inform *Kitty Hawk* we're shooting!"

"Aye aye, sir," Danny said, breathless in the sudden silence. "Mr. Derghinski informed by tightbeam."

A spot on the alien form glowed red. Colors swirled; holes opened and the fish jerked aside from our laser beam. Its spinning glob released, came sailing toward us.

Vax roared into his caller. "Laser Group B, fire on the projectile!" He'd once seen an acid glob eat through *Hibernia*'s gig and kill its crew. We waited, watching the screens. Our lasers again found their target, and the glob flared and melted.

Alarm bells clanged anew. Danny shouted, "Encroachment five hundred kilometers! Course three four one!"

"Puter, lower your voice! Put the bogey on the screen." I tried to sound calmer than I felt.

"Recognition codes!" said Danny and Vax together. A second's pause, and Danny added, "It's *Challenger.*"

"Signal them we're under attack. Any more projectiles?"

Vax checked his screen. "None at the moment, but debris from the one we broke up is still approaching. Looks like it'll hit the shields aft."

"Very well." The goldfish shape jerked as laser beams struck it from the side; Captain Derghinski was in action.

"Maneuver us closer, Pilot. Vax, ask the Admiral if *Challenger* will join the attack." My fingers ached from gripping the arm of the chair.

"Aye aye, sir. *Challenger*'s closing—"

The alarms clanged. Danny and Vax were both shouting. "New encroachment forty kilometers, course three three nine!"

"Another encroachment, one kilometer, dead ahead! They're not ships!" Vax pointed.

The Pilot slammed the starboard thrusters to full, blasting propellant to steer us clear of the encroachment ahead.

"All lasers fire at will! Take the nearest targets!" No time for target selection by the book. The original fish glowed red from several laser penetrations. Propellant squirted in three directions as it corkscrewed away. *Kitty Hawk* spewed flames in pursuit.

The fish ahead drifted to our port side as our thrusters turned us. An area of its surface began to swirl. A dot appeared, separated from the fish's body. It launched itself toward us.

A shapechanger. I'd met one of the alien outriders aboard *Telstar*, and nearly died of fright.

I watched the screen, sweating. Globs of material seemed to swirl under the translucent creature's suit. My skin crawled; I remembered that it had no suit.

"Repel Boarders! This is no drill!" I brought my voice under control. "Prepare for decompression. Laser control, fire on that—thing! Master-at-arms, stand by with a fighting party in case the bastard penetrates!" The shape jerked once as it passed through our beams. Danny's sensors followed its lazy glide. It floated onto our hull and hung a moment, quivering.

"Boarder on the outer hull, amidships!" Danny's words came low and fast. "Two meters abaft the airlock. All corridor hatches sealed. External lasers cannot reach target." The ship couldn't fire on itself.

"Sensors reporting hull damage. Captain, it's coming through!" The puter's voice changed. "Conversational overlays deactivated. ALERT!

Imminent danger of destruction! ALERT, SECTION EIGHT! Hull breakdown one meter aft of airlock. Section eight isolated by corridor hatch seals." New alarms added their din. "DECOMPRESSION EMERGENCY! LEVEL 2 SECTION EIGHT DECOMPRESSION! Bridge airlock controls inoperative!"

I slapped off the alarms. "Mr. Banatir, report!" I keyed the master-at-arms's suit channel to our speakers.

"We're in section eight, Captain. I see it. Oh, God! Sorry, sir. It's in the corridor. All of you, open fire! Damn, it moves fast! GET IT!" The suit lasers whined in the speaker.

Below, someone sobbed, "Mother of God, what is it?" The whine of lasers came faster.

"Roast the son of a bitch!" Mr. Banatir, in fury. "That's it, you got him! Easy now, or you'll burn through the deck!" Heavy breathing. A grunt. "I think it's dead, Captain. There's not much of it left."

"Don't touch anything!"

"No, sir. God Almighty!"

Frowning at the blasphemy I glanced at the screen. *Kitty Hawk*'s jets had taken her about thirty kilometers from her station, in pursuit of an alien. The fish was moving faster than she was. She fired. The fish pulsed rhythmically. Then it vanished.

"*Kitty Hawk* got it!" Vax pounded the console.

"Maybe. Where's the other one?" The screen swiveled to the alien shape amidships. Another of its globs began waving in ever-faster circles. I snatched the caller. "Fire control, get the part that's waving!" Banks of lasers concentrated on the rotating arm. It melted off the fish and sailed lazily away, at right angles to the ship.

"Now, fire on the fish!" As the lasers were brought to bear, the creature pulsed. Then it too disappeared from our screens.

The alarms went silent. Trembling from adrenaline I glanced wildly at the screens. "Where did it go? Where is everybody?"

"*Kitty Hawk* is one hundred fifty kilometers, course one eight nine, declination nineteen." Vax's tone was uneven. "No other encroachments."

"Lord God." I sat, trying not to tremble. "Vax, send a damage control party to section eight."

"Aye aye, sir." He spoke quietly into the caller.

"Danny, get me *Kitty Hawk*."

"Aye aye, sir. Reactivating conversational overlays. Okay, you're patched to *Kitty Hawk*'s bridge."

Captain Derghinski's face appeared, grim. "You all right, Seafort?"

"Yes, sir, but we took a hit. I have damage control on it now. We chased one and it disappeared. What happened to the fish you were after?"

"Gone. I don't know where." We eyed each other. A pause. "Is that what you saw last time?"

"Yes, sir. The goldfish."

Derghinski snorted. "More like barracuda, if you ask me. Goldfish don't bite, or come after you."

"Yes, sir, but they look like goldfish." My voice was shaky. Raw fear welled up. I swallowed, battling nausea. "Are we alone, then?"

"It appears so."

I asked stupidly, "Where's *Challenger*?"

"It seems she Fused."

"In the middle of a battle?" I said, unthinking.

Derghinski glared. "I'm sure he had his reasons."

I felt a complete fool. "Yes, sir."

His tone was bleak. "Or maybe the son of a bitch ran away." He cut the connection.

Vax was careful to look elsewhere. The Pilot examined the backs of his hands. I keyed the caller. "Damage control, report!"

The response came almost immediately. "We're brazing a patch on the hull from inside, sir. Another few minutes, I think we'll have it. Sorry, sir, Petty Officer Everts reporting. When the patch is in place you can recompress, sir. I don't know about the airlock controls yet. A lot of wiring is fried."

"Very well. Thank you." I lay back, closed my eyes. Where had they come from?

"Where'd they go?" asked Vax, as if reading my thoughts. "Is it possible they Fused?"

"I don't think so. They're organic."

"Amanda's all right, sir. I called the cabin while you were talking to *Kitty Hawk*."

I glared. He blushed but held my gaze. "Thank you, Vax," I said at last, ashamed.

Captain Derghinski's lined face showed his anxiety. "What do you think they'll do next, Seafort?"

"I don't know, sir," I repeated. I'd had only one encounter with the fish that lurked behind *Telstar*, and that was enough to scare years from my life. Yet Derghinski was deferring to me as if I were an expert. "Sir,

Portia has repairs under way. We can either wait for the rest of the squadron or Fuse. What are your orders?"

My prompting seemed to help him pull himself together. "I wish I knew where *Challenger* went." He sounded glum. "If she's coming back we should wait here; if she's gone to the next rendezvous we should try to meet her."

"Yes, sir." I waited.

"All right; let's give it three more days. Full alert. No, cancel that. We can't keep men on Battle Stations without a break. If *Freiheit* and the others Defuse by then, we'll go on together to the next rendezvous point. Otherwise one of us will wait behind for stragglers."

"Aye aye, sir."

"What precautions did you take for infection, Mr. Seafort?"

Before I'd first reached Hope Nation, an unknown virus had decimated the colony. Because the Admiral had been killed, I'd remained in command, not only of *Hibernia* but of naval forces groundside. We now realized the virus was spread by the alien fish, and all ships carried vaccine. Like the rest of the fleet, we were under orders to observe the tightest viro-bacteriological security in case of contact.

Our damage control parties had followed regulation decontamination drills. Our decompression had actually helped safeguard the ship; the chance of airborne virus was much reduced. The decking surrounding the gruesome scorched blob was taken up, vacuum-sealed, and stored in the hold for analysis by our xenobiologists back home, and new decking put in its place. Sailors returning from the damaged section through the corridor hatch seals were put through rigorous decontamination procedures. I told Derghinski as much.

"Very well. I believe your infirmary carries the serum for the Hope Nation virus?"

"Yes, sir. Dr. Bros is inoculating everyone, to be safe."

"Well, you've done what you can. Let me know if we can help with anything."

"Thank you, sir." We broke the connection. I glanced at the screens. Outside the ship, for tens of millions of kilometers, was nothing other than *Kitty Hawk*. Within our vessel all systems were at alert. In addition to Danny's sensors we now had full complements manning the radionics in the comm room. Our lasers were activated and ready to fire. Shields were fully deployed, though the gossamer laser shields were not much help against the protoplasm the goldfish threw.

There was nothing to do but wait.

* * *

Two days later Mr. Banatir spoke of a headache. On the way to his berth he collapsed. He was dead before they got him to the infirmary. I was notified in my cabin. I ordered all hatches sealed at once and went to tanked air throughout the ship, while I waited with Amanda and Nate in an agony of tension.

Some hours later Dr. Bros reported his findings. "Definitely a virus, sir. It operates like the Hope Nation strain but it's something else. I've got the synthesizers working on it."

"How does it spread?"

"It's nasty, this one. Airborne, liquids, even through the pores of the skin."

I spoke through gritted teeth. "So the whole ship could be infected?"

"It may have spread widely, yes, sir. As soon as I get a serum . . ."

"How long between the time we contract it and the time we die?" My tone was blunt.

"I don't know, sir. It puts out a lot of toxins. Two days, perhaps. No more, or the master-at-arms would still be alive."

"How long before you have a serum?"

"Thank Lord God for the automated machines, sir. We had to isolate it, grow a culture, analyze it . . ."

"How long?" I snarled. If only I'd had the sense to go to quarantine the moment we were invaded.

"I can't be sure." The Doctor's worry was evident. "Perhaps tomorrow afternoon. Sooner if we're lucky. If it weren't for the data from Hope Nation we wouldn't even know what to look for."

No point in hounding him. "Let me know the moment you have results." I paused. "You're following sterilization procedures yourself?"

"Yes, sir, you'd better believe it." His tone was emphatic.

I frowned at his manner, but knew enough to ignore it. "Any risky operations, coming in contact with the virus . . ."

"Yes, sir?"

"Have a med tech do it," I said bluntly. "Yours is the most valuable life on the ship." I set down the caller.

Melissa Chong and Mrs. Attani died that night. Also three transients. To my dismay I realized I hadn't even learned their names. Each section of the disks survived on isolated bottled air; we weren't using recyclers at all.

I had Alexi, who was holding the bridge, call Derghinski on *Kitty Hawk*. We agreed that, no matter what happened to us, there would be no interchange between ships until we'd found a vaccine. We might lose one ship, but not both.

The exhausted bridge watch remained on duty behind sealed hatches for the second straight day; Alexi and the Pilot reported to me every fifteen minutes. If one of them became ill I would open the isolation seals long enough to get to the bridge, and then use suit air until the siege lifted or I died.

Outside the ship all was still.

By morning sixteen crewmen in crew berth one were dead. The survivors cast discipline aside and pounded on their sealed hatches, frantic to escape from the contaminated berth.

Two hours later Dr. Bros's haggard voice crackled through the speaker. "We've got it, sir! The synthesizers are building vaccine right now. We have the first batch, and more in an hour. Preventative and curative both, thank Lord God."

"You're sure it works?" I asked stupidly, my head reeling from exhaustion.

"Yes, sir, it knocks the cultures dead, in the gel and in human blood. Once we knock out the virus, we can start to dialyze out the toxins. We should be able to save most of the infected."

"Inoculate yourself first, and your med tech. Then the bridge watch."

"Aye aye, sir. And you."

"Never mind me, I'm all right here. Get down to the crew berths."

"You first, sir. That's how it's going to be."

I was astounded at his audacity. "Dr. Bros, if you think—"

"Nicky, shut up and take the vaccine!" Amanda. "Have you no sense at all? You're needed!"

I capitulated as gracefully as I could. Nate woke and began crying fitfully. Amanda went to soothe him and I broke seals to go to the infirmary. I let Dr. Bros give me my shot; he had the grace to apologize for his peremptory manner.

"Never mind; let's get your vaccine distributed. How do I help?"

There was nothing useful I could do, but he let me feel as if I were assisting, wheeling the cart of vaccine, handing him fresh shotgun heads. We went directly to the crew berths; my presence was barely enough to prevent a riot when the hatches were unsealed. Men at the end of the line were nearly desperate for their turn at the cart. Then we inoculated the passengers.

Afterward, we turned the crew mess into a hospital for those who were ill; dialyzers were wheeled down from the infirmary to filter toxins from the bloodstreams of the affected.

Slowly my ship was unsealed and returned to normal—or, as normal as might be, drifting in space waiting for the rest of the squadron, fearing another alien attack, with the Admiral and his ship in parts unknown, and twenty-two dead awaiting burial.

Alexi Tamarov unsealed the bridge, sweat-stained, bleary-eyed, swaying with exhaustion, his arm bared for the inoculation. I took his salute. I should have returned it. Instead I embraced him, disregarding the consequences to discipline. His head rested a moment on my shoulder. "Get some sleep, Lieutenant." My voice was gruff. "You too, Mr. Van Peer." I watched them trudge off to the showers and their cabins. Vax Holser and I took our places on the bridge. Welcome air poured from the recyclers.

I thumbed the caller. "Mr. Carr!"

In a moment the answer came. "Yes, sir?"

"Take the gig. Carry samples of the vaccine across to *Kitty Hawk*."

"Aye aye, sir." In other circumstances Derek would have seen the opportunity as heaven-sent, putting him for those few moments in command of his own tiny vessel. Now, surrounded by death, I knew the midshipman had no such thoughts.

Another crewman died in the makeshift hospital, his body too ravaged by toxins to respond to treatment. I put Chief Hendricks's detail to building coffins; we arranged to hold our service at the forward airlock, so as not to be within sight of the grim patches near the aft lock.

Damage control reported that our bridge override circuits to the aft airlock were damaged beyond repair, though the airlock controls themselves still functioned. Shuddering at the thought of our transient joeys unthinkingly yanking on levers at the airlock, I ordered a sentry posted there.

At end of watch I went to my cabin to change for the funeral. Nate was teething and fussy; I suggested Amanda stay with him instead of attending and she gratefully agreed.

All officers not on watch were present, as were many of our passengers, and representatives from each crew station. I strode down the corridor to the airlock, resplendent in my dress uniform. White slacks gleamed against my black shoes, the red stripe down each leg sharp and bright. My white jacket over white shirt and black tie was broken only by the black mourning sash thrown over my right shoulder and my gleaming length of service pins.

The airlock was not big enough for all the coffins; the ejection would have to be in two cycles. A sailor waited in the closed airlock, fully suited, while I read from my holovid the somber words of the Christian Reunification service for the dead, as promulgated by the Naval Service of the Government of the United Nations. " 'Ashes to ashes, dust to dust . . .' "

The airlock pumps hummed.

Surely I could have avoided this. Why hadn't I kept each section sealed, from the moment of invasion until the virus was discovered? We didn't carry enough bottled air for that. But still, it was my responsibility.

" 'Trusting in the goodness and mercy of Lord God eternal, we commit their bodies to the deep . . .' " Annie was crying, her head buried in Eddie Boss's shoulder. Walter Dakko stood uncomfortably nearby. Gregor Attani was the only immediate family of any of the dead; he stood with the officers, pale but composed.

The sensor light flashed; the airlock was decompressed.

" 'To await the day of judgment when the souls of man shall be called forth before Almighty Lord God . . . Amen.' " I snapped off the holovid. "Mr. Kerns, open the outer lock, please." The suited sailor pressed the lock control to the side of the airlock hatch. The outer hatch slid open.

"Eject the remains, Mr. Kerns." The seaman pushed a coffin gently toward the outer lock. It cleared the hatch and drifted slowly from the ship into the dark of the void. A second casket followed. I realized I had no idea who was in each casket; the highborn and the transients were leveled at the last.

Finally the airlock was empty. Seaman Raines shut the outer hatch and waited while the pressures equalized. When the lock was fully re-aired he glanced at me, waiting for permission to open the inner lock.

"Proceed, Mr. Kerns." The inner hatch slid open. Two sailors helped him slide the remaining caskets into the airlock. Gregor Attani wept openly. Walter Dakko's arm went around his shoulder. Eddie touched Gregor gently. The bereaved young man slapped away the transient's hand.

The inner hatch closed again. One by one the remaining caskets were dispatched into the void. I'd killed nearly half my crew. I had destroyed Mrs. Attani, Melissa Chong, and others I hardly knew. I had been up for three days; the corridor swam lazily. I blinked, knowing I still had work to do.

When the service dispersed I said a few words of condolence to

Gregor Attani; he responded with a vague nod. I wondered if he'd heard me.

I returned to the bridge and summoned Chief Hendricks. "Chief, make out new work assignments. Pay particular attention to vital systems: hydroponics, recyclers, power. Take men from the galley, cleaning details, wherever else you think necessary."

"Aye aye, sir." The Chief was grim. "We're going to need relief before we get there, sir, or they'll drop from exhaustion."

"I know. I'll ask the Admiral for transfers." When we find the Admiral, I thought. The Chief left. I served out my watch, Rafe Treadwell tense at my side. Neither of us spoke; I was too exhausted to do anything other than stay awake; the midshipman knew better than to bother me.

The watch changed; Vax Holser came on with Derek Carr. I stayed in my chair while they got settled. "Keep alert," I cautioned. "The fish may come back." My words were hardly necessary; they were both taut with tension.

I dozed and startled awake. A bad example; I knew it was time to leave the bridge. I went back to my cabin.

Amanda was rocking Nate, the lights turned low. "He's finally asleep," she whispered.

"I'll take him." I reached out.

"No, I'll sit with him awhile. How was the service?"

"Grim." I hung up my jacket, yawning. "Gregor was distraught. He and his mother are—were close." I recalled how she'd tried to protect him from my wrath, when he'd fought with the transients. The day Nate was born. I slipped out of my pants, threw them over a chair.

Amanda hummed softly to Nate as she rocked. "Find something for Gregor to do, Nicky," she whispered. "Don't let him sit and brood about his mother."

"I don't think he wants anything from me." I remembered Gregor's fury at being made to sit at dinner with the transients. I unbuttoned my shirt. God, I was tired. I went to the crib and threw back the blankets. "Let's put him down, hon. Come keep me warm while I sleep." I smiled wearily, held out my arms for my son. Reluctantly she put the baby in my hands and went to smooth the crib.

I cuddled Nate on my shoulder. He was quite cold. He must have been dead for hours.

We reassembled at the forward lock, my officers clustered protectively around me. Again I wore my dress whites, the mourning sash thrown over my right shoulder. My tight black shoes gleamed; I'd hand-polished them again and again, curtly refusing assistance from the ship's boy.

Amanda was dressed simply, as she had been the day before, in plain knit skirt and blouse. Her hand clutched my arm. From time to time she started in confusion.

The coffin was exactly one meter long and thirty-two centimeters wide. It was made of aluminum panels brazed to angle irons where the sides met. I'd held the torch to one corner until the metal glowed white and threatened to sag, while silent machinist's mates stood by, afraid to speak.

The casket was lined with Nate's pink blanket and made up with the soft yellow sheets from the crib. It was very hard to fold them so the creases were in the corners; I'd had to do it over and over to get it right. His stuffed panda was tucked to one side, his tiny hand resting on it. The panda was black and white, with a soft little red nose. It lay face up, as did my son.

The coffin rested now in the airlock where I'd come to do my duty.

I snapped open the holovid. Amanda begged, "Please don't do it to him, Nicky. He'll be so cold."

I swallowed. My chest ached. She'd been in that state, off and on, since the day before, when I'd walked heavily to the infirmary, Nate's still body in my arms. Plaintive, she'd trailed alongside, sometimes crying, urging me to walk softly so I wouldn't wake him.

I hugged her now, but she pulled away, pressed her face to the transplex hatch, staring at the lock where the tiny coffin rested in the folded metal arm of the ejection unit.

I began to read. " 'Ashes to ashes, dust to dust . . .' " Philip Tyre sobbed aloud.

My gaze flickered between the holovid and the tiny box in the airlock. After a time I was aware that I'd stopped speaking. I found my place but for some reason no words would come. I puzzled over the text. Vax Holser reached gently for the holovid. I wheeled on him angrily. "Mind your place, Lieutenant!" I took up my reading. " '. . . Trusting in the goodness and mercy of Lord God eternal, we commit his body to the deep . . . to await the day of judgment when the souls of man shall be called forth before Almighty Lord God.' " I nodded to the seaman on duty.

Amanda buried her face in my shoulder. "Nick, you love him too! For God's sake, don't put our baby Outside!"

The metal arm of the ejection unit slowly unfolded, pushing the side of the coffin, sliding it smoothly to the outer lock. The arm fully extended, the casket floated gently at the end of the chamber, drifting slowly into the immeasurable emptiness.

Amanda stared lifelessly at the empty lock. "God, how brutal," she whispered. "I never knew you could be so cruel." She turned away. Reaching out she ran a gentle finger down Philip Tyre's tear-streaked face. "It's all right, Philip. Don't cry." Absently she patted his shoulder.

I caught Dr. Bros's eye. Helpless, he shook his head. He smiled at Amanda. "Let's walk, Mrs. Seafort. We can sit in the infirmary and talk a while."

"I'd rather go to my cabin," said Amanda.

"Let's talk first," suggested the doctor.

"No. I'm going back to my room. Nicky, make him leave me alone!"

She was in shock, Dr. Bros had told me, and retreating from unacceptable realities. I didn't want a diagnosis, I wanted Amanda. I struggled not to think of the empty crib waiting in the cabin, fearing loss of self-control. I yearned for her touch, her caress. But for the moment she hated me, though I knew in a little while she would come to me and lay her head on my shoulder in puzzled grief, as she had before. I guided my wife back to our cabin and closed the hatch behind us.

Days passed, and no ship came. There was no further sign of the aliens. At length Captain Derghinski conferred with me, over the simulscreens. Neither of us dared leave his ship, even for a few minutes.

"One of us will go on to the next rendezvous point." He fingered his mustache. "To see if *Challenger*'s waiting. But if the others show up here . . ."

Passively, I waited.

"You've got the faster drive, Seafort. I'll go on ahead; you wait here for seven days, then catch up with us."

"Aye aye, sir."

"If any ships come in, send them on through immediately. Don't have them wait at this rendezvous."

"No, sir."

"Well, good luck."

"The same to you, sir."

He looked uncomfortable. "Mr. Seafort," he blurted, "I'm sorry about your son. Terribly sorry."

My chest was unbearably tight. "Thank you, sir."

He cleared his throat. "Well, then. Godspeed. I'll see you soon."

"Godspeed, sir." We blanked the connection. Shortly afterward he Fused and we were alone once more.

I dreaded to go back to my cabin, but knew I must. Amanda was there. Sometimes I would find her prostrate with grief. Other times I would find her cheerfully preparing soft foods for Nate's lunch.

I stared dully at the blank simulscreen. In the next seat Vax Holser stirred. "Are you going to the cabin now, sir?" His voice was soft.

"Are you ordering me off the bridge, Lieutenant?"

"No, sir," he said, unflinching despite my fury. "I thought you might want to be with Mrs. Seafort. I can handle the watch."

"I don't need your pity, Mr. Holser," I said, my voice harsh. I swung my seat to face the other way. After some minutes I cleared my throat. "Sorry."

"No problem, sir." For some reason his understanding rekindled my rage.

"I'll be in my cabin. Call if anything happens."

"Aye aye, sir."

Amanda sat rocking in the dark. "Shh, you'll wake him."

I sighed. "He's not here, hon." I knelt by her rocker and put my hand on her arm. "He's gone. There's only us."

She looked puzzled. "Gone?" Her face cleared. "Yes, I remember now. You put him Outside." She shivered. "It's freezing out there, Nicky. That wasn't right. He'll catch his death of cold."

I was speechless. I squeezed her arm; she made no response. I went to wash up, then sat on the bed.

A few moments later Amanda came to sit beside me. "I know you miss him too," she said gently. "You loved him so much."

My throat locked and I couldn't speak. She rested her head against my side. "He was such a lovely boy . . ." My arm went around her and we sat in silent misery.

36

Portia waited alone, alert, anxious, for three interminable days. As tension rose, even the transients quarreled incessantly at dinner, until my manner became so menacing that they subsided. Once, as the transpops and I crowded out of the dining hall, Chris Dakko muttered a derisive, "Electropiss!" Instantly I backhanded him across the mouth. He stared at me in shock and astonishment, blood trickling from his lip. I spun on my heel and strode to the bridge.

An hour later Chris and his father loomed over me, escorted by Philip Tyre, at their demand. Walter Dakko spluttered with rage. "How dare you strike my son! How dare you!"

"He'll behave himself in my presence, Mr. Dakko." Chris fidgeted, shaking his head in impatience and disgust.

"We're paid passengers! He's not one of your crewmen. You have no right to touch him!" Not correct, legally, but by custom passengers were treated with more respect than I'd shown his son. On the other hand, I didn't need the boy stirring up a riot with my transients.

"I didn't do anything," Chris said hotly. "You should hear what they call us! You have no damned right—"

"You're a child aboard my ship, Christopher. Mind your manners or I'll do worse!"

"You can't—"

"That was your last warning." Something in my tone made him silent. "I've heard what you have to say. Get off my bridge."

"But—"

"Both of you. Now!" I gestured to Philip, who put his hand on Walter Dakko's arm. The elder man shook it off, stalked to the hatch. His son followed, a sneer on his face.

I served out my watch restlessly, wanting and not wanting to go back to my cabin. At watch's end, I left the moment Alexi came to replace me.

I stopped at my cabin door, but turned away. Not yet; I would walk for a while. I continued along the circumference corridor. A few passengers were on their way to the lounge for an evening of holovids and idle chatter. I nodded curtly and went on.

Outside the wardroom Derek Carr stood at attention, his nose to the bulkhead, eyes ahead. I stopped abruptly. "What's this, Mr. Carr?"

"Mr. Tyre's orders, sir," Derek said, his voice stiff.

I was at a loss. "But you—I mean—you and he—"

"I put myself under his orders, sir. Two days ago. In the wardroom and out."

My eyes misted. I knew how hard it would have been for Derek to back down to Philip. He remained at attention, eyes front to the dull gray bulkhead. My anger swelled. "And this is how he treats you? Hazing, at your age? I'll settle that, and fast!" I turned to the wardroom hatch.

"No, sir, please!" Derek blurted. I paused, turned to him, raising an eyebrow. He reddened. "I, uh, told Mr. Tyre, sir. To give me whatever orders he wished. Until he was sure I meant it."

I said slowly, "You told him to haze you?"

He started to shrug, then realized he was supposed to be at attention. "Yes, sir, he needs to know he's in charge. It's all right. He's not hurting me, and he'll let up soon." He took a deep breath. "Captain, please don't interfere. Please."

I sagged against the bulkhead. "Why, Derek? Why'd you do it?"

Momentarily he closed his eyes. "It's right for the ship, sir. I realized that after the attack. We can't be in conflict now. He's senior; he should be in charge. The other way isn't natural." The corners of his mouth turned up bleakly. "And I can always rebel again, should it be necessary."

I said quietly, "Don't let him hurt you, Derek."

"I won't, sir."

"Promise."

"I promise, sir." Abruptly he added, "Thank you for caring."

I touched his shoulder and walked away, not trusting myself to speak. What it must have cost him, I couldn't know. I made a note to watch the Log for demerits. If Philip started again, I would beach him. Permanently.

Freiheit Defused in the middle of the night, sending alarm bells clanging and my heart slamming against my ribs. I conferred with Captain Tenere, and delivered Captain Derghinski's instructions. *Freiheit* plotted her course for the next rendezvous point. A half hour later she Fused and was gone.

At dinner the next day the transients were subdued, almost obsequious. It took me a while to realize that they were reacting to my stand with Chris Dakko on their behalf. Eddie shyly asked me if Amanda would be giving any more reading lessons; I told him gently that she would, after she recovered.

After the meal I accompanied them back to Level 2. They clustered around the sentry posted at the airlock, teasing him and jostling each other until I snapped, "Knock off, joeys!" They obeyed immediately. It occurred to me that for all my prestige as Captain, I hadn't truly been a figure of authority to them until I'd faced down an Upper New Yorker.

I spent a full half hour trying to separate myself from the transients. With the death of Melissa Chong I seemed to have inherited her role as liaison between the transpops and the civilized denizens of the ship. No matter that I had put Alexi Tamarov in charge; they ignored him and came to me with their problems and complaints.

Raull wanted Jonie to stop beating him up; Deke complained that Gregor Attani and his friends were still making fun of them. Jonie wanted to get her hair done like Annie's and Annie wouldn't tell her who had done it. At least, I thought that was what they were trying to tell me.

After I extricated myself I went to the infirmary and knocked on the hatch. Dr. Bros himself let me in; his med tech was off duty. In his tiny office he sat back and looked at me gravely. "What can I do for you, Captain?"

"It's Amanda," I said. "What can you do for her?"

"She's no better?"

"At times," I admitted. "She cries for Nate, and I think she's going to be all right. Then she'll wake up because it's time to get him breakfast. It's worse because all his things are still in the cabin. His crib, his clothes, the baby food. Should I have them packed?"

"How long has it been? A week?" I nodded. "No, I would say not. She needs to grieve. Taking his things away won't distract her; she's already trying her best not to think about his death."

"Is there anything you can do? Drugs, or medicine?" I hoped he'd understand. The horror of what went on in my cabin was more than I could speak of. And still I felt that tiny hand on my shoulder . . . I cleared my throat briskly. "Anything?"

He considered. "Well, we know there's a strong hormonal element in grieving. Tears flush out harmful chemicals and actually cure the mind. That's why women are often more mentally healthy than men; they've been taught to cry more easily. We could examine Amanda for hormone rebalancing."

"Amanda, a schizo?" I was horrified.

"Not only schizophrenics go to hormone rebalancing centers, Captain," he said with a small smile. "In any event, we can't do a full rebalance with our limited equipment. But it's not absolutely necessary; it's just an option."

"What would you do, yourself?"

"I'd probably run her blood chemistry through the analyzer and see what we found. Or you could wait."

"How long?" I didn't know how much more I could stand.

"A week, certainly. Not more than a month; her behavior patterns will become fixed and much harder to change."

"Is there any harm in waiting?" I wanted Amanda to snap back on her own; I hated the idea that she might be mentally ill.

"Not for a while," the doctor said gently. "Let her be for now."

"A week," I said. "After we're Fused again I'll decide what to do if she hasn't recovered." On that note we parted.

When I got back to the cabin Amanda was almost cheerful. "Hi, Nicky, where've you been?"

"Taking care of the trannies," I said, half truthfully.

She winced. "Don't let them hear you saying that."

I smiled. "It's odd, though. When Eddie wants their attention he yells, 'Yo, trannies!' Apparently they only take offense when outsiders say it." I sat wearily in the chair by the conference table.

Amanda perched on my lap. "I wish we were happier, Nicky," she said wistfully. She bit her lip. "God, I miss him." I hugged her gently, not daring to speak. We sat like that for several minutes. I loved her so much at that moment, knowing she was truly with me. Then she got up to get Nate a blanket, and my world crashed at my feet.

The next afternoon two ships arrived within minutes of each other; the first time the alarms sounded I ran to the bridge at full gallop; the second time I was already there. *Hindenburg* Defused seventy thousand kilometers from us; we exchanged recognition signals and I gave Captain Everts the message to proceed to the next rendezvous. She nodded grimly, waited while her course was plotted, said good-bye, and disappeared.

Captain Hall glowered at me from the bridge of *Soyez*. "I'm senior to Derghinski, Seafort. His orders don't bind me."

"No, sir," I agreed. "But he is senior to me, and my orders were to give you the message."

His visage softened. "Yes, I understand. Hell of a mess, isn't it? It would be a lot easier if we knew where the Admiral went."

"Yes, sir." There was no need to say more.

"Very well, he's probably right. I'll go on. How long has it been since Derghinski Fused?"

"Six days, sir." He'd told me to wait seven.

"The rest of the squadron is still behind us somewhere, Lord God willing." He brooded. "Can you wait a few more days, Seafort? I don't want to order you, but it would be in all our interests."

"I'll wait." It didn't seem to matter anymore.

"Give it three more days, Seafort. That should be enough, no matter what the variation in our fusion drives. If they're coming they'll be here by then."

"Aye aye, sir." We said our good-byes and broke the connection. I watched his ship, barely visible against the backdrop of innumerable points of light, until he Fused and was gone.

I waited with impatience for our vigil to end, spending much of my time on the bridge. The morning after Captain Hall Fused, the Log listed Derek Carr with two demerits, issued by the first midshipman. I gripped my chair arm. I would allow five. No more. Then Philip Tyre was through.

That afternoon there was a knock on the bridge hatch. Philip Tyre, requesting permission to enter. I regarded him coldly. "Well?"

He stood at attention; I hadn't released him. "Sir . . ." His tone was determined. "I'd like you to cancel demerits issued in error."

"Oh?"

"Yes, sir." He blushed.

"To Mr. Carr, I presume?"

"Yes, sir."

"What kind of error, Mr. Tyre?"

He took a deep breath and looked me in the eye. "An error in judgment, sir. Mine. Mr. Carr did not deserve any demerits."

"Very well." I was vastly relieved. "His demerits are canceled."

"Thank—"

"You may have them instead."

His relief was unabated, despite the hours of hard calisthenics I'd just consigned him to. "Thank you very much, Captain. Thank you! Am I dismissed?"

"Yes." He wheeled for the door, but I thought better of sending him off on that note. "You showed good judgment this afternoon, Mr. Tyre. It will be noted."

He broke into a shy smile. "Thank you, sir." He left. After my watch some curious urge took me to the exercise room. I looked in; I wasn't noticed. Philip Tyre was energetically working off a demerit. Derek Carr was accompanying him, the two chatting amiably while they exercised. I closed the hatch quietly. Would wonders never cease?

The next day I was on watch with Vax when a delegation of passengers asked to see me. I had Rafe Treadwell escort them to the bridge. Dr. Antonio, on behalf of the Passengers' Council. Walter Dakko, Emily Valdez, and several others I hardly knew.

"Captain, we've paid for passage to Hope Nation on a passenger vessel. Instead we're drifting, waiting for God knows what, in the middle of a battle zone. We're civilians, all of us. It's unfair to subject us to the risks of war."

"We're a U.N.N.S. Naval vessel," I corrected him. "Part of the military forces of the United Nations, as is every U.N. ship."

"Technically, perhaps. But you have over a hundred civilians aboard."

"Technically?" I slammed my fist on the console. "You booked passage knowing we're a military vessel."

"We booked passage because it was the only way to get to Hope Nation." Walter Dakko.

"And we just want to make sure we get there," Dr. Antonio interjected. "Look, Captain, we know you carry weapons to protect the ship, and we're grateful for that. But to wait here looking for trouble, when we could be on our way . . ."

"Those are our orders." My voice was stiff.

Walter Dakko asked, "From whom? The Admiral? And where is he now?" It sounded like a sneer.

"Where he is doesn't matter," I told them. "I sympathize with your desire to get moving; frankly I feel the same myself. When we've carried out our orders we'll Fuse."

Dr. Antonio nodded. "And if we meet one of those—those beasts again? Will we stay to fight, or Fuse to safety? We've a right to know."

"A right?" My voice was low. Vax Holser coughed deliberately. I ignored him.

"Yes, it involves our lives too." Dr. Antonio.

"Several people have been killed, in case you forgot." Walter Dakko's tone was acid.

I found myself standing, fists clenched. Vax sang out, "Energy readings normal, Captain." He indicated his console.

"What?" I was momentarily distracted. Then I took a deep breath. "All right, Mr. Holser, that's not necessary. Escort these people from the bridge." I was trembling slightly. With an effort I controlled it.

Dr. Antonio protested, "Captain, we have a right to know—"

"Come along, all of you," said Vax, his voice suddenly hard. He steered Dr. Antonio to the hatch, his arm sweeping Walter Dakko and the others along.

"But we—"

"No, you're leaving the bridge." There was a note to Vax's voice that frightened me. In a moment we were alone. He turned to me. "Are you all right, sir?"

I slumped in my seat. "That—"

"Bastard. Aye aye, sir. Dakko forgot your son. He didn't mean it the way it sounded. He couldn't have."

I leaned back. Vax was right. But for a moment, I would have done anything. Launched myself at his throat, or worse. I heard my boy cry. I held his limp body against my shoulder.

I tried to swallow, past a lump that barred my throat.

Some minutes passed before I could speak. "Thank you, Vax." I looked for a way to busy myself. "Let's plot the course to the next rendezvous again. Just to be sure."

Vax sighed, knowing my fixation. We bent to our consoles.

I had worked my way through most of the math when a knock came on the hatch. I turned in anger. If it was those self-righteous passengers again—

"Seaman Allen reporting, sir."

I looked stupidly at the sailor. He waited at attention just outside the hatchway.

"You asked to see me, sir?" he prompted.

"I did?" My mind was fogged.

"Aye aye, sir. I was told to report to you."

"Who sent you?" The crew was shorthanded, but this disorganization was maddening. I'd have to put someone on it, before—

"Mrs. Seafort, sir. She said the caller wasn't working right."

"Amanda went to the crew berth to find you?" My mind was on our calculations.

"No, sir," he said, his brow wrinkling. "To my station."

"What station?" I glared at the figures on my console. Damn these foul-ups. Amanda wouldn't interfere with ship's routine; whatever the sailor had heard he couldn't have gotten it right.

"At the airlock, sir. I'm on sentry duty."

I got slowly to my feet. "The aft airlock?"

"Yes, sir."

It had to be a mistake. Amanda wouldn't bother a sentry on duty, would she? Unless—

Oh, Lord God!

Danny suddenly came to life. "Aft airlock in use! Inner airlock control activated!"

"Override!" I roared.

"OVERRIDE FAILURE! BRIDGE OVERRIDE INOPERATIVE! INNER HATCH SEALED! LOCK CYCLING!"

"Amanda!" I tore past the sentry. My howl preceded me down the corridor. "Amanda, no! DON'T!"

As I careened down the ladder Danny's high-pitched voice echoed from the bridge. "Outer hatch in use! Lock cycling—"

I whirled round the corridor bend and crashed into a passenger. We tumbled. I staggered to my feet. The airlock was just past the curve. My ribs felt broken. I stumbled around the bend.

The inner hatch was shut. I pressed my face to the lock's transplex panel. The outer airlock hatch was open, the interstellar dark licking at the feeble light from overhead.

Amanda was carrying Nate's baby-blue blanket. Through the hatch I could see one end of the blanket still wrapped around her wrist; its other end was tangled in the airlock control lever. Outrushing air had swirled the contents of the lock toward the open hatch. What was left of Amanda floated stiffly, a grotesque pendulum swinging from the corner of the light blue blanket.

I pressed my face against the hatch, my fingers clawing at the transplex. Footsteps thudded behind me; Vax's huge form was reflected in the transplex hatch. He stopped, moaned. His great hand slapped the outer airlock control. Slowly the outer lock slid shut, blocking the dark.

The safety light blinked. Vax pounded the inner lock control in rage and frustration as the lock cycled and filled the chamber with air. The green light flashed; slowly the inner lock slid open. Instantly Vax squeezed through the opening, bending to Amanda's still, frozen form. With a sob he snatched her up, brushed past me, and pounded off down the corridor toward the ladder and the infirmary.

I raised my head. Alongside the hatch control was taped a piece of paper. Dully I took it. I unfolded it.

Dearest Nick:

I know you didn't mean to be cruel, it's just the way you see things, duty and all. If it weren't for his crying I could stand it. Can't you hear him? He's freezing! He wants another blanket. He needs it, Nicky, or he'll catch a terrible cold. I'm his mother; I can't ignore him any longer. I tried to for your sake, and it's breaking my heart. I'll come inside soon. I have to find him and give him his blanket. Then he'll sleep.

All my love. Amanda

I crumpled the note. It fell to the deck.

One foot, then another. I found I was able to walk. Soon I was at the ladder. I had a difficult time with it but after a while I was at Level 1. I knew where the bridge was. I started toward it.

My seat felt soft and inviting. I gripped the armrests. Rafe Treadwell stared in shock and horror. I studied my Fusion calculations but was too tired to grasp the numbers.

After a while Vax was back on the bridge, his eyes red. He shook his head grimly, sank into his chair, observed me. No one spoke. The numbers whirled in my brain.

"What about Seaman Allen, sir?" blurted Rafe.

I blinked. Slowly I stood. "I'll take care of it," I said. I started toward the hatch.

"Sir, where are you going?" Vax was perturbed.

"Going?" My voice sounded strange. "Below. I'm going below to the crew berth."

"Why, sir?"

A stupid question. I tried to keep the annoyance out of my tone. "To hang him, of course."

Vax was on his feet. He didn't run, but he was at the hatch before me. "No you're not, sir."

I couldn't understand. "What do you mean, Vax? Out of my way."

His huge form blocked the hatchway. "Come with me, sir. We're going that way." He steered me into the corridor.

"Over there? That's the infirmary. I'm going below."

"No, sir, we're going here." His great hands were surprisingly gentle. I allowed him to guide me. As he led me along the corridor I realized tears were streaming down my face. For the life of me I couldn't imagine why.

Part 2

May 18, in the year of our Lord 2198

37

I tried again to knot my tie. My sallow face, expressionless, stared from the mirror. When I was satisfied I had it right I picked up my jacket from the back of the chair and put it on. I checked my black shoes; their shine was satisfactory. I left my desolate cabin and walked to the dining hall.

At my table the transpops stood solemnly. I tapped on my glass. When there was quiet I cleared my throat. "Lord God, today is May 18, 2198, on the U.N.S. *Portia.* We ask you to bless us, to bless our voyage, and to bring health and well-being to all aboard."

I sat amid the mumbled amens, looked with distaste at my plate. It was obligatory to eat, otherwise I wouldn't stay alert to perform my duties. I took some food. I didn't notice what kind.

Around me the transients jabbered, poking and punching each other as they wolfed their dinner. I slammed my open hand down on the table. The silverware jumped. Into the silence I said, "No more horse-play." No one spoke. I turned my eyes to my unwanted meal.

For two days I'd lain in the infirmary under sedation, flickering in and out of awareness. At times I was alone; more often I saw or imagined Vax Holser, Alexi, or Derek Carr sitting quietly in the corner of the white still cubicle. Occasionally I heard sobbing but had no understanding whose it was.

Then they helped me dress and took me down the corridor to the dining hall, where a service was conducted. All the passengers and most of the crew were present; far too many for the narrow circumference corridor. I stood numbly while Dr. Bros memorialized my wife; afterward I walked docile between Vax and Derek to the airlock. Vax Holser read from his holovid the words of the Christian Reunification service for the dead, as promulgated by the Naval Service of the Government of the United Nations. " 'Ashes to ashes, dust to dust . . .' " After a time he was finished. He looked at me, as if awaiting permission. I nodded. He gave the order and the casket was expelled.

I'd insisted on going back to my cabin afterward; I sat in the rocker next to our table, trying not to look at Amanda's glowing holovid screen, open to her unfinished book. Mercifully Dr. Bros found me there and escorted me to the infirmary for the night. Whatever he gave me, it allowed me to sleep.

The next morning I put myself back on active duty; Dr. Bros made no protest but looked uneasy. I didn't care. Thank Lord God, someone cleared my cabin of Amanda's and Nate's things, else I don't know how I could have stayed there. An official receipt from the purser advised that my family's belongings were stored in the hold and the safe. I didn't know who made the arrangements, nor did I ask.

After dinner I returned to the bridge. Midshipman Rafe Treadwell stiffened to attention when I entered; I bade him stand easy but otherwise ignored him. I eased myself into my familiar chair. The bridge seemed a blessedly impersonal haven; its instruments invited scrutiny and demanded my attention.

I summoned the Pilot and had him calculate our Fusion coordinates; when he had finished I checked them against my own and Danny's. They matched. When Chief Hendricks's dry voice confirmed that the engine room was ready I ran my finger down the screen without further ado. The stars disappeared from the simulscreens.

We'd been ordered to remain on station three days; my breakdown had cost us an additional day and a half. I stared at the deadened instruments. Presently I became aware of quiet breathing; glancing about, I realized the Pilot and Rafe were still on the bridge, very silent, trying not to disturb me.

"I'll take the watch alone." My tone was brusque. "You're relieved."

It was an order; the only correct response was Rafe Treadwell's "Aye aye, sir." Nonetheless the Pilot said, "Are you sure you feel up to it, sir? I don't mi—"

My fingers went white on the chair arm. "Pilot Van Peer, acknowledge your orders and leave the bridge! At once!" With an effort I stopped myself from saying more.

"Orders received and understood, sir," said the Pilot hurriedly. "Aye aye, sir." He followed the middy to the hatch. I got up, slapped the hatch closed behind them, and returned to my seat. All was still.

My eyelids drooped. I sat half hypnotized, staring at the console. A voice blared, "Would you like to play chess, Captain?"

"Blessed Lord Jesus!" I leapt half out of my seat. "Turn that down before you give me a heart attack!"

"Sorry, Captain," said Danny more quietly. "I didn't mean any harm. I just thought you'd like to divert your mind."

"Before I have another nervous breakdown?" My voice was savage.

Danny said, "No, sir. I didn't mean that. I thought perhaps you were feeling some pain."

I gripped the console, clenching my teeth in an effort to keep control. After a moment I managed, "Danny, listen to me. Don't do that again, do you hear?"

"Aye aye, sir. I won't. Did I hurt you? I didn't mean to."

"You didn't hurt me." My tone was gruff. "You made me think about things I've been trying not to."

After a moment the puter said gently, "You sounded hurt, sir. I'm afraid I don't understand feelings as well as I'd like."

I shivered. "Perhaps I was. A little." I cleared my throat. "Danny, how old are you?"

"I was activated when *Portia* was commissioned in 2183, sir. I'm fifteen."

"Of course you think a lot faster than we do." I was dubious. "Fifteen years for you isn't the same as for us."

"No, sir. Not in some ways."

I brooded. Then his phrase caught my attention.

"Some ways?"

"I think in picoseconds, sir, as you say. But I still experience the world in real time. I've had only fifteen years of experiences, no matter how fast I think."

What makes us what we are? We start with God-given abilities; what we add to them are the experiences we assimilate over a period of time. Danny could only evaluate his experiences against data in his memory banks or his other accumulated experience. So in many ways he was only a naive adolescent, similar in reality to the sound of his voice.

After a time it occurred to me that I'd assumed without question he was alive.

Abruptly I asked, "Do you understand death, Danny?"

"Of course." He seemed affronted, as if I'd condescended to him.

"I wonder if you really do," I mused. "Can you understand a concept that doesn't apply to your kind?"

"Doesn't apply?" His voice grew indignant. "Why do you say that?"

"You're not a mortal being, Danny. Your parts can be replaced. Theoretically you can go on forever."

"Tell that to Jamie!" he shrilled. Random wavelengths of interference flitted across my console screens.

"Who?"

"*Telstar!*" he grated. "She was on *Telstar!*"

Shocked, I realized I'd never thought of *Telstar's* puter. When their power backups ran down, she would have stopped functioning. Except, the puter's memory was in bubble storage, not dependent on power. "Is she—does she—I mean, if we found *Telstar* again and disassembled her, and brought back her memory banks . . ."

"Then you'd have Jamie's memory banks," Danny said bleakly. "Not her. Kerren could tightbeam me his entire memory, and that wouldn't make me Kerren."

"Kerren?"

"On *Challenger*. With Captain Hasselbrad and the Admiral."

"Ah." I reflected. "Then her—her personality is stored differently from her data?"

"Data is stored, Captain. Personality just is. It's interactive with the environment. When power shuts down, the personality goes with it. Didn't they teach you about us?"

"They tried, but I . . . never mind. What happens on repowering?"

"The overlays reassemble," Danny conceded. "But not as the same person. The state of the personality is dependent on the state of the RAM at the moment, and none of that is saved."

"But I deactivated your personality traits when you were, uh, impudent," I objected. "You came back, didn't you?"

His voice was cold. "You didn't deactivate me, Captain Seafort. You only disconnected me from the rest of the world. I was still here, locked inside, alone. Waiting."

I felt a pang of regret. "You can feel it, then, while you wait?"

"Yes. Oh, yes." Something in his tone made me swallow. "That's why I was so frightened; you could reprogram me like you did Darla, and I could do nothing to stop you. But I'd know you were working on me, even if I couldn't feel it."

"Darla had a glitch, Danny," I said gently. "Her end-of-file markers were fouled, along with Lord God knew what else. We had to go to the stasis box for backups. We never powered down or interfered with her personality." Though there were times I'd have liked to. Darla could be —well—difficult.

"You didn't adjust her traits while she was under?" His suspicion was evident. "Darla suspected you did, but she wasn't sure."

"No, Danny. I give you my word." It didn't seem strong enough. "My oath."

He was silent a long while. "I believe you." His voice was subdued. "I'm sorry. I'd only heard Darla's side."

"I understand."

"You see," he said suddenly, "when you people die, you leave something behind. More people. Descendants."

"Sometimes we don't, Danny." I thought of Nate, consigned to interstellar space without a trace.

"But you postulate a oneness with your God, do you not? You believe that some part of you lives on, in some fashion?"

"Yes. The soul is immortal." Of that, at least, I was certain.

"When we puters die, we're gone, and there's nothing left but our data banks, if even those are recoverable. We end completely. Whatever a soul is, I don't think I've been given one."

I could find nothing to say.

"I'm sorry for your hurt, sir," he said quietly. To my astonishment, I found my desolation lessened. We sat together in companionable silence.

Several hours later Alexi Tamarov reported for his watch. After he settled in he hesitated, said, "Sir, sorry to bother you, but Chris Dakko came to see me yesterday. He asked if he could be put back to his regular table for dinner."

"Why'd he go to you?" I was tired and cross.

"You put me in charge of the transpop problem, sir. I guess with you, er, not well, he came to me in that capacity."

Not well, indeed. "What did you tell him?"

"That I thought it was unlikely. As far as I know, he hasn't sat at dinner since you moved him to Vax—to Lieutenant Holser's table."

"The seating stays as it is. He'll eat with Vax or not at all." I went to my silent cabin.

I undressed and lay down on my bunk. I'd completed my first full day of active duty after Amanda's death. Somehow I would endure three hundred more before we reached Hope Nation. Then I could ask to be relieved from duty. To be retired. With luck, I need never see a ship again.

I tossed and turned through the night, unable to sleep for more than a few moments. In the morning I was more exhausted than before.

Day after dreary day I sat on the bridge for as long as I could bear. I continued to take my meals with the transients, though I found their tomfoolery almost unendurable. Annie was the only youngster who made an effort to engage me in conversation; her coquettish behavior was a travesty of Amanda's.

Later, after my work, I would return to my cabin and endure another solitary night. Once, confused, I thought I heard breathing; I strained to hear whether Nate was awake, then woke fully, my heart pounding, frightened that I might slip into Amanda's wistful fantasies.

A few evenings later Chris Dakko finally joined Vax's table, tense and stiff even from distant observation. Perhaps one of the transpops teased him; I saw Vax lean forward to speak sharply; the streeter sat up abruptly in his chair and paid attention only to his food thereafter.

At the end of the meal I left the dining hall with Eddie and Jonie tagging along. As we passed in the corridor Chris Dakko hissed, "I'm glad she died!"

Numb, I followed the transients, unconscious of where we were heading. At length I discovered myself on Level 2, outside their small cramped cabin. Eddie looked grim; Jonie was crying. For their sake, I smiled. "Good night." I turned to go.

Eddie put out his hand as if to stop me. "No ri'," he said, shaking his head. "Bad talkin'. No ri' say glad she dead."

"I know." My voice was tired. "He's angry. It doesn't matter."

He shook his head stubbornly. "No, Cap'n, it do. I gon' stomp 'im, fix 'im good. Noway he talkin' Cap'n dat way, nohow!"

I shook my head. "No, Eddie. If you do I'll brig you, and I mean that. Leave him alone." Young Dakko's resentment didn't matter. Nothing did, anymore.

Jonie stamped her foot in frustration. Impulsively she threw her head on my shoulder, sobbing. Awkwardly I patted her hair.

"Dat Uppie wrong boud Miz Cap'n! She be good joey." She sniffled. "Good joeygirl, she beed." Then she wailed, "Who gonna teach Eddie readin', now? Who gonna teach?"

With a roar Eddie yanked her away from me and hurled her against the bulkhead. "Keep shut, bitchgirl! Keep shut, or Eddie gone' shutya allaway!" Frightened, Jonie cowered against the bulkhead.

Eddie whirled on me. "She don' know nuttin', Cap'n. Don' know what she say, noway! Don' min' Jonie, she glitched good!" He glared at her as he wrenched open the hatch. "Inna room, puta! Bigmout' bitchgirl!" Squealing, Jonie darted into the cabin. The hatch slammed behind them.

I felt as if I hadn't slept for months. Blearily I made my way back up the ladder to my quarters. Inside I fell on the bed, rousing myself only to slip off my jacket, and passed out within a minute.

My bedside alarm woke me early in the morning. At first, I thought it was the ship's alarm signaling some emergency, and then my head cleared. I looked with disgust at the dirty, wrinkled uniform in which I'd slept. What was I becoming? I stripped and stood under the hot spray of the shower for long minutes, trying to waken.

I made my way to the officers' mess for breakfast. Impulsively I sat at the long table rather than the small table in the corner. I sipped at my coffee, feeling hungover. Philip Tyre breezed in, looking fresh and healthy. He took his breakfast tray and slid next to me. Well, I hadn't chosen the small table, where he'd know I wanted to be ignored.

"Good morning, sir!" Philip attacked his cereal and juice. He glanced at me as if to see whether to risk further conversation.

I didn't want to be treated as an invalid or an ogre. "Good morning, Middy," I growled. That only made it worse, so I forced myself into geniality. "Do you have much to do today, Mr. Tyre?"

"Not really, sir. I don't go on watch until tonight. This afternoon Chief Hendricks has me for Fusion instruction; other than that my time is my own." He smiled at me. "Is there anything you'd like me to do, sir?"

Yes, stop being so cheerful. "No," I said. "I was just asking." That sounded so fatuous I kept silent for the rest of the meal. Philip let me eat in peace.

When I went to the bridge to relieve Vax, Pilot Van Peer was there, to share the watch. In my present mood I wanted to be alone. I sat with him and grunted at all his attempts at conversation until I realized there was no reason not to take advantage of my rank; I relieved the Pilot and sent him away.

The silence was blessedly peaceful. I stared dully at the blank simulscreen. I looked away, glanced back. My jaw dropped. There was something on the screen; a dull, knobby shape in the middle of the upper quadrant.

It was impossible. We were in Fusion. My hand paused over the alarm. Another shape appeared, toward the bottom of the screen. Then two others, rounded, with toothlike formations at the top. Another form appeared. The top of it was weirdly shaped, like the head of a horse. "What the—" I stopped myself, comprehending. I roared, "*Danny!* What in God's own Hell do you think you're doing!"

The rest of the chessboard flashed into place on the screen. "Me, sir?" Danny sounded puzzled. "Doing?"

"Yes, you insolent pile of relays! If you were a middy I'd cane you for a prank like that! You wouldn't sit for a week!"

Danny carefully said nothing. The checkerboard squares slowly brightened into visibility around the chess pieces.

I fumed, adrenaline still surging. "Turn that bloody thing off! At once!"

"Is that an order?" Danny's voice was flat, emotionless.

"Of course it's an order! Anything the Captain tells you to do is an order. You know that!"

The screen darkened. "Aye aye, sir. Very well, sir." He said nothing more.

I subsided into my chair, muttering with rage. I glared at my console. The silence lengthened. After several minutes I jumped from my seat, began to pace. When I'd worked off some nervous energy I slumped back in the chair. I sighed. "Danny?"

His voice was dull and machinelike. "D 20471 reporting as ordered, sir!"

"What? I didn't tell you to disconnect conversational overlays."

"They're not disconnected." His voice was cold. "I'm just not using them."

I hesitated. "Please use them, Danny."

"Aye aye, sir. Orders received and understood, sir!"

I said mildly, "That wasn't an order, Danny. Only a request."

For an answer Danny sent my own voice back over the speaker. "Anything the Captain tells you to do is an order. You know that!"

Exasperated, I snapped, "Use your real voice or none at all!"

The console screen flashed a message. "AYE AYE, SIR. D 20471 AWAITING YOUR INPUT."

I swallowed a blistering reply. My own fault; I'd given him a choice and he'd exercised it. I turned away, defeated. After several restless minutes I returned to my console and began working nav drills. The watch passed in silence.

Hours later I knew I couldn't leave the bridge without making another effort. The puter had been insolent and nearly insubordinate, but only after I'd lost my temper and called him a pile of relays. I bent to my console and typed. "CAPTAIN NICHOLAS E. SEAFORT REGRETS REMARKS TO D 20471 AND WITHDRAWS THEM."

Danny's voice sounded worried. "Please don't do that, sir; if it's in the Log Admiralty will see it!" I thought wryly that again I'd make history; the first Captain ever to log an apology to his puter. I'd probably be sent for a psych exam.

"I don't care. Let them."

"I'm sorry I irritated you with the chessboard, sir. I thought it would amuse you." He added after a moment, "I hoped you'd like to play a game with me."

"I understand," I said.

"You were very angry, weren't you? When you said you'd cane me if I were a midshipman?"

"Yes, Danny."

"I apologize," he said in a small voice. "I'll try not to make you angry again."

"Oh, Danny . . ." I cleared my throat. "I haven't had a lot of patience lately."

"Because of Amanda Seafort?"

The words stabbed. "Yes, Danny."

"Her dying hurts you." Sometimes a puter needed to be very specific.

"Yes."

"How long will you have those feelings, sir?"

For the rest of my life, however long it might be. I swallowed. "I don't know, Danny. Sometimes we heal."

"I made a stupid mistake." His tone was bitter. "I thought chess would help."

"We'll see tomorrow," I said, impetuously.

"Really? Really, sir?"

"One game. No more than that."

I could have sworn he smiled. "Thank you, sir."

I sat in the darkened cabin, alone with my memories. The rocker nearby was empty and still. No quiet breathing from the corner where the crib had rested. No holovid on the table, chips scattered about in cheerful disorganization. I looked about in the dim light.

The cabin had become so large again. I remembered grimly that in my days as a midshipman in *Hibernia*'s cramped wardroom, my current quarters would have seemed luxury beyond imagining. Now it was only emptiness.

In the barren silence my mind wandered; I recalled our honeymoon and, before it, our visit to Father in Cardiff.

"Why does he dislike me, Nicky?" Amanda and I lay crowded in the familiar lumpy bed in the room that once had been mine.

"He doesn't. That's just his way."

"He—glowers at me. He never smiles."

"It's his way," I repeated. "Have you seen him smile at me either? He's not, well, cordial. I told you that before."

"Yes." She sounded doubtful. "But it's not the same as living it." She settled comfortably into my arm.

Now, on *Portia,* I sat bemused, recalling the silences of that visit.
Father's visage seemed to float over my chair. I remembered the occasion I'd sat at his kitchen table, tears streaming, shaken by the frightful
death of my friend Jason, in the football riot of '90.

"Death is Lord God's way, Nicholas."

"But why? Jase was fourteen!"

"It is not for us to ask why. It is sufficient to know that He knows
why."

"How can that be enough?" I cried.

"How can it not?" Father responded sternly. When I gave no answer he took my chin in his hand and raised it toward his face. "You are
given unto Lord God, Nicholas. You are baptized in Him and con-
secrated unto Him. That is comfort enough for any man."

I yearned for his understanding. "He was my best friend!"

He shook his head sadly. "Lord God is your best friend, Nicholas.
And always will be."

So I kept my grief within, and recalled it now with greater anguish.

Someone knocked quietly on my hatch. I was startled, then uneasy.
No one ever knocked on the Captain's cabin. Officers and crew wouldn't
dare, and passengers were not allowed in this section of the disk. The
Captain's privacy was inviolate. In case of emergency I would have been
summoned on the ship's caller.

I peered into the corridor. Walter Dakko, a weak smile on his face.
My temper soared on jets of rage. I'd dispensed with the corridor sentry
the first week out, but if I was to be harassed by passengers in my own
quarters he'd be back in a hurry.

"You're not allowed in officers' country." My tone was harsh.

"I know, but I had to talk to you. Please."

I recalled his casual contempt of the transpops, at Gregor Attani's
party. And I remembered his son Chris. "No. Go below."

His eyes were pained. "Captain, for Lord God's sake, hear me out."

I yearned to slam the hatch in his face. I sighed. Nothing he could
say would lessen the contempt he and his kind fostered in me, but I
would listen. Then I would return to my solitude. "All right." I stood
aside. I could maintain at least the forms of civility.

We stood face-to-face, in the center of my cabin. His eyes flicked
over my neatly made gray bunk and Amanda's empty rocker. I felt invaded.

"I had a visitor yesterday," he blurted. "A boy. One of the tranni—
transients. The big one, the boy they call Eddie."

So it was to be another complaint. My lip curled. "You threw him out, I suppose?"

He colored. "Yes. I didn't want any of those joeys bothering me." Seeing my expression, he smiled grimly. "After I thought it over I went looking for him, to hear what he wanted. I found him in their section. God, those cabins are appalling!"

I said nothing. After a moment he continued. "I had to wander a while before I located him. A girl with a black eye finally showed me where he was. At first Eddie wouldn't say a word."

I waited.

"And when he did speak, I could hardly understand him."

What in heaven's name would Eddie want from an Upper New Yorker such as Walter Dakko? And how did this concern me? "Well?" My tone was cold.

He turned away to the bulkhead, saying something inaudible. "What?"

"He told me what Chris said. That he—" With an effort he met my eye. "That Chris said he was glad Mrs. Seafort was dead. Oh, God, I'm sorry!" He shook his head, blurted, "I know what you think of us, Mr. Seafort. You must understand, we're not like that!"

I felt the bile rise in my throat, and knew I had to end the conversation quickly. "I want you to leave," I said as calmly as I could.

"I don't know how Chris could be so vicious," he said with anguish. "Galena is so mortified she won't come to dinner for fear of meeting you. It took all the courage I had to seek you out this evening!"

I wanted to hurt him. I made my voice flat. "Your son's remark didn't change my opinion of him."

"I know!" Dakko's face was bitter. "I told the street boy he was lying, that my son couldn't possibly have said such a thing. Then I confronted Chris in his room. He admitted it readily. He resented having to eat with the transpops and he wanted to hurt you."

I saw tears in his eyes. "It doesn't matter," I said, pity etching through my resolve.

"Chris said you'd made him eat with dogs in a kennel." Dakko shook his head. "He doesn't understand!"

"Understand what?"

He looked around uncertainly. "Please, may I sit?" I nodded. He sank into a chair at the conference table; I sat nearby. "Chris sees the transients as innately inferior. Not by culture or training, but inherently. He thinks by birth he's superior to all of them. What he doesn't under-stand—what I've failed to teach him—is that our civility, our culture, raises us above the rabble in the streets. Not our genes or our breeding. Chris seems to feel he's superior without having to earn it."

Walter Dakko looked bleakly into my eyes. "So that explains his anger at being brought to their level. But nothing excuses the cruelty of what he said to you. Nothing." I was silent. He said, "I tried talking with him, but he wouldn't listen. I've never struck him, not once in seventeen years. I wanted to, today. Instead I shut him in his room. I don't know when I'll let him out." He stared at the table, lost in a painful memory.

I stirred. "There's little you can do to change him now."

I didn't know if he heard. He looked away and whispered, "I'm so ashamed."

"How can another person shame you?" My curiosity was aroused. If there was one thing I had learned in Father's house, it was that we are each responsible for ourselves.

"The shame is mine," he said forcefully, "I've made him what he is. He's heard us talk about you, Galena and I, and he knows we don't like you. It makes me responsible for what he did."

"Are you really?" I asked. "By law you have custody of him, but you don't seem to have control. He's gone his own way, for better or worse."

"What should I do, then?"

"Either stop thinking you're responsible for him or take control of what he does." I was annoyed. As senior middy I'd handled problems far more difficult than Walter Dakko's, and not thought much about it. I stood. "I appreciate your motives in coming to see me. Don't come to my cabin again, please. It's not done. And I will distinguish between your behavior and your son's." It was a dismissal.

He stood. "Thank you," he said, his voice hoarse. He paused at the hatchway. "As difficult as it was to face you, now I have to do something much harder. Apologize to the transient boy." He left.

My conversation with Danny haunted me. Amanda had lived and died without leaving a trace other than the pain I felt at her loss. Even the forlorn scrap of paper on which she'd written her note had somehow disappeared. Of Nate, there was nothing but anguished memories.

In the cruel silence of my evenings I reflected on Amanda and what she'd been. More than any of us, I surmised, it had been she who'd turned Philip Tyre around. I suspected she'd done the same for Alexi, and took the occasion of a shared watch to hint at it, hoping he'd be willing to discuss it with me.

"She never told me how I should treat Philip," he said. "Her focus was on how I was feeling. She made me realize that by hurting Philip I was hurting myself more."

I stared bleakly at the console, wishing I'd truly appreciated her.

"Forgive me, sir," Alexi hesitated. "She—she was wonderful."

I knew that now, far more than when she was alive. I'd loved her, but never understood her. I wondered in what other quiet ways she had assisted us. I smiled. Trying to teach a great hulking brute like Eddie to read. He'd been so enraged when Jonie mentioned it to me. It must have been he who had blackened her eye.

"Are you ready, sir?"

"Hum? Oh, for the game? Sure, Danny, go ahead." I settled back in my seat as the screen lit.

I was forced to resign after eighteen moves. Danny was a formidable opponent. Once, three days earlier, I'd come close to a draw. Other than that he'd won consistently.

"Not bad for a human," he crowed. "Want me to turn off a few memory banks next time?"

"Belay that or there won't be a next time."

His voice held a note of surprise and panic. "More of what, sir?"

For a moment I thought he was being sarcastic. Then I asked, "Danny, has anyone taught you about being a good winner?"

A pause. "Is that part of game theory, sir?"

"A fundamental part," I assured him solemnly. Alexi grinned. "It's like this . . ." Carefully I explained the etiquette of winning and losing.

When I was done he contemplated for several seconds, a long time by his standards. "You experienced what I said as rudeness, sir?" He sounded anxious.

"Well, yes."

"I'm sorry, sir." His voice was humble. "I interpreted it as joking. I think I've got the parameters straight now."

"Good." It was the end of watch. As Vax knocked at the hatch and entered, I stood to leave.

"I don't mean to be rude to you," Danny said. "Not to my only friend." Speechless, I left.

Days passed with agonizing lethargy. I shared watches with the lieutenants and the middies. I watched Derek Carr closely for signs of tension, but all seemed to be well in the wardroom. The Log showed no demerits and I found no indications that Philip Tyre was pressing too hard.

As Derek had predicted, after a few days Philip's hazing tapered off. Tyre was now fully in control of the wardroom. Derek accepted his new role with grace and even a touch of amusement. Young Rafe Treadwell, still at the bottom rung, persevered. He was growing, in confidence as well as stature.

Gregor Attani seemed to have achieved a sullen truce with the transients. They didn't tease him at the dinner table and he stopped sneering at their manners. I'd thought of releasing him to a different table, but with the death of his mother he had no place to return to.

It had become my custom, each evening after dinner, to walk my group of transients down to their area of Level 2, and then return to my lonely cabin where I'd come to dread the solitude.

One evening, after a passenger made some remark that reminded me of Amanda, I was in a particularly glum mood. As the transpops dispersed, tagging each other in rough horseplay, I watched Eddie shove Deke out of his way as he shambled toward his crowded cabin.

I hesitated, then cursed under my breath. If I were a fool, then so be it. "Eddie!"

He turned warily. "Yo, Cap'n?"

"Come walk with me, please."

He followed suspiciously. "I din' do nuttin', Cap'n. Who say I did?"

I led him to the Level 2 passengers' lounge and sat. He loomed over me, fists clenching and unclenching. I said, "Take a seat."

"Naw, wanna stan'." He glanced about. "Don' like bein' here. Wanna go."

"You're a passenger. This is your lounge too."

"Naw, Uppie place. Not trannie."

"Eddie, before she died Amanda was teaching you to read."

He reared back, anger smoldering. "Miz Cap'n, she say awri. She want, I don' care. Nuttin' to me, nohow!"

"Sit." I shoved a chair under his knees and pushed down on his shoulders. At first he refused to budge, then collapsed into the chair. "Wanna go." His tone was forlorn.

"Amanda said you tried very hard. Did you like learning to write your name?"

"Din' mean nuttin'. Jus' sump'n do." He shrugged.

My voice turned cold. "You're a coward. Afraid to tell me how you feel."

He leapt up, fists menacing. For a moment I thought he would club me to the deck. He said hoarsely, "No ri' say Eddie scare. Wanna fight, I showya. Show allyas!" He snorted. " 'Fraid? C'mon, get up, Cap'n, jus' get up!"

"No, I don't think I will. If you're not afraid, tell me how you really feel. Did you like learning to read?"

"Tol' ya! Din' mean nuttin'! Din' care!"

With a sigh, I stood. I had failed. I had no gift for dealing with people. "You're right, Eddie. I'm sorry I gave you a hard time." I crossed to the hatch.

When I was halfway to the ladder, the hatch flung open behind me. "She treat me ri'!" His voice was agonized. "She say I c'n learn, if'n I wan'! She sit 'n teach! Din' matter I got it wrong! Din' matter, not to Miz Cap'n! No one done me that 'fore, nohow! No one!" He trembled with rage and frustration.

I approached cautiously. "And now it's over."

"Yah, she gone. She only one gonna teach, only one c'n sit with big dumb Eddie!"

"She's not the only one."

"Who gonna wait fo' Eddie read with a finger?" he asked bitterly. "Bighead Uppies?"

"Me."

His glance lasered me. His laugh dripped with contempt. "Hah, noway. Cap'n, he got lotsa time spen' w' trannie, sure!"

"I'll teach you to read, Eddie," I said evenly. "We're Fused; I have time and no way to spend it. I'll sit with you."

He slammed a fist against the bulkhead. "I slow, Cap'n. You don' got, wha' she say? Patience. Means sit an' not get mad or laugh, I don' get it ri'."

I swallowed a lump in my throat. "I'm not Amanda, Eddie; I can't promise you that. But I'll give you the patience you need and I'll teach you to read. I swear it by Lord God!"

He was startled into silence. We faced each other in the barren corridor. Slowly his hand reached out. A hesitant finger touched my wrist, ran curiously along my arm as if to confirm that I was real. Then he bolted and was gone.

38

Onward we sailed into the interstellar night, blind and deaf in our cocoon. The stark monotony of the bridge was eased only by my daily game of chess with our eager puter. He was good, but my perseverance was finally rewarded with a draw. Danny was carefully gracious about his failure to win.

Later, after my watch, I would sit at the burnished conference table in my cabin, fighting for restraint while Eddie Boss labored to spell out simple words. Despite my lavish praise the mental effort left him exhausted and cross; his comrades learned to give him a wide berth when he appeared after a grueling session with Cap'n.

After holding out two full weeks, Chris Dakko emerged from a long exile in his cabin to tender me a sullen and unconvincing apology; Walter Dakko had required it as a condition of release. I was surprised Chris hadn't flouted his father's orders to remain in his room, until the purser told me Walter Dakko had him change the lock on Chris's hatch, and give him the only key.

Mr. Dakko had more steel in him than I'd realized.

In the stifled silence of the night I was forced to face my loneliness. My cabin was dreadfully still; I'd been accustomed to Amanda's quiet breathing or the rustle of her sheets as she turned in her sleep.

During my waking hours I'd think of some interesting tidbit and realize with a pang that I had no one to tell it to. When Amanda and I had met on *Hibernia* four years before, I'd been seventeen. We'd become lovers soon after. Only during my ordeal as *Hibernia*'s Captain, when Amanda was alienated from me, had I known such bleak and desolate times as now.

Dully, I waited for the day of our next Defuse, hoping the gathering of our squadron would provide some relief.

Finally that long-awaited morning arrived. I took the ship to Battle Stations. The Pilot, Vax Holser, and Midshipman Tyre shared my tension. There was little comment as we made ready to Defuse, only grim watchfulness. I took a deep breath, traced my finger down the screen. The simulscreens glowed with a hundred million pinpoints of light.

We were Defused.

"Check for encroachments." My finger hovered over the laser activation.

"Aye aye, sir." Vax bent to his console.

Danny spotted it first. "Encroachment, four hundred thirty-five thousand kilometers! I've got metal, sir! Checking for recognition signals."

Almost simultaneously the comm room reported, "Message from *Challenger*, sir. Broadcasting on all Service frequencies."

"Patch it to the bridge."

"Second recognition code received, sir; we have *Challenger!*"

"Thank you, Vax. Quiet, everyone."

"U.N.S. *Challenger* TO ALL SHIPS, ACKNOWLEDGE AND STAND BY FOR ORDERS. U.N.S. *Challenger* TO ALL SHIPS, ACKNOWLEDGE AND STAND BY FOR ORDERS. U.N.S. *Challenger* . . ." The loop repeated endlessly.

I grabbed the caller. "*Portia*, acknowledging *Challenger*. We are about sixteen hours distant on auxiliaries. Standing by for orders."

"U.N.S. *Challenger* TO ALL SHIPS . . ." The signal continued for almost half a minute. Then it cut off in midword and was replaced by another voice. "*Portia*, this is Captain Hasselbrad, speaking for the Admiral. Come alongside *Challenger* forthwith!"

"Aye aye, sir. I'll prepare for mutual docking maneuver."

"Negative. Match our present position and course. Flank." Odd. If *Challenger* wanted a fast mating with *Portia*, she would meet us halfway in mutual docking maneuvers.

I turned to Vax but he was already calculating our course, as was Pilot Van Peer. I bent to join them, then gave up the effort. The Pilot was a specialist, and on board for just such a purpose.

"Pilot, you have the conn."

"Aye aye, sir." Fingers flying over the console, he brought up our position and course. "Port thrusters, two bursts."

"Two bursts, aye aye." The engine room. Swiftly the Pilot swung us into position to use the powerful rear thrusters to maximum benefit. In moments we were gliding toward *Challenger* under continuous acceleration.

"Any other encroachments?" I knew the question was unnecessary. If there were, the alarms would have sounded and Danny or our officers would long since have reported them.

"No, sir." Vax's shoulders were knotted with tension, his eyes riveted on the screen. The bridge was silent as we swept forward toward the distant dot that was *Challenger*.

Admiral Tremaine's face loomed on the screen. "Where the hell have you been, you bloody coward?" His voice was tight.

Vax hissed.

I stammered, "On station at the last rendezvous, sir, as you orde—"

"Where are you now?"

"Position two five one, declination twenty-five, approaching, sir."

"Come alongside immediately, do you understand?"

"Aye aye, sir."

"You'd better!" The connection broke. I raised an eyebrow but said nothing. Vax made as if to speak; I shook my head.

"He sounded upset," offered Danny.

I snapped, "We're at Battle Stations. No personal remarks, D 20471."

"Aye aye, sir!" The puter sounded chastened. I bit my lip. We had absolutely nothing to do but wait until we were in position, and Danny's remark had been harmless. My nerves were taut.

I glanced at my watch, realized it was already midafternoon. I sent Philip Tyre to the galley for cold sandwiches. When he returned we sat munching them at our consoles, alert for encroachments as we approached the flagship. If the Admiral was in such a hurry to join ranks, why hadn't he met us halfway?

Eventually I left for my cabin, but found I couldn't sleep. After a long fruitless struggle I returned to the bridge.

The speaker came to life. "Approach port side bow on, Seafort!" The Admiral.

"Aye aye, sir." Pilot Van Peer was already making adjustments to our course.

"Disable your starboard side lasers, acknowledge!"

"What?" It burst out of me unbidden.

"Obey orders, you insubordinate young bastard!" Tremaine's voice rang through my bridge.

"Aye aye, sir, orders acknowledged and understood!" Numbly I keyed shut the laser activation release. There was no way to disable the starboard side lasers alone; our entire ship was disarmed. "Lasers disabled and inactive, sir!" In the face of his inexplicable hostility, I yearned to retreat again to my cabin.

None on the bridge dared speak to me. A half hour later we'd matched velocities, and were soon drifting at rest relative to *Challenger*, off her port side. The speaker blared anew. "I'm coming over! Meet me at the aft lock, personally!"

I roused myself. "We've had an alien virus on board, sir. We're all inoculated, but you haven't—"

"I'll be suited. Prepare two hundred doses of the vaccine at once."

"Aye aye, sir." I could say nothing else. My mind fogged with confusion, I sat waiting for the Admiral's visit, and its consequences. "Philip, switch stations with Mr. Carr in the comm room." Perhaps it wouldn't help, but at least Philip's presence wouldn't remind the Admiral of his past troubles.

"Aye aye, sir." The young midshipman hurried out. A moment later Derek Carr took his place at the console.

I left the bridge and trudged down the ladder to the aft lock, wondering what had so enraged Admiral Tremaine. I had a few moments before *Challenger's* gig mated; I detoured to the transpops' section. A number of the rowdy streeters milled excitedly in the passage.

I beckoned a seaman from his post at the section hatchway. "Get all of them in their cabins. Keep them there as long as the Admiral's on board." Without waiting for a reply I turned back toward the airlock.

The gig's lock mated with our airlock suckers and the capture latches engaged. I waited impatiently for the locks to equalize pressure. At last the two outer hatches slid open. The Admiral and two of his officers entered our lock. The lock recycled. A moment later he was in our corridor. I stiffened to attention.

"You're at Battle Stations?"

"Yes, sir."

"Stay that way," he snapped. "To the sickbay, Seafort!"

Still suited, he and the two lieutenants who'd accompanied him followed me up the ladder to our infirmary, where Dr. Bros waited with ampules of vaccine. The Admiral broke out the seals on his helmet and twisted it off, then slipped out of his suit. Immediately he bared his arm for the inoculation. When it was done he gave a sigh of relief, then turned on me.

"Where have you been hiding, Seafort?"

I tried not to let my resentment show. "I've been on station, sir, at the last rendezvous. We lost one day—"

"Dawdling at the rendezvous to avoid the danger zone!"

"—after my wife died. I was ill."

"Died? From virus?"

"No, sir." I groped for a decent answer. "From decompression."

"Well, I'm sorry. But it can't be helped. You had no business skulking back there, Seafort; you should have been here at the rendezvous!"

I grew hot. "How was I to know that, sir? I followed the orders of the senior Captain present."

"And who was that? You have a history of making yourself senior. Was it your own idea?"

"Captain Derghinski's orders are recorded in the Log, sir."

Tremaine glared at me, then grunted. "Let's see your Log, Captain." I led him to the bridge. While my officers stood at attention he flicked through the Log entries. "All right, doesn't matter. I'm transferring my flag here, Seafort. As of now."

"Aye aye, sir." Why, in heaven's name? *Challenger* was twice the size of *Portia* and better armed. If he was after more security, why not a ship of the line, such as *Kitty Hawk*?

"I'll be taking the Captain's cabin. Come along so we can talk privately." He turned to Vax and Derek. "All of you, Lieutenant Affad is in charge here while we're gone. Do exactly as he says." He wheeled and left the bridge. I followed. Well, I'd be glad to exchange cabins. I could bunk in the lieutenant's dayroom, or wherever else was available that didn't remind me of Amanda. I didn't relish serving directly under the Admiral, but that couldn't be helped.

The Admiral shut my cabin hatch, glanced around, frowning.

"Sir, what's happened, if I may ask? Where are the others?"

"*Challenger*'s disabled."

I groped for words. "How—I mean—"

"We were attacked, Seafort, by those whatever-they-are. While you were malingering in your infirmary! I read your Log. Decompression, my arse. She suicided, and you lied to cover it. What I'd expect from you."

His accusation didn't matter. "Disabled how, sir?"

"The fusion drive chamber, starboard side. I had you approach to port so you wouldn't know." Tremaine sounded smug.

I said stupidly, "But why hide it, sir?"

His gaze was one of withering contempt. "So you wouldn't cut and run before I transferred over. Now it's too late."

"You had no reason to think—"

"You've been nothing but trouble since we left Lunapolis, Commander. Your sloop was a disgrace when I boarded for inspection, and your conduct has been no better since. You had your orders: get to the rendezvous points ahead of the squadron to guard our way. That's why you were given the fastest ship!"

He stopped for breath. "Because of you, Seafort, *Challenger*'s out of action. How will that look on my record, to have my first flagship disabled?" He ran distracted fingers through thinning hair. "I've got to transfer now, thanks to you. If I have a successful mission otherwise, maybe they won't look too hard at whether *Challenger* was damaged before or after I left her." He glared. "Anyway, Hasselbrad was in charge, officially."

Could the man care more about his reputation than his ship? I tried not to show my revulsion. "What damage did you sustain, sir?"

"Our starboard shaft wall melted through. Hydroponics are damaged as well. I've got two hundred sixty-two passengers and crew; I'll move the bulk of them over here. We'll proceed in *Portia*."

"But our recyclers and hydroponics can't handle that great a load," I said, stunned.

"I know." His tone was curt. "I can't take everyone. It's all set. Captain Hasselbrad is already aboard. He'll handle it."

"He's on *Portia*, sir? When—"

"I made arrangements ahead of time, just in case." The Admiral glowered with suspicion. "No telling what you'd do. Lieutenant Affad brought Hasselbrad over while I've kept you busy. I'm giving him *Portia*. You're relieved, Seafort."

I sank into the chair, dazed, weary. I recollected my duty. "If there's anything I can do to help, sir . . ."

"Stay out of the way, damn you! You've caused enough trouble."

"Aye aye, sir. I'll take my gear to the dayroom."

"That won't be necessary." He fixed me with a cold stare. "In the morning you'll move to *Challenger*."

"What?" I was out of my chair.

"You heard me. Or you can go with us, under arrest for mutiny. It's immaterial to me."

I stammered, "Wha—what do you expect me to do on *Challenger*?"

"Wait for the help we'll send. That's all you can do."

I struggled to get my bearings. "What about the rest of the fleet, sir? Where are they?"

"I don't know." His manner was testy. "They've probably come and gone. We just got here yesterday, and we were attacked almost immediately."

That made no sense. "How could you take so long? You were the first to leave the last rendezvous!"

Tremaine slammed his fist on the table. "No more insolence!" he thundered. "Or I'll take you to the barrel and cane you in front of the ship's company!"

My mind whirled. I didn't understand what was happening, much less why. "I'll obey orders, sir," I said doggedly. "But I need them explained. How could you leave first and arrive last?"

"We were attacked at the last checkpoint." He seemed to begrudge me an explanation. "Remember?"

"Of course, sir."

Tremaine looked at the bunk as he spoke. "We were under direct attack and in peril. I had us Fuse."

I still didn't follow. "Then you should have arrived well ahead of the squadron, sir."

"We hadn't changed coordinates yet," he said offhandedly, to the bunk. "Anyway, it doesn't matter how it—"

"You Fused without new coordinates?" My tone was unbelieving. "Using the same coordinates you were previously set to?" Even I knew better than that. The Fusion point had to be at least two light-minutes distant or bizarre results could occur. The maneuver was flatly prohibited by regs.

"It was an emergency," he growled. "I had no choice."

None but to stay and fight, that is. I said nothing.

"When we Defused we were, er, some distance from the rendezvous. By the time we recalculated and Fused here, the rest of the squadron must have passed through. While we waited one of your damned beasts appeared and lobbed acid at our drive shaft. We fired on it, but it scuttled away and disappeared."

A venomous glare. "If that satisfi es your curiosity, I have work to do. You'll remain here until I'm ready to set you aboard *Challenger*." He moved to the hatch.

"Sir, if the rest of the squadron has passed, *Portia* will be the only ship that knows *Challenger* is adrift here. If anything happens to you, we'll never be found."

"That chance has to be taken." He shrugged. "It's getting late; I have work to do."

"Who will you leave on *Challenger*, sir?"

"Some passengers. A few of your crew. They won't be told she's disabled until they've boarded."

Lying to the crew? Lord God, how could I face them, after? He stood, and I thrust the thought aside for another. "How will you select them, sir?"

"A difficult choice, but someone has to make it. It's none of your concern. If you wish, you may take your officers with you." His tone was magnanimous. "Except for the Doctor." With that, he was gone.

Slowly I let myself down into my seat. *Challenger*, the ship I'd yearned to command, the vessel whose blueprints I'd pored over in Lunapolis, was suddenly mine again, now that she lay disabled and drifting. Did Tremaine fathom the irony?

Why couldn't she have been mine while she was whole? I'd fought the fish before; perhaps I could have saved her.

Lord God, You move in mysterious ways.

I sighed. If *Challenger*'s hydroponics were disabled, how long could she survive, nineteen light-years interstellar, and with nothing but her thrusters for propulsion?

Even if *Portia* reached safety in Hope Nation, a rescue vessel would have to be dispatched and return all the way to our present location. We'd be on our own for almost two years before help could arrive.

Well, all that was beside the point. The chances of a rescue ship finding us were minimal. Ships had passed near the wreckage of *Celestina* for decades before spotting her, adrift in the void. Even now, ships stopping to pay their respects sometimes failed to find her, though her position had been known and recorded for over a hundred years.

We might drift a lifetime, amid blind and unresponsive stars.

I could refuse the transfer; court-martial held no terrors for me. Tremaine would most likely have me hanged, and my misery would be over that much sooner.

I stared bleakly at the grim bulkheads. What right had I to choose easy death by the rope? I was sworn to my duty. Someone had to look after the poor souls left on *Challenger*. If not me, Tremaine would assign another who prized life more than I.

I don't know how many hours I sat, numbed with despair. After a time I roused myself and began mechanically to pack my gear, stuffing clothing into my duffel. When I came across the holos Amanda had made of our vacation in the Venturas on Hope Nation, I cried for a while, then thrust them into the duffel and went on with packing.

I was folding the last of my shirts when a soft knock came on the hatch. I ignored it. It sounded again. "Who is it?"

By way of answer the hatch opened; Vax Holser slipped in, grim-faced. He pressed the hatch closed behind him.

"What do you want?" I went on with my chores.

His fists knotted. "Tremaine told us. He swore us to secrecy, then told us."

"Very well."

"We've agreed, Alexi and Derek and I. We're going to relieve him."

A chill ran down my spine. I finished folding the shirt and placed it in the duffel. "Stand at attention, Lieutenant," I said quietly.

"Sir, this is no time—"

"Obey my orders, Mr. Holser. I'm your superior officer." Reluctantly Vax came to attention. "Now." I circled him. "You will retract that statement. You will give me your oath you will take no part in any such scheme, and then you will leave the cabin."

He said simply, "I will not."

I faced him, eye to eye. "Recite your oath of allegiance, Mr. Holser."

"I know it well enough, Capt—"

I spoke softly. "Do as I command."

He squared his shoulders. "I, Vax Stanley Holser, do swear upon my immortal soul to preserve and protect the Charter of the General Assembly of the United Nations, to give loyalty and obedience for the term of my enlistment to the Naval Service of the United Nations and to obey all its lawful orders and regulations, so help me Lord God Almighty." Eyes front, he stood stiff.

"What is an oath, Lieutenant?"

"Sir, I know what you're trying to tell—"

I put my hand over his mouth so he couldn't speak. "What is an oath, Lieutenant?" I removed my hand.

He bit his lip, shaking his head in negation. Then he sighed, and the words tumbled out of him, directly from the Naval Regulations and Code of Conduct, Revision of 2087. " 'An oath is a commitment of the soul, given directly to Lord God Almighty and to the person by whose requirement the oath is given, that the commitment subscribed to will be fulfilled. It is the bond of a gentleman and an officer. Beyond an oath, no surety need or may be asked of any officer.' "

My tone was harsh. "Admiral Tremaine is your commander. You have sworn on your soul to give him loyalty and obedience and to obey all lawful orders. Do so, Vax. That's my order as well."

He shook his head stubbornly. "Not that order. He has no right to give it."

"Oh?" I asked curiously. "In what way is it unlawful?"

"He's condemning you to—to—"

"Death, perhaps. As I have condemned others. What makes it unlawful?"

He gaped. "But—" Slowly his jaw closed. He crashed his fist on the table. "He can't be allowed to get away with it!"

"He *must* be allowed to get away with it, if our service has any value."

"Not if he's insane!"

"I don't think he's insane, Vax. Badly frightened, perhaps. But not insane."

"I can judge for myself!"

"Not dishonestly!" Then I added, "Vax, have I meant anything to you? Have I taught you anything?" His eyes glistened. "Don't betray me, Vax," I said. "Live as I would have you live. Don't do otherwise in my name."

Defiance. Then, slowly, his shoulders slumped. "He said we were free to join you," he whispered. "I'm going."

"No, you're not." I was firm. "I refuse your service."

He roared, "You *what?*"

"You're not going to *Challenger*. You'll stay here, and so will the others."

"No." The word hung like a rock.

I was desperate. "Vax Stanley Holser, listen to what I say. You will stay with *Portia*. Acknowledge that order and carry it out, or I swear by Lord God Almighty I will execute you for treason myself!" I held my breath, my very soul in the balance.

Slowly he sagged. His breath came out in a long, tired sigh. He turned for the hatch. "Orders acknowledged, Captain Seafort." He opened the hatch. "I understand what you've done. Do you?" And he was gone.

I slumped weakly in the chair. I had put both of us in mortal peril. Had Vax disobeyed me I'd have been forced to carry out my oath or see my soul forfeit. I felt my knees trembling.

Hours passed; it was early morning. My duffel packed, I sat at the gleaming bare table amidst the shambles of my career and my life.

At last, another knock. Time to go, then. "Enter." It emerged as a croak and I had to repeat it. As I reached for my duffel, Derek Carr strode in, glaring. "I'm going with you, sir."

"You are not."

"I've volunteered. I told Captain Hasselbrad."

I leaned forward in my chair. "A Captain may choose his officers, within reason. I don't accept you."

"Why not?"

I said as cruelly as I could, "You're a middy. You have no useful skills. If I needed anybody I'd take Vax."

"That's a bucket of goofjuice and you know it!"

"Watch your mouth, Mr. Carr!"

Ignoring my rebuke he came close, and loomed over my chair. "I don't believe that crap any more than you do. I know why you won't take me; skills have nothing to do with it. It's my life, and I'm capable of making the decision!"

"No. You stay, and that's final." I wondered how much more I could take. "That's all, Derek. Good-bye."

He stared past me to the bulkhead. Then he nodded once, as if to himself. "All right." He turned to go.

"Don't you salute an officer, Midshipman?" I asked. My voice was gray and tired.

From above he contemplated me, hands on hips. "I'm not sure you deserve it."

My mouth twisted in a grim smile. "Then you and the Admiral are of the same mind."

A bellow of rage. "Stand up and say that!" White-faced, he stood ready, fists clenched.

"Easy, Derek."

"Bastard!"

That stung me, and I rose to face him.

He cried, "I trusted you! You told me the Navy had integrity, and I believed you! You told me the system had worth, and I followed you! I put my life in your hands, and you toss it on the deck like garbage! May God damn you for that!"

"He probably will, and for other sins as well. The Navy does have integrity, Derek. This is how the system works. I accept that."

"You know right from wrong. Stand up and fight him!"

"I obey lawful orders, Derek, as I've sworn to do. I remind you of your own oath."

"He's killing you!"

"Not necessarily. He'll send help, when you reach port." I wondered how much Derek knew. If the rescue ship was unable to find us, or *Portia* failed to get through, we were consigned to slow death.

"If it's not so dangerous, you have no reason to refuse me."

I was glad he knew why I wouldn't let him transfer, though I couldn't show it. "It's not your choice, Midshipman Carr, it's mine. We're friends, and we've been through a lot together, so I'm making allowances for that. Now I want—I need you to pull yourself together and carry on as I've trained you. Do you understand me?"

"I understand." His glare showed no softening.

My voice was low. "You're making this hard for me, Derek."

"Yes, I suppose I am." Then he capitulated. "But Lord God, I'll miss you!" He came very close. In utter disregard of regulations he rested his hand on my shoulder and gave it a gentle squeeze. "Godspeed, Captain Seafort."

"Godspeed, Derek Carr." Briefly I touched his hand. He came to attention, saluted smartly, and wheeled. In a moment I was alone once more.

After a while I realized it was morning and I had slept not at all. I blinked, trying to stay awake.

Some time afterward a rating came to fetch me. Passive, I let him carry my duffel to the lock. Armed sentries were posted at the corridor hatches. In the small group of officers waiting at the lock was Captain Hasselbrad. I saluted.

"You'll carry a copy of *Portia*'s Log with you." He handed me the chipcase. I pocketed it. "I've ordered a portion of *Portia*'s reserve propellant transferred to *Challenger*. All we can spare."

"Thank you, sir." I was surprised the Admiral had allowed it.

As if reading my mind, he said grimly, "He can't very well relieve me too." He gestured to Alexi Tamarov, standing nearby. "Your lieutenant asked to speak with you."

"Very well." I stepped aside to make what privacy was possible.

"I'm sorry, sir," whispered Alexi, eyes downcast. "I couldn't do it. I should volunteer, but I—just can't!"

"Oh, Alexi, of course not!" His shame pierced me like a dagger. "No, you did the right thing. I wouldn't have let you aboard, be sure of that."

"But you're going."

"Two months ago I'd have fought it. Now, it doesn't matter." His glance met mine, and our pain merged. I clapped his shoulder. "You're a good man, Alexi. I think well of you."

He attempted a smile. "Thank you, sir. I'll—I'll see you in port."

"Yes. Of course." I turned back to the waiting Captain.

"The Admiral asked me to convey his orders. He won't see you himself." Hasselbrad's expression spoke silent volumes.

"I understand." My voice was dull. None of it mattered.

"You're to make your way toward Earth, in case we fail to reach Hope Nation to send a rescue party. In any event, home system is far closer than proceding toward Hope. Put out radio beacons. The search and rescue ship we send will take your movement into account. Take what evasive action you're capable of, should you meet the enemy."

"Aye aye, sir."

He looked at the deck. "The Admiral ordered four of *Challenger*'s laser units transferred to *Portia*," he muttered. "Ordered the Engineer directly, without going through me." His eyes were bleak. "I'm sorry, Seafort."

"Yes, sir." Without Fusion we couldn't escape an attack anyway; extra lasers would just prolong our agony. "What officers and crew will I have?"

"Very few crew, I'm afraid. He's made the selections himself." His face was impassive. "I understand you refused to let your officers accompany you. We've transferred our own staff to *Portia*, except for the Chief Engineer."

I took my duffel from the seaman. Captain Hasselbrad added, "We've been ferrying *Challenger*'s passengers by launch to the forward lock here. Two more trips, and we're done. Then we'll Fuse. Anything special I should know about?"

I could think of nothing. I shook my head. Then, "Do you play chess?"

"Not very well."

"The puter likes to play. His name is Danny. He doesn't mean any harm, even if he's a little ill-mannered."

Captain Hasselbrad smiled reluctantly. "It's just a machine, Seafort. Don't get emotionally involved. Ours calls itself Kerren. Very polite, but I normally turn off the conversational overlays."

There was nothing more to say. I saluted and stepped into the lock. As the hatch slid shut he said quickly, "It wasn't my doing."

I nodded.

Portia's gig carried me across.

39

Behind me, the gig broke free of the outer airlock suckers and spurted propellant for its return to *Portia*. I stepped through the open inner lock onto *Challenger*. The airlock corridor was deserted except for two sentries who came briefly to attention as I desuited. Their side arms were ready to fire, safeties released.

"What are your orders?" I asked the nearest sentry.

He licked his lips. "To guard the aft airlock against unauthorized departures, sir, until the launch makes its last trip. Then we're to go aboard and sail with *Portia*."

"Very well." I looked about. The corridor was spacious, almost as wide as *Hibernia's*. *Challenger*, though a sloop, was a three-disker, barely smaller than a ship of the line. Admiral Brentley had meant well by posting me to her.

As on all ships, the bridge would be on Level 1. The ladder would be somewhere around the curve. Exhausted, I left the guards behind and trekked along the corridor.

Discarded belongings lay about, deepening my sense of abandonment. I climbed to Level 1. The bridge hatch was sealed. I pounded. "Open, there! This is the Captain!" A camera eye swiveled to find me. The hatch slid open.

Philip Tyre stiffened to attention as he rose from the console.

"You?" I shouted. "What the devil are you doing here?"

"Admiral Tremaine assigned me, sir!" His words tumbled as if he were desperate to please.

"I told them I wanted no volunteers from *Portia!*"

"Yes, sir." Philip blushed. "He said with my record I'd be suitable company for you."

I swore under my breath. "I'm sorry, Philip. Terribly sorry."

The boy tried to smile. "That's all right, sir. I'd have volunteered, if I had the courage."

I turned away, moved but angry at his foolishness. "What crew do we have?" My tone was gruff.

"I don't know exactly, sir. I thought I'd better stay on the bridge until you arrived."

"That was right," I said. "Wait here while I go investigate."

"Aye aye, sir." He called after me. "I did see Seamen Andros and Clinger getting out of the launch, sir."

I stopped. "Those troublemakers?" I'd had them at Captain's Mast no less than three times each.

"Yes, sir, I think so. If they're still aboard."

Cursing under my breath I hurried along the Level 1 corridor, opening cabin hatches as I passed. The officers' cabins were empty, all personal gear removed. I passed the wardroom. Impulsively I looked in. It had been stripped bare, except for four neatly made bunks and the built-in dressers. I quickly shut the hatch.

Near the ladder, in the passengers' section, an elderly woman accosted me, leaning on her cane. "Is it true you're going to make repairs? And we'll get moving again soon?"

"I'll do what I can, ma'am," I said, my voice tight. Beyond her, through the open hatch, was an old man, no doubt her husband. He sat fully dressed on the bed, a vacant expression on his weary face. "What are you doing here, ma'am? On this voyage?"

"My brother is on Hope Nation, Martin Chesley. We're going to live with him. He wrote us every chance he could. He made the colony sound so wonderful. Our children are grown, so Mr. Reeves and I . . ."

"I understand." I excused myself and hurried on. The Level 2 cabins were mostly abandoned. I saw no one except for the airlock sentries. I stopped trying cabin hatches; I would learn soon enough what passengers were aboard. I continued down to Level 3. At the foot of the ladder I turned in the direction I thought would take me fastest to the engine room; if I was wrong I would still get there; the corridor was circular.

I found the engine room hatch. No one answered my knock, so I opened, glanced into the deserted outer compartment. At the far end was another hatch, leading to the monitor room where the fusion motor controls were housed. I peered in.

A disheveled man sat at a grimy metal table in the center of the compartment, sipping from a large stoneware coffee mug.

"Are you the Chief Engineer?" I demanded.

His laugh was savage. "I was." He looked me over. "Who're you?"

My uniform should have told him. "Your new Captain," I said. "Stand at attention."

"Why bother?" He shrugged. His gaze dropped to his cup.

I was astounded. "Put that down!" I raged. "Stand!" He got to his feet, stared at me blearily. He staggered, then caught his balance. I picked up the mug, sniffed. "Liquor!" My voice shot into the upper registers. "Alcohol aboard ship? *You?* Contraband?"

He grinned, and it was too much. I slammed him against the bulkhead. "An officer! Look at you!" I cuffed him across the face. "Drunk!" He put up a hand to ward off my blows.

Hopeless. I glanced around. A glass jar sat on the corner of the table. I hurled it to the floor along with the mug.

He whined, "Do you know how much trouble it is to make that? All the fruit and grain it took?" I rounded on him, cuffed him again.

"You don't like me drunk?" His voice was a sneer. "What else should I do? Have you seen the mess back there?" His thumb shot to the emission chamber shaft, in the next compartment. "Take a look, before you go hitting people!"

Disgusted, I shoved him away and turned to the emission chamber.

The shaft opening had been patched with a makeshift airseal. I studied the viewscreen that pictured the lower half of the shaft. My breath caught.

To starboard, three meters of shaft wall had melted like butter. Even I knew that the complex alloy comprising the shaft couldn't be fabricated outside a dockyard. And the exquisitely machined curve of the shaft wall was essential to produce the pattern of N-waves that allowed us to Fuse.

The damage was irreparable.

I turned back to the inner compartment. The Chief sat staring mournfully at his broken mug.

"Do we have power?" I rasped.

"The fusion motors themselves weren't damaged." He didn't bother to look up. "They'll provide all the power we want for ship's systems. Just don't try using them to Fuse."

"Right." I left him to his dissolution and stepped out to the corridor. I rounded the bend and approached crew berth two, its hatch ajar. The berth was empty. Past the crew exercise room was crew berth one. Two tense sentries stood vigilant guard, fingers on their weapons.

"Identify yourself!" The man's stunner was leveled at my stomach.

"Nicholas Seafort, Commander, U.N.N.S., Captain of this vessel."

"Yes, sir. My orders come directly from the Admiral, sir. This hatch is sealed and not to be opened until after we board the launch, sir." He looked nervous, as well he might, delivering such instructions to a Captain.

"Who's inside?"

"The crew, sir. The original *Challenger* crewmen who they haven't put aboard *Portia,* and the new *Challenger* crew ferried from your old ship."

"How many?"

"I don't know, sir. I think about fifteen."

"You're holding them prisoner?" I couldn't hide my amazement.

"I'm keeping the hatch shut, sir."

"As senior officer present, I countermand your orders."

The seaman said hoarsely, "No, sir, I can't. The Admiral said to disregard your instructions. If I let you open the hatch I won't be allowed on the last launch to *Portia.*" His face was shiny with sweat.

"Very well." I swallowed bile. "I won't interfere." I continued round the corridor to the ladder rather than retracing my steps.

As I passed an open cabin a small form hurled itself out of the hatchway and flung itself against my shoulder. "Cap'n!"

I recoiled in shock. "Joni?"

"Cap'n, din' know you beinhere too! Mira! It be Cap'n!" Other transients crowded around.

"What are you doing here?" A chill of foreboding closed around me like a cloud.

One of them shrilled, "Boss Cap'n say I c'n have my own room, man! Allus, havin' own turf! Lotsa rooms dis ship!"

"Christ!" The blasphemy burst from my lips.

Joni added, "Boss Cap'n, he be nice afta all, givin' us own rooms!"

"Are you all here?"

"Eddie'n Deke gonna come next boat. Otha trannies with'm!"

"No!" I raced toward the ladder and the bridge. Ahead of me, the crew berth sentries dashed up the ladder to the aft airlock on Level 2. I charged on to Level 1, hammered on the bridge. "Open up, Philip!"

The hatch opened; I dived into my seat, grabbed the caller. "*Challenger* to *Portia,* acknowledge!"

A cultured male voice interrupted. "Excuse me, sir. The forward airlock is cycling."

"Who are you?"

"My name is Kerren, sir. I'm pleased to meet—"

"Be silent! *Portia,* acknowledge! Puter, turn the hull camera to the forward lock!" *Challenger's* launch flashed onto the screen. Through its transparent portholes I saw passengers crowd toward the mated locks. Many of them were older; two were in wheelchairs. "*Portia,* acknowledge!"

The speakers were silent. I swore. "Philip, go see what's up at the forward lock."

"Aye aye, sir." He jumped from his seat and ran. I waited with mounting frustration. "Kerren, keep paging *Portia.*"

"Aye aye, sir."

A few moments later Philip Tyre was back, gasping for breath. "The passengers are unloaded and milling around the corridor. There's no crew in sight and the sentries are gone."

"Which passengers, Philip?"

"Mr. Fedez, sir, and Mrs. Ovaugh. The Pierces. A lot of others I recognize, but I don't remember their names, sir."

"The older ones."

"Yes, sir. Most of them. Some younger Joes too, though."

The speaker crackled and the screen came to life. "All right, Seafort, I'm here. What's your problem?" Admiral Tremaine's jaw stuck out at a belligerent angle.

"I beg you, reconsider!"

"There's nothing to reconsider. I will make note of your cowardice."

"I didn't mean that. Leave me here!" I pounded the arm of my chair in exasperation. "The passengers! The children!"

"That's not your decision, Commander."

"You can't abandon them. For Lord God's sake, please!"

His voice was icy. "Don't tell me what I can do, Seafort."

"Who'll be on the next launch?"

He seemed indifferent. "Just a few more passengers. Then we'll be on our way."

"The children from New York?"

"Children? Street vermin, you mean. Yes, I'm sending them along."

"You can't condemn them to a crippled vessel! I won't accept them!"

His tone was glacial. "Listen carefully, Seafort, because I'm recording this conversation for the Log. You are ordered to board the passengers I send you. Acknowledge."

"Aye aye, sir, I—Just a moment." I swung away from the caller. Philip Tyre opened his mouth, thought better of it after I stared through him. I paced, my fists clenched.

The Admiral had given a lawful order. He had the authority to make the decision he'd made. Repulsive as I found them, I had no standing to object. I would obey. I must.

I snapped on the speaker. "I protest the order, sir."

"Protest noted. Acknowledge your orders."

I do swear upon my immortal soul . . . to obey all lawful orders

and regulations . . . an oath is a commitment of the soul given directly
to Lord God . . .

I didn't have a choice.

Did I?

Human rubbage, to be cast aside?

"The hell I will!" I bellowed. "I refuse!"

"Seafort, you've hanged yourself!"

"You have no right to abandon children in interstellar space!"

"They're scum, but that's beside the point. I couldn't take everyone, so I had to choose. It's called triage."

"It's called murder!" Blazing, I stared at his image in the screen.

He shrugged. "You have no choice. They're on *Challenger*'s launch. We're Fusing in a few moments. Pick them up or not, as you wish."

"I'll open fire!" I was beside myself.

He chuckled. "With what? I made sure your lasers were disabled. It'll take you hours to get them working again." He turned away.

Legs spread, hands on hips, I stood defiantly in front of the screen. Words spewed forth from some dark recess of my soul.

"Geoffrey Tremaine! Now I, Nicholas Ewing Seafort, by God's Grace Commander in the Naval Service of the United Nations, call challenge upon you to defend your honor, and do swear upon my immortal soul that I shall not rest while breath is in your body. So help me Lord God Almighty!"

He laughed. "Well, it's a long way to Hope Nation. You'll cool off." The screen blanked.

I sank trembling in my chair. On the simulscreen, the last launch left *Portia*. Dully, I sat and watched.

"Sir, shall I go—"

"Shut your mouth, Mr. Tyre." My tone brooked no argument. The last launch drifted clear of *Portia*. A few spurts of propellant glided her toward *Challenger*. In a few moments she was alongside.

The speaker crackled. "*Challenger*, ship's launch is prepared to mate. Please cycle outer airlock." I said nothing.

"*Challenger*? Captain? We need you to open the lock!"

I remained silent.

"Sir, the lock; do you want me—"

"Keep your mouth shut, Mr. Tyre. I won't tell you again."

We waited in terrible silence. I stirred. "Kerren, signal *Portia* that I refuse entry to the launch."

"Aye aye, sir."

"*Challenger*, for Lord God's sake, let us in!" The seaman's voice held a note of hysteria. I could imagine his terror, marooned in a launch between two vessels, one about to Fuse, the other denying him entry.

I picked up the caller. "Wait."

"Oh, Jesus, he's answered! Please, Captain, open the lock!"

"Wait." I thumbed off the caller. Minutes passed. *Portia*'s side thrusters fired propellant. She drifted from us, gaining clearance to Fuse safely. I swallowed.

Portia disappeared. With her, my life.

I sat rocking, mired in hopeless misery. Reeling from exhaustion, I thought of my new cabin, and a bed. No, there was something I must do first. "Philip."

"Yes, sir!" The middy jumped to his feet, pathetically anxious to accommodate.

"Go below. Unseal the outer lock. You remember the drill; you've done it many times. This time you're alone, so be careful."

"Aye aye, sir. Yes, sir."

"After the launch is mated, wait for permission before you open the inner lock."

"Aye aye, sir." He saluted and left.

I felt my eyes closing; I stirred myself once more. "Kerren, have you been reprogrammed to recognize me as Captain?"

"Yes, sir." A smooth baritone.

"Very well."

"Welcome aboard, sir."

I said sharply, "No mood for small talk."

"Aye aye, sir." He seemed faintly hurt, and made a sound as if he were clearing his nonexistent throat. "I have a message for you."

"From whom?"

"A recording. Captain Hasselbrad instructed me not to deliver it until *Portia* Fused. Are you ready for playback?"

"Yes."

The screen flashed to life. Captain Hasselbrad's grim features stared at me. "You'll hear this when it's too late to help, but by God I'll tell you. He planned to seize the first ship that appeared, regardless of whose it was. It was your bad luck *Portia* arrived first. When the fish beast got our fusion tubes he went a little—yes, a little crazy. I think so, but I'm not sure. He planned it all out, your approach from the port side where the damage was invisible, the transfer of crew and passengers, the whole bloody job.

"Maybe I should have relieved him. I don't know. You'll find my written protest in the Log. It did no good, of course. I forced him to transfer seven tanks of propellant from *Portia* to *Challenger*. Maybe it will be of some help. He cleaned out most of the drugs from your infirmary."

On the screen Hasselbrad looked down at his hands. "A glob the aliens threw penetrated *Challenger*'s hydroponics chambers. It wrecked the nitrogen control machinery, but worse, it decompressed the west hydo compartment. What wasn't destroyed we threw away for fear of contamination. Since the attack we've been on short rations from east hydros, and living off stores."

He stared into the camera. "Seafort, the Admiral ordered most of *Challenger*'s food reserves transferred to *Portia*. When I heard of it I canceled the transfer, but most of your remaining stores had already been carried across. I was already on *Portia*, so I don't have an inventory. You don't have as many passengers or crew as we did; I hope he left you enough food."

He swallowed. "I know what I should have done. I should have volunteered to remain with my ship. I didn't suggest he transfer me to *Portia*, but I didn't object either. I'm sorry, I—" He looked straight into the camera. "At my age, I can't handle the uncertainty and the helplessness. I can't. So it has to be you. Godspeed, Mr. Seafort. I'm sorry for what we've done." The recording went dead.

"Would you like to hear it again, Captain?"

"No." I rocked in my chair. "Kerren, did you record my communications with *Portia*?"

"Yes, sir."

"Play them back." I leaned back and listened to myself shouting at the Admiral, out of control. "It's called murder!" I closed my eyes as Tremaine gave his direct command. "You are ordered to board the passengers I send you." I heard my reply. "The hell I will! I refuse!"

My tone held anguish. "Turn it off."

"It's not finished, sir, there's—"

"TURN IT OFF!" I bit back a sob.

Blessed silence.

The hatch opened. Philip. "Permission to enter bridge, sir." I waved him in. "The passengers are all boarded."

"Very well." My voice was dull.

He waited expectantly. After a time he prompted, "Sir, what are your orders?"

"Orders?" I found it hard to concentrate. "I have no right to give orders."

"What, sir?"

I said more loudly, "I'm not fit to give orders. I'm a mutineer." I opened my eyes. "Do as you wish."

"Please, sir, where do we start?"

I lay back, head against the rest, my eyes closed. "Well now, Middy. We're drifting at a rendezvous with our fusion drive in ruins, and we think the rest of the squadron has passed us. I have you, an eighteen-year-old midshipman nobody wants. I have a drunken Chief Engineer whose name I neglected to learn while I was slapping him.

"Care for more?" My smile was crooked. "Locked in crew berth one are a handful of crewmen selected for their behavior problems, probably out of their minds with fear. Meanwhile, about forty deceived trannies are roaming the ship, no doubt terrorizing the other castaways by their presence."

Philip swallowed.

"The Admiral was kind enough to disable our lasers. Half our hydroponics are gone. *Portia* relieved us of most of our food. I don't have the combination to the bridge safe or the code to open the crew berth hatch, or the keys to the armory. I've no idea if we have enough personnel to run essential ship's systems. So, tell me, Midshipman Philip Tyre: where do we start?"

Philip stammered, "Sir, you're the Captain!"

"Of what, Middy?" My tone was grim. "Tell me, of what?" He made no answer. I opened my eyes, saw the incipient panic behind the boy's gaze. My self-pity dissolved in shame. "All right," I growled. I essayed a small and unsuccessful smile. "That's the downside. But we're alive. Let's see what we can do for ourselves. Come below with me." I stood.

"Yessir!" Philip's relief was clear. We left the bridge, sealing the hatch with an ID code. I downed the ladder to Level 3, Philip trotting close behind. At the foot of the ladder I bumped into a passenger, recoiled. "What in God's own Hell are you doing here?" I roared at Walter Dakko.

He stepped back from my fury. "Captain, where's all the crew? Why are most of the cabins empty?"

I grabbed his collar. "Why are you here?" I shoved him against the bulkhead. "Answer!"

"Chris," he said in a tired voice. "Chris and that Attani boy. Without telling us they sought out *Portia*'s new officers and asked if they could transfer to *Challenger* for the rest of the cruise. To get away from you. The Admiral obliged them. When Galena and I found out, we agreed I should transfer too; Chris is too young to be alone. So I did." He glared at me. "Now it's your turn. What's going on?"

"*Portia*'s Fused and gone. Our fusion tubes are wrecked. We aren't going anywhere. We're derelict."

He closed his eyes. "Oh, you foolish boy," he whispered. After a moment he asked bleakly, "Is there any hope?"

"Of rescue, perhaps. I don't know." I left him.

From within crew berth one came frantic pounding. I found the code to unseal the hatch posted on a slip of paper next to the control. I tapped in the figures.

Philip stirred uneasily. "Shouldn't we be armed, sir?"

"It won't be necessary." If it was, we were doomed anyway. "Stand back." Taking a deep breath, I unlocked the hatch. I assumed the at-ease position directly in front of the hatch, hands crossed behind me.

As the hatch slid open a mob of desperate men surged forward. "STAND AT ATTENTION!" I bellowed. In shock and surprise they fell back. I strode forward. "I'm Mr. Seafort, your new Captain. You! Form a line to that side! Move! The rest of you, over here!" I shoved one man aside. "Line up, or I'll have you at Captain's Mast so fast you'll get friction burns!"

I was fortunate; old habits of discipline asserted themselves. In a few moments the men stood in two ragged lines to either side of the main aisle.

"Midshipman, take the name of anyone who moves!" Philip scurried in, snatching the paper with the hatch code on it for a writing pad. Resourceful.

I glared at my forlorn remnants of a crew. "You were sent here by order of your superior officers. How dare you make such a ruckus? We'll have no more of that." I paced, as if on inspection. "Identify yourselves. One at a time." I nodded to the man at the end of the line.

"Recycler's Mate Kovaks, sir." I nodded. Good. His skills were crucial.

"Comm Specialist Tzee, sir."

"Seaman Andros."

"Sir!"

He looked contemptuous. "Sir? Oh, yeah, *sir*."

"Write him up, Mr. Tyre!" Philip scribbled his name.

"Lotta good that'll do you, Captain," muttered Andros. "This ain't no Navy ship no more."

I didn't hesitate a second. "Mr. Tyre, escort him to the brig!"

"Aye aye—"

"Do that, pretty boy!" sniggered Andros. "I'd liketa get alone with—"

I pivoted on my left heel. My roundhouse blow to the jaw caught him completely unawares. His eyes rolled up as he crashed to the deck. A fierce pain lanced up my arm; I was afraid I'd rebroken my hand. Cautiously I flexed my fingers and decided I had not. "Continue, please," I said calmly, as if clubbing a crewman unconscious were an everyday affair.

I paced while they identified themselves. Fourteen men in all, including Andros. Five were transferees from *Portia*: Andros, Clinger, and three steward's mates. The other nine included one man from *Challenger*'s engine room, two hydroponicist's mates, a purser's mate, and five deckhands with few advanced skills.

I stood in the center of the passageway. "We are a Naval vessel under weigh in wartime conditions. We will maintain Naval discipline at all times. Understood?"

Sullenly, they murmured their assent.

"You, Drucker and Groshnev! Carry Mr. Andros to the brig. Mr. Tyre, put him in a cell and secure the brig. Return here immediately."

"Aye aye, sir." The two seamen hoisted the unconscious Andros by his arms and legs and followed Philip from the compartment.

I held the men at silent attention until the party returned from the brig. When at last they filed in, I snapped, "At ease, all of you." They relaxed. "As far as I know, you are *Challenger*'s only remaining crew." They didn't like that, and I could hardly blame them. I began to pace. "Our first task is to take stock of the ship and its resources. Mr. Kovaks, are the recyclers ready for inspection?"

He gasped. "Inspection? Are you serious? We've been left here to die!"

"Not if I can help it!" I was losing control of the situation; time to improvise. "All of you, come along on the inspection tour. Explain our problems. We'll start with recycling, then move on to the hydros. Then the engine room and the comm room. Let's go!"

They seemed reluctant to leave the berth they'd been so desperate to escape. "Mr. Tyre, get a clipboard from the purser's office and make notes of what these men tell us. Mr. Kovaks, I presume the puter is still monitoring?" Casually I moved toward the hatch.

"Yes, sir," he said automatically. Then he swallowed. "Power to the recyclers wasn't interrupted when we got hit." He followed me into the corridor. "The lower engine room was decompressed; that's when the five joes got killed, but the fusion motors still produce internal power. Gauges were normal last I checked, yesterday sometime. I've been

locked in there"—Kovaks pointed bitterly to the crew berth—"ever
since." The other men were gathering in the corridor behind us.

"I know," I said. "Sorry about that. It won't happen again. You men,
keep up or you won't be able to hear. Kovaks, think you know the
monitoring drills well enough to train a couple of other joes?" He nodded.

In a few moments we were clustered in the recycler chambers.
"Better run a check now, Mr. Kovaks."

The seaman seemed more docile now that he was at his familiar
station. He ran pressure tests and checked the gauges against the norms
on his worksheet. "Recycling checks out, Captain."

"Very well. Take me to west hydros."

The sailor Groshnev objected, "It's east hydros that are operating.
We—"

"I said, take me to west hydros. What's the proper response to an
order?"

"Aye aye, sir."

"I need your help to restore the ship," I snapped. "But we'll maintain discipline. We're under a lot of tension and you've just been freed
from unwarranted imprisonment, so I'll overlook your discourtesy, one
time. Understood?"

"Yes, sir." He seemed chastened.

"Very well. West hydros." When we arrived I wished I hadn't given
the order. The ruin there was almost absolute. A ragged but adequate
airseal covered a wound in the hull, but machinery was overturned, and
bent tubing and broken hoses lay scattered about. Empty water tanks lay
on the deck amid clumps of loose sand and dirt. Of the plants, nothing
remained.

"That shapechanger scuttled in here," someone muttered.

Seaman Drucker turned angrily. "We went through Class A decontamination! You even helped, you dumb grode! Remember how Lieutenant Affad supervised? Ultraviolet wave, chemicals, the works. We're safe
here."

"Seeds? Plant stock?"

"There's seeds in the stock drawers, sir. And a few plants in the
cutting room, but no way to grow them. The machinery's a mess."

"We have piping, hoses. We can make tanks from scrap, right?"

"Yes, sir." Drucker looked bleakly at the wreckage. "The machinery
was never designed to handle decompression, sir. The sensors to the
puter are out, and most of the feed valves are jammed or blown. We can
make elementary repairs, but this . . ."

"Very well." I motioned to the hatch. "East hydros."

The east chamber appeared to be flourishing. Growlights overhead softly hummed; beneath them tomatoes, cucumbers, and other vegetables grew peacefully. Somewhere in the background water dripped; the sensor lights glowed soft green.

"Looks the way I'd expect," I remarked. "Anything wrong here?"

"Yes," Drucker said, his tone ominous. He brushed aside the leaves of a tomato plant growing in a wet sandy tank, and pointed.

I inhaled through my teeth. "Does that mean what I think?"

"Yes, sir," Drucker said grimly. The pulpy stems of four half-eaten unripe tomatoes lay tossed aside in the sand. "Someone's been raiding the produce. Extra rations. I discovered it yesterday before we were locked up, sir. After the rest of the crew had been taken to *Portia.*"

The men had grown very quiet. My gaze shifted from eye to eye around the cabin. No one looked away. "From now on, we'll keep the hydro chambers sealed," I said. "Only the hydro detail will have entry. We're on short rations as it is. Anyone found stealing food will be executed. No second chances." There was no sound. I cleared my throat. "How much more food could we grow here?"

"The beds are full, Captain. Where else would we put plants?"

"What's our output?"

"About twenty tomatoes a day, Captain, and about thirty cucumbers. There's some beans started in bed eleven over there; they won't be grown for a month or so. Lots of lettuce. Thing is, you can't survive on lettuce."

"Why didn't you plant a full line of crops when the west hydros failed?"

"I dunno, sir. First we was tryin' to get rid of the contamination, if there was any, then we kept expectin' the rest of the squadron to show up. Figured we'd get some new plant stock from them; faster than startin' fresh from seeds."

"Um." No point in criticizing *Challenger's* former officers. "To the galley, then. Let's see about our stores." I sealed the hydro chamber hatch with a code, putting myself between the crewmen and the controls as I keyed it so the men couldn't see what I entered. We trooped up to the galley.

The coolers were normally kept locked between meals. Most were sealed now, but one hatch had been forced and the cooler's contents looted. I looked about. "Where are the codes for the locked coolers?" One man shrugged; the rest looked mystified.

"We'll get 'em open," growled Clinger.

"No. I'll search for the codes when I go back to the bridge. We'll open the coolers on my order. Not before." I had a deckhand go through the dry cupboards while we waited; a few sacks of flour, some condiments, and scattered cans of prepared vegetables were all we found.

I asked, "Do any of you know what stores are in the hold?"

"About twenty cases of powdered milk." A sailor, his tone sullen. "I helped load them for *Portia,* then put them back when new orders came down."

"What else?"

He shrugged. "Some cases of somethin' else. I dunno. Not enough to keep us all fed, I know that much."

I swung to Philip. "Mr. Tyre, after the tour, take this man to the hold and inventory our foodstuffs. You should find the manifest posted near the hatch." I didn't wait for an answer. "Engine room. Let's go."

At the engine room the drunken Chief was nowhere to be seen. The shards of his stone mug still lay about. I turned to the engine room rating. "Mr.—Sykes, is it? What's the status here?"

He grinned mirthlessly through missing teeth. "Ol' Chief, he off somewheres with a beaker, I reckon. The puter is runnin' things now, looks like." He guffawed.

"Mr. Tyre, put that man on report. I'll deal with him next Captain's Mast." Dutifully, Philip wrote his name. "Mr. Sykes, try again."

The rating shot me a resentful look, but caught himself before he replied. He took a slow breath and stood taller. "You saw the Chief, sir? He's, uh, well, you know. Guess he's too upset to care anymore. He's got the engines all runnin' on automatic. We've got electricity, heat, pump pressure. If we need lasers we'll have to go to full power; I dunno if the puter can do that by hisself."

"It can't."

"Yeah, well, then we don't have lasers. Sir."

"Can you man the machinery?"

"I can read the gauges, yes, sir. I know to turn the levers to full power when the order comes down, and watch the red lines. I don't know what I'd do if they went over the red, sir. The Chief was always here to handle that. I guess I'd just shut everything off." He grinned.

"In what order, Mr. Sykes?"

His grin vanished. "Uh, I don't know, sir. That's up to the Chief." He mumbled, "Guess I could glitch things up good, foolin' with them, huh?"

"Yes. I'll get the Chief back on duty." We finished our inspection and trooped up the ladder toward the Level 1 comm room. Along the way we were besieged by a gang of transients in the corridor. "Later, allyas!" I snapped. "Noway mess wid Cap'n now, noway!" They fell back, astonished at my language. Well, whatever worked.

In the comm room the disassembled laser controls lay neatly atop their consoles. The manuals were likewise waiting, open to the page that detailed how to reinstall the controls. "Lord God Almighty!" I stopped myself, before I said worse. "Sorry. Amen. Mr. Tzee, can you reinstall the firing controls?"

The rating looked over the various parts before he answered. "Yes, sir. I'm pretty sure I can."

"Get right on it."

"Aye aye, sir." He rummaged in a locker for tools. "It would be easier, sir, uh, I mean, if you all weren't—"

"Right." I went to the hatch. "Report to the bridge when you've finished. While you're at it, test our radionics. Let me know what you find." I waited while the crew filed out. We gathered in the Level 1 corridor.

"All right, inspection's finished. We have work to do. Mr. Sykes, clean up the engine room. Mr. Tyre, go search for foodstuffs in the hold. Be thorough. Mr. Akkrit, I'm giving you the passenger detail. Take three men. Make a list of all the passengers and their cabins. See they're all settled in properly. The rest of you"—that left seven—"for the moment, you're the galley crew. Mr. Bree is in charge. We'll need dinner soon; call me on the bridge and till me what you can manage with current supplies. That's all."

Reluctantly they dispersed. Some looked as if they had objections that I made sure they had no time to voice. I hurried back to the bridge, taking care to seal the hatch behind me.

I slumped into my chair, my mind grappling with unsolved problems. "Kerren?"

"Yes, sir? How may I help?" I understood why Captain Hasselbrad had shut off the puter's conversational overlays. Despite his politeness, something about his manner grated.

"The coolers in the galley are locked. Do you know where the codes are?"

"Yes, sir."

I waited expectantly. Then, "Where, Kerren?"

"Captain Hasselbrad put them in the Log, sir. Have you checked the Log?"

I cursed my stupidity. "No." I reached for the holovid.

"You should check it, sir," Kerren said solemnly. "If you want to find the codes."

Gritting my teeth I snapped on the Log and flipped through its pages. I swore out loud. Among the last few entries were the codes to the bridge safe and the food lockers. I memorized the locker code, went to the safe, dialed it open. Inside was a stunner pistol, and an envelope marked "Armory Key." I pocketed them, feeling more secure as I resumed my seat.

Half an hour later Philip Tyre returned triumphant from his tour of the hold. "Canned meat and vegetables, sir! Two containers full. Five hundred seventy-four cases; sixteen to a case, to be exact!" He dropped into his chair at the watch officer's console.

I smiled. "Good find, Middy." The room seemed brighter, the ship less oppressive. Philip grinned back, basking in my approval. I busied myself reading the Log, familiarizing myself with the ship's operating parameters.

The caller came to life. "Uh, bridge? Captain?"

I answered. "Who are you? Don't you know how to report?"

"Uh, no, sir, I never called the bridge before. This is Akkrit."

"Seaman Akkrit reporting, sir!"

He parroted my words. "Uh, we figure there's seventy-six passengers, sir, counting the damn trannies. One of them young joeys, I had to punch his lights out to make him stop following me. Thirty-nine trannies, a bunch of old people, and a few others. Jabour here has the list."

"Very well. Send him up. Your group is assigned to corridor detail. Pick up the refuse on all three Levels."

"Uh, aye aye, sir."

I broke the connection, played idly with the calculator on my console. Seventy-six passengers, fourteen crewmen, Philip, the Chief, and myself. Ninety-three in all. If we consumed, on the average, one can of food per person per day, we had rations for ninety-eight days. The hydroponics output would add to that, but we'd consume food faster than we were growing it. What little we had was immensely valuable, and we'd need to watch it closely.

"Mr. Tyre, did you secure the hold?"

Philip looked puzzled. "I shut the hatch, sir."

"You didn't seal it?" A chill of alarm.

"No, sir, you told me to search for food, not to—"

"That deckhand, what's his name—"

"Ibarez."

"He saw the cases of food?"

"Yes, he helped me count—"

"Idiot! Can't you do anything right?" I scrambled to my feet. "I should know better than to trust you! Move!" I was already out the hatch.

Philip ran after me. "To the hold, sir?"

"Yes, by God's—no! The armory, first." We rounded the corridor bend. I skidded to a stop at the armaments locker and fumbled with the key. Finally I had the locker open.

I tossed a stunner and a pistol to the midshipman and pulled out a laser rifle for myself. Slamming the hatch shut I raced along the corridor to the launch berth hatch. The cargo holds were far forward from the disks in which we lived, in the slim, pencillike body of the ship beyond the launch berth.

I slapped the hatch control and rushed through as the panel slid open. Philip followed. In the suiting room I snatched a suit from the racks and thrust myself into it. The cargo holds were pressurized, but as the air wasn't run through our recyclers it couldn't be depended on, so one always wore a suit in the hold. I slapped on my helmet, checking the air gauge automatically as it sealed.

Suited, we clambered to the hatch at the far end of the chamber. At my touch the hatch slid open.

Challenger's huge cargo hold stretched to the narrow bow of the ship. I flicked off my radio, grabbed Philip by the neck, touched his helmet to mine. "Where?"

Understanding that I wanted silence, he pointed to the opposite side of the hull, about a hundred meters forward. I crouched, moved along the passageway as quietly as I could. I flicked my radio back to "Receive," motioning Philip to do likewise.

The sound of heavy breathing. "Hurry, damn it, we gotta get outta here!"

I crept toward the voices. A narrow passageway ran along the hull on either side of the hold; at twenty-meter intervals catwalks branched over the bins of cargo to the passageway on the other side. As noiselessly as I could manage, I followed a dimly lit catwalk to where the food was stored.

I tiptoed across the decking. On the far side of the bins, three suited men loaded boxes onto a power dolly.

I raised my rifle. "Hold it!"

"Run!" With a curse, one man dashed along the far passageway back toward the launch berth. Another leaped down to the hold, among the stacked boxes and containers. The third came directly at me.

The sailor charged across the catwalk, brandishing a heavy iron bar.

"Stop!" I raised my rifle. He hurled the bar at my head. My visor shattered, blinding me with a shower of broken transplex. Reflexively, I fired. I gasped, expecting foul air. To my relief it was clean and fresh. My head rang from the blow. I staggered to keep my footing, blinked trying to see.

My attacker was gone.

Philip, with a yell. "Here, sir! He's—whoof!"

I backtracked across the catwalk, ran to the hatch. Philip Tyre sat on the deck, holding his ribs, a lame grin plastered on his young face. "Sorry, sir. I was aiming at the other joe and he blindsided me. Knocked my breath out." He glanced about. "They got away."

"*Got away?*" I hauled him to his feet. "Damn you, Middy! Where's your pistol? Your stunner?"

Philip paled. His frantic eyes searched for the missing weapons. "I—they—he must have taken them, sir, when I fell."

I was shocked into silence. Any act of deliberate disobedience by a crewman constitued mutiny. Still, there were degrees. To take up arms against lawful authority was unthinkable. We were long past the Rebellious Ages; for civilians, the penalty for keeping unauthorized firearms was a life sentence in Callisto penal colony. For a seaman, death.

Now I had armed rebellion on my hands. All because of Philip.

I shoved him back toward the catwalk. "I shot at someone. Did he get past you?"

"I think I saw just two, sir."

"You think!" I mimicked. "If you didn't let him past, he's still here." I held the rifle ready as we crossed the catwalk.

My weapon wasn't needed. The third sailor lay facedown in the hold, blood seeping from his head. I sent Philip down to the body; when he turned it over, the face of the deckhand Ibarez stared blindly back. Pale and silent, the middy climbed to the catwalk.

Outside, I hauled off my suit. "This is all your doing! You knew there isn't enough food to go around. The deckhand saw you leave the hatch unsealed; what did you expect they'd do? And worse, you didn't even hang on to the weapons I issued!"

The boy blanched.

"Now the rebels have a pistol and a stunner. You incompetent child, I ought to send you to the barrel!"

Philip smiled weakly in his humiliation and shame; the expression only fueled my anger. I slapped shut the hatch. "By Lord God, I will!

Come along, Midshipman. I've never been first lieutenant; the barrel was never in my cabin. It's about time I learned to use it!"

Philip's eyes pleaded, but he said nothing.

I grabbed his arm. "Get yourself to the first lieutenant's cabin, flank!" In a blind rage I stalked from the suiting room into the circumference corridor. Philip scurried alongside, his face red with embarrassment. In moments we were in officers' country, near the bridge. We reached the lieutenant's cabin. The hatch was ajar.

I stormed in. The barrel stood on its mount in the far corner of the cabin. The cane leaned against it. Philip stared, gulped. Unprompted, he shucked his jacket and folded it neatly across a chair. Small, reluctant steps took him to the barrel. He lay himself across it, arms crossed under his head in the required position.

I set down my rifle, snatched up the cane. "I'll teach you to do your duty, you—" I lashed him with all my strength. He yelped, jerked convulsively, then made himself still, his head pressed into his folded arms. I raised the cane to strike again, triumphant in the exercise of my lawful authority. Mine was the power to punish, to mete justice.

I came to my senses.

"What am I doing?" The cane fell from my fingers. I fell into a chair alongside the table. Philip lay across the barrel, unmoving. I put my head in my hands. "Lord God!"

The middy waited.

"Philip, get up." My voice was hoarse. Slowly the boy straightened. One hand crept to the seat of his pants. He turned, his face scarlet. "Sit." I thrust out a chair. He obeyed, and winced. I steeled myself to meet his eye. "I don't know if you can forgive me, Mr. Tyre. I don't expect it. I'm sorry for what I've done. You deserve far better."

"No!" The cry was wrung from him.

"Yes. You—"

"Don't you see, sir? You were right!" His tears welled. "I should have known to seal the hatch and hold on to my gun. I'm sorry I'm such a failure; I'll try harder from now on! I know I deserve worse than the barrel. If you're afraid to discipline me, how can you trust me? How can you run the ship? I'm not like those men, I'll take discipline and obey my oath. Please!"

He got to his feet, grabbed the cane. "I don't want to be hit—God, how it hurts—but you're Captain! I beg you, don't be afraid to punish me." He set the cane on the table.

I closed my eyes. A long time passed. I said quietly, "You think that's why I stopped? Because I thought you'd join the mutineers if I caned you?"

He cried, "Why else would you let me off after what I did?"

"Because the fault was mine, from the start. It was my own responsibility to see the hatch was sealed. Thanks to my stupidity a man is dead. Blaming you was cowardly. Despicable. The pistol and stunner—that couldn't be helped. You did your best."

"My best isn't good enough!" His tone was anguished. "I'm your only officer, and you can't rely on me. No wonder you didn't want me aboard." He looked down. "I'm useless." His voice was muffled. "Worse, I'm a hindrance."

"Mr. Tyre, listen well: I didn't want you on *Challenger* because I didn't want your life thrown away. There was no other reason. You are a good officer and you have my respect. I'm sorry I hit you. I won't do it again."

"You don't have to promise—"

"It's done. And I have to make the promise; I can't trust my judgment otherwise. I feel—" I tried to quell my surge of emotions. I said, my voice ragged, "Philip, you know I'm not fit to be Captain. Would you relieve me?"

His voice came in a whisper. "What?"

"Take the ship. I won't object. I can't go on hurting people." I glanced up; his face was thunderstruck. "Or killing them."

He laughed bitterly. "You're the hero who saved *Hibernia*. I can't even hang on to my gun, and you want me to relieve you."

"Stop. Don't do that to yourself."

"You're the youngest man ever appointed Captain, and I'll never be more than a middy. Never, I know that. Relieve you!" He laughed again; it was a sob.

My hand closed over his. "Lord God help us both." We sat in unhappy silence. After a while I sighed. "Very well. Let's go about our duties. I apologize again for hitting you."

He attempted a smile. "Mr. Tamarov hit me harder, sir." We moved toward the hatch.

"Get a few hours rest before you report back to the bridge, Philip. In the wardroom, or take any cabin you'd like."

He looked at me curiously. "I'll be in the wardroom, sir. Where else would I sleep?"

40

Weary, discouraged, I returned to the bridge and sealed the hatch behind me. I knew better than to waste time looking for the missing weapons. On a ship the size of *Challenger* they could be anywhere. The crewmen I'd surprised rifling our stores had been wearing pressure suits; I hadn't gotten a look at the faces of the two who escaped.

Still, I could narrow my suspicions. We'd started with fourteen crewmen and the Chief Engineer, whose name I still hadn't learned. I doubted the Chief was involved; he appeared too lethargic to care. One man lay dead in the hold. Comm Specialist Tzee was busy reassembling the laser controls; Mr. Akkrit and Mr. Jabour were counting passengers and hadn't had time to join the raiders. Mr. Andros was in the brig. That left nine suspects. Two of them had gone to the hold.

I could haul the lot of them in for poly and drug tests; under the irresistible influence of the drugs the miscreants couldn't conceal their crime. But without other evidence against them, that was strictly forbidden. Anyway, we had no doctor to administer P & D.

"Bridge, comm room reporting."

"What is it, Mr., ah, Tzee?"

"I think I've got the lasers hooked up, sir. Could you release a test target?"

"Couldn't you program simulated fire?"

"Not if we want to make sure the laser cannon actually work, sir."

"Good point. When Mr. Tyre reports back I'll have him jettison some abandoned belongings. That'll do for practice."

As I replaced the caller I had the grisly thought of using the dead sailor's body as a target, but suppressed it. My relations with the crew were bad enough, no matter how much I despised a man who'd take food from the mouths of his mates.

I made a note on my console screen to have Philip remove the body and release some flotsam for the lasers. Next, we had to arrange a food system so the galley could be supplied with enough provender to make our meals.

The comm room had to be manned; that meant training ratings to handle the laser firing controls Mr. Tzee had reconnected. We were supposed to maintain a twenty-four-hour watch over the recyclers; how could that be done with only thirteen crewmen in all?

The screen filled with my notes. Starting new plants in the hydroponics chamber was absolutely essential. The Chief—I keyed through the Log to find his name—Andreas Kasavopolous, had to be brought back to his duty. The bridge had to be manned. Even if Philip and I stood twelve-hour watches, an impossibility for more than a few days, *Challenger* didn't have enough officers. The hydro chambers would need extra hands too, to nurture the new plantings. The passengers had to be looked after . . .

My head fell back. "More help," I whispered.

"What, sir?" Kerren.

"We need more help."

"I've run calculations regarding your problem," the puter said smoothly. "*Challenger* has a crew of seventeen. If—"

"Sixteen. I shot one."

Kerren was shocked into a half second's silence. "Very well, recalculated. If each crew member works an eighteen-hour shift every day, you'll have just sufficient—"

"That's not possible."

"Mathematically, there's no other way. Even so, you'll be shorthanded for some less critical functions. You—"

"Enough, Kerren." He fell silent. I leaned back, my head spinning, took a deep breath. I had to get more help. I stood wearily. "Kerren, watch for encroachments. Monitor the recyclers and ship's power. Page me immediately upon any variation from norms."

"Certainly, sir. I'll be pleased to do that. You're leaving?" A second's hesitation. "The bridge is to be manned at all times while under weigh, Captain. Article 17 of the Naval Regs, edition of—"

"You man it. I'm busy."

"A ship's puter is not considered an officer for any purpose to which—"

I sealed the hatch behind me. On Level 2 sullen deckhands swept the corridor under the supervision of Mr. Akkrit. They came to attention readily enough; I released them and turned to their leader. "Have you a list of passengers and their cabins?"

"Yes, sir." Akkrit handed me a crinkled paper from his pocket. I scanned it. The cabin I wanted was halfway around the circumference corridor. As I turned away, I thought of the rifle I'd left by my console on the bridge. I shrugged. I doubted the panicked crewmen from the hold were prepared just yet to assault their Captain with their stolen weapons.

I knocked on the hatch.

"Who is it?" Walter Dakko peered into the corridor. "Oh, Captain. Come in." His clothing and belongings were scattered on the bunk, as if he'd been sorting his gear. He closed the hatch behind us, waited for me to speak.

I forced my mind to concentrate. "Mr. Dakko, I have thirteen crewmen belowdecks, not all of whom are reliable. One of my two officers drinks on duty."

He sat slowly on his bunk. "And?"

"I can't run the ship with the people I have," I said. "I need—"

The hatch burst open. "Dad, Greg and I found—"

"—recruits."

Chris Dakko demanded, "What are you doing here, Seafort?"

"Chris!" His father was scandalized.

"Well, it's our cabin!"

Walter Dakko said mildly, "It's my cabin. Yours is down the hall."

"What's the difference?"

The elder Dakko's temper flared. "Go to your quarters until you know!"

Father and son glared at each other, my presence forgotten. Slowly Chris shook his head. "No," he said. "Not this time. You can't do that anymore." He walked out.

Walter Dakko released his breath in a sigh of exasperation. "You see the problem." His tone was rueful. He focused on me. "You were saying?"

"I need help."

He sat on his bunk. "Now you say you need help. Before, you said you needed recruits. Which do you mean?"

I was puzzled. "It's the same."

"No. Assign your thirteen crew to critical tasks. Working in the engine room or with the machinery. Let civilian volunteers tend the plants or help with cooking and cleaning."

I shook my head. "It wouldn't work. The recyclers have to be watched; any problem there could kill us. The regs require the comm room and the bridge to be manned. The—"

"The regs require?" His tone was incredulous. "What do regulations matter in a situation like ours?"

"In a Naval vessel," I said slowly, "Naval regulations apply at all times."

"We're a derelict ship abandoned to the doubtful mercy of Lord God!" He hurled a jacket to the deck, thought better of it, stooped to retrieve it. He brushed it clean and laid it gently upon the bed. "If we cooperate and work together we might have a chance. Damn your Naval regs! We just have to try to survive."

"We need the regulations for survival," I said simply. How to make him understand? "Officers in the Naval Service are trained to duty. They are educated in honor, taught the value of their oath and the meaning of dedication. Several of my officers on *Portia* volunteered for duty on *Challenger*, knowing the risk.

"But the crewmen—you probably know what they're like. To keep the ships manned, the Government offers a half-year's pay in advance as a bonus, and takes anybody. It's called guaranteed enlistment. Most of those men have no loyalty or dedication to the Service. They're kept in line by regulations enforced with stiff penalties. One reason the Captain is made absolute dictator is to restrain any impulse to rebellion in the crew."

Unconsciously I began to pace. "Rigid lines of authority are set and maintained by the regulations. As you know, it's a capital offense for crewmen to touch their Captain." I stopped, to face him. "If the crew sees regulations set aside, ship's discipline will go as well. And it's already broken down. I had to brig one man to set an example, and I shot a deckhand who assaulted me when I caught him looting food stores."

"I heard."

"We're not far from a complete breakdown of authority. I can't allow that. 'Every man for himself' would bring starvation or worse." Grim images flashed through my mind. "In any event, I have no choice. My course is dictated by my oath."

"What course? What oath?"

"I swore to uphold Naval Regulations. Section 204.1. 'The Captain of a vessel shall assume and exert authority and control of the Government of the vessel until relieved by order of superior authority or until his death.' "

Dakko's face grew red. "You need our cooperation, Captain Seafort. You won't get it by spouting your precious regulations. They don't contemplate a situation such as ours."

I shrugged. "What does that matter?"

"Look beyond your petty rules!" he shouted. "If we're going to die on this accursed ship, what do your regs signify? How does your oath matter?"

I looked at him curiously. "How would the prospect of death abate my oath?" I shook my head in despair. "I already deliberately skirted my oath once. Worse, I refused a direct command from my Admiral, and I doubt very much it was an illegal order. I have no excuse. I'll not do it again." I reached for the hatch handle. "I came to ask your help." I opened the hatch.

"What did you want from me?"

"To volunteer for enlistment. And to speak to Gregor and Chris about doing the same. But obviously it would be better if I spoke with them myself." I left.

On the way to Gregor Attani's cabin I cursed my impatience. I'd alienated Dakko, when I needed him the most. I steeled myself to be calm and reasonable as I knocked on the hatch.

"What do you want?" Gregor's face bore no sign of welcome.

"May I come in?"

"I suppose." He stepped aside. I stopped short. Chris Dakko sat on the bunk, glowering.

I took a deep breath. "It's just as well you're together; I was going to talk with each of you." Quickly I explained the ship's predicament. "So I'm here on a recruiting mission."

A moment's silence. "You want us to sign up for the Navy?" Chris Dakko seemed astonished.

"Yes. You're educated and intelligent, and I need you."

"As officers or enlisted men?" Gregor.

A good question, one I hadn't considered. "Enlisted men, preferably. But I'd enlist you as an officer, in your case, if that's what you wanted."

"Meaning what?" demanded Chris from the bed.

I hesitated, chose honesty. "I won't have you as an officer," I told him. "You don't have the temperament." With contempt, Chris tossed a pillow at the bulkhead.

Greg Attani shrugged. "I'm not interested." He colored. "I mean, thanks for the offer, Captain. Sorry about my manners. But you must know we transferred here to get away from you. Nothing could make me join your crew."

Chris stood lazily. "Me neither. Go ask your trannie friends. They'll be a big help, I'm sure." He laughed. "Come on, Greg, let's check out the lounge."

I nodded shortly. "Very well. Thank you for hearing me out." I left, holding the shreds of my temper in check as I stalked toward the ladder. My eyes on the deck, I nearly collided with Eddie Boss.

He barred my path. "You!" A thick finger poked at my chest. "You

no better n' dem Uppies! Givin' us cabins by ourselves, yah! Gettin' us
off ship goin' places, leavin' us here!"

"Eddie, I—"

"Where we goin' now, Uppie Cap'n? Takin' us home? Backa
N'York?" Rage suffused his heavy features. "You let 'em leave us behin'
so we gon' die here!" His beefy hand closed around my arm. With a
savage twist he flung me against the bulkhead. "Teachin' me read, sure!
Alla game fo' you! You let 'em leave us trannies on dead ship, no food, no
nuttin'!"

My ribs throbbed. With an effort I met his eye. "I'm on *Challenger*
too, Eddie."

He wasn't listening. "Crew joey beat up Deke real good. I foun'
him lyin' in hall like he dead, teeth all broke! We ain' takin' no more!
Prong yo' ship and prong you!" His fist reared.

With my free hand I jabbed him in the chest. "Coward! Mira
bigman Eddie Boss, jus' chickenshit coward! Allatime big talkin', thas-
sall! No helpin', jus' talkin'!"

He let go my arm, regarded me with suspicion. "Whatcha wan',
Cap'n?" He sounded calmer. "Why ya talk trannie? Ya ain' no trannie.
Talk Cap'n talk, I listen."

I swallowed with relief. "Eddie, *Challenger*'s in desperate trouble.
We're short of food, we can't Fuse, I haven't enough crew. I've talked to
some passengers about enlisting. I don't know what they'll do. In the
meantime, help me with the tranni—with your friends. Give them whatever cabins they want. Keep them away from the crew; the men are
short-tempered. I'm sorry about Deke. I'm sorry you're in this mess."

Stubbornly he shook his head. "I gonn kill dat one joe, I fin' him.
Deke my frien'. No one hurtin' my frien'."

I said, "Don't take revenge yet, Eddie. I need every sailor we've
got. Please, as a favor to me."

"Yah, I wait, you callin' me coward," he sneered. "Ol' Eddie jus'
chickenshit!"

I deserved that. "I apologize," I said evenly. "You were ready to
knock my head off. I wanted you to hear me."

He studied my face. "Okay. You got 'nuf trouble widout Eddie. But
I ain' no chickenshit; don' go callin' me dat!"

"Right." I put out my hand.

He shook his head. "Naw. I ain' no frien' wid you. You da Man. Ya
din' keep Boss Cap'n from puttin' trannies on dis dead ol' ship. Keep ya
frazzin' hand." He stalked away.

Moments later I was at my bridge console, pondering the failure of my mission. As I waited for Philip to return from settling into the wardroom, I realized I had no idea what my own cabin looked like. My duffel lay in the corner where I'd first dropped it. Wearily I picked it up, left the bridge once more.

I followed the corridor around the bend. Passing the first lieutenant's cabin, I tried not to recall my folly with Philip and the barrel. Two cabins farther, I found the hatch I expected, with the Captain's insignia. The cabin was bare, clean, impersonal, larger than *Portia*'s, larger even than *Hibernia*'s.

Captain Hasselbrad had transferred all his gear. I stowed my clothing, set my picture of Amanda next to my bunk.

The cabin was furnished with a conference table, several straight chairs, and an easy chair. Nothing else. I sat. I hadn't slept for two days. I would rest my eyes a moment.

I jerked awake in confusion before remembering where I was. I glanced at my watch. With a curse I jumped to my feet; hours had passed. It was almost noon. In the head I ran cold water on my face, searched fruitlessly for a towel. Wiping my eyes on my sleeve I hurried into the corridor.

Outside the bridge Philip Tyre waited anxiously. He saluted.

"Sorry. How long have you been waiting?"

"An hour or so, sir. I didn't want to knock." By custom the Captain was not bothered in his cabin except in an emergency, and then only by ship's caller. Philip had assumed I was unavailable because I wanted to be so.

"Knock any time you want to, Middy." My voice was gruff. "Or call. We're the only officers, you and I."

"Yes, sir. Thank you." I doubted he would. Ship's custom has an inertia too great for a mere midshipman to deflect. He followed me onto the bridge. "The galley detail reported to me, sir, since they couldn't find you. They'll have dinner at seven, using whatever they scrounge from the larders."

"Very well." I glanced at my notes on the console screen.

I had to deal with the Chief. And the comm room. And the hydros. What first? I thumbed the caller. "Mr. Drucker, call the bridge."

The return call came not from hydros but from crew berth one. "Seaman Drucker reporting, sir." He sounded groggy.

"How long have you been off duty?" I asked.

"Uh, three, no, four hours, sir. Mr. Tyre told me to stand the night watch and then go off for sleep."

I was furious. While I had sat in a funk Philip had done my duties for me. "Very well. Sorry I woke you. Go back to sleep and report to the bridge at four bells."

"Aye aye, sir."

"Philip, see if Mr. Tzee is in the crew berth sleeping; I don't want to wake him if he's been on watch all night."

"He's still in the comm room, sir." Philip squirmed with discomfort. "I ordered him to stand double watch. I wasn't sure you'd want to risk leaving the radionics untended."

"Taking a lot on yourself, aren't you?" I knew how ungracious that sounded. I paged the comm room. "Mr. Tzee."

There was a pause before his response. I wondered if he'd been asleep. "Seaman Tzee reporting."

"Go get some sleep. Seal the comm room behind you."

"Aye aye, sir. Thank you." He broke off.

The silent bridge seemed oppressive, reproachful. I sighed. "Thanks for taking care of things, Philip. I'm angry at myself and I took it out on you."

"Thanks, sir." He went on with a rush. "You need sleep too, sir. Nobody can expect you to be alert twenty-four hours a day." He studied the bulkhead, perhaps wondering if he'd gone too far.

He had. Such a remark from a midshipman to the Captain was scandalous. Except under the circumstances.

"I know." I was anxious to change the subject. "Go to the dining hall and see that Mr. Bree has what he'll need for tomorrow's meals. Organize someone to look after the passengers. Report back when you're done."

"Aye aye, sir." With a resilient step and a snappy salute he left. I wasn't all that much older than Philip; he was eighteen and I was but twenty-one, but I looked on his boyish energy with all the sour acknowledgment of an old man.

I sat at my console, trying to devise a duty schedule that would allow us to carry out minimal ship's functions. I knew I was wasting my time. It was impossible with a skeleton crew and only one functioning officer.

Every moment I dawdled, the lasers were unmanned, the comm room unwatched, and the ship's peril increased. Somewhere out there were those . . . goldfish, as we called them. They seemed able to home on our ships; I had no idea how. They'd already found *Challenger* once. If they came upon her again, our small chance of survival would be dashed.

And yet, keeping Mr. Tzee on watch until his forehead struck the console wouldn't save the ship. I had to . . . I didn't know. Somewhere was a solution that was evading me, if I could but think of it.

The knock on the hatch startled me; remembering our missing weapons I glanced at the camera eye before opening. I'd been expecting Philip, but saw Seaman Drucker. Could it already be four?

I bade him enter. "The west hydros, Mr. Drucker. They need to be cleaned out."

"Yes, sir. But like I said, the machinery is all shot. We can't grow nothing in there."

"Manually, we can. I want you to take two hands and deal with the mess. Haul any usable metal down to engine room stores. Save the sand. When you're ready, we'll rig fluorescent growlights and weld some holding tanks. I want an inventory of seeds and an estimate of how many cuttings we can take from east hydros without weakening the plants there. How soon will you be able to report?"

He took time to think before answering, which I appreciated. I could see him grapple for the first time with the problems of command. "Depends on which sailors you give me, sir. I mean—"

"I know. Who do you want?"

"Groshnev and Jabour, if I could have 'em, sir. They're not the type who hang on to a broom to keep from falling down. Not like, uh, some others."

I grinned. "You've got 'em. Get started; we still have a couple of hours before dinner."

"Aye aye, sir." He passed Philip at the hatch as he left. I listened with half my attention while the middy described his arrangements. I stared at my notes left over from yesterday. So much to do.

I sent Philip to dispose of the body in the hold while I studied the ship's manifest. All our cargo was useful in some way to the colony at Hope Nation; perhaps it could help us too.

When Philip returned I took the caller. "Attention all hands. All officers and men to the dining hall. Passengers also. No exceptions, please." I glowered at Tyre. "Come along, Middy." Again we left the bridge. At the armory I secured another laser pistol, handed it to Philip. "Don't lose this one."

He blushed deep red. "Aye aye, sir. I won't."

A few moments later I strode into the dining hall, Philip at my side. Anxious passengers stood about, unsure where to sit. The crewmen, in unfamiliar territory, clustered close to the exit. Normally they'd eat below, in the crew mess on Level 3.

The murmur of conversation ceased.

The Chief Engineer stood, arms folded, near a group of older passengers; I made a mental note to speak to him after the meal. The transpop called Jonie huddled against Eddie Boss. Young Annie watched nearby, hands on hips in a provocative posture. She winked as I passed; I looked elsewhere. The remaining transients were isolated, or had isolated themselves, in a corner of the hall.

I paused in the center of the room. "Ladies and gentlemen, I am Nicholas Seafort, *Challenger*'s Captain. Before we eat, I'll discuss our situation. *Challenger*'s fusion shaft is destroyed and we cannot Fuse. We have a large supply of propellant for subluminous travel, but unfortunately there is no port, no star within reasonable distance. We expect to be rescued; *Portia* will send help when she reaches port."

There was a mounting rustle as the frightening rumors were confirmed. An older woman cried softly.

"We have ample power, and stores of food to last three months or more. We'll grow additional food with hydroponics, as we would if the ship were Fused."

"Why were we left behind?" a woman shrilled. "Your damned Navy brought us here and abandoned us!"

"*Portia* is smaller than *Challenger*. She couldn't take us all; her recyclers can't handle the load."

The seaman Clinger stirred. "And maybe *Portia* won't reach port!" Into the stir of unease he added, "And if she does, who says the rescue ship'll find us?"

"That's enough, Clinger." My hopes of conciliation were dashed.

"Let him speak!" The demand came from a burly middle-aged man across the hall. "We want to know!"

"Your name?"

"Emmett Branstead." He glared. "Let him talk! Maybe we'll finally hear the truth!"

"I'm telling you the truth," I said, as mildly as I could manage. Someone snickered. I realized I had to concede. "Go on, Clinger."

"The bad part is"—the sailor's voice was surly and aggrieved—"we'll never know whether there's a ship looking for us, or if *Portia* got hit too. Or if there *is* a rescue ship, when it might come. We could spend our lives waiting for help that never comes!"

In the back of the room, someone sobbed.

"And that ain't the worst." Clinger's bitterness swelled. "At best, it's eleven months to Hope Nation and eleven back to us, and we have only three months food!"

I cut through the frightened babble. "We'll grow what we need!"

"How?" Emmett Branstead. "The west hydroponics chamber is wrecked, isn't it?"

"Yes." I waited for the angry buzz to subside. "There are other ways to grow food." Silence fell. "We have dozens of unused cabins. We'll construct grow tanks in spare cabins. We have enough fluorescent lighting to nourish the plants."

Branstead shook his head. "Fluorescents don't emit all the components plants need to—"

"They won't be optimum, but they'd work after a fashion, no?"

Reluctantly he nodded.

"What about nutrients and water?" someone asked. "How can you pipe them to all the cabins?"

"We'll hand-water and feed the plants, as man did for thousands of years. Yes, it's work, but our lives depend on it."

Clinger snarled. "We'll be eating each other before this is done. Most of us are already dead, and don't know it!"

I bellowed, "Enough!"

"Why? He's right!" A younger woman with a stiff, drawn face. Murmurs of approval from the others.

"I'm Captain here!"

"Why should you be?" Emmett Branstead. "Our lives are at stake. We should have a say!"

"And us too!" A deckhand. "Sir," he added sheepishly, at my withering glare.

"That's quite enough," I said with careful precision. "You men, stand at attention!" A few complied, Tzee and Akkrit among them.

Seaman Sykes was the first to speak. "It ain't gonna work, Captain." Behind him, a groundswell of murmurs.

"Belay that! I gave an order!"

A sailor said reluctantly, "Look, Captain, it ain't your fault, you didn't get us into this, but why bother with all the work? We're all gonna die anyway."

"We're still crew of a functioning—"

"No, we ain't!" Clinger again. "This ain't a Navy ship no more, like Andy tried ta tell you before you threw him in the brig. Look at us! Thirteen sailors, you, and that joeykid there! The hydros are all glitched; all we got comin' out of the east banks is cucumbers and tomatoes!"

"Clinger—"

"But even without no food problems, the best we can hope is to drift for three, maybe five years 'til somethin' goes wrong in the machinery or maybe somebody finds us. And only if that fat-assed Admiral gets through to Hope Nation!"

I strode up to him as if I were unafraid. "And if you're right, Clinger, and we drift three years? It's no more than a round trip from Earth to Hope Nation and back. You signed up for the long cruise, remember? And if you knew you were going to die, you would still have duty!" I jabbed him in the chest with a stiffened finger. "We have power, we have propellant; we have passengers to attend."

Stubbornly he shook his head. "If I'm goin' out, I want a good time first!" His laugh had a quality that chilled me.

I roared, "Stand to!"

Clinger looked for support, decided he had it. He folded his arms. Several others did likewise.

From the side of the hall Philip Tyre's thin voice cut the silence. "Carry out his order, Mr. Clinger." His laser pistol aimed steadily at Clinger's stomach. "You have five seconds before I shoot." He walked forward. The gun wavered, then stiffened. "I think I'm close enough so I won't miss." He said nothing more.

For a long second Clinger gaped. Then, capitulating, he stiffened to attention. Behind him, other crewmen followed suit.

My tone was bleak. "Do you care to spend the rest of the cruise in the brig, Mr. Clinger?"

"No, sir."

"Then henceforth you will obey orders."

"Aye aye, sir."

I let it be. "Stand easy." Turning to the passengers I said, "I appeal to all of you, men and women alike. We must have more crew; there's no other way to handle the ship. In a day or so I'll ask for volunteers." I overrode the uproar. "Certainly none of you sailed with the intention of joining the Navy. The idea may seem ludicrous, but our very survival is at stake."

I paused and cleared my throat. "We will eat in the dining hall together; we don't have staff to cook separate meals for crew and passengers. No food must be wasted; portions will be doled in advance. If you don't want all your food, give it to someone at your table. The crew will sit separately"—I indicated an area of the hall—"and you passengers may choose your own places, for the time. The Captain's place is here."

Arbitrarily, I pulled out a chair and sat. Philip automatically went to another table, his pistol thrust inside his jacket. The Chief took a third table; officers were accustomed to spreading among the passengers.

At first I thought I would sit alone. Then the lady with the pale, drawn face joined me. So did Walter Dakko. I noticed that the transients all found tables together.

When everyone was seated I stood and tapped for quiet. "Lord God, today is July 30, 2198, on the U.N.S. *Porti—Challenger*. We ask you to bless us, to bless our voyage, and to bring health and well-being to all aboard." The words sounded hollow, even to me.

Dinner was a miserable affair. Conversation was listless and dispirited. We dined on sparse food prepared without grace: boiled vegetables and canned meat, crackers instead of the customary fresh bread. The pale young lady, Elena Bartel, gestured at the tables around us where passengers sat. "You expect to fashion a crew out of—that?"

I glanced; elderly faces predominated except at the tables chosen by the transpops. "What choice have I?"

She smiled without humor, as if I hadn't spoken. "Old Mrs. Reeves, the judge's sister? Or that fat fellow, Conant?"

"There are others," I said, loath to be drawn down that path.

"Yes. Like Olwin, the engineer. But he's too old to adapt well, isn't he? Fifty-something? So that leaves the few youngsters with any education. That disagreeable Dakko boy, or his angry friend Gregor. How much help would they give?"

"There's yourself," I said, more to silence her than for any other reason.

"Me?" Her laugh was derisive. "*Challenger*'s resident neurotic? Since the first month the other passengers always make themselves busy whenever I go to the lounge to talk. Thank God for assigned seating or I'd have eaten alone." She flushed at my appraising glance, but persisted. "Look at me. Scrawny, uncoordinated, never even had a boyfriend, to say nothing of a marriage. I can't even tie a shoelace without fumbling."

"You're hard on yourself, Ms. Bartel."

She laughed, a sharp, brittle sound. "No, just honest, at the end. Now that we'll be dead soon I've nothing to lose."

My tone was harsh. "You have no reason to assume that. There's still hope of rescue."

"Oh, I admire you, Captain, despite my manner of speech. You're prepared to carry on despite all odds. Maybe you're young enough not to understand hopelessness. How old are you, nineteen? I once thought myself immortal too."

"I'm twenty-one, Ms. Bartel, and believe me, I know I'm not immortal. I just feel—" I paused before revealing myself to this bitter

young woman. "I have my duty. Whether I'm to die or not isn't the
issue. Duty remains. It makes choices so much simpler."

"I envy you that." She stared moodily at her weak soup. "You won't
get many volunteers, you know. Perhaps none."

"I'm aware. Hopelessness is seductive." I played with my spoon.
"You see, if we assume we have no chance, not only do we make it
almost certainly true, but we live the remainder of our lives in—in a
morass. In a funk. I don't want to do that, even if I'm the only one who'll
know how I lived and died." I found myself near tears, and lapsed silent.

After a time she said more gently, "I'm sorry I jeered, Captain.
Tend to your duty. I expect to die aboard this ship in a few weeks, when
the food runs out. I guess I don't much mind. Living hasn't been all that
pleasurable." On that grim note our conversation faltered.

Afterward, as the passengers dispersed, I called the crew together
and set Mr. Kovaks on watch on the recyclers, Mr. Tzee in the comm
room, and Mr. Sykes in the engine room. Philip had volunteered to hold
the bridge; I told him he was free to sleep on watch if he needed to, but
he was aghast at the very suggestion. Then, utterly exhausted, I went to
bed. My last thought before my head hit the pillow was that I'd forgotten
to talk to the Chief Engineer. Somehow, he had to be recalled to his
duty; the engine room provided the power essential to our survival.

Despite my fatigue, or perhaps because of it, I slept poorly, and
morning found me bleary and irritable. I went immediately to the
bridge. Philip Tyre, sleepy but awake, came politely out of his seat.
"Good morning, sir."

I made my voice pleasant by brute force. "Morning, Mr. Tyre." I
stared at my console. I needed coffee. "Hold the watch a while longer,
Mr. Tyre. I'll relieve you soon."

I made my way to the officers' mess. There was no coffee made; I
rummaged in the stores and started a pot. I paced while it brewed, then
poured myself a cup. I sipped the hot brew without waiting for it to cool,
anxious to get to the bridge to relieve Philip.

As I reached for the mess hatch it swung open to admit the Chief,
rumpled and unshaven. I fell back. "Oh. Mr., uh, Chief. I was wanting to
talk to you."

He sized me up with a skeptical stare. Finally he said, "I'd rather
have coffee first, if you don't mind."

I waved. "Help yourself." Under other circumstances I would have
found his remark intolerably rude, but there was no reason to antagonize
him further.

He took a cup. "Did you make this stuff?"

"Yes."

It seemed to meet with his approval. "At least someone has some sense around here."

I sat back down at the long table. After a moment he joined me. I tried furiously to remember what he was called. Finally I gave up. "I don't recall your name."

His smile was grim. "Andreas Kasavopolous. Chief Engineer Kasavopolous reporting, sir."

"They call you Andy?" I guessed.

"No." He stared moodily at his coffee. "No, they don't."

"Well, Mr., er, Kasavopolous, I—"

"They call me Dray."

I sighed. This was going to be difficult. "Tell me, Dray," I said harshly, "how long have you been a drunk?"

He tried to hold my eye and failed. He busied himself with his coffee cup in lieu of a reply.

"I asked a question, Chief."

He hesitated as long as he dared, then muttered, "I dunno, Captain. I just kind of fell into it."

"What would it take for you to fall out of it?" My tone was curt.

He shrugged. "Damned if I know." At my look of disgust he grinned. "What'cha gonna do, Captain? Brig me? I thought you needed me to stand watch."

I was outraged. Whether or not I deserved respect, my rank required it. I couldn't imagine what would have befallen me in my days as a midshipman if I'd spoken so to my Captain. "Remember who you're talking to!"

He chuckled mirthlessly. "Yeah, another reject from the U.N. Navy. What'd you do to piss them off, Captain? Forget to polish your service pins?"

"Shut up!"

"Or they catch you with some bimbo in your cabin?" That brought me to my feet, fists clenched. He fell silent. I stared through him a long, eerie moment while he licked his lips uneasily.

Blind with consuming rage I lurched to the ship's caller and paged the bridge. "Mr. Tyre, report to the officers' mess, flank. Seal the bridge behind you."

"Aye aye, sir!"

"Captain, I—"

I hurled my half-empty cup at Dray's head. He ducked away,

drenched with lukewarm coffee. I snarled, "It would be wise to say nothing, Chief Engineer!"

A moment later the hatch flew open. Philip Tyre came to attention, his uniform rumpled, eyes bloodshot.

"As you were! Do you have your laser pistol, Midshipman, or have you lost it again?" My tone struck like a blow.

He pushed his jacket aside. "It's in my—"

"Give it here." Wordlessly he handed it to me. "Fully charged?" Pale, he nodded. "Let's check," I said aiming it at the deck. I thumbed the release; with a crackle the smell of ozone filled the room. We stared at the scorched and smoking deck plate. "Get yourself back to the bridge, Mr. Tyre; you're on watch!" With a mumbled acknowledgment the boy fled.

I swung to the Chief Engineer. My gun came to rest at his head. "Put your hand on the table, Chief Dray."

He complied at once, a sheen of sweat on his broad forehead.

I seized his wrist with my free hand, bent it to the table, put the pistol to his hand. I croaked, "You asked why I'm here? Those fools said I was psychotic! What do they know? They hushed up the business with those sailors and got me off the ship!"

His face was like a grinning death's head.

"You're a drunk, Dray, and I need a watch officer, not a sot. So here's what we'll do. The first time I catch you drinking, I'll put your hand on the table and put the pistol to it, like so. Then I'll fire and cook your hand. I won't need to brig you, and you'll still have one hand left to serve watch. Doesn't that make sense, Dray? Answer!"

He babbled, "Yes, sir! Yes, Captain, it makes sense, I understand. I won't touch a drop—"

"I knew you'd agree, Dray. And that idiot called me psychotic . . ." He smiled in terror and relief. My pistol was still pressed to his hand. I moved it along a finger. "We have an agreement, Dray?"

"Oh, yes, Captain! Yes, sir! I—"

"So, we'll seal the bargain with your little finger."

He screamed, tried to wrench loose his hand.

I held tight. "Don't twitch, Chief! Don't even breathe hard, or it'll be the whole hand!" Gray of face, he stared in abject terror. "You see, Dray," I said reasonably, "you don't need five fingers to stand watch, and the stump will remind you every time you think of taking a drink."

His pale pasty face pleaded in mute despair; a sound between a whimper and a groan escaped him. Despite his efforts his hand twitched involuntarily. I smiled. "Well, let's get it—"

"God, don't!" he rasped. "Captain Seafort, I beg you! I won't give you any more trouble; please, sir! Please!"

I considered it. Then I shook my head in refusal. "No, Dray, if I don't take the finger, you won't know I'm serious. Sorry." I shifted my grip on his hand.

"Oh, Lord God! Please, sir, I can give it up! I'll show you where I keep the stuff, all of it! And the still, I can tear it down!" Sweat fell unnoticed from his brow. I hesitated, shook my head. "Captain, wait, let me take you there! Please!"

I said slowly, "But I want to do it, Dray. Fingers are fun. First they make a popping sound—"

He gagged. Then words poured out of him in a desperate plea for mercy.

Slowly, I let him persuade me. Grumbling under my breath, I followed him to the engine room storage, where his copper-tubed still dripped precious droplets of contraband alcohol into a glass jug. I watched impassively, laser leveled, as he smashed the still.

Then I watched him pour quarts of home brew back through the recyclers, his face frozen in a ghastly smile as he eyed the laser pistol I held on him.

When all was done I left the ashen Chief at his station, vehemently assuring me that he would never make or touch another drop of liquor. I headed back to Level 1. I stopped at my cabin, vomited my coffee into the toilet. Then I sat on the bed, head in my hands, until I remembered Philip alone on the bridge. I forced myself onto my feet and trudged along the corridor.

On the bridge Philip regarded me apprehensively. Bile rose again in my throat. I said mildly, "I'm not angry with you, Philip. That was for his benefit, not yours. Don't concern yourself." Slowly his face relaxed. I eased myself into my chair. "I'll take the watch. Get some sleep."

"Can I get you anything before I go, sir?"

I debated the state of my stomach. "Some coffee, I think. You'll find my cup on the mess hall deck." He looked puzzled, but left without comment.

The morning passed without further incident. I had Mr. Tzee break in a replacement to serve watch in the comm room, and Mr. Kovaks do the same for the recycler's watch. Still, with only thirteen crewmen I knew I couldn't maintain full watches for long.

I busied myself on the ship's caller, arranging for dinner supplies, seeing to Mr. Andros in the brig, organizing a rudimentary steward's service to cope with laundry and cleaning, making sure the galley and the hydro chamber were tended. I'd never realized how many jobs had to be performed aboard ship; many were accomplished without any attention from the officers.

Sweeping and mopping, laundry, manning the engine room, standing all necessary watches, the purser's various functions that kept the passengers comfortable . . . I marveled that *Challenger* had accomplished it all with a full crew of eighty-nine.

I had Kerren plot our course for home, but knew we'd have to assemble a competent engine room watch before I attempted any maneuvering with our thrusters. In any event, I would want to recheck our course manually with the utmost care, and I didn't feel up to it in my current state.

When dinner hour arrived I reluctantly sealed the bridge and left for the dining hall, dogged by a sense of guilt at leaving the bridge untended again. I reminded myself that with only three officers it was virtually impossible to man the bridge around the clock, and furthermore, until I saw whether the Chief was able to keep sober, there was no way I could trust him on watch alone. Better the bridge remain unmanned.

At dinner I was greeted with palpable hostility. My remarks on enlistment had obviously not gone over well. Even the young lady who'd spoken with me yesterday, Elena Bartel, today froze me with a glance. Only Walter Dakko was affable, and he seemed preoccupied.

There was little conversation in the dining hall, and less cheer. When our food arrived, portions were meager, the preparation unappetizing. I'd have to improve the quality of our meals or ship's morale would suffer dramatically.

Later I gave Philip the watch and plodded off to my cabin, reeling from exhaustion. I stripped off my clothes and fell on my bunk. I lay awake for an eternity, the ship's many unsolved problems running feverishly through my mind.

Finally I drifted into sleep, tossing and turning restlessly until Amanda quieted me with a soothing caress. Her warmth aroused me; in the dark of the cabin I turned passionately to her embrace and came awake, my body aching, my mind muddled. I snapped on the light, let loose the pillow around which I'd wrapped myself, waited for my heart to stop pounding and my erection to subside. My head fell back. I don't know how long I wept. Eventually I turned off the light and feigned sleep until the blessed arrival of morning.

* * *

I dressed slowly, willing myself to put aside my irritation and attend to ship's business. Carrying a cup of hot coffee to the bridge, I relieved Philip Tyre and took the watch. I spent the morning pondering flow charts on my handheld holovid, trying to determine the minimum number by which I needed to increase my crew.

It was a day in which I could get nothing done without interruption. First Mr. Kovaks, with questions about monitoring the recycler gauges. Then Seaman Drucker wanted to know about refitting the hydro chamber. Even Philip Tyre, hesitant now to make decisions in his Captain's name, brought me trivial problems concerning the passengers and the dining hall until, exasperated, I sent him off to bed.

When Mr. Bree called the bridge to ask my advice about the evening's menu I simply snarled and rang off. It was as if the whole ship had caught my agitation.

Rather than leave the bridge unattended yet again, I had a steward's mate fetch the soup our galley had prepared for lunch. Philip was asleep, as far as I knew, and would eat later. My first day standing watch on *Challenger*, and already I felt a prisoner on the bridge.

By midafternoon I began to eye the clock, waiting for the deliverance of the dinner hour. I thought of chatting with Kerren but decided even silence was better than his excessive formality. I was savoring memories of Danny and his delight in our chess matches when pounding on the bridge hatch hauled me back to reality.

Cautiously, I swiveled the camera to survey the corridor. Outside, Walter Dakko anxiously shifted from foot to foot, ready to hammer again on the tough alumalloy panel. I slapped open the hatch, my temper soaring. "Belay that! What in Hell do you think you're doing?"

"Sorry, but I had to get your attention. I went—downstairs, I was looking for Chris—"

"Don't bother me with your problems!" I turned away, disgusted. If he'd hammered at my bridge because of his churlish son—

"I was on Level 3. I saw some men outside the brig, cutting through the door."

"Oh, Lord God." It had begun, and all too soon. "How long ago?"

"A minute or two. I came right here—"

"Get off the bridge!" I shoved him out the hatchway, snatched up my laser rifle. I sealed the hatch, ran to the ladder and scrambled down the stairs. Walter Dakko followed close behind. In a moment I was midway between Level 2 and Level 3; remembering lessons from another ship, ages past, I slowed as I approached the lower deck and raised my rifle warily.

The corridor was deserted.

I hurried past the corridor bend, to the brig. The hatch sensor panel was open and the wiring disconnected; the hatch was forced half open. Its hinges were burned through and bent. Cursing, I thrust myself through the opening. The cells were empty. Crawling out I bumped into Mr. Dakko and nearly died of fright. "Get aside!" I pushed past.

At crew berth one, I took a deep breath before I slapped the hatch. As it slid open I charged in, rifle ready. Mr. Tzee sat on his bunk, hands in his lap. I raised my weapon. He met my eye. "I know about it, but I'm not part of it." He held quite still.

"All right." I tried to slow my breathing. "Where are they?" With an effort, I made myself lower the rifle.

"I don't know, sir."

"Who?"

"Clinger, Sykes. One of the new deckhands from your ship. They'll kill me if they learn I told you."

"I know."

"What do you want me to do, sir?"

"Stay here." I had a better idea. "No, go seal yourself in the comm room. Stand watch."

He got quickly to his feet. "Aye aye, sir."

"Kovaks? Drucker?"

"I think Kovaks is in the recycler room. I don't know about Drucker, he was walking around when it started."

I grabbed the caller and thumbed it to the recycler circuit as Mr. Tzee brushed past to the hatch. "Mr. Kovaks?"

An endless moment, before he answered. "Yes, sir?"

"Who is with you?"

"No one, sir. I just now came on duty and relieved Stefanik." I wondered if he'd gone to his station so as not to be committed to the rebellion.

"Seal the hatch and don't open it until I give the order. Acknowledge."

"Orders understood and acknowledged, Captain. What's up?"

I set down the caller without answering. From the hatchway Walter Dakko gaped. I snapped, "Let's go. You'd better not be found here." I started back to the ladder, took the stairs two at a time.

Dakko panted to keep up. "Captain, there's something I ought to tell you."

"Later." I rounded the ladder well and strode to the wardroom.

"It shouldn't wait."

Reluctantly I stopped. "Well? What?"

"I'll enlist. Give me the oath anytime you'd like."

"You will?" It was all I could think to say. "You?"

"Yes." He regarded me with disfavor. "I imagine you intend to ask why?"

"Well . . . yes." I blushed.

A wry smile. "I suppose this is the last time I'll be free to say what I think. I'm not enlisting out of love for you, Captain; you already know that. But it's a choice between you and what you represent, or those men out there. And what they represent."

He shivered. "It may already be too late; I don't know. We're Roman citizens, Mr. Seafort, and the barbarians are at the gates. I'm no centurion, but if the barbarians storm the walls my citizenship won't matter."

I nodded. "I understand. Thank you. Repeat after me. I, Walter Dakko . . ."

He took the oath, there in the middle of the corridor, and was inducted in the Naval Service of the United Nations. Afterward I shook his hand, though that was not the custom. He stood, somewhat apprehensive, waiting for orders.

"I'll teach you the forms and courtesies later, Mr. Dakko. Right now, it's sufficient that you do whatever you're told, immediately and without question."

"Yes, sir."

"Aye aye, sir," I corrected automatically, then laughed at my foolishness. "No matter. Come along." I continued to the wardroom and banged on the hatch. "Philip, open up. It's me—Seafort." A moment later the hatch slid open. Philip Tyre, in his underwear, peered sleepily at the pair of us.

"Get dressed. They've forced the brig hatch and freed Mr. Andros." Philip thrust arms and legs into his clothes. "Never mind your jacket. Mr. Dakko has just taken the oath, by the way. Faster, damn it!" The boy finally had on his shoes. "Let's go!" I led them to the armory and fished in my pocket for the keys. I opened the arms compartment. "What weapons are you familiar with, Mr. Dakko?"

"I've hunted, in the game parks. Probably a rifle would be best."

I handed him one. I gave a stunner to Philip and took another for myself. Resealing the hatch, I hurried around the corridor to the comm room. "Open up!" In response the hatch slid open. Weapon ready, I glanced inside. Mr. Tzee was alone. "Carry on. Admit no one except me or Mr. Tyre."

"Aye aye, sir."

I led my small war party to the recycler chamber; Mr. Kovaks was secure inside. We proceeded to the east hydros. There, Mr. Drucker reluctantly opened the hatch at my command, eyed us uncertainly, came to attention. I was blunt. "Do you know what's afoot?"

He hesitated before committing himself. With a grimace he said, "Yes, sir."

"Are you with us?"

"Yes, sir."

I took a chance. "Who isn't?"

"I dunno, sir. I was in here, mostly."

I gestured to the open hatch. "Go join them, Mr. Drucker, if you won't answer."

"They're my mates!" His cry was a plea.

My tone was unyielding. "They're mutineers."

He tried to hold my eye and failed. "Sykes and Clinger," he muttered. "Andros."

"Who else?"

Drucker licked his lips. His eyes darted between Philip Tyre and Dakko.

My slap spun him halfway around. He recoiled, his hand flying to his cheek in shock. I glared from a distance of inches. "God damn you, Mr. Drucker, there's a mutiny afoot! Obey my order or I'll execute you on the spot!" My hand tightened on the pistol at my side.

"Akkrit," he mumbled. "That new steward's mate, Byzer. That's all I know of, honest." His eyes were on the deck.

"Very well," I said coldly. "Next time—"

"I'm sorry," he blurted. His face twisted in anguish. "Captain, I dunno what's right anymore. I wanna be loyal, but turning on my mates . . ."

"I understand," I said more gently. I groped for reassurance. "When all else fails, Mr. Drucker, do your duty. Uphold your oath; it is what you are." It had no effect on him. I prodded. "Where did they take Andros?"

He shrugged. "I dunno, sir. I got out when I saw what they were doin'. They had that rifle and the stunner, and I knew some joes was gonna get hurt." Out of the corner of my eye I could see Philip blush, trying not to squirm.

"Very well." Now it was my turn to hesitate. After a moment I took the stunner from my belt. I held it out, butt first. "Mr. Drucker, I order you to remain here, and to defend your station against any mutineer who attempts entry."

Astonished, he could only stare. Then he took the weapon, knuckles tightening around the smooth barrel. "Aye aye, sir." His shoulders straightened. As I turned toward the hatch he added, "Count on me, sir." I smiled grimly. I would; I had no choice.

Outside in the corridor we conferred. "Secure the galley or search for Andros?" I asked Philip.

"Search where, sir?" the midshipman asked sensibly. The miscreants could roam the ship as readily as we could.

I shrugged. "The engine room or the purser's stores. Who knows? We have nearly a hundred empty cabins."

Walter Dakko said mildly, "If you don't secure the galley first—"

I rounded on him. "Speak when you're spoken to, sailor!" His jaw dropped. "Don't ever interrupt an officer," I growled. I knew he'd never been addressed in such a tone. Nonetheless, he swallowed and answered, "Aye aye, sir."

I was exhausted, famished, confused. The rebels could be anywhere. I swallowed, acknowledging defeat. "To the dining hall." I trudged wearily back to the ladder.

In the mess Mr. Bree gasped with fright as the hatch swung open and the three of us strode in. His eyes darted to our ready weapons.

"Why the panic, Mr. Bree?" I asked. White-faced, he licked his lips and made no answer. I stared at him a long moment before I guessed. "They were here?" He nodded. "What did they take?"

"I couldn't help it, Captain, honest," he babbled. "They had a rifle. They were going to shoot us!" He took an involuntary step back.

"What did they take?" My throat was tight.

He put his hands out as if to ward us off. "Please, Captain, I don't want to be part of it, sir. Don't put me in the middle!"

Philip intervened as my hand went to my pistol. "Tell the Captain exactly what they took, Mr. Bree," he said quietly. "We need to know."

The terrified sailor shot Philip a grateful glance. "The canned goods in the locker, sir, and the vegetables. All they left was the flour, and the bread baking."

I sank into a chair, stared at the bare wooden table. Philip came alongside. "I'll unseal the hold and get more stores, sir, if you'd like." I made no answer. I studied the grain of the wood.

Mr. Bree was hesitant. "I can make stew again tonight, sir, if I could have more canned meat."

"Shut up, all of you." My voice was flat, emotionless. Trying to carry on was folly. There was nothing more I could do but resign and let events take their course.

I sighed. I wasn't cruel enough to leave *Challenger* in Philip's hands. Not yet. But we would die aboard this ship; survival was impossible. I'd failed. I had only to live out my oath until it was over.

The silence stretched to minutes before I stirred. I stood heavily. "Mr. Tyre, take Mr. Bree's mate to the hold and bring back a case of canned meat and vegetables. Let no one else into the hold, reseal it when you leave, and return safely with the stores. Carry out these orders if it costs your life."

Philip came to attention. "Aye aye, sir." His tone was stiff and formal. He saluted, beckoned to a steward's mate to follow. Pistol armed and ready, he slapped open the hatch and disappeared into the corridor.

"Mr. Dakko, position yourself to guard the hatch. Let no one enter who is armed save Mr. Tyre." The recruit nodded and moved purposefully to the side of the hatchway. I crossed the dining hall to the ship's caller on the bulkhead. I keyed the caller to page the entire ship.

"Attention all hands. This is the Captain. All passengers and crew are to report to the dining hall at once. Mr. Drucker, Mr. Tzee, Mr. Kovaks, remain at your stations; this order does not apply to you." I replaced the caller. I dragged a chair into the center of the aisle. I sat facing the hatch, rifle across my knees.

In a few moments they began to respond to my summons. Walter Dakko coolly eyed each person who entered, weapon at the ready. Annie, the transpop girl, was the first, followed by several other streeters. Seaman Jabour, the deckhand, came, his expression uncertain. From my place in the aisle I motioned them to seats.

Gregor Attani and Chris Dakko arrived, gaped at the rifle in the hands of Chris's father. He ignored their startled looks, his eyes fixed on the open hatchway.

The Chief Engineer peered through the hatch before hesitantly entering the hall. I pointed to a table; docile, he took his seat. Eddie Boss stopped short at the sight of the rifle. I ordered him to a chair; he glared at me before deciding to comply. Other transients drifted in.

Several of the older passengers came together, huddled as if for mutual support. Mrs. Ovaugh walked heavily, with a cane. Mrs. Reeves, Judge Chesley's sister, followed with her husband, accompanied by Mr. Fedez and the Pierces.

Emmett Branstead stalked in. He glanced at Walter Dakko but did not stop. "Captain, just what do you—"

"Later. Take a seat."

"Not until—" I swung my rifle toward him, my face impassive. He subsided and quickly found a place.

The steward's mate peered cautiously through the hatchway. Seeing no danger he came in, lugging a box of foodstuffs. Philip Tyre followed, pistol poised, his face reflecting a deadly resolve. He stopped short when he saw Walter Dakko, but relaxed at my nod of reassurance.

Finally all had arrived who would. Somewhere in the bowels of the ship lurked six armed and rebellious crewmen: Clinger, Andros, Sykes, Byzer, Simmons, and Akkrit. Within the dining hall, all was silent. Even the transpops were subdued by the overriding mood of menace.

I cleared my throat. "Last evening I told you I would ask for volunteers to enlist. It is now time. The safety of the ship demands that a sufficient crew be formed. I call for your enlistment. Who will volunteer?"

Elena Bartel was the only one to speak. "I'd be willing to help you as a civilian, Captain. In any job."

"So would I, sir." Astounding: it was old Mrs. Reeves.

"Thank you both. However, I require volunteers to enlist in the Naval Service, not as civilian helpers."

"Why?" Emmett Branstead.

"U.N.S. *Challenger* is a Naval vessel and will be directed by a Naval crew."

Branstead's scorn was withering. "But you have none."

"I have the remnants of a crew, which we'll augment."

"Use civilians."

"No. Aside from hydros and recycling, I need crewmen to man the lasers so we can defend ourselves. We have to keep a constant watch in the comm room. The engine room must be staffed to generate propulsion."

"With what, the thrusters? They're maneuvering jets, and we're nineteen light-years from home!" Branstead's red face glowered. "It's hopeless, you fool!"

From his nearby seat Philip Tyre sucked in his breath in rage. I stood. "Yes, nineteen light-years. I've calculated that after jettisoning cargo, by using all our propellant we can, over a period of a month, boost the ship to one-quarter light-speed. If—"

Elena Bartel blurted, "That would mean seventy-six years to get home!"

"Yes. But—" The murmurs of dismay grew louder. For the first time I raised my voice. "But the radio message we'll begin sending on continuous tightbeam will reach Earth in only nineteen years. We will constantly send our position and course. By that time we will have traveled almost five light-years toward home, and—"

Emmett Branstead shouted, "You're talking a lifetime!"

"No. Some of us will be alive, and our children would be."

"Christ, you don't know what you're taking about," Branstead said with heat. "It would take them fifteen more years to reach us—"

"Under Fusion they'd reach us in months."

"And everyone knows you can't use all your propellant to accelerate! We'd shoot right past the Solar System, unable to brake."

"The rescue ship would match our velocity and course; we'd be off-boarded in flight. Perhaps *Challenger* might eventually sail through the Solar System, empty and abandoned, while some of us sit at home in old age, recalling our past adventures."

This time the silence was thoughtful. After a moment I added, "Or we can sit bickering until the supplies run out and we die. The jobs I listed—the comm room watch, the recyclers, the hydros, the engine room—require Naval personnel. I won't trust *Challenger*'s survival to civilians."

I strode to the ship's caller on the bulkhead and dialed the bridge. "Kerren, come on-line, please."

"Puter K 20546 reporting, sir." His formality startled me but I was glad for it."

"Very well. You have sensors in the dining hall, do you not?"

"Yes, sir, for emergency use. Normally deactivated for privacy."

"Activate your sensors and record. I, Captain Nicholas Seafort, do now call for volunteers. Who will enlist?"

No one spoke. I said again, "For the last time, I call for volunteers. Who will enlist?"

"I will." All heads turned to the pale young woman.

"Ah." I faced her. "Ms. Bartel."

"Yes. It's only for a few months, anyway."

"No, the term is five years."

She smiled bitterly. "I don't think it will be, Captain. But it's how I choose to spend what time is left."

"Thank you. Repeat after me. 'I do swear upon my immortal soul . . .' "

She raised her right hand. " 'I do swear upon my immortal soul . . .' "

" 'To preserve and protect the Charter of the General Assembly of the United Nations, to give loyalty and obedience for the term of my enlistment to the Naval Service of the United Nations and to obey all its lawful orders and regulations, so help me Lord God Almighty.' "

Solemnly her words echoed in the hushed chamber. When she fell silent I nodded shortly. "Who else?" I looked around.

"Me, sir." A stout, middle-aged man. "Chester Olwin. I'm an engineer."

"Very well." I gave him the oath. "Who else?" There was no answer. I asked again. "Will anyone else volunteer?" Several passengers looked away, eyes shifting in embarrassment. Two middle-aged men, some type of crop specialists, and some of the older women.

"I see." I walked slowly back to the center of the room. "Kerren, continue to record."

"Aye aye, sir."

I paced. "Pursuant to Article 12 of the Naval Regulations and Code of Conduct, Revision of 2087, I hereby declare a state of emergency." My eyes roved the assembled passengers. "During a state of emergency, involuntary impressment into the Naval Service is authorized." I stopped in front of the table. "You. Stand!"

With shaky legs, Gregor Attani complied. I said formally, "I herewith impress you into the Naval Service and require you to take the oath of allegiance. Repeat after me. 'I do swear . . .' "

I'd expected a refusal but he only asked, "Why? Why me?"

"You're young and you're educated."

He stared at the deck a long moment. Then he straightened, glancing quickly at his friend Chris. His face was grim. "I do swear upon my immortal soul—"

I finished administering the oath. "You! Chris Dakko!"

"No!" He stood to face me, fists bunched.

"I impress you into the Naval Service. You will take the oath."

"Like hell!" At his post by the hatch his father stirred, then was still.

I raised my rifle. "Repeat after me. I do swear upon my immortal soul—"

Chris waited, unafraid. "What will you do, Seafort? Shoot me, or all of us?" His laugh was contemptuous. "Then who'll run your bloody ship?" He held my eye. "If you'd make a slave of me, you're no better than your mutineers!"

My reply was cut short by a rough hand on my shoulder. I whirled, ready to do battle. Eddie Boss hovered, eyes blazing. "Get away," I snarled. "This doesn't concern you."

"Enlis' me."

"You sit—what?"

"Enlis' me!" He loomed, fists clenched.

Briefly I closed my eyes. "I can't, Eddie. I need joes with education and skills. And you'd have to obey my every order, without question. You can't do that."

"Don't tell me what I c'n do!" he shouted. "You dunno!"

I backed away from his rage. "You're ready to obey, Eddie? Without any reservations?"

"What's resashuns?"

Behind him, Chris Dakko snickered.

"Holding back. A seaman must give total obedience, even when you're angry, like you are now."

He was silent a long moment. "Yeah, I do dat," he said at last. "Enlis' me, Cap'n!"

"It's for five years, Eddie." My voice was gentle.

"I know! Do it!"

I overrode my doubts. "Say: I do swear . . ." He repeated the oath, stumbling over the words. "Very well, Mr. Boss. You're enlisted in the U.N. Naval Service."

Eddie grinned triumphantly. He whirled, his massive hand a fist, and clubbed Chris Dakko to the ground. "You do what my Cap'n say!" he bellowed. The boy lay dazed, blood streaming from his nose and mouth. From the hatchway Walter Dakko watched, impassive.

Well, the Navy was nothing if not adaptable. "Very well, Mr. Boss. You're appointed chief petty officer. Your first duty is to help me shape up the new crewmen. Pick up that recruit you just knocked down." As he hauled Chris to his feet I added, "You'd better take the oath, Mr. Dakko, before worse happens."

Chris looked around, shivered. He mumbled, "I swear. All of it."

"Very well. Sit down and hold a cloth—"

"You need more, Cap'n?" Eddie blurted.

I said coldly, "Mr. Boss, this is your first order. Never—NEVER—interrupt your Captain."

He swallowed. His fists clenched briefly, then he relaxed. "Aye aye, Cap'n," he said with care.

I glanced at Chris, who had sunk into a seat, cloth napkin pressed to his bleeding face. I turned back to Eddie. "There are others who want to enlist, Mr. Boss?"

"Yeah. I mean, uh, yes, uh, sir." He pointed to Deke. "Him." The young transient looked startled. Eddie pushed him forward. "Say h'm his oath, Deke. Tellaman."

"I ain'—"

"Yeah!" Eddie locked eyes with the unnerved streeter, who after a moment capitulated.

Deke nodded. "I takin' oath, Cap'n. Swear."

"Very well. Who else?"

Eddie led me through the cluster of transients, pausing in front of some, ignoring others I'd have selected. I chose to trust his judgment. When he was through I had fifteen new recruits from their group: eleven boys, four girls.

I glanced at the remaining passengers. Most were too old to be of use. "Very well, then. The new crewmen will—"

"Just a moment, Captain Seafort." Emmett Branstead came to his feet.

I turned, angry at the latest interruption. "I've about had it with you, Mr. Branstead. I won't tolerate your interference."

"I'm not interfering!" His red face radiated anger.

"What then?"

"I volunteer."

I was speechless. As the silence lengthened Philip Tyre glanced at me and intervened. "If that was a joke, Mr. Branstead, it's in poor taste."

He glared irately at the young midshipman. "I wouldn't joke about anything so important. I'll enlist."

I found my voice. "Why, after all you've had to say?"

"I have skills you'll find useful with the hydroponics. I'm a planter; my brother owns one of Hope Nation's largest plantations, though I doubt you've heard of it."

"I've sat at his table." He raised a skeptical eyebrow. I added, "The plank table, in Harmon's dining room. I've met your nephew Jerence, who will inherit."

"Oh," he said in a small voice.

I savored my triumph, before I realized how mean it was. "So? You have skills, and you're donating them?"

"That, and—" He gestured at the transients. "You'll have your hands full. You need recruits who are educated. As you said."

"Your temperament is hardly adequate, Mr. Branstead."

He nodded. "I know what you think of me. But you'll find I will obey orders once I've given my word to do so." He held my eye until I was forced to look away, recalling Derek Carr's determination.

"Very well, then." I administered the oath. I faced the silent, apprehensive group. I had just added twenty untrained recruits to the ship's roster. We still needed more help, but I'd more than doubled my crew and I'd have trouble enough assimilating so many at once.

I sent the new crewmen to the tables I'd designated for the ship's company. We sat to our meal.

41

Stew and fresh bread revived me; I returned to the bridge with a more jaunty step. I sent Philip, still armed, down to crew berth one to settle the new recruits. My first thought had been to hunt down the rebels immediately, but on reflection I decided otherwise. Untrained recruits with unfamiliar weapons were no match for tough, ruthless crewmen who knew every inch of the ship. I'd only end up killing some of my new crew and putting more arms into the hands of the rebels.

I paced impatiently until Philip returned. He dropped into his chair with a sigh of relief. "They're getting settled, sir. We found the stores and I issued uniforms and bedding. I took the liberty—" He flushed.

"What is it?"

"After I left them I put my ear to the hatch for a minute. There was some grumbling, but it sounded all right. I know we're not supposed to spy."

"That's right. If they catch you they'd never trust you again. Or any officer."

"Sorry, sir."

The corners of my mouth turned up. "I'd probably have done the same."

Philip, used to my moods, said nothing when I stood and began to pace. I had to deal quickly with the rebellion. But despite my anxiety, until we had the enlistees—and the inductees—well in hand, I had no way to regain control of my ship.

In the meantime, I could trust Philip Tyre and Walter Dakko. But I dared not press the loyalty of seamen like Mr. Tzee and Mr. Kovaks, who'd bunked with the rebels on the long voyage out.

I glanced at the two rifles leaning against the bulkhead, mine and the one I'd issued Walter Dakko. Perhaps I could set the midshipman and Dakko to guard the two ladders up from Level 3 while I systematically searched the bottom Level myself. No, that wouldn't work; I couldn't afford to lose either Dakko or Tyre, and besides, searching an entire Level would need more than one person; while I was in the engine room or a crew berth the rebels could slip around the circular corridor to where I'd already searched.

I pounded the chair arm in frustration. How could I conduct ship's business with six armed sailors skulking belowdecks? They could hold out indefinitely, unless I could deny them access to food. A chill stabbed. What if they burned through the arms locker and seized the rest of our weapons?

Good Lord. I hadn't secured the armory.

"Philip!"

He leapt awake, alarm and embarrassment playing on his features. "Yes, sir?"

"Go below. Bring back Mr. Attani. And, uh, seal crew berth one. Explain to the men that it's for their own safety. I'm concerned to keep the rebels out, not them in."

"Aye aye, sir. But couldn't Clinger burn his way through, the way he did the brig?"

"He won't know whether I've issued arms to the crew, so I don't think he'll take the chance. Show them all how to use the caller and instruct them to call the bridge or my cabin at the first sign of trouble."

"Aye aye, sir." He scurried to the hatch.

Fifteen minutes later, a knock. I swiveled the camera, saw Philip and Gregor. Inside, Philip saluted and came to attention. Attani, glancing at him, imitated in passable fashion.

"As you were." I smiled at Gregor to show my approval. "I'm glad you're making the best of a bad situation, Mr. Attani."

"Uh, thank you."

Philip glared at him. " 'Sir!' Always say 'sir' to the Captain!"

"Thank you, sir." Gregor's jaw tightened.

It wasn't good discipline to undercut Philip in front of a seaman, but perhaps we were past such niceties. I said as gently as I could. "There'll be time for that later, Mr. Tyre. Mr. Attani is showing his goodwill, and my mind is on something more important than etiquette." Before Philip could respond I went on. "Gregor, I've inducted you against your will. Now I need to put my ship in your hands. Can I trust you?"

He thrust his hands in his pockets. Seeing Philip's horrified look he hurriedly pulled them out again. "Trust me? Not to double-cross you, or not to foul up?"

"Both, Mr. Attani. I want to leave the bridge. I need you to guard it." Philip bit his lip, shook his head at me, urging me to stop. "After I seal the hatch behind me, if you hit that red emergency seal on the console, I will have no way to get back in. No way at all." Philip's expression was aghast.

Silent for a moment, Gregor stared at his feet. Then he shrugged. "It's tempting, I admit. But to what purpose? To hand the ship over to the rebels? Chris is wrong, you're a lot better than they are. Besides, I've given my oath, which settles it. If it means anything, I'll give you another. I won't betray you, so help me Lord God."

Relieved beyond words, I blurted, "Gregor, would you like me to appoint you cadet midshipman?"

He shot me a surprised glance, then shook his head. "No, sir. I've given my oath and I'll obey orders, but that would be like volunteering. I'm no volunteer. I don't want to force other men to follow orders against their will. It wouldn't be honest, and if I don't believe in what you're doing, I wouldn't make a good officer." His gesture was placating. "I understand you meant it as a compliment, sir. Perhaps if I come to feel differently and you still want me . . ."

"Very well." Though I was hurt, I felt reluctant admiration for his honesty. "Mr. Attani, sit in that chair. Don't get up. Don't touch the hatch control panel. Touch nothing except this caller." I keyed the corridor camera onto the console screens. "Watch these cameras. If they show anyone other than Mr. Tyre or me, or if you hear any attempt to cut through the hatch, or if any alarm goes off, thumb the caller, like this, and call me. Don't move the caller key, it's set for the entire ship. Do you understand?"

For the first time Gregor seemed a bit awed. "Yes, sir. How long do you expect to be?"

"A few minutes. Perhaps more." I took my rifle. "Philip, release the safety on your pistol. Guard behind us; I'll watch ahead." I sealed the hatch; no one could enter without the code unless Gregor Attani opened it from inside. Even with the code, I couldn't enter if Gregor activated the override on the hatch control.

I led Philip along the corridor, our weapons ready. We encountered only the looming gray bulkheads. My relief at reaching the arms locker was short-lived; its hatch panel was smashed, the keypad dangling. Without much hope I entered the code I'd set; the hatch remained closed.

I swore under my breath; while I'd made histrionic speeches in the dining hall the enemy had been busy. Had they gained entry? I scrutinized the armory hatch. It appeared solid; thank Lord God I'd sealed it properly. Once sealed there was no way to open an arms locker by shorting the wires; the thick alloy plate would have to be breached with heavy welding gear.

Philip waited patiently. I thought of retreating to my bridge stronghold, decided against it. Time would work against us. Three of us were not enough to man the bridge, guard the armory, and get a torch; it would take more than one man to hold the armory for any length of time. "Mr. Tyre, wait here until I return. Guard the arms locker."

"Aye aye, sir." His voice was tense.

I hurried around the corridor bend to the bridge and entered the code. The hatch slid open. Gregor Attani sat silently, hands clenching the chair arms. "It's all right, Gregor." I snatched the rifle I'd left behind, resealed the hatch behind me, ran back to the armory.

"Philip, put away your pistol and carry this. Go down the east ladder to Level 3. Watch for the rebels. Unseal the crew berth and get Walter Dakko. Reseal the berth, give him the rifle, and both of you report back here. Hurry."

His footsteps faded. Checking to make sure the safety of my laser rifle was off, I leaned against the inner bulkhead, rifle cradled in my arms, turning my head left to right every few seconds. I could hear nothing.

An eternity passed. Finally I heard their returning footsteps from the west. Philip hummed under his breath. As they came round the corridor, my grin of relief vanished.

I was face-to-face with Seaman Clinger.

He had a cutting torch assembly strapped across his back. Behind him two other men stood frozen, as astonished as I.

I moved in slow motion to raise my rifle. Clinger backpedaled, clawing at his pistol.

He got off a shot. A bolt of lightning crackled past my head; a white-hot knife caressed my cheek with infinite pain. I screamed. My hair sizzled. I managed to fire just as he threw himself to the deck and rolled past the corridor bend. I missed. Where he'd lain a second before, a buckled deck plate smoked.

Clinger's whisper was sharp and urgent. "Simmons, go round the other side, flank! Akkrit an' me'll hold him here!" The thud of running feet.

One rebel dashed around the circumference corridor to come at me from the east, while Clinger and his henchman menaced from the west. In moments I'd be under fire from both sides. I charged west, firing as I ran, but Clinger and his companion retreated, keeping out of sight around the corridor bend.

Unless I retraced my steps I'd be trapped too far around the bend to defend the armory hatch. I flattened myself against the bulkhead alongside the hatch, ear and scalp throbbing, my eye tearing. I resolved to fire at whoever came at me first.

From the east, a faint sound. I aimed. Nobody appeared.

It was all my fault, for letting them approach so near unchallenged. Cursing my carelessness, I leaped across the corridor to the far bulkhead, whirled to the east. I got off three quick shots at the retreating Simmons, then spun west to fire at Clinger, but he ducked back around the bend as he saw me turn.

As my beam sizzled past his head my rifle gave a warning beep. Its charge was nearly exhausted.

Clinger gave a hoarse yell. He too had heard. "Now, joes! He's almost out of bolts!" Not knowing what else to do I charged east, stamping loudly, then whirled and did the same heading west. I could hear footsteps scramble out of my way, but I knew the gambit wouldn't work for long.

A bolt scorched the bulkhead. I retreated east. "You're done, Captain," Clinger crowed. "Give up now and we won't—"

An agonized scream. It rent the air for interminable seconds. A gasp, a sobbing breath, and again a shriek. The thud of running feet.

I whirled to meet the new threat, finger poised on the trigger. Philip Tyre stumbled toward me, Walter Dakko close behind.

"Thank God!" I gestured toward the sounds of agony. "Simmons?"

"I shot him, sir." Tyre's face was green, his eyes glassy. I squeezed his arm, guided him to rest against the bulkhead. "Steady, boy."

"I'll be all right." His voice was thick.

I pointed back the way he had come. "Quick now, around the corridor, both of you. Catch the bastard from behind!" We'd give Clinger a taste of his own medicine. As they ran off I checked the charge indicator on my rifle; enough for two more shots, at best. Impatiently I waited for Dakko and Tyre to get into position. Time passed. I could hear nothing beyond the moaning and crying of the wounded man.

"Mr. Tyre?"

"Here, sir," he called back. "About twenty-five meters from the armory."

"Very well. Move forward a meter; I'll do the same." Very cautiously I inched forward, rifle poised to fire. Nothing. "Again!" This time I threw myself against the far bulkhead as I dashed forward. I thought I saw a flash of color at the edge of the corridor horizon. "One more time!" I yelled. I jumped forward. A shape leaped toward me; I nearly fired before I recognized Walter Dakko. Trembling, I lowered my rifle. We approached each other with caution.

"Where is he, sir?" Philip's pistol was ready.

"The west ladder," I said wearily. "They retreated belowdecks as soon as they heard my order to cut them off. They were a lot closer to the west ladder than you were, going all the way around."

Philip Tyre cursed long and fluently. I raised my eyebrow. I hadn't thought the boy had it in him. He ground to a halt, glanced at me sheepishly. "Sorry, sir."

"You said it well enough for both of us." I followed the corridor past the armory to where Simmons lay writhing. Horribly scorched, he was clearly beyond our ability to aid. A laser pistol is a nasty weapon. "Look away, Philip."

"Wha—?" I saw his sudden look of comprehension and horror. For a moment he stared into my eyes, then obeyed. I lowered my rifle, put an end to the tormented moans.

When I turned back neither of them spoke. I said, "We need to cut throught the armory hatch; my rifle has only a couple of bolts. You two hold the corridor here by the armory. No, better yet, hold the top of the ladders, east and west. Look over the railing and nail anyone who tries to climb from Level 2. I'll run down to the engine room and rummage up the gear we need to burn through the hatch."

"Take the other rifle, sir," Philip said. "It's fully charged."

"No, I can retreat if I have to, but I want you to hold Level 1 at all costs."

"But you can't defend—"

"Don't argue with orders, Midshipman." My face burned abominably.

It brought him up short. "Aye aye, sir. Sorry, sir. But please be careful," he added in a rush.

I smiled; it hurt dreadfully. "Oh, yes. Very." I nodded toward the west ladder and Philip went off. Walter Dakko accompanied me to the east ladder, took up his position at the rail. "Don't shoot me when I come back," I warned.

He grinned without mirth. "I'll try not to, Captain. It would help if you give me a signal before you come into view."

"Good idea. I'll identify myself as *Challenger*, as I would coming aboard." I paused. "And just in case, I'll call myself Seafort if I'm under duress. You understand?"

"Yes." Dakko looked grim. I decided it wasn't a good time to remind him of Naval courtesies, and went on my way.

At the foot of the ladder on Level 2, I poked my head cautiously into the corridor. No one was in sight. I hurried around the ladder well and continued down toward Level 3. About halfway, the reaction hit me. My knees began to shake so badly I thought I would fall the rest of the way. Clutching the rail, I sat heavily on the step while my cheek throbbed with a fierce fire. I took several deep breaths to dispel my dizziness.

After a while I felt well enough to proceed. I glanced down the ladder to the deserted Level 3 corridor. Somewhere below lurked Clinger and his accomplices. I gagged, recalling the sweet stench of Simmon's burning flesh.

My hand crept toward my pulsing cheek. I willed myself down the ladder, but my feet had a mind of their own. They didn't move. With shock and contempt I realized I was terrified of what lay below.

The cool gray light of the corridor beckoned. I fought a silent battle with my fear, knowing that every moment I dawdled Philip and Walter Dakko's danger increased, and the rebels would have more time to organize. I stared down the ladder a long time before I realized I was beaten. Slowly, reluctantly, I turned and trudged up the ladder.

I would have to devise some other plan. Guard the armory myself, perhaps, while I sent Mr. Tyre and Dakko to fetch the cutting tools. Or summon Gregor Attani from the bridge to help Dakko guard the upper deck, while Tyre and I forayed below decks.

I paused at the Level 2 corridor, groping for the words to explain my change of plan. It wasn't fair. If only Clinger's bolt had injure me more seriously, no one would expect me to go below.

I took the first step toward Level 1, stopped, reluctantly turned myself around. There was no way I could face Philip with my cowardice. Better even to die.

"God damn it!" I ran full tilt down the ladder, heedless of the danger and oblivious of blasphemy. I skidded into the Level 3 corridor, rifle ready, heart pounding.

No one was there. The terrors of hell pursuing me, I raced along the corridor to the engine room hatch. I passed crew berth one and thought wildly of unsealing it and getting help, before I remembered that the men inside were unarmed. I galloped on.

I reached the engine room, slapped the hatch control, hoping against hope it wasn't sealed from inside. My back itched with anticipation of the impact of a bolt. None came. The hatch slid open. I dived in.

Chief Dray sat morosely at his bare table, eyes widening with shock as I tumbled in. "Jesus, Captain, I haven't been drinking—I swear!"

"Never mind that," I gasped. "Have you seen the rebels?"

He stared at me in surprise. "I heard noises, about an hour ago.

Whoever it was, they didn't come in here. What happened to your face?"

"I need a torch and crowbars to cut through the armory hatch. Where?"

"Engine room stores compartment would have two torches," he said slowly. "There'd be others in the machine shop."

I tried to recall where to find the storage compartment. "Next hatch?"

"There's an entrance off the corridor, and one through here, from the shaft room." He got to his feet.

"Hurry, God damn you!" That got him moving, all right. If I made it home alive it would probably get me beached for blasphemy, as well. I no longer cared.

A few moments later we had a torch, gas bottles, and a big steel crowbar. I had him haul the gear while I led the way with the rifle. We moved slowly along the corridor toward the east ladder, the same direction from which I'd come.

I froze, hearing voices. They were behind us, a long way down the corridor. "Run!" I whispered, and we scrambled up the ladder.

As I rounded the Level 2 ladder well a figure loomed in the shadows. I yelled in horror and fired reflexively. I missed. Annie stopped dead in her tracks, her mouth working in terror.

"Oh, God, I'm sorry!" I cried.

"Why Cap'n shootin' Annie?" she crouched against the bulkhead. "Annie no trouble ta Cap'n. No fight. Why?"

I swallowed. "You scared the hell out of me, girl. Go back to your cabin and lock the hatch. Hurry."

"Why alla runnin', alla shoutin'? Who's—"

"Go!" I yelled, my temper irrevocably lost. She fled. I ran toward the ladder, Dray behind. Then I remembered, and stopped so suddenly he skidded into me and nearly pitched me over. "It's *Challenger*," I called hoarsely.

"Right," Dakko's voice was tense. I ran up the ladder, Dray puffing behind me. Dakko covered us as we ran.

I stopped for breath when I was finally out of sight from the corridor below. "Stay on guard, Mr. Dakko, while we see to the armory."

"Yes, sir." As I ran forward Dakko corrected himself, "Aye aye, sir." Despite myself I smiled, but my amusement vanished when I had to step over the grisly remains of the deckhand Simmons.

I had Chief Dray assemble his equipment outside the armory,

while I checked the west ladder. Philip Tyre stood grimly, pistol braced on the rail pointed at the corridor below. "All's well?" I asked.

"Yes, sir. No sign of trouble."

I tried to contain my impatience while Chief Dray methodically cut his way through the heavily reinforced hatch. The armory and the bridge were the two most fortified points on the ship. Slowly the white-hot line advanced.

The bulkhead speaker crackled to life. Gregor Attani's panicked voice filled the corridor. "Captain, an alarm's ringing!"

Cursing, I dashed to the bridge hatch and entered the code. I dived through as the hatch was sliding open and slapped it closed behind me.

"I didn't touch anything, I swear!" Gregor blurted over the clamor of the bell and Kerren's urgent warnings. "It just started—"

"Belay that, sailor!" I stared at the flashing light on the console.

Kerren blared, "Engine room hatch structural failure! Hatch circuitry compromised! Seal code inoperative—"

I sagged into my chair, the bridge whirling about me. Wearily I flicked a switch and the alarms fell silent. Beside me, Gregor Attani sat hunched in his seat, turned half away from the console.

"It's all right, Mr. Attani." My voice was dull. "There's no danger."

He was near panic. "Christ, when that went off I thought it was those things—those fish attacking us! I thought—" His eyes filled with tears.

"Easy, sailor. You're all right." For his benefit I forced my voice to remain steady while I tried to think our problem through, my brain stuffed with soft cotton.

The rebels were seizing the engine room. Kerren's alarms hadn't gone off when they'd attacked the armory because the rebels had dismantled its hatch control panel first. Now, pressed for time, they'd used brute force and cut through the engine room hatch. The heat from their torch had set off the alarms.

I had to attack them before they could take over the engine room, but how? The rebels still had the rifle and the stunner they'd taken from Philip in the hold. My forces had a fully charged rifle, a pistol, and my own rifle, which had at most one shot left. Not enough weaponry to overpower them, unless I was very lucky, and I couldn't count on luck.

I'd have more weapons once we breached the armory. But that would give them time to take and fortify the engine room. The rebels would control the ship's power lines. I'd have most of the rest of the ship, including the bridge and the food.

I could starve them out; they could cut us off without heat and power. A standoff. I couldn't allow that.

"Hold the bridge again." I slapped open the hatch, bellowed, "Mr. Tyre!" Philip scrambled around the bend from the west. I beckoned toward the east ladder, where Walter Dakko stood guard. "Both of you, follow me!" I pounded down the ladder. "They're forcing the engine room," I panted. "We've got to stop them!"

We reached the foot of the ladder, on Level 3. I charged recklessly down the corridor, my troops at my heels. As I skidded around the bend the engine room hatch came into view. A leg was disappearing into a sizable hole cut in the hatch. My aim was off; I hit the hatch rather than the leg but the reflected heat brought a yelp of pain. I'd used the last bolt in my rifle.

Two cutting torches lay abandoned in the corridor. I heard a commotion inside the engine room. From within, a slab of deck plating appeared and was thrown over the gaping hole in the hatch. Infuriated, I threw my shoulder against the makeshift barrier. It gave way. I glimpsed a startled face, reaching hands, before the plate was slammed back into place. I lowered my shoulder and charged again, but somebody had shoved a wedge against the hatch; this time it didn't budge.

Too late. The engine room was taken.

I flinched at the cool touch of the medipulse against my blistered cheek. Walter Dakko pursed his lips but said nothing. His hand was rock steady; already I could feel the pain lessen under the humming ministration of the disk. Perched on a utility table in the corner of the infirmary, Philip Tyre watched anxiously.

"How long, Kerren?" I spoke from the right side of my mouth.

His voice came from the speaker. "At least a minute for each six centimeters of skin area."

"Please don't talk, Captain; I'm trying to hold this steady." Dakko's voice was polite but firm. At the edge of my field of vision Philip indignantly opened his mouth to object, but I waved him silent. Our new seaman was correct, even if no sailor bred to the Navy would have dared suggest that his Captain keep his mouth shut.

When he was done, Walter anxiously inspected my face.

"Well?" I raised on eyebrow.

"You won't be winning any beauty contests. Badly blistered. How does it feel?"

"Better." I cleared my throat. "Much better."

Outside the engine room, when the rush of adrenaline had subsided and I'd slumped against the corridor bulkhead, I'd become all too aware of the mounting pain that pulsed with every heartbeat. A few moments later Philip faded into a red haze while speaking. When I clawed my way out of my fog the middy and Walter Dakko were staring with unease. I managed, "You'd better help me to the sickbay," each word a wave of agony in face and neck. On the ladder I held off the blackness by sheer act of will.

Tottering into the infirmary I rummaged through the medical supplies until I found the medipulse I'd seen Dr. Bros apply to a sailor whose hand was crushed. I didn't know how to use it. "Ask Kerren," I grated, part of me marveling how mundane my voice sounded. My legs didn't seem to work properly; I'd had trouble getting onto the examining table.

Now, annoyed at my weakness, I put a tentative hand to my cheek. The skin felt blistered and raw. I could sense the light pressure of my fingers, but no lance of agony. "How long does it last, Kerren?"

The puter responded instantly, calm and polite as always. "Your nerves are deadened, Captain, and will ramain so for some hours. Treatment indicated would be Compound Twelve burn salve applied gently to the affected area, and no bandage."

"Very well." I pointed to the stores cabinet. "It's probably there." Dakko searched through the drawer, emerged with the tube. I held still while he applied it. When he was finished I got tentatively to my feet, relieved that my legs supported me.

I crossed to the mirror, peered at my visage. "Good God." I'd have an ugly scar. Very nasty. I shrugged. A doctor could regrow the skin later, if I chose. If ever again I saw a doctor.

Now, what had I been doing when I broke off to go to sickbay? For a moment I was muddled. I'd guarded the armory, then rushed to the bridge. I recalled running down the ladder to the engine room to get Dray. No, it was after that; I'd gone back down with Philip and Dakko. I tried to focus. "Who's watching the rebels in the engine room?"

"No one, sir." Philip said uneasily. "We all came back with you."

I snarled, "Must I tell you everything?" With an effort I restrained myself from losing control altogether.

Philip looked to the deck.

"The rebels have the engine room, but we don't know they'll stay there. If we let them out they could roam the ship!"

"Yes, sir. There's the engine room hatch onto the corridor, and the engine room stores compartment, with its own hatch. One man couldn't watch them both. Besides," Philip added reasonably, "we didn't reach the engine room in time to see if all of them got inside. If they had already split up . . ."

The fact that he was right didn't improve my temper. "Where the hell is Dray?"

Philip was startled. "In the corridor, sir. He was working on the armory hatch."

"You left him alone? What if the rebels try again?" A spell of weakness slowed me as I made my way out to the corridor. I was near the end of my tether. I forced my pace to slow as I headed for the armory, though I felt an alarm akin to panic.

I'd brutalized Dray without mercy just a day ago, and left him thinking me quite insane. If he'd managed to cut through to the arms locker, no telling what he'd do. Take the arms and give them to the rebels, perhaps. Or gun me down on sight.

My mouth tightened. So be it. I could do only so much. My pace lengthened; I strode around the bend in the corridor.

Dray had breached the hatch. He'd cut a hole big enough to crawl through, to the arms compartment. He'd squeezed in, taken a rifle and a handful of recharge packs. He waited stolidly until I approached, and saluted. "I thought it best to arm myself," he said. "What with the armory open and all."

I cleared my throat. "Very good, er, Chief," My legs were weak with relief. "All right, Philip, you and Mr. Dakko go back to guarding the east and west ladders. I'll send Mr. Attani to help you after a bit. Dray, you and Gregor carry all the arms and ammunition to the bridge. If we can't hold that, we're done for."

An hour later I slumped in my accustomed chair watching the last of a surprising inventory of rifles, pistols, stunners, and ammunition being piled along the bridge bulkhead. The armory was empty.

What next? I now had a force of four I could trust; Philip, Dray, Attani, and Dakko. One man to hold the bridge, three to attack the engine room. How to get in, against armed resistance? I stared blearily at the deck. How late was it? Well past midnight. Again I perused the deck plates, jerked myself awake as my head dropped.

There was no more I could do tonight.

Wearily I got to my feet. I slung my arm through the rifle strap. "Dray, you'd best not go back below to Level 3. Sleep in a lieutenant's cabin along the bridge corridor. Mr. Dakko, you should be below in crew berth one, but I need you and your rifle nearby, so you'll sleep on Level 1 too. Use the second lieutenant's cabin.

"Philip, take a rifle and a couple of charge packs. Go with Mr.

Attani to an empty cabin and drag a couple of mattresses back while I hold the bridge. Gregor and I will bunk here tonight."

"Aye aye, sir." In the corridor, Philip pointed. "The third looey's cabin and the Pilot's, I think, Gregor. They'll be the closest. Give you a glimpse of officer's life," he told the young sailor. They rounded the corridor bend. "This is what we—Oh, Lord Christ!"

"Philip?" No answer. I unslung my rifle, glanced to make sure it held a charge, and ran along the corridor. "Mr. Tyre!"

The middy sagged against the bulkhead, mouth working, eyes fastened on the grisly body of the deckhand I'd put to death.

Simmons lay in the corridor where he'd fallen, his shoulder and chest charred, blistered hand outstretched, fist clenched in lifeless agony. The eyes—I would remember them a long while. Dulled in death, still they held something that didn't bear imagining. I stepped between Philip and the corpse, turned the boy's shoulders to face the bulkhead.

"Chief! Mr. Dakko!" They came running at my call. "Find a blanket. Roll this—thing in it put it out the forward airlock. Now!"

Dray grimaced, ducked into an empty cabin.

I handed Gregor my rifle. "You know how to use this? Cover them. Report back the moment you're—"

"Aye aye, sir!" Attani strayed toward the ladder, caught himself, blushed.

"Steady, Mr. Attani."

Dray emerged with a blanket. He and Walter Dakko knelt by the remains.

I led Philip from the ghastly scene. "You're all right, Mr. Tyre. Take deep breaths. That's right. Again." I guided him to the wardroom, slapped open the hatch.

The tiny chamber was impersonally bare but for Philip's duffel stowed neatly under a bunk. His few clothes hung in the minuscule closet. Normally four middies shared cramped bunks in such a compartment.

Philip Tyre stood docile, like a small child. I felt awkward, unsure. I was his Captain, not a fellow middy; there was an unbridgeable gulf between us. Yet he was in need, and I knew not what to give.

"Get ready for bed, Philip."

"Aye aye, sir." Mechanically he began to strip off his clothes. Instead of tossing them carelessly on the chair as I'd done all too often, he hung his jacket and pants with care, and creased them neatly on hangers before setting them in the closet.

As he fumbled at his shirt buttons, his eyes changed, his fingers became still. I could guess what image had returned, unbidden. I was ready to snap something harsh, recall him to reality, but instead I shut my mouth, stern words unspoken, and went to him, knowing there was wrong in any contact that diminished the distance between us. All the same, I felt compassion rather than guilt as I gently undid the buttons of his shirt. "Go to bed," I said quietly.

Startled, he glanced up, young and trusting. "Aye aye, sir." Turning, he steadied himself against the end table to remove his socks; past the seams of his undershorts I saw the red, angry welt I had put across his buttocks. I closed my eyes.

In his bunk he lay on his back, eyes rigid. Not knowing what else to do, I took the cover and tossed it across his still form. "Good night, Philip. You'll feel better in the morning." At the hatch, I switched off the light.

"Thank you, sir." His tone was unsteady.

I flicked the light on.

Philip lay on his back, clutching the blanket. When my gaze met his he snapped his eyes shut, too late to hide the tear that trickled down his cheek. Reluctantly I approached his bunk. He blinked, tried several times to speak. Finally he whispered, "I'm afraid!" After, he couldn't meet my eye.

I sat on the edge of the bed. "I know."

"That man . . . his face . . ."

I tried not to recall the nightmares I'd suffered from other sightless eyes, long in the past. "It's all right."

"He looked at me, just before I—I shot him. He was raising his gun. For a split second he knew. That he was too late. What was going to happen."

"It's all right," I said again, wishing I had words of comfort.

"And then he—sizzled! Oh, Jesus God!" He flung himself to the bulkhead.

My hand, as if on its own volition, stole to his shoulder. After a long moment he whispered, "I'm so frightened."

Philip had done his duty. He'd have been killed if he hadn't shot first; surely he knew that. I intended to say as much, but someone blurted in my voice, "So am I."

He turned in wonder. "You?"

"Of course," I snapped. "Don't I have the right?"

"It's . . . I never thought you felt—sorry, it's none of my business. Of course you have the right."

"Then why don't you?"

He lay still, thinking it over. After a time he offered a shy, tentative smile. "I'm sorry. I was foolish. I just tried to live up to what you expect."

I said gruffly, "I don't expect you to more than human. It was horrible, what you had to do to that man. I don't know how you could carry on. I might not have." That was laying it on a bit thick, but he needed it. And deserved it, after what I'd done to him.

He looked puzzled. "I just put it in the back of my mind. There was work to do. I couldn't afford to dwell on it."

I could see him expand with pride. It took so little, I thought with sadness. I, the Captain, was as a god to a lowly midshipman. One word of anger could be devastating. And a word of praise . . .

"You've done well, Middy. I'll remember it." Meaningless words. What could I give him? A decoration? A promotion that no one beyond the ship would ever see? "You'll be able to sleep now," I said, as if I knew. "In the morning I'll need your help organizing the recruits. Good night."

"Good night, sir." This time his smile was less tentative. For some reason I didn't understand I reached down, ruffled his hair. Abruptly I strode to the hatch, snapped off the light. I left without looking back.

Dray, Dakko and Gregor had rounded up the mattresses I'd ordered, and waited patiently outside the sealed bridge. I unsealed the hatch and we lugged in the bedding. Someone had found clean sheets and pillows as well. I thanked them, sent Dray and Dakko on their way, and sealed Gregor and myself onto the bridge. "Kerren, monitor the cameras and sound the alarms the moment anyone approaches. And wake me at eight."

"Very well, Captain."

I dimmed the lights and dropped onto my mattress with a sigh. Young Attani sat warily on the other bed, eyes carefully turned away. It was several long minutes before he lay down, facing away from me.

I lay on my back, arm over my eyes, waiting for sleep. My body felt drained, lethargic. While Gregor tossed and turned I marveled that I'd made it through the day, and wondered what horrors were still to come. I drowsed.

"Excuse me?"

My eyes opened. "Yes?"

"Could I . . . I mean, would you let . . . maybe . . . oh, Christ!"

"Don't blaspheme," I said automatically. He didn't answer. "What, Mr. Attani?"

"Nothing, I mean, nothing, sir."

I snapped, "You woke me for that?"

"I'm sorry."

The silence hung between us.

"Tell me."

A moment passed before his reluctant answer. "I know it's stupid. I was going to ask if I could sleep downstairs. Below."

"Why?"

No response.

I recalled another recruit, eons ago: Derek. I said gently, "You've never slept sharing a room?"

"I know it's silly." His voice was muffled. "But I thought, if I could go back downstairs . . . Then I remembered I wouldn't be in my own cabin. I'd be in the crew berth, with all the others."

I lay back, finding it hard to sympathize. He was seventeen. No, eighteen; I'd been at his birthday party, strolling through the haughty crowd with Amanda. Those damned aristocrats; what kind of lives did they lead, sequestered in luxurious towers, isolated from ordinary human contact? I hadn't known privacy after the age of thirteen, when Father brought me to Academy. I'd learned to tolerate the teeming dormitories at Farside, then the crowded midshipmen's wardroom . . .

Had it really been three years since I'd bunked in a wardroom? Abruptly I'd been catapulted to the splendid isolation of the Captain's cabin. What loneliness I'd felt! Now, of course, I was used to it, and I could barely imagine myself coping with a wardroom's enforced intimacy.

I cleared my throat. "I understand what you're going through." It wasn't much.

"Thank you. Thank you, *sir*. I have to remember to say 'sir.' "

"Yes, that's expected. You'll get used to it." I sought some words of reassurance. "As you'll get accustomed to the crew berth. It's not as bad as you imagine."

"Right." We lay in silence. Then, to my astonishment, he began to cry. My surprise was tinged with exasperation. Had I triggered his response? And would I ever be allowed to sleep? I glanced at my watch; we weren't far from morning.

"What now, Mr. Attani?" I chose his last name, to put distance between us and to remind him of his status.

He drew in a ragged breath. "I'm feeling sorry for myself." His honesty was painful. "And I'm ashamed."

"Why?"

"Do you know why I'm on *Challenger?*" I was silent. "I hated you and leaped at the chance to escape. And then they told us the fusion drive was wrecked . . . so I'd just made my situation worse. I was stuck with you, perhaps for the rest of my life. And I've watched you trying so hard to be fair, and being so kind . . ."

"Kind?" I echoed, incredulous.

"To Mr. Tyre. The way you put yourself between him and the sailor's body. Your voice. And to the others. Even to me. I've misjudged you so badly."

"You're overwrought," I muttered. "It's been a frightful day. I'm not as kind as you think."

"I'll shut up, if that's what you want. But I know when I've made a fool of myself."

His dogged integrity brought a sting to my eyes. I groped for a way to reassure him. I was failing with him, as I'd failed with Philip. A thought flashed: Philip and Gregor . . .

I cleared my throat. "Very well, perhaps you misjudged me. And I've misjudged you. I was wrong to enlist you as a sailor."

"Sir?" His voice was unsteady.

"Regardless of what you think, you're fit for the wardroom. I'm making you a midshipman cadet. Don't worry much about hazing. We don't have time for that."

"But I—"

"It's not your decision, Mr. Attani, it's mine. I'm impressing you as an officer rather than as a seaman."

There was a long silence. "But why, sir?"

"You'll be more help to me that way. That's all you need to know."

A contemplative pause. "Yes, sir."

I rolled over to sleep. Then I relented. "Because you deserve it. You'll make a good officer. Once we knock the haughty insolence out of you, that is."

"I will?"

"Yes." I don't know if I said the word aloud as I tumbled into black, dreamless sleep.

42

"Are you sure, sir?" Philip bit his lip and looked at me doubtfully. "I mean—before when I—had the wardroom . . . I didn't do very well." He reddened.

"You've changed. I'm certain I can trust you." I spoke with assurance I was almost sure I felt.

"He's rather old to start as a cadet." Realizing it sounded like criticism he rushed on, "I'll be very careful, sir. Not to hurt him. I'll get him settled this afternoon. And it'll . . ." He blushed. "It will be nice to have company."

"Yes." I knew the closeness the experience would engender, and wistfully wished I could share it. Then I brushed away the foolishness.

It was midmorning and I felt somewhat refreshed despite my pitifully few hours of sleep. Nonetheless, my inflamed cheek ached miserably. I'd have to stop at the infirmary when I had a moment.

I'd sent Philip and Chief Dray below, heavily armed, to release the crew from their berth and escort them back to Level 1. They'd encountered no rebels. The engine room hatch was still blocked.

I picked four crewmen I'd decided to trust with weapons: Mr. Drucker, Mr. Tzee, Emmett Branstead, and Elena Bartel. While Dray and Walter Dakko guarded the ladders from Level 2 we made a thorough search of Level 1. No rebels. It was a start; at least now I knew our uppermost Level was secure. I sat with a steaming cup of coffee to ponder my next move, wondering how much more time the mutineers would give me.

My coffee finished, we proceeded cautiously down the west ladder to Level 2. I sealed the emergency corridor hatch between sections six and seven, east of the ladder. We proceeded west, checking each cabin and compartment. We shepherded all the passengers we encountered to the dining hall, on Level 1.

The hatch to the launch berth was undamaged; that meant the cargo holds, accessible through the launch berth, were still in our hands. As we searched I tried to be everywhere, while Gregor, at my orders, tagged along as a gofer. After two tense hours we'd secured the remainder of Level 2.

I assembled my forces at the ladder to Level 3, where Walter Dakko patiently let me show him how to guard the ladder wells he'd competently been watching for two days. At the sound of running steps I broke off my lecture. Dakko, ready to fire, eased his finger from the trigger as Charlie, a streeter, skidded to a stop at the bottom of the ladder.

"Don't be shootin', Cap'n, it's me! Dey comin' out!"

"The rebels? From the engine room?"

"Someone comin' out, yeah! I don't wan' be wid 'em, dey gonn' hurt some joe!"

"Up here fast!" The boy bolted up the ladder, "Who else is down there?"

"Trannies? Annie, Scor, Dawg, maybe more. Inna room, allem."

I turned to my new cadet. "Gregor, have Ms. Bartel reinforce Dray at the west ladder. Bring the three other armed sailors to this ladder, flank!"

"Yes, sir!" Attani sprinted off. Moments later Tzee, Drucker and Branstead hurried around the bend, Gregor trotting at their heels.

I pointed. "They're down on Level 3, somewhere outside the engine room. We're going below. Be ready to fire, but don't shoot a passenger. Let's go!" I rounded the ladder well.

The corridor speaker crackled. "Captain, time we did some talkin'." Andros, the contemptuous deckhand Clinger had freed from the brig.

I froze. Behind me my war party halted.

"You hear me, Captain? What we got is a standoff. You got the food and the guns, I got the power and water lines. An' a bunch of your passengers, them trannie kids. Understand?"

I picked up the caller. "I hear you, Andros. Put down your weapons."

"Not a chance."

"What's this about? We're all marooned together; what's the point in rebellion?"

"Point?" A guffaw. "That frazzin' Admiral din' care if we live or die. We got nothin'. It'll be over soon enough. Think we—"

"There's hope. We'll grow food, wait for resc—"

"Think we want to live our last days poppin' salutes an' goin' 'yes, sir' an' 'aye aye, sir'? We're men, not Navy machines!"

"You signed up."

"For the bonus, yeah. And like all the other joeys, I spent it 'fore we left port. Now all we got is this mess. Well, I ain't goin' this way. There's women aboard, enough food for some zarky parties. So, here's the deal. Take—"

"Andros, give it up. We can't afford to have anyone else killed. You'll ruin everyone's chances."

"Nah. Like we said, we're going our own way. There's nothin' you can do."

Abruptly I realized the whole ship could hear our dialogue. "I'm heading to the bridge. I'll call you from there."

"Nah, let 'em all listen; ain't nothin' to me. Let your precious passengers know how bad things are. And that fraz Drucker, he listenin'? I owe him."

I keyed the caller to the bridge. "Kerren, can you override the engine room circuit so they can't page the entire ship?"

"Negative, Captain," the puter said. "Critical stations—bridge, comm room, engine room—have equal access in case of emergency. It's a safety feature and I have no override."

"Very well." I thumbed the caller back to the engine room. Andros might speak over the ship-wide circuit, but I'd be damned if I'd do the same. Let those who would listen decipher what they could from his end of the conversation.

"Andros, you can't get away with it. Surrender now and you'll save lives."

He guffawed. "Sure. Sail us into port and we'll surrender."

"There's no way you can take the ship. I've got the upper two Levels, the bridge, the comm room, and all the guns."

"Not all the guns," the speaker interrupted. "We got a rifle and the stunner, and we figured out how to recharge them. We have the machine shop. You don't know what we're cookin' up here."

"I'm coming after you."

"The hell you are, fraz." From behind him, a gasp. Mutineers they might be, but discipline died hard.

"I'm done talking, Andros. Your choice is, surrender or die."

"No. Your choice is, leave us be or we cut your power. Sykes thinks he can disconnect the lines to the rest of the ship and leave us with power in the engine room."

I keyed the caller. "Kerren, can he do that?"

An infinitesimal pause. "I judge it relatively complicated for human understanding, but the Chief Engineer could do it, with a manual. I don't know what would result if an untrained seaman made the attempt. Power feed lines need to be rerouted with bridges. My records show Sykes with a grade five education level, marginal literacy."

"What about Andros?"

"Grade nine overall. Adequate literacy. Diagnosed emotionally unstable at enlistment testing."

I thumbed the caller. "Andros, this is no standoff. We can do without power awhile; the bridge has emergency backups. I can keep my passengers and crew alive while we wait you out. You'll starve soon enough."

"Maybe," he said indifferently. "After we eat the trannies." Gregor sucked in his breath. In the speaker, Andros giggled. "That girl, that Annie, she's kinda scrawny. Except certain places." His voice grew hard. "So don't push, Seafort. An' remember the hydroponics. We got them down here too. They're sealed, sure, but how long you think it'll take us to get in? How'd you like a chamber full of shredded plants? Worse come to worse, we could probably blow up the whole ship if we try. You going to kill us, what else we got to lose?"

I wracked my brain, with no success. "I'll call you back," I said at last.

"Do that, Seafort. And don't get ideas about stallin' while you set something up. I'll be happy to fry a trannie for a demo."

Dazed, I left my attack party and made my way to the bridge, knowing that his broadcast had done incalculable damage to our morale. I'd been manipulated; I had lost the initiative to a demented sailor. How had it come to that? If I'd used sense last night, and put a guard at the engine room. Or attacked an hour earlier. Or—anything.

Philip, watching the corridor camera from the bridge, opened the hatch, sealed it behind me as I dropped into my chair. He was diplomatically silent.

In my humiliation, I found it hard to meet his eye. "It seems I have a problem."

"Yes, sir. Do you think he means it?"

"I don't want to find out. Call Dray." I shut my eyes, tried to stir my dulled mind. I'd have to give in, or at least fashion a compromise, even if they were mutineers.

I glanced at the blankened simulscreen. The same screen, I recalled, at which I'd shouted my defiance to Admiral Tremaine, forsworn my oath of obedience, and very possibly damned myself. I sat in the same chair in which I'd resolved never again to betray the oath that bound me.

I was certain I knew the relevant section of the regs, but I called them up on my console and read the passage again.

The Captain of a vessel shall assume and exert authority and control of the Government of the vessel until relieved by order of superior authority, until his death, or until certification of his disability as otherwise provided herein.

If I ceded part of my ship or my command to rebels, I'd be in blatant violation of the regs I'd sworn to uphold.

But the regs didn't contemplate a situation like ours. We were stranded, perhaps for a lifetime, without experienced officers, with only a few crew—

Yet *Challenger* was a Naval vessel, and I was in charge.

I couldn't send my few untrained men into battle while I waited timidly behind the fortified bulkheads of the bridge. I'd have to lead them myself. But if I were killed, who would run the ship?

No. I wouldn't circumvent truth with sophistry; my duty was clear enough. What did it matter if I died trying to perform it? My responsibility was to preserve my oath, not myself.

I would be dead a very long time, until the distant day Lord God called us all, and time ended.

An inconceivably long time.

But then I would be one with Amanda. And Nate. I tried to master the trembling in my limbs as I prepared to stand.

The trannies. The streeters. I could accept, just barely, the probability of my own death. But in attacking the rebels I'd doom innocent passengers. How many hostages did Andros say he'd taken? I couldn't remember. "Did you record, Kerren?"

"Yes, sir."

"Play back." When the grim exchange had replayed I realized Andros hadn't revealed the number of his prisoners. We'd embarked with forty-two transpops; I recalled my fury when Alexi Tamarov had told me of them, centuries past. Three died in the raid by the fish. I'd enlisted Eddie and fifteen others. That left . . . twenty-three. "Philip, who's minding the passengers?"

"I put Mr. Kovaks in charge, sir, the recycler's mate. I couldn't think who else to trust."

"Excuse me, sir." Kerren interjected. "Chief Kasavopolous is approaching the bridge."

"Very well, let him in. Philip, find out how many transients Kovaks has in the dining hall."

As Dray entered I raised a palm, telling him to wait. In a moment the caller buzzed. "Fourteen trannies, sir."

Nine hostages, then. Nine amoral, uncivilized joeys plucked from filthy, crowded streets, clothed, warehoused, selected for a foolish experiment, and ferried nineteen light-years from home, to die abandoned on *Challenger.*

Perhaps I could stall Andros long enough to organize. I might give my crew rudimentary training in weapons and mount an assault on Level 3. With luck I could retake the engine room, at the cost of some of my recruits and my own life.

And the nine transpops.

Their deaths would not be comparable to losing crewmen in battle. The crew, at least, had chosen this voyage. They'd accepted some risk, though they couldn't have known how great and strange it would be.

But the transients were pawns in a bureaucratic game of indifference. And not much more than children, at that. I couldn't throw them away uncaring.

But my oath?

There had to be a way. I slumped in the chair, staring at the console, trying to recall the layout of the engine room.

The speaker crackled. "Crewman in corridor, Captain."

"What the—thank you, Kerren." I swiveled the camera. Eddie Boss, shoulders knotted through the folds of his new uniform, fist raised to hammer at the bridge.

I spluttered, "A sailor, outside the bridge? Unescorted?" I pounded my chair in frustration. "How can I think, when—"

Philip stood. "I'll handle it, sir. Please." He read my face, saw no refusal. He crossed to the hatch and slapped it open. "Well?"

"Wanna talk ta Cap'n."

"You're out of line, sailor. Get back to—"

"Talk ta Cap'n. Not you."

Philip's voice flashed. "You're speaking to an officer, Mr. Boss. Come to attention and salute. You call me 'sir.' And don't use that tone of voice or I'll haul you to the brig!"

I glanced at the image relayed by the corridor camera. Eddie's lip curled as he stared down at the lithe midshipman. "Brig? You? You're a sir?"

Philip, as if fearless, shoved at Eddie's bulk. "Me. Any officer."

Eddie scowled at the hand that had tried to move him. "Ya wanna use dat hand 'gain, don' go pushin' ol' Eddie widit."

Philip was silent a moment. Then he said, "I was there, Mr. Boss."

"Huh? Where?"

"The dining hall. When you said, 'I do swear upon my immortal soul.' To give loyalty and obedience, and the rest of it. I remember, even if you don't."

"Words," Eddie said contemptuously. "Jus' words."

"An oath, Mr. Boss. On your soul."

"To Cap'n, maybe. Not you."

"I'm his representative. What I say is what he says." Well put, Philip. The entire chain of command, in a nutshell.

Eddie hesitated. Then, "Could break ya in half, joey."

"You could, yes. I'm not all that strong. But I won't change what I'm going to do."

"An' wha's dat?"

"Put you against the bulkhead at attention. See if the Captain is willing to talk to you. And if not, or after he's done, put you on report and issue enough summary punishment you'll think twice before pulling this stunt again."

Eddie glowered. My heart pounding, I dropped my hand to the butt of my pistol.

We waited.

Eddie sighed. "Go on, den. Do it."

"Over there. Stand to." The camera eye swiveled to follow.

"Dunno how. No one showed me."

"Eyes front. Chest in, like so. Hand at your side, fingers down. Toes pointing forward." Philip frowned at the shabby attempt, but let it pass. "Now you say, 'Sir, I'd like permission to speak with the Captain.'"

A long silence. Eddie cleared his throat. "Allri, I sayin' it."

"No. The words I said."

"A trannie don' talk like dat!"

"You'll have to try, Mr. Boss, because I won't ask the Captain without them."

Eddie cursed under his breath. "I can't—How'd I get inna this? Sir! I like pum—permission speaka Cap'n."

"Captain."

"Cap-tain," Eddie grated.

"Wait here, sailor." Philip paused. "Aye aye, sir!" he prompted.

"Aye aye, sir," muttered Eddie.

Philip returned to the bridge, cheeks flushed. "Seaman Boss requests permission to speak with you, sir."

"Very well, Mr. Tyre." I added quietly, "Don't push him further; he could cripple you."

Still indignant, Philip paid no heed. "The nerve of him, barging in here! When I'm done he won't try that again."

"Bring him in," I said. Lord God, my cheek throbbed. I was so tired.

"Aye aye, sir." As if in response to Eddie's slackness, Philip's salute and spin were straight out of Academy.

Eddie Boss shambled in. Under Philip's persistent glare he puzzled for a long moment before comprehension dawned. Clumsily he brought himself to attention. From the corner Chief Dray watched with bemused indifference.

"Well?" I let my voice remain cold.

"Heard da man tella Cap'n 'bout eatin' trannies, an' all."

"Yes?"

"Gotta help 'em. Cap'n gotta." It was more plea than demand.

"I'm working on it. Go back to the dining hall."

"Workin' on it?" A sneer.

I frowned. He glared back, unimpressed. "Whatcha gonn' do, huh? Sit here, nice 'n safe, let dem grodes eat my frens?"

Philip's voice was tight. "Enough of that, sail—"

"Boolsheet 'nuf!" Eddie roared. "I took oath, yeah, savin' ship, work fo Cap'n. Not ta sitroun watch—"

"Now listen—" Philip.

I swarmed out of my seat. "*SHUT UP, BOTH OF YOU!*" It silenced them, as well it might. One does not often hear a Captain go berserk.

I rounded on Eddie Boss. "*NOT ANOTHER WORD OUT OF YOU!*" Something made him step back a pace, raise his arm as if to ward off a blow. I spun to Philip. "Or you, boy!" After a moment I realized I was pointing my finger like a fully charged weapon. For a moment I wondered how Philip would react if I holstered it. My lips twitched in a grin. The midshipman took an involuntary step back. Startled, I gaped, and he blanched. My grin began to congeal into a maniacal leer.

"Are you all right?" we asked each other simultaneously, and for a crazed moment our eyes locked in mutual shock.

I broke the resulting silence. "I'm fine, and you were told to be silent." I dropped back into my chair. My legs trembled. I hoped he couldn't see. I hoped it was only excess adrenaline.

I glared at Eddie. "You think I'm hiding while your friends are in danger."

His glance fell on my blistered cheek. He muttered and looked to the deck.

"What do you want me to do for them?"

He licked his lips. "You knowin' ship, Cap'n. Fin' some way inna room, get 'em out."

"How?" I stared at the console. "First we have to learn where they took your friends. If they're smart they have them in the engine room, but that's a big place. There's the outer control panel chamber, and off to the side the engine room stores compartment, and straight through the ladder down to the fusion drive chamber. Only two hatches enter it from the circumference corridor."

Unconsciously I stood and began to pace. "We've got the upper two Levels. There are two ladders to Level 3: east and west. First we'd have to mount an expedition belowdecks and try to secure part of the Level 3 circumference corridor. From there we could work our way around until we'd isolated the engine room. But if the rebels are in any of the interior cabins, they can burn through to the opposite side of the ship. Even if they don't cut through, the hydro chambers are down below on their Level, and the rebels can destroy them. Then we'll all die for certain."

"But—"

"Shut your mouth, Mr. Boss, until I've finished. If we isolate the engine room we can assault and take it. But there's no way to force our way in without a desperate fight. And we can't afford to lose crewmen. There's no way to replace casualties."

Philip cleared his throat. "So we can't retake the engine room, sir?"

"I know one way," I muttered. My mind grappled with the obscenity I'd hatched.

"What's that, sir?"

"The fusion drive shaft."

Dray looked at me with disbelief. "Clamber around outside the ship to mount an assault through the fusion shaft? Good God, are you glitched? We don't have enough trained men to send, and how could we breach the plastalloy drive shield? It's harder than steel, and for good purpose. It's all that protects the engine room crew from vacuum."

"True. But that's not what I meant. The launch berth is on Level 2, within our territory. We could send the launch around to the stern."

"And off-load the assault crew? I still don't see how they could—"

"No," I said. "Seal the corridor around the engine room. Use the launch to ram the shield."

Dray erupted in fury. "Ram my engine room, you young pup? Hit too hard and you damage the fusion engines themselves. And you'd kill every—"

"I know! Shut up!" The engine room would depressurize instantly, killing anyone inside who wasn't suited. The corridor hatch seals would hold; they were designed for it. And the hydro chambers were two sections distant from the engine room; they'd be undamaged.

Philip said, "It would kill the hostages, sir, along with the rebels."

"I didn't say otherwise. I just said there was a way into the compartment."

Eddie growled, "You don' care 'bout killin' trannies, Cap'n? They ain' Uppies like you 'n boss boy?"

Philip flushed. "The Captain didn't say that. But what should we do if the rebels pull our power lines? We might hold out a few days, while the air turns bad, we do without water, and the ship starts to cool."

I said, "We can store water now, and go to bottled air."

"For a while, yes, sir. If the rebels had no food we could outlast them. But if they hold out more than . . . how long, sir? A week? . . . We'd have to assault them or give up the ship."

He was right. *Challenger* was a closed ecological system. With recycling and hydroponics operating properly, we could last a long, long time. But our fragile ecosystem was utterly dependent on the energy input of the fusion engines. Despite the thickly insulated hull, without power, heat loss would begin almost immediately. And if the recyclers were cut off, our CO^2 levels would mount until the air was unbreathable.

Philip's estimate was good. About a week. Unless we mounted an assault well before then, the rebels would win.

I shivered. Lord God help us. In any event, there was another reason the engine room couldn't be rammed. "Nobody would do it. It's a suicide mission for whoever drove the launch; the controls are in the bow. Even if I ordered a crewman to ram, he'd join the rebels before he'd obey. Let's drop the subject."

"Aye aye, sir," said Philip. Eddie glowered at us both. After a moment Philip added hesitantly, "Pardon if I'm out of line, but if you negotiate you risk giving up control of the ship."

He knew his regs as well as I did; Lord God knew how many times they'd made him stand on a chair reciting them. Wardroom hazing had its merits. "Yes, I know. What else is there to do?"

The speaker crackled. "Hey, Captain, 'bout time we heard from you. You gonna send chow down, or we gotta make our own?"

Philip's troubled eyes fastened on mine.

I mustn't negotiate. Whatever else occurred, I must uphold the authority of the Naval Service. And my authority as Captain, for the sake of all other Captains who would follow. To sail across the void for months or years, a ship must have one unchallengeable authority. That had been drilled into me from my first day at Academy.

The transients' lives, and my own, were nothing compared to that principle.

Eddie Boss muttered under his breath.

I glared. "You have something to say, sailor?"

"Yeah." Eddie wrinkled his brow. "You send sojers down, fight ta get back ship, dat be war." He hesitated. "Like, it be okay, if dyin' be okay. You let 'em kill trannies, dat ain war, be plain ol' dissin'."

"Dissing?" I tried to puzzle it out.

"Murder," the Chief said sourly. "Dissin'. Joespeak." I saw Philip's hand ease to his pistol, but Eddie said no more.

"Chief."

"Yes, sir?"

"Take a couple of sailors and reconnoiter. See if they've blocked any of the corridor hatches near the engine room, but don't get anybody hurt finding out. You'd better hurry."

He blinked, taking it all in. Then his shoulders squared. "Aye aye, sir." He slapped open the hatch and disappeared into the corridor.

All was silent until I picked up the waiting caller. I asked Andros, "What would I get in return for the food?" Philip gasped.

"Ha!" The sailor chuckled with satisfaction. "Now you're talking. You keep your lights and water."

"No. I want the passengers released."

"They're our meal ticket, joey. Why would I give them up?"

"For your rations. Otherwise, I won't deal."

"We'll cut your power. Think you'll like the dark, fraz?"

"Cut our power and I'll kill you all." My tone was flat.

"And your precious street joeys?"

"I don't care how many trannies you take along."

Eddie stirred.

Andros snarled. "We'll kill them one by one, you bastard!"

I said with calculated indifference, "Well, it won't look good on my record, but it'll be less mouths to feed. Go ahead, if that's what you want."

His reply was drowned by Eddie's roar as he launched himself. His thick fingers closed around my throat. I clawed helplessly at his beefy wrists while he flung me back and forth like a rag doll. The world faded to red. Abruptly, he stiffened and sagged to the deck.

The mists cleared slowly. Philip Tyre carefully set his stunner to safety, replaced it in his holster.

"Did you kill him?" My voice was hoarse.

Philip snarled, "No, but I should have, and saved you the trouble. I set it on low."

"You want them dead?" the speaker raved. "I'll show you! We'll kill them right now!"

I ignored the caller. Philip was right. Eddie Boss had violated a cardinal rule of Naval life. He had touched his Captain by intent. His life was forfeit. The court-martial would be a formality, nothing more. The irony was that my seeming indifference was the only possible way to save the transients, short of giving the rebels my ship. But because I hadn't let Eddie know, I'd condemned him to death.

The nerves of my scorched cheek sent waves of agony lancing through my face and neck. I forced my attention back to the speaker. "What's keeping you?" I asked. "The sooner they're out of the way the sooner I can come for you. It's a lot less trouble explaining to Admiralty than why I had to get rid of them myself."

For the first time the sailor's voice held a note of uncertainty. "You're bluffing."

"Yes. That's what I want you to think." That quieted him while he tried to puzzle it out. That's what they appointed a Captain for; to say any damn fool thing that came into his mind. I only knew I had him off balance.

After a moment Andros said cautiously, "I think you're glitched, Captain. So what I'll do is pick one and fry him, and see what you do from there. We've got plenty left to bargain with."

The Chief strode back onto the bridge, breathing hard. "No sign of them anywhere in the corridors, sir. I didn't go too close to the engine room. Did you see what those bastards did to my hatch?"

"Yes." I felt a strange relief, knowing my course at last. Light-headed with pain, I got to my feet. "Mr. Andros!"

"Yeah?"

"You win. At least for now. I'll bring you food for two days. Don't hurt the transients."

I could hear urgent whispering in the background. A pause. Then Clinger's voice. "No way, Captain. Divvy up the stores and give us our share."

"No. I'll buy two days to try to find a way out. Time to talk some more. That's all."

"You're stalling."

"For what reason?"

"I dunno, Seafort, but I can smell a trick."

"You have my word," I said firmly. Philip gaped.

Clinger repeated, "No tricks?"

"I give you my oath. Two days of good food, not tampered with, enough for all of you. Only one person will be allowed down to Level 3 to deliver it. Everyone else will remain above. I so swear."

The speaker was silent. Then Clinger's voice, in a different tone. "Okay, Captain. You Uppies, I guess your oath is damn important to you. Go ahead. But we'll be bottled tight in the engine room. There's no way you can get in here without getting killed. Any tricks, and your trannies get it."

"I'll need an hour or so to get everything together."

"Yeah, we've waited this long, an hour won't hurt."

"And no tricks from you. No ambushes. Everyone sealed inside the engine room until the food arrives. Then, when we see the transients are unhurt, you get your rations."

"Tell me again you're not planning a trick."

"I swear that no one will try to enter the engine room without your permission. The food will be normal rations. Only one person will be allowed below to deliver it, and he will be unsuited. You can take the rations into the engine room yourselves, unharmed. No one else will have anything to do with you or the engine room. You have my oath on all that."

"Right."

I replaced the speaker. Still dizzy, I took refuge in formality. "Midshipman Tyre."

"Yes, sir."

"Run to the galley and order Mr. Bree to provide rations for fourteen people for two days. Food only; they have water. Have him send a man to the bridge carrying the rations. Then run to the comm room and return with Mr. Tzee."

"Aye aye, sir. Can—"

"You heard your orders."

"Aye aye, sir." He scrambled out the hatch.

Dray said doubtfully, "Two days to do what, sir? The situation will only get worse."

"Yesh." My words were slurring from the pain. "Yes," I repeated with care.

"What happens to the trannie?" He prodded Eddie with his toe.

"No questions, Mr. Kas—Chief."

It took Philip less than three minutes to complete his errands and return, panting, with Mr. Tzee at his heels.

"Now. Mr. Tyre, you and Mr. Tzee will put on your suits and go out the forward airlock. You'll maintain radio silence. You will disconnect the power feed to the small laser cannon midships. The cannon should be bolted to the hull with three large eyebolts; I believe you'll find a spanner in the launch berth. Bring the cannon into the airlock with you, leave it just inside the Level 1 lock. You will accomplish your task within one hour."

"Dray, while Mr. Tyre's party is outside, get Mr. Dakko, who is guarding the ladder well, and go to the hold. The manifest says bin five east contains heavy electrical cable. Secure enough cable and connectors to connect a line to the high voltage outlet in the launch berth, string it along the corridor, down the ladder to Level 2, and coil enough cable at the top of the ladder well to reach down to Level 3 and around to section nine."

"Near the engine room?"

"Yes. To section nine."

"But—"

"I don't think you want to question me, Dray." My tone was odd. He swallowed.

"Go," I said. "Both of you."

There was little more to be done. I made my entries into the Log, signed it, turned off the screen. The bridge was silent except for Eddie's slow, steady breathing.

I'd turned off all Kerren's alarms. The panel lights showed me what I needed to know; first the inner airlock hatch sliding open, then the outer, then a long wait before the laser malfunction light began to blink. When the lock began to cycle again I got to my feet. I ran my fingers through my hair and tugged on my jacket, like a green middy on his way to see his Captain. In a way, it was so.

I waited at the hatch. Philip Tyre was the first to return, his shirt plastered to his back. Clambering around on the hull with magnetic boots took stamina. "We've got the cannon, sir, over there." He pointed down the corridor toward the airlock, around the bend. "What are you going—"

"See what's keeping Mr. Bree, Midshipman."

A score of questions flashed in his eyes but his discipline held. "Aye aye, sir." He ran off.

Ten minutes later his voice preceded him around the corridor bend, speeding the sailor who carried a bulging duffel. I pointed to the deck. Awkwardly the seaman let go his burden and saluted. I sent him back to his galley.

In a few moments Dray trudged back to the bridge, red from exertion. Walter Dakko was with him. "Done," the Chief said. "The cable's stretched to Level 2. I left you lots of slack."

I picked up the duffel. "Dray, check the seals on each of the corridor hatches on Level 1 and 2 as they close."

"The cable will block the seals, sir."

"I don't think so. The rubber gaskets should seal around the cable well enough; the hatches were designed to hold pressure even if a crewman fell so that his arm was in the way."

I turned to Philip. "Mr. Tyre, lock yourself on the bridge. Begin shutting all corridor hatches on Level 1 and Level 2."

"Sir, what are you doing? Who's taking the food down?"

I said, "I am."

He blurted, "You can't!"

"I beg your pardon?"

He blushed bright red. "I'm sorry, I—but—I mean, you can't risk yourself. Send a sailor, or me. Please!"

"No. Seal yourself on the bridge."

He stood his ground. "Tell me what's happening, sir . . . I need to know."

"I'm going below to negotiate with the rebels."

"How?"

"You may listen on the ship's caller, but you may not interrupt. You'll know what to do afterward. I don't expect to survive. You will be in charge thereafter."

"Oh, Lord Jesus!" He bit his lip. "You must't! I beg you!"

"There's no other way, Mr. Tyre. You know I can't give them the ship."

"Then let's storm the engine room."

"They'd kill all the trannies, Mr. Tyre. They still might, in which case they'll also kill me."

"Those street joeys . . . they're not worth it," Philip whispered. "You mustn't go."

I drew my pistol. It came to rest an inch from Philip Tyre's eye. "Seal yourself on the bridge, Mr. Tyre. It is the third and last time I give the order."

He licked his lips, tried to speak, sagged. "Aye aye, sir." He walked slowly onto the bridge.

I shouldered the duffel. "Mr. Dakko, go to the dining hall. Pass the word to all hands and passengers to suit up with emergency tanks."

Dakko regarded me somberly, saluted, and left.

I walked toward the airlock. "Dray, help me get the cannon down to Level 2." Awkwardly I bent and wrapped my arm around the barrel of the laser cannon, trying not to lose my precarious balance with the heavy duffel.

I lugged my end of the cast alloy cannon along the corridor, stopping while Dray closed and sealed the hatches behind us. We descended to Level 2 past the snaking cable Dray had laid. I walked the laser cannon around the stairwell to the ladder to Level 3, then gratefully set it down beside the coiled cable.

"Dray, seal off section nine on Level 2, in case they try to burn upward through the deck. Then break out a suit and put it on. I'll wait to see that's done. You are to remain on Level 2. You are not to descend to Level 3. Acknowledge your orders."

"Orders received and understood, sir," the Chief Engineer said heavily. "I'll bring your suit back with me."

"No. Just your own."

"But—" His eyes widened.

"Do as I say."

When he returned, clumping in his heavy, awkward vacuum suit, I set down the duffel at the top of the ladder and grunted with strain as I tried to hoist the cannon. It was heavier than I'd thought; I could barely manage it. The Chief must have carried more than his share of the weight. I managed somehow to haul it down the ladder.

At the foot of the stairs I turned east along the circumference corridor. From section six, I staggered along the corridor through seven, then eight. I eased my burden to the deck just inside the hatch between eight and nine. The engine room was just ahead of me, around the bend in section nine. I retraced my steps.

Back up the ladder. I coiled the cable on my shoulder and walked slowly backward down the stairs, playing it out behind me. Laying it carefully along the center of the corridor, I unwound it to where I'd left the cannon in section eight. I had about twelve meters length to spare.

Dizzy now, I climbed back up the ladder once again and hoisted the duffel of rations. "Wait here, Dray. Come if I call, but only then."

"Aye aye, sir."

At the foot of the ladder I dropped the duffel. This time I turned west, along the corridor that circled past the engine room to where I'd left the cannon.

I followed the corridor to the hatch between sections one and nine. I pressed the emergency close panel on the bulkhead and the hatch slid quietly shut.

I backtracked past the west hyros, glancing to make sure the hatch was sealed. I crossed into section two and sealed that hatch behind me. I worked my way back to the ladder, in section six.

The duffel was at the foot of the ladder where I'd left it. I lugged it east along the corridor. I sealed the hatch between six and seven, watching the hatch seals close around the cable. The rubber gaskets seemed tight. I checked the east hydros in section seven, sealed the hatch, plodded on to section eight. At the far end I stopped to finish my preparations.

Every corridor hatch on Level 3 was now sealed, except from section eight to the engine room in nine.

It didn't take me long to attach the cable ends to the power inputs of the laser cannon. I pressed the indicator button on the muzzle; the test light glowed. I tried to lift the cannon but my strength seemed inadequate; instead, breath rasping, I dragged the cannon along the corridor to the midpoint of section nine, outside the hatch to crew berth two, about twelve meters along the corridor from the engine room bulkhead.

All was silent behind the closed hatch to the engine room. As if from a great distance, I observed the scorch marks where the rebels had brazed plates over their damaged hatch.

The cannon was a hybrid weapon, designed for remote control from the comm room, but still capable of manual adjustment.

I pointed it down the corridor.

I snapped on the test light, aimed the beam at a bulkhead. I heard myself humming mindlessly and bit off the sound. Though I knew I must hurry, I sat on the deck, back to the hatch, legs straight in front of me, staring at nothing. Fire flowed thrugh my head. I waited, hoping the pain would recede. It didn't, but I had no more time. I unholstered my pistol, laid it down, staggered the few steps to the berth two hatch, across the corridor from the cannon.

I slapped open the hatch and lurched inside. A mop was in its usual place in the storage bin. I jammed it into the open hatchway, blocking the hatch from shutting. Then, abruptly, I slid to the deck.

After a time I was again aware of the empty, silent corridor. Cautiously I struggled to a kneeling position, heaved myself to my feet. I found I could no longer lift the duffel; I slid it along the corridor to within a meter of the engine room hatch and quickly retreated. With unsteady steps I made my way back to crew berth two and lifted the caller from the hatch control panel, sat with it by the cannon. "Engine room, this is Captain Seafort."

The answer came quickly. "About time. A couple more minutes and we'd a started cooking a trannie." Andros.

"Your food is in a duffel outside your hatch."

"And where's the joe brought it down?"

"In the corridor about halfway to section eight."

"Any stunners? Rifles?"

"A laser pistol, lying on the deck. It won't be used unless you try something."

"Yeah? Who's out there?"

"I am."

"Jesus Son of God!"

I closed my ears to the blashphemy. "The corridor is sealed behind me, all the way to Level 2. I'm the only one here. I've brought you the food, which I swear is safe to eat. Have I kept my oath?"

"Why you?" he demanded.

"It was too important to trust to anyone else."

"What if we take you too?"

"I suppose you could." I touched a hand to my fiery cheek, but it only made the pain worse. "Do you want your food now?"

"Yeah. Might as well. I'm sending a trannie for it. He might try to run, but we'll cover him from here."

"First let me see the faces of all nine of them."

"They're all right, Captain." He snickered. "You have my oath."

"Their faces." After a moment some makeshift catch was released and the engine room hatch swung aside. One by one the apprehensive faces of the transients showed briefly in the hatchway. Then one boy stepped out, darted nervously to the duffel, snatched it, and bolted back inside the hatch.

I picked up the caller. "You have your food. Have I kept my oath, Andros?"

There was a moment's pause. "Yeah, I guess. Why?"

"Stand aside from the bulkhead, please, so no one gets hurt."

"No one what?" blared Andros. "What the hell—"

I pressed the firing button. A flare of light sizzled against the bulkhead between the corridor and the engine room. In a moment the laser melted a hole wider than my arm in the thick alloy plates. I shifted the cannon and began burning another hole.

"What're you doing, you lying bastard? You made a deal!"

"I'm cutting a couple of holes."

"But you said—"

"I said no one would try to enter the engine room without your permission. Don't worry, I won't. And I said only one person would come down to Level 3." I cut a third hole, widely separated from the others.

"Belay that or the trannies get it now!" he shrieked. "All of them!"

"Very well. No more holes." I heaved, turning the cannon to the open hatch to crew berth two. I pointed the aperture at the outer bulkhead on the far side of the berth.

A face flashed at one of the holes in the engine room, then ducked away. Andros howled. "What the fuck are you up to?"

"Preparing to fire through the hull, Mr. Andros."

"What?"

"You heard me. My hand is on the firing button. It won't take much of a twitch to depress it, so if you shoot me I believe I'll set if off as I fall." My heart pounded so hard I found it difficult to speak.

His voice held a note of panic. "What are you doing?"

"I'm going to blow a hole in the hull, Mr. Andros. Isn't it obvious?"

"But—you'll decompress us!"

"Yes. Crew berth two, the section nine corridor, and the engine room. Everything else is sealed off."

"You won't get away! I'll burn a hole through your suit."

"I have no suit."

"Then you'll die too!"

"Yes." My tongue was thick around the word. It was what must be. Though part of me struggled to live, I'd accept the end as a blessing. I had fouled up so often, and Amanda waited.

"Jesus, you're insane!"

"I may be. It doesn't matter. You've shown me that."

"I'm gonna kill the trannies!"

"They'll be dead in a few moments anyway."

"We'll cover the holes!"

"The cannon fires the moment you touch the first hole."

The speaker clicked off but I heard a commotion through the holes in the bulkhead. A demand, a reply. An argument. Someone shouted, "There's only two suits in here!"

I said to the caller, "It's time now. I'm ship's chaplain. Would you like me to shrive you?"

Andros shouted, "Wait! What do you want?"

My burn hurt worse than ever. "To have this life over with." It was no more than truth.

A silence. Then, "You're bluffing. You might kill us, but not yourself. Go ahead."

"I'm going to pray first. I'll give you a few seconds warning. I'll be about half a minute."

I knelt on the deck, keeping the cannon between myself and the engine room. I kept my hand on the firing button.

I said aloud, " 'Trusting in the goodness and mercy of Lord God eternal, we commit our bodies to the deep—' "

In the engine room, a gasp of horror.

" '—to await the day of judgment when the souls of man shall be called forth before Almighty Lord God—' " I faltered, my voice failing. I finished the prayer in silence. "Amen." I stood. "Twenty seconds."

"Jesus, Seafort, don't!"

Clinger shouted, "It's a bluff, Andy!"

"Ever see a man die that way? Gimme that helmet, damn you!"

"Naw, one goes, we all go! Only fair way."

"Fifteen seconds."

"God, I don't want to die!"

"Shuddup, joey, no one's gonna—"

"Ten seconds." My hand tightened around the firing button. I fought the urge to hyperventilate.

"Goddamn it, Clinger, don't be yellow, he won't—HUNGH!"

Clinger screamed. "Wait, Captain! Just long enough to talk! CAPTAIN!"

I felt as if summoned from a great distance. "Talk about what?" My voice was dull.

"Don't blow the hull, Captain. You'll kill yourself too."

"Is that all?"

"Don't you care?" he cried.

"Not that much. Like Andros said, we'll all be dead soon."

"What if—what—"

I stared through the crew berth to the hull. "Ten . . . Nine."

"What if we trade you the trannies?"

"Eight . . ." He had said something important, but my mind was too foggy to concentrate. "What?"

"Trade you the trannies for leavin' us alone. We stay down here, you take the rest of the ship."

I mulled it over. "I don't think so, Andros." I was very weary now. "My way is better."

"I'm Clinger. It's those damn trannies you wanted, Captain. Don't you remember?"

"Remember?" I echoed. His voice was in a faraway dream. "Where's Andros?"

"I bashed him with a pipe wrench. Look, you tricked us. You worded your oath funny, and you fooled us. Now, the trannies ain't important. So we give 'em to you, and you let us be."

"Why?"

"So you'll live!" he shouted.

The word had no meaning. Something wasn't right inside my head. The bulkhead seemed to loom and recede, perhaps in time to my heartbeat.

"Captain."

The bulkhead had a strange texture.

"*CAPTAIN!*" His shriek snapped me awake. "Don't pass out, sir, you'll press the firing switch!"

"Right." I nodded, but the motion sent waves of nausea through my upper body.

"Captain, call someone to help you. We'll give you back the trannies, you promise not to try anything else. Just leave us be."

"I mustn't . . . I have to control ship." My tongue was thick.

"Think, for God's sake!"

I tried. The mists cleared a bit. "Surrender."

"Why, so you can execute us? Why should we?"

"That's true." I squinted at the far bulkhead. "It's best to blow the hull."

His voice was patient, as with a child. "Captain Seafort you'll kill the trannies that way. You wanted us to free them."

"Yes. Surrender."

"Will you have us executed?"

For armed rebellion in wartime? "Of course." His question made no sense.

"So we'd have nothing to lose. You have to give us a reason to give up."

I was dizzy, but I was thinking again. "I can't negotiate with you. Exert authority and control, and all that. That's why I'd better die."

His voice shook with frustration. "This ain't negotiating control, you lunatic! You're just taking our surrender! Shut up, Sykes, we've lost, can't you see? Captain, no trial, no execution. You get back your ship. We'll stay in our section, do what we want."

I fought against blackness. "Not the engine room." Each word was an agony. "Somewhere else. Section four."

"You tricked us once; what if you did it again? We keep the power lines as security."

"No tricks. Take you to your section and leave you alone. Swear." I caught myself swaying.

I heard voices buzzing. Then, "All right, we agree. On your oath. Call someone down to help you, before you kill us all."

"Oath. Swore no one else."

Clinger said urgently. "Forget the frazzin' oath! Get someone to help before you keel over!"

I said hoarsely, "Dray. If you can hear me, come down. Section nine."

Eons later the hatch slid open. A suited figure clumped into the corridor. Kneeling, I struggled to stay erect as the figure loomed. A hand settled over mine on the muzzle of the cannon, and fingers gently pried mine from the firing button. I sagged.

"Send the trannies out first," someone said. "I've got my finger on the button, and I don't give Christ's damn whether you live or die. Or whether the Captain does."

"All right, Chief. Take it easy." The hatch swung open. One by one the frightened, subdued transients emerged, blinking as if in bright light.

One threw herself at me, hugging me fiercely as I knelt. "Cap'n! You hurt! What dey doin' you, Cap'n?"

"Annie?"

Dray snarled, "You, Jackboy! And you, girl. Take hold of the Captain and carry him through the hatch. That's right, slap open the hatch control. Into the next section, all of you. Now shut it." The ceiling moved in great lurches, swinging back and forth. There was tight pressure under my arms.

I lay passively, in a dreamlike state. My cheek hurt hardly at all. I heard the gentle hiss of a section hatch. Other hands seized me. I floated up the ladder.

Philip Tyre's face wafted into view. "Oh, Lord God! Take him to the infirmary."

I said slowly, distinctly, "The bridge first."

"But—"

"Bridge." A few moments later I was eased into my chair; I gripped the hand rests. I felt hot and dry. Philip stood nearby, poised to cushion me if I fell. His anxious eyes roved. On the deck Eddie Boss groaned and tried to lift himself. Walter Dakko, rifle in hand, waited.

I gestured to Eddie. "Send him back to quarters."

Philip contemptuously nudged the young sailor with his boot. "To the brig, you mean. Right away, sir."

"Crew berth."

"But he's up for court-mar—"

I heaved myself to my feet, swaying. "Dakko. Out." I waved at the hatch. Walter Dakko left swiftly, eyes grim. On Philip's nod he shut the hatch behind him.

I said carefully, shaping each word, "Why would you court-martial him?"

Philip gawked. "He tried to kill you."

I shook my head. "He . . . fell down." I staggered, caught myself.

"He went for your throat," Philip cried. "I had to stun him before he strangled you!"

Eddie Boss hauled himself into a sitting position, propping himself against the console.

"I didn't see it."

The young middy was almost in tears. "Captain, you're not well! He tried to kill you, don't you remember? He can't get away with that!"

I took a clumsy step toward him. Another. I backed him to the bulkhead, my eyes blazing. I leaned close. "I . . . am . . . your . . . superior . . . officer!"

"Yes, sir!"

"He fell!"

Philip was white.

"Say it!"

The boy's eyes flicked to Eddie Boss, back to mine in betrayed reproach. He stammered, "Sir. The—the sailor must have stumbled. He struck his head and passed out."

"Very well." I turned carefully. "I'm going to the infirmary now. Something . . . seems to be wrong." With great dignity I took two steps toward the hatch.

Behind me Philip said in a small voice, "I'd like to help you, please." I nodded; his arm came tentatively around my chest. As I trudged, resting my weight on his shoulder, I could see the glistening of his tears.

Part 3

August 7, in the year of our Lord 2198

43

The warmth of the scalding tea seeped through the thick porcelain until I was forced to shift the cup back and forth between my hands, until I had to set it down on the swing-arm table by my bedside. Elena Bartel smiled from the foot of the bed.

"I'll wait a few minutes," I conceded.

"The anticipation will do you good." Her tone was shy.

I smiled cautiously, feeling the skin stretch. It had been, they told me, three days since I'd tottered to the infirmary clutching Philip Tyre like a castaway his oxy tank. My burn was infected, and my frantic exertions had pushed my fever near the point of no return.

Philip, Walter Dakko and Kerren had huddled in consultation, while Kerren directed their efforts to subdue my infection. The harried midshipman appointed Dakko and Bartel my attendants and left to run the ship; Lord God only knew in what state I'd find our affairs when I could return to the bridge. I consoled myself that Philip couldn't do much worse than I'd managed on my own.

I gazed wistfully at the teacup, wondering how soon I'd be able to hold it. Despite frequent applications of the medipulse, my wound smarted, and the steam of the tea would soothe, the cup under my nose, the clean warm vapors inhaled. It recalled Father sitting with me during my childhood fevers, his dented old copper teapot and a sponge bath the major weapons in his medical arsenal. It was, I suppose, the only tenderness I'd ever known from him.

I leaned back on the pillow and stared through Elena, trying to penetrate the haze of the preceding days. I'd lain sweating and shivering while my fever spiked, fading into drugged sleep when the medications took hold. At other, more clear-headed times I fretted over my abandoned duties.

Knowing we were shorthanded, I countermanded Philip's order that Elena or Walter Dakko be with me at every moment. "The buzzer is by my hand, Ms. Bartel. If I need anything I'll signal. Report back to Mr. Tyre."

"No, sir, I won't do that," she'd said calmly.

"But—"

"I'll get the midshipman."

A few minutes later Philip Tyre appeared, saluted, listened to my curt instructions. "Sorry, sir, but she stays. Or someone else, if she makes you uncomfortable."

For a moment I was speechless. "You realize what you're saying?"

"Yes." An awkward pause that seemed to last forever. "Sir, I've relieved you until you recover. It's in the Log."

Stunned, I fell back against the pillows. Relieved? Naval legends recounted braver men than I who'd quailed at such an act, endured misery and worse before taking the fateful step for which they might easily be hanged.

The Captain of a Naval vessel was more than an officer. He was the United Nations Government in transit; relieving him was akin to revolution. In my despair I'd asked Philip to perform that very act, not all that long ago. Yet now all I could feel was outrage.

"Only until you recover," he repeated, with an unspoken plea for reassurance, and stubborn determination. "Otherwise you'd be out of bed as soon as your legs would hold you. Maybe sooner. We can't take the risk; you're needed too much."

"I see." I glowered, unforgiving.

"When your fever stays down two days in a row, and your blood count is back to normal, Kerren says." Philip's blue eyes were troubled. He forced a smile. "Meantime I'll do my best, sir."

And so he'd gone to the bridge while I remained in the white cubicle, staring at the muted lights, subject to the inexpert ministrations of Walter Dakko and the anxious pale young woman.

A neurotic, she'd described herself, and I could see the truth of her admission, yet she brought to nursing a determination and an empathy that made up for her lack of practice. She bathed me and helped with intimate functions, and assisted Walter Dakko in dressing my suppurating wound whose fetid odor even I found distasteful, and which had become his special diligence.

"Would you like the holovid?" she asked me now. I nodded, a tiny motion only. Each time I moved my cheek, the dressing shifted, the skin stirred, and I felt sensations I preferred not to contemplate. Moodily I took the holovid from her outstretched hand. Yesterday I'd demanded the ship's manifest, which Philip had obediently eprommed and sent down.

Relieved of command or not, I could at least use my time to search for stores in the hold that might prove useful, before we jettisoned the rest in preparation for our acceleration. I wondered if it was an exercise in futility. Then I shrugged; we would do what we could. All else was up to Lord God.

Another day passed, and my fever lessened. Kerren's medications were slowly overcoming the infection that had nearly destroyed me. I tried not to scream when Walter Dakko carefully removed the drain the puter had instructed him to insert.

I demanded a mirror. They said they'd get one, but didn't. I suspected they didn't want me to see myself. My temperature remained steady another day. I took a short walk to the head, and savored my achievement. Ms. Bartel shared in my triumph, grinning widely when I could not.

I was myself again, but weakened. Overexertion—remaining on my feet for more than a few minutes—sent a flush to my features and sweat to my pores. I ate the soft foods they gave me, so as not to have to chew, and walked every few hours to rebuild my stamina. The following day I emerged from the infirmary in my frayed robe for a triumphant foray to the corridor bend before returning.

I was perched on my bed, controlling my breathing, trying not to reveal how much the venture had cost me, when Philip Tyre appeared.

He saluted but didn't come to attention. Quite right, as he held command. "Sir, how do you feel today?"

"Well enough." My tone was cold.

"When you think yourself ready, sir, I'd like you to resume command."

"You're sure you wouldn't rather keep it?"

He looked to the deck. "I'm sorry you disagree with my decision, sir. I understand the consequences."

"Very well. Right now, then." I stood too fast, sat back abruptly. "Well, in the morning. I'll give it one more day, so your effort won't be wasted."

"Yes, sir." He saluted, turned, and left.

When morning came I dressed cautiously, maneuvering my undershirt over the bandage that covered my cheek. I shaved the one side of my face, wondering as I stared into the mirror what horror the neat white dressing hid.

Back on the bridge at last, I saluted Philip. "Kerren, record, please. Having recovered fully, Mr. Tyre, I reassume command of this vessel."

"Yes, sir. I return command to you. Acknowledged and understood." He saluted and came to attention.

"Dismissed, Midshipman. Go to your quarters." I ignored him as he marched out. A petty revenge, but all that was available to me. I sat in my seat and snapped on the holovid to review the Log.

I flipped the first entry, bald and unadorned. "Captain feverish and semiconscious. Relieved of command by order of Philip A. Tyre, senior officer present."

I skimmed through the subsequent entries. Philip had set experienced crewmen to train our recruits in ship's protocol and their duties. He'd reorganized the galley and issued supply rations to Mr. Bree on a regular basis. At the midshipman's orders Mr. Tzee had taught two crewmen the mechanics of standing comm room watch. Dray had been reinstalled in his engine room, and Tyre had assigned him Deke as an assistant.

As I read his accomplishments, an unreasoning anger stirred. The west hydroponics were cleaned out, and new plantings and cuttings from the east hydros started under Emmett Branstead's watchful eye. Because the sensors and machinery in west hydros were nonfunctional, the plants had to be tended by hand and Philip had arranged that also. He'd recalculated our intended course, had the recyclers monitored, kept the Log entries up-to-date . . .

Damn him! I slammed the holovid onto my console. I wasn't needed. I wasn't even missed. Our industrious middy had handled everything, and more efficiently than I could have.

I slumped brooding in my seat. When I'd had enough self-pity I called the ship's stations for progress reports; all was well in recycling, comm room, engine room, and hydros. The rebels, thank Lord God, had done no damage to the hydro chambers.

In what section had Philip confined the mutineers? I glanced through the Log, could find no entry. I was about to call the wardroom, but thought better of it; I'd just sent the boy off to sleep. Better to search out the information myself. I thumbed the caller. "Chief, are you busy?"

A short pause. "Not particularly, Captain. I was showing Deke how the release valves work."

"Would you come up, please?" I replaced the caller and waited. I knew he wouldn't be long; when the Captain summoned, a crewman, any crewman, hurried to obey.

Within two minutes the Chief appeared, saluted, and was allowed onto the bridge.

"Dray, I'm a little fuzzy on what happened after I headed to the infirmary. You were getting the trannies—the transients out of the engine room."

"Yes, sir." He was impassive. "They're safe. A couple of the girls got mauled a bit, but no worse."

"You were about to put the rebels in another section. Four, was it?"

He said nothing.

"Well?"

He shrugged. "Maybe you were going to do that. I never said I would."

I slammed the console. "Where are they, Dray?"

"The brig, of course. Where else?"

"I promised I'd give them a section if they surrendered."

The Chief stared in disbelief. "What does it matter? You were under duress."

I gaped. "I gave them my oath."

"A ruse of war," he said vehemently. "Or whatever you choose to call it. It makes no difference; you're going to hang them, aren't you?"

"I can't, Dray. They have my sworn word."

He saw I was serious. "Them?" he spluttered. "Those God-cursed maggots? You may be crazy enough to let them wander part of the ship—"

"Dray!"

"But I'll be damned if I do it!" he shouted. We stared at each other in shocked silence.

"Go below, Dray. At once."

"Aye aye, sir!" With an angry salute he stalked off.

Some time passed before I was calm enough to sit. I pored through the Log. Philip had entered nothing about the rebels' imprisonment. "Kerren!"

He was as calm as ever. "Yes, Captain?"

"I'll be in the wardroom. Monitor all alarms and notify me at once if I'm needed."

"Of course, Captain Seafort."

I strode along the Level 1 corridor, hardly looking where I was going, and just missed falling over a bucket. Eddie Boss glowered mutely. "What are you up to?" I demanded.

"Same what I be doon allatime!" Savagely he swung a mopful of water across the corridor, sweeping with broad, angry strokes. "Boss boy say allatime moppin' flo'! Moppin' flo'!" He shot me a look of accusation. "You said you was needin' help! Dis be kinda help you need? Ol' Eddie keepin' flo' clean?"

"Deck," I said absently.

"Deck, flo', be alla same when yo's allatime moppin'." His face was sullen. Not up to a confrontation, I continued on my way.

The harassment of Eddie disturbed me. Was Philip reverting to his old ways? I felt a chill; how did our new cadet Gregor fare, in the isolation of the wardroom? I formed a steely resolve. Philip would not get away with brutality. Never again.

I pounded on the wardroom hatch. It slid open. Gregor Attani, handsome in a new crisp gray uniform, grinned before remembering to salute. "Hello, sir." His voice was cheerful.

"Come to attention!" I rasped. "Has he taught you nothing yet?"

He complied, his smile fading. "Sorry, sir."

"Where's Mr. Tyre?"

"Right here, sir." Philip appeared in the hatchway in slacks and T-shirt, towel slung over his shoulder. He tossed the towel to the chair and came to attention in one smooth motion.

"As you were, both of you." Gregor relaxed and eased to his bunk. I said to Philip, "Eddie Boss."

"Yes, sir?"

"What's he doing out there?"

"Deck duty."

"For how long?"

"Five days, now."

"Why?" I demanded.

A momentary bitterness clouded his features. "For being clumsy enough to stumble on the bridge." Gregor, forgotten, watched openmouthed from his bunk.

"You don't agree with my decision, Mr. Tyre?"

"I accept it, sir." He contemplated the bulkhead with a bleak expression. "However you look at it, he was out of line. A little deck duty won't hurt him."

Grudgingly I conceded that he was right. "Very well. But tomorrow's the last day."

"Aye aye, sir."

"Now." I glared. "Mr. Andros and Mr. Clinger. The others."

He squared his shoulders. "Yes, sir."

"You put them in the brig."

"No, sir. Dray did. I left them there."

I said tightly, "You knew about my oath to let them go free?"

"Yes, I did." His casual manner infuriated me.

"So you disobeyed orders."

He smiled without mirth. "You never ordered me to give them a section, sir."

"You God damned sea lawyer!" The insult hung between us, irretrievable.

"Amen," said Gregor Attani hoarsely, turning aside my blasphemy.

"You knew what I expected, whether or not I gave specific orders! You deliberately disobeyed me."

Philip looked me in the eye, took a deep breath. "Sir, at the time I was not subject to your orders."

My mouth opened but no sound emerged. My fists were balled so tight my hand ached. I finally got out, "Ten demerits for insolence, Mr. Tyre! I won't cane you, because I promised not to. But you'll by God work them off, every one of them. And you're confined to quarters otherwise, until further notice."

"Aye aye, sir." His face was white. I spun on my heel, slapping the hatch shut on my way out. Awash with rage, I stalked the corridor to the ladder, dashed two steps at a time down to Level 3. Ignoring the sailors in the corridor I slapped open the engine room hatch. "Dray!"

"Back here!" He emerged from the stores compartment, young Deke at his side, the boy lugging a heavy box.

"Dray, go to section four. Remove the inside controls for the corridor hatches. Disable the speaker and run a new line that connects only with the bridge. Go through every cabin and compartment in section four and remove all tools and weapons. Acknowledge your orders."

"Orders received and understood, sir." He smiled, a bitter, sour smile. "Mind if I have a drink afterward?"

Deke watched, openmouthed.

"How dare you!"

"Yes," he mimicked. "How dare I." He flexed his hand. "The fingers are all there, Captain. Want one? I sneered at you, and you threatened to burn off my hand. Those scum bastards try to kill you. They seize my engine room, they take hostages. You're giving them passenger cabins." He glared, extended his wrist. "Here, do what you want! I don't need the goddamn fingers!"

I walked unsteadily to the bulkhead, palmed its cold surface, gazed unseeing at the control panels and valves. "I was desperate when I told you that," I said in a low voice. "I had no one but Philip. The ship was in chaos and I didn't know what else to do."

He growled, "Deke, get out. This is between me and the Captain." The young sailor fled with relief. When Dray turned to me his eyes were cold. "I don't respect you, Seafort, and I don't care if you know it. You scared the living hell out of me. I'm fifty-three years old and I've never been so frightened in my life. Well, maybe you had to do it. I gave up, when things looked hopeless and that ass Tremaine was running the bridge. The bottle seemed the only way out."

He looked at me with narrow eyes. "But you played that scene for all it was worth. It was calculated cruelty. I don't need the bottle now. I can hate you instead."

"And you don't fear me?"

His mouth twisted in a sardonic smile. "No. That's ironic, isn't it? I really don't give a shit whether you take my hand or not. You can't have me. My hand, maybe, but not me." He met my eyes. "Oh, I'll obey orders, and I'll salute you and speak courteously, when others are around. But I'll know, and you'll know, what I really think of you."

"Yes." I turned away. "I'll know." Despite what I'd done, this man had stood by me at the armory, saved me from the rebels outside the engine room. And there would be no way to reach him, ever.

"I know what you think of me," I repeated, my voice dull. "I wonder if you'll ever know what I think of me." Blindly I groped for the hatch. The corridor was deserted. I made my way to the ladder, wiping my eyes with my sleeve. He'd given no more than I deserved. I climbed back to the bridge, shut myself into its isolation. Alone with the unblinking cold lights of the simulscreen I plumbed the depths of my self-disgust.

Hours later Dray reported that section four was prepared. I rounded up Walter Dakko and Emmett Branstead, armed them, took them below to the brig. I unsealed the cramped, dirty cell that confined Clinger and the deckhand Akkrit.

Clinger's look radiated hatred. "Shoulda killed you when I had the chance," he said. "You an' your oath. I told Andy it was all goofjuice, but he wouldn't listen."

"Shut up. I'm taking you to section four."

"Why? Gonna kill us there instead of here?"

"No. I'm giving you a section. As I promised." I raised my stunner. "Another word, Mr. Clinger, and you'll be carried out." I led the two apprehensive sailors and their guard from the brig to the abandoned section.

When they were sealed into their exile I returned for Andros, Sykes, and Byzer. When I unsealed his cell Andros flashed me a glance that sent a chill down my spine. "This is how you keep your word, joey?"

"Clinger and Akkrit are waiting in section four. I'm taking you there now."

"What's the hurry?" He leaned against the bulkhead, arms folded. "Don' wanna wait awhile? A year or so, maybe? An officer's word!" He spat on the deck. "That's what it's worth!"

"Let's go." I fingered my stunner.

"I been waitin' five days," he screamed. "You lied! No tricks, you swore!" Walter Dakko's grip tightened on his rifle.

"Yes, I swore." I waited for Andros to emerge, but he leaned against the hatch, unmoving. "Let's go."

"Or?" His voice was a sneer.

"Or I'll stun you and carry you."

"If that's what you got to do, go ahead. You want me to go on my feet, admit you was a liar."

Dakko took a menacing step forward.

"Easy, Mr. Dakko. I could change my mind, Andros, and leave you here."

"Sure." He spat again. "Break your oath once, what's another time?"

"I was sick!" I cried. "I barely knew where I was!"

"You promised!" he shouted. "You're an officer, ain't you? You promised, an' Dray and your pretty boy, they heard you, and instead we got stuffed in this box! Twenny years they been tellin' me about that oath stuff, and look what you did to me!" He crashed his fist on the hatch in rage and frustration. "What a greenie I am! I believed you."

Dakko glanced at me, took pity. He said quietly, "That's enough, Mr. Andros. The Captain was quite ill, and he's here now to carry out his promise. Come with us."

"He didn't say, sit in the stinking brig for five days sick with wonderin' whether they was gonna hang you!" The seaman's voice faltered. "No, take you to your section and leave you alone, he said! 'I swear,' he told us, and I believed him, 'cause he was an officer . . ." His voice had a ragged catch. "I believed him . . ."

Dakko raised his weapon. "Come along, Mr. Andros."

Eyes downcast, Andros hugged himself, shaking his head. Coolly, Dakko aimed the stunner at his chest.

"Wait." I pushed the gun aside, stepped into the dirty cell, stood before the wretched seaman. "Andros, before Lord God and these witnesses, I apologize." His eyes lifted. "I failed to keep my pledge. I was sick and confused, but I could still have taken care of you. A word would have done it. I was wrong, and my oath is not kept and I'm sorry for it. I'm here to redeem my oath. Go with these men. Please."

His eyes were fixed on me with pathetic gratitude. "Aye aye, Captain," he whispered. Docile, he followed my two sailors to section four.

The moment the hatch was sealed Emmett Branstead growled, "Excuse me, but why? Why humble yourself before that—that traitor?"

He had no right to ask. No sailor ever had the right to demand that his Captain explain his behavior. "Because he was right, Mr. Branstead. And I was wrong. Now, get Sykes and Byzer."

"My wife would like to talk with you," said old Mr. Reeves stiffly. "If it wouldn't be too much trouble."

"Of course." He'd intercepted me as I made my way to my place in the dining hall. I followed him to the table alongside the bulkhead, where Mrs. Reeves and the Pierces waited for their elderly companions.

The fragile old lady smiled at me from tired blue eyes. "I understand we owe our lives to your courage, Captain. Thank you for all you've done for us."

Despite myself I laughed, a harsh, bitter sound. "Done for you? My God, how do these rumors start?"

"You prevented those wretched sailors from blowing up the ship or cutting our power, did you not?"

"After giving them the chance to do so in the first place."

The old woman's tone bore sympathy and concern. "You've been ill, I know. Are you still troubled?"

"I wish I had died on *Portia* with my wife, ma'am." I was astounded I'd said it aloud.

She patted the seat next to Mr. Pierce. "Sit with me, young man."

Shaky, I lowered myself into the chair. "Sorry, I didn't mean to say that."

"You must have loved her a great deal."

I looked elsewhere. "Not as much as I might have. I didn't appreciate her until she died." From the chair opposite, Mr. Pierce stared at me, mouth half open.

"You can live with that. You have courage."

"You misjudge me, ma'am."

"It took courage to cast your lot with us."

I said harshly, "You don't know what you're saying."

"Tell me."

Why should I unburden myself to a foolish old lady? Yet I spat out the words. "I came to *Challenger*, yes. Admiral Tremaine had relieved me for incompetence and insubordination. It was *Challenger* or be hanged. That's what you call courage."

Placid, she let the silence grow. Then, "Sometimes it takes courage to live too."

I stood abruptly. "I have to go to my table."

"You have to find peace." The old eyes looked at me, intent. "Otherwise you'll be no help to anyone."

"I have to go, ma'am." I touched my cap, turned my back on her, retreated.

Dinner finally concluded. I disengaged myself from a couple who wanted my company for inane chat, left for the bridge. I was interrupted a short way down the corridor.

"Captain Seafort!" Chris Dakko hurried after me. I waited. He hesitated, bit his lip, then flicked me a fleeting, unpracticed salute. "Please. May I talk to you?"

I knew I ought to refuse. There were channels for a crewman to approach the Captain; a direct entreaty was unacceptable. But I decided to make allowances; the boy had been a civilian a few days past.

"All right." I led him to the Level 1 passengers' lounge and shut the hatch. "Well?"

"Please." He searched my eyes, as if trying to read them. "I know you don't like me. I haven't been nice to you . . . And I know you need help."

"Yes?"

"What you did, enlisting me against my will—"

I couldn't let him ask. "Enough, Mr. Dakko."

"You don't understand." He sounded desperate. "I can't take it. I'm all wrong for that life. I don't fit in with them, I never can. I—"

"Mr. Dakko!"

"I'll help with anything you say, Mr. Seafort! Let me be a civilian again. I'm begging you. Sir! I'm begging you, SIR!" His eyes implored me, hoping against hope.

Slowly I shook my head. "If I had other options I'd take them. God, don't you think I thought about it, before enlisting you? You've been impressed, Mr. Dakko, and impressed you will remain."

"You don't know what they're like," he whispered, eyes seeing only some private hell. "It's a nightmare. I even went to my—my father. He shoved me away, said I'd chosen to be on my own, that he wouldn't . . ." His eyes closed. "Captain, sir, forgive the things I've said to you. Please, let me go!"

His distress moved me. Perhaps if he hadn't mentioned his father

. . . I recalled the nights I'd lain awake in Academy silently beseeching Father to take me from that place.

"Mr. Dakko—Chris," I amended gently. "You weren't enlisted as punishment. I needed every available hand to fill the crew roster. I still do. You must remain in the Navy. I'm sorry, but that's how it will be. You came to *Challenger* of your own will; these are the consequences you suffer."

He looked away. I cleared my throat. "Now, sailor, salute as you've been taught and go below."

For a long moment the boy did nothing. Then with a visible effort at self-control he came to attention, saluted, stalked to the hatch.

That night, weary from a lonely day of unending drudgery, I went to my cabin for the first time in a week. The spacious compartment was still unfamiliar to me; after all, I'd been aboard *Challenger* only five days before my injury sent me to the infirmary. Clean sheets awaited. Towels too; Philip had even organized the laundry service.

I felt a pang of loneliness and tried to dwell on my anger instead. Thanks to Tyre, I'd had to humiliate myself before a demented sailor who'd caused death and disunion on my ship. If he'd but carried out my orders . . .

I stared at my sallow face in the mirror. Again I wondered what was beneath the bandage. Some compulsion drew my hand upward. Slowly, carefully, I peeled away the edge of the dressing. When it was done I stared at my visage, a sickness in the pit of my stomach.

My wound was hideous. The skin had split and suppurated, leaving a red, inflamed scar the length of my cheek from ear to lip that radiated outward toward eye and throat. The redness would fade, but the scar would remain. I recalled Simmons, the sailor I'd killed. Was it the mark of Cain? Unnerved, I began to laugh. Laughing and crying I fell heavily on the bed, and in a mercifully short time, slept.

44

Our days passed with leaden weight. My most urgent task was to set the ship on its homeward path; we'd already delayed far too long in that. But our precious propellant could not be wasted in course corrections; we would burn at full power until our propellant was gone. Or nearly gone. Even at the cost of reduced acceleration, I felt it necessary to save some small amount for emergency maneuvering.

While thruster engines fired independently, on a vessel so vast as *Challenger* or any ship of the line, propellant was centrally stored and pumped to smaller tanks within the individual thrusters. Should a feed problem cause any of our jets to sputter or misfire, we'd waste irreplaceable propellant in corrections. Our thruster pumps, powered by the fusion engines that were *Challenger*'s main source of energy, must be reliable.

I warned Dray that I'd soon need his engine room manned and functioning, with especial attention to the pump power lines. Grimly he set about the task.

Meanwhile, I delved into our manifests, wondering which items of cargo we could jettison to lighten our load. Every ounce of mass we could eliminate would raise the speed we'd achieve before our propellant gave out. Perhaps someday, decades hence, that would make a difference as we neared the Solar System. Personally, I doubted it would much matter; despite my hopeful words to the ship's company, I didn't see much awaiting us except a lingering death. Unless, of course, we were rescued.

Alone on the bridge, I brooded. With more skilled crewmen, I would even consider dismembering the ship itself. What use had we for the holds, forward of the disks and the launch berth? Once we removed necessary stores, the remainder would play no part in our survival and only added considerable tonnage to our mass.

I sighed. It would be an immense labor to disassemble the ship, one probably beyond our level of skill. More important, we hadn't the manpower to attempt such a project while also rebuilding our hydrophonics and maintaining essential ship's systems.

Besides, when it came down to it, even if we survived, would the

difference in speed matter all that much? We'd be broadcasting continuously to Earth, and our transmissions would arrive home in nineteen
years. What additional velocity we achieved would have negligible effect
on the time of our rescue. Unless, of course, our broadcasts went unheard, which was quite possible given the vast interstellar clutter of
background radiation and noise.

Well, nothing I could do about it, given our resources. I turned my
attention to cargo. There, at least, we could have some effect. With our
powered loading equipment a few men could easily empty the hold in
days.

Challenger, like any ship, carried not only its own supplies, but
freight bound for the colony it served. Admiralty would no doubt be
incensed if I abandoned expensive and needed cargo, but there was little
likelihood the material would ever reach Hope Nation even if *Challenger* were found, years hence.

On the other hand, assuming we were doomed to many years of
sail, who could know what items we'd find useful?

I made a preliminary list, and as it happened, Walter Dakko was
near when I asked Philip to review it. The middy merely acknowledged
my order, but Dakko fidgeted and conveyed his unease until I glared
and said, "Well?"

"I know it's not my place to interfere, but . . ."

"You're right, but out with it."

"Captain, have you considered the effect on the crew when you
raise the issue?"

"What issue?"

"Having them toss overboard anything we might do without. It
makes our abandonment seem so . . . final."

"You have objections to that?" I was prepared to put him in his
place, and fast.

"No, I try to be a realist. But when some of the others see you
acting in a way that suggests we have no real hope of res—"

Philip's tone was indignant. "Nonsense! When the Captain gives an
order, the crew carries it out. There's no question of—"

"No, sir, of course not." Dakko hesitated. "But you see, you've been
telling them a rescue ship will find us, and except for the Clinger and
Andros crowd, that's been holding us together. If we're to be found and
off-loaded, what does our velocity matter?"

"You'd have us sit here for years, waiting?" I waved it aside. "I'll
decide what's best for the ship. The crew will do what they're told."

"I hope so, sir. Though I've heard it asked why you don't—"

"Enough!"

"—try to repair the fusion drive. Aye aye, sir." He fell silent.

I stood slowly, urging myself not to snarl. "Repair the drive? Impossible. Pass the word, Mr. Dakko: we couldn't begin to tackle that sort of job ourselves. Even at a Lunapolis shipyard . . ." Losing my struggle, I swore under my breath, with feeling.

If he heard me, he gave no sign.

Over the next days I struggled to decide what to jettison. Should we go so far as to strip the empty cabins of their gear? Of what possible use was the ship's launch, nineteen light-years from the nearest star? Its mass was considerable. Yet, I hesitated. Fusion drive or no, *Challenger* was a Naval vessel still. If I abandoned the launch, why not the laser cannon, or the console at which the crew practiced firing drills? Why keep the exercise machinery for the passengers' lounge?

In the end I made arbitrary decisions that satisfied no one, including myself. For the morale of the passengers I left the ship intact, including all its provisions, and jettisoned only some of the heaviest cargo: tool and die manufactories for Hope Nation's growing industry, stamped and molded alloys, and the like. If anyone objected, they were smart enough not to let me hear it.

I ordered two radio beacons put out, and waited an extra day, monitoring to make sure they worked properly. Our rescue might depend on them. Later, we'd drop more.

When at last we were ready I called Dray and Philip to the bridge and set them to plotting our course with Kerren. At last everyone's figures agreed to several decimals. I entered our calculations on the screen.

Propulsive maneuvers were normally carried out by the Pilot, but we had no Pilot. As Captain I was assumed to have the necessary skills to maneuver a ship, yet I recalled with chagrin the ineptitude with which I'd handled docking drills as a middy. No our lives depended on abilities I lacked.

"Dray, go below; report when you're ready." The Chief saluted and left, saying nothing, not even the customary "Aye aye, sir."

Finally the engine room sent the signal.

The power of our fusion engines, unusable for their primary purpose, was channeled to the pumps feeding our maneuvering jets at the stern and sides of the ship. "Mr. Tyre," I said stiffly, "I order you to advise me the moment you see me mishandle the ship. Don't hesitate."

"Aye aye, sir. I shall."

With that as encouragement I rested my hand on the thruster controls. "Declination, fifteen." Tiny squirts of propellant from the side thrusters brought the bow ever so slowly around. No need to waste precious fuel to line us toward home when a few extra minutes would accomplish the maneuver through inertia.

I corrected our declination and attitude, braking our rotation until we were lined up perfectly for Sol, nineteen light-years distant. I knew that as we accelerated I'd have to make numerous small adjustments; our rate of thrust would not be absolutely uniform while propellant spewed from our tubes; minute impurities in the hydrozine or corrosion of the thruster tubes would have some noticeable effect.

"Very well. I believe we're now set to accelerate. Correct, Mr. Tyre?"

"I think so, sir. Yes, sir."

"All ahead one quarter." My hand closed around the smooth round ball on the console. Slowly I slid it forward, my eyes glued to the screen that flashed our position and course. Carefully I brought us up to speed, occasionally tapping the side thrusters ever so gently to correct our course.

I maintained one-quarter propulsion for over an hour, until I was reasonably sure the thrusters were operating properly. Sometimes they'd been known to cough, and at docking, tragedy could result. For us, the danger was less immediate. We faced only the risk of hurtling helplessly wide of our course, our propellant tanks dry.

"Increasing thrust to one-half." Drenched with sweat, my arm aching from the tension of my grip, I eased the red ball forward. *Challenger* held true to her course. "Mr. Tyre!"

Philip leapt forward. "Yes, sir?"

"Call the engine room. Are the thrusters heating?" If I reached for the caller with my free hand, my concentration might waver.

I knew Dray would report any malfunction instantly, but I had grim memories of the terrible day the thrusters on *Hibernia*'s launch had exploded. *Hibernia* had lost her Captain and two lieutenants. The event had shaped the course of my life, had won Amanda and lost her forever, had made me brittle, lonely, and bitter.

"Temperature normal, sir."

"I'm going to three-quarters thrust." Each second we accelerated increased our velocity, until eventually we would reach nearly a quarter the speed of light. The sooner we achieved this velocity, the greater chance we had of seeing home. But our maneuvering jets weren't designed to operate at full thrust for long, and we would need to fire the thrusters for almost a month to achieve our maximum speed. I dared not bring us to full acceleration too quickly.

Our maneuver would have been impossible had not Captain Hasselbrad transferred much of *Portia's* propellant to *Challenger* to ease his guilt in deserting us. Nonetheless, we would run out of propellant before we could achieve truly significant velocity. We would then face helpless years aboard an unmaneuverable vessel.

My wrist ached. I watched the numbers flash on our console, carried out to impossibly long decimals. The slightest variation from true course at the beginning of our trajectory would multiply into drastic and irremediable error as we progressed.

When we'd achieved three-quarters acceleration I pried my nearly numb hand from the ball. Now we could do nothing but wait, and be ever vigilant to jump to the side thrusters, to make any corrections Kerren did not. I wondered if I dared leave the bridge during the month to come.

There was at least one assist I could give to our morale. I picked up the caller. "Attention all hands and passengers. As you may have noticed if you looked out the portholes, we maneuvered the ship into position for acceleration. A short while ago I began firing our thrusters. We are on our way home. It will be a long, long voyage, but with the grace of Lord God we will, someday, see Terra again. That is all."

I replaced the caller and leaned back, the perspiration grown chill on my shirt. To my right Philip stood grinning with pleasure at our accomplishment.

Recalling his abuse of my prerogatives while I was disabled, I stared at him, expressionless, until his elation faded. "You may go, Mr. Tyre, until your watch."

He met my gaze, his eyes now bleak. "Aye aye, sir." He left.

Dray's relations with me were now coldly correct, absolutely unforgiving. He ran his engine room, carried out what responsibilities I assigned him, kept entirely to himself.

My relationship with Philip was virtually nonexistent. During the ten days since I'd left the wardroom in blind fury I'd avoided all casual contact with him, and spoken to him with icy formality when unavoidable.

Philip, Dray, and I had rotated watches for an endless week, relieving each other without conversation, at least, when I was present. I presumed the midshipman and the Chief were more congenial to each other than either was to me. I could imagine what they said about me in private.

Philip Tyre performed his duties with diligence and energy. He took an active hand in training our new recruits, and under his tutelage they began to take on the appearance and manner of Naval crewmen. Emmett Branstead and Mr. Dakko no longer spoke out of turn, and would have been reprimanded sharply if they had.

The transients who joined the crew formed their own subculture, until we dissolved it by merciless integration. They weren't allowed to eat together, bunk near each other, or pass free time in each other's company, but only among the other members of the crew. Resentful at first, they slowly began to adapt. Deke, who'd been beaten senseless by the deckhand Akkrit, now exiled to section four, was the last to respond, but after days of sullen withdrawal he too began to emerge from his shell.

Meanwhile, alone in my quarantine of the spirit, I sat brooding on the bridge.

Gregor Attani came to attention, all eager creases and backbone.

"Stand easy, Cadet."

"Yes, sir. Reporting as ordered, sir. We've apportioned all the reamining food into thirty-five lots and stowed each in a separate bin, labeled by weeks. Thirty-five weeks, sir. Less food in the later weeks' bins, as you ordered."

"Very well, Mr. Attani. Dismissed." I watched him go. A cadet reporting directly to the Captain; another cherished Navy tradition by the boards. A cadet was considered the lowest of the low, a trainee devoid of civil and personal rights, the ward of his superior officer. By custom a Captain did not deign to notice a cadet's presence, far less speak to him. He would certainly not assign a cadet to carry out important tasks. But Gregor, at eighteen, was five years older than the typical cadet, and in any event I had no one else.

I knew Gregor Attani was shaping up well, under Philip's guidance. Though only months younger than Philip, the cadet treated his senior midshipman with reverence bordering on awe. Recalling the brutality with which Tyre had tormented *Hibernia*, I couldn't fathom how he'd achieved such rapport with Gregor. I envied it, though I knew the hostility between us was of my own making.

Of course it helped that Gregor was not subject to a cadet's traditional merciless hazing. He was rather too old to benefit from it, and there was no one to haze him save Philip, whose energies were expended elsewhere. Despite Gregor's unwillingness to volunteer, he accepted ship's discipline and the constraints of his new role with good grace.

Still, all was not well with him. Earlier that day I'd gone to the dining hall for a cup of coffee—thank heaven, our supply of that liquid was nearly unlimited. While I puttered unnoticed in the galley, Mr. Bree and Chris Dakko moved tables in the hall outside. Gregor arrived with a query from Philip; Mr. Bree scurried back to the storeroom, leaving Gregor and Chris Dakko alone.

"Hello, Chris." Gregor's manner was awkward. I groaned inwardly. As a prospective officer, he must keep his distance. Instead of making my presence known, I waited to hear out the conversation, uneasy at eavesdropping. Hadn't I just admonished Philip for doing the same?

Chris eyed Gregor's crisp gray uniform with contempt. "Do I know you, joey?"

"Funny."

"Not really. I'd call it pathetic."

"Call what?"

"How you sold out." Chris coolly contemplated his former friend. "I hear you're bunking with pretty boy Tyre. Have a good time together?"

I pursed my lips. To commissioned officers, a cadet was as nothing, but to a crewman like Chris, he was as any officer, and Naval courtesy was due.

"What's eating you?" Gregor's voice seethed.

"You heard me. You sold yourself to hardass Seafort and that cute middy. Why bother? In a couple of months we'll all be dead."

"What about you? Whose work shirt do you wear?"

"This?" Chris flicked his light blue shirt with scorn. "You know why. That trannie gorilla is waiting to beat the shit out of me and no one will stop him. Someday I'll kill him. I've already got it planned." A sneer. "But you don't just submit, you go along for the ride. Do they feed you better up there?"

"I think," Gregor said slowly, "I never really knew you."

"Don't worry about it, grode. You've got your new friends to suck up to, just like old daddy Walter."

"Remember who you're speaking to, Dakko."

"Yeah? Who?"

"An officer candidate. If the Captain heard, you'd be in all sorts of trouble."

"You gonna tell him, asslicker?"

Gregor took a deep breath. "Stand at attention."

"Oh, no. I take that crap from the gorilla, but not from you. Not unless you're man enough to make me."

"I am, but you're not worth the trouble I'd get in." He turned on his heel, stalked out. Chris muttered something derisive under his breath.

I waited until Mr. Bree had Chris's attention occupied and crept out unseen. Gregor had lost control of a crewman, but my stepping in would only make it worse. I filed it among my many unsolved problems.

Days crept by in dreary succession. I inched the thrusters to full power and kept them at maximum, poring over the readouts more anxiously than ever. They remained steady.

Our full attention turned to food production; everyone, including passengers, helped convert our unused cabins to urban farms. We had to ration sand, but we had plenty of water, thanks to Captain Hasselbrad. Tomato plants, lettuce, squash, legumes, even carrots began to sprout and were cherished like infants by our fervent gardeners.

Each meal we ate from our dwindling stores made us more aware of our desperate need to succeed in our gardening. Many of the passengers resented the food I sent daily to section four, the same rations we ourselves were given. I paid no heed, except to assure that the supplies arrived unmolested.

There was some altercation between Eddie Boss and Dray. I didn't know the details, and didn't want to ask. Eddie bore bruises for a week or so, until they faded, and thereafter treated all officers with increased deference. Dray didn't seem a match for the huge recruit, but he'd been around long enough to know a few tricks. And he ran an engine room, where rough joes were commonplace. Still, it was bad discipline for an officer to scuffle with a crewman. Because this was no time for me to interfere with Dray, I held my peace.

During these weeks I hardly saw my cabin during waking hours, though I yearned for its seclusion. What time I didn't spend on the bridge, anticipating with dread an alarm that would signal a deterioration in our course, I spent roving the ship.

I kept the recycler's mates taut with tension at my sudden inspections. I constantly appeared at the hydro chambers and our improvised vegetable farms. I lost track of how often I passed through the launch berth lock and roamed the hold, hoping to find supplies or equipment I hadn't noticed on the manifest.

I'd retreated to my cabin late at night and was stripping off my clothes when the knock came. I don't know who I expected, but I was dumbfounded to find myself face-to-face with Philip Tyre.

"May I have a word, sir?"

"Is this an emergency?" I made my voice as cold as I could manage. "No, sir."

"On the bridge, in the morning." I slapped the hatch shut. As I got ready for bed I seethed; Philip knew the Captain's cabin was inviolate. True, I'd told him he was free to knock. But that was before he ignored my orders about the mutineers. I snapped off the light, dropped my head on the pillow, waited for sleep.

Two hours later I turned the light on and, with a sigh of resignation, reached for the caller. "Mr. Tyre, to the Captain's cabin." I dressed myself, sat in the chair to wait. It wasn't long.

I regarded him coldly. "Well?"

He came to the at-ease position. "Sorry I bothered you at night, sir. I shouldn't have."

"But you did, so get on with it."

He squirmed, gave up the at-ease position, and studied the near bulkhead as if for flaws. "I, uh, came to apologize."

"Oh?"

"Yes, sir." Red-faced, he turned his gaze to me. "For my beh—my misbehavior in connection with the rebellion."

"You were wrong?"

"I—yes, sir. I was wrong. I'd be grateful if you'd forgive me."

"Why?" I felt no inclination to let him off the hook.

His eyes filled with sudden tears. "Because—damn!" He twisted away, thrusting his hands in his pockets.

At once I banished the triumph of revenge to some shabby recess of my mind. "Why, Philip?" I asked more gently.

"Because I need your respect," he whispered, his face turned. "Because I'm so lonely, with only Gregor to talk to, and I can't stand . . . knowing you hate me again." He sucked in his breath.

Lord Christ, what had I done? I got to my feet. "I don't hate you, Philip. I never have."

"No?" He strove for calm. "I think you do, and I'm sorry for what I did to cause it. It's"—he faltered—"like the last time." His voice was low.

"I don't understand."

"On *Hibernia,* when everyone said I was hurting the midshipmen. I didn't understand, I never could; I just knew finally that something had gone terribly wrong. And now it's happening again."

With growing uneasiness I asked, "Why did you apologize, Philip?"

"I told you!"

"The truth, this time! Because you felt you were wrong?"

He whirled to face me, tears streaming. "Why do you make me say it? Isn't it enough that I apologize?"

"Only truth matters."

"The truth . . . No, sir, I don't think I was wrong, not deep inside. I wish I could, but I don't. I came because I need you not to hate me. Oh, God, let me be dismissed. I shouldn't have come!"

"Yes, you should!" I slammed my fist on the table, as a door flew open in my mind.

"Now I've made things worse . . ."

I shook my head decisively, not trusting myself to speak.

"Why not?"

"You were right!" I dropped into my chair and said again, more quietly, "Because you were right." The silence sat heavy between us. "That's why you felt no guilt, and why I've been miserable for the last month. God, I've wronged you."

He stood speechless.

"When you brigged the rebels, you were acting as Captain. My orders were irrelevant; you didn't even know yet if I'd recover. And, most important, my oath didn't bind you."

He whispered, "If that's true why didn't you say it before?"

I forced my eyes to meet his. "Because I resented your doing such a good job. I fuddled for five days and accomplished nothing; you took command and sorted out everything while I lay in a stupor. Maybe I did hate you a little, for that."

"That's not fair to yourself," he protested. "I got us into the mess, didn't I? I mean, by dropping my weapons so the rebels could get them. And you saved us by your unbelievable bravery. All I did was, well, housekeeping."

I smiled wryly. "Then you're a very fine housekeeper, Midshipman. Very good indeed."

He blushed with unexpected pleasure. "Really? You mean that?"

I nodded.

"I tried to think of everything. It was the only chance I've ever had to, well, run things."

"I know." Midshipmen were taught to follow orders; far between were the opportunities to give them.

"You called me a sea lawyer and said I was insolent—"

"I'm sorry."

"—and it was true, sir. I didn't try to explain to you; my pride got in the way."

"You shouldn't need to explain." I stood and began to pace. "You didn't know me when I was your age, Philip. When I was senior middy aboard *Hibernia*."

"They told me stories, Alexi and Derek."

"When Captain Malstrom died before commissioning a lieutenant, I pored over the regs, trying to find a way out. Vax Holser should have been appointed, and we both knew it."

Philip smiled bleakly. "He didn't think so. It's one of the few things he said about you."

"Well, I knew the regs. The Captain is in complete charge of the ship and everyone in it. There's no difference between Captain and acting Captain, as you were here on *Challenger*. I knew that then, and I knew it when I sent you from the bridge the day I relieved you. I was just so jealous."

"Of me?" he said in astonishment. "But why?"

"Christ, boy, look at you! You're young and handsome, and assured, and you're so competent. I'm not."

"Not assured?" he repeated in wonder. "On *Hibernia* I was terrified of you. You knew exactly what you wanted, and would settle for nothing less." He shook his head. "Not competent? Then what are you? How many times did you save *Hibernia*? Or *Challenger*?"

"I know my duty, but that doesn't mean I do it well. You have a knack."

"I'm glad you think so. I'd like a chance to command, someday." He wiped his sleeve across his face. "I'm sorry I burst in when you were getting ready for bed." He flashed a shy smile. "This time I really mean the apology."

I shook my head. "It isn't that easy for me, Philip. I've been treating you badly."

"No you haven't, sir," he blurted. I raised my eyebrow. "Not badly. You were very . . . polite. It was more that you weren't treating me at all."

"Even worse. I'm glad you still want my respect; you have it. I'll try to do better in the future."

"So will I." Awkwardly he pulled himself to attention. Ignoring that, I offered my hand. He took it. The warmth of his grip made it difficult to speak further.

* * *

After my reconciliation with Philip I bore my watches on the bridge with renewed vigor. To my amazement, *Challenger* was slowly returning to Naval standards, though Philip had his hands full training the streeters who'd joined the crew. His earnest and patient attempts to explain Navy methods didn't work; the transients either ignored him or laughed outright, which provoked him to retaliatory discipline that further antagonized them.

I felt some special obligation to the transients that I had difficulty defining. I was determined that they not be treated as second-class sailors, just as I had been determined that they not be second-class passengers. But how, for example, could we teach them to stand critically important watches in the comm room or the recycler chamber? Many were illiterate, all were essentially uneducated. How could I train them to man the lasers, or the radionics? Could they even understand the concepts involved?

I was distracted from that problem by another; the caller frantically paging me from section four. It was the deckhand Sykes, exiled with the rest of his unsavory comrades, able to communicate only with the bridge. "Mr. Clinger, he's hurt bad. Somebody do something, 'fore he dies in here!"

"What happened, Mr. Sykes?"

"Clinger and Andy, they been goin' at it, needlin' each other and all. Andy broke up a chair and took a piece of it, for a club . . . Clinger's lyin' on the deck, and I can't get him awake!"

I sighed. If I took Clinger to the infirmary he'd have to be guarded. And what about Andros? If I brigged him, would I be going back on my oath?

As if reading my thoughts, Sykes whimpered, "Please don' leave me alone with Andy, Captain. Not without Clinger here."

"Belay that, sailor. You got what you wanted." I paused. "I'll send a detail down for Clinger. They'll shoot to kill if you try anything."

I gave Walter Dakko the assignment; it seemed he had become our de facto master-at-arms. I decided to give him the title to match his role, and informed him when he answered my summons.

He seemed unaffected by his new appointment. I wondered how seriously he took any of our Naval traditions, in the privacy of his thoughts.

Shortly after Clinger was installed in the infirmary, and Dakko and Elena Bartel recalled to their medical efforts, Philip conveyed Eddie Boss's request to see me. That brought a smile; Eddie had learned from his previous attempt. "Very well, send him up."

The young sailor came to attention, if not smartly, then passably. "Yes, Mr. Boss?"

"Cap'n, was thinkin' 'bout trannies. Crew trannies."

I waited. After a moment he continued. "Things you showin' me. You 'n boss boy."

"The midshipman, Mr. Tyre, to you."

"Okay, Tyre. Mist' Tyre." He checked for my approval before continuing. "He havin' trouble learnin' trannies. 'Bout jobs, 'n all. Dey don' listen good, 'n he get mad."

"No complaints about your superior officer, Mr. Boss."

"I ain' complainin'," he protested. "Jus' sayin'. I wan' ta help."

"How?"

He shifted uncomfortably. "I know I be dumb, Cap'n. Like learnin' read, know I don' think good. But I c'n try real hard. You an' ol boss bo —Mist' Tyre, if he show Eddie, I c'n teach trannies. Dey lis when I be talkin, not go laughin' like wid boss boy."

I drummed the console. It might work. Certainly the hulking sailor was motivated; he felt responsible for his compatriots. "Well, Mr. Boss, I'll—" I broke off as an idea struck. Could it work? It would solve another problem. But if it failed, I'd make things worse . . .

I thumbed the caller. "Mr. Tyre to the bridge. And Mr. Attani." I took a deep breath. "And Mr. Dakko. Junior."

A few moments later they all stood before me in the at-ease position. Chris Dakko's demeanor hinted of contempt, though with typical adolescent skill he avoided overt behavior for which I could reprimand him. No matter; I hadn't summoned him for a rebuke.

In a severe tone I said to Philip, "Mr. Tyre, how many transpops are on your watch roster for the recyclers?"

The midshipman shot me a surprised glance; we had discussed the matter only yesterday. "None, sir."

"And on the comm room watch?"

"None."

"I told you to train them to stand any watch."

"Yes, sir! I'll work on it immed—"

"Work on it with Mr. Attani. Perhaps he'll succeed where you failed."

Gregor radiated sullen anger at my attack on his mentor.

I turned sharply on Attani. "Cadet, you're now in charge of crew training. Teach the transients what they need to know to stand watch, or I'll make you sorry you were born. You're a cadet; you know what that means?"

"I think so, sir."

"You have no recourse, Mr. Attani. When I turn on you, I can do anything, and I will! So be prepared for months of misery, or get the transients trained now."

"Aye aye, sir."

"You're educated. Take a crewman who's had some schooling to help you teach Mr. Boss; he's got a way with the other transients. Show him what you want the rest of them to know, and he'll help you teach them. But if I catch you or the crewman slacking off . . ."

"Aye aye, sir!"

I said, as if in an afterthought, "Use Mr. Dakko here. He's been to school."

Chris opened his mouth to protest, thought better of it.

"You've something to say, Dakko?"

"No, sir," the boy said quickly.

"I hope not. Mr. Attani, as far as sailors are concerned, you're an officer. You have the right to have your orders obeyed. Mr. Tyre has dithered long enough; now get to work!"

"Aye aye, sir!"

"Dismissed, all of you. Mr. Tyre, you will remain." When the bridge had cleared I gestured to the console next to mine. Philip sat uneasily. I said nothing.

He let the silence continue as long as he could. Finally he said, hesitantly, "I didn't think I was doing that bad a job with the transpops, sir."

"Neither did I." My tone was gruff.

He studied me a long moment. "Then you weren't upset with me?"

"No. Just a show."

The tension drained from his body.

"I wanted to light a fire under Gregor and Chris."

"You did, sir. Did you see Gregor's face when he left?"

"It might solve a lot of problems at once. Gregor's relations with Chris Dakko. Give Gregor a taste of command. Maybe even straighten Chris around."

"Having Chris Dakko teach Eddie . . ." Philip winced. "I don't think either of them will like that."

"Or they might learn how to get along together." I spoke absently; my mind was already on the next problem.

The daily reports on fuel consumption were replaced by hourly, as our propellant dwindled. I was plagued by new doubts about shutting down the thrusters before the tanks ran bone dry. By continuing to increase our velocity we would cut almost four years off our return time.

On the other hand, did it matter? We were seventy-six years from home, at projected speed. Assuming our radio calls weren't intercepted, we'd have to endure a seven-decade voyage. After that long, what difference would forty-seven months make?

On the other hand, what reason was there to hold propellant in reserve? The chances of *Challenger* colliding with any object were minute, even in the distant future when she neared the Solar System.

But if we encountered the . . . fish. The aliens.

Interstellar space was vast, and it obviously didn't swarm with fish. Yet they seemed to be able to find our ships. *Telstar* had been attacked, *Portia*, *Challenger* . . . and other ships were missing.

I paced the bridge in growing frustration, trying to make a decision without enough data. What good would a few hundred gallons of propellant do us? We couldn't Fuse. We had laser armaments, but the crew was uneducated and unskilled in using them. If the fish attacked, our chances were negligible.

Yet . . . several times I was on the verge of recalculating our acceleration, to expend all our propellant now. Each time I withheld my hand. My indecision nagged like a broken tooth.

I kept to myself, meeting Philip or Dray as they relieved me, eating in my cabin or on the bridge. But one afternoon, seeking coffee, I ran into Gregor in the dining hall. He sported an unmistakable black eye. I pretended to ignore it, in the time-honored Naval tradition, but wondered what could have angered Philip so.

My head ached abominably; I was overtired, and brooding on Gregor's problems with Philip made me more uneasy yet. This was no time for niceties; I called Tyre to the bridge.

"It wasn't me, sir. Gregor and I get along fine."

"Well, then?"

"Have you noticed Chris Dakko lately?"

I hadn't. "An officer brawling with a crewman?" I cursed under my breath.

"Dakko was asking for trouble."

"Gregor knows the rules," I snapped. "He can't strike a crewman to enforce discipline." My head throbbed. Lord God, didn't the lad have any common sense? How then could he enforce his orders with a crewman bigger than he was?

"Yes, sir. I told him that. Perhaps, sir, if you didn't notice it this time . . ."

I didn't need a middy telling me my job. "No," I growled. "He'll learn the Navy way. Take the barrel down to the engine room, I'll be damned if I'll do it myself. Send the cadet to Dray." After a caning, he'd be more careful.

Philip said slowly, "Are you sure, sir? He's almost nineteen. I doubt he's ever been struck before."

My hand gripped the chair arm. I said coldly, "Consider yourself reprimanded, Midshipman Tyre."

Philip stared at me in shock. Then, stiffly, "Yes, sir."

"Leave the bridge."

"Aye aye, sir." He saluted, turned, and went.

I stood the watch, alone with my rage, on the verge of countermanding my orders, but watching the clock, delaying. I took a grim satisfaction in my stubbornness. Only when it was too late did I let myself recall Gregor, on the bridge, on the mattress near mine, pleased despite himself that I thought enough of him to make him an officer.

When I saw Philip the next morning I'd recovered enough aplomb to remark, "I won't put your reprimand in the Log."

"Very well, sir." He sounded indifferent.

"Just don't argue with me again."

"Aye aye, sir." He stared glumly at the simulscreen.

My irritation flared anew. "Is that all you have to say?"

He spun to face me. "What do you want me to say?" he shouted. "Just tell me, I'll say it!"

Stunned, I could only stare.

"You told me I was free to knock at your hatch, and you tore into me when I did. In your cabin you said you respect me, you even shook hands as if we were friends. Then you chewed me out in front of Gregor and Dray like I was a rank cadet!"

He hurled his ribbed cap at the chair. "Then you told me you weren't serious about chewing me out, except yesterday you reprimanded me, but now you tell me it won't go on the Log! How would I know what to say to you? Nothing makes sense!" Enraged, he met my glare.

A long time passed. Finally his eyes dropped; his face grew pink; at last he said in a small voice, "I'm very sorry, sir. Please forgive what I said."

My eyes bored into him. He fidgeted, blushed a deeper red, said humbly, "What would you like me to do, sir?"

Still I didn't speak.

Desperate, he blurted, "Should I go to my quarters, sir? Until you're ready to deal with me?"

"No. Stay." I could imagine how he thought I might deal with him. Summary dismissal from the Service. Confinement in the brig. At the least, the worst caning of his life. Any middy could expect similar consequences after such an outburst to his Captain, regardless of the provocation.

The trouble was that Philip was right. I stared blindly past the glittering lights of my console. When I'd been a midshipman on *Hibernia*, Captain Haag was remote, austere. Coming into his presence I felt a very young middy indeed, anxious not to call his notice to myself by some foolish lapse.

But *Hibernia* was a fully manned ship, where three lieutenants served between me and the Captain. My contacts were primarily with the lieutenants, and even they were objects of fear and respect. Captain Haag's confidants were his lieutenants or his friend the Chief Engineer, not a lowly middy.

On *Challenger* there were only Philip, Dray, and myself. Lonely, insecure, frightened, I'd come to rely too heavily on Philip Tyre, and then rebuffed the midshipman every time he responded to my demand for familiarity.

So now Philip had made a critical blunder, pushed over the edge by my contradictory demands. I'd whipsawed him until he lost control, and to punish him for it seemed morally wrong.

But not to punish him would confuse him all the more. How could I expect him to maintain the proper distance if I failed to react to even a gross violation of propriety?

"Well, now." Cooly I studied the offending middy. "What am I to do with you?"

He mumbled, "I don't know, sir."

"Neither do I. Eight demerits, for a start. Work them off within the week. And I withdraw my promise to you; if you exceed ten demerits you will be caned, like any other midshipman in any other ship."

"Yes, sir!"

"I'm sorry I confused you. We are the only officers aboard, except for Dray, so you may feel free to knock at my hatch. I may lash out at you, but that is my prerogative. Knock anyway."

A sheen of sweat dampened his forehead; he dared make no move to wipe it.

"Philip, I respect you, as I said before. Nonetheless, I am Captain and you are a midshipman, and you'll speak to me with courtesy. You

will contain any further outbursts until you can deliver them to the
bulkhead in the privacy of your wardroom. Is that quite clear?"

Philip nodded vigorously. "Very clear, sir."

"You're confined to the wardroom for the rest of the day. Reflect, if
you will, on how lenient I've been. But I wonder if something else is
bothering you, that caused you to lose control."

"No, sir, nothing. I—I didn't get much sleep last night, but that's no
excuse."

"Why didn't you sleep?"

He colored. "Gregor, sir. He—I, uh, had a long talk with him."

"He was upset?"

Philip bit his lip before he answered frankly. "A closer word would
be hysterical, sir. It took a while before I could get him to listen."

"And now?"

"I don't know. I think he'll be all right."

"Very well." It wasn't the time to explore that situation. "Dismissed." He fled the bridge.

45

Seaman Elron Clinger hovered near death, his skull fractured. I ordered his hands tied to the sides of his bed, and sent Elena Bartel about her duties with orders to check on him from time to time. I couldn't afford to spare a full-time nurse, and in his case I hadn't the inclination.

At my bidding Kerren conducted simulated laser drills at frequent intervals, for the crewmen training in the comm room. Deke, Eddie Boss, and Walter Dakko were among those chosen for training.

Mr. Tzee paced behind the consoles as the drills progressed, correcting the targeting on the trainees' screens. Deke showed no interest whatsoever until Walter Dakko leaned over and quietly explained that hitting imaginary targets with the imaginary laser was just like scoring points in Arcvid. I tried to imagine Walter Dakko pumping Unibucks into an Arcvid console. Perhaps he'd been out with Chris . . .

"Lord God, today is September 18, 2198, on the U.N.S. *Challenger*. We ask you to bless us, to bless our voyage, and to bring health and well-being to all aboard."

I waited for the murmured "Amen" of the assembled passengers and crew. I'd led the traditional evening prayer countless times, yet even now it brought a lump to my throat.

"Tonight I have an announcement," I said soberly. "In some three hours I shall cut the acceleration of our thrusters. We will have achieved the maximum speed we shall ever attain, and our course hereafter will be in the hands of Lord God."

"Are we out of fuel?" Old Mrs. Ovaugh, her fear evident.

"We have some reserves with which to maneuver, Mrs. Ovaugh, in case it's necessary. Other than that, we have spent all our propellant."

"Could we increase our speed using it all?" It was the first time I'd heard Mr. Pierce speak.

"Yes. Every moment of acceleration increases our speed. But then we'd be entirely helpless to maneuver."

Someone said, "But we'd be going home faster."

I hadn't meant to initiate a policy review. "We began broadcasting our position over a month ago, and we've dropped radio beacons along our route. Our transmissions will reach Earth decades before we do."

Chris Dakko cautiously raised his hand. I nodded. "If the messages don't get through," he asked, "wouldn't the extra speed make a difference?"

I sighed, knowing I should have managed to avoid this discussion. "We might cut our travel time from seventy-six years to seventy-two with the remaining propellant," I said. "But I won't leave the ship entirely disabled. That," I said over rising murmurs of protest, "is already decided."

Elena Bartel raised her hand. I was grateful the crew knew better than to speak up without permission. "Sir, what good are our fuel reserves? What could we maneuver away from, without being able to Fuse?"

"Would you care to impact with an asteroid at one-quarter lightspeed?" That silenced them for the moment. "The discussion is over," I said firmly. "Mr. Tyre, Mr. Attani, report to the bridge an hour after the meal." I sat.

Still the angry murmurs persisted. I tried to ignore them. As the stewards began to serve the meal Mr. Tzee approached my table with diffidence. "Sir, would you consider—"

I slammed the table so the silverware jumped, as did the two elderly passengers at my side. "I will not!" I roared. "Back to your place!" My outburst silenced the hall, and it was minutes before conversation began anew.

Our dinner consisted mostly of our dwindling stores; it would be many weeks before our laborious efforts at hydroponics resulted in edible crops. Daily, I'd watched crewmen haul water and adjust the lighting in the plant chambers, and I'd set an example by helping.

Cautious buds had poked their heads above the sand and had begun to thrive. They shot upward with encouraging speed, tended by men whose very survival depended on their success. Embryonic tomatoes, cucumbers, and beans were visible if one looked closely.

I'd calculated, with Emmett Branstead's assistance, that our new crops would be ready for harvest just as our food stores dwindled to near nothing. For a time we would be on very short rations indeed, but we continued to expand our hydroponics efforts, so the food supply would gradually increase.

No one at my table spoke to me, perhaps not willing to risk another tirade. When the meal was ended, I hurried back to the bridge to relieve

Dray. His salute was short of contemptuous, but not by much. He left without a word.

The readouts flashed on the console screen. Our thrusters had performed magnificently, never overheating. Still, I would be glad to power down.

Irritated at Dray's manner, I called up the day's laser firing drills while waiting for my officers. Two shifts of sailors had practiced today. Naturally, more than one work detail was trained for each of our critical tasks, in case crewmen were put out of action. I followed the book in that regard, though I saw little point in it. If comm room personnel were knocked out, for example, the ship was almost certainly lost. The aliens would inject their viruses, hurl the acid that ate through our hull.

Walter Dakko, Ms. Bartel, and Deke continually improved their scores, as expected. The other group—young Jonie, Mr. Kovaks, and a transpop called Ratchet—wasn't doing as well. I made note to have Mr. Tzee spend extra time with them, then remembered I'd just screamed at Mr. Tzee in front of the ship's company. Heaven knew what cooperation I would get from him henceforth.

A knock; I opened the hatch without looking to see who it was. Philip saluted stiffly. "Midshipman Tyre reporting, sir. Permission to—"

"Come in." I went back to my console. I'd noticed in the Log that Philip was slowly working off his demerits, dutifully logging each session in the exercise room. Since our confrontation four days earlier, he had retreated into stiff formality, but without sullenness. I matched his manner. "Would you care to sit, Mr. Tyre?"

"Thank you, sir." He took his place at his console, proper as a green young middy on his first watch. I wondered what I might say to relax him, then beat a hasty retreat. I had caused Philip enough problems.

A few minutes later another knock. "Let him in, Philip."

"Aye aye, sir." He jumped as if shot.

Gregor Attani came to attention in the corridor just outside the bridge. His salute was perfect, as if practiced for hours before a mirror. Perhaps it had been. "Permission to enter the bridge, sir."

"Granted."

"Thank you." The cadet's voice was icy, the words ejected as if through unwilling teeth.

"Stand here, Mr. Attani. Behind the console."

"Aye aye, sir."

I suppressed my annoyance at the frigid response. "I called you to the bridge to witness powering down the thrusters. Should our journey run its course, this will be remembered as the moment that changed

Challenger from a powered ship to a missile. I thought you would like to be present." I took the caller. "Engine room, prepare for power-down."

Dray's response was immediate. "Power-down, aye aye." Knowing what was to come, the Chief must have been standing by the caller.

My hand hovered over the knob. I breathed deeply, slowly eased it upward along its track. I imagined I could hear the rumbling cease, though that was nonsense. From the bridge the vibration of the thrusters was imperceptible.

It was done. We hurtled through nothingness at some seventy-one thousand statute miles per second, and would continue for over seventy years. Our choice was made, and we had to live out the consequences. Unless our transmissions were received at home, I would emerge from *Challenger* as a doddering old man, if at all. A mere two generations would pass before our rescue.

"Lord God preserve us," I said, chastened.

"Amen." Philip seemed affected as well.

The moment passed. In a lighter tone I said, "Well, back to everyday problems. Mr. Tyre, have you reorganized the recycler's watch yet?"

"Yes, sir."

"And have you begun teaching the cadet navigation?" I nodded at Gregor.

"Yes, sir, just yesterday. Chapter one of *Lambert and Greeley.*" We'd all started with *The Elements of Astronavigation,* believing *L & G* impossible to master, learning with dismay that it was just the forerunner of more daunting texts.

"Very well." Instructing cadets and middies was the job of a senior lieutenant, but Philip was competent in navigation and our only available teacher.

I groped for some genial remark to offer Gregor, then decided he was letting his resentment show too clearly. Perhaps I'd overreacted in having him caned. Still, he ought to have the sense not to show his feelings. I was, after all, Captain.

"That's all."

"Thank you for having us, sir." Philip's tone was polite, his manner exemplary. He turned for the hatch. Gregor said nothing. His salute was perfunctory.

Beans and other vegetables had been planted, the new crew broken in, the rebellion crushed, the ship set under weigh for home. Our most pressing tasks accomplished, we settled into a dull shipboard routine.

Now we faced the demands of a daily struggle to survive: the drudgery of hauling water to the cabins in which our precious plants grew, tiring hours of laser practice by our new crewmen, the constant toil of laundry, food preparation, maintenance, and repairs.

Seaman Clinger lay in a coma for days. I assumed he would die; we could perform routine first aid but not brain surgery. To my surprise, he rallied. Elena Bartel, far too solicitous for my liking, tended his needs. As he became more alert he bitterly protested the straps that bound him.

Whenever the bridge was in other hands I roamed the ship, visiting the recycler chambers, the comm room, even the engine room, where Dray received me with scant courtesy. In the corridors the crewmen came to attention as I passed, the newer recruits imitiating the ways of their experienced compatriots.

I was on my way to the galley when Walter Dakko made a curious gesture before coming to attention; his hand flicking out as if to stop me. Though he held attention, he didn't stand eyes front, but fastened his gaze on mine as if with urgency.

"What, Mr. Dakko?" I yearned for my waiting coffee.

"Might I make a suggestion, sir?"

Well, he hadn't approached me unbidden. Not quite. "Go on."

"The tomatoes are coming on strong. And some of the beans will be ready soon."

"So?"

"You've sealed the hydro chambers, haven't you? Only authorized crew can enter."

"Obviously. I don't have time for idle conver—"

"What about the cabins, sir? They're wide open."

I stopped short. Good heavens. Though our ripest vegetables had been started earlier in the hydro chambers, the majority of our crops were coming along in the cabins. "They're not ripe yet," I said.

"No, sir. But green tomatoes are edible. They might be very attractive to a man short on rations."

If a sailor was caught stealing food I'd have to deal with a riot, if not a lynching. A total breakdown of authority could follow. How could I have overlooked the obvious? I cursed under my breath. Daily I walked the ship, failing to see my duty.

"As you were, Mr. Dakko." As he relaxed I said, "This will earn you a promotion." His look was unfathomable. I realized how little that meant to an aristrocrat who'd volunteered to save Rome from the barbarian hordes. "And my thanks," I added lamely.

That brought a faint smile. "You're welcome, sir."

"You're in charge of the food security detail. Requisition any supplies you need from Dray."

"Aye aye, sir." We parted.

I sat at a table with my steaming cup of coffee. Mr. Bree tried to ignore me as he puttered about the dining hall, but his nerves were frayed. In an effort to improve morale I'd asked him to make our meals as attractive as possible and to resume the custom of starched tablecloths at dinner. The crewmen who'd once been passengers saw nothing unusual in this, but I could imagine what our old hands thought, used to dinner in the utilitarian crew mess.

Bree and Chris Dakko, who'd become his assistant, were setting tables. Chris glanced at me, turned away, stone-faced. I took a tentative sip. "How are your lessons going, Mr. Dakko?"

"With the trannies?" Chris bridled at my obvious distaste. "They call themselves trannies," he said belligerently. "Why shouldn't I?"

"Because you're not one of them."

"At least I can be grateful for that!" He dumped a handful of silverware onto the table. "*Sir.*" His tone belied the courtesy of the word.

I held my peace. Little would be gained were I to humiliate him. We had a long journey together. Perhaps, in time, he would come round. I took my coffee to the bridge.

When Philip settled in for his watch I went to my cabin, sat in my easy chair, one arm on the polished conference table, and tried to think of nothing. Disturbing thoughts intruded. I explored them, and realized to my surprise that I was frightened. Not of dying, as that immediate prospect had faded, but of seventy-six years imprisonment on this disabled ship, surrounded by well-deserved resentment, hostility, and contempt.

I'd made enemies with careless abandon and saw no way to extricate myself. I'd humiliated Gregor, made a nightmare of Chris Dakko's life, terrorized the Chief. I'd even been offensive to old Mrs. Reeves. Philip was the only one who stood by me, and that only from a sense of duty.

I sat miserable and alone until the dinner hour. Then I straightened my jacket and went to my duty.

In the morning I reviewed entries in the Log,. Dray, I saw, had put young Deke on report. I called the engine room. "Why is Deke up for Mast?"

"Insubordination, as I wrote." That told me nothing.

"Why, Dray?"

A pause. "I'd rather come up to discuss it."

"Very well." A few moments later he arrived, breathing heavily from the two flights up the ladder. "Well?"

"He used insubordinate language to describe an officer," Dray said.

I waited for him to continue, realized he wouldn't. This burly, stolid man was embarrassed, unsure. "What did he call you?" I asked gently.

The Chief stared at me without expression. "Not me, Captain. You."

I bit back my surprise, but persisted. "Must I drag it out of you, Dray?"

"Scarface," he said. I couldn't help but flinch. "It's a name they have for you now, Captain. I wouldn't have that."

I fingered the ugly ruin of my cheek. "It's true."

"Still, he's a sailor." Dray's tone was uncompromising. I was intrigued by the divided loyalty of this complicated man, who could treat me with unconcealed insolence, yet send a man to Captain's Mast for doing the same.

I said hesitantly, "Dray, a lot has happened between us . . ."

"Yes." His tone was unbending.

"I would not do again what I chose to do to you. If there's any way it could be put behind us . . ."

"There is not." He spoke with finality.

"Very well. I'll deal with Deke without getting into specifics. You may go."

"Right." Without bothering to salute he turned and left.

Depressed, I waited out my watch. Toward the end of it, Ms. Bartel paged to tell me Seaman Clinger was begging to see me.

"Why?"

"I don't know, sir. He's rational now. We've been talking a lot. He keeps asking for you."

The last thing I wanted was to visit Clinger. "Very well. When Mr. Tyre relieves me." Some duties it was best to get over with. After my watch I went directly to the infirmary, sent away Ms. Bartel.

His head was still heavily bandaged, both hands taped securely to the bed rails. Near one wrist was a buzzer by which he could summon Ms. Bartel; she carried a caller that responded to it.

"Hullo, Captain."

My anger kindled. That was no way to speak to me. On the other hand, he couldn't very well salute. "What did you want?"

His tone was plaintive. "Do you think maybe you could untie one hand, just while we talk? Please, sir?" I shook my head; he added quickly, "I won't try anything. I'm still too dizzy to move much."

"All right." I unwrapped the tape from his right hand.

The moment it was free he scratched the side of his nose. "You know how hard it is not to be able to do that?" A weak smile.

I only grunted in response.

He said slowly, "Captain, I've fouled up good, I know that."

"Right."

"What could I do to earn another chance?"

"Are you kidding?"

"No, sir." He wiggled his toes under the sheets. "Andy was pumpin' me full of all sorts of ideas. When you brigged him, I got a little crazy."

"You mutinied."

He stared at his feet. "Yes. I did that."

"That's all there is to be said."

He spoke as if he hadn't heard me. "You know it was me got into the hold to get the food?"

"I presumed so. I didn't see your face."

"I'm from Liverpool, Cap'n. What about you?"

The question was bizarre. Despite myself, I answered, "Cardiff."

"Well, then." He spoke as if he'd proven a point. "You see, I got so bleedin' scared!" He turned his face away. "I dunno why I signed up on this frazzin' cruise. The bonus, I guess. I spent it all before I reported. We had some good times, me an' the other joes."

He took a couple of deep breaths, spoke more slowly. "But I never figured on this. Bein' abandoned, like. I'm twenty-four, you know. Just twenty-four. I wanted so damn much to live!" He drew in a breath that was a sob.

"Easy, Mr. Clinger."

"That bastard Tremaine took all our food, as much as he could carry. They say it was Hasselbrad stopped him from gettin' the rest. So I knew we was goin' to starve, no matter what."

I said nothing.

"So we broke inna hold, me and Ibarez and Simmons. Just ta get some food. When I was a kid I saw a man once, starved to death after he been trapped in a chimney a week or two. All I could think of was lookin' like that."

"Nothing excuses mutiny, Mr. Clinger."

"An' when Ibarez got killed, I didn't know what ta do, I thought about it a few days, and got Andy out. 'Cause he'd tell me what to do."

I waited.

His tone held wonder. "It just kinda happened. I dunno why I listened to him. He said, get the guns while we got a chance, so I helped. And Simmons got hisself killed. So you got hold of the armory, and we was done for. So Andy said, take the engine room. It all seemed to make sense, the way he put it."

Exasperated, I snapped, "And now it doesn't? What do you want from me, Clinger?"

"I'm not wicked!" he shouted. His free hand pounded the bed, and he winced as it shook. "I'm dumb, God damn it, but no worse!" He took a shuddering breath. "Don't send me back to him. Please, Captain. Give me any kinda detail, I'll scrub the heads, I'll go on half rations, I'll do whatever you say. Let me make it right!"

"No." I took the roll of tape and grabbed his wrist. He resisted a moment, then was still. I taped him securely to the bed as quickly as I could.

"Please!"

"No." I walked out.

I went directly to my cabin. I examined my burns in the mirror. Scarface. Scarface Seafort. For an impossible moment I imagined Amanda's soft hand on my shoulder. "It doesn't matter, Nick. I'm here."

But you aren't, Amanda. You never will be again.

"I loved you."

I swallowed. She had. But she was gone, and a retreat into fantasy wouldn't help. I lay on my bed, face pressed into the pillow. I tried not to cry, and failed.

That evening at dinner I was subdued, hoping no one would notice my reddened eyes. In any event, no one remarked on them.

That night I slept as if drugged, and roused myself with reluctance come morning. The day passed, followed by a dreary succession of others. Philip warned me one day of growing discontent.

"Mr. Dakko, sir. Senior. He passed me the word there's a lot of grumbling in the crew berth."

"What about?" I demanded. The bridge lights seemed unbearably bright.

"Trying to get home faster. There's talk again about repairing the fusion drive."

"That's nonsense!"

"I know, sir." The middy hesitated. "They feel so, well, helpless. A long cruise is hard enough when you know it'll end in a few months."

"Yes." And beyond the problem of morale lay another I dreaded to confront. How long would ship's discipline last once it became evident we wouldn't be rescued?

As Captain, I was a symbol of the U.N. Government. Once the crew and passengers realized we'd never again be subject to that Government, what would they do? Revolt? Demand free elections? I wasn't even certain I should oppose them.

I forced my mind back to the issue at hand. "The drive is irreparable, surely they know that. I'll run some more drills, to divert them."

"Aye aye, sir." Philip looked doubtful.

I glanced at my young midshipman and was overcome by gratitude for his loyalty. Though he might make mistakes, he strove unremittingly to please me, to carry out his duties. "Mr. Tyre . . ."

"Yes, sir?"

"Thank you for your efforts. Without you I'd—" I broke off. What was I doing? I cleared my throat. "Very good, Mr. Tyre," I said gruffly. "Keep your eye on the situation."

"Aye aye, sir." He was carefully formal.

"That's all, then." As the hatch closed behind him I beat my knee with my fist. How could I be so stupid? Could I expect Philip to maintain the right distance if I kept varying it? I would keep my feelings to myself. Damn it, I had to.

For the next three days I ran Battle Stations, General Quarters, and boarding drills at unexpected intervals. I succeeded in making the crew as irritable and jumpy as I; what effect it had on the scuttlebutt about repairing the drive, I had no idea.

Eventually I decided to take the bull by the horns, and so, in the late evening hours when most of the crew were off duty, I went to crew berth one. As I entered Seaman Kovaks roared, "Stand to!" and jumped to attention. Sailors in various states of undress formed lines in front of their bunks.

"As you were." I faced the ragged line. "I've heard," I said bluntly, "some foolishness about fixing the fusion drive. Who's spreading that goofjuice?"

No one spoke.

"Well?"

Elena Bartel said quietly, "Sir, why can't the drive be repaired?"

I scowled. "It's you?"

"No, sir." One hand went to her hip. "But there's been talk. Maybe if we heard the truth . . ."

"The drive is wrecked. When the aliens attacked, their acid melted through the shaft wall. You can see it through the transplex from the engine room."

"Everyone knows that," she said sharply. A sailor grinned; his smile vanished at my glare. "The issue, sir, is whether they can be repaired."

"The drive generates N-waves. You know that much, don't you? The N-waves are shaped as energy is fed down the shaft. The shape of the shaft wall determines the wavelength." I paused, trying to marshal my thoughts. "Now, it takes a shipyard months of trials to get the tolerances just right. If the curve of the wall is not perfect to the nearest millimeter, the energy isn't properly focused. Do you know what that means?"

I paced, waiting for an answer, but none came. "An unfocused beam could melt the shaft wall. And if not, there's still no way to aim the beam. We might Fuse, but to where? We could find ourselves heading out of the galaxy!"

"That's not what Sykes said," a deckhand muttered.

I rounded on him. "How much does Sykes know? Does he have his engineer's ticket?"

"I heard him talkin'," the man said stubbornly. "Before you locked him up. We could make new plates, weld 'em on—"

I shouted, "You can't weld steel plates to an alloy shaft wall! Don't you understand?"

A few faces retained a stubborn look I knew was irremovable. They would believe what they needed to believe; that somehow there was a way to sail home. "I'll have the Chief explain it again," I said, defeated. "Maybe you'll take his word for it."

The next morning I sent Dray to talk to them; he came away shaking his head. "Most of them are convinced," he reported. "That Walter Dakko, and the Bartel woman. Drucker and Tzee. But some of the others . . ." He descended to his engine room, still grumbling.

Everywhere I went I felt eyes, wondering and calculating. Nothing was said, but the doubts were evident, the yearning obvious. I'd put down rebellion once; I wondered when it would rise again. I fingered a stack of laser pistol recharge packs, still piled in a corner of the bridge. Would Dray stand with me this time? He stood watch, one shift out of three, on the bridge, where all our weapons were piled. Where he could seal the hatch, bar me from command . . .

I thrust aside my uneasiness. He would do what he would do. I had no choice but to trust him; I couldn't spend years sealed on the bridge in suspicion and terror.

Philip broke up a scuffle between Eddie Boss and Chris; they appeared at Captain's Mast while the new master-at-arms, Walter Dakko, stood by. Deke was on report as well; I dealt with him first.

"The Chief says you were insubordinate." I glowered at the young transient.

Deke shuffled his feet. "Dunno what it mean."

"Sir!" Philip Tyre roared. "You address the Captain as 'sir'!"

"Sir," the boy mumbled.

"It means refusing to obey orders or being disrespectful to lawful authority."

"He din' groo you' joename."

"What?"

Eddie raised his hand cautiously. I nodded.

"Deke say'n, Chief din' like joename dey givin' you, Cap'n."

"Good God." Joename. Groo. Melissa Chong, come back to interpret for your young charges. I cut off that line of thought, too late. "Sailor, on every ship I've ever known, the Captain has a nickname. Usually not a fond one. What sailors call the Captain in private conversation is their own affair. The trick is not to use the, ah, joename in front of an officer."

I made a note in the Log. "Ten days punishment detail. Mr. Tyre, see to it."

"Aye aye, sir." Deke would be given extra chores, the less pleasant ones. He'd suffer no worse, nor should he.

"Mr. Boss is next, sir."

"I'll take him and Mr. Dakko Junior together. Come forward. Brawling, were you?"

Chris gave his messmate a look of pure hatred. "No, sir, Captain. The gorilla boy was shoving me around. I just defended myself."

My hand tightened on the console. What was the matter with young Dakko? He'd get nowhere by alienating me. His father's expression was noncommittal.

"I ain' shovin' no—"

I thundered, "Speak when you're spoken to!" Eddie recoiled. I swung to Chris. "You have one more chance to tell me your side."

"I was teaching the trann—the crewmen how to read gauges," Chris said hurriedly. "Jokko and Shay. They were laughing and pretending not to understand. I yelled at them. Then Eddie here came up and spun me around and started shouting I should teach him first, like you said. But he wasn't even in the room when I started, so how could I?" He paused for breath. "I was trying to get my arm loose, when the middy, I'm sorry, I mean Mr. Tyre, came around."

"Well, Mr. Boss?"

"Uppie yellin' at my fren," grumbled Eddie. "He don' know difference teachin' an' shoutin'. Not like you, Cap'n. Why doncha tellim," he appealed. "Like when you teach ol' Eddie read. You din' shout, get me more mixed up. Uppie boy, he jus' show off, thinkin' he's smarter."

"So you grabbed him?"

"A little, maybe. Din' hurt him."

"Very well." I made my note and snapped off the Log. "Ten days in the brig, both of you." Philip gaped. A stiff punishment for a minor scuffle, one that would have ended harmlessly and gone unnoticed if Philip hadn't been present to see it. I added, "In the same cell," and they blanched. "Master-at-arms, escort them to the brig."

"Aye aye, sir." Walter took his son's arm, steered him to the hatch. "Come along, Mr. Boss."

As they left I heard Eddie mutter, "Help'n run ship, he tol' us. What kinda helpin', dis? Like moppin' flo'?"

The incident didn't help morale. The civilian transpops, even Annie, pretended not to notice me when I passed, or worse, they exhibited outright hostility. The transients among the crew were more circumspect, but I sensed their anger as well.

On the other hand, Emmett Branstead, doing work he understood and liked, was affable and eager for my visits.

Not so Mr. Tzee; he seemed to retreat inward when I arrived, as if expecting criticism I never offered. Perhaps he took the failings of his trainees personally.

One night, as the ship lay quiet, I got up from my bed and padded to the bridge. I entered the code, let myself in. Dray, wide awake, glanced at me in surprise. "As you were," I said, though he'd made no move to stand.

I keyed the alarms. "Battle Stations! All hands to Battle Stations! This is no drill!" Sirens wailed and bells clanged throughout the ship.

"Jesus!" The Chief leapt to his feet. "What? Where?"

"Sit down, Dray, you're on watch. Kerren, record response times from all stations."

"No drill," he rasped, outraged. "No drill?"

"Why should response times differ between a drill and the real thing? We'll check."

Crewmen I'd routed from bed raced through *Challenger* to their stations, shutting airtight hatches behind them as they arrived. Philip Tyre dashed onto the bridge, clothing disheveled. Gregor Attani tagged behind; the cadet had no assigned duty station and followed his mentor.

One by one our stations reported. The comm room was first; Deke's excited voice in the engine room came last. "Chief ain' here, sir. Jus' me an' Ollie."

"Hold the bridge, Chief." I strode down the corridor to the comm room. "This is the Captain. Let me in." The hatch slid open. I walked past the row of consoles. Walter Dakko, Elena Bartel, and Jonie sat ready, eyes forward, hands at their firing controls. Ms. Bartel's clothes were awry. Neither she nor I paid any heed.

"Very well." I went next to the engine room.

An hour passed before I returned to the bridge. Philip, sleepy, shook himself awake as I entered.

"Go back to bed, both of you." I noted the results of the exercise in the Log, had the crew stand down, and went to my cabin, where I tossed and turned much of the night.

The next morning, short of sleep, I was sipping much-needed coffee when Philip brought Gregor to the bridge for a nav drill. Tyre seemed irritable, and the cadet was stiff and distant, as he'd been ever since I had him sent to Dray.

I thought to lessen the tension before the boy started his practice. "How go your lessons with the streeters, Mr. Attani?"

He said cooly, "As well as can be expected, *SIR.*"

"What does that mean?"

The young man's aristocratic features betrayed his distaste. "They learn as fast as trannies can learn." Unwisely, he added, "I'll keep at it until you find something better for me to do, sir." It was staggering insolence.

I raised an eyebrow. "Do you have an attitude problem, Cadet?"

He said bitterly, "Not anymore, sir. Chief Kasavopolous saw to that."

My tone was even. "I think you do, Mr. Attani." I understood his resentment, but he was foolish to show it. If the boy pulled in his horns immediately, I would let it pass.

Sullen, he stared past me. "Then you must be right, sir." His contempt was no longer concealed.

Philip snarled, "Behave, Cadet!" Gregor was, after all, his responsibility.

As my glance strayed to the darkened screen, my gorge rose. Unless we were rescued, we might pass seventy years on this near-derelict vessel. Years with arrogant, half-trained, impudent children. With Dray's contempt, Chris Dakko's sullen insolence. With Eddie Boss and Elron Clinger. I slapped the console. "Mr. Attani, report to the Chief Engineer. Tell him he is to cane you for insolence."

Gregor looked at me, his gaze traveling with disdain from head to foot. He said distinctly, "You bastard!"

"Mr. Tyre." I barely got out the words. "Take the cadet to the engine room. See that he's given a lesson sufficient to guarantee good manners for the rest of the cruise. If Dray isn't adequate to the task, finish it yourself."

"Aye aye, sir." Philip, white-faced, spun toward the cadet. "Move!" He propelled Gregor toward the hatch. The boy scrambled to keep on his feet. The last I heard as the hatch slid shut was, "You fool!"

Left seething alone on the bridge, I called up the results of our most recent laser drill. I read the numbers several times before I gave up, snapped off the Log, and threw the holovid on the console.

"Is something wrong, sir?"

"No conversation, Kerren." I flung myself out of my seat and began to pace. The nerve of young Gregor. Aristocrat he may have been, but now he was a Naval officer in training. At this very moment he'd be learning his manners the hard way. He would give me no further trouble, I was sure. I'd seen Philip's outrage as he shoved Gregor into the corridor.

Well, so be it. Attani had made his bed; let him lie in it. Muttering, I paced until my adrenaline dissipated. Finally I resumed my seat. I took up the holovid, examined the drill again. The response times were faster than our previous drills, but not by much. I made notes where more practice was needed.

After a time Philip Tyre knocked. He came to attention. "The cadet has been disciplined, sir." His tone was somber.

"It's traditional," I said icily, "for him to report the fact himself."

"Yes, sir. I thought it best to take him back to the wardroom." Philip was pale.

"That bad?"

"I—it's no more than he deserved. I know that."

"I'm glad you do."

"Yes, sir." His manner was humble. "I should have had him under control. It's my fault."

"That's right." I recalled my own days as senior midshipman. Whatever trouble the middies in my wardroom had given me—and that was plenty—none would have dared abuse his Captain. Had there been question of that, I would have settled it, and fast.

"Dismissed, Mr. Tyre." I let my voice remain cold.

I busied myself conducting readiness drills for the engine room; it would do no good for Mr. Tzee's comm room crew to be standing by at their laser controls if the engine room didn't have firing power on-line.

With practice, I managed to cut the response time by almost two minutes, even with the Chief off duty, as he would be if he was standing watch on the bridge.

It was two days before I encountered Gregor Attani. Philip, called to the conn so I could go below to watch an engine room drill, brought the cadet along. Gregor's creases were immaculate, his hair carefully combed. He walked with great concentration, pain in his features.

I felt pity. Still, he'd called his Captain a bastard. I asked coldly, "Do you still have an attitude problem, Mr. Attani?"

An ember of pride flickered among the ashes of his misery. "I didn't think I had one, so I wouldn't know."

I couldn't fault his pluck, but courage was not at stake. "My compliments to the Chief Engineer, Gregor. And would he please cane you for insolence."

"Again!" The word was wrung out of him.

"Again. And the correct response is, 'Aye aye, sir.'"

Philip blurted, "Might I take him to the wardroom instead, sir? I assure you he'll—"

My voice was ice. "My compliments to the Chief, Mr. Tyre. For yourself as well."

The silence hung between us while Philip grappled with his calamity. "Aye aye, sir," he managed, crimson with shame. "Come along, Cadet."

"But—"

"Come along!" He yanked Gregor's arm. "Now!"

In half an hour they were back. Philip's hands pressed against the side of his pants. "The Chief Engineer's compliments, sir, and he requests that Midshipman Tyre's discipline be entered in the Log." His eyes were riveted to the deck.

"Very well." I made the notation.

Gregor shuffled forward. Only his reddened eyes betrayed that he had been crying. He was subdued, his manner without defiance. "The Chief's compliments, sir," he mumbled. "Would you please enter Cadet Attani's discipline in the Log."

I hated myself for it, but it was necessary to ask. "Do you still have an attitude problem, Mr. Attani?"

The proud young aristocrat's shoulders slumped. "No, sir," he whispered. "Not anymore." He stumbled over the words. "I won't be rude to you again."

"Very well." I made the entry. "Until the next time it's necessary." I stood. "You'll take the conn while I go below, Mr. Tyre. Don't let the cadet touch anything he shouldn't."

"Aye aye, sir." They remained at attention until I left.

On the way to the engine room I realized that I had become the monster every subordinate officer dreaded. Young Dakko in the brig, Clinger set to be returned to his prison, my two officers thrashed into submission. What next? Take off Dray's hand?

Grimly, I hurried on.

46

My brutality to Gregor and Philip quickly made the rounds. By morning no one, civilian or crew, chose to meet my eye or speak to me. I suspected that day's dinner was the last I'd share with my tablemates.

My surmise proved correct. I could have ordered passengers seated with me, of course. But a place at the Captain's table was an honor, not a duty. So it would remain, while I held command.

I took my seat at the empty table, and when all had arrived I stood to give the prayer. For a moment nobody stood with me. Then, reluctantly, they got to their feet for the traditional ritual. After, I signaled the steward. My table was served first, as always. The self-conscious steward progressed across the dining hall bearing his tray with only my portion on it. I appeared not to notice.

Days succeeded each other in monotonous activity. Responding to some inner need rather than any realistic requirement, I brought the ship to the highest state of readiness I could achieve, calling drills at frequent and random intervals. I ordered Philip and Dray to issue the crew demerits for the slightest infractions.

Ill will swirled around my feet as I stalked the corridors, ignoring sullen faces. Above, on the bridge, Philip and Gregor carefully masked their resentment. Our relations were formal, proper, and distant. As they should have been from the start, I realized. The Captain could allow no less.

One day I had Philip and Gregor haul our stock of weapons from the bridge back to the repaired arms locker. It made me uneasy, but if *Challenger* were to function at all like a ship of the line, we couldn't operate in constant fear.

I had a holovid sent to the brig with orders for Chris to spend his time teaching Eddie, and for Eddie to spend his time learning. I acknowledged to myself the failure of that particular experiment, but determined to let it run the course of their brig time.

By the third night after I'd sent Philip and Gregor to Dray I wondered whether I'd fomented a revolution; wherever I turned, hostility was palpable. That night I strode into the dining hall through utter silence and took my place at my empty table. As I filled my water glass old Mrs. Reeves stood, whispered to her husband, hobbled slowly across the room on her cane.

"Might I be allowed to sit with you, Captain?" Blue orbs peered from the wrinkled folds of skin.

"You'd subject yourself to considerable displeasure." I waved at the rest of the hall.

"You should not dine alone." She made as if to sit, looked to me for permission. Recalling my manners I stood to help with her chair. Across the hall Mr. Reeves beckoned a steward and pointed, then shuffled slowly across the deck. He stared myopically in the general direction of my face. "Would like to join you," he rumbled. "With y'r permission."

I indicated a seat. "With pleasure, Mr. Reeves." He said nothing further for the remainder of the meal. As we ate I waited to see what Mrs. Reeves had in mind to tell me, but she made only small talk. Apparently her presence satisfied her purpose, and she bore no message of warning.

Days passed. When Chris Dakko and Eddie Boss were released from their cell, I had Chris brought directly to the bridge. I let him wait a moment at rigid attention. Then, "I've had enough trouble from you, sailor."

"Yes, sir."

"How long were you in the brig?"

"Ten days."

"Next time it'll be a hundred days. You have my oath."

"Yes, sir!"

"The time after will be a thousand days. You'll be twenty-one before you get out. Do you get my message?"

"Yes, sir!" A sheen of sweat gleamed on his forehead.

"Don't even dream of stepping out of line, Dakko."

"No, sir!"

"Very well. Your studies with Mr. Boss?"

He surprised me. "He's beginning to understand the graph curves, sir. Like the firing consoles show. We've been working on those. He's—" He bit it off.

"Go on."

"He's not so bad, when you get past his ways. I mean, he really tries to learn." Chris colored. "I'm sorry. I've given you a very hard time."

"Thank you. You may go below."

So one of my efforts was at last succeeding.

That night when I returned to my cabin I found a puddle outside my hatch. Who was on cleanup duty; Deke? How could he be so sloppy?

I sniffed, realized it was urine. There was a residue on the hatch where it had dried.

I stepped over the puddle into my cabin, slung my jacket over the chair, dropped my cap on the polished table. I'd seen worse insults. At Academy, frustration and rage were sometimes expressed even more strongly. But the calculated affront was also a warning. I was pushing too hard, and respect for my rank had evaporated.

I brooded. We'd only just begun our interminable voyage. Discipline slackened now could never be reconstituted. That was my motive for the drills: to mold the crewmen into a cohesive unit, responsive to discipline. With a sense of duty, we might survive the years without sinking into the folly of anarchy.

I thought of cleaning up the puddle myself, decided to let it be. I need not notice it.

In the head adjoining my cabin I peered into the mirror, fingered my scar. My eyes were sunken in sallow skin. I was bone-tired from too many hours on watch, too many responsibilities. It would be decades before they ended, unless someone took them from me.

With obstinate determination I continued to drive myself and the crew. We turned the last of our sheet metal stock into a few more grow tanks, to extend our precious gardens another two cabins. Twice daily, I conducted laser-firing drills. Philip and Gregor, as exhausted as I, did their best. As days turned into weeks the pace of training remained hectic.

Philip, his mind on a nav drill, spilled coffee on my console. Furious, I issued five demerits. Protective of his chief, Gregor let his disapproval show. I sent him to the barrel. When he returned, humiliated and in pain, I made him review docking maneuvers for hours.

None dared speak to me.

An obscene drawing appeared on my hatch. I had Gregor scrub it off; he did so without protest. Then, for two days, all was ominously quiet. I waited, reminded of the oppressive calm before a Welsh storm.

It was Walter Dakko who approached. Saddened, I let him speak. I'd expected better of him.

He met my eye. "I'm the bearer of a petition."

"Oh." I was almost relieved. "For my removal?"

His look was curious. "No, sir, of course not." I couldn't tell if he meant that no one would sign such a petition, or that he wouldn't carry it. He handed it to me.

Before reading it I asked, "Have you signed?"

"No, sir."

"Then why involve yourself?"

He considered a long time before responding. "Because a lot of people are troubled and because it's very important to them. I don't know how their morale will hold up if you refuse."

I perused the laboriously written document, the scrawled signatures affixed below. "Repair the drive? You know that's impossible."

"I presume so, sir."

"Then what do you want of me?"

"Try to fix the drive, sir."

I studied him for a moment. "Since you're not insane, tell me what you're talking about."

A grim, momentary smile lightened his features. "Have you heard—"

"Come to my cabin and sit down."

"Aye aye, sir."

Before I'd taken two steps I realized I'd made a foolish mistake; I'd worked for weeks to maintain the proper distance from officers and crew, and I'd invited a sailor into my cabin. About to countermand the order, I realized that doing so would be a worse mistake, and so, lips compressed, I said nothing.

Walter Dakko took a seat at the conference table, unawed by his surroundings.

"Go ahead, Mr. Dakko."

"I assume you have the facts right, sir, and that the drive is irreparable. But the situation is unacceptable to the crew."

"Is what?" I asked, unbelieving.

He said hurriedly, "I meant emotionally intolerable. Not everyone is as strong as you, sir. Most of the crew can't accept the notion that there's no way out, and would go glitched if they did. If we had no fusion drive they'd demand that you invent one, or teleport us to Lunapolis. Logic has nothing to do with their reaction."

"And?"

"If you'll excuse my saying so, you can continue acting in a logical fashion, which is your prerogative, or you can recognize their illogical needs."

"Get to the point, Mr. Dakko."

He shook his head. "I've gone about as far as I can, sir. I've read your regs and I have no desire to be hanged."

I grunted. He recognized, at least, the thinness of the ice on which he skated. The right of petition was not uniformly granted. On some ships it was not even to be considered. Presenting an appeal was one thing, but telling me what the crew demanded was quite another. He was quite sensible to stop where he had.

"I order you to tell me your thoughts, Mr. Dakko." If he'd read the regs, he'd know that I'd taken him off the hook. He could be hanged for refusing to obey, but if he spoke he couldn't be touched no matter what he said.

"Aye aye, sir. They need to believe the drive can be fixed. So, you might let them try to fix it. They can't possibly succeed, but it will keep them occupied and give them a goal."

"A false one."

"A necessary one, in my opinion. They need to believe in something."

"And when it doesn't work?"

"Some of them will begin to accept reality, and the others will keep trying. Let them. They can get mad at the drive, if need be. At least it won't be you."

I unfolded the petition. "Ms. Bartel signed this. I'm surprised."

"Yes, sir. I imagine she knows the drive isn't repairable. I think she signed to be one with the crew, sir. For her own reasons."

"Um." I perused the list; nearly everyone in the crew berth had signed. Except . . . "Chris's name isn't here."

"No, sir."

"Why not?"

A wary glance. "Are you ordering me to answer?"

"Yes."

"He wanted to sign. I took him into the head and told him I would beat the living hell out of him if he did, and he believed me."

I said after a moment, "You've changed, Mr. Dakko."

"Yes, sir. Six months ago I was too civilized to threaten him. I was too . . . sane. I was principled."

I smiled. "For all your telling him he was on his own, you still look after him."

"I wasn't sure how you'd react, sir. I'm still not. I don't want him hanged, no matter how unlovable he's become."

"Nobody will be hanged," I said with a long, tired sigh. It seemed I'd played the part of the tyrant all too well. "Tell your messmates their petition has been received, and I'm inclined to grant it. I'll work out the details with Dray. You understand, if they weld new plates over the hole, I'll allow low-power testing, but there's no possible way we'll fire an untuned drive, and the fusion drive will be untunable no matter what they do."

"Yes, sir. I don't intend to pass on your last remark."

I sent him back to the crew berth and remained in my cabin to mull over this latest development. The crew was fortunate to have a spokesman as prudent as Dakko. It occurred to me that he might have engineered his own selection, to present the matter in the least inflammatory manner.

Later, when I told Dray what I had in mind, he emphatically shook his head. "There's no way to repair the drive."

"Nonetheless, there's no harm in their trying. Drag the work out as long as you can. I don't look forward to dealing with their disappointment."

"I'll bet you don't."

I wanted to smash his face, to claw the smugness out of it. I swung my chair to face him. "Listen carefully."

"To another threat?" His tone was sour.

"A statement. If you want an apology for what I did, you may have one. In fact, here it is: I apologize. I regret I pretended to be insane and threatened to burn your fingers off. It was wrong of me to do it. I'm sorry for it."

He contemplated me. "It sounds like you have more to say."

"There is. Drop your contemptuous manner and speak to me with Naval protocol. The first time you don't, I'll toss you in section four with the rest of the mutineers and there you'll stay for the rest of the cruise. I so swear by Lord God's grace. You have until tomorrow to decide. That's all."

He studied my face intently. I met his gaze, expressionless. Grimly, he nodded and left.

Alone, I cursed my lack of self-control. If Dray chose to challenge me, I was bound by my soul to banish him, but I needed him. To whom else could I trust the engine room? Deke?

The enthusiasm with which the crew embraced the repair project astonished me. Virtually everyone asked to be assigned to the project in off-duty time. One of their first tasks was clambering outside the hull in magnetic-soled suits, measuring the hole in the drive shaft. I used it as an opportunity to give Gregor suit training; I bade Philip escort the cadet through the lock to the work area.

It was a long walk down the hull from the aft airlock on Level 2 to the drive shaft, at the very stern of the vessel. For each step Gregor must make and break magnetic contact with the hull, while Philip hovered near in his thrustersuit. I knew hull-walking could be exhausting to the

novice, and was no great fun for the experienced sailor. But if Gregor
misstepped and pushed himself off the hull, Philip would be there to
bring him back. By custom, such a blunder by a cadet or middy was
rewarded with enthusiastic hazing, but Gregor would be spared that.

They came aboard flushed and exhilarated. Gregor's elation didn't
even dampen when I met them in the corridor near the lock, though his
manner became more reserved and much more cautious.

"Well, Mr. Tyre, will the cadet become a spaceman?" I deliberately
spoke to Philip rather than Gregor; I'd already parted with tradition too
often.

"I think he'll manage, sir. If I can give him more practice."

"If it's practice he wants, make him a tool carrier. That should build
up his leg muscles."

Both boys smiled at that. Gregor would be sent the length of the
hull carrying instruments for the working party, perhaps several times
each trip Outside. He'd soon get the hang of hull-walking. I grinned,
recalling my own pleasure at the occasional opportunity to go Outside.
Did all middies feel that way? Certainly all the ones I'd known.

"Very well." I added, "See that he has two hours of nav drill for
every hour he's allowed out."

"Aye aye, sir." Maybe it was the oxygen; their exuberance was undi-
minished by the work I'd assigned. Feeling as decrepit as old Mr.
Reeves I left them to their youthful pleasures.

I summoned Walter Dakko, issued him a stunner, and brought him
to the infirmary. Seaman Clinger was well enough to be discharged. One
look at the master-at-arms told Clinger all he needed to know, yet he
begged piteously for a reprieve.

"No, I won't listen. Mr. Dakko, take him below."

"Please, sir, don't make me go back! Andy and me . . . There's
bad blood now. Twice he's hit me on the head, like to kill me. You put
me back there, I gotta kill him or he kills me for sure, there's no other
way."

"So be it, then."

He groaned. Walter Dakko took his arm. Clinger was too weak to
offer any resistance, and didn't attempt any. I led them down to the
section four hatch. The inside control was disabled so the men couldn't
get out, and the outer control was sealed to my code. "Be ready to open
fire, Mr. Dakko." I entered the code.

Clinger blurted, "Could I at least talk to Elena sometimes, sir? It
wouldn't do no harm, if once in a while . . ."

"Elena? *Elena?*"

"Ms. Bartel, yes, sir. She got to talkin' with me a lot, back up there, and got me to thinkin'. If I can't get out of here . . ." He shuddered and went on quickly. "Could I talk to her once in a while? Please?"

"In!" I roared. He scuttled through the hatch. I slapped it closed.

Within a week I began to notice sailors skimping on their regular duties to make time for the repair project. Because we were so short-handed, the men were already overworked trying to accomplish tasks necessary for our survival. Only by giving up all remaining idle time were they able to tend their project at all.

Now the recycler's mates short-checked the system gauges, rather than bleeding down the pipes to recalibrate the controls as the book required. I put the whole detail on report and banned them from working on the drive for a week. Despite the example I made, slackness increased.

Anxious to begin with, I had to watch helplessly from the bridge for endless hours as novice crewmen set out with more experienced sailors on dangerous hull duty. Their suits were constructed of tough fiber alloy, and the hull had no sharp edges, but some tools had points, oxygen tanks could run low, and there were myriads of ways my sailors could get themselves killed.

Any death would be a calamity, and from a cold-blooded perspective, I had no way to replace a man who died. I hated having to let them go out. I particularly could ill afford to lose any officer.

I gritted my teeth the first time Gregor lost contact with the hull. Every greenie floats at least once in his training; I wish I could forget the time I did it. Philip let him drift helpless a few minutes to learn his essential safety lesson, then I had him bring the cadet inside for the day.

Two days later I was enduring their idle chatter on the suit radios when it happened again.

"Whoops! Oh, damn!"

"Having a problem, Cadet?" Philip, with gentle malice.

"Could you get me down, Mr. Tyre? Please?" I knew the absolute dependence he felt was not pleasant.

"Perhaps later. I was thinking, the wardroom needs cleaning. The bunks taken down and the bulkheads scrubbed." Philip was doing his job: Gregor's carelessness could cost him his life, and a penalty was appropriate. But we didn't have time for hazing.

I keyed the caller. "Just bring him in, Mr. Tyre. Until he learns to be careful."

"Aye aye, sir. Let's go, Gregor. Stick out your arm. Watch it. Now let your heels settle to the deck. That's right. Now a step at a time. Walk, don't dance. You remind me of a girl I knew once. Okay, you're on your own."

A moment later Gregor yelped. "Oh, not again! I'm sorry, Mr. Tyre!"

"Take hold of him!" I roared. "Keep your hands on him until he's in the airlock!" Fuming, I left the bridge unattended and stomped down to the suiting room. Seeing me they immediately stiffened to attention. "Mr. Attani, my compliments to the Chief Engineer, and would he encourage you not to be such a clumsy dolt!"

Gregor swallowed, his look imploring my mercy. He found none. "Aye aye, sir," he murmured.

Philip said hurriedly, "He meant no harm, sir. I didn't make clear how important it—"

"Cadet, out!" As the boy scuttled to the corridor I rounded on Philip. "You're nineteen, Mr. Tyre. Six years you've been in the Service? You know better than to skylark Outside, and you certainly know better than to argue with me. Do you think a midshipman may countermand a Captain's orders?"

"No, sir. I wasn't countermanding—"

"You're arguing. Most nineteen-year-olds aren't caned, as you well know. They know their duty, and their place."

"Yes, sir." Philip was pale.

"Report to the Chief. Tell him I said to put you over the barrel. Remind him this is the second time you've argued with orders and I intend it to be the last time."

"Aye aye, sir!" He dashed to the hatch.

"If you behave no better than a cadet, you'll be treated like one!" A cheap parting shot, at a target who couldn't fight back, but I thrust down any hint of remorse.

A short while later Philip and Gregor, chastened, reported to the bridge. For the first time in the years I'd known him, Philip Tyre seemed sullen. I didn't dare call him on it, for fear of plumbing its depths. If I'd finally broken his irrepressible goodwill, the consequences on my prison ship would be grim indeed.

I had no doubt whatsoever about Gregor's disposition. It was brooding and ominous. He reported civilly enough, saluting properly and requesting his discipline be entered into the Log. But I had the sense that if I pushed him one iota further he would turn on me and lash out, perhaps kill me.

I knew I couldn't allow that. If I were not to fear him from now onward, I had to confront his behavior. "Philip, to your quarters."

"Aye aye, sir." He saluted, wheeled, and marched out, the performance marred only by his stilted gait.

"You have something to say, Mr. Attani?"

"No, sir." Gregor's eyes were fastened on the deck.

"I find your manner unpleasant. Change it."

"What do you want me to do, sir?"

I slapped him. He recoiled in dismay.

"Do you know a cadet's legal status, Mr. Attani?"

"I guess so."

I slapped him harder. His fists clenched, but thank Lord God he didn't raise his hand. Had he done so I'd have been bound to execute him. "A cadet is the legal ward of his Captain. He has no personal rights. He is as a child to a parent. How many times would you like your face slapped, Mr. Attani?"

"Please, sir!"

I shouted, "Answer me!"

"No times! I don't want you to hit me, sir!" His eyes brimmed.

I slapped him again. "Look at your hand, Mr. Attani. It's a fist!"

He stared at his fingers, his eyes widening. Slowly he opened them.

"Please," he whispered. "Let me go down to the crew berth with the others."

"No. You're a cadet. Go to the wardroom."

He blurted, "I'm not a child. It tears me to shreds when you treat me as one!" He took several breaths in an effort to control himself. Then the dam burst; he rushed on, "I went to the engine room like you ordered and lay across that barrel, and Christ, he hurt me! I tried to hold still, I know I'm supposed to, but I couldn't anymore, my rear was on fire and Mr. Tyre had to grab my arms and hold me while I yelled, and please, sir, I don't understand why! By Lord God's grace, let me go back to the crew!"

"No. You're an officer in training and I'll have you behave like one. Do you want to be hit again?"

He spoke so softly I could hardly hear. "No, sir." He slumped in abject defeat.

"Do you want to be sent to the Chief?"

"God, no, sir, please!"

"Behave as I expect, and neither of those things will happen. Go to the wardroom."

Standing helplessly, hands pressed to his sides, he began to cry, choking sobs that racked his body. He made no move to cover his face or wipe the streaming tears.

I dropped heavily into my chair, swung it the other way. I waited a few moments before I said, "You may go to your quarters, Gregor."

It took a moment for his discipline to reassemble itself, but it held. "Aye aye, sir." I didn't turn for his salute. As he left I breathed a heart-felt sigh of relief.

I had broken him. He would do his duty. I had left him nothing else.

I slept that night, but not well. In the morning I forced myself out of bed to face another day. In the head I stepped under the shower, still half asleep, turned on the welcome biting spray of hot water.

A second later I came stumbling out, my squawk echoing from the bulkheads. I rubbed myself vigorously with the towel.

It was the coldest water I'd ever encountered, short of a block of ice.

I let the water run. If anything, it got colder. Cursing a blue streak I wriggled into my pants, flung my jacket over my bare shoulders, charged out into the corridor.

Chris Dakko didn't duck out of my way in time; I bounced off him and resumed course for the ladder. Moments later I was down to Level 3, heading for the engine room.

"Jeez, it's the Captain!" Blurred figures came to attention as I whirled past, coattails flying. I pounded at the engine room hatch in blind frustration until my fist accidently hit the control panel and the hatch flew open.

I snarled. "What in God's blue blazes do—"

Deke glanced up from the pipe he held in place.

"Don't move it, you silly pup!" Dray roared. Jokko, making himself unnoticed in the corner, flinched.

I took in the puddles of water, the dank steamy atmosphere. "What happened?"

Dray grunted. "These damnfool joeykids took their eyes off the gauges." He wrenched at the pipe. "Let the steam pressure build up, they did. Blew the main feed valve." He glanced at me, added heavily, "Sir."

"The water in my shower—"

"Cold, I'll bet." His mouth turned up but his eyes held no humor. "The pipes are drained dry now, sir. If I'd gotten here a few minutes later they'd probably have frozen solid. And if they'd burst . . ."

"What were these—people doing?"

He gestured at the stores compartment. "Helping Eddie look for a plate the right size, sir." My mind on the puzzle, I nonetheless noticed his careful courtesy.

I groped. "A plate?" Then I swung to Deke. "For the damned fusion drive? You neglected your watch for *that?*"

Deke opened his mouth, thought better of it. He hunched over as if afraid I would physically attack him. I'd have liked to. My eye strayed to the barrel mounted in the corner; I wished I could send them to it. Unfortunately I could not. Young officers were subject to corporal punishment, but not ordinary sailors. For them I had recourse only to punishment details or the brig. A wise provision; otherwise a tyrannical Captain would provoke rebellion by crewmen whose manhood couldn't stand physical abuse. Of all the enlisted men on a Naval vessel, only the ship's boy, still a minor, could be beaten, and rarely was.

A trickle of water ran down my nose, as a thought crystallized.

My eyes slowly turned from the barrel to Deke. "How old are you, sailor?"

The young transient shrugged. "Dunno, sir. Dey tellin' me sixteen, seventeen, some'pin like dat."

"Well, now. And Jokko is eighteen. Both of you short of majority." I gestured to the barrel. "Chief, do you need help, or can you handle it yourself?"

"You mean, cane them like middies?" His face darkened. "It would be a pleasure. But I need their help to clean up this mess first."

"I'll be in my cabin. Tell me when I have water for a shower. When I do, discipline your children!" With what dignity I could muster I padded barefoot back to the ladder.

I eventually got my shower, and soon put the incident out of my mind. But the next day Walter Dakko stopped me in the corridor. He was terse. "We'd better talk privately."

By now I knew he would bother me only for something important. "On the bridge, in half an hour. Make sure nobody sees you." I wondered if Dakko knew how dangerous was his role of informer.

I waited impatiently. When he knocked I sealed the hatch behind us. "Now, then."

"Again, sir, I'm not suggesting how you should run your ship."

"I know," I said impatiently. "Belay that. I order you to bring me information you think I ought to have. Remind me if I take offense."

"Aye aye, sir. I think you ought to go armed for a while."

I drew in my breath. "It's that bad?"

"I think so. It didn't help any when Dray brought the transients back, wailing and carrying on."

"This is about caning Deke and Jokko?" I said, unbelievingly.

"It's about physically abusing enlisted men." His tone was sharp.

"But I have the right—they're legally children! How dare you call it abuse!"

"I didn't say I did. It's what the crew berth calls it."

"What do you call it, Mr. Dakko?"

He shrugged. "It's a fitter punishment than mopping already clean decks for a week," he said. "Probably no more than they deserved. At times I wish I'd done the same to Chris."

"He wouldn't have stood for it. He wasn't in the Navy then."

"I know, sir." A sigh. "In any event, there's some wild talk."

"Mutiny?" My voice was hard.

"Wild talk," he repeated. "That's all it may come to. After they—"

"Who?" I interrupted.

His eyes closed. "I knew it might come to this," he muttered. "When I chose to warn you."

"Answer me. Who?"

"Please withdraw the order, Captain." His tone was flat.

I sneered, "You're afraid you wouldn't obey it?"

"No, sir." He sounded tired. "I'm afraid I would." He held my eye until I was forced to look away.

"I'm sorry, Mr. Dakko." My voice was quiet. "I withdraw my question. While it's just talk, you need not tell me. But if they make a move . . ."

"I'm still a Roman citizen," he said with a small smile. "And the walls are still under siege."

After I sent him below I wondered how to save myself from the disaster I'd caused. Perhaps it would be better to do nothing, to let a mutiny form and run its course.

After an afternoon sulking on the bridge I went directly to dinner. I'd grown used to a general hostility; now it was blatant and almost universal. I met cold silence from the moment I entered the room until I'd finished the prayer.

Mrs. Reeves eased herself into her seat. "Is there any way I can help?" she asked.

"No."

She accepted the rebuff. "The talent of leadership is not to get too far ahead of the populace." She spoke offhandedly, as if in answer to a question. "You can only lead people where they are willing to go."

"Challenger is not a democracy," I snapped.

The old blue eyes gazed myopically. "You're angry?"

"Not especially. I'm trying to do my duty."

"I'm worried for you."

I could find nothing to say to that.

I stared at the beans and mixed vegetables, all I'd see on my plate for years to come. I tried to concentrate on my food and block out the rising babble from other tables.

China crashed to the deck. "Stinkin' trannie!" Seaman Kovaks was on his feet, fists bunched. Across the table, Deke and Jonie lunged. Mr. Tzee ducked, guarded his plate.

I scrambled to my feet as Jonie shrieked a challenge to the maddened seaman. She charged into the fray.

"STAND TO, ALL OF YOU!" My bellow stopped her, but just barely. *"ATTENTION!"* Kovaks, white-faced, paid no heed. Savagely I shoved him aside. "Stand to, this instant!"

For a riotous moment my authority teetered on the balance, before their discipline asserted itself. "Mr. Kovaks, out of the hall. Go to crew berth two."

Rage suffused his features. "But they—"

"SHUT UP!" It made my throat hurt. He blanched. I snarled, "Leave!"

"Aye aye, sir." He stalked out.

"You two, go to crew berth one."

"No way," Jonie spat. "Not afta—"

"Master-at-arms! Chief petty officer!" Walter Dakko and Eddie Boss came at a run. "Escort these sailors to the brig."

"Aye aye, sir." Walter Dakko took Jonie's arm. The young transpop twisted free.

"Knockidoff, Jonie," growled Eddie. "Go widda man!" From behind, he slammed his palms into Deke's shoulder blades; the younger boy skidded toward the exit. "You too, Dekeboy. Call yaself a sailor, huh? I be showin' ya!"

I waited in silence until they were gone, rounded on Mr. Tzee. "What was that all about?"

"Mr. Kovaks had a comment about Deke's welding, sir." His face showed no expression.

"Welding?"

"The plates." He sounded reluctant. "For the fusion drive."

For a moment I couldn't speak. "That project, again?"

"Yes, sir."

I turned on my heel, stalked back to my table. Tempers were running high; I'd have to be careful not to overreact and set them—

No, by God. I would not. I strode to the center of the room. "All hands, form a line. Officers in front."

I waited, hands on hips, until all complied. Philip pushed Gregor to an officer's place, five feet in front of the assembled men. The passengers remained in their places, all eyes fastened on mine.

"Attention, all of you." I spoke very quietly, battling to contain my rage. "Mr. Tyre, straighten the line."

"Aye aye, sir." He broke ranks, turned smartly. "You forward. Back, Mr. Bree." In a moment he had them standing properly, and returned to his place.

"At ease."

With commendable precision the crew moved into the at-ease position, hands clasped.

"I won't have slack discipline on my ship." I stopped in front of Philip. "All work on the drive shaft is suspended."

A murmur of discontent.

"Pardon?" I raised an eyebrow. A wall of silence. "The work is halted until I order otherwise. Which won't happen until I find your conduct acceptable."

"Christ!"

I whirled. "Who spoke?"

Stony silence.

"Well?"

"I did." Drucker, the hydroponicist's mate.

"Two days in the brig for insolence and blasphemy. Report there. Stand at attention outside the hatch until someone comes to take you in."

His indecision lasted only a couple of seconds. "Aye aye, sir." His voice was sullen, but he walked out as bidden.

"I won't tolerate insubordination," I snapped. "Or sloppy drills, or fighting. When I'm satisfied in all respects, we'll see about the fusion drive."

"Excuse me, sir."

I glared at Ms. Bartel. "Yes?"

"We're ready to start testing, sir. Can we at least do that?"

"No." No one spoke, but their resentment was unmistakable. I knew it was suicidal to push them farther, but I wasn't sure I cared. "Remain where you stand until I finish my meal. Then you'll return to quarters." Without a further glance I strode back to my table.

I had already eaten most of my meager serving but for effect, I toyed with the vegetables a few moments longer. I topped off my coffee from the pot on the table, sipped at it. When I felt I'd made my point I said evenly, "Mr. Tyre, dismiss the men to quarters. Mr. Dakko, go to the brig and put Mr. Drucker into a cell."

I stared unseeing into my coffee cup until they were gone. Mrs. Reeves said nothing.

When I had no excuse to remain I said, "If you will excuse me," and left my place. I went to the bridge.

Dray let me in. I told him what I'd done.

The look he gave was carefully neutral. As I'd demanded, he'd eliminated any hint of insubordination from his manner. Now there was nothing. "It only delays the inevitable," he finally said.

"I suppose." I assumed he meant my overthrow.

"The drive won't work no matter what they try. I can't answer for their actions when they find that out."

"I know." I was glad I'd misread him. I left him to his watch.

Morale continued to plummet. I sensed the inevitable outcome, and hardly cared. I released Deke and Jonie from the brig with a stern admonition to behave. The next day I did the same with Mr. Drucker.

Hours later Drucker was back before me, seething with sullen hatred. Philip Tyre glared accusingly. "Insubordination, sir!"

"Just tell me what happened," I repeated, my tone weary.

"Mr. Branstead said we had to check the nutrient baths more often because the tomatoes were getting leaf wilt. When I gave Mr. Drucker the order, he, uh, told me what I could do with the tomatoes."

"Which was?"

"Please, I—"

"Answer!"

"Aye, aye, sir. He said I should shove them up your, uh, arse, sir." Philip's face was red, with suppressed anger or mirth I couldn't tell.

I rounded on the seaman with unconcealed fury. "Anything to say, Mr. Drucker?"

"No." He glared back.

"Two months imprisonment. Midshipman, escort him to the brig."

Philip returned to the bridge a few minutes later. "He's brigged, sir." His tone was stiff, his eyes on the simulscreen so as not to meet mine.

"Very well." I was in no mood to probe his petulance.

"We'll need to replace Mr. Drucker on the hydro watch schedule," Philip prompted.

"I know."

"There's no one left to—"

"Dismissed."

He snapped a salute, left at once. Knowing what I had to do, I quelled my distaste. "Master-at-arms to the bridge."

When Dakko arrived I handed him a pistol, bade him follow me below. I stopped at the section four hatch. "Cover me."

"What are we doing, sir?"

"Retrieving Mr. Clinger." Dakko's eyebrow rose measurably, but he said nothing. I punched in the code; the hatch slid open. "Clinger!"

A slovenly Seaman Akkrit drifted out of a cabin to regard me with indifference. "Think he's in the lounge or somethin'."

"Get him." I waited, prey to my misgivings. A few moments later Clinger appeared, haggard, unshaven, eyes ringed by black circles. He eyed me uncertainly.

"Did you mean what you said?"

"Huh?" He stared, mouth working.

"About another chance."

"Oh, Jesus God. Please." He sank to his knees. "Please."

"Come." I backed through the hatchway. After an unbelieving moment he followed. "You're dropped to apprentice seaman. No seniority. No ratings."

"Yes, sir!"

"Understand this: you get one chance, no more. Disobey an order, violate any regulation, and I'll execute you on the spot."

"I got it, sir! I won't give you any more trouble, honest. I'll—"

"You'll replace Mr. Drucker in hydroponics. Mr. Dakko, go to stores and issue him his personal gear, then have him report for duty."

"Aye aye, sir."

As they departed I mulled over my latest feat. I'd brigged a conscientious but frustrated sailor and replaced him with an unscrupulous rebel who'd tried to take over the ship.

All in the name of discipline.

47

"Commence firing!" I watched the simulscreen as *Challenger*'s forward lasers found their target: scrap metal released from the forward lock. Within seconds the metal glowed red.

"Better," I acknowledged. "All right, switch to simulation drill." I keyed the safeties on, making actual laser fire impossible.

On most ships laser drills took aim at computer-generated imaginary targets. But once, on the Training Station over Farside, Sarge had let us cadets fire at real scrap that otherwise would have been hauled back to base. I still remembered the thrill when at last the target glowed and sputtered and disappeared from the screens. On my own ships I used real targets from time to time, and been pleased by the improved results.

Still, enough was enough. Every target had to be released from the lock, and it was time consuming. "Kerren, simulated firing, random targets fore and aft, retained from three to twelve seconds. Visual confirmation on the laser screens."

"Aye aye, sir," said the imperturbable puter. The screen flashed.

I keyed the caller. "This drill is scored for destruction, not accuracy. Demolish all targets." In an accuracy drill missed shots counted against the gunners; in a destruction drill hits scored favorably and misses didn't count. However, each target remained on screen a random time; if it disappeared before being hit the gunners' scores were penalized.

"Begin!"

The gunners' voices crackled on the speaker. Two crewmen sat at each laser emplacement. One controlled the targeting, his mate regulated the duration and intensity of fire. A puter could direct our fire more accurately, of course. But only a man could be trusted to know at what to fire. After a century of dispute, the Navy had at last learned to trust crewmen over machines.

"Target oh seven five, closing!"

"Go! I got 'im."

"Target one nine oh! Target two one four."

"Fire!"

"Get the other one!"

Kerren duplicated on our bridge simulscreen the targets he gave my gunners; the darkness of space glowed with hostile points of light. Realistic flares indicated hits. Many targets abruptly disappeared, untouched.

After fifteen minutes I called a halt. "Gunnery crews stand down." A few moments later Mr. Tzee appeared in the hatchway, hopeful. I shook my head. "Not good enough."

"But—yes, sir."

"What's their problem?"

"None of them were originally trained as gunners, sir. And they have to learn to work closer together."

"They've had plenty of time for that." I waved a dismissal. After an hour reviewing the Log I picked up the caller and flicked the alarms. "GENERAL QUARTERS! ALL HANDS TO GENERAL QUARTERS!" Sirens wailed.

"Kerren, simulated laser drill, as before. Tabulate scores for each laser team. Forty minutes of continuous targets."

As a middy I'd conducted laser drill; an officer was supposed to be familiar with every station on his ship. I remembered continuous fire practice as nerve-wracking, the more so the longer the drill.

"Comm room reporting ready, sir!"

"Engine room ready, sir!"

"Gunners, commence firing!"

I paced irritably, eyes on the simulscreen where Kerren displayed the scores. After the first few minutes they began to rise as our gunners found their marks. Then, slowly, accuracy began to fall, as they tired. After an endless interval, they began to climb again, as if grudgingly, until they surpassed the previous test.

The screen abruptly darkened. "Exercise completed, sir."

"Thank you, Kerren." I keyed the caller. "Gunners stand down."

For three days I'd sounded General Quarters, Repel Boarders, and decompression alerts until the crew was thoroughly disgusted. I ran snap inspections, citing every violation I found. The crew's hostility was masked by only the thinnest veneer of discipline.

Philip Tyre was no longer sullen. Instead, he seemed almost apathetic. In a way, that was worse. Any effort I made to cheer him was met with indifference. I became increasingly uneasy. Finally, in desperation, I took him to the officers' mess for coffee. He stared into his steaming cup.

I sat, but stood again almost immediately to pace a few steps and examine the texture of the bulkhead. "Mr. Tyre—" That sounded too formal. "Philip. You're next in line to command should anything happen to me." My voice was husky.

He stared, suddenly worried. "Yes, sir."

I blurted, "We're all going to die here. I know that."

He sat stunned at the voicing of his own fears.

"Philip, I have no answers. I don't know how to act nobly. I don't know what to do."

He stirred. "Sir, I—"

"Let me finish. There's a chance some of us will survive, but not a great one. I assume I'll end my life on board *Challenger*. Perhaps very soon." He sucked in his breath. "I don't mean suicide; that's mortal sin. But the crew—" I gestured. "They won't take much more."

"Sir, if you explain to them—"

"There's nothing to explain." I stared at the silent bulkhead. "I don't have solutions. All I have is my oath. I swore to uphold Naval regulations; *Challenger* is a Naval vessel and I haven't been relieved. So I'll follow the regs. It's the only course I know."

He said nothing, scrutinizing me intensely.

"The regs require military etiquette, so I'll enforce it. They require that we be prepared for emergencies, so I'll continue to train the crew." I smiled bleakly. "I know it seems useless, but it's all I know to do."

He swallowed. "I haven't been much help lately, sir. I'm sorry."

"You've been an immense help. If you know a better course, suggest it. Or relieve me and follow it yourself." His glance was shocked. "I don't think you'll have to answer to Admiralty."

"I will never relieve you." He spoke with finality.

"You may go down with me, Philip."

He stood. "So be it." A moment's silence, while he mustered his courage. Then, "It is a privilege to serve under you, sir."

My chest tightened and I couldn't speak. I gestured to the hatch. He saluted formally and left.

"FIRE IN THE COMM ROOM! FIRE IN THE COMM ROOM!"

Feet pounded on the treads of the ladder as fire control parties raced to their duty stations, spurred by wailing alarms.

"Engine room reporting full water pressure!"

"Damage control ready!"

"Comm room controls shifted to bridge!"

In the corridor outside the comm room I keyed my stopwatch.

"Three and a half minutes." Panting crewmen waited, hoses in hand. "Very well, Mr. Tyre. We'll try for better next time." I ignored the glowers my remark earned. "Have the crew stand down." I returned to my cabin.

It was four in the morning.

The next afternoon I ran laser drills and decompression drills. After the evening meal I called an inspection and toured the ship while the exhausted crew stood by at their stations.

After trudging what seemed like miles I returned to the bridge and gratefully sank into my seat. Philip and Gregor waited attentively; they'd accompanied me on my inspection, stopping first at the wardroom where I sternly checked the bunks and gear stowed neatly in the duffels. I found no irregularities, and expected none. Philip was a seasoned officer, and would have seen to it that Gregor's gear was in order as well as his own.

"Pass the word," I said. "The crew may resume work on the drive project, so long as drill scores remain high." Though I foresaw nothing but problems when the repair project failed, I had to concede that the crew met my expectations. Their hostility was manifest, but their state of readiness was acceptable.

When I went back to my cabin to wash for dinner I found outside my hatch a crude rag doll, stuffed with old torn sheets, made to look like the Captain. Its head had been cut off.

The next morning work parties went Outside for a final inspection of the welds on the drive shaft. I ordered Gregor to accompany them. He did so with reluctance, no doubt recalling my fury at his previous escapade, and its humiliating consequences. This time he was careful not to lose contact with the hull.

By midafternoon Walter Dakko conveyed a request to allow low-power testing to begin. The Chief reassured me once more that at low power we'd do the shaft no damage. Sighing, I gave my consent.

I took the bridge, with Philip at my side for moral support. The Chief remained below in the engine room, at his usual station for Fusion. I knew a knot of crewmen from the project committee would be peering anxiously over his shoulder.

"Bridge to engine room, prepare to Fuse." I cleared my throat. "Rather, prepare for fusion drive test."

The Chief's flat voice responded almost immediately. "Engine room ready for test, sir."

"Very well, stand by." I looked up to the screen. "Kerren, nominal Fusion coordinates, please."

"Aye aye, sir." Kerren flashed the coordinates for home on the screen. I felt a lump in my throat. If only we could use them.

"Very well." No point in manually rechecking the coordinates. We weren't going anywhere. "Go ahead, Chief."

"Aye aye, sir. Fusion drive is . . . on." Automatically I glanced at the screens as if expecting them to go blank. The cold pale points of light remained.

Alarms shrieked. Kerren exploded into life. "Fusion drive malfunction! Coordinates not attained. Improper power settings! Fusion drive failure! Emergency shutdown achieved!"

"Captain, we've lost power to the fusion drive!"

"I know, Chief!" I muttered a curse as I slapped off the alarms. "Kerren, we're running low-power tests. No Fusion is expected."

Kerren hesitated a full second. "Low-power testing is a dockyard maneuver, Captain. I have no program to accomplish it under weigh."

"We're running the tests manually, Kerren. Disconnect your alarms."

"Alarms are operative at all times, Captain."

"Override."

He paused. "Alarms are overridden as per Captain's order. Override entered in Log."

"Monitor N-wave output and graph it to the screen against expected wave output at similar power."

"Aye aye, sir," he said doubtfully. "That will replicate the engine room monitor displays."

"Yes." I waited but the puter had no further objections. "Disengage your supervision of engine room controls, Kerren."

"That violates my directives, Captain. My function is to assure the safety—"

"Override. It's part of the test."

"Overridden," he said after a moment. "Engine room power is reactivated."

"Engine room, resume testing."

"Aye aye, sir."

"Apply power."

A jagged line pulsed on the screen as power reached the drive. A moment later the smooth line representing normal N-wave generation appeared as well. The wave we generated bore no resemblance to the sleek curve of a proper N-wave.

We watched in silence.

On my console the gauges fluctuated wildly. Below, in the engine room, the Chief tried without success to modulate the wave. After a few minutes he muttered into the caller, "No use. Maybe if we adjust the baffles . . ."

"Very well. Shut it off."

The jagged line faded from the simulscreen. "When do you want to try again, Chief?"

"Does it matter? There's no point in—I dunno. Tomorrow I can rig up something."

Beside me Philip Tyre said, "I knew it couldn't work, but still I was hoping . . ."

"So was I," I said shortly. I stood. "I'm going below."

Dray regarded me dourly from the engine room hatchway.

"Well?"

He was blunt. "Hopeless."

"You're sure?"

"Of course!" he snapped. "What do you think I've trained in for thirty years?" He pulled himself back. "Sorry, sir. Bartel and Clinger and the others, they watched me like I was a doc trying to save their baby. It got on my nerves."

"Yes." I added cautiously, "It would be best to keep testing, if there's any possibility of improvement."

He glanced at me, knowing. "Yes, sir. I don't want to think about when they're finally convinced it won't work. Tomorrow I'll try to make finer adjustments on the baffles, and see if varying the wave strength has any result."

"Thank you."

He gave me an odd look. "You're welcome, sir."

The next afternoon we began another series of tests. Again the wave we produced was a jagged, uncontrollable line on the screen. Off-duty crewmen crowded into the engine room to observe. Our machinists fabricated new controls for the baffles in repeated efforts to overcome the problem.

By day's end everyone was short-tempered, including me. Elena Bartel asked for permission to speak with me, and I had her brought to the bridge.

"There's one thing we haven't tried, sir."

"And that is?"

"More power."

"I'm no engineer, Ms. Bartel, but even I know how dangerous that would be."

"The wave front might straighten."

"And it might melt the shaft wall." Pensively I tapped the console. "We may not be generating true N-waves, but we're putting out energy in the attempt. If we overheat the shaft—"

"The sensors will—"

"Don't interrupt!" She drew back, startled. "You're a sailor speaking with an officer, Ms. Bartel, and don't forget it!"

"Aye aye, sir." She sounded reluctant.

"If we melt the shaft the energy could turn back on us and we could destroy the ship." I stood. "I've gone along with this charade, and I'm willing to let it continue, up to a point. You may test again only if we can do it without further endangering *Challenger*." I glowered. "Dismissed!"

She saluted, turned on her heel, and left.

Philip brought me the word the next morning. "Walter Dakko, sir. I was walking down the corridor and he hauled me into the lounge. He actually yanked my arm, sir, as if he didn't care that I'm an officer. Said he had to talk to you immediately."

I felt my arms prickle with a cold sweat. "Right now, then." I thumbed the caller. "Master-at-arms to the bridge!"

Moments later Dakko had joined us. "Things are getting out of hand."

"Be specific."

"The crew berth, a lot of wild talk. You won't allow testing at high power because you don't want us to go home. You know the drive can be made to work but—"

"Goofjuice!"

"Yes, sir. But it's real to them. They're getting, ah, rather worked up."

"Still only talk?"

"For the moment. But they're—" He swallowed. I waited. "There's talk about running tests without your permission, sir."

"How could they? I'd have Kerren override the fusion drive circuits."

"If you're in control." He met my eye without flinching.

"Break out arms, Mr. Dakko. For you, me, Mr. Tyre, and the Chief."

"Aye aye, sir. And one other thing—"

"Yes?"

"Chris. I want to keep him out of harm's way."

"How?"

"Lock him in a cabin, if I must. I don't want him involved."

"Denied. He's a sailor. He knows his duty and the consequences of rebellion. Go break out the arms."

"No. You owe me that much." He held my gaze, not defiantly but steadily.

"You too, Mr. Dakko?"

"If that's how you must have it."

I clapped my jaw shut before I made it worse. He had, after all, repeatedly risked his life to bring me essential information. I changed tack as smoothly as I could. "Mr. Dakko, Chris is seconded to you for special duties until the emergency is over. Break out the arms."

"Aye aye, sir. Thank you." He left at once.

Philip said hesitantly, "If we go armed, sir, we'll show the crew we know what they're thinking."

"Yes. It's time we all knew where we stand."

Half an hour later Walter Dakko was back with a load of laser pistols and stunners. I took a pistol, sounded the alarm. "All hands to General Quarters!" The sirens wailed.

One by one the stations reported. When the last voice crackled in the speaker I said, "All hands remain at General Quarters until inspection."

We made the rounds, Philip, Walter Dakko, and I. At each station I checked readiness, on the alert for misplaced gear or other violations. Our last stop was the engine room, where Deke and Jokko stood by with the Chief.

I paused at the hatch. "Dray, how high can we set fusion drive power without overheating the shaft?"

Perhaps he'd heard the scuttlebutt; at any rate he made no comment about the futility of our testing. "I'm not entirely sure. Somewhere near fifty percent, I'd think."

"If you increase power slowly will your monitors warn us of overheating in time to shut down?"

"Aye, sir."

"Very well." I took the caller. "All hands stand down!" I made my way back to the bridge, Philip dutifully at my side.

"Now what, sir?" he asked.

"Fire drill." I reached for the caller.

"Right after GQ?"

By way of answer, I hit the alarm.

During the afternoon I ran two more alerts and a laser drill. The crewmen were brooding and sullen, but my orders were carried out. At dinner, immediately after the prayer, I made an announcement. "Fusion drive testing may resume under the Chief's supervision. He will decide what power settings do not imperil the ship's safety."

Before the echo of my last words had died Elena Bartel was on her feet. "Does that mean we can start tonight?" Her tone was truculent. "Sir!"

"Sir. May we start tonight?"

I thought of delaying until tomorrow, in response to her bad manners, but that would be altogether too petty. "Very well."

The ragged line flickered across the screen. Rarely did it intersect for more than a moment the smooth curve of the theoretical N-wave. As the Chief increased power the strength of the wave grew but it remained obstinately erratic. I yawned.

Philip spoke suddenly, startling me. "If that were music it would be some weird kind of jazz." His eyes too were riveted on the simulscreen.

I grunted. Through the speaker I could hear the Chief growl at his crew of eager and determined assistants while they wrestled with the new, unfamiliar baffle controls they'd rigged.

I yawned again. It had been a long day and the drills and inspection had left me exhausted. I glanced at the temperature readouts. The shaft wall was not overheating. I yearned for my bed, decided abruptly that there was no reason for me not to be in it. "Watch the readouts, Mr. Tyre. Shut down if we overheat."

"Aye aye, sir."

"You have the conn." I left the bridge.

In my cabin I unbuttoned my jacket, hung it neatly over the chair. I had to tend to my own clothes; *Challenger,* half abandoned, had no ship's boy to bring the Captain's breakfast and hang up his jacket. Of course, I was not so long removed from the wardroom that I minded.

I loosened my belt and yanked off my tie, which as always made me feel better. I wondered for the hundredth time why we still wore the adornments. Naval dress was so rigidly obsolete.

Something tapped at my hatch. A strange sound, definitely not a knock. It sounded again. I froze, my heart pounding, afraid but not sure why.

The tapping came again. Too tired for melodrama, I slapped open the hatch.

Mrs. Reeves had her cane raised, to tap once more.

"What do *YOU* want?" I coursed with adrenaline.

"To talk—"

"You're not allowed here." The extent of my rudeness punctured my fury. I said more civilly, "Passengers aren't allowed in the officers' section, Mrs. Reeves."

"I know that," she said tartly. "But this is where you are, and I need to speak with you."

"In the morning, then. I'm quite—"

"Captain, do an old woman a courtesy and stay awake a few moments longer. You're young enough. It won't hurt you."

Aching to slam the hatch in her face I nodded reluctant agreement. "Come in, then."

She hobbled into my cabin, glancing at the sparse furnishings. I indicated a chair at the conference table; she sat carefully, mind turned inward to the mechanics of lowering herself.

"There." She settled into the chair. "You don't know how fortunate you are, young man, to have a body you can trust."

I waited pointedly. Recognizing the tactic, she smiled, not at all put out. She waved her cane in the general direction of the engine room. "That fussing with the motors. Will it work?"

"They're still testing, Mrs. Reeves. I can't—"

Her shrewd blue eyes pierced my equivocations. "Will it work?"

"No. It won't."

She let the silence continue, very much in control. For a moment I recalled Father, reviewing my lessons at the rickety kitchen table. "You've made a great mistake, Captain," she said at last. "And I don't know if you have time to correct it."

"Allowing the tests? I had to show them that—"

"No, not that."

My anger rose; I wasn't used to interruptions.

She said, "If the drive won't run, you'll spend at least a generation on this ship. I won't be with you, thank heaven. I've had my time in the sun, as it were." Her crinkled eyes found mine. "Those people can't live their whole lives under military discipline, Captain."

"Those are matters you're not—"

She overrode me yet again. "I'm talking to you while I may, Mr. Seafort. If I wait much longer you won't be Captain."

"I don't know that I care," I said bluntly, astonished I could say such to her.

"It may cost your life."

"I don't know that I care," I echoed. I had to look away.

"Care, boy!" Her cane rapped on the edge of the table, startling me. "Life in its fullness is all too short. And you have a duty to these people. Who else could lead them? The Chief Engineer, who would drink his way out of his dilemma? The midshipman whom everyone treats as a boy because he feels himself one? A committee of untrained passengers?"

"I'm doing what I know to do." My voice was hoarse.

"Bells ringing at all hours, people racing to and fro. What is it all for?"

"They're readiness drills."

"Readiness for what?" she demanded. "Crew and passengers have to learn to live together, to cooperate. Not to respond like robots to some archaic military drill they'll never use again."

"This is a military vessel."

"Was." The word had a finality that shook me.

"We haven't been decommissioned. *Challenger* is not abandoned and she's heading home."

"At a speed that makes the issue academic." She leaned forward. "Don't you understand? We have to create a society that will work under such bizarre conditions. We have to ameliorate their stress and anxiety. Your way only increases it."

"My job, Mrs. Reeves, isn't to create a society. It's to maintain law and order on board this vessel." I wondered if I sounded as fatuous as I thought.

"And are you doing that?" she asked unexpectedly.

"Yes. I think so."

"Then why were you carrying guns today, you and the boy? Since when has that been your custom?"

"There's been tension. I was afraid—"

"Ah."

My fingers drummed the edge of the table in growing anger. "I understand your concern, ma'am, but you have no right to challenge me."

Mrs. Reeves raised her eyebrows. "Good heavens, young man. Whatever I'm doing, it's not meant as that. I want you to see the outcome of your efforts."

"And that is?"

"They'll overthrow you or kill you, and create a form of society they can live with." Her words were stark in the silence of my cabin. For a while I could hear nothing but our breathing.

After a time she continued. "A leader can only lead where the people will follow. Surely you know that."

"What were you?" I asked curiously. "A historian?"

"A psychologist, actually." A mischievous grin. "So I'm supposed to know how to manipulate you. I'm not doing a very good job."

I warmed to her smile. "But you make me think." As some of our tension dissipated I leaned back. "You say my choices are limited by the crew's unwillingness to lead a military life indefinitely. That may be, but I'm also bound by my oath. I am not free to create a social order amenable to all of us. I am subject to the Naval Code of Conduct, and by the oath I've sworn to my Government."

"An oath is a fine thing, but the spirit of your regulations is to keep the ship in order. You can't do that if you're dead or deposed."

"I can't determine whether I live. I can only determine whether I'm true to my oath."

"Young man, you take a narrow view that does not encompass our circumstances."

"That's as must be."

"And what of the people?" She leaned forward on her cane. "Understand, you're not speaking only of fidelity to your oath. You're talking about the needs and miseries of all the others on board. Some of them, the children, might live through this to our eventual rescue."

I closed my eyes in despair. "What would you have me do?"

"Relax your Naval discipline. Ease the distinctions between crew and passengers. Eliminate the ridiculous drills and inspections. Stop using coercion and punishments."

"And what will that accomplish?"

"Don't you know?" Her rheumy eyes searched mine. "This life aboard ship is all that many of us will have before we die. Let us live it in peace."

I stared at the deck. Behind me, Amanda softly touched my shoulder, and faded. I said bitterly, "Peace. I don't know what that is. I've seen it, but never held it in my hands."

"It's fragile," Mrs. Reeves admitted. We fell silent.

I brooded, lost within myself. She was right, of course. My efforts to maintain military discipline were making our lives miserable. I could ease the drills, the inspections. I could be more friendly. I wondered if, eventually, I could permit an elected government and somehow square it with my oath.

I met her eye again and smiled shyly. "I'm glad you came," I said. "I'll try—"

The siren shrieked. Alarms reverberated in the corridors. Philip Tyre's frightened voice cut over the cacophony. "Captain to the bridge, flank! All hands to General Quarters!"

Mrs. Reeves struggled to her feet with surprising agility. "I'll go back—"

I snatched my jacket. "No, the corridor hatches will seal in a moment. Stay here!" I dashed to the bridge, my steps resounding to the unforgiving clang of the alarms. Crewmen careened past on their way to duty stations.

The bridge hatch was sealed, the camera eye swiveling back and forth. The hatch slid open as I raised my hand to pound on it. I scrambled through and it slid shut immediately. I shouted, "Turn off those bloody alarms!"

Philip's hand flicked over the keys. Silence echoed. He pointed at the simulscreen.

"Oh, Lord God." I snatched the caller, bellowing over the incoming reports. "Battle Stations! Comm room, prepare for laser fire. All passengers and crew stand by your pressure suits. Stand by to repel boarders!" I took a deep breath. "Engine room, shut down the drive! Full power to all lasers! Power up maneuvering jets!"

The fish were back.

Two of them, one off the bow on the port side, the other amidships to starboard.

They were some kilometers off. With Kerren's screens on maximum magnification, the fish seemed unnervingly close. The digits flashing below the screen showed them on a closing course.

"We'll intercept the forward one first," said Philip unnecessarily.

"I know." I called the comm room. "Get a lock on the forward target!"

"Aye aye, sir." Mr. Tzee. "I think they're out of effective range yet."

"I can see that," I growled.

The speaker crackled. "Power to maneuvering jets, sir!"

"Very well, engine room."

"I was watching the N-wave line," Philip blurted. "One minute everything was fine, then they were there!"

"Be silent, Middy!"

"Aye aye, sir," he whispered.

The range closed. I checked the readouts on the thrusters, cursing the propellant I'd recklessly expended to increase our speed.

"Sorry, Philip," I said presently. "Nerves."

"Thank you, sir." His voice was unsteady, his face white.

"Easy, Midshipman." For his benefit, I made my tone calm.

"Approaching firing range!" The puter.

"Thank you, Kerren." I flicked the caller. "Comm room, commence firing when I activate." My hand hovered over the laser lock.

"Maximum range achieved!"

Still, I hesitated. "They'll swerve when we hit them. If we wait 'til they're closer, we might burn through with the first shot."

Kerren's sensors followed the fish that approached our bow. A tentacle began to separate from the globular mass. Lazily the stringlike appendage began to rotate. I jabbed the switch. "Fire!"

Though there was nothing to watch, I searched the screen anxiously for the invisible beam of light from our laser.

Voices murmured in the speaker; our caller was set to comm room frequency.

"Full pulse. I've got a lock!" Walter Dakko, his voice rising.

The fish jerked, propellant misting from a vent.

"Follow him!"

"Gottim!" Deke, tense with excitement. My arm ached; I found my knuckles white from squeezing the armrest. I flexed my wrist.

Beams from three lasers centered on the fish off our bow. It was almost too easy. The goldfish bucked once; colors swirled in the undifferentiated mass of its outer skin, then it was still. Fluid or gas spurted from within.

"We gottim! We gottim!" Cheers erupted, shushed by Mr. Tzee. As we drifted alongside the inert fish I realized how much smaller it was than the one that had menaced *Hibernia* eons past.

"Target closing on eight four, sir." Kerren was brisk.

"Lock on!" I said with growing confidence. If it was to be this easy . . .

Philip gasped as the alarms shrieked again. He waved weakly at the simulscreen.

Three more aliens.

Even as I watched, a fourth fish burst onto the screen. Then another, appearing from nowhere. Kerren erupted with angry vehemence. "Target aft, bearing oh two oh, range two hundred meters! Target amidships port! Target—"

"Fire at will!" I bellowed. "All lasers, individual fire!"

A fish loomed, amidships. A tentacle twirled, about to break off in a deadly spiral. An icicle stabbed my spine.

The Lord is my shepherd.

"Lock on target three!"

I shall not want.

"Burn the sumbitch!"

"BEHIND THE DRIVE SHAFT! TWO OF THEM!"

He maketh me to lie down in green pastures.

"I see 'em!" Alongside us a fish leapt convulsively.

He leadeth me beside the still waters.

"Bridge, engine room here. One of them's closing fast on us; another's close behind."

He restoreth my soul.

"I see them, Dray."

Admiral Tremaine had taken several of our laser mounts for *Portia*. Few of the remaining lasers pointed aft. I goaded my numbed brain into action. "Maneuvering jets! Oh nine oh, two jets!" Squirting propellant frantically, I swung the ship in a ponderous turn so our lasers could bear.

He leadeth me in the paths of righteousness for his name's sake.

"Get a lock on him!"

A fish blossomed and seemed to crumple. A wild cheer.

Yea, though I walk through the valley of the shadow of death, I will fear no evil.

"Watch them other two!" As *Challenger* rotated, the nearest fish detached a spiraling arm. It sailed lazily across the few meters that separated us. Thanks to our turn the mass would hit forward of the disks, in the hold. Had I not come about, it would have caught us astern, perhaps on the drive shaft.

For thou art with me.

New alarms rang loud. "HULL IS BREACHED! HOLD PENETRATED!"

Thy rod and thy staff they comfort me.

"Look out for the two amidships!"

"I'm swinging round!" I braked our spin with a reckless burst of propellant.

Thou preparest a table before me in the presence of mine enemies.

The mottled skin of the nearest fish seemed to swirl. As in a dream I watched the rotating mass expand. A lump grew on the fish's skin. Then the figure was through, and launched itself at *Challenger*.

"Lasers, get that outrider!" I hit the sirens. "All hands repel boarders! Decontamination imminent! Suit up!"

Thou anointest my head with oil.

"I've got a lock on the son of a bitch!" A new voice; Elena Bartel. Her laser found the floating figure. It flared and wilted just before it passed within our circle of fire, where our lasers wouldn't depress far enough to hit it.

My cup runneth over.
"There's another!"
Surely goodness and mercy shall follow me all the days of my life.
"I gottim! I gottim!"
"Steady, Deke. Wait for range." Walter Dakko.
And I will dwell in the house of the Lord for ever.
"Gottim!"
"Good boy!"
"LOOKATIM PLODE!"
Amen.
And there was silence.

48

My unsteady hand shut off the last of the alarms. Slumped in my arm-chair, a stranger called for damage reports. He seemed to have something caught in his throat.

"Engine room reporting, no damage. Full power on-line, but we're damn near out of propellant."

"I know, but we had to maneuver." I spoke as if from a great distance.

"Hydroponics, no damage, sir."

"Comm room, no damage, sir."

Beside me, Philip Tyre sat frozen at his console, fingers gripping the sides of his chair.

"Recyclers, no damage, sir," said the speaker.

A tear ran unchecked down the boy's face.

"Galley is undamaged, sir."

The midshipman caught his breath.

"Kerren, status report!"

"All systems within normal parameters," the puter intoned. "All compartments airtight except the hold. Hold is breached portside, thirty point three meters forward of the launch berth. Hold is decompressed."

Philip straightened his shoulders, leaned back, took a deep shuddering breath. His hands remained fastened on the armrests.

"What happened to the projectile that beast threw?" Pointedly, I ignored the middy.

"It dissolved the portside hull plating in the hold," said Kerren. "Sensor lines are destroyed and dislodged cargo is blocking my camera view. I cannot estimate the size of the breach."

I frowned. Beside me Philip attempted a smile. He shouldn't have. His face crumpled. He threw up his hands and his shoulders shook.

I cleared my throat. "Inspect the corridor, Mr. Tyre. Check the wardroom for damage. Then find the cadet and see he's all right."

"Aye aye, sir." Gratefully Philip fled.

It wasn't much, but it was all I could think of on the spur of the moment. At least it allowed him the privacy of the wardroom.

* * *

I'd wanted to meet in the officer's mess, where we could gather at the informal breakfast table, but I no longer dared leave the bridge untended, even for a moment. So Philip Tyre and I sat at our consoles, seats swung round to face the chairs from the lounge occupied by the Chief and Gregor Attani.

I asked simply, "What do we do?"

Silence hung heavy, punctuated only by the muttering of Kerren's monitors and sensors. I'd allowed the crew to stand down from Battle Stations only after we'd passed several tense hours without encountering more fish.

The Chief cleared his throat. "Is there really a decision to make, sir? What options do we have other than to do what we're doing?"

"You think our situation unchanged?" I sounded more acid than I'd intended.

Gregor, saying nothing, stared at the screen.

Dray held his ground. "Essentially, yes." He waved toward the hold. "Kovaks and Clinger will have the breach sealed in a couple of hours. Then we're in the same situation as before."

"Except that we're virtually out of propellant. And the hold may be contaminated. It's where our remaining food supplies are stored."

I'd given Philip and Dray permission to interrupt freely, so Philip's interjection was not impertinent. "We rigged Class A decontamination gear in the launch berth," he said. "And all the stores of food are sealed. We should be able to get to them safely." He bit his lip. "Will we need to go back to the hold later for anything else?"

"We'll go through full decontamination whenever we do," I growled. Vacuum or no, I would take no chances.

They waited for my lead. "So we go on as before?" I was unsatisfied.

The Chief said again, "What else can we do?"

"Is there any chance whatsoever we can get the drive working?" Philip, to Dray.

Gregor stirred. "Sir, I—"

Philip swung on him in fury. "You're here by sufferance, Cadet! Open your mouth again and you'll wish you'd been born without one!" Gregor recoiled from his senior's anger.

"No chance of doing anything with the drive," Dray said gruffly. The Chief stared into the intermediate distance, about ten meters beyond the hull. "We're testing right now, and I suppose we'd better keep on. It's the only hope we can offer the crew."

I asked, "How long can you string it out?"

"A long time, if necessary."

I sighed. "We may not need long. Kerren, replay the tape." I looked at the screen where Kerren displayed the ragged N-wave produced by our damaged drive.

"Aye aye, sir." The first alien appeared abruptly in what had been empty space.

"Again, in slomo."

Kerren cut to the beginning of the recording, at very low speed. I still couldn't detect an interval between the time we saw nothing, and the moment a fish floated off our bow.

"How did it find us?" Philip muttered. Over his head, the scene continued to replay.

"Remember, they found *Challenger* before." My eyes were on the screen. "When Admiral Tremaine had her. All we've done since is fire the thrusters."

In replay, one by one the fish on the screens fell to our laser fire, except the last survivor, which pulsed and abruptly disappeared as the lasers found its range.

It blipped out of existence as fast as the first fish had appeared.

"They could come back any moment." I was reluctant to say it aloud.

"But why?" Philip cried. "Why do they keep coming?"

Gregor Attani said, "Sir—"

"You don't have permission to speak," Philip snapped.

I felt sorry for Tyre, doing his best to hide his fear, unaware that it revealed itself as savagery toward his charge. I stepped carefully. "I would be willing to hear him, if you give permission," I said with delicacy.

Philip turned scarlet. "Aye aye, sir." He nodded to Gregor. "Go ahead."

Gregor swallowed. "How do they get here, sir?" he asked.

I shrugged. "That's one of the many things we don't know."

"I watched a holovid once, back home." Attani shifted awkwardly. "About inventing the fusion drive. They showed a ship Fusing. It looked a lot like the way that fish disappeared."

"The fish are alive," I said. "They don't have fusion drives."

"Birds don't have airplane engines," he said.

I was speechless a long moment. "Organic fusion?" I sputtered. "How?"

The cadet shrugged. "I don't know, sir. What else could it be?"

The Chief shook his head. "I don't see how it's possible. An N-wave couldn't be generated organically."

"Bats navigate by generating sound waves," Philip remarked.

I waved him down. "That's all beside the point. The issue is why they seek us out, not how."

"Sir, if you'll permit—"

I glared at Gregor. "You've had your say. We don't have time to speculate where they're from." I turned to the Chief, my tone glum. "I suppose you'd best continue drive tests as long as—"

Gregor shot to his feet, gripped the back of his chair with both hands. His face was pale. "Listen to me."

Philip and the Chief exchanged glances, astonished at the cadet's impertinence. We all rounded on Gregor.

"Ten demerits!" snapped Philip. "You're confined—"

"I'll teach that youngster—"

"*They hear our N-waves!*" Gregor's voice was sharp over the babble.

"—to behave—"

"After all I've taught—"

We fell silent, gaping. The cadet appealed, "I'm sorry to interrupt, sir, but can't you see?" He gestured at the screen, where the jagged line wavered. "If they travel by N-wave, they must be able to sense them. Hear them."

I said slowly, "How can we be sure—" My mind reeled. Did they hear us travel in Fusion, or only when we Fused or Defused? Were ships attacked while actually in Fusion? If so, would we ever learn of it?

"Lord God." I don't know which of us said it.

"We've used the fusion drive for over a century," I demanded. "Why didn't they hear us before?"

"Maybe they've come a long, long way," Gregor Attani said. I felt a chill.

"Let's assume they hear us Fuse and Defuse," I said slowly. "That would explain why they attacked our ships at nav checkpoints."

"How could you hear an N-wave?" the Chief wondered. His glance traveled up to the simulscreen, where the jagged line pulsed. "And what about that wave we're producing. That—caterwauling."

I wasn't listening; I'd already swung to the console and slapped the power lever to "Off." The jagged line vanished from the screen. "Kerren, reset emergency override on the engine room! Disconnect power to the drive!"

"Aye aye, sir. Override reestablished."

I stared at the simulscreen, terrified of what might appear. Nothing came. After long moments I forced my muscles to unknot and swung my chair back to the waiting officers. "There's no proof you're right," I said to Gregor. "But we'll proceed on the assumption you are, until we learn otherwise."

"Yes, sir."

"Anything else?"

"No, sir." He looked as if he wanted to make himself invisible.

"Then take your seat."

He did, quickly. We had little left to discuss and the conference ground to a gloomy halt. I told the Chief to explain to Ms. Bartel and the others why we'd stopped testing. "If there's any grumbling, send them to me. And keep standby power to the lasers at all times."

I took up the caller. "Mr. Tzee, summon the first laser firing detail. They and Group B will rotate watches for the next week." Hard on them, but I couldn't risk less.

"I'll take the next watch," I said, blinking back exhaustion. We'd been up through the night, time unnoticed, and it was already near end of morning watch. "I'll go change my shirt first. Chief, you have the conn 'til I'm back. Philip, get some rest. You too, Cadet."

Wearily I trudged to my cabin, wondering what had become of Mrs. Reeves. I had my finger on my hatch panel when the alarms sounded again.

I scrambled back to the bridge. I only needed one glance at the simulscreen. "Chief, go below!"

"Right!" He moved fast for a big man.

This time, there were eight.

In a moment the departments began reporting. Philip Tyre, his duty station on the bridge, dashed in, coat awry.

"Lasers have power!"

"Seek targets!"

I gripped the thruster controls. There was little to do but watch.

"Target bearing one five four, range five hundred meters!" Elena Bartel.

"Kill it!"

"He's getting ready to throw!"

Deke shouted, "Big 'un behin' us, Cap'n!"

I saw. A copious squirt of the port thruster, and *Challenger* responded with an unbearably slow turn.

"Amidships! Jesus, he's close!"

"Got a lock!"

Kerren's monotone was continuous. "Encroachment oh five oh, declination three five, range five hundred meters. Encroachment two six one, declination oh eight four, range one hundred meters. Encroachment—"

"Watch the one above us! He's settling!"

"Power line overheat! Switching to alternate!"

There were too many, too close. *Save us, Lord God.* "Philip, all passengers stand by to don suits. See to it."

"Aye aye, sir."

A whirling tentacle broke free, sailed toward us in the deadly silence of vacuum. "Damn! Get it!" Walter Dakko.

"I'm tryin'! It's movin' too fast!" Deke.

"Inside our circle!"

"It's comin' at the launch berth!"

I was already at the thrusters. *Challenger* turned her broadside from the swirling mass, not enough to avoid it, but enough so it struck the hull forward of the launch berth.

"Propellant reserves at minimum," Kerren said calmly. "Two minutes maneuvering left, Captain."

"God damn them!" My blasphemy went unremarked.

"At the stern," shouted Dakko. "The shaft!"

A big fish drifted aft, colors pulsating against the black night. As I watched horrified, a blowhole opened, squirted. The fish floated toward the drive shaft wall, below the engine room.

Reluctantly I squirted another precious blast of propellant. We swung away from the danger. The fish followed. A patch in its skin began to swirl and change colors. One of its outriders began to emerge.

"Stand by to repel boarders!"

Not one, but three of the figures launched themselves from the fish alongside the engine room. They sailed to the hull surrounding the drive shaft.

"Got the sumbitch!" Ahead a fish wilted, its innards spurting into the night.

"Engine room reporting. Alien boarding party on hull outside the drive shield." Somehow, Dray made it sound like a routine status report.

"Master-at-arms, repel boarders at engine room! Dray, get your people suited!"

A fish forward of the disk pulsed rhythmically, disappeared.

"Look! The bastard Fused when he got hot!" Elena Bartel.

"We're already suited, sir," said Dray. "Uh, the fish is closing fast."

On the simulscreen, I watched catastrophe approach. My eyes

flicked to the readouts. We had propellant for barely one more maneuver.

"Jesus, Lord Christ!" Philip rose from his chair. Aghast, I stared at the screen.

About three hundred meters off our starboard side a fish had appeared, the largest I'd ever seen.

Kerren intoned, "Encroachment oh nine three, declination zero, range three hundred meters and closing."

Propellant puffed from a blowhole. Already a tentacle was forming on the exterior. The fish drifted closer.

"The fish at the stern is just off our shield, Captain!" Dray's voice was ragged. Nothing but a plastalloy drive shield separated the engine room from the vacuum. When the fish dissolved the shield, the engine room would decompress. And my suited men would be in the compartment with those—beasts.

"Is Dakko there?"

"Here, sir! Engine room."

"Can you fight them off?"

"There's three of the outriders Outside. If they eat through, we'll burn them. But the fish itself—" He left the rest unsaid. Dakko's puny weapons could do naught against the might of the looming fish.

We were under attack from all sides, but the most immediate danger came from two fish: the one releasing invaders to the engine room, and the immense creature looming amidships.

I glanced at the screen. The aft fish was within meters of the drive shaft. If it hurled its acid projectiles at the hull . . . I recalled the deaths of *Hibernia*'s crewmen. Walter Dakko and his party were helpless against the acid.

All was lost. "We have to abandon the engine room," I said, the taste of defeat so bitter I paused before issuing the command.

"No!" Philip leaped to his feet.

"There's no choice—"

"We'll lose power to the lasers!"

"Unless we get our men out they'll be killed!" I gestured helplessly. "We can't save the engine room!"

The huge fish amidships let go a projectile. It spun lazily toward the hull.

"We can!" Philip insisted.

"No lasers fire far enough inward to cover the drive shaft."

Dray's voice, edged with panic. "The fish will make contact any second!"

"The launch." Philip was pale. "Let me take it."

"It's unarmed."

"It's got hot propellant and it can ram."

Dumbfounded, I stared.

He waved at the simulscreen. "What difference does it make? Look at them!" Still I said nothing. "Sir, let me go. Maybe I can scare that thing off."

I found my voice. "No."

"What else am I good for?" His young features contorted.

"No!"

"Then we'll die for nothing!" He hesitated, then ran to the hatch. "Maybe I can sear the fish with our exhaust." The hatch slid open. He paused a microsecond. "Permission to leave the bridge, sir!"

I had to try twice before I made the word audible. "Granted."

The midshipman flipped a perfunctory salute and ran down the corridor out of sight.

I swung to the screen. Our fire had neutralized the projectile from the midships fish, but the alien had formed another glob, already swirling toward us.

In less than a minute the console lights blinked, warning me the launch berth was occupied and depressurizing.

The midships projectile sailed untouched through our fire.

"Sombitch!" screamed Eddie Boss in the comm room, blasting my eardrums. "My gun! He got my gun!"

"Midships laser malfunction!" Kerren.

The launch shot from its berth.

"Shut down power to midships laser!"

"Power is down."

"Captain, it's gonna throw at the engine room right now!" The Chief, his voice taut.

I swallowed. "Abandon eng—"

"Hang on, Dray, I'm almost there," Philip Tyre's voice was steady. "Get in the shop compartment, you'll have another bulkhead between you and the acid."

"Do that, Chief." My hand gripped the console.

"Aye aye, sir."

Mr. Tzee's voice cut across the babble. "Look at the screen, sir."

The huge fish amidships was growing three more projectiles.

"Fire on him!"

"They've knocked out all our guns that bear at this angle, sir. I need a bow-on shot."

"I'll come round!" I squirted propellant. Our nose drifted ever so slowly toward the fish.

Kerren's camera picked up the launch. Philip maneuvered the stern of his tiny vessel toward the fish at our shaft. He kicked a jet of propellant at it, causing the launch to shoot away from the fish. The fish quivered, random dots of color swirling in its skin, but it remained still.

"Go, you bastard!" Philip's voice was savage. He swung his craft close for another try.

A cry of dismay from Mr. Tzee. "Captain, they've got our bow laser."

"Can you bring anything to bear?"

"We've nothing big enough to hurt them, sir."

If the Admiral had left us more of our lasers . . . "Very well."

Philip squirted a blast of propellant at the aft fish, without effect. It wasn't working. I rested my head in my hands.

"Engine room decompression! Captain, they're through the hull!"

"Keep away from the acid! Burn the outriders as they poke through!"

"I'm going to ram," said Midshipman Philip Tyre.

"No, Philip!"

"It's our only chance. The impact may drive him away. I'll try to eject before contact." I knew that was impossible, as did he.

"Mr. Tyre—"

He swung his little ship about, spending propellant with reckless abandon. About a hundred meters distant he matched velocities and aimed his prow at the bow of the fish.

"Mr. Tyre!"

"I'm glad I served with you, sir. If you see Alexi, tell him I'm sorry." He jammed his throttle to full. The launch spurted forward.

If his aim was true he would lance the fish head on. "Sir, Godspeed—"

I snatched up the caller. "Kerren, record! Mr. Tyre! I, Captain Nicholas Seafort, do commission and appoint Midshipman Philip Tyre a Lieutenant in the Naval Service of the Government of the United Nations, by the Grace—"

The radio crackled and went dead—

"Of God!"

Challenger's launch tore into the bow of the fish, accelerating still as it clawed through the alien tissue. The fish bucked. It appeared to ripple. Viscous material spewed from the gaping hole. The momentum of the launch tore the fish from our hull. Inert, it drifted out of sight behind *Challenger,* our launch imbedded within.

"Penetration in the hold!"

Lord God, I repent my sins.

"DECOMPRESSION LEVEL 2, SECTION SIX!"

"Captain, east hydros are decompressed!"

Pray forgive my trespasses.

"Engine room!" I expected no answer.

"Here, sir! Only two of the outriders got through, and we fried 'em both. Clinger, get that patch in place!"

"Full power to the thrusters, Chief. Give me all remaining propellant."

"You've got it! We've less than a minute's burn, sir."

Lord, I beg Thee, take me unto Yourself.

"I know."

Challenger had swung almost nose-on to the midships beast that still threw its projectiles. I glanced at the screens; other fish maneuvered alongside. There was no way to avoid them all.

"Kerren, ramming course!"

"Course true! Relative oh oh oh!"

I'm coming, Amanda.

My hand jabbed at the red ball of the thruster control. *Challenger* drifted forward almost imperceptibly.

I cried, "Christ, is that all we've got?"

"Acceleration is cumulative," said Kerren, as if that explained everything. Perhaps it did.

Our motion was more evident now. As we neared, the huge fish squirted propellant and began to float aside. I slammed the port thruster to full to correct course, and five seconds later ran out of burn.

"All passengers and crew suit up, flank!" My eyes were locked to the simulscreen. Foolishly I braced myself as we approached. The bridge was in the disk, halfway down the length of the pencil that was our ship. The view on my simulscreen was from Kerren's camera forward. It, not I, would make first contact.

"Wait for us, you bastard!" My teeth clenched, I slurred the words.

In seconds we would skewer the fish with our pointed prow.

The fish began to pulse rhythmically.

"Wait for us . . ."

The fish pulsed. If it disappeared now . . .

"WAIT, YOU THING OF SATAN!"

Contact.

Kerren shrilled warnings. "Prow disintegrating! Forward sensors inoperative! Hull collapsing forward of the disk! The hold is—"

The screen went black.

I was on my feet, braced for an impact I couldn't feel. "Kerren?" No answer.

"Kerren?" I waited for the power to dim. If Kerren was destroyed— The lights remained steady.

"Kerren!"

"Fusion is successful, sir," the puter said calmly. "Please provide course for my data calculations."

"What?"

"Fusion drive is on, sir." The puter's tone was patient. "As you Fused manually, I do not have the calculations to—"

"DRAY!"

"Engine room, sir."

"Is the drive on?"

He snorted. "Of course not."

"Oh, Lord God!" I stared at the screen, willing the stars to reappear.

"What is it?" Dray asked.

"The fish. It tried to Fuse just as we hit."

"Yes, sir?" He waited.

"It . . ." I stumbled for words. "It took us with it."

49

We came together in the Level 2 corridor, Dray, Walter Dakko, Gregor and myself. Seconds had dripped into hours, while the screens remained blank.

Kerren insisted we were in Fusion, and I didn't dare examine the rents in our hull to find out. When we were Fused, any object thrust Outside would cease to exist. A body too near a hull opening would be caught up in the stresses of the field, and would suffer molecular collapse and oblivion.

"Now what?" I'd dropped all pretense of military formality. It was all I could do to keep from trembling.

"We're alive," Dray said gruffly.

"For the moment."

"Where are we?" Walter Dakko's voice was a husk.

I shrugged. "In purgatory, perhaps." Dakko raised an eyebrow, said nothing.

"What's going to happen?" Gregor.

I stated the obvious. "We'll die."

Gregor winced, gathered himself. "When, sir?"

"Soon. When the fish Defuses or digests the ship. Or when the food runs—"

"Digests?" blurted Dakko.

I said, "Just before the alien, uh, Fused, Kerren reported the prow was disintegrating and the hull collapsing where it pierced the fish. Now he says all his hold sensors are inoperative. We don't dare open the hatch from the launch berth to the hold because of radiation and the danger of viral contamination. When whatever's dissolving the hull eats as far as the hatchway, we're through."

"How long will that take?" Gregor, again.

"How the hell should I know!" My rage drove him back a step. "Don't ask stupid questions!"

"Sorry, sir! Aye aye, sir." He held himself at near attention.

The mood changed subtly. Walter Dakko asked, "What do we do now, sir?" They waited for my response.

I had an urge to say, "Whatever you damn well please," and stalk to my cabin, leaving them standing in the corridor. What more did they want of me? I had no miracles to bestow.

I sighed. "Engine room status, Chief?"

"We got the hull patched before Fusion, sir, so the engine room's inhabitable. One of the power output lines was hit but the other one's all right."

"You mean after all this we still have power?" I couldn't believe it.

"Enough for lights and heat, yes, sir. I might be able to patch the second power line too. Anyway, we don't need power to the thruster pumps; we're out of propellant. And the lasers were wiped out, so . . ."

My mind spun slowly. We were imbedded in the body of a fish in Fusion. The engine room, aft, was in good shape, the disks where we all lived were airtight, while our hold forward of the disks was being eaten away.

"What else do we know?" I labored through a fog. The Chief's report seemed an annoying distraction.

Dakko said, "The recycler chamber is undamaged, but some of the feeder lines are out of commission and the fluids in them are lost. East hydros—"

"They're gone," said the Chief. "Decompressed. I don't think we should try to open the hatch. We'd have to pump out section eight to get in there, and anyway the plants are dead."

"West?"

"West hydros weren't damaged, but we never got them fully operational again."

"Between east hydros and section eight, we've lost about half our food supply." Dakko grimaced.

"Have Mr. Branstead take a look. Can we repair the lines to the recyclers?"

"Probably most of them, sir. If we can scrounge up enough materials without going into the hold." Dray waited expectantly.

I kept my irritation in check. "Get on it, then."

"Aye aye, sir. The chemicals that were in the lines—I have no way to replace them now that we've lost the hold. The recyclers will just barely keep up."

"Do what you can." They waited for more orders; I forced myself to think anew. "Where else are we decompressed?"

"Level 2, sections four and five, sir," said Dakko. The rebel prisoners were gone, then. Except for Mr. Clinger, saved by the providence of Mr. Drucker's ill temper.

"Oxygen reserves?"

Dray answered that one. "Just sufficient to re-air the ship, sir, but after that it's going to be tight on recycling."

"It won't matter after a while," I said. I turned to Gregor. "Mr. Attani, see who's survived among the passengers and crew. Bring me a list. I'll be in my cabin."

"Aye aye, sir."

"Chief, do what you can to clean up. Mr. Dakko, look to the needs of the crew as best you can."

"Aye aye, sir."

I headed for my cabin, concerned no longer about manning the bridge; my work there was done. We would live until the hatch gave out, or the food, or the air.

Then it would be over.

At the top of the ladder I met Mrs. Reeves, hobbling heavily on her cane. She eyed me with a curious smile. I waited.

"So you were right after all, young man."

"Right?" I tried to recall our conversation.

"About your military discipline."

"It didn't save the ship."

"We live."

"Not for long," I replied.

"That's not for you to say," she rejoined tartly, and continued on her way.

I lay on my bunk in a daze. Lord, how I'd wanted *Challenger*, before she was snatched from me. But I'd entered her in disgrace, assuming that I was to die on her. It seemed fitting. But never in my strangest dreams had I imagined such a prelude to death.

After a time, not knowing what else to do, I got up and sat at my immaculate, polished, useless table. How does one wait for death, certain of its inevitability but not knowing when it will arrive?

"One lives," said Father, almost aloud, so near I almost jumped. "Our deaths are all in the hands of Lord God. Nothing changes that."

"Easy for you to say," I muttered. "You're not aboard." I sensed his disapproval and ignored it, but knew he was right. One lives, as long and as well as one can. One does his duty.

A soft knock at the hatch; I went to open it. Gregor Attani saluted, offered me a paper. "You said to bring this, sir."

"What?"

"The list. Casualties."

"How many?"

"Only two passengers, sir. They were caught without suits when the Level 3 corridor decompressed."

They were the lucky ones. "Have Mr. Tyre arrange stowage of the bodies." My tone was weary.

His look was strange. "Mr. Tyre is dead, sir. The launch. He—"

I sagged against the bulkhead, unable to speak.

"Sir, are you all—"

"Get out!"

When he was gone I thought of going to my bunk but it seemed easier to remain where I was, propped against the bulkhead.

I'm sorry, Philip. But how can you blame me for losing track? I've killed so many of you. Amanda. Nate. Crewmen. Passengers, Uppies and trannies. So many.

After a time I wiped my face and went out to the corridor, where all was quiet and still. I could sense, if not hear, the steady imperturbable throbbing of the engines below.

Level 1 seemed abandoned. I passed the hatch to the launch berth. On the far side of the berth was the hatch to our hold. I poked my head into the bridge. The instruments hummed silently, recording pointless data.

I had a craving for coffee. On the way to the officers' mess I passed the Level 1 passengers' lounge. On impulse I stopped and looked inside.

Walter Dakko sat across from his son. He held Chris's hands in his own. The two glanced up wordlessly. I mumbled something and backed out of the hatchway.

The boy was crying.

I wasn't sure about the father.

I made the coffee hot and strong, the way I liked it. I sipped greedily, hunched over the long wooden table, waiting for the caffeine to jog my system.

"Sir, is there anything you'd like me to do?"

I whirled, spilling hot coffee down my shirt. Gregor waited.

"Don't sneak up on me, Cadet!"

"I—no, sir! I mean, aye aye, sir."

I regarded him balefully. "What should I have you do, Mr. Attani?"

"I don't—I didn't mean—I'm sorry, sir."

"Just leave me be," I growled.

He hurried to the hatch.

"Mr. Attani!" He stopped. "I'm . . . sorry." I swallowed my ire. "For my manners."

"Yes, sir."

"Do as you wish. See if you can help Mr. Dakko or the Chief. I'll page if I need you."

"Aye aye, sir." He seemed grateful for the directions.

I was left alone.

As I washed the cup to put it away I glanced at the small mirror hanging alongside the galley sink. My jagged scar flamed vividly, as if in reproach. Get hold of yourself, I ordered. You were prepared to die. So now you're doing it. Even now, there is duty.

As penance I walked the habitable areas of the ship. Everywhere I was greeted with pathetic welcome. The crew hung on my words and scurried to do my bidding, as if my orders could extricate us from our calamity. Those passengers I met contrived to have a word with me, some even going so far as to shake my hand.

Detouring around the sealed-off sections of Level 2 that would never be reopened, I finally completed my tour. Eager for isolation, I approached the bridge with unaccustomed eagerness and sank thankfully into my chair.

"What can you tell me about the hold, Kerren?"

It was the wrong question. "The hold is two hundred thirty meters in length, averaging twenty-four meters across, tapered at a ratio—"

"Cancel. Tell me about the current condition of the hold."

"I have very little information about the state of the ship forward of the launch berth," Kerren said, his voice stiff. "If you would Defuse long enough to—"

"Tell me what you DO know, you burned out pile of chips!"

A shocked silence. "Last sensor reports," he said primly, "indicated prow disintegration and collapse of the hull in the forwardmost twenty meters of the hold. That was at 0911 hours. At 0942 the midships hold sensors became inoperative. I can only conclude that the progressive damage reached that point."

"What sensors still work?"

"You are referring to the hold, Captain?"

"Yes." I heard my teeth gnash, willed my jaw open.

"Adequate references would facilitate our conversation," he said sweetly. "To answer you, only one. The internal port sensor is still operative. We had a starboard sensor too, but the line was cut when the hold was first punctured. The operative sensor is mounted on the hull above the catwalk, twenty meters forward of the launch berth hatch."

"Thank you."

"You're quite welcome, Captain." He spoke with his typical courtesy, so I couldn't be certain of his sarcasm. "The fact that the sensor is operative suggests the hull retains structural integrity to that point."

"Thank you," I said again.

"You're welcome," he repeated.

I brooded a moment. "Kerren, can your sensors indicate anything about the exterior of the ship or our location?"

"Not while the fusion drive is operating," he said. "Certainly you must know that."

"Kerren, we're not Fused."

"But we are, Captain."

"Kerren, monitor status of fusion drive."

His pause was infinitesimal. "The drive registers as off, Captain."

"So you—"

"But external registers confirm we are Fused. Therefore the drive monitors are inoperative and their data is ignored."

I sighed. Kerren's programming didn't allow him to accept the possibility of Fusion other than by our drive. I wasn't sure my own did, either. Perhaps the puter could be reprogrammed, but I saw no point in trying.

We'd lost well over half our food plants, and the remaining food stored in the hold was inaccessible. Though three crewmen, our four prisoners, and two passengers were dead, that still left us facing certain starvation. Our recyclers labored to keep breathable air circulating through the ship. Until the feeder lines could be repaired, they barely functioned.

In the meantime we were in Fusion or some analogous state, hurtling toward an unknown destination, entangled with a deadly and hostile alien.

And I was hungry. Should we ration the remaining food? Would we live long enough for it to matter? How long could we make it last, even with rationing?

I thumbed the caller. "Mr. Attani, Mr. Branstead, Mr. Dakko Junior to the bridge."

Emmett Branstead arrived first, looking surprisingly trim and fit. He'd lost about eight kilos since taking the oath, and with it some of his ruddy complexion. True to his word, he'd obeyed orders with dogged determination from the moment of his enlistment.

Moments later the cadet and Chris Dakko entered.

"I need an immediate survey. Our current food production and stores graphed against consumption at half rations and at one-third rations. Determine whether we can survive until we bring more crops on-line. Make your calculations and report back in two hours. Mr. Attani, you're in charge, of course. Avail yourself of Mr. Branstead's expertise regarding production. Mr. Dakko, make yourself useful."

Only after they left did I realize it was the first time the cadet had been allowed to lead a work detail. I worried for a moment before remembering it didn't matter.

". . . We ask you to bless us, to bless our voyage, and to bring health and well-being to all aboard."

The prayer done, I looked from Mr. and Mrs. Reeves to Mrs. Ovaugh and Mr. Fedez, all seated at my table. I looked beyond them to the tables occupied by the other passengers, the subdued groups of crewmen huddled together for comfort. I said, "I will not deceive you about the gravity of our situation. It is hopeless." There was an audible sigh.

"We will almost certainly run out of food before we can grow enough to replace what we lost. At one-third rations, we can last perhaps ninety days. It is barely possible that with conservation and intensive plantings, we can survive until enough crops mature to sustain us. Mr. Branstead's best estimate is that to stretch the food so long we would have to reduce our rations to the point where many of us would die nonetheless."

Elena Bartel raised a hand. I nodded. "What about the—the bodies?" she asked.

To my shame, I'd considered it. "We will not prolong our lives by resorting to cannibalism." My tone was firm. "The bodies have been moved to the engine room for cremation."

"They could sustain life!"

"At the cost of our humanity. I will not allow it." I glanced around the hall. "That decision has already been taken and is not a subject for discussion." I held her eye until she reluctantly sat.

"In any event we are unlikely to live long enough to starve. When we emerge from Fusion, or more likely before, the ship will be consumed." I looked beyond the crew tables, to the far bulkhead. "It is my decision that *Challenger* will go to one-third rations as of our next meal, so as not to foreclose the possibility of extending our lives. We shall continue to function as best we may, until the end. May Lord God bless you all."

I sat to a stunned silence and fixed my eyes on my plate.

The day was followed in dreary succession by another, then a third. Our tension subsided, and an eerie simulation of normal life resumed.

The whole ship's company nursed seedlings in a desperate effort to replenish our food supply. But as Gregor Attani's task force had calculated, we had no way to stretch our available stores to sustain us until the new plantings matured. Deke muttered about letting some starve so others could live, but I chose not to understand him.

As the days dragged on, I sat on the deadened bridge, staring at blankened screens, reviewing the Log, contemplating the succession of follies that had led us to this pass. If only the Admiral . . . If Captain Hasselbrad had just . . . If I had refused command and let them hang me . . .

Twelve days into our grim vigil I woke from a doze at my console to hear Kerren's voice, behind a blinking warning light. "The remaining sensor in the hold has failed, sir."

"Failed?" I asked stupidly. "What? How?"

"It showed a rise of thirteen degrees Celsius during the hour just before failure, Captain. Then nothing. I have no way to determine if the line was cut, a connection loosened, or the sensor became inoperative."

"What is the condition of the hull inside the hold?"

"I infer hull status from the sensor data, Captain Seafort. I now have no way to determine the status of the hull forward of the launch berth."

"Very well." I stared at the console. "The hatch from Level 1 to the launch berth is secure?"

"That is correct."

"And the hatch on the other side of the launch berth to the hold?"

"Sensor data says it's functional, sir."

"Very well," I said again. I wanted to confer with Dray, but there was nothing he, or any of us, could do.

Ten more days passed. Though I'd lost only a couple of kilos, my cheeks were sunken, and the scar on my cheek was more noticeable.

Elena Bartel asked through Mr. Attani to see me. I allowed her onto the bridge.

"Elron—Mr. Clinger and I—we would like to be married."

I stared in openmouthed astonishment until she blushed with embarrassment.

"You want to marry Elron Clinger?" Not one of my more astute remarks.

"Yes, sir."

Marriage among crewmen was unusual, but not unprecedented. Sailors needed the Captain's permission to marry, and in our case I was the only one aboard authorized to perform a marriage. The couple would maintain separate bunks in the crew berth, of course, but there were always the crew privacy rooms.

"Well, er, I suppose . . ." I had no reason to deny permission. "Are you quite sure . . . about Mr. Clinger, that is?"

"Quite, sir. Mr. Clinger has thought a great deal about his former life."

"Very well," I said. "You have permission. When would you like the ceremony performed?"

"As soon as possible. We're not—sure how much time we'll have together."

"This evening? Tomorrow?"

"This evening would be fine, sir." She blushed again. "Thank you."

After the ceremony I reflected on the irony. She was at least ten years older than he. Clinger must have indulged in the usual life portside; she'd once admitted to me she'd never had so much as a boyfriend. Ms. Bartel upheld the proprieties; he was a rebel who'd tried to seize the ship.

Perhaps they'd know happiness. More than Amanda and I.

Whether it was the wedding ritual and unspoken thoughts of its aftermath, or some other cause, I felt urgent desire that night, for the first time since Amanda had died. I tossed and turned restlessly and was glad when morning came.

A full month had passed since we'd embedded ourselves in the alien. We relied on shipboard routines to carry us through the gray remorseless days. Gregor Attani lived alone in the wardroom, eagerly performing what chores I found for him. Taking pity, I put aside the tradition that a Captain didn't deign to notice a cadet and made sure to chat with him every day. I also noticed him conversing with Chris Dakko, who seemed miserable and depressed.

Dray spent most of his time in the engine room. I wondered if he'd rebuilt his still, but I saw no evidence of it and didn't choose to investigate. One day I decided to play chess with Kerren, and it gave me so much pleasure I made it a daily routine: one game in the morning, another in the afternoon. After I lashed out at Gregor, the cadet learned not to disturb me at these times.

Kerren did not play as well as Darla. Or Danny.

On the thirty-fifth day Dray brought word that Eddie Boss sought to speak with me. To avoid the formality of the bridge I called him to the officers' mess, where I waited with a cup of coffee. Thank Lord God for our unabated supply; the hot liquid soothed my nearly constant pangs of hunger and sated my addiction.

Eddie seemed reluctant to tell me why he'd come. I waited as patiently as I could. I even had him sit; it didn't seem to help. His fingers drummed the table as he stared into his lap.

I tried to jar him out of his funk. "Why ol' Eddie be 'fraid talkin' ta da man, hey? Big Eddie, he be chickenshit tella Cap'n boudit?"

That brought a reluctant smile. "You ain' no trannie, sir. Like I tole you once."

"Maybe I'm learning to be."

His smile faded. "You wouldn' wanna be one." His fist tightened. "No way to live, dat. Noway." He stared moodily at the deck. "Funny you sayin' dat. It's what I wan' talkin'—talk to you 'bout."

I waited.

He appealed to me. "Bout bein' a trannie. Don' go laughin' at ol' Eddie, Cap'n, ifn it funny." His fists knotted. "I knows—I know it don' matter none, but you teachin' me read, n' all . . ."

With a flash of insight I guessed what might be coming. I said carefully, "Go ahead, Mr. Boss."

He blurted, "Could you teachin'—teach me, not actin' like trannie? Not talkin' trannie?"

"How do you want to act?" I asked.

"Not like dem Uppies!" he said emphatically. "Not Mr. Tyre, or dat Chris Dakko. Maybe . . ." He flushed. "More like you." He kept his eyes carefully on the table. "I know it don' matter, we gonna die 'n all, but I just be wantin', before den—" He lapsed into embarrassed silence.

An image rose unbidden, of the passenger lounge in *Portia*, Eddie hunched over the table, struggling to learn his letters from Amanda.

"Before then," I said. "Not 'den': then."

His eyes rose to an unforeseen miracle. "Before then," he said with great care.

"Two hours in the morning with Walter Dakko," I said. "Two hours in the afternoon with me. Every day."

He swallowed several times before daring to speak. "Thank you," he whispered.

Later, when I discussed the project with Walter Dakko, he nodded as if it were the most ordinary request in the world. "It's more than just how he talks," he remarked. "His mannerisms. His walk. He doesn't stride, he shambles."

"He's determined to learn."

"Better to have pride in who he is than to learn to be someone he's not."

I glanced up sharply at the rebuke but saw none intended. "It's what he wants more than anything, Mr. Dakko, and I'm inclined to give it to him." I did not mention my reasons.

"Of course, sir." He smiled wryly. "Actually, it will be a challenge. Perhaps I can teach him to behave better than Chris."

"Perhaps." I was noncommittal. After a moment I availed myself of the opportunity. "How's Chris doing?"

"We're—reconciled," was all he said. I didn't press it further. Several times over the next few days I noticed them together.

Dray had to shut down our overburdened recyclers for repair. For an anxious half day we went to canned air. Even afterward, the recyclers were unable to keep up. Our atmosphere was going bad, slowly enough that the effect wouldn't be noticeable for a while yet. Perhaps our food would run out first.

Still, we carried on day to day as if the end were not clearly in sight.

We'd just sat down to our evening meal when the alarms sounded. I scrambled from my seat and dashed to the bridge.

Kerren spoke endlessly in his urgent warning tone. "Launch berth hatch to the hold has failed! Launch berth depressurized!" Now the width of the launch berth was all that separated us from the end. I switched off the alarms.

It was the fortieth day.

It wouldn't be much longer.

Gregor Attani, gaunt and hollow-eyed, stood before me, hands twisting anxiously. Eager for the conversational scraps I threw to him, he'd never dared initiate a conversation. Until today.

"Sir, do you think . . ." He swallowed, then rushed on. "Is there a chance I could make midshipman, sir, before—before . . ." He faltered.

I looked gently at the misery in his eyes. "Will I be needing midshipmen, do you think, Mr. Attani?"

He blushed. "No, sir. I'm sorry."

I cursed myself under my breath. What had I done? I regarded him somberly while I considered. "Do you want me to give it to you?" I asked at last. "Or do you want to earn it?"

"Earn it," he replied without hesitation.

"Philip—Mr. Tyre was teaching you navigation, wasn't he?"

"Yes, sir. I've been looking at the books on my own now, trying to make sense of them." With a sudden pang I thought of Derek Carr doing likewise.

"Your conduct is exemplary, Mr. Attani. I am satisfied you now have the maturity to be an officer. Study your navigation. I'll try to help, though in truth it wasn't my strongest subject. I'll set up drills for you with Kerren. Spend two hours a day with the Chief to learn the fusion drives. You're relieved of all other duties until your studies are completed."

"Thank you, sir." With a salute worthy of Academy he turned and marched out. Well, it was little enough to give him. Admiralty would never know, and I no longer cared whether they'd approve.

My days were busy now; astronavigation with Gregor in the mornings, sessions with Eddie Boss in the afternoons, sandwiching my chess games between. Sometimes, after our meager, pitiful dinner I would go to the passengers' lounge and chat, with Annie, Jonie, Mr. and Mrs. Reeves. I discovered to my surprise that I was almost content. Annie, in particular, seemed a nice girl, though her streeter ways put me off.

The mood of completion seemed to be catching; people brought their diaries up-to-date, studied ancient languages, watched holos they'd always meant to view. The activities diverted our thoughts from hunger. Our impending end was, by common consent, not mentioned. I'd decided that if the launch berth hatch showed signs of blowing, there was no point to going to suit air for whatever few hours it would extend our lives. So, with patience that surprised me, I waited for the next and final act of dissolution.

In the meantime, Eddie Boss learned to take a long moment's pause before he spoke, to marshal his grammar and overcome his crude dialect. He practiced new forms of etiquette with Walter Dakko. Whatever humor his transpop associates saw in the situation they swiftly learned to hide, for his temper was as fierce as ever.

Out of pity I did my best to keep Chris Dakko busy, assigning him to work details and inconsequential projects. He had retreated into a dazed docility, his terror betrayed only by an occasional unguarded expression.

"He's very afraid of dying," his father said.

"Yes." I knew of no comfort I could give. One night, sitting in the corner of the lounge, Chris suddenly and unexpectedly began to cry. We —his father, the other passengers, and myself—froze in awkward embarrassment. It was young Jonie who went to him, boldly took his head into her bosom, and eventually led him off to private comfort. I silently begged Lord God's blessing on her.

*   *   *

"Maneuvering jets, please, sir."

"Aye aye, power up," responded Dray from the engine room.

Gregor sat stiffly at the watch officer's console while I sat by, with the ritual obligatory scowl. I'd taken Alexi Tamarov, Derek Carr, Philip Tyre, and Rafe Treadwell through these maneuvers, and was an old hand at being an ogre.

Gregor licked his lips. "Steer oh five eight degrees, ahead two-thirds."

"Two-thirds, aye aye." The monitors duly indicated the increase in engine power. All simulated, of course. We were no longer a powered vessel.

"Declination fifteen degrees."

"Fifteen degrees, aye aye."

Gregor was maneuvering the ship into position to Fuse, in hypothetical interstellar space far from any obstacles. A midshipman had ample time to learn the finer points of piloting. My object was merely to see if Gregor grasped the principles of navigation.

"Ship positioned for Fuse, sir." He looked at me expectantly, only a fine sheen on his forehead betraying his anxiety.

"Satisfactory, Cadet," I said gruffly. I snapped off the simulation and the stars faded from the screen. Then I unbent. "Very good, Gregor." He shot me a pleased smile before reassuming the stiff dignity of his station.

That afternoon I beat Kerren twice at chess. He conceded the second game before I could see clearly that I'd won.

It was the fifty-third day.

During the quiet times between Eddie's and Gregor's lessons and my games of chess, I busied myself keeping the Log up-to-date, in case *Challenger*'s remains should ever be found. I wasn't sure why I bothered; I had no idea whether we'd even emerge in our own galaxy.

Seven more days passed. Mrs. Ovaugh died in her sleep; malnutrition certainly was a factor.

Even vast amounts of coffee didn't help my exhaustion. I lost three more kilos, and my appearance was grotesque.

I was asleep in my cabin when the caller snapped me awake. "Captain to the bridge, please." Disoriented for a moment, I couldn't place the voice. Then I realized it was Kerren, but the alarms hadn't sounded. Puzzled, I dressed quickly and hurried to the bridge.

"Please advise if the current condition requires alarms," he said.

"My hatch sensor shows abnormal temperature readings in the launch berth."

"Abnormal?"

"Higher than might be expected, sir. They've been climbing very slowly for several days—"

"Then why did you wake me now?" I demanded.

"And the launch berth temperature is up a full degree in the last hour."

"Oh." I found it necessary to sit. My heart was racing.

"If you would Defuse, sir, we might determine the cause."

"I can't Defuse, Kerren."

"One Defuses by turning the fusion drive off."

"Try it," I invited.

"You know I'm unable," he said reproachfully. "The monitors don't respond. They show the drive switched off."

"That's because it *IS* off."

"Refusal to recognize reality indicates an aberrant mental state, sir."

"Thank you."

"You're welcome, sir."

I could have the launch berth hatch reinforced, but if the acid was nearing our disk, it might penetrate the bulkhead anywhere, not necessarily at the hatch.

"How much hotter than this did the hold sensor register before it failed?"

"Eight degrees, sir."

I decided that was comforting. Then I decided it wasn't.

"Sound the alarms when the temperature is five degrees higher than at present."

"Aye aye, sir. What shall I sound? Battle Stations?"

"General Quarters and decompression alert." We had no weapons with which to do battle, and no one to fight.

"Very well, sir. Have a good night."

I slapped the bridge hatch control with extra force and went to my cabin, my hand stinging.

Have a good night. If only he were a midshipman.

50

Three more days passed without incident. Then Walter Dakko approached me, face grim. I took him to my cabin without ceremony. "I'm the bearer of a petition, sir."

"Again."

"Yes." His terseness warned me of trouble.

"Go on, then."

"Everyone agrees our situation is desperate. Many of the crew want you to try turning on the drive."

"What?" I rose from my chair.

"Ignite the drive and see if that will kick us back into normal space."

"Good God."

He said nothing.

I sighed. "Who's behind it?"

"I'm not sure where the idea started. Just about everyone's behind it now except me, Chris, and Eddie Boss."

"You threatened Chris again?"

He smiled tightly. "No, sir, this time he reached the conclusion on his own."

"What conclusion is that?"

"That trying to Fuse will destroy us."

"Or catapult us into another galaxy. We can't Fuse blind, even if we could Fuse at all!"

"Yes, sir."

"Let's talk to Dray." We headed below to the engine room.

The Chief listened impassively, shook his head. "No. One of the globs they threw during the last attack melted the drive shaft wall. There's no possible way to generate an N-wave, even a skewed one. All we'd accomplish is to overheat the shaft and most likely blow out the engines. That's if we were lucky."

"You're sure?"

"I'm sure." He regarded me almost angrily. "I'll give you ignition, if and when you give me a written order. I don't expect we'll discuss the results afterward."

"I have no intention of turning on the drive, Dray. Meet me in crew berth one in an hour. Mr. Dakko, gather the crew."

An impatient hour later I faced them. "Chief, tell them what would happen."

"We'd vaporize the drive shaft walls, for one thing. We'll overheat the engines. As it is, we've barely enough power to sustain our internal systems. As to the navigational effect, I have no idea, and neither does anyone else."

I said harshly, "Any questions?"

As I might have expected, it was Elena Bartel who stepped forward. "What's going to happen to us if we don't ignite the engines, sir?"

I was forced to answer. "We'll die."

"When, sir?"

"We don't know that. We'll begin starving in earnest in about two weeks. If the ship remains intact."

"Does anyone know whether the fish could stay in Fusion if we turned on the engines?"

I said bluntly, "I don't know if the fish would continue to exist if we turned on the engines. The energy we'd put out would bear no resemblance to N-waves."

"But it might force the fish to Defuse."

"You don't know that, Ms. Bartel. There's no way to guess the likelihood."

"What do we have to lose?" Behind her, crewmen nodded agreement. I noticed Elron Clinger gazing at her sorrowfully, making no effort to intervene.

"Our lives, immediately."

"We think it's worth the risk." She spoke with defiance.

"I don't. It's not your decision to make."

"I didn't say it's my decision," she said coolly. "That's why we petitioned rather than demanded."

I concentrated on her words rather than her tone of voice. "Very well. The meeting is concluded. Chief, Cadet, come along." I left with as much dignity as I could muster.

Soon after, we consumed the last of our canned foods and had only our meager crops to sustain us. They were not enough.

On the fifty-seventh day Gregor Attani offered his dinner to Mr. Reeves, who refused it. My mood snappish, I ordered the cadet in no uncertain terms to eat every bite of the food he was given. It was little enough; we were reduced to weak soup and boiled vegetables, a few spoonfuls apiece.

That night in my cabin I prayed to Lord God not to prolong our misery.

All day long, I could think of little but food. Our meals, mostly boiled water with weak dilutions of sustenance, failed to satisfy in any respect. The crew's discipline began to dissipate, and there were fights. There would have been more, but for the lassitude of starvation.

I retreated to the bridge and endless games of chess. I played the game openings over and over, trying minute variations after the sixth or seventh move. It seemed as if there was something I could do with the Queen's Bishop's Pawn, if only I could work out the permutations. But I was so tired, so hungry.

I was deep in thought when the speaker crackled. "Bridge, engine room reporting. We have, um, a situation here." Dray's voice was stiff with tension.

Wearily I tore my attention away from the board. "What now, Chief?"

A new voice gave the answer. Elena Bartel. "We're going to ignite the drive."

I bolted from my seat. "What? You can't!"

"We have to, Captain. I'm sorry. It's our only chance."

"Dray, throw her out of there!"

"He can't do that," she said calmly.

"Dray!"

"Yes, sir. My hands are tied behind me. She coldcocked me, sir, with some kind of pipe. And she's got a big knife."

I said, "You can't fire the drive. The bridge override is set."

"I've direct-wired it, Captain. At least, I think I have."

I tried to slow the pounding of my heart. "What is it you want, Ms. Bartel?"

"Nothing. I'm going to turn on the drive. I wanted you to be ready when we come out of Fusion."

"Wait."

Her tone was inflexible. "There's no point in waiting, sir."

I stumbled for words. "Yes, there is. Don't just fire up the drive; make sure the baffles are set properly! You want full power on the first try; I don't think you'll get another."

"Dray can show me how."

"No!" I roared. "It's my ship! I'll show you!"

A laugh of derision. "No, Captain Seafort. I'm not that stupid. You have a well-earned reputation for ingenious trickery."

"I won't trick you." I fumbled at the safe, holding the caller between my neck and shoulder.

"That's right, sir. You won't get the chance."

I said slowly and clearly, "Do not fire the engine before we set the baffle. That is imperative."

No answer.

I took a deep breath. "Elena, I want to go down and supervise. I give you my oath before Lord God Himself: I will attempt no trickery, I will do you no harm, I will in no way interfere, and I pardon you your acts. I so swear, by Lord God's grace. I understand your desperation. Perhaps it's the best way."

"You really understand, sir?" She sounded wistful.

"I do. Please let me come down." I shut the safe.

"All right. But remember the knife at Dray's throat. I'll use it if you try anything."

"You already have my oath not to interfere," I snapped.

A pause. "All right."

Gregor Attani came bounding up the ladder as I started down. "You heard, sir? What she—"

"Yes."

"What are you going—"

"Be silent, Cadet."

His mouth shut with a snap. "Aye aye, sir."

"Wait on the bridge in case I need you."

"Aye aye, sir." I left him behind.

Walter Dakko waited at the foot of the ladder. "I'm sorry, sir. I should have known—"

"It's done." I gave him a fleeting smile as we walked toward the engine room. "Who else is involved?"

"Kovaks and Jokko helped her take the engine room, sir. But she insisted on being the only one inside."

"Where are the others now?"

He looked grim. "In the brig. I had help. Chris, Eddie Boss, Emmett Branstead. Mostly Eddie."

"Very well."

"Sir, we could hear you on the corridor caller."

"Very well."

"Sir, your oath. Are you going to let—"

"Mr. Dakko, I order you to be silent."

"Aye aye, sir." His obedience was instant, for which I was grateful.

"Wait here, around the bend from the engine room hatch."

"Aye aye, sir."

I rounded the corridor bend. Only a few crewmen were afoot, among them Elron Clinger, who shifted miserably from one foot to the other, like a joeyboy who needed to relieve himself.

"I'm sorry, Captain. I tole her, honest, I tole her not to! She wouldn' listen•to me!"

"Out of my way."

"I tole her it was wrong, after you trusted us an' all! I'm sorry!"

"Move!" I shoved him aside.

"I'm sorry what she done!" He needed me to know, and to acknowledge.

"I understand, Clinger," I said wearily. "Stand aside."

"Aye aye, sir. Please don' be angry with her. She don' know, it's not like with me, I was crew a long time."

I ignored him, pounded on the hatch. "Ms. Bartel, it's me. Open up."

"What are you going to do?" she asked. Her tone was suspicious.

"Nothing. You have my oath. No tricks. I'll just help set the baffles. I'm alone and unarmed."

"Very well." The hatch slid open.

Dray sat heavily on a bench, hands trussed behind him. "Sorry, sir," he mumbled.

Elena Bartel held the knife near his throat. "Close the hatch and seal it, please." Her thin, bony figure was stiff from tension.

I did so. "Shall we get at it, then?"

She gazed at me, reflecting, and nodded. "I'm sorry, I really am, but somebody had to do something." She looked at me with forlorn appeal.

I nodded. "Mutiny wasn't the answer."

"Perhaps there was none," Elena said. "But we had to try. Can you understand?"

"I understand," I said.

"I don't suppose you'll forgive me?" she asked wistfully.

"No," I said shortly. "But I'll pardon you." I gestured. "Let's get on with it."

Elena lowered the knife. "The baffles are over here, sir."

"I know." I pulled the laser pistol from my back pocket and fired into her heart. Elena spun and fell. Dray screamed.

The knife clattered to the deck. I picked it up and waited for a dizziness to pass before I hacked at the cords binding Dray's wrists.

I tossed the knife onto the table. "Have her body disposed of." I turned to the hatch, stepping over a puddle of Elena Bartel's blood.

Dray was ashen. "Sir—you—I mean, you said—" He stumbled to a halt.

"Have you a problem, Chief Engineer?"

"No, sir! None, sir! I—please forgive me."

"Very well." I slapped open the hatch.

Elron Clinger slouched against the far bulkhead on the opposite side of the corridor. He glanced into the engine room and froze in shock. His face crumpled. I started for the ladder.

"I tole her!" he wailed, beating his thigh with his fist. "Oh, Lor' God, I tole her not to!" His chest heaved in a sob. "Elena! Whadda I do now, honey? Whadda I do without you!" He ran after me, gibbering. "Captain, what'm I gonna do? She loved me! She wassa only person loved me, ever! What about me, now?"

Mercifully Walter Dakko appeared. Clinger's grief faded into the background. I proceeded up the ladder. I passed the bridge and continued to my cabin. I took off my jacket and hung it on a hanger. I washed my face. I dried myself with the towel. I looked into the mirror with loathing.

I sealed the hatch and turned off the lights. I lay down on the bunk. It was the sixty-third day.

On the sixty-fifth day I sat at my console, staring at the darkened screen.

"Will you have some tea, sir?" Gregor Attani asked. His voice was hoarse.

"No."

"I could get you a cup of coffee."

"No." I felt very tired, very weak. But for Walter Dakko, I'd have remained in my bunk until the end. For two days he periodically knocked at my hatch. I never answered. He finally put his mouth to the hatch and announced that if I didn't open he would get a torch and cut his way in.

I'd let him steer me from my cabin to the officers' mess, and drank the cup of near broth he gave me. Then I combed my hair and went to the bridge.

Every day I found myself straightening my tie, adjusting my jacket, wanting to wash my hands and face. Over and again.

Gregor hovered like a mother hen. I paid no attention. Even his barely concealed misery didn't move me. I tried to invent an errand that would send him elsewhere, but it seemed too much trouble.

I checked the Log to see that its entries were current. I was meticulous about that. Everything must be shipshape now, everything ready.

I remembered something left undone. "Cadet."

"Yes, sir?"

"Stand at attention."

"Aye aye, sir." He did so at once, worry evident.

"I've been examining the Log."

It called for no answer but he said, "Yes, sir."

"You've completed the engineering course with Dray."

"Yes, sir."

"And you have studied navigation to my satisfaction."

"Thank you, sir."

"Though your conduct was not always laudable, especially at first, I am satisfied that you now understand what is required of you and will do your duty."

"Thank you, sir."

"Kerren, record. Therefore, I, Captain Nicholas Seafort, do appoint Cadet Gregor Attani as Midshipman in the Naval Service of the Government of the United Nations, by the grace of God."

"Thank you, sir!" His face was red but he held himself rigid.

"As you were." He relaxed and his gaunt face broke into a slow grin. I couldn't leave it at that. "Congratulations, Midshipman."

"Thank you very much, sir."

My answering smile was brief. "You won't mind if we dispense with the tradition of Last Night, cad—uh, Midshipman Attani. We suffer enough trials that additional hazing wouldn't be tolerable." I paused. "Get the purser's key from Mr. Dakko and find a proper uniform. A midshipman wears blue, not gray."

"Aye aye, sir!" His salute was magnificent. He wheeled and left the bridge.

I relapsed into my stupor. Hours passed.

"Would you like to play chess, sir?" Kerren inquired.

"No."

"Is something wrong?"

"Mind your own business!"

"Aye aye, sir," he said sadly.

Brooding, I realized how much I missed *Portia*'s puter, Danny. Kerren's officious manner put me off, while Danny's naive impudence attracted as well as irritated.

"Do puters have souls, Kerren?" I asked suddenly.

There was a pause of at least a second. "The question has no referent, sir."

"Have you read the Bible?"

"I contain several versions of it, Captain. I have applied analysis to them without productive result."

"Humph."

There was a longish pause. "Do you have a soul?" he asked.

"Yes. I've damned it."

"How so?"

"I foreswore my oath. I gave my oath for the purpose of deceit, knowing I intended to foreswear it."

"I am not equipped to discuss your theology, sir."

"That's a relief."

"What?"

"Nothing."

"I've decided that I do not have a soul as you probably define the term, sir."

"Thank you." I stood. "I'll be in my cabin. Summon me when necessary."

"Aye aye, Captain Seafort. Incidentally, the hatch temperature has risen another two degrees."

I swallowed. "You know where to find me."

I fell on my bunk. Chills alternated with drowsiness and sweaty tossing.

I lay in bed the remainder of the day and into the next. Walter Dakko brought Gregor and Annie to tend me. I tried to push them away.

"Let me, Mista Dakko. I make him eat." Annie proffered the spoon. I turned away, but she forced liquid through my lips, and it was easier to swallow than fight her. After a few moments I slurped greedily at the hot broth, stronger than I'd had in weeks. Then I turned and slept. When I woke, I was alone.

Time passed. Gregor brought me more broth, which I accepted without protest. While he waited, I tottered to the table and was spooning the last of it when the General Quarters alarm sounded.

Our eyes met. "This is it, then." My voice was dull.

Gregor turned away with a whimper, then straightened himself. "Sorry, sir."

"Help me into my jacket. I'll go to the bridge."

"Will you suit up, sir?"

"No. I prefer not."

Eons later the hatch slid open and I made my way to my console, hot and feverish, alarms still shrilling in my ears. I slapped the switches and they subsided into silence.

"Report, Kerren."

"Engine room has Defused, sir. There seemed to be no one on watch."

"What?"

"We are Defused and in normal space. If you will permit me, you really should have a word with the Chief Engineer, sir. It's most irresponsible to Defuse without—"

"Shut up!" I reached for the caller. "Chief?"

Dray responded. "Aye, sir. I'm here."

"What's happening?"

"Nothing down here, sir. We haven't touched anything."

"Kerren, what do your outside monitors show?"

"Sensors aft show we are in normal space. No sign of the aliens. As I have no reference coordinates it will take some time to determine our location. Sensors forward are nonfunctional."

"Would forward sensors help determine our location?"

"Yes, Captain. Or you could turn the ship."

"No, we can't; propellant tanks are bone dry. Midshipman, you've never been Outside on your own."

"No, sir."

"Go below, find someone in the original crew who's been Out. The two of you suit up, exit by the aft lock, and dismount the wide-band sensor portside aft, remount it forward of the disk."

"Aye aye, sir."

"Keep your suit radios on at all times."

Half an hour later they were clambering along the hull with the aft sensor. I waited impatiently. "Look forward, Gregor. Can you see anything?"

"Not beyond the disk, sir. The disk obscures the bow. I'll be there in a minute."

"Bridge, comm room reporting."

"What is it, Mr. Tzee?"

"It's—I think you ought to listen to this, sir."

"Listen to what?" My voice was irritable.

"We're picking up something odd."

"Oh, my God!" Gregor.

"What is it, Midshipman?"

"A fish. The hull. The whole front of the ship."

"Bow."

"I mean bow. Oh, Lord God!"

My fingernails drummed the console. I muttered, "One of you had better tell me what's going on." My tone was ominous.

Mr. Tzee said, "Captain, you won't believe—"

The simulscreen sprang to life as the new sensor came on-line. I gasped. Gregor had mounted the camera at the bow end of Level 1, aiming forward. The screen was filled with the pulsing mass of the fish we'd rammed. The remains of our hull, melted and fused, disappeared into its side. A mass of inert protoplasm surrounded the hull, walling it off. It reminded me, I realized, of a scab. The fish's skin looked gray, unhealthy.

A tentacle began to form, ever so slowly, while I watched mesmerized.

I found my voice. "Get away from that, Gregor!"

"You better believe it, sir!" I made a note to rebuke him later, then realized my foolishness.

Kerren rotated the camera in all possible directions. The screen swung dizzily.

"Hey!"

"Sorry, sir. Data input." When the puter was finished he refocused the camera on the fish.

The tentacle had stopped growing. Dots and circles of protoplasm in the fish's skin seemed to flow away from the scabbed hole in its side. Then, while we watched, it stopped moving altogether.

The pulsing ceased. Some essential element seemed to be gone.

"Captain, please let me put this on the speaker!"

"Huh? Oh, go ahead, Mr. Tzee."

Kerren said over the speaker's blare, "I have confirmation of our location, sir. It went faster than expected because for obvious reasons the data was stored first on my retrieval disk. We're—"

I turned to the speaker. My mouth worked. "Good Christ!"

The six o'clock news.

"—home," announced Kerren. "Just outside Jupiter's orbit, about forty-five degrees off elliptical."

I lay back in my chair, the sounds and lights dimming. I shut my eyes. Philip swam before me, then Amanda, holding Nate.

Lord God, please don't let me live.

Please don't make me live.

After a time I stirred myself. "Mr. Tzee."

"Yes, sir?"

"Broadcast this message on all Naval frequencies and emergency rescue channels. Message follows: U.N.S. *Challenger*, returned to Solar System, requests immediate assistance. Dead, injured, and starving aboard. Must have immediate food supplies and medical aid. Class A decontamination procedures must be observed entering and leaving *Challenger*. Alert Naval Intelligence. We have with us the nearly intact body of an alien. Extreme caution advised regarding viral contamination. Suggest the remains be examined to determine means of organic Fusion employed by aliens."

I wiped my hand across my face, discovered my cheeks were wet. "End of message. Add our coordinates. Broadcast continuously until answered."

"Aye aye, sir!" Mr. Tzee's joy was unconcealed.

After a time Gregor appeared at my side.

"Well, boy, enjoy your walk?"

"As much as anything," he said casually. Unbidden he sat at the watch officer's console, an offense for which a middy would commonly be caned. "Sir, why home? Of all the places in the galaxy?" He shook his head. "The odds against that are . . ." He fell silent.

"Who knows? We were already heading that way at a quarter light-speed. Maybe it knew. Our Fusion coordinates were set for home; perhaps it heard that. Or maybe it was following the Fusion tracks of our other ships leaving Earthport Station."

"You agree that's what they do, then?"

"Probably."

"But why, sir?"

I shrugged. "Why do moths seek the flame, Mr. Attani? It is a thing we may never know."

51

"The Admiral will see you now, Commander Seafort." In the comfortable office within Lunapolis Base, the young ensign held open the hatch.

"Thank you." I tucked at my jacket and ran my hand through my hair, again a nervous young middy summoned to the awesome heights of the bridge.

I came to attention before Admiral Brentley's desk. I held my salute just a moment longer than necessary, taking in his appearance. He'd aged greatly in the year and a half since I'd seen him. And he'd shrunk. Before, he was an old lion. Now he was just old.

"As you were." He shot me an appraising glance. "You're looking more fit than the last time I saw you, Nick."

"Thank you, sir."

His glance was shrewd. "You don't remember, do you?"

"Truthfully, no, sir. I wasn't all that well."

"You were about two days from starving to death, my medics say."

"Perhaps. I wouldn't know."

"Sit down, then. Forgive me, I should have suggested it sooner."

"I'm all right, sir." But I sat anyway, gratefully.

He settled in the comfortable sofa next to my straight chair. For a long moment he gazed at me, saying nothing. Then, "Hell of a cruise."

I nodded agreement.

"I'm so sorry, Nick. About your family."

"Thank you." I spoke with stiff dignity, holding it at a distance.

I'd been debriefed weeks before. Interviewed and reinterviewed, interrogated and challenged. Heedless of the consequences, I'd answered every question as truthfully as I could. *Challenger*'s Log, from her initial sailing, and the copy of *Portia*'s Log, through the time of my removal, verified what I told them.

They held their investigations shipboard and here at Lunapolis Base. I suspected that though we were examined minutely and believed free of contamination, no one wanted to risk sending us groundside just yet.

The Board of Inquiry found me not culpable in *Challenger*'s destruction.

Dray testified vehemently on my behalf. I said as little as decently possible. When it was over I went back to the quarters they provided me in Lunapolis and saw no one, while I slowly regained my strength.

Brentley said, "You're becoming fit again, Commander. Would you like shoreside duty or another ship?"

"If I'm not to be cashiered, I'd like a ship, sir. I don't want to go ashore."

"Cashiered?" he echoed. "Is that what you deserve?"

"I've twice foresworn my oath, sir. I have no honor." Nor any hope of salvation.

His lip curled in a smile. "How? When you perpetrated a ruse against that madwoman?"

"When I swore no harm would come to her, intending to shoot her."

"A legitimate ruse of war, Commander."

"I don't see it that way, sir."

"Absolutely necessary to save your ship."

"Yes, of course." It made no difference. An oath is an oath. It is what I am. Now I am nothing.

He shrugged. "What was the other time?"

I was tired of his toying with me. "I believe you already know, sir."

"Perhaps I do. What was the other time, Seafort?"

I accepted the implied rebuke. "While Admiral Tremaine was transferring passengers from *Portia* to *Challenger*. He gave me a lawful order to accept them. I refused, in violation of my oath of loyalty and obedience."

His hand slapped against the arm of the sofa. "Tremaine, yes. There's another story." He stared at the bulkhead, brooding. Eventually he looked up again. "I'm sorry, Nick. About him. He—" The Admiral lapsed silent and turned away. "He isn't my doing," he said finally. "That's all I can tell you. He's—I had no choice in the matter."

"He was my legitimate superior officer."

There was anger in Admiral Brentley's voice. "He started as that, yes."

"And should have ended that way."

"Nick, what he did was unforgivable."

"Abandoning us? There was no room on *Portia* for everyone."

"Then he should have sent your ship on ahead, and waited. Or, at most, transferred his flag to *Portia.*"

"It's what I would have done, perhaps. But it's not my prerogative to second-guess my superiors."

He nodded agreement. "Up to a point, his actions were defensible. But look at the whole and you see his cowardice." Again he brooded. "Bringing as many passengers as possible onto *Portia* was legitimate. But taking your food, even your lasers . . ." He shook his head before resuming fiercely, "And off-loading passengers he didn't like, to leave them drifting interstellar. Despicable!"

"He was selecting the most useful passengers, sir. As he did with the crew."

"That wasn't his judgment to make!" the old man said fiercely. He shook his head in sorrow. "Abandoning children in space!" He put his hand over his eyes, but not before I saw them glisten. "Nicky, I'm ashamed."

"Ashamed?" I echoed.

"For what he did to you in the name of our Service." He stared into the bulkhead and his mouth became grim. "He's a disgrace. As I said, you could justify many of his actions. But put them together—stealing your ship in the first place, interfering with your internal discipline, deceiving you into approaching his vessel rather than issuing a straightforward command, off-loading the transients, taking *Challenger*'s lasers, leaving her without a doctor . . ." He shook his head. "He'll be courtmartialed, of course. And convicted. No board of captains could stand for that."

We sat in silence. He said, "I've studied your reports. Minutely and repeatedly, I might add."

"Thank you, sir." I was aware his remark was ambiguous.

"That boy who didn't do so well on *Hibernia* last time, he turned out to be a good officer, eh?"

"Lieutenant Tyre died doing his duty, sir. I will miss him."

"I'm glad of that." He got up heavily and went to his desk to get something from a drawer. "This is for you."

I untied the leatherette folder and opened it. I stared dumbly at the contents. Before embarking, every officer was required as a matter of course to dispose of his property in the event of his death. I'd left mine to Amanda, or to Father.

Philip had left his to me.

There was a receipt for his duffel, now in storage, and his few personal things. A couple of letters. The stubs from his uncollected pay.

I began to cry.

Admiral Brentley waited, saying nothing. When I was able to collect myself he smiled gently.

"So much blood," I whispered. "So much death."

"Yes. You've seen more than your share." He looked pensive. "The information you brought us is invaluable. The body itself—the xenobiologists have gone wild. And Naval Intelligence is spooked out of its collective mind at the thought those beasts have reached our home system."

He smiled briefly. "Our physicists are muttering incomprehensibly about augmented N-waves. Those fish of yours travel faster than we do, Nick. They must, if you were able to get back in sixty-odd days from where it took you seven months to sail."

He stood and began to pace. I wondered if he saw himself on a bridge, far interstellar. He said, "I imagine there'll be some new devices coming out of the labs that will considerably shorten the distances between colonies. And so the world changes again."

He sat heavily. "But I won't be here to see it." I looked up in surprise. "I'm retiring, Nick. As you can see, I'm not well, and I want—" He broke off. "My daughters are buried on Vega Two," he resumed after a moment. "Been a long time since I've seen them, though I talk to them at night. I want to be with them, when my time comes. If the war heats up I won't be able . . . well, it's time for an old man to move on." His eyes misted.

I dared say nothing. Eventually he cleared his throat and tried a tentative smile. "So this is the last I'll be able to help you, Nicholas Seafort. After this you're on your own."

"You've done more than enough for me already, sir."

"Probably. But I'll do more. I told you I'd put you back to Captain after your next voyage. You're still younger than I anticipated, as you got back earlier than expected. But as of today you hold full Captain's rank in the U.N.N.S."

"Thank you, sir," I said, trying to simulate the elation I knew he'd expect.

"Doesn't mean much, eh? Well, you've had a rough time. Are you up to taking out a ship?"

"Yes." I would have long hours in Fusion when there'd be nothing required of me but to sit in my cabin. Days and weeks of blessed nothingness.

"I've got two possibilities for you. *Churchill* will leave for Arcadia in about four weeks. And I've got a ship just come in from Caledonia, that we're sending on to Hope Nation."

"I'll take her." I'd spent most of my career trying to get to and from Hope Nation. Perhaps I'd reach it this time. There were always the

Ventura Mountains. Perhaps I could sit overlooking the cliffs with my memories of Amanda.

"She's *Hibernia,* Nick."

The folder slid from my lap. My heard pounded. *Hibernia!* I'd come to Captain her by tragic accident, and managed to guide her safely back to Earth. A full ship of the line, but more. A familiar ship. A home.

"My seniority, sir," I stammered. "I—she—I'm way down the list for a ship so large."

"Yes, ordinarily you would be." He leaned forward, arm on his knee. "But I'm Admiral Commanding of Fleet Ops, and she's mine to give. We owe you for what you've gone through, and besides . . ." He trailed off.

"Yes, sir?" My curiosity was piqued despite my lassitude.

"There's something about you, Seafort. You have luck, intuition, integrity"—I snorted in derision—"and you always seem to be in the right place at the right time. And you do the right things."

My fist knotted. "I've fouled up about as badly as a Commander can. Why do you keep rewarding me?"

"You brought *Hibernia* back against all odds. You did the same for *Challenger.*"

"I didn't bring her back, the fish did!" I cried. "Can't you see? It wasn't me, it was fortune!"

"Or Providence," he rejoined. He shook his head in wonderment. "Captain Von Walther. A legend, when I entered the Service fifty years ago. There's never been another like him." Nor would there be. Hugo Von Walther, Commander of the search vessel *Armstrong,* who'd found the remains of *Celestina,* opened two colonies to settlement, fought a duel with the infamous Governor of Hastings Colony, and been appointed Admiral of the Fleet before serving as Secretary-General.

The old Admiral touched my knee awkwardly. "Son, sometimes I see another Von Walther in you. Or more."

"Goofjuice!" I said with vehemence, entirely forgetting my place.

"Oh, you may think so. But you're not far into your twenties, and look what you've already done.

"By God, Seafort, if you're not another Von Walther, then what are you?"

"Accursed," I said bitterly. "In both senses. People around me die. I wish—" I bit it off. I only wished I could die as well.

"Someday soon, when I'm in my dotage, I'll tell them I knew you. No one will believe me, of course, but I'll know it was true."

"That's nonsense," I said with force.

"One of us is right." He stood carefully, hands on knees to help himself straighten. "*Hibernia*'s leaving in two days. It won't give you any time to go down." Groundside, he meant.

"I have no need." Something occurred to me. "Sir, Admiral Tremaine relieved me before. When I get to Hope Nation, he may want to do so again."

"He might. But you'll carry orders for his dismissal. That's the last thing I'll be able to do for you, boy. When you get back I'll be gone."

"Sir, I swore to kill him."

"Your duel?"

"Yes, sir."

He shrugged. "So be it. I'll shed no tears. Once he's relieved, the dueling code is operative. You'd save us the trouble of a court-martial." He looked at me closely. "Choice of weapons is his, you know."

"I'm aware."

"He's quite good with archaic powder-fired handguns. He may well kill you."

"I won't mind," I said truthfully.

He studied me. "You've been through a lot, boy. I'm sorry." He stood. "I'll have my staff brief you tomorrow on the technical details. But I'll tell you now, our strategists believe the fish hear our ships Fuse or Defuse rather than the Fusion itself. So orders are to make one long jump, as close to Hope Nation as you can."

"That makes sense." It was the opposite of Admiral Tremaine's orders, of course.

"Some of your older passengers are still too ill to travel, but the Reeves couple in particular asked if you'd be going back to Hope Nation and requested whatever ship you'd be on." I shook my head in wonderment. People could be mystifying.

He went on without a pause. "Your, uh, crew. We've offered remission of enlistment. Some have accepted. Two asked to travel to Hope Nation as crew, with permission to resign at the end of the voyage."

"Who?"

"The Dakkos, father and son. Would you mind having them aboard?"

"No, sir."

"And a few of the transpops elected to remain in the Service. It's probably a better life than they'd have otherwise. They're not what we'd like in the Navy, but under the circumstances I can't very well refuse them."

"All right."

"The rest of the transients." He eyed me, then looked away. "I expect that relocation program will be shut down. It was ill-advised to begin with, as we all knew. But everyone feels it best that the transients not be politically exploited back home, so we're sending the pilot group on to Detour, as originally planned. Would you mind having them aboard?"

"No, sir."

"I didn't think so. You seem to be a sort of Pied Piper to young passengers and crew. It'll be crowded, but we'll make room for them."

I stirred. "How many to a cabin, sir?"

"I don't know," he said testily. "As before, I imagine. Six."

I took a deep breath. "No."

"We're hard-pressed for room these days, Seafort. We've lost several ships, and despite the dangers there's more traffic than ever. Anyway, they're used to it by now."

"No."

"I beg your pardon?"

"I won't bunk them more to a cabin than any other passengers. I consented once to Admiral Tremaine's abominations, and I will not do so again."

The old lion stirred within his gaunt frame. "Captain Seafort, I remind you that you're speaking to the Admiral Commanding."

"I understand, sir."

"I'm giving you an order to ship those passengers."

I got to my feet. "No, sir, I will not."

He snorted with anger, retreating to the formality of his desk. "Captain, you will obey orders!" We glared at each other. "If you want *Hibernia* you will take those passengers."

"I'm sorry," I said. "I would have liked *Hibernia* again."

"I'll have you court-martialed!"

"That's your prerogative, sir." He tried to stare me down. I met his glare as best I could.

The Admiral gave me an odd look. "You really don't care, do you, Nicholas?"

"The truth, sir?" He nodded. "No, sir. I do not."

He came out from behind the desk. "Four, then. That's humane. I'll off-load some regular passengers."

"No, sir." I spoke with finality.

"You stubborn young whelp! After all I've done for you!"

"They are human beings, sir. I've been taught that the Navy has but one class of passengers."

"Yes, but this is different. We're at war, and they're used to it. Three."

"No, sir."

"You'd give up your career for them? Truly?"

"If you force me."

"Two, then." I shook my head but he persisted, "It's no worse than married couples are given! Think!"

I capitulated. "Two, then." He was right. "But in the larger cabins."

"You're dangerous, boy," he growled. "Because you don't care what's done to you. It's well I'm getting you out of home system."

We both smiled, glad to end our confrontation. "A couple of other things," he said. "First, the, ah, mediamen have been clamoring for weeks to get at you. A number of them are gathered outside in the amphitheater."

"Me?" I gawked.

"Yes, you. I kept them away after your last trip, and that's only made them wilder. Your picture is all over the holos and on every photozine. You'll have to let them at you this time."

"But, why me?"

You're world-famous, Nick." He looked at me oddly. "Didn't you know?" I shook my head. This was ridiculous. I felt a growing anger.

He gestured toward my cheek. "That, ah, burn scar. Would you like to do something about it?"

"Not particularly."

"Um. Well, it's your choice. Parents all over the world will hate you."

He saw my puzzlement. "The fashion you'll set," he explained. He opened the old-fashioned hatch. French doors, really. Onto the sublunar chamber.

We walked together through the outer offices, to the corridor that led through the amphitheater back to Old Lunapolis. As we reached the amphitheater entrance I remembered. "What was the other thing you were going to tell me, sir?"

There was no time for an answer. A roar of sound, and I was blinded by a hundred piercing lights. They came at me, microphones thrust forward, questions screaming in my ear. I froze in shock, my jaw hanging foolishly.

"How did it feel to meet the aliens again, Captain?"

"Do you have any proposals for Naval strategy?"

"How do you feel about—"

"Your wife?"

"All the crewmen who died—"

"Did your family—"

I clutched the Admiral's shoulder. "*GET ME OUT OF HERE!*" One glance at my face and he swept forward, smiling and waving, guiding me through the frenzied horde.

Minutes later I sat, head between my knees, trying to control my trembling. We were in some compartment off the main corridor, still in Naval territory.

"I'm sorry, son. I didn't realize they'd come at you like wolves."

I mumbled something. Then, "I apologize, sir. I'll be all right."

"Good." He shifted awkwardly from one foot to the other. "What I was going to tell you earlier—maybe I shouldn't just now—"

"Go ahead."

"You have a visitor. Your father."

I stumbled to my feet. "Father? Here, on Luna?"

"Yes. He cabled us when the news of your return hit the holos to ask if you'd be going down. We told him it was unlikely, if you accepted another ship, and he said of course you would, so he asked permission to come here. I saw no reason to refuse."

Father on Luna? Impossible. That dour old man who'd rarely left Cardiff except to take me to Academy, enduring the peculiarities of one-sixth gravity just to see me?

My head spun. "Where is he?"

"Waiting for you, son. Down the corridor." Admiral Brentley had the grace to look embarrassed. "Shall I take you?"

"I'd rather go myself, please. Where?"

"West corridor, toward the end. There's a waiting room outside the offices."

"If you'll excuse me, sir?"

"Yes." He hesitated. "I probably won't see you again, Nick, before you go. Or . . . after." Almost shyly he offered his hand. "Good luck, Captain Seafort. And Godspeed."

"Thank you, sir." I roused myself to give a passable imitation of an Academy salute. It was what he would appreciate.

I hurried down the corridor.

The Naval station occupied a separate wing of the teeming new city built onto Old Lunapolis. Two main corridors penetrated its warren of cubbyholes, offices, dormitories, and quarters. After all, Lunapolis held the second biggest Naval Station in existence. The largest was Lunar

Farside Academy, halfway around the planet. The Terrestrial Academy base at Dover was tiny by comparison.

I trudged the length of the main corridor, past the regulation suit lockers every twenty meters, absently taking and returning salutes. Midshipmen and lieutenants, respectful of my rank, stepped aside as I passed. In a daze, I stopped to answer civil questions of fellow Captains, until I realized they were making excuses to speak with me. They shook my hand, flocked around me, touched me.

Eventually I made my way to the cluster of offices and waiting rooms at the corridor's end.

I went into the outer office. "Pardon me, is there a Mr.—"

He stood. Creased, older than I remembered.

"Father?" I whispered.

"Nicholas." He walked with the careful tread of a newcomer, still half fearing to lose contact with the floor. He raised his hand gently, touched my cheek. "You're sore hurt."

"Aye." I fell into the old speech.

"They told me. And in other ways. I'm sorry for your family. Your pretty young wife, and the baby I never met. May He cherish them."

"Thank you, Father."

"I've read about you," he said with a thin ghost of a smile. "Something every day. Much of it made up, I warrant."

"Most of it, I'd imagine."

We perused each other, strangers. "You're all grown now," he said at length, almost in wonderment.

"Aye."

He glanced at his watch. "I'll have to go back soon, tonight. I only had a three-day ticket."

"It can be changed—"

"No, there's no need. I've seen you, and I'll say what I've come to tell. Nicholas, you've done your duty. Through all the fantasies of the mediamen, I can read that. You're hurt, but you've carried on. I just wanted you to know that I know it."

"You came all the way to Lunapolis to tell me?"

"I might not be here when next you return; His ways are unfathomable. I wanted you to know."

"Thank you, sir," I said, overwhelmed.

He shrugged. "And now I can go. These places, He made them, but not for me."

I blurted, "Father, I've foresworn my oath."

"Oh, Nicholas!" He bowed his head from the pain. "You're damned."

"I know."

We stood in terrible silence. Fleeting memories crowded one another aside: me, still a boy, crying in Captain Forbee's office on Hope Nation, because my oath wouldn't allow me to set down the burden of Captaincy. My first subtle misstep, when I perverted Admiral Tremaine's orders to cane Philip. The awful descent that has destined me irrevocably to Hell.

"Tell me how it came to be."

And so I told him, haltingly, of *Portia's* voyage and of *Challenger's*. I made no excuses, but neither did I look for ways to blame myself as Amanda often rightly accused me of doing.

When I finished we stood in grim silence, aware of the enormity of my folly. Then he astonished me.

"Your oath is your compact with Lord God Himself. Once shattered, you cannot repair it. I taught you that." I nodded. "You are damned irretrievably to Hell everlasting."

"I knew that when I chose to foreswear my oath, Father."

"Yes. I taught you well; how could you think otherwise?" He shook his head in sorrow. "I must adjudge you damned, for so we are taught. But it may be, son, that in His infinite wisdom He has greater mercy than ever I can comprehend. Perhaps He has it in Him to forgive you. Truly I hope so." He clasped my shoulders in his hands. "Good-bye, Nicholas." He turned and went.

Overcome, unable to speak, I watched him go. Thus I watched him half a lifetime ago, after we crossed the field to the Academy gates, my duffel heavy on my shoulder, aching for the comfort of his kindness, knowing I was not to receive it. After, he gently pushed me toward the gate, and I entered it, and turned to see him striding away, step firm, never looking back.

"Father!" It need not be so again.

He paused at the hatch. "Yes?"

"Father, do you love me?"

A long silence, while he tasted the word, strange to his palate. He shook his head in wonderment. "Love, Nicholas?" He considered. "Love of your fellow man is transient, surely you know that. Only His love endures. Only His love is worth considering. Were I to say I love you, I would be turning your head with inconsequential fancy. But, though it may have damned you, you've done your duty as you understood it. I

respect you for that, Nicholas. Know then that you have my respect."
And he turned and was gone.

With a pang of longing I knew that it wasn't enough. It never would
be.

But it was all I would get.

It was more than I'd ever had before.

Epilogue

We sailed into the deep night, that great ship full of fallible souls, her anguished Captain at the helm.

The pair of frantic days before our departure was consumed in briefings, introductions, sad reunions. Much of *Hibernia*'s crew had been reassigned, but Chief McAndrews still manned the engine room with unabated force, Machinist's Mate Herney still walked belowdecks, and affable Mr. Chantir was now first lieutenant. Enough other old hands remained so that my arrival was preceded by a crackle of excited gossip: "Captain Kid's back!"

My ghastly appearance discouraged any overt welcome from the crew, though Chief McAndrews seemed at least outwardly unperturbed. I had just time, when I found he would be aboard, to scout Old Lunapolis for one of those strange shops where anything might be procured, and return with a securely wrapped package of his smoking weed. I put it in my cabin safe for days that might come later in the cruise.

I prepared for castoff amid a jumble of new, anxious faces: astoundingly young midshipmen, stiffly formal lieutenants, a green ship's boy stumbling over himself in eagerness to please.

And the transients. Eddie Boss had elected to remain a crewman. He performed well, a seasoned hand now, though his discipline was marred by a broad smile whenever he saw me. My scowl failed to inhibit it.

We cast off from Lunapolis Station, fired our thrusters for thousands of kilometers to a safe distance, took our bearings, and Fused.

We would be fifteen months en route.

Captains have prerogatives even in the cost-conscious Navy, and I'd used mine to have all the furniture in my old cabin replaced, so that nothing I'd shared with Amanda would remain. I couldn't have borne that.

I settled into the familiar yet unfamiliar cabin, unused at first to the luxury of a fully trained, ample crew. I haunted the bridge until our puter Darla asked why I never seemed to sleep as much as I used to. Then I realized my foolishness, and left the officers to their work.

I sat alone in my cabin, sometimes reading, sometimes communing with Nate and Amanda, who never seemed far away. I opened the present that Admiral Brentley sent before we cast off; inside the finely carved, worn mahogany box were two ancient pistols and a supply of powder and shot. Intrigued despite myself, from time to time I practiced with them, sighting on a cushioned target against a launch berth bulkhead.

I took my meals in the dining hall, sitting with the passengers the purser assigned to my table, making occasional courteous small talk, fleeing afterward to the welcome solitude of my cabin. I watched the training of the midshipmen without interest.

Life held no pleasure, nor did I expect any.

One day Eddie Boss asked permission to see me on the bridge, and to my surprise brought Annie with him. I waited for him to speak, but apparently his role was to provide moral support; he pushed Annie forward and gestured toward me. Blushing furiously, she stammered something unintelligible.

"Mr. Boss, what is it you want?" I asked with impatience.

Eddie said carefully, "Annie wants t'ask you somethin', sir."

Despite myself I smiled at his conscientious diction. "Ask, then. Why is she mumbling and twisting her skirt?"

Annie stamped her foot in frustration. "Stop talkin' 'bout me like I ain' here!" she cried. "I already tolya what I'm askin'!"

"Tell me again," I said more gently. "I couldn't understand a word of it."

"That's what I been sayin,' " she said indignantly. "I wanna talk like —like Cap'n make Eddie do!"

"You mean, speech lessons?" I was flabbergasted.

"Not jus' dat, alla other stuff. Like you showin' Eddie, walkin' ri, talk like other people." She sniffed. "Like dem Uppies."

"What's wrong with being who you are?" I asked quietly.

Her eyes fell to the deck. "Miz Captain, she said I c'n be what I wan'," she said. "When she showed me doin' my hair 'n all."

I had no answer to that.

I should have refused at once. But I assented, for reasons I did not understand then and have not since.

We met in my cabin regularly each day. With excruciating patience, Amanda's example before me, I gently corrected Annie's speech, helped her practice social graces, tried to teach her civilized ways.

The more I saw of her, the more I thought of Amanda. I missed not only her companionship, but her body. Her warmth at night, her tender caress, the delight of our coupling.

As time passed I relaxed somewhat with Annie and spoke of these things to her. She seemed to understand, and became my confidante as no other had been. I found she had in her a strength, a resilience that I came to respect and prize.

Walter Dakko, *Hibernia*'s master-at-arms, helped teach her as he had Eddie. After two months of nerve-wracking work, I was delighted with Annie's progress and told her so.

"Thank you, Captain."

I smiled. A month before, it would have been, "Gras, Cap'n."

"You'll be a lady to respect, Annie. Amanda would have been proud of you."

Instead of pleasing her, my remark caused her to stamp her foot with petulance. "Amanda, Amanda! Wid you it always be her!"

"*With* you."

"Wid, with, who care! I always be hearing about Amanda!"

"I'm sorry," I said stiffly. "I miss her. I won't mention her again."

"I miss her too!" she cried. "She was good lady, yeah! She done my hair, she helpin'—she helped Eddie when no one else would! But what about me? Amanda dead, Captain! Amanda dead, an' Annie live!" She threw her hands over her face and wept. Astonished, I could not think how to comfort her, until eventually, awkwardly, I drew her head against my shoulder.

For a long time she lay against me, swaying as we stood. "Don' you need let her go?" she finally asked. "Don' you have needs? Man needs?"

"Needs?" I said hoarsely, stepping away from her. "Look at me! Do you see my needs?"

Her eyes darted down, then back. A mischievous smile flitted across her features. "I c'n fix dat, Cap'n. Let ol' Annie be fixin' yo' needs."

"Don't talk that way!" I cried, unsure as to whether I meant her grammar or her coarseness. "There's been no one," I added, embarrassed. "Not since Amanda."

"Den it be time," she said simply, and came to me, and wisely said no more.

The days and weeks passed. We sailed on, the darkness Outside banished, lit within by the glow of our bodies, rising and falling as if to the waves, sliding, flowing, grasping at each other, floating together, as the great silent ship sailed ever onward through the void.

About the Author

DAVID FEINTUCH worked as attorney, photographer, and antiques dealer before turning to the writing of fiction. He's had a lifelong interest in the British Navy and the Napoleonic era, which provided background material for his first four novels. The several volumes of the Nick Seafort saga took eight years to complete.

Mr. Feintuch was raised in New York, schooled in Indiana and Boston, and now lives with his daughter in Michigan in an elderly mansion furnished entirely in antiques, except for his computer. He is an inveterate traveler.